MASSACHUSETTS

A Novel

Also by Nancy Zaroulis

FICTION

The Poe Papers
Call the Darkness Light
The Last Waltz
Certain Kinds of Loving

NONFICTION

Who Spoke Up? American Protest Against
the War in Vietnam 1963–1975
(with Gerald Sullivan)

MASSACHUSETTS

A Novel

NANCY ZAROULIS

FAWCETT COLUMBINE · NEW YORK

A Fawcett Columbine Book
Published by Ballantine Books

Grateful acknowledgment is made to the Industrial Workers
of the World (IWW) 3435 N. Sheffield, #202, Chicago, IL 60657
and P.O. Box 40485 San Francisco, CA 94140,
for permission to reprint "Bread and Roses" by James Oppenheim
which appeared in *Industrial Solidarity.*

Library of Congress Cataloging-in-Publication Data
Zaroulis, N. L.
Massachusetts: A novel / by Nancy Zaroulis.
p.   cm.
ISBN 0-449-90586-1
1. Massachusetts—History—Fiction. I. Title.
PS3576.A74M37   1991
813'.54—dc20   90-82332
CIP

Design by Holly Johnson

Manufactured in the United States of America

First Edition: April 1991

10 9 8 7 6 5 4 3 2 1

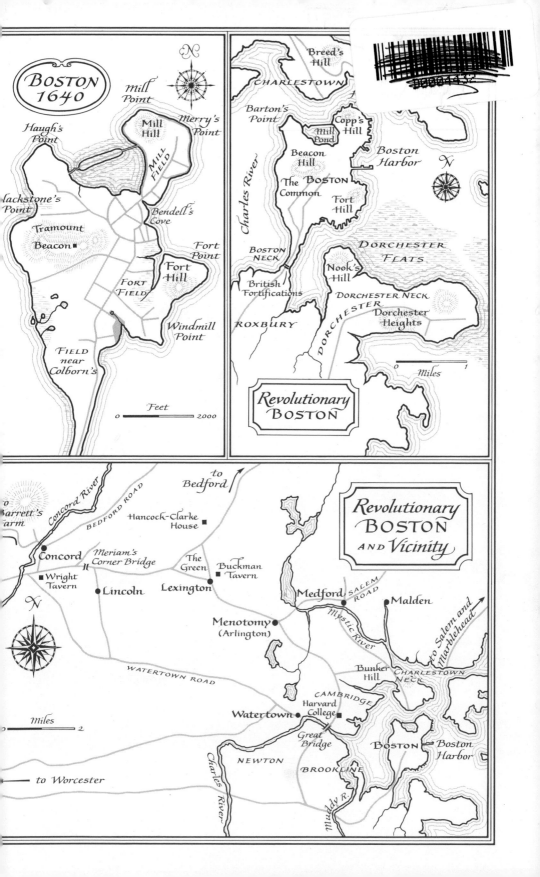

For Jerry
and for Alex and Katherine

Always with Love

ACKNOWLEDGMENTS

Many people helped me during the writing of this book. I am particularly grateful to my editor, Kate Medina, for her intelligent and sensitive reading of the manuscript, her wise counsel, and her unfailing sympathy and understanding for what I was trying to accomplish. Jonathan Karp and Olga Tarnowsky were also very helpful.

I am indebted also to Leona Nevler, Vice President, and to Susan Petersen, President, of Ballantine/Del Rey/Fawcett Books, who had faith in me from the start; without their support, *Massachusetts* would not have been written.

And my agent, Roslyn Targ, has been a friend for many years.

During the research for the book, library and historical site staff everywhere were of great assistance. Accordingly, my thanks to the following institutions and individuals:

The African Meeting House, Beacon Hill
Arrowhead Farm, Pittsfield
The Boston Athenaeum, and particularly to Jill Erickson, Trevor Johnson, Jan
    Malcheski, and Sally Pierce
The Massachusetts Audubon Society, and particularly to Elizabeth Wood
The Boston Public Library, and particularly the staff of the microfilm collection
The Brookline Public Library
The Bunker Hill Monument, Charlestown
The Codman House, Lincoln
The Franklin Institute, Boston, and particularly Michael Mazzola, President
The Isabella Stewart Gardner Museum, Boston
The Robert H. Goddard Collection, Clark University, Worcester, and partic-
    ularly Dr. Stuart W. Campbell, University Archivist
The State Library of Massachusetts, and particularly Patricia Hewitt
The Minuteman National Historical Park, Lexington
The Museum of Fine Arts, Boston

Old Deerfield Village
Old Sturbridge Village, and particularly Dennis Picard
The Peabody Museum, Salem
Plimoth Plantation, Plymouth, and particularly Nanepashemet of the Wampa-
    noag Tribe and Carolyn Freeman Travers, Research Librarian
The Thomas Crane Public Library, Quincy, and particularly Mary Clark
The Quincy Historical Society of Massachusetts, and particularly Hobart Holly
The Shirley-Eustis House, Roxbury, and particularly David Mittell, Jr., Exec-
    utive Director
The Thoreau Country Conservation Alliance, and particularly Thomas Blan-
    ding, President
The Thoreau Lyceum, Concord, and particularly Anne R. McGrath, Curator
The Library of the University of Massachusetts at Boston, and particularly
    Chris Roberts
Widener Library of Harvard University

and to:
Tish Burnham, Prof. Thomas N. Brown, Prof. Anthony Carrara, Edgar J. Dris-
coll, Jr., Sara Ehrmann, Prof. Lawrence Kaplan, Michael Kenney, Peter H.
McCormick, Dr. Stanley Remsberg, Grant Rudnicki, Richard Rust, Prof. R. J.
Schork, Zoe Sleeth, Mary Ann Sullivan, Timothy Sullivan, Kenneth Tatarian,
Prof. Gerald Volpe, Alex Zaroulis, and Katherine Zaroulis

Finally, a word of thanks to my family. As they have always done, they gave
me their loving support during the writing of *Massachusetts*. I am especially
grateful to my husband, Gerald Sullivan, who undertook much of the extensive
historical research necessary, spending long hours in the labyrinthine stacks of
Widener Library and the airier precincts of the Boston Athenaeum. He has
served faithfully as reader, listener, and advisor whenever I needed a sympathetic eye and ear, and his love and encouragement have helped me every day
from the inception of this book to its final word.

CONTENTS

PART I

SAINTS & STRANGERS

THE REVELLS

Bartholomew Revell
(1608–1689)

m.

Susannah Hatherly
(1615–1692)

Jedediah
(1637–1695)   *Nine others*

m.

Catherine Mayhew
(1642–1741)

Isaac   *William*   *Lydia*
(1664–1725)   (1667–1695)   (1669–?)

m.

Elizabeth Chauncy
(1676–1711)

Benjamin
(1701–1792)

THE GRIFFINS

Phineas Griffin
(1650?–1679)

x.

Rebecca Sparhawk
(1649–1692)

Remonstrance
(1680–1729)

m.

Charity Tyler
(1684–1765)

Abraham   *Ten others*
(1701–1750)

And for the season it was winter, and they that know the winters of that country, know them to be sharp and violent, and subject to cruel and fierce storms, dangerous to travel to known places, much more to search an unknown coast. Besides, what could they see but a hideous and desolate wilderness, full of wild beasts and wild men—and what multitudes there might be of them they knew not.

Of Plymouth Plantation
William Bradford

1. PILGRIMS

1

All night he had lain awake, feeling the roll of the sea, listening to the creak of the ship, the snap of the sails, the sounds of his fellow passengers as they coughed and muttered and moaned, children crying, now and then a few words of prayer: "Save us, O Lord, and lead us to safe harbor!"

Now, toward first light, his restlessness overcame him. He rose from his narrow space—about the size of a coffin, he thought—and climbed the ladder to the deck to see the day come: another day tossing on the vast sea, riding the huge swells that so often had threatened to swamp the little ship, a speck of canvas and wood carrying a hundred souls toward a new Jerusalem in the wilderness.

He balanced himself on the heaving deck and drew the cold air into his lungs. As cold as it was, it was better than the fetid air below. He looked up. He saw the lookout aloft in the rigging, a little monkey of a man. He breathed deeply again, and he thought he smelled a new smell—something different from the sour salt smell of the sea. He saw a flutter of wings near the foremast: a sea gull. His heart leapt as he understood: like Noah's dove, this bird was a sign from God.

A tremendous shout began to rise from within him, but he stifled it as he heard the lookout cry instead: "Land ho! On the starboard bow! Laaaand ho!"

He looked. At first he saw nothing, but then—Yes! There—a thin line at the horizon between the gray sky and the darker gray of the water. Land! They were saved!

And then he shouted it, too—"Land ho! Land ho!"—and he heard his cry echo and re-echo down through the ship as the other passengers began to stagger up on deck to see for themselves the miracle (for so it seemed) of their deliverance: "Land ho! Land ho!"

2

He was a likely lad, wiry and strong, just past twelve and not yet full-grown, but giving promise of good height and good health and strength—and intelligence, too, for his eyes missed nothing that might help him to survive. They were dark blue, as blue as the sea on a calm fair day, and his hair was golden-brown, the color of the sun on the Thames at Rotherhithe.

He had been given to John Carver in London the year before, after his parents died; his brothers and sisters had gone elsewhere. When he learned that Carver was preparing to make this voyage to the New World, he had been frightened at first, hearing tales of the wilderness, of fierce savages; but he knew that his prospects in England were not good, and the excitement of the thing had come to him—to venture out to the rim of the world where, Carver assured him, he would not drop off. Captain John Smith had made the voyage, and had drawn a chart for them to follow.

"Yes, sir," he said then; "I will come with you."

Carver was a stern man, not given to showing affection (for he'd had no children of his own), but now he smiled and said, "Well, Bartle, you will be a good right hand to me as we perform God's errand into the wilderness."

3

It was full day now, sunshiny and brisk, the wind strong from the northwest. He could see high bluffs; gulls swooped and curved overhead as if in greeting; the little ship creaked and groaned as she beat her way along, her sails snapping in the wind as every turn of the glass brought them nearer to their landfall.

"Well, Bartholomew Revell, are you ready to set your feet on firm ground?" It was John the cooper, a sturdy, steady young man whose skill would be invaluable in their settlement.

"Yes." In fact he could hardly wait; they had been on the ship for weeks, since the summer.

They stood by the rail on the crowded deck; everyone who could walk had come up to see.

And now, their destination in sight, Carver led them in a prayer of thanks; that done, Bartle watched as Carver, together with Elder Brewster and Mr. Bradford and Captain Standish, went to confer with the ship's captain. Something was wrong, it seemed.

"We are far off course, Master Jones." Carver pointed to Captain John Smith's map of the New England coast as he spoke. "Hudson's River, we thought—the northern parts of Virginia, as we agreed. We are too far north. Our patent is for Virginia, not here."

Jones nodded. "But the winds have made your course for you, it seems."

"Can you get us farther south?" Bradford asked.

"I will try. But I promise you nothing. It is a miracle that we have gotten this far."

And so he gave the orders to turn the ship south. But the wind shifted, too, and came contrary, and the tide ran against them. The leadsman was frantically working his lines, sounding the bottom, for while Smith had mapped this shore, he had not given its depths. This ship drew two fathoms. Soon the lookout cried a warning—"Shoal water!"—and the leadsman went on, faster and faster, "Twenty fathoms! Sixteen—fourteen—sixteen—ten—"

Impossible to go on. If they continued, they would bleach their bones on this coast.

And so they were forced to turn back—to retrace their course to where they first saw land. Master Jones took a few of them into his cabin and pointed to the map to show them where they were: Cape Cod, so named because of its abundant stock of fish.

"I cannot go south," he said. "We will founder."

They understood: this would be their place. Winter was coming on; they must make a settlement.

Carver accepted for all of them: "It is God's will."

For a moment they bowed their heads, thanking God for their deliverance. Then, looking landward, Edward Winslow said: "It looks a wild and savage place—full of wild beasts and wild men."

To which Jones replied: "This is a harsh land in winter. You must build your shelters quickly."

When word of their decision filtered down through the ship, dissension arose among some who had come as servants:

"Is that Virginia?"

"It is not."

"Then we need not keep our agreements, since they have not kept theirs. We were promised Virginia."

Bartholomew heard the mutterings of discontent, and he wondered how his master and the others would silence them. He did not care where they were, as long as they were on dry land; he hated being cooped up on the ship, he wanted to begin the great adventure, life in the New World.

Carver and the others withdrew to confer for a time, and then they gathered in Master Jones's cabin. They had a document newly written; Elder Brewster read it aloud:

"In the name of God, Amen. We whose names are underwritten, the loyal subjects of our dread Sovereign Lord King James . . ."

Bartle spied John the cooper. "What is it?" he said. "What are they doing?"

"It is a compact—a covenant. To prevent a mutiny, I think. They will all sign."

And so they did, Elder Brewster calling out the names as each man stepped up to write: "William Bradford; John Carver; Edward Winslow; Isaac Allerton; Myles Standish; Samuel Fuller . . ."

But still some of the servants muttered discontent. The leaders needed more authority, and so Brewster said to Carver: "Will you serve as Governor?"

"If they wish it. Wait—before you speak—"

Bartholomew watched as Carver went on his knees to pray. Then he rose, and nodded to Brewster.

"Good friends," said Brewster, his glance sweeping around to encompass them all: the chief men in the cabin, the company watching from the deck. "Master Carver has consented to serve as our governor. Let us confirm him so."

Bartholomew felt a little thrill as he heard the men's voices: "Aye."

"Opposed?"

No one spoke.

"Done," said Brewster. Then he stepped out onto the deck to lead them in a prayer: "Have mercy on us, O Lord, as we begin thy task. We are poor and weak. We have no welcome here. We have no home . . ."

Bartholomew's head was bowed, but he ventured a glance around. The leaders, all save Captain Standish, were devoutly concentrating on the words; Standish looked openly bored, anxious perhaps to get on with their work. Bartholomew had heard that Standish was a Papist, but he could not believe it; no Papist would join this voyage. Others of the chief men who were not Separatists were attentive to Brewster's words, but hardly uplifted—Mr. Allerton, Mr. Hopkins, Mr. Martin—and John Billington, who, like the servants, had not troubled to hide his discontent.

". . . We are in thy hands, as thou art in our hearts. Help us in our labor, blessed Lord, that we may truly say we are God's Pilgrims in the New World . . ."

Mrs. Allerton, big with child, looked sad and suffering, as if her time was on her already; and Mrs. Bradford wept openly, not troubling to hide her tears. Her husband did not seem to notice: his head was bowed, his eyes shut. Perhaps the women had not wanted to come, thought Bartle. Many of the Separatists had lived in Holland in recent years, having escaped persecution in England. Bartle had heard that life in Leyden was good for them: they could worship as they pleased, without threat of prison or death from the authorities. The men had decided to leave because they and their children were growing too Dutch, and of course the women had to do as their husbands commanded. He turned his head slightly to glance at the servants in the rear. They seemed not sad but angry; perhaps they would mutiny yet.

He looked once more at the barren coast. The New World was rumored to be one vast forest towering to the sky, but he could see no big trees here, only stunted, dwarfish pines and low scrubby bushes behind the long stretch of sandy shore. Master Carver had let him look at the map. They were at the very tip of the Cape; it curved around like a fist to make the harbor where they had anchored.

Suddenly he shivered, and not from the cold. He closed his eyes tight and whispered his own fervent prayer: *"Merciful God, help me to survive in this place. . . ."*

4

"Wheeeeeee!"

Bartle ran down the beach, laughing, shouting, the cold wind whipping his cheeks crimson. He stumbled once or twice, for he did not yet have his land legs, but he was steadier than the Billington boys, who staggered as they tried to keep up with him.

The *Mayflower* lay at anchor in the little harbor. On the beach the carpenter and his men worked at putting the shallop back together—the small boat that would serve them when the *Mayflower* returned to England; it had been dismantled for the journey. Beyond the dunes, at a little freshwater pond, the women washed clothes and bedding while two sentries stood guard.

Bartle threw himself down on the cold damp sand, and soon the Billingtons joined him. They carried handfuls of shellfish.

"Here—we found mussels, Bartle. Have one."

But Bartle shook his head; raw mussels were no treat. Francis Billington pried out the slimy flesh and stuffed it into his mouth; then another, and another. Bartle understood: they were all tired of their diet of ship's biscuit and dried fish.

From down the beach he heard the sounds of hammering as the men worked. They could not even begin their exploration until they had the shallop to survey the coast; the repair would take four or five days, the carpenter said.

But when he returned to the ship, he found that Captain Standish was unwilling to wait that long. He would go tomorrow, he said, and take a party with him.

"If you meet the savages," said Carver, "you will need the shallop to escape."

"We will be well armed. There is a danger, but there is a greater danger waiting here, doing nothing. We must settle before Master Jones leaves us."

Captain Standish was a short, red-haired man with a quick temper and no sufferance for fools. Further, he was a military man with a thorough mastery of the *Manual of Arms*; he had been a soldier of fortune in the Low Countries. Already he had announced that once they had settled, he would hold regular drills.

Bartle gazed in envy as the men made their plans to explore. He longed to go with them, and as the meeting broke up, he caught Carver's eye.

"Well, Bartle? Nothing to do?"

"Sir, Captain Standish is taking a party ashore."

"Tomorrow, yes."

"And do you think—" His boldness terrified him, but he forced himself to go on. "Do you think that I might go with them?"

"Exploration is man's work, Bartle."

"Yes, sir. But I am nearly a man."

A smile twitched at Carver's thin mouth. "So you are. Well. I will speak to the captain and vouch for you."

The next morning Bartle arose in the dark and put on his shoes and his jacket, ready to descend with the others into the longboat. Sixteen men, they were, including Bradford and Hopkins, Allerton and both the Winslows, three of the servants—but not those who had shown malcontent—one of whom brought his dog, a mastiff who seemed as glad as all of them to be free of the confines of the ship.

They disembarked near the pond and walked to the far side of the spit of land, where the great Atlantic waves pounded on the beach. The day was cold and cloudy; the wind blew strong, nearly sucking breath away. The little captain, splendid in his shining armor, marched them along at a brisk pace until suddenly his voice rang out: "Halt!"

Ahead, on a low, wooded rise, they saw five or six Indians and a dog. When the Indians saw the white men, they turned and ran back into the trees, whistling for the dog.

"Come on!" cried Standish, and he set off at a run toward the place where the savages had disappeared. The men plunged into the trees behind him—a poor sort of forest, small, stunted trees, undergrowth that slowed their pace. Branches whipped across their faces, blinding them, and vines and roots tripped them as they stumbled along. After a while the captain gave the order to halt and held up his hand for silence. They listened, but they could hear nothing save the rustle of wind in the trees and, from the beach, the rumble and pounding of the surf. The savages seemed to have vanished into thin air.

The captain ordered them on. All day they tramped through the forest. They saw no more savages, no wild beasts. That night they slept near the beach, and the next day they went into the forest again. They had nothing to drink, only a small bottle of Holland gin, and they were parched with thirst, their faces and hands scratched and bleeding, their clothing torn by the maddening thick growth. Bartholomew envied the captain his armor, as heavy as it would have been to bear.

At last they stumbled on a spring and crowded around it. Bradford knelt, cupped his hand and drank. Bartle admired his bravery; no one drank water, not ever. Water was dangerous, it made people ill. But now he saw Bradford's pleased, surprised expression: "It is good!"

Bartle was very thirsty. He knelt and scooped up a handful and swallowed it. It was cold and sweet—delicious, as he imagined the finest wine might taste. He moved away to let some of the others have a turn, and then moved in and drank again.

After they had rested awhile, they went on. They came to a high bank near the shore, with a meadow beneath and many mounds of sand.

"They can't all be graves, can they?" said Hopkins, kicking at a mound. "Else they've had a visit of the plague."

"Dig into it, then," said the captain. "Perhaps it holds their treasure."

In short order Bradford lifted two ears of multicolored corn. "A treasure indeed!"

"Could we plant it?" said Allerton.

"Certainly we could," said Bradford. His face was suddenly grim, as if he were thinking of the weeks and months ahead. They must see to planting as soon as possible in the spring, or they would starve. He bent and began furiously to dig out the whole cache. "And we shall!"

Soon he found a woven basket filled with the strangely colored corn, and they hauled it out. If they met the savages, they would somehow make them understand, with gestures, that they wished to trade for it.

"Look!" One of the men, digging independently, came running up with a large iron kettle.

Bradford examined it. "Captain Smith did not write in his book that the savages were ironmongers," he said.

"It was left by a French trader, no doubt," the captain said. "Bring it along. If we meet a savage, we'll offer to pay for it."

But the kettle was heavy; the man soon tired of carrying it, and so he left it behind.

Back in the forest they followed a narrow trail. The day was cold, but the sun shone bright, and soon they were warm with their exertion. They were not as cheerful as the day; they felt the presence of the savages all around them, as if a thousand eyes watched them from behind the trees, from the depths of the undergrowth. Bartholomew's heart was pounding, and not entirely from walking fast. He wondered if—

"Whoa!"

A sudden thrashing up ahead, and then, after a shocked silence, a burst of laughter.

"Here's a fine young buck for the savages, men!" cried the captain.

They crowded around to see. There was Master Bradford dangling upside down, one foot caught in a trap—a rope of twisted vines. They couldn't help but laugh, even as they hurried to cut him down.

"It is a devilish invention, is it not?" Winslow said. He examined the snare as he helped to ease Bradford to the ground. It had been concealed underfoot: to catch a deer, perhaps.

"Yes," said Bradford, shaking himself together, checking to see that his musket had not been damaged. "They are clever people. The Lord has been good to remind us of it."

So Bradford was not harmed, but only warned of how cunning their adversaries were. When the company returned to the ship, he made light of it for his wife's sake; still, she was horrified to hear of his mishap, and he took her aside to comfort her.

The children crowded around Bartle to hear of his adventures while the men talked to the adults. The Billington boys were especially envious; they were rough, restless lads, and in their idleness the Devil had found work for them, for Francis had set off a keg of gunpowder in his father's space below decks and had nearly blown up the ship and everyone with it. The Billington boys had become violently ill on the mussels and clams they had gorged that first day on the beach, and had been soundly beaten by their father for their gluttony. Bartholomew had felt sorry for them then, but now he turned away angrily, not wanting to talk to Francis any longer. Playing with gunpowder!

The shallop was repaired at last, and again a party went out to explore, and again Bartholomew went along. The little boat sailed down the shore, smoothly enough at first, but then a wind sprang up and they could not land. But they were so eager to get on with their task that they jumped overboard and waded in; the water was not deep, but it was freezing cold, and they were soaked through and badly chilled. Bradford said later that many of them first caught their sickness there, the sickness that would take so many in the end.

All that day it snowed; and when they made their camp that night, they froze, coughing in their sleep, their still forms drifted over with snow. But when the shallop returned for them the next day, they said that they would go on, they had no time to rest, to wait for a clear sky.

They returned to the place where they had found the corn—"Corn Hill," they called it—and dug some more, ten bushels in all, which they would use for seed. These they loaded on the shallop; then they went on, and soon came to another clearing and more mounds of sand. Again they began to dig—and then Bartholomew had the fright of his life, for as they pulled aside a woven mat, they saw a canvas bag, and in the bag was the skeleton of a man with some flesh still on the bones, and some hair still on the skull, and the hair was yellow.

"Aaaahhh . . ."

And the bones of a little child, buried with the yellow-haired man, and a string of fine white beads, a knife, a pack needle, some bowls.

"And who was this poor creature, buried with his child?" Bradford said.

"A sailor," said Jones.

"If they had killed him as an enemy, they would not have buried him so carefully," said Winslow.

"Shipwrecked, perhaps," said Jones.

"And not too long ago. You did not hear of it, Master Jones?"

"I hear much, but not everything."

They covered the bones; they went away. Bartholomew felt tears in his eyes, and he knew that they did not come from the cold wind blowing off the water. To die here, alone, friendless—and the child!

When they returned to the ship and told of their strange discovery, many took it as a bad omen: did it mean that they should explore further, and not settle here? They argued back and forth:

Winslow: "It is a good anchorage at the river."

Jones: "If you get the equipment, I've seen enough whales here to bring three thousand pounds for their oil."

Bradford: "Whaling's a skilled job, and we're none of us trained for it."

Winslow: "Without whaling—consider what we would have at Corn Hill: good fishing, a fertile soil, a healthy place, easy to defend."

Deacon Fuller: "There are too many savages about, Master Winslow. We would be constantly under fear of attack."

Winslow: "Defense would be easy on the hill."

Standish: "But consider: if you fortify the hill, and stay there, you need to haul up every drop of water. Pure and good though it may be, there is none on the hill."

Carver: "We must settle."

Fuller: "If we make too hasty a choice, we risk having to live with it."

Standish: "Or die."

Master Jones, impatient, put an end to it. "Mr. Coppin!"

The first mate stepped forward. "Yes, sir."

"You have sailed this coastline before, with Captain Gosnold. Can you help them?"

"There is a place—a good harbor on the far side of this bay. I have seen it. We called it 'Thievish Harbor' because we trucked with some wild men there, but they would not trade fair. They stole a harpoon from us."

"Can you take us there?" said Carver.

"If my memory serves me, I can."

5

And so once again they set out, and they landed south of Corn Hill. A stiff wind froze the blowing spray on their coats into coats of iron. They were perishing with cold; two of them fainted. Bartholomew's hands and face were numb; he thrust his hands inside his coat, but the coat was wet and his hands did not warm. As they landed they saw Indians on the beach working at something. When the Indians saw them, they danced wildly up and down and then ran away. Captain Standish decided not to investigate, but to build a fire and settle for the night on the beach. In the distance they could see the small red glow of the savages' fire, but none came near.

In the morning they went to see what the savages had been working on. It was the carcass of a big black fish—a Howling Whale, as it was sometimes called, *Globicephalus melas*.

"Should we take some of the meat?" Winslow asked.

"It does not look fit to eat," said Standish. "Leave it. Faugh! I'd need to be closer to starving than I am now to eat that flesh."

They went on exploring. They found another graveyard, but they did no digging. Late in the afternoon they made a little barricade, set a watch, built a fire, and settled down.

In the middle of the night they heard a great cry from the watch: "Arm! Arm!" The savages were howling, he said—listen! At once they leaped up, seized their muskets, and began to fire. Then they stopped to listen. They heard nothing but the wind.

It was a wolf, perhaps, one of the sailors said. He had heard a wolf howling once in Newfoundland; an 'orrible thing, a wolf's cry.

They tried to go back to sleep, but Bartle was awake for a long time, straining his ears, listening for the cry of the wolves—or the savages.

In the morning when they were at their prayers and breakfast, all of a sudden they heard the savages yell: "Woach! Woach!"

They had already taken their muskets to the shallop, and now, despite the danger, Winslow and Allerton and a few others made a dash to retrieve them. They ran back to the barricade, charged their pieces with powder, and began to fire. Still shrieking, the savages ran away. Bartholomew's knees went to water and his heart was pounding. *O Lord protect us—!*

Bradford stepped outside the barricade and pulled a handful of arrows from the coats hanging there. "I'll send these back to England with Master Jones," he said, "so that they may see how in this first encounter we are attacked."

"And how we survive," Winslow added.

Bartholomew glanced at Carver, who had sunk to his knees—not in weakness, but in prayer. He closed his eyes and said a brief prayer of his own, thanking God for sparing them. Then he hurried to help the men load the shallop in preparation for another day's exploring.

They sailed across the bay, a brief voyage, but almost more perilous than the one they had just endured at sea. The wind rose; the rudder broke; the mast broke; they were nearly dashed to pieces on the sharp rocks by the shore, and it was only by the most valiant effort, the men pulling hard at the oars, that they were saved from disaster. At last, as darkness fell, they landed at a wooded shore in calm water.

The next day dawned fair and still, and when they awoke they saw that they were on an island in the harbor that Mr. Coppin said he remembered. Safe from the savages, they took that day to rest, to warm themselves in the mild December sun; the next day being the Lord's Day, they said their fervent prayers. Finally, on the third morning, they ventured out again, and at last they came to their place to settle. They stepped out onto the land—good land, with a brook close by, and a hill to fortify.

"Here," said Bradford; it was not a question.

"Yes," said Carver. He caught Bartholomew's eye and he spoke again, more firmly. "Yes. Here."

"And we will call it—"

"New Plymouth, for the place from which we sailed, back home."

6

"How did she die?" Bradford said.

Elder Brewster put his arm around the younger man's shoulders and led him away from the company clustered on deck: the two men were like father and son, long companions in adversity. "Into the water," he said. "She was gone before we could reach her. We cried out, but we were too late. We could not retrieve her."

And so the news that they had found their place to settle was overshadowed by this sorrow: Mrs. Bradford dead, and probably, some said, of her own will.

Even though Bradford was surrounded by members of the company, he seemed terribly alone. They stood by him for a while, letting him feel their sympathy; then they moved on. They had no time to stop for Death, not even when he took one so close to them as Dorothy Bradford.

Master Jones sailed the *Mayflower* across the bay and anchored it in Plymouth Harbor. They would live on board ship while they built their houses.

On Christmas Day a great storm blew up, so that the men working on shore could not get back to the ship for two days. Christmas was a heathen invention; they paid no heed to it, but went on building—a Common House first, for storage and shelter, and then little "English wigwams," crude huts of branches and turf.

But God had not finished testing them yet. Even before they made their place, they began to sicken and die. Solomon Prower died, and Mr. Martin. Mrs. Allerton, poor soul, began a hard labor and gave birth during the storm; her child was stillborn, and she died, too, not long after. Degory Priest died, and Moses Fletcher, and John Goodman; Edward Tilley and his brother John, and John's wife Bridget; James Chilton and his wife (but his daughter Mary survived). . . .

On shore, the men cutting timber for the Common House found skulls lying thick on the ground. Many of the men were sick unto death, and they thought that they must be digging in their own graveyard; some of them could hardly walk, but still they kept on, sawing their logs and hauling them to where others had dug the foundation.

John Crackston died, and Edward Fuller; Mrs. Sarah Eaton died, and Richard Gardiner and three of Master Jones's sailors. When the Common House was finished, some of the sick were transferred, and it became a pest house and then a charnel house as people kept on dying.

One bitter night the thatch on the roof caught fire, and the sick had to be carried out on pallets. The guns were saved, and the barrels of gunpowder, but Bradford lost some books, and others some clothes.

Mr. William White died, but his wife Susanna survived, and their little son born on board ship in December; he was called Peregrine, which means Pilgrim. Edmund Margeson died, and John and Alice Rigdale. . . .

Coppin, the first mate, went urgently to Master Jones: "We must leave, those of us who are going back, we cannot stay a day longer. We will all die if we wait until spring."

Carver intervened: "*We* will all die if you do not wait. We need the ship for shelter."

Coppin: "Our contract was to deliver you here, Mr. Carver. No more. We could have left the day we landed you—and we should have! We have no contract to stay and die."

Jones: "Enough, Mr. Coppin. Mr. Carver, how soon will you be finished building your houses?"

Carver: "I don't know. So many are sick—"

Jones: "Yes. As we are. In truth, Mr. Coppin, we have little choice but to stay. I do not have a crew that can sail the ship. Three more are sick since yesterday—fifteen since Christmas. We must stay until they recover."

Coppin: "And if they do not?"

Master Jones had no answer for that.

Each morning, Bartholomew awakened in his place with the Carvers on board ship and said his morning prayers with them before he and Carver set out in the longboat to work at the settlement. Bartholomew would go into the woods with a few others and select a fine straight tree to cut, and then set to with the saw. The clearing was getting bigger; soon, when the spring came, they would plant around the stumps. When a tree was felled, they lugged it to the shore where their settlement was building; Captain Standish had ordered a platform for his cannon, which they built as soon as the Common House was done.

But one day Gilbert Winslow asked Bartle to come along to hunt waterfowl, since their food was running very low, and Carver gave his permission. Gilbert was a clever lad, just twenty, Mr. Edward Winslow's younger brother, but not a member of the Leyden congregation. He would be glad of Bartle's sharp eyes, he said; a lad of twelve would be of more use hunting than lugging logs.

It was a clear day, not too cold, the sun warm enough to feel like spring, a day when the ice over the Town Brook would thaw a little before freezing up again. They walked through the trees to a swampy place, frozen now, where reeds poked up through the ice and winter birds pecked for sustenance. The trick was, Gilbert said, to conceal yourself and stay very still so as not to startle the waterfowl; that was why it was best to go on a mild day like this, for if you stayed very still on a very cold day, you would freeze.

They crouched in the brushy cover. They were well away from the settlement, far enough so that they could not hear the rasp of the saw on wood, nor the hammers pounding; once Bartholomew thought he heard a distant shout, but it did not come again.

They waited. Gilbert crooned softly, hardly whispering: "Come on now, we've hungry bellies to feed." His flintlock was charged and ready; ceaselessly the two of them scanned the landscape, looking out for their quarry.

A movement so slight that it might have been a breeze fluttering a branch caught Bartholomew's eye. Then his brain registered what he had seen; then some part of it dismissed it: *No!* Then he saw another movement, and another. . . .

His mouth went dry; he could not swallow. He went weak all over. He was aware that Gilbert had glanced at him, then looked in the direction he was looking, where silent shadows passed through the cover of the trees, their dark skins blending into the landscape: a dozen savages, at least, going toward the settlement.

In a moment they were gone—without sound, without trace. Bartholomew, whose heart had stopped, felt it begin to beat again. Gilbert was as white as the snow that lay on the icy swamp. He held up his hand to warn Bartholomew to keep quiet; then he moved his head to signal that they should rise and move away. All thought of waterfowl gone, they stepped carefully, silently, until they were well away, and then, heedless of noise, they began to run.

They tore through the forest as if they were chased by the Devil, and burst into the clearing where Captain Standish and a few others were working.

"Savages," cried Gilbert. "Get your guns! Savages!"

At once the men dropped their tools and seized their muskets and ran to the settlement, where the captain called out his orders: "Around the Common House! Form a line! Load and ready to fire!"

A great commotion arose, children crying with fear, and women, too, everyone herded into the Common House. Bartholomew would have liked to stay outside and fight, for all that he did not have a musket or a flintlock, but an order was an order, and so he went in.

Outside, the men stood at attention, awaiting imminent attack. It did not come. An hour they waited; two; three. The settlement was as silent as if Death had already struck; not a sound except the occasional wail of one of the younger children, and one brief, protesting outburst from Francis Billington—"I want to fight the savages!"—followed by a sharp *thwack!* as his mother boxed his ears.

And so the day passed. The men stayed at attention, scanning the forest. They saw no enemy; they heard only the wind and the sound of their own harsh breath, one or another coughing despite their efforts to smother the sound. The sun crossed the sky and descended in the west, casting a rosy glow over the winter landscape. Finally Captain Standish approached Gilbert Winslow.

"Are you sure you saw them?"

"Yes, sir. Bartle saw them, too."

Waiting inside, Bartholomew felt a little thrill when he heard his name; he hoped that the captain would call him out to question him, too. The Common

House was stuffy and dark, and the long hours endless, tedious—a fearful, nerve-wracking tedium that left him exhausted even though he had done no work at all.

The door opened a crack: it was Gilbert, beckoning him. Gladly he went out into the winter twilight; promptly he answered the captain's questions and waited while Standish contemplated him as if he held the answer to their dilemma.

Then: "They may wait until dark to attack."

This was a new horror that Bartholomew had not thought of. He would never sleep peacefully again if he thought the savages would wake him!

At last the captain set a watch of four men and dismissed the others. He sent two men to fetch the tools that had been left in the clearing, but soon they returned to report that everything had been taken. "Thieving bastards," muttered the captain, but he did not dwell on his anger. He had more important affairs to tend to: provision for a larger watch both day and night—and the immediate beginning of military drills. That was why they had brought him along, to see to their defenses. Well, he was doing so. And what he needed most was a fort. As soon as their houses were made, they would start to build it.

7

That week Mrs. Edward Winslow died, and Mr. and Mrs. Mullins; their little son Joseph was very ill. Bartholomew went to see him; he was lying in the Common House tended by his sister Priscilla.

"Well, Joseph, I saw a spouting whale this morning, out in the bay. When you are well again you can help me watch for them, and perhaps we will take one."

With a great effort the child focused his eyes on Bartholomew and tried to speak. But all he could say was, "Yes."

Priscilla tried to spoon a little food into his mouth, but he could not swallow. She did not look well herself, Bartholomew thought: her hands were shaking, and although she was just eighteen, deep lines of fatigue and grief on her face made her look like a woman of forty.

"I will watch with him," Bartholomew said, "if you want to rest."

"No," she said. "I can rest after he— I can rest later."

Her voice was flat—dead, Bartholomew thought. He remembered the time when his parents had died; he wanted to tell her that he understood her grief, but he did not know how. She had been a pretty girl, he thought, bright and merry, filled with hope when the voyage started; now all the light had gone out of her.

Joseph had gone to sleep. Or—

Suddenly, with a cry of despair, Priscilla threw herself across his small, still form. "Joseph!" she sobbed. "Oh, Joseph! I am so sorry! Please forgive us! Joseph!"

Mrs. Brewster hurried over to console her. "Hush, child! There is nothing to forgive. It is God's will. Hush!"

But Priscilla would not be comforted. "Why does God want to take him?" she sobbed. "He is all I have. Why can God not leave him with me?"

"We cannot question God's will. He has a purpose for everything. Hush, now."

And she led the despairing girl away. Bartholomew, after one last look at little Joseph, turned away and went outside to make himself useful. So many had died, and there was no end to the work left to the living.

Ann Fuller died, and Thomas Tinker and his wife, and John Turner and his two sons. And then Captain Standish's wife Rose died, and the captain, burdened as he was with protecting them all from attack, went into the forest to grieve alone.

They had a cemetery now, filling fast, and some wanted to put markers on the graves. The captain forbade it.

"Just a small marker," said Edward Winslow; he choked back his tears, grieving for his wife.

"No," said the captain, more roughly perhaps than he intended. "No. It is dangerous enough to bury them. If the savages see how many we have lost . . ."

So they went out secretly at night to lay the dead to rest, the sound of howling wolves in their ears, and no stones marked the graves. By the end of winter nearly half their number had died, and many who lived, lived nearer death than life.

Always, they knew they were being watched. One day, to their astonishment, they saw two painted braves atop the hill across the Town Brook. The Indians signaled for the white men to come to them.

"Should we go?" said Carver.

"No," said the captain. "Signal them to come here."

But the braves would not cross the brook, and so the captain and Mr. Hopkins went across to them, laying their muskets on the ground as a sign of peace. Slowly, cautiously, the two white men walked up the hill. As wary as they were, they were glad of a chance, at last, to meet some of the inhabitants of this place; if nothing else, they wanted to truck for food.

In the settlement the others anxiously watched them go; Mrs. Hopkins, terrified, clutched the baby Oceanus to her breast and tried to keep from crying. But as the white men reached the crest of the hill, the Indians suddenly bolted down the other side, out of sight; many of their brethren awaited them, for the whites heard a great commotion and shouting before they all vanished back into the forest.

"They are cowards—they will not meet us," said Hopkins.

"Not cowards. Cautious," said the captain. He turned to look back at the half-finished settlement—a poor little scattering of huts around the Common House, a weak defense against an attack. "We must have more cannon."

The next day some of the ship's crew lugged a minion and saker across the beach from the shallop and mounted them, under the captain's direction, onto the newly built cannon platform. Until the fort was built, they would give at least the illusion of strength; one blast from the three-inch mouth of the minion would frighten the savages well enough, they thought.

But the best defense would be the fort, and the captain admonished them, every day, to get on with it.

8

"Bartle! A savage!"

It was Francis Billington, yelling at the top of his lungs, and at first Bartholomew paid no attention, for the Billington boys were not above crying false alarm. But one glance at the boy's face told him that Francis was not lying, and he seized his hoe and ran with the others from the field to see their visitor.

The Indian strode down the street of the little settlement as if he owned it. He was magnificent—tall and well muscled, his shining red-brown body covered only by a loincloth. His coarse black hair hung in a single braid down his back; in it he wore three eagle's feathers. He carried a bow and a quiver of arrows. He moved with an animal's grace, and he held his head high; he was not afraid of them. So fearless was he, in fact, that he strode right up to the door of the Common House and would have thrown it open but for two men who stopped him. And then at once the men meeting inside, hearing the commotion, came out. Before the governor or anyone else could say a word, the Indian thrust out his right hand; and he nearly dumbfounded them when he said:

"Welcome! I am Samoset!"

They could not believe their ears. A savage who spoke English?

The governor was the first to recover from his astonishment. Extending his hand, he said: "Welcome. I am John Carver."

"You make good settlement here. You meet my people?" Samoset gave the governor's hand a hearty shake.

"No. We have seen them, but—"

"People live here all dead. You give me beer, I tell you."

Word of the visitor had spread like wildfire; people who had fled to the safety of their houses now began to emerge, overcome by curiosity to see what they had so long dreaded—a savage! That any savage could speak English was beyond their imagination, and they whispered to themselves as they wondered: was this the Devil masquerading in some way to trick them?

The governor dispatched Stephen Hopkins to fetch some of their small stock of brandy and a little food. "And bring the red horseman's coat, so that we may give him a present!"

The men ushered Samoset into the Common House, where they sat in a circle to await Hopkins's return. The door was open, and Bartholomew and the others crowded around to peer in. It seemed to Bartholomew that there was a gleam of laughter in the Indian's eyes, as if he enjoyed the sensation he made. At last Hopkins returned, pushing his way through the crowd. Graciously, as if he were one of the King's courtiers, he served the visitor, and made a great show of presenting the coat to him. Samoset seemed to like it; he put it on at once, and fortunately it was not too bad a fit. Then, as he ate and drank, he began to talk again.

"Now you say, how I know your speech? I come from Pemaquid—north of here. I meet many fishermen of English. We talk. I am sagamore of Algonkian."

They hung on his words as if he spoke Revelation. Even now, hearing him, they could hardly believe their ears. Truly this was God's mercy, to send them a savage who spoke English!

"There is another who speak better. I bring him. And I bring Ousamequin—Yellow Feather—you call him Massasoit. Sachem of Wampanoag. Chief of all tribes here."

The governor nodded gravely. "We would be honored."

"You fight Nauset people when you come," Samoset went on. "Nauset big fighters." He began to laugh. "You good fighters, too. You frighten Nauset with loud noise." He laughed and laughed at this joke; and after a moment the white men began to laugh, too.

All day they sat in the Common House with their visitor. He showed no inclination to leave, and they were reluctant to ask him to do so for fear of offending him. When night fell, they offered him a place to sleep in Hopkins's house; he accepted with somber dignity, as if he were conferring a favor on them by consenting to stay. All night Hopkins and Mr. Eaton, the carpenter, sat by the fire keeping watch. They did not think that Samoset was the advance of an attack, but they could not take the risk, however small, that he might be. They gazed at him in wonder as he slept peacefully, covered by the red horseman's coat. Truly, he was a miracle!

In the morning he went away, but the next day he was back with his companion who, just as he had promised, spoke better English—a miracle twice over!

This brave's name was Tisquantum—Squanto for short. Like Samoset, he was tall and well built, covered only by a loincloth, bearing himself with great dignity. He wore a necklace of bear's claws and carried a bow and a quiver of arrows. After exchanging greetings, he told them his story.

"Yes, my lords, I went to England with Captain Weymouth after his exploration many years ago. I came home again with Captain Smith. Then I was kidnapped by Captain Hunt. He took me and many others. Some Nauset people, too. He sold me as a slave in Spain. I escaped to England, and came home again on Captain Dermer's ship. I was of the Patuxet tribe. They lived here; they cleared these fields. They all died of the white man's sickness. When I came back from England, last time, all were dead."

So this savage had suffered the loss of his family, too, Bartholomew thought.

He and the others stood behind the circle of white men and two Indians and listened, fascinated, to the incredible tale that Squanto told.

"When you came," said Squanto, "the Nauset people feared you. This is why. Three years ago a French ship was cast away in a storm on the shore of the Nauset. The Nauset captured the sailors, they used them horribly, they made slaves of them and sent them from one sachem to another to make sport of them. I will not tell you all that they did. It is too unhappy. But when you came, the Nauset were frightened. They thought you came to avenge the French. So they fought you."

More wonders! "We never knew of them," said Master Jones.

"It is good they did not capture you, too," said Squanto.

Bartholomew remembered the morning at the barricade on the beach, when the savages had shot the men's coats full of arrows. *What if they had won?*

Squanto paused then, and lifted his head to listen. Bartholomew heard nothing, but Squanto obviously did. He signaled for silence; then, in one graceful movement, he stood. The others followed as Squanto led the way toward the Town Brook. Then, halting, he lifted his hand as if in benediction: "Massasoit!"

And there on Strawberry Hill stood Massasoit and sixty braves. None of the white men had ever imagined such a sight. Sixty!—but in their massed formation, in their warpaint, carrying their bows and lethal, bone-tipped arrows, they seemed as hundreds. Massasoit's face was painted dark red; he wore a wolf skin slung over one shoulder and a chain of white bone beads; he carried a knife and a tobacco pouch.

Samoset and Squanto walked to meet him, and while they were gone the governor murmured to Bradford and the captain: "A large force—three times our strength."

"But we have guns," said the captain grimly. His face was hard and drawn with worry under the gleaming curve of his helmet; he stood so erect in his armor that he looked taller than he was, and Bartholomew thought that any savage must be impressed by this fearsome little man.

Samoset came back to report: "Massasoit want you come over."

"I would rather have him come here," replied Carver. "Ask him to lay down his arms and come to us."

"He will not. He want you come to him."

"Tell him— No. Wait." Carver turned to the others to confer. This impasse must not be allowed to stand, and yet—

Edward Winslow stepped forward. Like Standish, he wore full armor. Carver spoke with relief: "Yes—Winslow! Can you be our ambassador? I want him to come here to us. It is important that he do so."

"Gifts, perhaps?" said Bradford.

"Yes. Exactly. Allerton! Go to the stores. Get brandy, and an ornament or two—the copper chain with a jewel in it—and some knives, and ship's biscuit. Edward, you will present them to Massasoit, and tell him—you will phrase it well—tell him we wish to be his friends and make a treaty of peace with him. You have your sword? Good."

A strange pair, crossing the brook and climbing Strawberry Hill: Edward Winslow in his shining armor, and Samoset in his loincloth. As they left, the governor called to the captain: "Can you prepare a guard?"

An honor guard, which Standish would have ready when Winslow persuaded the chief, as they were all sure he would, to cross over the brook and come into the settlement.

With everyone else, Bartholomew watched, fascinated, as Winslow parleyed with Massasoit. Back and forth they spoke for some minutes, with Squanto translating; as Winslow said later, he thought that it all would come to nothing. Massasoit was pleased with what they gave him, but he wanted more: he wanted Winslow's armor. He did not ask it as a gift: he would truck corn for it. Only by assuring Massasoit that King James himself, the great king across the water whose country Squanto had seen, sent his greetings and wanted to make a treaty of friendship—only then was Winslow able to persuade Massasoit to drop the subject of the armor and enter the settlement. But Winslow stayed on Strawberry Hill, under guard as a hostage.

And so at last Massasoit came to them, down the hill and across the brook, accompanied by Squanto and twenty of his finest braves. Captain Standish, with great pomp, had his guard ready to receive them, with pounding drum and silvery trumpet making a flourish. Tall and stately the Indians marched, escorted by the captain into Stephen Hopkins's house. Fourteen braves awaited Massasoit outside, impassive under the stares of the settlers. Governor Carver, William Bradford, and William Brewster went in to join the chief. They sat by the fire on a green rug and some cushions; above them was the sky, for the house was not finished, it lacked a roof. A sudden silence as the drum and trumpet ceased; then the bargaining began.

First the governor and Massasoit kissed hands. Then they drank from a pot of brandy. Those who were close by saw that Massasoit broke into a great sweat, but whether it came from the brandy or from fear, they did not know. Then the chief took his tobacco pouch, filled and lit his pipe, smoked it, and passed it to Carver.

Squanto translated to him as the governor spoke: Welcome, Massasoit. We wish to live in friendship and make a treaty of peace with you.

Massasoit said that peace was his wish also.

Carver said that if any people took from the other, each would restore what was taken.

Massasoit said that if any men warred against his people, the white man would come to his aid; and he would do the same for the white man.

Carver said that when Massasoit's men came to Plymouth, they would leave their weapons behind.

This gave Massasoit pause. He looked around the room, at the faces of his braves, the faces of his new allies. For a long moment he hesitated. Then:

Agreed. Further, he would tell all his neighbors and allies that this treaty had been made, that they would know of it and not harm the white man.

Done! cried Carver. With God's help they would live in peace.

9

On a bright April morning Master Jones set sail for home. The settlers gathered on the shore by the longboat where he and his crew were preparing to row out, one last time, to the ship anchored in the harbor. The shallop would remain for fishing and exploration. It was a sad day, for while Jones and his men were with them, they knew that if the thing seemed impossible—if too many died, if the settlement could not be made—they could always go back. Now each must decide: Stay? Or return in defeat?

There were only five women now, and all of them wept as Jones and his men shook hands and received their wishes of safe voyage.

But no one elected to go with him; all would stay. They were determined souls, Jones said; they would survive.

He climbed into the longboat with his men, and they rowed away to the ship. The settlers watched as the sails unfurled; then the anchor rattled up, the sails caught the wind and the ship turned and headed east. The cannons boomed a salute. Those on shore remained watching until it vanished beyond the horizon. Some cried; some prayed; the governor stood apart, his face drawn and tired. He did not look well, Bartholomew thought. He was not a young man, and the rigors of the winter had taken their toll.

But they had no time to mourn the ship's departure. Planting season was upon them, and they needed to set out their crops.

Squanto came to help them, not only with the planting, but with every other task.

"Go with him, Bartle," said Carver. And so, liberated from the drudgery in the fields, Bartholomew and a few others trooped after the tall, dark man whom they called a savage—wise savage, to teach them how to survive!

Squanto led them to the shore, where he trod the wet sand, showing them how to work eels out: "You can live from the sea and the forest until you harvest your corn," he said. "The shore is rich with eels. You step like this— so—and they come up. They are fat and sweet; they will feed you well."

And he bent and pulled the long, wriggling eel out of its hole, and laughed to see their amazement.

Then he took them into the forest. "You can find good food here," he said. "Ground nuts and strawberries and raspberries, sorrel and yarrow, leeks and onions—gather them up, and live on them while you tend your corn."

By the Town Brook he showed them how to build a weir. "The fish will come up the brook to spawn," he said. "You can use buckets to catch them, but it is better to build traps. You will have plenty of fish to eat, and to plant with the corn, for these are old grounds and will not give a crop without fish."

Then, in the cornfields, he showed them: "When the leaves of the oak tree are as big as a mouse's ear, put your corn in hills, three or four seeds in each one. Then put on three fish, like the spokes of a wheel. The fish will feed your corn as your corn feeds you. You can make meal with your corn, and pudding and bread. But you must guard your cornfields, for the wolves will come to dig up the fish. You must set a guard day and night until the stalk is half a man high and the fish is gone."

How wise he was, and how generous with his knowledge! He moved through the landscape like a child of nature; the sun glinted off his bronzed skin as his moccasin-shod feet trod swiftly and silently through the forest. Bartholomew thought that Squanto must be the wisest man he had ever met—wiser even than Master Carver or Elder Brewster, whose knowledge of Scripture was unsurpassed, but who had little idea of how to survive in this wilderness.

And then one day as Bartle and John Carver were working in the fields, planting corn as Squanto had instructed, Carver collapsed. They carried him to his house; soon people crowded in, and Bartle understood that it was the deathwatch. Carver lay on his pallet, pale and barely breathing. Mrs. Carver wept; Dr. Fuller stood by. He had bled Carver, with no sign that bleeding had helped. "If he lives," Fuller said, "it is God's will."

"And if he dies?" said Bradford.

"That, too."

A great cry came from Mrs. Carver just then as she threw herself across her husband's still form. "No! John! Don't leave me here alone!"

To no avail: he was dead.

Bartholomew helped to carry the body to the burying ground; he stood at attention as the volleys were fired in the governor's honor. Master Carver had died of a sunstroke, Dr. Fuller said. Afterward Mrs. Carver withdrew into herself and would not speak to anyone. She sat in a daze all day, not moving; when Bartle or her maidservant brought her food or drink, she would not touch it, and when Mrs. Brewster beseeched her to rest she paid no heed.

The next day the men elected William Bradford as their governor. He said that he would serve, but since he was still weak from his sickness, he needed help. Isaac Allerton agreed to serve as his assistant.

Bartholomew did not know Mr. Allerton very well. He seemed a sharp man, a canny man, always bustling about on some business or other. But soon Bartle came to know him better, for Mrs. Carver followed her husband into the grave, and Bartle went to live with the Allertons.

10

That spring was starving time: they had only the sea's bounty to live on, too few eels and mussels, and otherwise lobsters and clams—disgusting food that many of them could not eat without vomiting. Lobsters were trash, Squanto said, wrinkling his nose in distaste; he refused to eat them. Bartle did eat them, but only because there was nothing else.

The corn grew, just as Squanto promised. One night the guards caught one of the servants, half starved like everyone else, stealing into the fields to eat some of the half-grown ears. The guards tied him to the whipping post and gave him thirty lashes, and after that no one tried to steal corn again.

Not long after, Captain Standish took a party of men in the shallop and explored up the coast. They sailed into the great bay of the Massachusetts, a name that meant "place of the great hill." Here they found a fine, deep harbor for shipping. When they disembarked they met a few natives who led them into the forest to see the grave of Nanepashemet, the king of the Massachusetts tribe. This grave was an enclosure fifty feet across surrounded by a palisade forty feet high. Around it was a breast-deep trench; a bridge led across the trench to the place within, where the king lay buried in his house.

Later they met some women of the Massachusetts wearing splendid beaver coats. Do not bargain with these women, said Squanto; simply take the coats, if you want them. The Massachusetts are bad people, he said; they want to do harm to the white man. But Bradford insisted on a fair trade; the women had done no wrong, he said, and he would do no wrong to them. And so the women stripped themselves naked for a handful of beads, and then, giggling and chattering, they quickly gathered branches to hide their nakedness. They were more modest than some English women, Winslow said approvingly. The furs would go to pay their debt, Allerton said, for the Plymouth settlement was not only a religious community, but a business venture financed by the Merchant Adventurers in London. Furs and fish would erase their debt, and shipments of clapboards, too, perhaps; certainly they would not grow enough crops to send back to pay what they owed. The corn had grown well enough, but their seed brought from home—barley and wheat and peas—had all died, they did not know why. The seed had rotted, perhaps; or perhaps someone had bewitched it, the servants muttered.

Nevertheless they had a good enough crop to increase their ration to a peck of corn each, every week. And now they would have a Harvest Home—a celebration to mark their first year of survival.

They sent a few men to shoot fowl—turkeys, ducks, partridges—and they invited Massasoit to join them. He appeared with ninety braves. By now they knew the Indians' habit of gorging themselves on whatever food was at hand; they saw their entire ration for the next year vanishing in this one feast. But Massasoit saved them: he sent his braves to kill deer, and they brought back five.

Bartle helped to roast the deer on a spit over an open fire. Nearby, some of the women stirred big pots of venison stew. Deer meat was tasty, all the more so because in England it was forbidden the common folk. The nobility kept deer parks; any commoner who tried to shoot a deer was punished. Here it was for the taking.

When they sat down to eat, they were all astonished at how much food there was—not only the roasted meat, venison and turkey and water fowl, but boiled eels and clams; wine from wild grapes; sallet herbs from their kitchen gardens, cabbages and carrots and onions and beets; dried fruits gathered from the wild, strawberries and gooseberries and cherries and plums, some of them cooked in dough; and pompion sauce—a dish from the Indians. And corn, of course, which was to be a staple of their diet, roasted on the ear, or ground and made into pudding or baked into corn cakes. Now Squanto showed them a new way to eat it. He husked some kernels which he put into an earthenware bottle, and he laid the bottle in the coals. When shortly he took it out, they saw that the kernels had popped into little white balls as big as the end of his thumb.

After their meal, Captain Standish entertained them with a military drill. He marched his men smartly back and forth, and then he ordered a demonstration of weapons. Bartle watched longingly. How he wished that he was old enough to join the captain's company! After the men had fired their guns, a little commotion arose: some of the Indians wanted to have guns, too, and they offered to trade for them.

"Now watch," said Giles Hopkins, who stood near Bartle, grinning to see the fine display. "The captain is no diplomat, but now he must tell them that he cannot give them guns. They will be angry."

Bartle watched as the discussion went back and forth, but at last Massasoit intervened and his braves gave it up. To restore harmony, Master Winslow organized games. "Ho—Bartle! Come on! We'll have a race!" They went down to the beach, where Winslow paired off whites and Indians. Bartle's opponent was a young man of twenty or so—he found it difficult to tell an Indian's age— with an eagle's feather knotted in his hair and stripes of dark red on his cheeks.

"Go!" Winslow cried, and Bartle ran as hard as he could; he felt his heavy shoes pounding on the damp sand, he felt the cool air tear into his lungs. In the distance he heard cheers, whether for him or his opponent he could not tell. In moments it was all over, the Indian winning by a good fifty feet. But no matter: everyone laughed and clapped Bartle on the back, and he understood that winning was not the point. The object of the race—of all the games they played that day—was to show friendship: they were forming an alliance with these people, in the face of unknown threats from all the tribes whom they had not yet seen.

For three days they feasted and celebrated with Massasoit and his men. On the third day, Bartle was assigned to roast the last deer. He looked for someone to help him put it onto the spit; he saw John the cooper and hailed him. "John! Can you help me?"

But John shook his head; he was bent on some more important task. Bartle watched as he went to speak to Priscilla Mullins. He had a determined look on his face, as if this were something that he had long wanted to do and had finally made up his mind to do it. He stood beside her, bending to her and then motioning toward the forest, as if he wanted her to walk with him there.

But she would not. She shook her head, slowly at first and then more sharply. Bartle understood: the women did not like the forest, they never went there. At last John gave up, but he stayed by her; he would not leave her side. Bartle found someone else to help him with the deer.

The sun set. In the autumn darkness their bonfires glowed like ruddy jewels: small points of light on the wilderness shore.

2. THE CITTY UPPON A HILL

1

In the deepening dusk of an October day in the year of our Lord 1635, Bartholomew Revell strode up the Broad Way in the Town of Boston in the Massachusetts toward the house of the merchant John Coggan, where he lived. He moved with the confident air of a man who is sure of his place in the world. He was middling tall, and well-muscled from years of hard physical work. His face was thin, with deep-set dark blue eyes, high cheekbones, and a beaky nose above his wide mouth and long, strong jaw. His hair, the color of antique gold, just touched his collar; his red wool cap kept it from falling annoyingly into his eyes. He was roughly dressed in leather breeches and doublet, a woolen shirt underneath; his hands were none too clean, for he had worked hard all day unloading a shipment of goods into Coggan's lighter and bringing them in to the merchant's warehouse by the wharf. Now, satisfied of a good profit (a small part of which would be his), he swung rapidly along the muddy way, noting the last light in the western sky and the beacon atop the Tramount silhouetted against it.

The Tramount's three hills, and Fort Hill by the water, and Windmill Hill at the North End, loomed over the little settlement like great, brooding beasts; if they stirred, angry, they could push the raw little houses, and the meeting house, and the governor's mansion, into the sea without a trace. Boston existed in their shadow—with their consent, it seemed. And yet they were useful, for the windmill ground their grain, the fort protected them, and the middle hill of the Tramount wore its crowning beacon—a tar bucket on a tall pole—set a-fire to summon help when it was needed: from Dorchester and Rocksborough, from Newtowne and Watertown and Linn, from Winnisimmet, from Charlestown just across the river. Trouble could come from the French, in Canada; or from the Indians nearer by; it could even come from England, the mother country herself, jealous of her control over her colony.

As Bartholomew passed the small wooden houses that lined the way, he saw, here and there, the light of candles within, or hearth flames where the evening meal was being prepared. Once at an unshuttered window he saw a woman holding her child in one arm, stirring a huge kettle with the other; the scene so quickly glimpsed gave him a curious turn in his heart. He would like to marry, he thought, but despite the steady influx of newcomers, he had not yet met a woman who appealed to him.

As he went on he was conscious of the sound of his heavy shoes thudding against the ground. It was full dark now, and the dark of the moon as well, so that he had only starshine to see by. A cold night, the wind from the northwest: winter was near, the long, bitter New England winter when people clung to their firesides and sickened and died, and many of them dead not from sickness, but from depression and melancholy, defeated even before they began to make their place in this harsh land. He could hardly remember winter in England, he had left so long ago, but he heard every year the complaints of new settlers about the long, white, frozen time between the golden autumn and the first faint greening in the spring.

A gust of wind struck him full on, blowing dead leaves into his face and momentarily blinding him. And then, before he could see again, he heard an angry voice coming at him out of the darkness: "Ho! William Miller! Stop!"

Before he could reply, a heavy fist struck the side of his head and he staggered, caught off balance.

He righted himself. A tall, heavily built shadow of a man lunged at him. He stepped aside, avoiding the blow; instinctively he hit back, but his fist merely grazed the side of the man's head.

And now the man swung at him again—and missed—and Bartle swung back—and connected—and the man stopped for a moment, breathing hard. "Y' canna' steal from me, William Miller," he said. "Dog! Shittabed!" He lunged again, and this time his hands fastened on Bartle's throat.

"No! I am not—" But the words—the very breath of his life—were being choked out of him. He struggled to loosen the man's terrible death grip, but the vise on his throat grew tighter and tighter and he could not break it.

"Ho! Break it up! Break it up now!" More figures out of the darkness, wrestling the man away, freeing Bartle.

He caught at the rail of a fence. The evening star careened across the sky; the earth tilted under his feet as if he were back on the *Mayflower*.

Two husky constables held his attacker, and two others gripped him. Before he could offer a word of explanation, they pulled him away, carrying him and his attacker both to the jail, newly built and never lacking for tenants. They chained him to the wall by his arms so that he could not even reach his aching throat to rub it. In the dim light of the rush lamps he peered at the other man, chained likewise. He was a rough, uncouth-looking fellow with black hair and a pockmarked face under a stubble of beard. His small piggy eyes glared at Bartle, while under his breath he kept up a continuous stream of abuse. "Ye'll not get out of this so easy, William Miller. That ye'll not. I'll ha' my money from ye—"

"I am not William Miller," said Bartle. His voice came in a hoarse whisper from his throbbing throat. For the moment they were alone, but then there was a commotion at the door and one of the constables came back.

"You'll go before the magistrate in the morning," he said.

Bartle started to protest that he was guilty of no crime, but the constable cut him off. "Don't bother tellin' me," he said. "My job is to lock you up. His mightiness'll deal with y' in the morning."

And so Bartle spent a miserable night with no company but his bellicose companion. He wondered what John Coggan thought; his employer was a meticulous man, attending to every detail of his considerable business, and naturally he would wonder why Bartle did not appear.

Bartle shifted a bit, trying to find a comfortable position; he was sitting on the dirty straw, his arms spread-eagled and growing numb. He was sure that in the morning, when he spoke to the magistrate, the man would understand that this was no trouble of his making and let him go.

But he was wrong. The magistrate, Richard Bellingham, was entrusted by the governor to keep order and punish wrongdoers. This he did with a vengeance. He peered at Bartle from sharp, canny eyes and questioned him sternly.

"Name?"

"Bartholomew Revell."

"Occupation?"

"Merchant's assistant."

"Name of the merchant?"

"John Coggan."

At this, Bellingham paused and gazed at Bartle for a moment. Yes: he recognized this young man; had seen him often, in fact, for John Coggan was the busiest merchant in the settlement. Then: "Will he vouch for you?"

"Yes, sir."

His attacker's name was James MacPherson. He was a seaman passing through and therefore, like all such, an object of deep suspicion. The magistrates wanted no pollution of their settlement from transients, who were not allowed to stay for more than three weeks. MacPherson thought he had been in the colony for about a week; he could not say for sure.

Bellingham moved swiftly to the issue at hand: who was the guilty party here? Two men fighting, no witnesses save the constables who broke it up.

MacPherson stood sullen and mute. Bellingham cocked an eye toward Bartle. "Well?"

"He set on me, sir."

"Hmmm." Like the governor, Bellingham was a man of deep religious faith. That faith centered on the Old Testament rather than the New; mercy had little part in it. Punishment was good for the soul—anyone's soul.

"MacPherson? What say you?"

A silent shake of the head; then: "No, sir. He went for me, mindin' my business as I was."

In the end they sent for Coggan, who vouched for Bartle to no avail: Bartle had been caught fighting, disturbing the peace, and he would have to be punished for it. Twenty-four hours in the stocks, said Bellingham. There was no right of appeal.

The stocks were set in the marketplace near the meeting house, the center of the settlement. People came by to have a look at Bartle, and small boys threw stones at him, and mudballs, and clots of dung. They jeered at him, and taunted him by name, for many people knew him. The day was warm: an Indian summer day. Soon Bartle was parched with thirst, and hungry, too, for he had had no supper the night before. A trickle of muddy sweat ran down his face. He glanced at MacPherson, imprisoned in another set of stocks beside him; but MacPherson was dead to the world, in a fair way to strangle himself as he dangled from his neck and hands.

Bartle told himself that by this time tomorrow he would be free to go about his business again—his and Coggan's. It was a prosperous business, and Bartle had a good share in it.

The sun rose in the sky, hotter and hotter. Bartle's throat was increasingly dry and raw. He shut his eyes; seeing the sun beating on the dusty marketplace made him even thirstier.

"Here—drink this."

A female voice. He opened his eyes. She stood before him holding a pewter cup filled with beer. She held it to his lips, tipping it so he could drink. It was cold and tangy—the best beer he had ever tasted.

"Thank you, mistress." He peered at her; she was silhouetted against the sun and he could not see her face clearly. He thought she was smiling at him, but he was not sure. He had no idea who she was.

2

Bartle had gone to Boston in 1631, a year after its beginnings. What he found was a rough little settlement at the edge of the harbor. The place was nearly an island, connected to the mainland by a long neck that was often submerged in stormy weather; what little land there was to build on was cramped around the several hills.

He found, too, that Boston had suffered very nearly as much as Plymouth during the first winter: almost half the company had died, and those who lived were so ill—and so frozen in the harsh New England cold—that they could hardly move, let alone do the work needed to make a settlement.

John Winthrop was their governor: a devout Puritan, a lawyer shrewd enough to bring their charter with him, thereby assuring at least partial independence from the financial backers of their corporation. Winthrop came across in the *Arbella*, one of the eleven ships of their fleet carrying nearly a thousand passengers. They intended to settle at Salem, where a preliminary group had landed with John Endicott in 1628. But Salem was unsatisfactory; or perhaps Winthrop disliked the place because his son, Henry, drowned in a creek there not two weeks after they arrived. And so they came into the Massachusetts Bay, to Charlestown, where several hardy souls had made their houses a few years before.

Charlestown lacked water, however; and so at last they dispersed. In August of 1630 some of them came to Boston—or Shawmut, as it was known: "fountains of living water." They were invited to settle by its sole white inhabitant, the Reverend William Blackstone. He was an Anglican minister who, seeking solitude, had built a house on the western side of the Tramount. A good spring flowed nearby, he said; and because the Shawmut peninsula had few trees, it was free of those three great annoyances of the wilderness forest, "Woolves, Rattle-snakes, and Musketos."

Like all men of his type, Winthrop had a vision, and he labored every day of his life to see it fulfilled. While the company was still on board ship, before he ever knew of Shawmut, he had with strange prescience preached a lay sermon: "We shall be as a Citty uppon a Hill," he had said. "The eyes of all people are upon Us, so that if we deal falsely with our god in this work we have undertaken, and so cause him to withdraw his present help from us, we shall be made a story and a by-word through the world."

The Reverend Blackstone soon grew to regret his generosity; so many people poured in that, despite the fact that his house was well away from the main settlement, he felt cramped and besieged. And so he picked himself up and rode away on a white bull, and sold Boston to John Winthrop for £30—more than the island of Manhattan had cost the Dutch, but a bargain all the same.

Bartle had brought with him a letter of introduction to the merchant John Coggan. He caught up with Coggan on the Town Dock, and when he told who had recommended him, Coggan put down the load he had been carrying and held out his hand in greeting.

"Roger Conant! How do you know him?"

"I've lived with him in Salem and Beverly these past eight years," said Bartle.

"Did y'come over with him?"

"No. He came to Plymouth, where I was. In '23. And in '24, when he left, I left with him."

With no hard feelings toward Bradford or the Allertons, he might have added; but when Conant offered him his chance to leave Plymouth, he had been glad enough to go—to try a new place to see what it offered.

"And now you've come here looking for work?"

"Yes, sir." Again, no hard feelings; but it had been time to leave the Conants.

Coggan was delighted. He was a busy man, and he desperately needed help.

"You can start now," he said, "and we'll talk terms later." And without another word he heaved the load of beaver skins into Bartle's arms and motioned toward his little warehouse at the head of the dock.

3

John Coggan believed what Bartle told him about the fight: the magistrate had made a mistake, Bartle had committed no crime. "He did you an injustice, true," Coggan said, "but you have no way to make it right. Best leave it be. Lucky he didn't fine you into the bargain."

Bartle realized that this was good advice; the authority of the magistrates was absolute. He might have taken the matter to the General Court, but the proceedings would have been lengthy, costly in time and money both, and the outcome far from certain.

And besides: the Lord worked in mysterious ways. Perhaps his misfortune would turn out to be the best fortune he had ever had.

Boston had a few thousand people; it was not difficult, in the days that followed his release, to discover the identity of the young woman who had brought him a drink. Her name was Susannah; she was the daughter of William Hatherly, a modestly successful merchant who had brought his family over only the month before. They lived near the Mill Pond.

One evening a week later, when Coggan let him leave work early, Bartle walked around to the Hatherlys' house. Their servant girl answered; then William Hatherly himself came to the door.

"Yes?" Although he had seen the young man in the stocks, he did not recognize Bartle now—clean-shaven, his hair neatly dressed under his beaver hat, a clean white linen shirt under his good wool coat.

"I have come to thank you, sir," said Bartle, "for your daughter's kindness."

Hatherly knew who he was, then; ever alert for his children's welfare, he had taken the trouble to inquire around the town: tell me about Coggan's assistant; what's he like?

And everywhere he had had the same answer: a fine young fellow, one of the most likely young men in the Colony. The stocks? A mistake, probably. So now Hatherly was not so hostile as he might have been, and he asked Bartle to come in and take a bite to eat.

In the Hatherly family were two brothers older than Susannah, two sisters younger, and a little boy not five years old by the look of him. Mrs. Hatherly heaped a wooden trencher with roasted fowl and a generous helping of stewed pumpkin and cornmeal mush; Mr. Hatherly filled a horn cup with beer and motioned Bartle to a seat. Bartle glanced at Susannah. She stood behind her mother with her eyes modestly downcast; she was very pretty, dark-haired, rosy-cheeked. She glanced at him: she caught his eye and smiled, showing an enchanting dimple; then modestly she looked down again.

Bartle felt a curious sensation in the region of his heart. He realized that Mr. Hatherly was saying something that he had missed.

Hatherly saw that Susannah was blushing, and Bartle, for all his courteous replies, kept looking at her as if he could never tear his eyes away. Hatherly smiled to himself. When the young man took his leave, he invited him to return the next day but one—"Don't come tomorrow. We'll be at Mrs. Hutchinson's. Have you heard her meditations on the Word?"

"No, sir." Bartle knew who Ann Hutchinson was: a woman who held religious meetings at her home in the evenings. At first she had admitted only women, but lately men had been welcome, too.

"So, daughter," said Hatherly when Bartle was gone. "You will not die barren after all, from the looks of him."

To which Susannah did not reply, but blushed more furiously than ever, and clapped her pretty, dimpled hands over her ears to shut out the laughter of her brothers and sisters.

For his part, Bartle lay awake half the night in Coggan's loft, listening to the rain beat against the house, shifting once or twice to avoid the leaks in the thatched roof. He held Susannah in his mind's eye like some rare treasure; over and over and over again he gazed at her sparking dark blue eyes, the wisps of dark hair that showed beneath her spotless white cap, her pretty red lips, her plump, shapely form under her modest dress.

Even if her father had forbidden him to call again, he would have gone to see her; nothing could have kept him away. As it was, he understood that Mr. Hatherly looked on him favorably, and so he had no hesitation in going as often as he could—three or four evenings a week. Still he was not satisfied, for like every other family, the Hatherlys lived cheek by jowl in their little house, the front room serving as kitchen and parlor and sleeping quarters for the parents, the back room and the loft for the children to sleep in, and no privacy anywhere. On the evenings when they went to Mrs. Hutchinson's meetings, Susannah went along. After a month of visits, Bartle still had not spoken a word to her alone.

One Thursday afternoon, therefore, after the Reverend Cotton's weekly Lecture, he called for her and asked if she would like to walk out—up the Tramount, where there was a splendid view. With a glance at her mother for permission, since her father was attending to business at the Town Dock, she took her cloak from the peg and followed him out.

It was a mild day toward the end of November, one of those last, lingering autumn days that never failed to deceive the newcomers: with such weather so late in the year, how could the winters be as bad as people said? A warm sun shone in a milky blue sky, making them glad of the little breeze from the southwest. As they walked away from the settlement toward the three hills, past the Common with its grazing cows, Bartle glanced down at her. She walked steadily along, looking at the path before her, her hands folded into her dark green cape. Her rosy face had a happy look; a little smile played at the corners of her mouth, and once, passing a pair of women whom she knew, she sang out a greeting to them, enlivened by a laugh because she was happy and she did not care who knew it. The women stared after her—after the pair of them—and then put their heads together. Little happened in women's lives in the Bay Colony; therefore they must get what entertainment they could from their neighbors' affairs.

Halfway up Beacon Hill Bartle took Susannah's hand. The thrill of that touch sent an alarm tingling through him—he had never felt such a thing, but he understood well enough what it meant. When they reached the top, she was panting more than he.

She leaned against the tall pole that held the beacon; gradually she recovered her breath. She did not look at him; she kept her eyes modestly down. But all the same, she let him keep her hand, so small and soft in his big hard callused paw, and she did not even flinch when he enclosed hers with his other. She let him; and at last, her smile fading now because of the seriousness of the moment, she ventured to look up at him, to speak to him without saying a word, to let her lovely eyes linger on his.

He longed to kiss her, but he did not dare, not even here where they were alone, for prying eyes were everywhere, and here at the top of the highest point in Boston they were plainly visible to anyone who cared to look. Kissing in public was a crime; only last month a man had been whipped for kissing his wife while standing on his own doorstep. And so, after a moment, he broke the spell and turned away; he gazed at the panorama spreading beneath them, beyond Cotton's Hill and over the huddled rooftops of the little settlement, the Town Dock, the barques and ketches at anchor, and to the mouth of the inner harbor where lay Castle Island with its fortifications, and the Governor's Garden planted with its orchard years ago by Roger Conant; then beyond to the island-studded outer harbor, to Spectacle Island and Thompson's, to Long Island and Deer Island and, to the northeast, over the mud flats between Noddle's and Governor's, to Nahant and Linn. From beyond the Mill Pond and Charlestown flowed the Mystic, and from the west the Charles came past New-towne; south beyond Dorchester lay Big Blue Hill; then, as he completed the circle, he saw the arm of Nantasket curled into a fist enclosing the harbor—a miniature Cape Cod.

He wanted to tell her what promise this place held for those who knew how to work it, how to make it give up its riches—wood from the forest, fish from the sea, and always buy cheap and sell dear so that at the end of the day you had a profit to show.

The fairest land in all the world, it seemed to him just then; and because he did not know how to speak to her, how to bring her into his vision of what it could be—for him, for both of them—he stood holding her hand in the warm autumn sunshine and dreamed his private dream, and tried to think how to tell her that he wanted her to be a part of it.

4

Ann Hutchinson was a woman of rare spirit and ready wit who claimed to have a direct communion with God. Therefore she did not need ministers to preach false teaching to her. She did not believe what the ministers taught: a

Covenant of Works—laboring all one's life to gain God's grace, which might in the end, at the Day of Judgment, not prove sufficient to get into Heaven after all. Her own Covenant of Grace, she said—personal knowledge of God's love—was all anyone needed to be saved from the flames of Hell.

Because that was the great question—the problem that tormented them all: how did one know that a place in Heaven awaited?

How did one know that one's life had been sufficiently blameless? How did one know that one's works were sufficiently good?

The ministers were no help. They preached fear and trembling—walking the narrow path of righteousness. Ah, but was the path narrow enough? Was one's righteousness strict enough? Did God even see it—take note of it, mark it down in one's favor in His great ledger, the final account book, tallying up the saved, the damned? One to the left, to Hell; one to the right, to Paradise . . .

Of course there were some—the leaders of the Colony, mostly—whom everyone assumed were saved: and those men themselves were sure of it. Winthrop, Dudley, Bellingham; the new young man for whom everyone had such great hopes, Sir Harry Vane; the Eliots, the Saltonstalls, the learned Reverend Richard Mather, the ministers Cotton and Wilson.

And yet . . . who knew for certain? The flesh was weak, opportunities for sinning lay all around, sure traps for the unwary. Only recently the General Court had passed the sumptuary laws: severe restrictions on dress, prohibitions against new and immodest fashions, against gold and silver threads and laces, against slashed clothes (save one slash in each sleeve and another in the back)—and against any man wearing long hair, which was a vanity that the Massachusetts Bay Colony would not tolerate.

Some said that the legislation had an economic motive: the less the Colony imported from the mother country, the quicker it would become self-sufficient. But most people saw the act for what it was: an attempt to keep the population upon the straight and narrow path to righteousness—particularly the women, who were so much weaker in spirit than the men, so much less able to understand what God wanted. If they could not keep themselves from sinning, the General Court would do it for them.

And now came Mrs. Hutchinson, in the very month that the sumptuary laws were passed, spreading her transcendental message, telling people that they could experience communion with God all by themselves, just as she did; they did not need the black-coats to tell them what God wanted.

This was a dangerous idea—more dangerous even than the ideas of the Reverend Roger Williams, who believed that women should wear veils. Worse, and more to the point, he preached strict separation from the Anglican Church—not a Puritan belief—and denounced the validity of Winthrop's charter, and argued for the separation of church and state. For these heresies he was summoned from his post at Salem to the General Court, but he would not come. He took to the woods in the middle of winter rather than face the ministers at Boston; eventually he fetched up in Rhode Island, a place which would, in time, become a veritable sewer of heresy, refuge to all manner of misfits—Baptists, Quakers, the scum of the world, and none of it welcome in the Massachusetts Bay.

Mrs. Hutchinson knew the Reverend Williams's fate, but she was not afraid: she had her faith to sustain her. She was a clever woman, the wife of a merchant, the daughter of a minister who had educated her far beyond the learning of most women. Further, she was a midwife: she had helped birth many new lives into the world, and women trusted her.

The authorities, on the other hand, were suspicious of Mrs. Hutchinson from the moment she arrived. Watch her, they said: she is dangerous.

And because she was considered dangerous, so were people like the Hatherlys, who went to hear her.

5

One bleak February day Bartle had a stroke of luck. Josse, the eldest Hatherly son, put his head into Coggan's store in the middle of the afternoon and greeted Bartle with a smile and a twinkle in his eye. "If you can get away, there's someone at the house who'll be by herself for a bit. She'd be glad of company."

Coggan was at the dock. Since the store could not be left unattended, Bartle ran next door and called for Coggan's eldest son, just twelve, just home from his classes at Master Pormont's. The boy looked none too happy, but he came.

Susannah was alone, as promised, sitting by the fire and sewing a shirt. She was not surprised to see him—far from it, since it was she who had sent her brother on his errand. Her father was at his business; her mother was at a neighbor's lying-in; her brothers were at work; her younger sisters and the little boy were spending a week with their uncle in Rocksborough.

Bartle did not waste time with words. The moment he stepped inside he drew her to him and kissed her red lips, her soft pink cheeks, her white throat with its little pulse throbbing just at the edge of her high-necked dress. Blood rushed to his head and he heard his heart pounding until he thought that both his heart and his head would burst. In all the times that he had imagined this moment, he had not dreamed that it would be so. How could he? He had never kissed a woman before; he had hungered—for what, he did not know. Only now, crushing her in his arms, did he understand what it was that he had wanted so desperately—to make her one with him, to bind her to him for all time.

And how strong she was! How tightly her arms went around his neck, drawing him down to her, clinging to him with an ardor that matched his own. He had not dreamed that a woman could be passionate, too, as hungry for him as he was for her. He put his hand on her breast and felt its fullness underneath the soft wool of her dress, the rigid nipple that he longed to suck—he reached up for her hand and guided it down to his straining member—sweet agony! If her hand inflamed him so, what would the luscious enclosure of her soft, sweet body do?

In the end it was he who drew back, he who raised his head and gasped for air like a drowning man. Her face was rubbed raw from his stubble of beard, her cap had fallen off, her lustrous dark hair half undone down her back—if anyone should discover them!

"I will speak to your father," he said. His voice was choked; he was surprised that he was able to speak at all.

"Yes," she said. "Speak to him—when?"

"Tonight—today! Do you—will he say yes?"

Foolish man: he did not yet know how a beloved daughter can twist an indulgent father around her finger. "Yes," she said. She smiled at him with absolute certainty, sure of her power.

William Hatherly was surprised only that Bartle had waited so long to ask for Susannah's hand. The whole family—the entire town, for that matter—knew that the two were in love. That, of course, would have mattered little if Bartholomew Revell had been an unsuitable match; but he was eminently suitable, lacking only church membership to make him nearly the perfect son-in-law—not a little thing, to be sure, but it would come. Each man in his own time. Most of the Colony, in fact, were not church members, although the magistrates decreed that everyone attend services. Some did; some did not. Had everyone decided to go to church, the little mud-walled meeting house could not have held them all.

Still, a man must not think that he was getting William Hatherly's daughter too easily, and so when Bartle came to him, he put on a stern face and eyed the young man warily.

"What have you to offer?" he said. "My Susannah must have a good home, a good husband. I will not see her live in poverty."

Of course Bartle had expected this interrogation, and he had his answers ready. "I am nearly five years at Mr. Coggan's," he said, "and all that time I have had a share of his profits. This spring I will have a quarter share in the London shipment—a hundred pounds and more."

Hatherly's eyebrows rose slightly. It was a much higher figure than he had expected. "Indeed? And you've no debts?"

"No, sir. I know I don't appear to be a gentleman, but I'll wager I have more estate than many a man dressed finer than I am."

Which was true enough: a suit of armor and a fine white ruff like Governor Winthrop's were often deceptive; Hatherly had heard rumors, in fact, that the governor's affairs were not so well run as they might be, since Winthrop spent all his time on matters of state and left the management of his plantations to a steward.

"You plan to stay in Boston, of course." Hatherly wanted no adventurer taking his Susannah into the wilderness—or, worse, back to England.

"Yes."

"And go on your own?"

"Yes. It needs connections—an acquaintance with merchants in London, even if only by trading. They are coming to know me because I work for Mr. Coggan. In time they will deal with me direct."

Hatherly nodded approvingly. What Bartle said was sound and sensible; he would not set up for himself until he was sure that he could succeed alone. With the constant influx of newcomers needing supplies, even the most dim-witted man could not but succeed—even given the price limits imposed by the court. Too great a profit was seen as contrary to Christian teaching; the merchants were forbidden to exploit the needs of the new settlers by charging too much, and wages were regulated as well.

"Very well," he said, smiling at last. "You shall have her." He paused; both men knew that they were not done yet with their bargaining. "As for her dowry . . . a portion to match your own." It was a generous offer, but hardly too much for the apple of his eye.

Both men were very pleased. They shook hands; Hatherly shouted for Susannah—for the entire family, who had waited in the back room. A bottle of brandy appeared; everyone drank a toast. Susannah kissed her father, then Bartle, then her brothers and sisters; lastly she embraced her dear mother, whose company she was about to enter—the company of married women, privy to all the secret knowledge of life and birth and death, the joys and sorrows of bearing a family and caring for it.

Later, when Bartle departed, Susannah stayed with him a moment outside the door. Clear and cold—bitter cold, for February was the coldest month. The night sky was filled with stars, more stars than any man could ever count, so thick in places that they crowded out the sky.

They kissed. Her mouth was soft and warm, her response to his embrace quick and eager. How he loved her! And as he made his way to Coggan's over the frozen, muddy way, he thought that he was the most fortunate man in the world, and he wanted nothing more than to work—for her, for the two of them, for the family that would come.

6

That summer of 1636, John Gallop of Boston, sailing through Narragansett Bay, spied a boat near Block Island that he knew belonged to John Oldham, the noted Indian trader. He saw several Indians on the deck, but no sign of Oldham. When he cried a greeting, the Indians, instead of answering, hurriedly descended into their canoe and paddled away. Gallop and his son decided not to give chase; instead, they boarded Oldham's pinnace. They found Oldham lying dead. He had been butchered, hacked to death and his parts cut off.

Gallop was as hardened as any man to life in the wilderness, but this mass of mangled flesh was too much even for him. He felt his gorge rise, and he staggered to the rail and vomited. He knew that he and his son were in peril of their lives: the savages who had murdered Oldham would not hesitate to kill again.

The colonists lived in constant fear of an Indian uprising—a concerted blow by all the tribes against the frail little margin of white settlement huddled along the coast. If this affair was the warning of such an attack, the authorities in the Bay needed to be alerted at once. The drifting boat, the calm sea, the wide blue sky—it was a landscape of peace and beauty, and yet this bloody mess before him spoke louder than any shouted warning of the horrors that lay in wait. Oldham had been a trusted friend of the Indians, he had traded with them for years. If they could kill him, no white man was safe.

The governor that year was Sir Harry Vane, a charming young man and a Hutchinsonian. He had only just come over. The older settlers—Winthrop, Dudley, Bellingham—did not like him; further, they did not trust him to govern wisely.

When Sir Harry heard Gallop's tale, he ordered John Endicott of Salem to take a party of ninety men to Block Island and exterminate every Indian brave and capture the women and children.

Endicott did so. Then he proceeded to Connecticut and began to slaughter Indians there.

7

In August Bartle bought a piece of land out toward Merry's Point in the North End and hired a carpenter to build a house. It was the same as every other house in Boston save for John Winthrop's, which was very grand, and William Coddington's, which was made of brick. It had a front and back room surrounding a great center chimney of wattle and daub, a loft above, a cow barn in the rear, plenty of space for a garden and a small planting of apple trees. To Bartle and Susannah it was the finest house ever built.

The banns were read before the middle of September, and at the end of the month Governor Vane married them.

Afterward the Hatherlys hosted the wedding feast. Bartle was intoxicated—not from the wine and the good dark English beer, but from love. He could not take his eyes from her; and she, loving him as well, felt nevertheless a little pang of regret that she was leaving her parents and the security of their household to go even the short distance away to entrust herself to him.

But it was only a brief regret—only a last farewell to her girlhood. And when the time came for the guests to see them to their new home, she walked gladly in the warm autumn dusk over the bridge at the mill to the fine place Bartle had built for her. A garland of sea anemone had been placed over the door, and the new-laid wide board floor was strewn with dried herbs. The cupboard was filled with pewter and crockery, the wide hearth hung with ironware, the great bed in the corner fitted out with her mother's best quilt over the new straw mattress.

At last they were alone. They stood together, suddenly self-conscious, getting used to each other. They heard the cry of a loon from the marsh; then an owl hooted in reply. Bartle embraced her, kissing her sweet, soft face, her warm lips. After a while, as her mother had instructed, she bade him turn away while she undressed and put on her nightshift. Then she was ready for him—for him, and for whatever it was that he must do to her to make her truly his wife. She did not fear it: she had heard all the garbled, giggled hints and rumors that girls are fond of exchanging, but still she knew next to nothing. She did not care: she trusted her husband to do what was right, and she would obey him as she had promised to do.

His hands trembled so that he could hardly hold her. They lay together in the sweet-smelling bed and touched each other like two strangers. What is it, she wondered: what will happen? She lay beside him, submissive, not knowing what to do; then slowly she felt her love for him overtake her, and she felt her body open to his.

Man and wife, they loved each other all that night in their small wooden house on the shore of the vast continent—how vast, no one knew—within sound of the ocean's great waves, vulnerable to plague and massacre and wild beasts of the forest.

None of that mattered. Here they were safe, here they were together.

8

That fall, Endicott's reprisals bore bitter fruit, and now at last, it seemed, there was to be a war with the Indians.

On a bright blue day in October Bartle was on his way to the Town Dock when he saw Isaac Allerton, with whom he had lived at Plymouth, and whom Bartle had not seen in more than ten years. After an exchange of greetings, Bartle asked what brought the older man to the Bay.

Allerton's face, which had brightened briefly at seeing how well Bartle looked, darkened as he hunted for words to tell his news.

"I'm just on my way to the governor. We've had bad news. John Tilley's been killed. No—not the man who came over with us to Plymouth, although he may be a relation. The Pequots took him north of Saybrook, in the Connecticut Valley. His murder is bad enough. But the way they killed him—" Allerton's voice broke; he looked away while he brushed a tear from his eye. "We heard they cut off his hands and feet, and tied him to a stake while they flayed his skin off and put the hot coals next his flesh. It was three days before he died, and never a cry escaped him."

Bartle thought of Squanto, and of the sachem Massasoit, who had always been their friend. But they were Wampanoags. The Pequots were different: warlike, jealous of their territory.

The General Court was deeply concerned at Allerton's news; in fact they were so alarmed that they sent for help to Roger Williams in Rhode Island, whom they had hounded out of the Colony only months before. But now they asked him to treat with the Narragansetts, among whom he lived, to ask them to remain loyal to the English and not to join forces with the Pequots.

Within days, Williams sent a delegation of Narragansetts to Boston to sign a treaty of peace. To show their good faith with the English, they promised to send a present, and shortly it arrived: forty fathoms of wampum and the hand of a Pequot warrior. But the English knew that they were not safe even with the Narragansetts' promise of help. Williams had reported that the Pequots promised to use witchcraft to defeat the white man, and the power of the Devil was a threat to be reckoned with.

Over the next few months reports trickled into the Bay: English were being killed, picked off in Indian raids, one here, two there. The Indians fought by stealth, by surprise attack on isolated settlers; they never came on in a proper style of military assault.

Winter came. The whites in the Connecticut River Valley—the front line— watched night and day against an attack, but it did not come. Snow lay deep over the fields and in the forest; the smaller rivers froze; the settlers clung to their hearths and listened for the blood-curdling sound of a war whoop. They heard nothing. The Pequots stayed in their camps.

But in April, in planting time, nine whites at Wethersfield were massacred as they worked the fields. Their deaths made a total of thirty English killed since Oldham's murder.

The English mobilized; in the Bay the General Court ordered a call-up, a troop of 160 men from the various towns. But it was Connecticut men who had the first victory: allied with the Mohegans, they ordered Chief Uncas to prove his loyalty. He did so: he exterminated a small band of Pequots, bringing back four heads and one prisoner who was known to the English as a spy.

The white men gave John Tilley his vengeance: they tied one of the prisoner's legs to a stake, put a rope on the other, and pulled him apart. Then, because he still lived, they shot him. The Mohegans roasted him; then they ate him.

9

"You must not tell her," Mrs. Hatherly said to Bartle. "Such news—such terrible thoughts—can harm the baby."

To their joy, Bartle had gotten Susannah with child almost at once. She was to be brought to bed some time in early July. Bartle never tired of looking at her: she had grown as plump as a setting hen, and she bloomed with good health. He could not do enough for her—fetching her dinner, doing half her chores, forbidding her ever to climb the ladder to the loft. He heartily agreed with his mother-in-law: his wife must know nothing of atrocities, nothing of Chief Uncas and his cannibals. But she found out anyway—how, he never knew—and she went a little pale, and sat down hard on the bench by the fire, the color draining from her face as she questioned him. "Is it true? Did such a thing really happen?"

Brusquely he forbade her to speak of it; he wished that he knew of some charm to work on her, to exorcise the image from her mind. Nothing mattered now, except that the child be born safely. She must not worry about Indian attack, he said. The Pequot War was far away, in Connecticut; no savage would harm them here in the safety of Boston. The narrow neck that was their bridge to the mainland was well fortified; no Indian could breach it. And then, when he saw that she was still afraid, he began to tell her stories of his youth, in Plymouth: of Squanto's teachings, of Winslow's successful treating with Massasoit, of the Harvest Home at the close of the Colony's first year, when ninety braves came to the feast.

He sat beside her; she rested her dark head on his shoulder. He could see the soft rise and fall of her swelling bosom beneath the gray stuff of her dress, and the larger swelling at her abdomen that was their child. He would kill and roast a hundred Indians, he thought, to keep her safe. Damned devils! Could they not understand that they had no hope, that the whites were fated by God to make this land their own?

In late May the English massacred several hundred Pequots at Mystic Fort in Connecticut: they set the Indian camp on fire, and they shot those who tried to escape. Most—women and children, as well as men—were burned alive within their wigwams.

The General Court set aside June 15 as a day of thanksgiving. The Pequot chief, Sassacus, was still at large, but his life was worthless; he would be captured or killed soon enough. Already the neighboring tribes were helping to exterminate the Pequots: to prove their good faith with the white men, whose hot-mouthed weapons they so greatly feared, they sent in Pequot heads by the dozen. And in August the Mohawks got Sassacus, and they sent his scalp to Hartford. The remaining Pequots—women and children, mostly—were parceled out to the other tribes; some were taken by the English as slaves.

From this war the English learned much: to better fortify their settlements; to cooperate among themselves; to use the red men as scouts, but not to depend on them for fighting; to keep a monopoly on weapons—never, never give a gun to an Indian! And, perhaps most important of all, to divide and conquer: to make allies of as many tribes as possible, so that the savages would kill each other, and so do the white man's work for him.

10

One hot night toward the end of June, Susannah woke with a cry. At once Bartle sat up; usually he slept heavily, but the past few weeks he had been wakeful, as if some part of him was always listening for the call that now had come.

He lit a candle; anxiously he peered at his wife. She was perspiring, her hair in dark tangles across the pillow, her plump face pale, her eyes large and dark with worry.

"Shall I call your mother?" he said.

"No. Wait. She said that sometimes there is a false alarm, particularly with the first birth."

This he knew, but not much else. Birthing was women's work; the very thought of it terrified him. Susannah would have the best of care, he knew: not only her mother, who was wise as all women were in such matters, but Mrs. Hutchinson as well.

He took her hand, but she pulled away; it was too hot to touch him, too hot to lie under even a light coverlet. She threw it off; she lifted her nightdress and fanned herself with it. He caught a glimpse of her enormous abdomen. He shuddered. Nothing could stop the process now, she had to go through with it, she had to make that journey down into the Valley of the Shadow of Death that all women knew so well. Men died in war, women in childbed; Death walked hand in hand with life, and it was no wonder that people fought about the way to get to Heaven, the way to sidestep Hell.

Susannah moaned. It had been ten minutes, at least, since that first pain; but still she would not let him fetch help. "Let them sleep awhile longer," she said. "This is only the beginning."

Slow pains came to her till dawn; then they stopped. Nevertheless at breakfast time Bartle hurried to his in-laws'. Mrs. Hatherly set at once to gathering the provisions she had laid by—a few pieces of the baby's linen, a basket of food and bottles of groaning beer for the women who would be in attendance. "Go to Mrs. Hutchinson's," she said. "I doubt she'll come right away, but she might just want to look in."

The town was beginning to set about its business on this bright, hot summer's day. Already the cowherd was gathering up his flock to walk them to the Common, and the hogreeve was on the prowl for stray swine; boys were in the gardens, weeding; a steady stream of men was heading toward the Town Dock; from a distance Bartle heard the first clanging from the blacksmith's shop.

He found the Hutchinsons up and about. Mrs. Hutchinson smiled at him and said that she would be along shortly, as soon as she had fed her younger children. Bartle did not like Mrs. Hutchinson. He hoped that she would not go into a trance while she was midwifing, and drop the baby, perhaps.

By the time he returned to his house, Mrs. Hatherly had already arrived. She was sponging Susannah's face; then she got Susannah to her feet and tried to help her walk. But Susannah gave a great cry and nearly fell, so Mrs. Hatherly helped her back to bed and gave her a little beer, which soothed her.

Mrs. Hutchinson arrived shortly, bringing the birthing stool and a packet of herbs. She was calm and cheerful; birthing was her business, and she went about it in a businesslike way. First off, she told Bartle to leave. She never wanted men around when babies came; they interfered.

Soon some neighbor women came in, and the birthing party—always a convivial event—became a roomful of gossiping females. Any one of them was ready to help if necessary, but there was little for them to do, and so they stood by, giving Susannah moral support. Each of these women had had many children; the very sight of them cheered her, for they had survived the trial that she was now undergoing; and if they had survived, so would she.

Mrs. Hutchinson busied herself with her herbs, boiling horehound with a little wine. Before she held it to Susannah's lips she put her hands on the laboring woman's belly. The child within gave a great, wrenching heave; Susannah screamed.

"Hush, Susannah, you must not cry out. You only lose strength by it. Take deep breaths. Each time a pain comes, breathe out—hard—and push the baby along."

She lifted the cup to Susannah's mouth. "Drink this. It will help quicken the birth."

Susannah drank. It did not taste like wine; the herb had given it a bitter flavor, and it trickled down her throat like fire. Her body was on fire, too—she was soaked with perspiration, burning up. The pains were coming quicker now, tearing her body apart. If the savages caught her and cut her apart, she would feel no worse pain than this. Again, and again—*aaahhh!*

Their faces hung over her; she saw her mother, and Goody Samson, and Mistress Coddington. She clung to her mother's hand, but then she let go—she did not have the strength to hold on. Mrs. Hutchinson stood by. The faces blurred; everything was in fog. I am dying, Susannah thought; she tried to think of a prayer, but she could not. Voices faded in and out. Then, quite clearly, she heard Mrs. Hutchinson say, "It is time now. Get her up."

Their hands grappled with her. For a second or two the pain lessened and she understood what they did: they wanted her to get onto the birthing stool. She could not. Part of her body was being torn away, and if she moved she would sustain a great wound, she would bleed to death. But they were stronger than she. They lifted her; they put her on the stool. It was a little three-legged thing, no seat. The women gathered around, a circle of watchful faces—members of a secret sect overseeing the initiation of a new member.

Her mother and Mrs. Coddington held her upright. She felt the lower part of her body tear itself apart; any moment now it would fall away. The room was close, the rank smell of bodily fluids intermingling with the sharp scent of the herbs. If only they would let go—if she was to die, let it be in her bed, not falling onto the floor like an animal at their feet.

Mrs. Hutchinson knelt before her; she spread Susannah's legs and reached underneath. Susannah wanted to kick her away, but she had no strength. If Mrs. Hutchinson went away, perhaps the pain would stop; it was Mrs. Hutchinson who made her suffer. Down and down—harder and harder—she felt their hands gripping her. *Let me go!* And then Mrs. Hutchinson pulled—*aaahhh!*—but they did not hear her scream, for now they gave a great triumphant cry of their own.

It was born! Still joined to her by the thick slimy rope of flesh, but born and safe and well. A boy—thank the Lord.

Skillfully Mrs. Hutchinson wrapped him in a cloth and gave him to someone to hold while she cut the cord. Everyone was craning to see, clucking and chuckling like a flock of hens. Susannah heard the baby's cry, and she felt her heart respond. She wanted to hold him, but they would not let her.

Instead Mrs. Hutchinson was giving her another bad-smelling thing to drink—*faugh!*—and then she bent over her, kneading her abdomen. "We must get the afterbirth, Susannah. Then you can rest. See—he is a beautiful baby, you can hear how he cries, so strong and healthy. You must suckle him at once, you have plenty of milk to make him grow—there." She reached down, retrieved what she sought, examined it briefly and threw it into a dish. Then they got Susannah back into bed, and her mother washed her face and gave her another drink—cool water, this time, the sweetest drink Susannah ever tasted—and under all their admiring gaze she suckled her child. A little red mite, he was, but perfectly formed, tiny hands grasping at the air, tiny mouth pulling at her nipple, a soft pale down over his tiny skull. She could see the steady pulse throbbing at his crown. First fruit was the strongest, her mother had said, and indeed it seemed to be so. She had never known a joy to match what she felt now, holding him in her arms. Her firstborn!

They had sent for Bartle, and now he came in, a lone male in this company of females: he seemed out of place here in his own house. The women were at the table eating the dinner that Mrs. Hatherly had prepared for them; they greeted him cheerfully and went on with their meal.

Bartle bent over his wife; she saw his anxious face relax into a smile. "It went well?" he said.

"Yes," she said. Already she was forgetting her torments, so glad was she to have pleased him.

The baby had fallen asleep at her breast. Her mother came and took him away; Bartle gave her a kiss; and then she slept. The long summer twilight darkened the room; the women went home.

They named the baby Jedediah. The next day the Reverend Wilson baptized him, sprinkling his head with a few drops of the precious water that would keep him safe.

11

That fall the ministers of the Bay Colony held a synod at Newtowne to stamp out heresy. For twenty-four days they met. They wrestled with eighty-two opinions—blasphemies and errors—and nine unwholesome expressions.

To strengthen them in their resolve, the Reverend John Wilson told them a marvelous tale lately brought in from Watertown: a mouse and a snake had met in mortal combat there, and the mouse had triumphed. They took it as evidence of their own eventual triumph over the arch snake, Satan.

In the course of their deliberations they wrestled also with their brother, the Reverend John Cotton, who was a supporter of Mrs. Hutchinson. In the end they were too strong for him, and he capitulated; he acknowledged his errors—and hers; he saw the light.

In November the General Court arraigned Mrs. Hutchinson for criticizing the ministers. The theological details of the case were obscure then, and were to become well-nigh incomprehensible as time went on, but theology was not the point. The point was power.

They put her under house arrest in Rocksborough for the winter; then they summoned her followers and disenfranchised them and took away their weapons. John Winthrop gave the order; he acted, he said, on the instructions of the clergy.

12

"They've done it!" Bartle and Susannah were at supper when her father burst in. He was distraught, panting for breath, his graying hair windblown. When they sat him down and gave him a drink of beer, they saw that his hands shook.

"What, Father? What is it?" Susannah knew that it must be something very serious, for he neglected to ask to see the baby.

"Mrs. Hutchinson is under arrest! No Hutchinsonian man may vote until he repents and disavows her! And every one of her followers is to turn in his gun to Captain Keayne."

There was a shocked silence. Then Susannah asked: "What will you do, Father?"

"Do? What can I do? I must obey, or else we will have a civil war. And that of course is what John Winthrop fears, and the ministers along with him. They fear that Mrs. Hutchinson—or her followers—will overthrow them. And so they have moved to prevent it."

Bartle said little; Hatherly would make his own decision, he needed no advice from his son-in-law. But later, pondering the issue before he went to sleep, holding Susannah in his arms as he listened to the night wind whistle around the house, the watch crying the hour, he thought that surely God must not want His children to spend their time quarreling one with another. The Hutchinsons, on the one hand, and the ministers and the magistrates on the other, all had a common interest, after all: they had a new land to build, a fresh start at a new life. Why waste strength on these disputes? What mattered if one got to Heaven by Grace, another by Works?

And, pulling her closer, he thought: this is all that I want. Let others fight over the will of God: leave me out of it. I will work for my wife and children (for Susannah was with child again); if God wants to punish me for lack of devotion, I will run the risk. All I ask is a full belly and a good snug roof over my head, a portion to leave to my children, a place to live in peace.

That winter some of the Hutchinsonians left the Bay Colony; others confessed their errors and were allowed to vote and carry their weapons again. William Hatherly was among those who stayed. On the bitter December evening of the day he made his confession, he walked home in a daze; he hardly responded to his wife's anguished questions, he was unable to eat what she put in front of him. From that day he was a broken man.

13

The following March Mrs. Hutchinson was tried on thirty counts of an ecclesiastical indictment. She attempted to save herself: she admitted error, she humiliated herself before her enemies who so hated and feared her. But she was one woman against many men, and her followers had been rendered impotent.

The ministers showed her no mercy. They had to vanquish her to save their own souls: hatred for a troublesome female aside, they risked God's wrath—not to mention control of the Massachusetts Bay Colony—if they did not silence her and cast her out.

They found her guilty. The Reverend Wilson, with her old friend and pastor John Cotton looking on, read to her her excommunication:

> "Therefore in the name of the Lord Jesus Christ and in the name of the church I do not only pronounce you worthy to be cast out, but I do cast you out; and in the name of Christ I do deliver you up to Satan, that you may learn no more to blaspheme, to seduce and to lie; and I do account you from this time forth to be a Heathen and a Publican, and so to be held of all the Brethren and Sisters of this congregation and of others: therefore I command you in the name of Christ Jesus and of this church as a Leper to withdraw yourself out of the congregation."

As Mrs. Hutchinson left the church, only one friend went with her, a comely young woman named Mary Dyer.

"Who is that?" someone asked.

"Oh," said another, "it is the woman which had the monster."

The monster! What business was this, then? Instantly John Winthrop went to dig it up where it had been buried. In the cold March night he and his companions stood around the little grave. Their faces were illuminated by the light of a flaring torch; and perhaps it was those leaping flames that made them look so like fiends, like the Devil's henchmen. Their eyes gleamed, their nostrils flared; some of them dribbled little trickles of spit from their trembling lips. Silently they urged the servant on; and when he removed the last spadeful of earth and reached in to lift out that pitiful bundle, not a man present had any pity at all, not for Mary Dyer, who had borne it into the world, not for the monster itself—for it was that, misshapen, grotesquely deformed.

The servant held it for them to see. Eagerly they crowded around. For certain, this was the Devil's spawn—dear Lord in Heaven, what a loathsome thing it was! One or two, weak in the stomach, turned away unable to bear the sight; but Winthrop was made of stronger stuff. He stared at it as if he would imprint the image on his brain for all time; he seemed fascinated by it, as if it appealed to some dark part of himself that he could not reveal to the light of day. A smile that was more nearly a sneer twisted his mouth. Yes—a monster! Brought forth by Mary Dyer, the friend of the Jezebel, Ann Hutchinson! He was not surprised: the Devil worked as mysteriously as God, and sometimes it seemed that the Devil's work was plainer to see. All women were the daughters of Eve, and any one of them liable for punishment for Eve's great sin.

Only recently he had had word of another troublesome woman, the wife of the governor in Connecticut. She had fallen away into madness, it seemed, and all because her husband was too lenient with her. She read books all day, and wrote many books, too, instead of tending to her housework. Her husband had not done his duty, had not punished her—and so the Lord had punished him by driving his wife mad.

Shortly Winthrop gave the order to bury the monster again. Then he dismissed his companions and returned to his house to take up his pen. For he was an assiduous writer: not only of government business, but of letters also, and, more important, a diary that would one day fill many volumes. He wrote in it with a curious lack of discrimination, great events jostling small, the vagaries of human nature taking their place alongside affairs of state. He loved to record sins of the flesh, and (even more interesting) mysterious bewitchments. Thus he wrote of the strange case of the sow that gave birth to a walleyed shoat; a half-witted fellow in the town, having a similar walleye, was arrested and questioned. He admitted his guilt with the sow, and so they hanged him.

This night, Winthrop thought for a long time; then with all the considerable eloquence at his command, he wrote:

> It was a woman child, stillborn, about two months before the just time, having life a few hours before; it came hiplings 'til she turned it; it was of ordinary bigness; it had a face, but no head, and the ears stood upon the shoulders and were like an ape's; it had no forehead, but over the eyes four horns, hard and sharp; two of them were above one inch long, the other two shorter; the eyes standing out, and the mouth also; the nose hooked upward; all over the breast and back full of sharp pricks and scales, like a thornback; the navel and all the belly, with the distinction of the sex, were where the back should be, and the back and hips before, where the belly should have been; behind, between the shoulders, it had two mouths, and in each of them a piece of red flesh sticking out; it had arms and legs as other children; but, instead

of toes, it had on each foot three claws, like a young fowl, with sharp talons.

The next day Winthrop sent a warrant of arrest to Mrs. Hutchinson. The day after that she and her family and a few friends, including Mary Dyer, boarded a boat at the Town Dock and made their way to Aquidneck in Rhode Island, where like so many others they took refuge near Roger Williams.

In time, after her husband's death, Ann Hutchinson left Rhode Island—after a quarrel with her followers there, some said. With her family she made her way into Long Island, where, in 1643, they were all murdered by Indians.

In April the Town of Boston and many of the towns surrounding were frightened by a great earthquake. Plates and tankards fell to the floor, house walls cracked open, chimneys fell, people in the streets were knocked to the ground, and some of them watched in horror as the earth opened at their feet in long, jagged fissures.

The wrath of God! For surely such an event was a sign of wrath, it could not be anything else.

But why was God angry with them? What had they done to incur His displeasure?

Could the earthquake possibly have to do with— No. Such a thought was ridiculous. God was not angry because they had sent Mrs. Hutchinson away. On the contrary, they were sure that He had wanted them to act so.

It was a great relief—and a sure sign of God's love—when a printing press soon arrived, for now the word of God could be more widely disseminated. But it was secular things that first came off the press: the Freeman's Oath, and then an almanac.

And then at last the ministers, the Reverend Richard Mather most prominent among them, labored over what would be the first book printed in the New World: a new version of the psalms (not better, but new); and Stephen Day over at the College, where the press had been set up, pulled the type and carefully inked it and fed in the precious sheets of sturdy paper, and brought it out: *The Whole Book of Psalmes Faithfully Translated into English Metre.*

Loudly they lifted their inharmonious voices:

> "The Lord to me a shepherd is,
> Want therefore shall not I."

That winter Indian slaves, the remaining captives of the Pequot War, were sold throughout the Massachusetts Bay. Mindful of his growing family (for Susannah had given birth again, and was pregnant for the third time), Bartle bought one to help her with her work. Twelve Indians had no buyers in Massachusetts; they were shipped for sale to the Bermudas.

3. SILVER AND GOLD

1

At the turn of the decade the Boston merchants were making good profits.

Six months into 1640 every one was hurting, and some were bankrupt.

Immigration had stopped. The Puritans had come to power in England; dissenters no longer needed to flee to the New World.

And without the endless stream of immigrants to the Massachusetts Bay wanting to buy the necessities of life, the merchants of Boston were ruined.

As the depression deepened, they grew desperate, and they looked about them to see how to survive.

2

"I must have those needles, and the ax and the saw," said the farmer, "and I'll give you these five bushels of corn for 'em, and the barley I'll throw in free."

They stood in Bartle's selling place by the wharf. It was the autumn of 1640, harvest time, and from all around the countryside men were coming in to trade, not just on market day, but every day of the week. They needed to get their business done before winter made travel difficult.

Bartle shook his head. "I can't use your corn, Goodman Fiske. I've no one to trade it to here, as you know."

"Take the cow, then. She's a good milker, you'll trade her right off."

"No. I've no market for cattle, either."

"Keep her over the winter. We'll have new settlers in the spring, and you'll get good hard cash for her."

A year ago, around the time that Bartle had left John Coggan to go on his own, a cow had sold for £20. Now £4 was the usual price, but even at that, a cow was hard to sell. Certainly feeding her over the winter would wipe out any possible profit.

"No," said Bartle. "I've no use for a cow."

Fiske looked desperate. "I need those supplies," he said. "Give me credit and I'll pay you next year."

This was not possible, as both of them knew. No merchant in his right mind gave credit to a farmer.

Bartle turned away. Such haggling was a waste of time.

"Wait!" Fiske caught at his arm. "What about my land?"

"I have no use for land."

"You will, if new planters come in. But it won't come to that. Take a mortgage on it in exchange, and I'll pay it off by next year."

Suddenly Bartle felt sorry for this man—a man with a family to provide for, just like himself. Perhaps it was because on this day, Susannah was giving birth again: their fourth child, and two of them living. When a man had a family, he would do anything to provide for them, even mortgaging his land.

And so he agreed, and he gave Fiske the goods he wanted: nails, and an ax and saw, and skeins of thread, and a packet of needles, and an iron cookpot. He told himself he should be glad of any customers at all, given the state of business.

Shortly he went home to get his dinner and, more important, to see how Susannah did. Walking up the Broad Way from the dock, he nearly tripped over a rooting pig. She and her kind were an endless source of annoyance, breaking out of their pens and wandering into the neighbors' gardens seeking to satisfy their seemingly insatiable appetites. A good deal of the authorities' time was taken up adjudicating bitter feuds that started over marauding swine; once, in Charlestown, the owner of a trespassing pig was shot and wounded by the man whose land it had violated.

Bartle's mother-in-law greeted him at his door. She was all smiles, and in her arms she held a tiny red mite wrapped in flannel. "A girl," she beamed. "Isn't she beautiful?"

Bartle looked at her and said that, yes, she was, but in truth he was more interested in Susannah: how had she done?

"Wonderful well. Come and see for yourself."

As glad as he was to have the yearly arrival of a new child, he always dreaded the thought that he might, one time, lose Susannah. He could not imagine it. She had become so much a part of him that he could not contemplate a world without her. So while he always hoped for the birth of a healthy child—what man did not?—he always prayed that Susannah would survive the birth. He was not a praying man, but he could not but believe that God heard him at those times.

She was awake, tired and rather pale, but glad to see him. He bent to embrace her. He knew that the women gathered to help were watching him, but he did not care. His Susannah was safe and well; nothing else mattered.

Meanwhile the pig, which had escaped from its pen at Goody Sherman's, continued happily on its way. It meandered down toward the Common, snuffing out edible morsels as it went: sometimes odds and ends it found in the street, sometimes more substantial fare. Every now and then it found a way into someone's garden. With an air of innocence it walked right in, snuffing furiously, chomping relentlessly. It sampled a little pumpkin at the Reverend Cotton's, and a few beans at Governor Winthrop's, where it also munched down a windrift apple.

By and by it wandered into Captain Keayne's cornfield, and here it found Nirvana, for the captain had been so busy with his business affairs (he was a leading merchant of the town) that he had not yet found the time to organize his harvest, and now all his crop of corn lay open to any marauder bold enough to take it. Moreover, since corn had become a medium of exchange, the General Court had passed a law forbidding it to be fed to pigs. This pig had never tasted anything so delicious!

At once it set to work. By the time the captain's servants discovered it, it had gobbled down nearly a bushel. After a considerable struggle, the servants managed to capture it and put it into the captain's pigpen, where his own pig lived.

Captain Robert Keayne was a man who not long before had been censured both by the church and the General Court, and heavily fined as well. Two hundred pounds they had ordered him to pay, and all because they said he was making too much profit selling precious imported goods to a captive market. Prices and wages were fixed; no man could charge above what the law allowed. Keayne had been distraught—more by the fine or the censure is not known—and had tried ever since to walk more righteously. Now, day after day, he cried the pig around the town: who has lost a fine fat sow?

No one came forward. The pig lived happily in the captain's pen. Well fed and contented, it showed no sign of missing its former master—or mistress; it never tried to wander again.

At last came slaughtering time, and Captain Keayne set about killing his own pig. No sooner had the last blood dripped from the creature's carcass than Goody Sherman came forward to accuse him not only of keeping her pig, but of killing it as well.

The captain denied that he had killed her pig.

Goody Sherman insisted that he had.

The captain denied it more vehemently.

The case was brought before the elders of the church, and Captain Keayne was cleared. So Goody Sherman went to litigation.

The Quarter Court at Boston found for the Captain and awarded him £3 for costs and £20 from Goody Sherman and £20 from her boarder who lived with her in her husband's absence—under suspicion of adultery, said Captain

Keayne, and had the man, a merchant named George Story, up before the governor on account of it.

Story found a witness who admitted having perjured himself, and in Goodman Sherman's name he brought the case again, this time before the General Court. The plaintiff was heard; then the defendant; back and forth it went for seven days. It was remembered—and held against the captain—that he had been chastised as a hard dealer, censured by court and church alike. On the other hand, *in equali jure melior est conditio possidentis:* possession is nine points of the law.

The case dragged on for months, and the months became years. At last the matter was settled in favor of Captain Keayne. This made the common folk unhappy; the magistrates had looked after their own, they said, and had obstructed justice. People murmured and muttered so loudly against the authorities that the governor tried to pacify them, to no avail.

And so at last the members of the General Court saw that because of the case of Goody Sherman's sow, the people's faith in them had been severely weakened, and they moved to restore it.

The court would sit in two houses, they said: upper and lower. Each house must agree before an order became law.

This arrangement—the bicameral legislature—was the first such in the New World.

The people were satisfied; this was more equitable, they said, and their muttering died down.

It is not recorded if Captain Keayne ever dined on Goody Sherman's sow— that wayward pig who wandered into history.

3

Hard times changed for the better, after a while. A ship came in to Boston Harbor from the Barbados. Her captain was looking to trade two dozen barrels of sugar; he thought that his masters would be happy to get some hogsheads of dried and salted codfish in return.

The coastal trade picked up as well. The planters in Virginia planted their best cash crop: tobacco. They were happy to trade it for corn and wheat and peas.

Bartle decided to make a little venture. With the remainder of Susannah's dowry and her inheritance from her father, who had died not long after Mrs. Hutchinson was banished, he had enough to subscribe to a tenth share in a new wharf going up at the North End just beyond the Mill Creek; at the head of the dock he built a small store and warehouse.

One bright spring morning he took little Jed to see the men building the wharf. The boy was almost five years old now, a sturdy child with hair the color of ripe wheat, and dark blue eyes like his mother's. The streets of the town, ordinarily so busy, were quiet today, for everyone had flocked to the Common to see an execution: a man and a woman being hanged for the crime of adultery. Bartle might have gone himself to see it, but he would not take Jed; the child had seen a hanging several months ago and had had bad nightmares afterward.

At the site, Bartle greeted Valentine Hill, the chief proprietor of the wharf. The air was tangy with the smell of the sea and filled with the cries of gulls sweeping and soaring over the harbor. Three ships rode at anchor and one was off-landing. If trade picked up more, as many merchants thought it would, the dockage and storage fees here would pay back his investment within the year.

A stranger stood with Hill, and now Hill introduced him: Thomas Penhallow, master of the *Trial*.

"We are filling Master Penhallow's hold for Barbados," said Hill. "Will you take an eighth share?"

"What tonnage?" Bartle rested his hand on Jed's head as he spoke; he was aware that the child was listening. Good: even if he did not understand now, one day he would.

"Fifty."

Bartle hesitated.

"You still use John Coggan's agents at the fisheries, do you not?" said Hill. "Barbados will buy all the fish we can send, and corn and flour and peas—and wood, no doubt, Master Penhallow? Pipestaves and clapboards?"

"Aye," said the captain. He pulled at his pipe. "They'll buy anything. They work their plantations from dawn to dark, they've no time to grow food and no wood to speak of. And they'll be happy of a new market for their sugar." He grinned, exposing the gaps between his blackened tooth stubs.

"Sugar—and molasses," said Hill. "We've a steady market for rum here— and at the fisheries, too. We'll take all the sugar and molasses they can send us, eh, Bartle? And we'll have it made into rum—why, we'll have a dozen distilleries here before you know it."

Bartle considered. He did not know Master Penhallow, and he did not like to do business with strangers. A merchant was at the mercy of his captain, roaming the high seas, to do honest trading for him.

On the other hand, Hill trusted the man, and Hill was no fool.

"Very well," he said. "But a tenth share only—in fish. If it goes well, I'll send more the next voyage."

Satisfied, they shook hands all around. Then Bartle and Jed went to inspect the wharf. It was a few feet longer than it had been the day before. Slowly, steadily, the workmen were pushing it out into the harbor; when it was done, it would hold warehouses and selling places, it would serve as their lifeline to the great world, a long slim finger thrusting seaward, beckoning their riches.

4

The fish that Bartle sent to the Barbados brought him a good return, and so on Captain Penhallow's next voyage he sent not only fish but corn and peas as well.

Captain Penhallow brought back not only sugar and molasses, but cotton and tobacco and several pounds of ginger.

Bartle sent out cattle and biscuit as well as the staples of fish and grain. He got back sugar and molasses and tobacco and cotton, and some hard currency—Spanish *dolars* and a few silver bars.

And so the trade grew, year after year, voyage after voyage, until Boston became known as the mart town of the West Indies. There was no end of profit, it seemed: any man with an eye to the future could see that Boston merchants would make their fortunes in the Caribbean. True, buccaneers were a constant danger, and more than one Bostonian had been ruined by those predators on the Spanish Main. But the profit was too alluring; they would take their chances not only with pirates, but with the weather, too—their little barques and ketches prey to the hiracanos that swept the southern waters every summer and fall.

But as good a market as the West Indies were, there was a better one. The northern fisheries supplied so much fish that even the Caribbean settlements could not take it all. And wood—where could they sell all their wood when the West Indies could take no more?

A merchant named George Story—the same who had been so helpful to Goody Sherman fighting for her sow—decided to make an experiment. He shipped 8500 clapboards to the Atlantic Islands.

He brought back a shipload of wine, on which he made a nice profit: rum was a harsh drink, a deathly drink, and people were glad to get wine from the Azores, and, later, trading salt fish as well as clapboard and pipestaves, from Madeira and the Canaries as well.

One day when Jed was in the store with Bartle, word came that the *Rainbow*, a barque of a hundred tons, had been sighted coming up the Nantasket Roads into the harbor. This was a ship on which, the year before, Bartle had sent salt cod and pipestaves to the Azores. He had long since given up hope of ever seeing her again—not that he thought the captain dishonest, but he assumed, since the ship was so long overdue, that she had met bad weather and had gone down. Such things happened; so far he had been lucky, he had never lost a ship, but he knew that his luck could not hold forever.

Now here was Captain Fessenden home again, after all this time. Bartle was so delighted that he laughed aloud. "Come on, lad, we'll see her come in!"

It was a bright summer day; the harbor was filled with barques and ketches and sloops; on every wharf the dockers bustled to and fro, loading goods, unloading goods; in the storehouses merchants dickered with their captains, toting up bills of lading, figuring their profits.

Captain Fessenden was a fat, florid man; he hauled himself up the ladder to the wharf, sweating, panting, and held out his plump hand to Bartle.

"Master Revell, a good day to you."

"We had given you up," said Bartle. "What happened?"

"Aye," said Fessenden. They walked back along the wharf to Bartle's store; Jed, who was tagging along behind, watched with fascinated eyes as Captain Fessenden got his land legs. "Aye, it was a difficult time. We broke orders, and for a time I thought we'd get a proper punishment for it. But the Lord was with us."

Broke orders! Bartle stared at him. What was the man talking about?

Captain Fessenden held up his hand. "I know—I know. But you understand, we cannot always foresee— Look. It was like this. Señor Velasquez gave us bad wine. Sour stuff—you couldn't have sold it here for anything. So I had the good fortune to meet a London man before I set sail home, and he told me to go to Guinea. I could trade it there, he said."

"Guinea! Where—"

"The coast of Africa," said Fessenden. Suddenly he seemed uneasy; Jed watched him as he perspired freely under his tall-crowned hat. His eyes, which always looked at you straight, wavered a little.

"Well?" said Bartle. They were in the store now, surrounded by the smell of spices and tar and tobacco.

"So we went there," the captain continued. "And we traded the wine."

"For . . . ?"

"Blackamoors. We took them to the Barbados. As soon as word got around that I had Negroes on board, the planters came running. I could have filled my ship with sugar and molasses twice over if I'd had the room. They'll pay anything to get slaves. They are desperate for them. They work them to death there, I've heard. A slave who lasts five years on the sugar plantations is a rare one indeed."

Bartle was silent for a moment. From the wharf they could hear the cries of the workmen, the rumble of cartwheels, the shrieking of the gulls. Then: "I don't like trading in human souls."

"Faugh! Blackamoors aren't human—leastways, they don't have souls, no more than an Indian. Their own people catch them and sell them—but not for sour wine. We were lucky this time that they took that bad stuff. But I'll tell you what they want: rum! If I can take a shipload of rum to the slave traders in Guinea, I'll make a fortune for us both, Master Revell! Mark my words if I don't. They'll do anything for rum—and we have more rum than fish, more rum than wood. There's your profit, Master Revell! Rum to the slave coast, Negroes to the West Indies, and sugar and molasses back home to make into more rum. See what a neat triangle it is? Mark my words if it don't show you double the profit of anything you've traded before."

Bartle did not give his approval at once; he thought about what the captain had said, he looked to his account books and made his calculations.

A week later he had word that another ship in which he had a half interest had gone down, all hands lost and the cargo as well, one day out on the voyage home from Jamaica. It was a heavy loss, upward of £500. That night Susannah told him that she was pregnant again.

They had seven children now—seven mouths to feed, seven children to bring up and see safely into adulthood. And now an eighth, and undoubtedly more after that. Bartle had seen merchants ruined—sharp traders like himself, good honest hard-working men brought down by the whim of fate, the loss of a valuable cargo throwing them into bankruptcy.

He had worked too hard, he had survived too long, to risk such ruin for himself. The next day he summoned Fessenden and told him that he had ordered five hundred hogsheads of rum from the local distilleries; Fessenden could take it to Guinea, and he could bargain there for whatever cargo he needed to trade in Barbados.

Fessenden clapped him on the shoulder. "That's right, Master Revell! You won't regret it!"

On the day that Captain Fessenden sailed, Jed stood with his father at the end of the wharf and watched as the sails went up on the *Rainbow*; he heard the captain's shouted orders, he saw the great white sheets fill with the wind, he saw the ship turn and head down the harbor, past the Castle and the Governor's Garden, threading her way through the islands and out to the open sea where, like a great bird, she would skim across the bosom of the water to those hot, sunny, exotic ports so far from this tiny settlement. And when she came home again—as they devoutly prayed she would—she would bring a profit greater than any they had yet seen.

5

At ten years old Jedediah was a good boy who studied hard at the Latin School and often earned the praise of his teacher, Master Woodmancy. If he continued so, the master said, his father should consider sending him to the College over in Cambridge. True, Harvard was not Oxford; it was only a single building abutting a cow pasture in a rude little settlement in the wilderness. Nevertheless it offered a good education, the best of the Latin and Greek corpus, logic and rhetoric and that most helpful little text, *Hebrew in XXIV Hours*.

Bartle had hoped that Jed would join him in trade; you did not need a university degree to make a profit on a shipload of rum or fish and pipestaves. Most boys went to Harvard to prepare themselves for the ministry. Bartle knew that Susannah would be delighted to have her firstborn become a minister, but he himself had no enthusiasm for it. There was no money in it, for one thing; and no excitement (that he could see, at least)—they stuck you into a country congregation in the middle of the wilderness, and there you stayed, never seeing town life from one year to the next, preaching and studying—for what? No: a man needed a call from God to become a minister, and that he was sure Jed did not have.

Jed was a tall boy for his age, a little stringy, but he would fill out. His deep-set dark blue eyes reflected his intelligence. He was interested in everything in the world: he loved to go down to the wharf on off-loading days and watch the seamen bring ashore the barrels of goods from far away; he loved to stand by his father's side and listen to the hard bargaining that went on. He was particularly pleased when Bartle let him count wampum: the strands of white and blue-black beads seemed to give him a curious kind of pleasure. Once, seeing the boy arranging the lengths just so, Bartle had asked him why he took such care.

"Because they are beautiful," Jed replied, "and they make a beautiful pattern."

Bartle did not know what to make of it. Wampum was wampum, nothing more—"peage," the medium of exchange because barrels of corn and fish were too unwieldy, and hard coin almost impossible to come by.

But once, as he readily admitted, he was glad of Jed's keen eye: a white man from Connecticut had dyed the less valuable white beads and tried to pass them off as dark blue worth twice the price. When Jed pointed out the counterfeit, Bartle threw the man out of his warehouse and warned him never to return. Good lad, he thought. No, he didn't want to lose him to the ministry.

One evening in the early summer of 1648, shortly before Jed's eleventh birthday, the family was assembled for the evening meal—all except Jed.

Susannah, big with child again, sat opposite Bartle; standing dutifully on either side of the oak trestle table were the children: Edward and Elizabeth and Matthew and Mary and Richard and Francis. Susannah understood God's mercy in blessing her with this flock; still, this pregnancy had been a hard one, she had bled off and on during the entire time, and now, a month or so before she was to be brought to bed, she was bleeding still. She understood that God might call her at any moment, and she would need to leave these children—and this husband—whom she loved so well. But she had been trained to love God more; she would accept His will.

Bartle's face was stern; he was hungry, he wanted to begin the meal—and were was Jedediah?

At last they heard footsteps pounding up the path. His thin face pink from running, Jed stepped into his place beside Edward and murmured an apology. But he did not look contrite; on the contrary, his eyes sparkled as if he had some delightful secret. Susannah was ever alert to the alluring dangers that lay at every hand in a port town like Boston—grog shops and sailors with fantastical stories to tell and exotic trinkets to lure a child with—and now she watched him closely. "Why are you late?" she asked.

"I was at Mr. Hull's place."

"Mr. Hull—the merchant?" said Bartle.

"No, sir. His son. He has set up shop."

"What kind of shop?" said Bartle.

"He is a master goldsmith. He let me watch while he made a silver tankard. He says that he might want an apprentice."

Bartle exchanged a glance with his wife, and suddenly he felt his age. He was forty years old, and now here was his eldest son ready to go away from home.

"Will you come with me tomorrow, Father, to see him? He makes very beautiful things."

John Hull was a small, square man about thirty years old who looked like an ordinary man—a merchant, perhaps; and in fact he had shares in many ships. Like artists in all ages, he could not make a living on his work, no matter how fine it was; his trading ventures kept the wolf from the door.

But somewhere inside him lay a rare talent, for he made handsome things: tankards and caudle cups and porringers and standing cups of elegant proportion, delicately chased and finished, they gleamed in the dark interior of his shop.

No serious business was transacted that day. Both men understood that this was an exploratory visit: the signing on of an apprentice was far too serious a matter on both sides to be done in haste. And in any case Bartle was not enthusiastic; he would lose his eldest son for years, no matter that he would live and work less than a mile away from home. But he saw the look on Jed's face as he examined the gleaming products of Hull's industry, and he heard and understood what Hull said: "I think he has an eye for it, and that's an important thing. And he has good hands—he's not clumsy like so many. Of course you can never tell for certain until you start to work with the metal, but I think he shows promise. Think it over. No hurry. I've another lad to see tomorrow, in any case"—a statement that brought a worried look to Jed's face.

To Bartle the life of a silversmith promised only tedium—shut up indoors for hours on end, crouching over a bit of hot metal, ruining your eyes. But there! Men were different from each other. He could not find it in his heart, if the boy really wanted it, to say no. And certainly Jed, having once learned his trade, could take shares in trading ships, too, just as Hull did. Nothing would prevent him from going partners with Bartle, even if he could not give his full attention to the business.

As the men talked, Jed wandered over to a shelf and stood before a small standing cup—an inverted bell-shaped cup on a stem shaped like a turned baluster on a stair; the stem rested on a circular base. How did it happen?—a mess of silver coinage, or perhaps an old tankard or two, melted down in the crucible, shaped on a block, hammered, softened in the fire and hammered again, until at last the artisan's skilled hand produced this lovely cup. He wanted to make such things. He did not know if he could, but he felt that he would never rest until he tried.

On the way home Bartle said, "You understand that it is a binding agreement."

"Yes."

"So it's best that you not make a mistake."

"I'm not. I want to learn—I want to do what Mr. Hull does."

Bartle sighed. "In any case, if it doesn't work out, I imagine I could get your release." Then, thinking that for his son's sake he should be more optimistic, he said, "When you've learned the craft, I'll order a porringer for your mother. She'd be very proud to have a piece by Jedediah Revell."

At the evening meal the younger children looked at their eldest brother with new respect. It seemed a wonderful thing—and rather intimidating, too— to be going away from home. For Jed would live with the Hulls and be able to visit home only rarely; the life of an apprentice, even with the kindest of masters, was busy from dawn till long past dark, and he must be at the master's beck and call every minute.

But they could see that Jed was set on going. He had never seen a painting, had never heard a note of music save the psalm-singing at the meeting house. But he had a love for beauty, an aesthetic sense that had been awakened at Hull's establishment and could not now be put away; the silversmith's art called to him, even so young, as the sea called to other boys, and he was determined to go to her.

At first Hull gave Jed only menial tasks: washing the Spanish coins that people brought to be worked into tankards and cups; stoking the charcoal fire to keep it at the proper level; sweeping out the shop. Mostly, however, he commanded Jed to watch. "See how I do. Once the metal is hot I need to work quickly. And no mistakes, else you have to heat it too often, and that dulls it, you don't get the proper finish."

Jed longed to try for himself, but he knew that it was no use asking: Hull would let him try when he thought best, and not before.

Months passed—nearly a year. At last his turn came. He gripped the tongs and pulled the melted mass of metal from the crucible and quickly hammered it flat. Then he pressed it over the cup mold and began to hammer out its shape. Hull said nothing; he watched as Jed worked. Soon Jed realized that the cup was lopsided, one side thicker than the other. He tried to hammer down the thicker side and found that he had no place to put the extra metal; he could not work it around. In a surprisingly short time the metal had cooled and hardened so that he could not work it at all. He put it back into the fire, took it out, hammered again—still unshapely. He trembled with frustration. He could see in his mind's eye the shape he wanted to achieve, but he could not make his hands produce it.

At last Hull took pity on him and reached for the misshapen cup. He looked at it as if it were worthy of inspection, although both of them knew that it was not.

"It takes a while to get the feel of it," Hull said. "But you've made a start. Here—" He thrust the cup back into the crucible, withdrew it, and with astonishing speed hammered it into a graceful shape. "Y'got to master the metal— let it know that you will have what you want from it. It'll come."

The next month he let Jed try again, and this time the shape that Jed saw in his mind came a little closer to existence. "Not bad, boy," Hull said. To Jed, those words were sweeter than high praise. Not bad!

Many masters beat their apprentices to get work from them, but you could not beat a boy into becoming a master goldsmith. Either he had the gift or he did not: no amount of physical pain could put the talent into him. So there was no question of beating, no question of any kind of punishment: if Jed were destined to become a goldsmith, he would show it fairly soon; if not, Hull would dismiss him and take on someone else.

At the end of Jed's first year Hull went around to see Bartle. "I'll keep him, Master Revell," he said. "He's a good worker, and more important, he has an eye, and hands that will make what he sees—some day."

Naturally Bartle was pleased at this information; when he told Susannah that night what Hull had said, her eyes lighted up and she smiled delightedly. "It is God's will," she said; if Jed was not to become a minister, she was glad that God had given him the chance to do what he had the talent for.

In the fall of 1652, the authorities took a bold step: they established a mint, and they put John Hull in charge of it. They knew that only sovereign states were entitled to make coinage, but they ignored that fact. The future of the Colony depended on trade. Trade was impossible without coinage—a convenient and standardized method of payment. Wampum was too bulky; corn and fish and livestock were impossible; Spanish *dolars* were undependable. Massachusetts would have her own coin; they asked Hull to make it.

He built a small mint house next to his shop, and there he designed his die: a shilling coin, the obverse stamped with a crude pine tree and MASATHUSETS, the reverse with the date: 1652.

When the first lot of coins had been stamped out, Hull picked one up in his stubby fingers and held it for Jed to see. "There you are, boy! A pine-tree shilling, coin of the realm!"

It was a crude thing, not perfectly round, but well suited for its purpose. The next year Hull made another issue, this time decorated with the willow tree; the date, however, remained 1652. To prevent clipping, he added a beaded border.

The merchants were pleased with the new coins; no one cared that their minting was illegal. The Puritan Protector, Cromwell, struggling to control all of England, had more pressing problems than the insubordination of one colony.

Illegal? Mind your own business! We are the Colony of Massachusetts Bay: we will do as we see fit, as God guides us to see fit—and we will brook no interference from anyone!

6

Summer 1656. A fine season, crops ripening in the sun, the harbor and the bay calm and free of storms, easy entry for the scores of trading ships that came, ever more often, to enrich the merchants of Boston. A fair little town by the sea, minding its own business.

And yet the Devil lurked: Beware!

The citizens of Boston searched their hearts, trying to understand God's will. One thing they knew for certain: He wanted them to stay pure, free of heresy; in whatever form Satan appeared, he must be cast out.

Thus they did God's will when they hanged Mistress Ann Hibbens for a witch. She was the widow of William Hibbens, a pillar of the community; and she was the sister of Richard Bellingham, a leader of the Colony since its earliest days, a magistrate once or twice elected governor, a wealthy man. But when Hibbens died, and her sons were away on business, a covetous neighbor started muttering against Mistress Hibbens. She had a fine farm out beyond Muddy River that the neighbor wanted for his own. What was more, she was a crabbed, quarrelsome creature. Some years before, she had accused a carpenter of over-charging her. When she would not withdraw the accusation, she was hauled before the church elders, accused of bearing false witness, and expelled from the church. Robert Keayne, mindful perhaps of his own troubles with the authorities, made a record of her trial for posterity.

Mistress Hibbens, in short, was a woman who did not readily bow to authority—a dangerous woman. So when her neighbor's cow died and his children sickened, he knew where to lay the blame.

And so the authorities arrested her and tried her for witchcraft. All Boston went to see her hang, or nearly all. Her brother said not one word in her defense. He knew what a woman should be—young and beautiful and compli-·ant, like his new wife—and his sister was not any of those things. He sat in his fine house in Winnisimmet, across the water from the North End, and shut his eyes and ears to his sister's troubles.

The citizens of Boston, ever watchful, felt that it was particularly impor-tant, just now, to show God that they kept the faith, for only within the last week a fresh plague had been visited upon them in the shape of two women who spouted a new heresy: Quakerism. For their pains, the women languished now in the gaol. From their dark, damp cell they could hear the cry of the crowd—the blood cry—as Mistress Hibbens swung. For all they knew, they might hang next: the authorities had roughly searched their bodies for signs of witchcraft, thrusting their prying fingers into the innermost recesses of female privacy, stripping them bare for all to see while they looked for the Devil's mark. No mark had been found, no more than any had been found on Mistress Hibbens; but that had not stopped her hanging today, and it

would not stop the hanging next week, or the week after, of these two interlopers.

Bartle was in his store, arranging a new shipment of cloth upon the shelves,
when a man's form darkened the open door.

"Good day to you, Master Upsall," Bartle said.

"A bad day, indeed, Master Revell." Nicholas Upsall was a man of some
threescore years and more, a leading citizen of the town. He was agitated, out
of breath. From his pocket he fished an oak-tree shilling—the newest mintage—
and put it on the counter.

"A length of the sad kersey, if you will," he said. He had a queer look to
him, Bartle thought—a kind of defiant glare.

"A new dress for Mistress Upsall?" said Bartle, more in the way of pleasant
conversation than any great desire to know the sumptuary habits of the man's
wife.

Upsall snorted. "She picks her own finery," he said. "She's making this
into summat for—" He caught himself. "Not for her," he finished. Without
looking at the cloth, he picked it up and went out, leaving Bartle with a sense
of unease.

That evening his children came home to report that they had been to the
gaol to see the Quakers. It was common gossip, they said, that Master Upsall
was sending in extra food to the women and that the authorities were very
angry with him for doing so. So, Bartle thought: Mistress Upsall would be up
half the night, no doubt, laboring over the cloth her husband had bought, and
when she was done, the Quaker women would be decently clothed.

The town was in an uproar over the two prisoners. Cast them out! Get rid
of them before they infect us with their foul beliefs!

In short order they were put on a ship for Barbados, where there was a
Quaker colony. The people of Boston breathed easier: a narrow escape!

But no sooner had the two Quakers been banished than eight more appeared. People felt that they lived in a nightmare: why was God punishing
them with this plague of Quakers?

The miserable eight were clapped into gaol while the authorities combed
their baggage for erroneous books and hellish pamphlets. At times like this the
Puritan fathers must have regretted their decree that every person be literate;
with a literate population, books and pamphlets were terrible dangers. The
decree for universal literacy had nothing to do with benevolence and everything
to do with self-interest. When the Massachusetts School Act was passed in 1647,
it was specifically worded: to thwart "that ould deluder, Satan," who "keepe
men from the knowledge of Y^e scriptures . . ."

So every man—and many women, too—could read the Word of God: but
if they could read the Word, they could read hellish pamphlets also.

Over at the College, Stephen Day worked the printery. From the little
press had come, so far, only good things like the Freeman's Oath, *The Bay
Psalm Book*, and *The New England Primer*, which was used in every school,
teaching not only the alphabet but Puritan belief as well:

In Adam's fall
Wee sin'ned all. . . .
Job feels the Rod,
Yet bleffes God. . . .

And now was to come the greatest effort of all: John Eliot's translation of the Word of God into the Algonquian tongue. What a work this was!—to bring to the savages sitting in darkness the light of God's Word! James Printer, an Indian himself, had been taught to set type to help produce this enormous work, and a skilled printer, Marmaduke Johnson, had been brought from England to supervise. Shortly after he arrived in Massachusetts, Johnson married.

When the authorities learned that he had another wife whom he had left behind in the old country, they were stretched to the limits of their considerable ingenuity to know how to deal with the case. They settled it by letting him go on with his work—and Eliot's—simply overlooking the fact that the man who helped to produce the *Up-Biblium God* was an adulterer who more properly should have been put to death. The Indian Bible was dedicated to Charles II—an offering from the Colony of Massachusetts Bay. It was presented to him by Robert Boyle, the founder of the Royal Academy. Boyle never actually had the chance to put the heavy volume into the monarch's hands, for the ceremony was interrupted; but no matter. The gesture had been made—and acknowledged.

In such ways, the written—or printed—Word was well and good, and all to the glory of God.

But sometimes, as in the case of the hellish Quaker pamphlets, printed material, or even words written down in ink, could pose the utmost danger to the peace of the Bay. For words conveyed ideas; and ideas often led to nothing but trouble. Ordinary people were not supposed to have ideas; they were supposed to follow the ministers' teachings.

Already books had been burned in the marketplace at Boston. In 1650 William Pyncheon, a founder of the Colony and the founder also of Springfield in the Connecticut River Valley, where he had gone to set up a fur trade, wrote a little pamphlet on his ruminations about Christ burning in Hell for the sins of mankind. Pyncheon did not believe that Christ had gone to Hell, and he said so. When the General Court got hold of his pamphlet, they burned it and demanded that Pyncheon present himself for chastisement. Instead, Pyncheon and his wife slipped out of the country and made their way back to England.

Eventually the authorities became so exercised about the dangers of a free press that they set up a licensing board—and a good thing, too, for not long after, fully half of Thomas a Kempis's *The Imitation of Christ* (a Roman Catholic treatise) was set into type before the licensers got wind of it and put a stop to it.

In the case of the Quakers and their books and pamphlets, the authorities debated among themselves while the interlopers sat in the gaol. For eleven weeks they sat; then the authorities bundled them on board a ship back to

England—the same on which they had come—and instructed the captain to take them or forfeit a £500 bond.

By now the magistrates were thoroughly aroused to the dangers of Quakerism, and they passed strong laws to protect themselves. Any Quaker found in the Bay Colony would be whipped, imprisoned, and banished. Any citizen who gave house room to a Quaker would be fined forty shillings an hour. Any Quaker returning after banishment would have his ears cropped and his tongue bored with a hot iron. Worst of all, any man who brought a Quaker into the Bay would be fined £100.

7

"One hundred pounds!" exclaimed Jedediah. He stared at his father as if Bartle had taken leave of his senses. "You have no right! It is my profit as well as yours that you risk, and I say no!"

At anchor in the harbor lay the Revells' ship, the *Increase*, a hundred-ton barque just come from the Barbados with a fine load of sugar, molasses, and tobacco. She brought human cargo as well: three Negroes and two Quakers. The Negroes were young and strong, two boys and a girl. They would be sold readily enough, for there was hardly a house in Boston, among the better-off families, at least, that did not have a Negro slave. The Quakers, a gray-haired couple, were more of a problem: they claimed that God had told them to come to Massachusetts, no matter what the authorities did.

When the *Increase* came in, Bartle and Jed went out to meet her. The captain, a reliable man who had worked for Bartle for years, was at a loss to explain how he had taken on the Quaker pair, but he ventured the opinion that they seemed harmless.

"Harmless!" Jed was only twenty-three, but already, Bartle thought, he had the air of a much older man. "We will see how harmless they are when we pay the fine! It will come out of your pocket, Master Rogers, not ours!"

Rogers shrugged. "Very well. I will not put them ashore here. We will find a passage to Newport for them, no doubt."

Newport would not be far enough, Bartle thought. Even now in Boston gaol lay Mary Dyer, who once had been Ann Hutchinson's friend and champion. In the past few years she had met Quakers coming to Rhode Island and had converted to their faith. And she, too, had insisted on coming into the Bay, and had been expelled, and now had come back again, risking execution.

Father and son returned to their wharf in silence. It was a mild October day, the sun sparkling on the water, the harbor alive with activity, goods coming in, goods going out—the busiest harbor in North America, it was. Jed's face was grim as he sliced the oars into the water, as if—as if he were whipping someone, Bartle thought.

In truth Bartle was a little in awe of his eldest son. The boy—no longer a boy now—was a handsome young man, taller than Bartle but somewhat resembling him, with dark gold hair and dark blue eyes that sometimes seemed nearly black. Throughout the town of Boston he was widely admired as a hard trader but an honest one, and a skilled artisan as well. He got rid of a shipment of hats and spices as neatly as he produced a handsome pair of candlesticks or a finely chased porringer or caudle cup. He had nothing of the artist about him—no delicate temperament, no shrinking from the affairs of the marketplace. And yet he was indisputably a very fine goldsmith. He had finished his apprenticeship with John Hull five years before. Hull had asked him to stay on as a partner, but Jed had decided to join his father in trade, and so next to the shop they had built a small room where Jed could make his silver pieces. He practiced one trade as easily as the other, and stood in a fair way, Bartle thought, to get rich at both. He had an apprentice of his own now, a tall, thin boy from Watertown.

They pulled up to the wharf and climbed the ladder. "Remember Upsall," said Jed; and without another word he turned and strode away.

He was right, Bartle thought, and not only in the matter of the fine. Poor old Upsall, who some years before had taken food and clothing to Quakers in the gaol, had lost everything for his pains—had been hounded out of the town, banished into the wilderness in the middle of winter. No: those Quakers on the *Increase* would not land. He and Jed had worked too hard to endanger everything they had for a couple of lunatics.

The following week Mary Dyer was hanged on Boston Common. Once before, the willful woman had been led to the gallows and, with the rope around her neck, sat on the steps with a blindfold over her eyes while her two male companions were executed. At the last minute the authorities reprieved her and sent her back to Rhode Island. But she was determined, apparently, to force them to kill her, and so she returned to Massachusetts. It was her fault, not theirs, that she was to die today!

The drummer beat his mournful dirge as the little procession made its way from the gaol to the Great Elm. The people stood hushed and filled with awe—for it was always an awesome thing to see a body hanged, and to know that the soul within went not to Heaven, but to the eternal flames of Hell. There were some in the crowd who thought that Mrs. Dyer should not hang, but they kept silent lest they themselves find a noose around their necks.

Jedediah took his younger brothers and sisters to the Common that day to watch the proceedings. When little Prudence, who was just seven, started to cry, Jed silenced her. It was God's will that Mrs. Dyer be hanged, he said. Prudence gazed up at him, her round little face streaked with tears, her big dark eyes shining with wonder. As young as she was, she understood that God's will must be done. Still, she could not bear to watch; and when Mrs. Dyer's body dangled from the rope, she hid her face in Jed's coat and shut her ears to the swelling voices of the crowd.

Mary Dyer was the last Quaker hanged in Boston, for Puritan rule in England was finished, and so inevitably Puritan influence waned in the Bay. Charles II ascended to his father's throne in 1660, and he forbade that any of his subjects should be executed for their religious beliefs. So Governor Endicott and the General Court did what they could to suppress the Quakers: they passed new laws against them, notably the Cart and Tail Act, which mandated that any Quaker caught within the confines of the Bay Colony be tied to a cart's tail and whipped through the towns to the border. But the Quakers, undaunted, kept coming; as late as 1675 the General Court proclaimed a Day of Humiliation to repent, among other things, the failure to suppress Quakers—and the failure, as well, to suppress the wearing of long hair, which was a Stuart abomination carried across the water.

Meanwhile, a new flood of immigrants from England began to pour into the Massachusetts Bay.

8

One summer day in 1662 two customers came into Jed's silversmith shop: a middle-aged man and a young woman. They were newcomers: Jed had never seen them before.

"Mayhew," rumbled the man. "Samuel Mayhew, at your service, young master. This is my daughter, Catherine. They tell me that you are the best silversmith in Boston. Is that so?" Master Mayhew was a stout, red-faced man with wide blue eyes and a head of tight gray curls.

Before Jed had a chance to answer, Mayhew went on to describe exactly what he wanted: a tankard and bowl in a matching design as a surprise for his wife. He produced a pouch of well-worn Spanish silver—pieces of eight—and miscellaneous English and Dutch coins: these Jed would melt down, and from them, plus whatever silver he would need to add, he must make the finest things—the very finest, mind!—for Mrs. Mayhew to display on her oaken press cupboard.

"And mind you do your best work," Mayhew went on, "or Catherine here will say it's not good enough, and we'll send it back to you."

During all this the young woman had said not a word. No matter: already Jed was intrigued by her, not only because she was a beauty, but because she had a delicacy, a refinement, a purity of feature, that seemed oddly out of place in the rough and tumble of this small plantation in the wilderness. In the dark interior of the little shop she seemed like a slim white flame. Her hair was very blond; her wide eyes as blue as the larkspur that bloomed in the countryside in springtime. Her small, short nose, her sweetly curved cheeks, the pale blue vein throbbing at her temple underneath skin so fine and white that it seemed that it would tear if you touched it—ah, but she was a lovely thing! Her voice, too, when she finally spoke, was exquisite, a silvery voice that uttered every word in a gentle, tentative way. Compared to the harsh, rough voices of some of the Boston women, it sounded like the high, sweet notes of a set of miniature bells.

"We've only just come across," said Mayhew, "and I want her to be happy. Ha! Happy in this wilderness—but still, it's better here. You don't know, you've not been across, have you? No, too crowded back home, and an unpleasant climate since we have the Stuarts again. So I made up my mind to come over, and here we are. We're living in Ship Street. Come to call on us. I can see I was directed rightly." He broke off to examine a beaker on a shelf. It was about eight inches high, engraved with a design of trailing flowers. With a glance at Jed for permission, he picked it up and held it for his daughter to see. She nodded.

"There, Catherine! A handsome piece, is it not? Do you approve of Master Revell?"

She did not glance at Jed; rather, she nodded slowly, not smiling. "Yes, Father. He seems . . . perfectly satisfactory."

"Good!" Mayhew gave a little laugh as he returned the beaker to its place. "I must say, I never expected to find work like this in the Massachusetts Bay. You trained with Hull, sir? Yes. Hull is a craftsman. Nothing the matter with that, but craftsmanship isn't good enough for Mrs. Mayhew. This is more like it. Shall we say . . . three weeks? Yes. Bring them around, and we'll give you a good dinner."

For two weeks Jed worked on his new commission. To the coins that Samuel Mayhew had brought, he added five ounces of silver from his own stock. He engraved an M on opposite sides of the bowl; the first and last strokes of the letter trailed off into a design of leaves which encircled the rim. The piece rested on a simple circular foot. The tankard, about six inches high, had a hinged lid; its handle was a head of a lion at the hinge, curving into lion's paws where the bottom of the handle joined the tankard. On the bottom of both pieces he put his mark: ⟨R⟩ .

He looked at his work with a critical eye, what he had come to think of as that critical artist's eye without which no artist could work, and he knew that these were the best pieces he had ever made. In this self-appraisal there was no hint of pride, no puffing up of his self-importance. He knew that God had given him his gift for a purpose. In making beautiful objects, he was fulfilling God's plan for him.

He did not take the pieces immediately to Samuel Mayhew. He put them on the shelf in his shop where he could look at them, and from time to time, during his busy day, he stared at them, evaluating them, separating himself from them to look at them critically: were they the best he could do?

They were: he could not have made them better had he tried a hundred times over. Shining and perfectly formed, they glowed like satin; the design etched into their surface was as fine as lace; taken in the hand, they balanced with a satisfying heft.

At last he delivered them to the Mayhews' house. As promised, they gave him a good meal. To his unutterable disappointment, Catherine was not there, and for the first time in his life his appetite failed him; he could hardly swallow a mouthful.

9

"What's the matter?" said Bartle, irritated. "Are you under a spell?" He had spoken to Jed three times now and received no reply.

They had finished their supper; the younger children had gone to bed, the two next eldest to Jed were visiting neighbors. Susannah was at a birthing.

"I was thinking," said Jed with an embarrassed laugh.

"Thinking! What about?"

Jed rose from his seat by the fire and reached for his hat and coat. "I'm going to check the lock on the shop door," he said. "I told Jeremuth to fix it, but I want to make sure."

Bartle sniffed, exasperated. Something was wrong with his son, and he was put out that the young man did not confide in him. On the other hand, at twenty-five Jed was old enough to solve his own problems; Bartle knew that the time had long passed when he should interfere.

It was a cold October night, the wind blowing hard from the west. Jed held onto his tall beaver hat to keep it on his head, and winced as the gusts drew tears from his eyes. He liked his creature comforts; only the most pressing errand would have drawn him from the fireside on a night like this—and it was not to check the lock on the door of his shop. The lock was all right; he had inspected it that afternoon.

He headed down Ship Street, which ran around the edge of the North End by the water. When he came to the Mayhews' house he stopped. In the distance he heard the cry of the watch: "Seven o'clock and all's well!"

Lights gleamed around the edges of the shutters; from within he heard the sound of laughter, voices raised in repartee. How he longed to be inside! He pictured her: sitting at the table, perhaps, speaking in her silvery voice, smiling on—who? a young man?—her lovely face alight. Perhaps, this night, that young man, whoever he was, would speak to her father; perhaps an offer of marriage would be made—and, worse, accepted.

It had been a month since he took the silver pieces to Samuel Mayhew. In all that time, he had seen Catherine perhaps four or five times, but always at a distance, always in the company of others. Every night as Jed lay in his bed next to his brothers, he tormented himself by conjuring up her image: the pure gold-and-white of her, the sound of her voice, the sweet glance of her blue eyes.

He had never imagined that a woman could be so beautiful—like a work of art, like a creature too delicate, too exquisite for the rough life of Boston Town.

And yet—here she was, and what was he doing about it?

He did not want to make a mistake—to put her and her father off by too bold, too crude an approach. No: the thing had to be done carefully—properly. He had known from the beginning that he would have to ask for help; now, tonight, he made up his mind to do so.

He stood shivering in the wind. The moon had risen; the harbor was a sheet of rippling silver, marked with the dark shapes of vessels at anchor. From the taverns by the docks he could hear the sound of sailors singing, raising their voices in drunken chants. It seemed impossible that those uncouth creatures were members of the same species as Catherine Mayhew.

The next morning he called on his friend Thomas Knollys, a young man his own age whose father, like Bartholomew Revell, was a merchant. Knollys' store was near the Town Dock—a few minutes' walk which would not tire a healthy man; nevertheless, Jed was breathing hard when he arrived.

"Well, Jedediah! I'm glad to see you! Where have you been?" Thomas Knollys was a small, plump fellow with a head of auburn ringlets; his rosy face beamed out at the world from above his neat white collar as if he had made up his mind to enjoy his time on earth—a sharp contrast to the usual Puritan severity of the Massachusetts Bay. Thomas loved a good joke, a hearty meal— and, on occasion, a visit to Dermin Mahoon's brothel. This recreation Jed had refused to share: he wanted no part of the "French disease" that flourished in such places.

"Busy," said Jed shortly. "Can you spare a minute?" The clerk, a sharp-eared fellow, was listening; Jed steered his friend outside and walked down the wharf.

"What is it?" said Thomas. "Secrets?"

"In a manner of speaking. I want to ask a favor of you." He dreaded that Thomas would laugh at him; somehow he needed to convey the seriousness of his request.

"Well, ask away. What is it? Great heavens, man, you look like Death! What's the matter?"

"I want— Do you know Samuel Mayhew?"

"Stout fellow? Gray hair? Merchant? Yes, I've seen him. He's got a family— ah!" Thomas beamed. "Now I have it! You want me to stand in for you!"

It was the custom for the young men of Boston to engage a surrogate lover when they decided to go courting. The surrogate delivered the favors—flowers, sweetmeats, perhaps a ring—and conveyed the messages of eternal devotion; then, when the young lady had been properly wooed—properly prepared, so to speak—the lover himself stepped in to gain the final reward.

"Which one?" said Thomas. "Mary is the elder. I think that they will want her to marry first. But she is not, ah, so very beautiful. Oh, yes, my friend, you needn't look so. I have to look out for a wife, too, you know. And I have seen her—the younger one. Catherine is her name, is it not? Yes. Yes, indeed."

His plump face was wreathed in smiles; no man loved a little joke more than Thomas Knollys. "Well? Am I right? You want me to stand in for you with Catherine Mayhew."

Jed felt the hot blush rise over his face; he could not stop it. "Yes," he said, more curtly than he had intended. "I do."

"And what is to be my initial offering? A fine silver ring from your workshop?"

Jed thought not. A ring was much too forward. Flowers would have been the thing—a bouquet from his mother's garden. But it was late October; flowers had bloomed their last weeks before. "I think—a spray of dry Rosemary." Rosemary meant remembrance; and even the dried flowers carried a haunting fragrance, as haunting as Catherine's image in his mind.

"Good," said Thomas. "Bring your little present around and I will deliver it—with an appropriate speech, of course." He grinned at Jed. "And if I succeed, mind, I want an invitation to the wedding!"

That very evening Thomas went on his errand to the Mayhews' house. The family was at home. Thomas had met Master Mayhew in passing at the merchants' gathering place at the Town House; now he reintroduced himself and explained that he had come, not on business matters, but on an errand of mercy. Thomas was a fluent fellow, always ready with a pretty speech; in no time at all the Mayhews understood that something serious was under way. For a moment Mary held her breath: could this be her chance at last? Mary had no doubt that one day she would find a husband, but she hoped desperately that she would not have to wait too long. At twenty-three, she was already by way of being overripe.

But Thomas turned almost at once to Catherine, and so Mary stifled her disappointment. He made an elaborate bow; from the bosom of his coat he withdrew the sprig of Rosemary and, with a graceful little flourish, held it out to her. "Fairest lady, would you accept this small token from one who dares not present himself, so smitten is he by your beauty? You would honor him if you would take it, you would let him know that his esteem is not altogether rebuffed." (Thomas had gone to the College, where he had been intensively exposed to rhetorical flourishes.)

Catherine had no idea that the Massachusetts Bay Colony contained a man who could speak so elegantly. With a smile that very nearly captured Thomas's heart, she held out her hand; her long, slim fingers took the spray of dried herb as if it was a jewel. "Thank you," she said. "You speak not for yourself, but for someone else? If he is as courteous as you, I would be pleased to know him."

The elder Mayhews exchanged a glance: must we hold Catherine back from a good match simply because Mary is not spoken for? They thought not. They had known from the beginning that finding suitable husbands for their daughters would be a chancy thing, since they had heard that Boston, and indeed all of the Massachusetts, was populated by uncouth rustics with no notion of civilized behavior. All the same, business opportunities being so good, they had decided to come over, leaving their two grown sons to handle the London side of the business. If all else failed, the girls could always return to England to find husbands.

And so Mayhew smiled at Thomas and clapped him on the shoulder. "May we know whom you represent, Master Knollys?"

"Not yet," said Thomas. "It is the custom here to, ah, treat courtship as if it were a diplomatic mission—as indeed it is. In time, I assure you, he will make himself known."

The Mayhews were impressed. Knollys came from a good solid merchant family; undoubtedly his friend did also. And so when he asked permission to call again, it was promptly given.

"Well?" said Jed. He had been too unsettled to wait until morning for a report of the mission; he waited for Thomas at his own store, passing the time by polishing a platter that was already as bright as a newly minted shilling. "What did they say? What did *she* say?"

"Success, my friend." Thomas grinned, pleased with himself. "They gave me permission to call again. The lady herself accepted your token most graciously. She's curious, I think—and that's the best thing for you, it will keep you foremost in her thoughts, wondering who you are. Now: what's my next step?"

Jed did not want to push; and according to Thomas's report it seemed that his rather modest offering had been the wise way to proceed.

"I don't know," he said. "Tell me again what you said to her."

Thomas tried to remember; at last he gave an approximation of the little speech he had delivered.

"That's it!" said Jed after a moment.

"What?"

"You're clever with words. You must have thousands of extra words in your head left over from the College. You can compose a poem for her! I'll copy it over, of course"—he had a pretty hand, better than Thomas's—"but I'm no good at making verses. I saw the almanac last year. They put three or four of your poems in. Mistress Bradstreet herself couldn't have done better." Anne Bradstreet was a wonder, like a two-headed calf: a woman who wrote poetry!

Thomas sighed. He might have known that he was letting himself in for a long, time-consuming business. And yet, he was a firm friend; he would do what Jed asked, and gladly.

The poem, when he composed it, turned out to be an elegant sonnet that owed much to the poetry of Robert Herrick. With great care Jed copied it onto a fair sheet and folded it into an intricate design. He did not seal it, for his stamp was the same as his goldsmith's mark and would identify him at once.

Catherine thought that the poem was charming. As she listened—for she insisted that Thomas read it aloud—her lips curved up into the sweetest smile that Thomas had ever seen. He heard his voice catch; he paused, cleared his throat, and went on. Pay attention! This was a business affair!

His good report encouraged Jed to think of a more extravagant offering. He made up a small parcel of his best ribbons and a length of fine Brussels lace; such fancy-work was forbidden the lower orders, but people of property, people like the Mayhews and the Revells and the Knollys, were allowed to wear it.

But he should wait at least a week before he sent Thomas again, he thought, else the fair Catherine would become bored—would begin to expect his offerings as a matter of course, and so value them less. Jed was a merchant born and bred; it did no good to flood the market, for then the value of your merchandise dropped, sometimes never to rise again.

10

Catherine Mayhew knew that she was pretty; she knew that she turned men's heads in the marketplace when she walked out. She had no doubt that some day, probably not far off, she would make a match, and while she loved her sister, she had no intention of passing up a good husband merely in consideration of Mary's feelings.

As the winter drew on, Catherine grew more and more intrigued by Master Thomas Knollys and his offerings: who was courting her? She wanted to be sure that he was a man who—if she accepted him—would be able to provide her with a comfortable home filled with fine things, handsome furniture and a good Turkey rug on the table, ample silver and brassware and pewter in the press cupboard, silk dresses and a maid to help her into them. She had no illusions about herself: she knew that she would be unhappy as the wife of a poor man.

Mary was not so choosy. Shortly after the first snow, to all their surprise, she found herself a suitor: a young man with a Master of Arts degree from the College who had been called to the pulpit in the frontier town of Lancaster and wanted a wife to go with him.

"Lancaster!" Mrs. Mayhew was appalled. She hurled reproaches at her husband. "You see what you have done! Mary will be as good as dead if she goes into that wilderness!"

Catherine shuddered, even as she pretended to be happy at her sister's news. She would miss her; worse, she would worry about her, for Mary's life would be drudgery from dawn till dark, lonely and poor—but Mary was determined, and so, in the middle of February, she married the Reverend John Talbot and went away with him.

In the rush of excitement at the wedding preparations, Catherine had had to put off the visits of Master Thomas Knollys. Now as she received him again, she thought that it was time that he reveal whom he spoke for, and she told him so.

"Ah—yes, indeed, I can well understand that you wish to, ah, see him in the flesh, ah, and I will convey to him your request. . . ."

But he did not. Again and again he went to see her, always with some excuse, until Catherine began to suspect that he spoke for himself, after all, and not for that mysterious gentleman whose offerings he claimed to bring.

Always he returned to Jed with a good report: she liked the bottle of plum preserves, she admired the poem (for there were many poems, always composed by Thomas). "Just one more visit, or two at the most, and I think she will be ready to receive you."

Thomas did not confine himself to visits to the Mayhew house. As the spring came, he sometimes offered his arm to Catherine to walk out awhile. This was perfectly acceptable behavior; all young couples did it.

And so one day Jed saw the two of them strolling down the Mall next to the Common. They were laughing, heads together, sharing some private joke. It was late afternoon of a mild spring day; the trees wore a gauzy green veil, only a hint of their leafing out; the sky was milky blue, the breeze a soft breath from the south. Suddenly Jed wanted to speak to her—to make himself known to her. In the narrow rutted lane just ahead, the cowherd prodded along his flock; and so while Jed could see Catherine and Thomas well enough, he could not get to them. The cattle, aching to be milked, blocked his way; they lowed and shuffled—stupid beasts!—creating a regular traffic jam. Thomas was waving his hands, telling a funny story, no doubt, for Catherine laughed again. It seemed that Master Knollys was performing his duties altogether too well; he was making progress in his suit—but for whom?

Jed turned and ran down a side street, nearly slipping in the mud. He would meet them at the next intersection—but then a stray dog ran in front of him and he tripped and fell into the muck. Disaster! He was covered with the stuff from head to toe. He could not possibly present himself to the young lady in such a state. Defeated, he picked himself up and made his way home, resolving to speak to Master Thomas Knollys at the first opportunity.

"When do I see her?" It was the next morning, and Jed was in Thomas's store the moment it opened.

"Oh, I don't know." Thomas smiled at him, and to Jed it seemed an insufferably self-satisfied smile. Then Thomas made a graceful little wave of his hand, as if to indicate that Jed's request was trivial—of no matter.

Jed was aware that he was trembling. He could not erase from his mind's eye the image of the two of them, Catherine and Thomas, heads together, laughing. "I have waited long enough to present myself—too long. I will see her today."

"I do not think—"

"I do not care what you think!" The clerk turned to stare. "I think that you have betrayed me!"

Thomas paled. "I have never—"

"I have been a fool. I have asked you to do what I could not do myself—I have asked you to see her, to speak to her, day after day, and not want her for yourself!"

"Jedediah—" At heart, Thomas was an honest man; he could not deny that his friend spoke the truth. With no intention of betraying Jed's interests, he, Thomas, had become altogether too fond of Catherine Mayhew.

The Revells, father and son, had a busy day that day: the *Reliance*, one hundred tons, had arrived from the West Indies, and they needed to supervise its unloading. Ordinarily Jed enjoyed this work, for it was only when the ship came home that a merchant had a chance to see his profit. All day he worked beside his father ordering the haulers with their ox-drawn carts as the hogsheads of sugar and molasses were unloaded, the bales of tobacco taken to the shed, the wooden crates of miscellaneous items—nails and ironware and fancy goods— delivered to the store. But this day the hours passed slowly; they would never be done, he thought. And while he worked here at the wharf, who knew what mischief Thomas Knollys was doing?—for he had taken a dislike to his friend, he thought that he would never trust him again. He must see Catherine!

At last they were done, the captain's bills of lading checked and rechecked, the seamen given their pay and a ration of rum, every jot and tittle of the cargo accounted for. Curtly, Jed announced to his father that he would not be home for supper. Bartle, somewhat taken aback, thought to question him, and then thought again and held his tongue. Something was ailing the lad—but there, he was a lad no longer, and he would have to work out his problems for himself.

It was not yet dark when Jed hurried toward Ship Street, and many people were still abroad. A woman in a long blue cloak and tall-crowned hat walked ahead of him. All women, at a distance, looked more or less alike in their voluminous clothing, and yet—

He hurried on. He caught up with her, peered sideways at her face.

Quite properly, she paid no attention to him. Her chin lifted a bit higher, her pace quickened.

"Excuse me—"

He might not have existed.

"You know who I am. I am Jedediah Revell. Your father commissioned two pieces of silver from me."

A flicker of her eyes toward him, nothing else. They were nearing the drawbridge over the Mill Creek; the light was fading fast, she wanted to get home before dark.

"If I could speak with you for a moment, there is something that you must hear—"

She stopped so abruptly that he nearly collided with her.

"Well?"

Amazing, the gratitude he felt toward her for even this grudging attention.

"Master Knollys has been paying court to you these past weeks."

"And what business is that of yours, Master—ah—"

"Revell. Jedediah Revell. You know me. You came into my shop last year."

"I do not remember." She moved on; instinctively he caught at her arm under the heavy cloth of her cape, but she pulled away at his touch.

"Please. You must listen to me. Master Knollys was acting for me."

And now, indeed, she paid attention to him. She stopped again, right in the middle of the bridge, and stared up at him as if he was her worst enemy.

"You!"

"Yes. He was my surrogate."

"Was!" Even as she stared at him, she knew he spoke the truth—this tall, lean, sharp-looking young man, not unattractive, but so serious, so intent, so different from jolly Thomas, who could always make her laugh, whose visits she had begun to look forward to. She had long since convinced herself that Thomas acted for no one but himself—and she had not minded, she had gone along with the little play, enjoying it, enjoying him: Mistress Thomas Knollys, she had thought—not a bad name. Thomas was rich—richer than her father, even; he could give her everything she wanted, and a good laugh in the bargain.

"Yes. I have dismissed him. I should have done so long ago, and I beg your pardon."

Catherine had been warned before she left London that the ways of the colonists were not the ways of Old England; but this—this was insufferable! To play with her as if she were a toy—a football, tossed back and forth!

"You shall not have it." She moved on, her chin higher than ever. She was shaking with fury. She would show him—and his friend, too! They laughed at her, no doubt, behind her back!

"Wait. Please. I cannot tell you how sorry I am. I know I should have spoken sooner."

She blinked, fighting back her tears. The world was a blur just then, but if she could not see, she could hear well enough, and in his voice she heard a note that gave her pause. Like most women, she was more or less uneducated, but she was not stupid; and she, like Jed, had inherited something of her father's shrewdness.

For the last time she halted; what a journey it had been, starting and stopping! She could see again; she could see him. She did not exactly take pity on him, but she did have a certain curiosity, stronger, just now, than her anger.

"Very well, Master Revell. You shall have my pardon after all. But only a conditional one. Come to call on me, and we will discuss it further." Had she been in better humor, she would have laughed at him; but this—this was her future at stake, it was no laughing matter!

He went to her that night. She sat by the fire, awaiting him. In the ruddy light her pale skin glowed pink; her hair shone like silverspun gold. She wore a dress of some soft, pale stuff that shimmered in the light of the flames. She had been working at a bit of embroidery; now her long, slender fingers let it fall. Her great blue eyes gazed at him steadily; she was in control of herself, and she knew exactly what she would say to him.

The servant who had let him in disappeared, as instructed; her parents, as instructed also, had done the same. For all her delicate appearance, Catherine had an iron will, and she was determined to handle this matter herself. Playing with her! She would show them who could play—and win!

Instead of asking him to sit down, she stood up; she felt more dignified that way. She bade him good evening; she was glad that her voice was steady.

"Well?" she said. "What did you want to say to me, Master Revell?"

"I want to ask you to marry me." There—like lancing a boil, his words cut cleanly through the poison of their misunderstanding.

As steady as she was, she was not prepared for that—not so soon—and right away she was a little off balance. "To marry you . . . ?"

". . . to beg your pardon, yes, and to understand—"

"Understand . . . ?"

". . . and to know that it was I who courted you—"

"Through your friend—"

"Yes, but only because I—"

"Lacked the courage—"

". . . did not want to press you. . . ."

He had had his speech prepared, had forgotten it—and now he was making no headway, he let her interrupt him at every word, he was a fool!

He stared at her as if he would devour her. How many nights had he imagined this meeting? And now his time was slipping away, he could not find the words he needed.

Hardly knowing what he did, he took her hands and raised them to his lips. He had not even taken off his cloak. She thought fleetingly of a magnificent eagle she had once seen, swooping down from the sky, all fierce and brown-gold in the sun. He was like that, she thought.

"Aaahhh . . ."

He enfolded her; he drew her to him and held her so close that she could feel him tremble beneath his thick layers of clothing. Her head spun; she clung to him to keep from falling. What pardon now, what talk of forgiveness? She had wanted him to beg her, she had thought to keep the upper hand, and now here she was, holding onto him for dear life to keep from swooning.

She lifted her face; he bent to kiss it—her lips, her eyes, the soft pale skin hot under his sudden passion. And then, she did not know how, she kissed him in return, she opened her mouth under his, she felt as if she could never stop, never tear herself away—ah! What thought of Master Thomas now?

11

They were married in August. The governor performed the ceremony—old John Endicott, still a hard, hard man, a zealous Puritan who saw no way but his own, and no recourse but banishment or death—often the same thing—for those who disagreed with him. Endicott's greatest claim to fame had come not long after he arrived in Massachusetts, when, at the behest of the Pilgrims at

Plymouth, he had taken a party of men to dislodge the notorious Thomas Morton and his maypole from Merrymount. Morton and his men had drunk and fornicated with Indian women, but more to the point—and much more dangerous—they had traded guns to the savages. That had been in 1628, two years before Winthrop came over and settled the Bay; the white presence in New England had been so fragile, so endangered, that Morton could not be allowed to stay.

Since marriage was a civil ceremony, not a religious one, Governor Endicott could not object to the fact that the Mayhews were Anglicans. His greater objection was to their finery; he frowned at Catherine's gown, gold lace and slashed sleeves and a bodice cut so low he could see her bosom. No woman should show her arms, let alone her breasts. He spoke of his displeasure to the Reverend Richard Mather, and the next week that worthy preached a sermon on the subject of women's immodesty. Perhaps Roger Williams had been right, after all, Endicott said: women should be veiled, hiding the shame of their sex.

For a wedding present, Jed made for Catherine a pair of silver candlesticks and a silver sugar box. Samuel Mayhew was pleased at that; he was pleased with everything about his new son-in-law. Thomas Knollys had been, he thought, too frivolous. The Revells were steadier: they had a reputation for hard work, more or less fair dealing—and luck, without which no one could succeed.

The night before the wedding he had drunk toasts with Bartle for a long time, until both of them were very merry indeed; they had agreed on everything in the world, on politics, on religion, on the King—splendid fellow, Bartholomew Revell! And his son, too! Bartle offered Samuel shares in his next ship; Samuel offered Bartle an introduction to his sons, his agents in London.

Samuel's gift to the newlyweds was a new house next to his own, in Ship Street in the North End. From the front door Catherine could look out onto the harbor at the ships that crowded in from Spain and France, from Holland and Italy and Portugal—all the flags of the world could be seen there. The shoreline bristled with wharves; sailors roistered through the town at all hours, keeping the watch busy; you could buy anything you wanted in the Boston shops, filled as they were with goods from all of Europe.

And the town itself was growing by leaps and bounds, so crowded now that even farmland in Muddy River or Rocksborough was becoming scarce. Only a few years before, with a large bequest from the merchant Robert Keayne, a Town House had been built at the marketplace, with chambers above for the meeting of the General Court, and an open place below for the selling of produce and merchandise. There were, by now, a few brick houses in the town, but most were still made of wood, unpainted save for their red trim, huddled together, steep-roofed and high-gabled, the way houses stood in northern European towns. Even here, with all the space in Cambridge and Charlestown if not in Boston, houses went up cheek by jowl because they were built that way at home.

Home! Where was home, to a man New England born? Not London or Canterbury or York or Lincoln; home was here, on the thin little fringe of settlement on the edge of a wilderness whose end no one knew, not even the savages who lived in it.

Catherine did not allow herself to be homesick. She had been in New England for more than a year; she was beginning to forget what her brothers looked like. She would never forget England, of that she was sure—the gentle countryside, the excitement of the great city of London; but she would not mourn for it. Perhaps she would even return some day; people did that, she knew. And Boston was not so bad, after all: or so, at least, she told herself.

When she learned that she was pregnant, she was pleased. She knew well enough that you could die, giving birth, but she could not imagine dying—why, she had hardly begun to live!—and so she did not fear it. Dying happened to other people, not to her.

She rather enjoyed her pregnancy. Jed doted on her; her father and mother ran over at all hours to see how she did, to bring her a little delicacy, figs in wine, sugared almonds, or a plum cake or bit of gingerbread. Her mother-in-law, too, was solicitous: obviously the Lord had intended that Catherine be Jed's wife, or otherwise she would not have been; as she accepted every work of the Lord's, Susannah accepted that.

One day in January when the cold gripped the settlement like an iron fist, the harbor frozen over, ink freezing in the inkwell, a man dead of cold in the cage for Sabbath breakers, Jed and Bartle came in together, stamping their feet, rubbing their hands and noses and ears—Lord, Lord, what cold! They had, it seemed, a present for her. Catherine, who had been drooping a little—no one had warned her how tiring pregnancy was—brightened at once. She loved presents. What is it? she wanted to know. Don't keep me in suspense. What have you brought me?

When Jed went to the door, she realized that they had made someone wait outside. In this cold!

A small figure wrapped in a dark cape stood before her. Fanned by the brief, bitter gust of wind, the fire blazed up for a moment; Catherine saw two great dark eyes staring at her. And now, as Jed unwrapped the cape, pulled back the hood, Catherine was astonished to see a face as dark as the eyes; black crinkled hair pulled into a topknot; a thin face, trembling lips—dear heaven, a blackamoor!

"Captain Gridley brought her in last week," said Jed. "She has been staying at Mother's until we could get her cleaned and fed up a bit. She was frightened at first, and would not eat; but now I think she's more accustomed to us. She seems quite bright; Mother said that she learns quickly. She will be of great use to you, we thought."

Catherine was delighted. "What is her name?"

"She has none yet," said Bartle. "None we know, that is. So you can name her yourself."

Catherine had been sitting in bed to keep warm. Now she swung herself up, found her black Morocco leather slippers, and heavily, not yet accustomed to her burden, stepped to where the girl stood by the fire. Sitting down on the bench, Catherine said, "Come here, child. How old are you?"

No answer. The small figure stood immobile, the great dark eyes staring in the expressionless face.

"About fifteen, we think," said Jed. "She's stronger than she looks. We could have sold her for ten pounds, at least."

Catherine was not accustomed to thinking of other people's feelings. Her wants, her desires, centered largely on herself. But now—how strange it was— it occurred to her to wonder what this girl was thinking: what she felt. Was she sad? Angry? Would she resent being put into lifetime service? Did she even understand that that was to be her fate? Suddenly Catherine took the girl's hands in her own and smiled at her. How cold the child was!

"Now, Missy," she said, "would you like to live with us? And I will teach you—oh, everything! How to cook, and sew, and spin—would you like that?"

And, looking up at the men: "That is what I will call her: Missy."

And so they knew that Catherine would keep their gift, and they were pleased that she was happy with it.

Still the girl made no reply. A tear welled up and spilled down her thin cheek, and then another. Catherine—and Jed and Bartle, too—took it for an answer: she would accept her fate.

As the winter wore on, day after day of cold and snow and ice making it difficult for her to get around as she grew ever bulkier, Catherine amused herself by teaching the little slave all that she had promised to do, and more. As Bartle had said, the girl was quick to learn. Within a month Catherine could trust her to make a passable pot of baked beans and pretty good hasty pudding, and to sew a reasonably straight seam. Spinning was more difficult, but Missy kept at it, and by the time the baby came she could draw out a thread almost as fine as Catherine's.

The girl learned to speak a little, too, and to sing from the *Psalm Book* more or less on key. She slept beside Jed and Catherine's great bed. At first Catherine had intended to have her sleep in the shed with the indentured girl; but in the middle of the first night, the girl had come in to report that the black child was having nightmares, screaming in her sleep, and Catherine brought her inside and put her on the floor beside her, where she slept quietly. After that, Missy never went back to the shed.

When Catherine's baby was born in May—a two-day torment that made Jed despair of the life of both mother and child—Missy stood at Catherine's side the whole time, helping in whatever way she could but mostly just holding Catherine's hand and wiping her sweat and tears. And when the torment was over and the baby was sucking well at Catherine's breast and Catherine herself was somewhat recovered, Missy looked down at the little creature and put out her finger to its tiny fist; and when the baby instinctively grasped it, Missy smiled.

"See," she said. "He strong."

Catherine was astonished. The girl was actually pretty when she smiled!

And from that day the child—a boy whom they named Isaac—was Missy's delight: she bathed him and held him and crooned soft, mysterious sounds to him—the only thing that she could not do was feed him, but as he grew and began to take solid food, she could do that as well.

Catherine did not mind. Caring for a baby was indescribably tedious. You endured long months of discomfort while you carried it, and you went through the pains of Hell when you delivered it—and then you were, in effect, its servant for years and years until it grew up. She knew well enough that the ministers said that it was women's fate to bear children, and to bear them in sorrow; and she knew that women who were barren were somehow ashamed (only married barren women, however; the shame was otherwise when an unmarried woman gave birth—so you had to belong to some man before it was all right to fulfill women's purpose, it seemed). Women's fate or not, the ministers had no idea what it meant to bear a child. She had done it, and probably she would have to do it again—a thought that gave her the cold sweats; and so for the moment she was content to let Missy care for the child as much as possible.

Susannah did not think that her daughter-in-law was wise to entrust the precious baby to a black slave. She did not like to meddle, but she visited as often as she could and watched closely as the girl went about her business. Missy seemed frightened of her scrutiny; she sidled away when Susannah came near, and her hands trembled so that once she nearly set the house on fire trying to light a lamp. Once, when Susannah came in, Missy refused to give her the child: she sat as if transfixed, clutching him in her arms, staring up at Susannah with wide, frightened eyes as if she was bewitched. Susannah had had to forcibly take the baby from the girl's grasp—and then he cried pitifully, she could not quiet him. Susannah had heard that blackamoors were agents of the Devil. This girl did not seem devilish—and yet, who could tell? Satan laid his traps, and the unwary fell into them.

Susannah began to take a dislike to her daughter-in-law. Surely it was unnatural not to want to look after your own child—and, worse, to allow an agent of Satan to care for it? And surely Catherine was too vain—too concerned with her worldly possessions? She had a new dress for every day in the week; she had jewelry and gold lace and many pairs of shoes; she had recently ordered bed hangings of a rich brocade that cost a fortune; and her manner was becoming increasingly haughty and cold—not the proper deference to her elders that young people ought to have.

The last straw fell when Catherine announced that Jed was building a fine new house near John Hull's, not far from the Common—a house with four rooms below, and a proper second floor instead of a loft, and enough land for a big garden and a few fruit trees.

"You'll have Jed bankrupt!" exclaimed Susannah; she had not meant to speak so abruptly, but the words popped out of her mouth before she could prevent them.

And then did she regret her hasty speech! Catherine wept and stormed, she claimed that her mother-in-law had never liked her, that she had always held a grudge against her. Susannah, torn between irritation and alarm, managed to calm her after a while with soothing promises that Catherine did not believe for a minute—the old sow! In the midst of the trouble, Susannah learned that Catherine was pregnant again—and that might be the cause of her moodiness, her greed to have as much of life as she could, as quick as she could. For now, this second time, she heartily believed that she could die, and that she probably would. She knew now what it was to birth a child, and nothing that her own mother or Susannah or any other woman could say to her comforted her. She lived in terror of the day she was to be brought to bed; and if her loving husband chose to distract her with a new length of cloth, or a pretty bit of silver—or even a grand new house which he could well afford—it was no one's business but her own.

Such a belief—that people's affairs were their own and not the larger community's—was Anglican, not Puritan. And so, even though she now understood why her daughter-in-law behaved as she did, Susannah felt constrained to talk to her minister about her worries over the young woman's conduct.

Recently the Reverend Increase Mather had been much troubled by the falling away of the younger generation in the Bay Colony. They were too worldly by far; they seemed to have forgotten why their fathers settled the place—to worship God in their own way, and to suffer no man to tell them different. The merchants of London who financed the venture had cared for nothing but profit, and so the two sides, God and Mammon, had always been in conflict; and now, it seemed, with the triumph of the Stuarts, God's purpose was being forgotten altogether in the new rush for worldly gain, and He might well punish them all on both sides of the water for their iniquity.

So Mistress Revell's questions, her tales of her daughter-in-law's behavior, struck a nerve in Mather's tormented soul. He gave her a copy of the Reverend Michael Wigglesworth's great poem, recently published from the press at Cambridge: "The Day of Doom."

It was Increase Mather's belief that Wigglesworth had composed this opus partly to gain forgiveness from God for having at the age of fifty-two, and against the advice of every minister in the Bay, married his teenaged servant girl. She was not even baptized! Everyone had been shocked—scandalized. It was not fitting, it was not seemly—and yet Wigglesworth had done it, and had gone on preaching to his flock over in Malden, telling them how to behave themselves. Now had come this mighty work, a warning to everyone to toe the line in the face of God's all-seeing, jealous wrath.

Mather had to admit that it was a wonderful thing, that poem. Two hundred and twenty-four verses warning sinners that

> Your gold is brass, your silver dross,
> Your righteousness is sin. . . .

He would not have minded writing such a poem himself. He admonished Susannah to read it aloud to her daughter-in-law. But when Susannah tried to do so, Catherine scrunched her eyes shut and drew her pretty mouth down into a hard line and clapped her hands over her ears and threatened to tell Jed that his mother was persecuting her. To add to the insult, Missy giggled softly at Susannah's discomfiture.

Catherine knew that Jed would take her side, for as much as he respected his parents, he adored his wife. The new house was only the beginning of what he would do for her, for he was prospering far beyond his expectations. There was no end of a market for cod and timber and rum, it seemed; and every shipload of wine and sugar and tobacco that returned brought him new profits. And only last month one of his ships had come in bearing treasure: a pirate ship had attacked his own, and his captain had won the fight, taking all that was on the pirate ship, killing the pirate captain, and bringing back seven filthy prisoners in chains. Jed had stood in his warehouse watching in amazement as the trunks of gold and jewels and silver bars were opened and counted—a treasure indeed! He had slept there that night, keeping an armed guard with his father and three other men; even the honest merchants of Boston in New England might be tempted by such a haul.

So he could well afford to give Catherine her fine new house, and her silks and laces and jewels, and anything else that she wanted. He had even offered her a sedan chair, but she had declined it; such a thing was too showy even for her.

Jed knew that married couples often grew apart, even though they were bound to each other for life. And so he was somewhat surprised to discover that he loved Catherine far more now, two years after their marriage, than he had at the beginning—and certainly he had loved her excessively then.

And now, as she grew near her time once again, he could not do enough for her. He hired another maidservant so that Missy could devote herself exclusively to Catherine; he bought the finest food he could find—lemons and limes, strawberries and peaches, butter and white-flour bread, the best Canary wine. Every day, as the new house went up, he brought the horse with its wide, comfortable sidesaddle so that Catherine could go to inspect—a carriage would have jolted her far too much. On days of bad weather he went himself and reported back to her: the black-and-white tile floor was complete; the diamond-shaped glass panes had arrived; the carved wooden mantel had been set in place.

When Catherine complained of being too tired to sit in meeting all the Lord's Day, Jed insisted that she not go. Once—and only once—the tithingman had rapped her head when she nodded off during the sermon; she had been so angry that she very nearly got up and walked out there and then. She had consented to go to the North Church, she said, because it was Jed's church. But she was an Anglican, and she would not suffer the insults of the stiff-necked Congregationalists any longer.

Jed acquiesced; he would have acquiesced to anything. Only let her live, he thought; only let her be by my side forever. Her pale hair had darkened a little, but it was still like finespun gold; her skin was still pure and white, faint blue on the eyelids, faint pink on the lips. Kissing her was like kissing a flower, soft cool petals touched by the morning's dew.

A month before her time, when the new house was complete and they were finally settled in, Jed proposed an idea that would, he thought, help to pass the last, difficult days of her pregnancy—and would also, in the unthinkable event of her death, give him some tangible remembrance of her.

"He has painted Mrs. Freake and Baby Mary," he said. "I would like to commission a portrait of you."

Catherine was amused by the idea, and it appealed to her vanity. She had seen portraits in England—magnificent pictures in which the artist had captured rich silks and velvets, the glow of gold buttons and jewelry—how handsome and imposing men and women looked in portraits!

"Is he a talented man?" she said. "Did he get their likenesses?" Although, God knew, Mrs. Freake was hardly a beauty; perhaps he had improved on Nature.

"Talented enough," said Jed. He had no idea of what a proper portrait should be; but the picture he had seen had been pretty good, he thought: better than nothing.

The artist was a tall, thin man; he spoke little, but he had a keen eye. Catherine felt somewhat uncomfortable in his presence, as if she were stripped naked, but she sat for him contentedly enough, a smile on her pretty face, her hair elegantly dressed in ringlets down the sides of her cheeks and pulled into a topknot behind, covered with a wisp of lace cap. She wore a low-cut dress with a wide lace bertha; its big puffed sleeves were caught above and below the elbow with velvet ribbons, and the rich blue brocade skirt was open at the front to show the white silk underskirt. A necklace of tiny gold beads encircled her long white throat; gold rings adorned her fingers.

Because of her delicate condition, she sat rather than stood. The artist had agreed to use his skill to paint her as herself: not swollen in pregnancy, but thin and elegant. He would not let her see the painting as he worked on it; he brought it with him each day when he came, and carried it away with him again when he left. She was aflame with curiosity: she could not wait to see herself.

At last he was done. He insisted that he would not let her see it before he showed it to Jed, and so she needed to wait until her husband came home to see what the artist had done with her. With a little flourish he took off the piece of canvas covering it. Catherine was so shocked that she could not speak. Stupid wretch! What had he done to her? She looked like—like nothing! Like a carved skull on a tombstone! Like the woodcut of the Reverend Richard Mather that some crude provincial workman had made for that worthy's biography!

And yet it was not a bad likeness: her delicate features, her fine golden hair, her graceful, long-fingered hands. But the thing was stiff and plain, like a child's drawing: the artist had not had the skill to make a portrait that was lifelike and glowing with texture; he had worked in two dimensions rather than three, so the portrait had a flat, unskilled appearance.

Catherine ran to her great canopied bed in the back room and flung herself, weeping, on the soft down-filled mattress. She was mussing her dress, but she did not care. Her great belly prevented her from lying face down on her stomach, which was the proper pose for such a tantrum; she lay on her side and buried her face in the pillows and refused to yield to Jed when he came to comfort her. She would not look at him; she would not speak to him. She was humiliated for life—and it was all his fault!

At last, exhausted, she fell asleep. The artist had long since departed with his pay, leaving the portrait propped on the mantel. He thought it was quite good, the best he had done. It never occurred to him to sign it—an odd omission, for all craftsmen signed their work.

Jed thought that the portrait of his wife was splendid, and he insisted on hanging it in the front room where every guest could see it—just this once, he went against her wishes, for she wanted to throw it into the fire. He made her promise that she would not do so some day while he was at the warehouse or in his shop.

Eventually she grew accustomed to it. Not many women, after all, had their portraits painted—and most women in the Massachusetts Bay were either provincials, born on this side of the water, or women who in England never even saw a portrait, let alone had one painted. They did not know the difference between good and bad, between glowing life on canvas and this stiff, unlifelike production. She had so many compliments on it, so many envious glances from her neighbors, that at last she came to think highly of it, and even to tell people that it had been her idea to have it done.

The baby was born a week later: a girl. She had no strength to suck—no strength to cry, even. She lay quiet and pale, hardly breathing, her eyes closed. In a month she was dead. Susannah, with all her experience in childbirth, had known at once that the infant would not live, but she had not had the heart to say so—more for Jed's sake than Catherine's, if the truth be told.

"There will be others," she said, trying to comfort him as best she might. "The best thing you can do for her is give her another. A woman needs a baby at her breast to feel right in this world."

Jed agreed; and yet they both knew that Catherine was different from other women: she seemed to lack, somehow, the maternal instinct. She made it quite clear to him, in fact, that she was not prepared to bring another child into the world just yet, and she refused him his marital rights for weeks afterward.

This was a crime against Nature, as both of them knew; he could have taken the matter to the General Court, had he been cruel enough. But of course he was not. Only recently he had heard about a woman in Plymouth who, having borne nineteen children, had hanged herself when she was pregnant with her twentieth. So one way or another, pregnancy was dangerous: he would not force Catherine to endure it again until she was ready. And so he abided by her wishes and patiently waited, night after night, until she was ready to give herself to him again. Night after night he held her in his arms while she sobbed herself to sleep; day after day he kept an eye out for any small thing—a new book from London, a pretty piece of cloth—that might amuse her. And when at last she recovered and let him couple with her again, it seemed as if he was taking her for the first time, so sweet it was, and in the ecstasy of it he forgot that he put her at risk, he forgot that in loving her so, he might lose her.

The next year she bore a boy, William, who lived; then a girl, who did not; and then at last, to her great joy, a girl who was so strong and healthy that no one had any doubt that she would survive, and so she did. They named her Lydia.

That was in 1669. By that time, Jedediah Revell and his father Bartholomew were among the richest men in the Bay. Of course they took losses like everyone else: ships lost at sea, a cargo of sour wine that they could not sell, hogsheads of fish improperly cured and stinking to the heavens—but all in all, they were favored by fortune, and they prospered well.

Catherine was as pampered and petted as any woman in the world. No woman at the court of the King himself had a more comfortable life. Her little slave, Missy, was at her beck and call; she had an indentured woman to look after the children, and another to do the cooking and cleaning; a hired man lived at the family's farm in Muddy River with two others to help him tend the crops, so in town they kept only a small kitchen garden and a few fruit trees—none of which Catherine had to care for. Her father had died the year before Lydia's birth, but her mother was still alive.

There was only one thing, in fact, that Catherine regretted, and that was that her sister Mary lived so far away in Lancaster—thirty miles away, too far for Mary to come to Boston more than once a year, and sometimes not even that. Catherine missed Mary more and more, but there was no hope, it seemed, of ever living close to her. Mary's husband was in his place for life, for once called, a minister stayed with his flock until death; and certainly the Revells were not going to go into the wilderness.

So the years passed, with only that one disappointment. The children grew; Jed got richer and richer; one month, one year, slid comfortably into the next until, before she knew it, little Isaac, her firstborn, was nearly eleven years old. Already Jed was talking of sending him to the College; sometimes he wished that he had gone there himself. Almost certainly the boy would join the family business, but no matter: education never hurt a man, and the business would be there for him when he was ready.

But then, like everyone else from time to time, Jed had a run of bad luck, and he decided to make a business trip.

"To London!" Catherine stared at her husband, astonished. "Why must you go to London?"

"We are losing our trade. We must find new agents there—the ones we have are cheating us, sending too little, or bad quality. Last month we had a shipment of wool that was so filled with moth that they flew out like flies."

While the Revells traded much with the Wine Islands and the Barbados, still, like all Boston merchants, they depended on London for manufactured goods.

London had been devastated several years before by a great plague and fire. The reports of it had been appalling: the dead carted through the streets, people fleeing to the countryside in panic, leaving all their possessions behind, only to lose them in the conflagration. Trade had not yet recovered—hence, perhaps, the unreliability of Jed's agents there.

Jed shifted uncomfortably in his high-backed great chair. He had known that Catherine would be upset at his news—not only because she would be left alone, but because, as she did not hesitate to tell him, she wanted to go with him.

"Why can I not come, too? I would love to see London again! As you very well know, besides my brothers, I have cousins there, uncles and aunts . . ."

But perhaps not: who knew how many had died in the plague? And besides—

"This is not a trip for pleasure," Jed declared. "I must be free to concentrate on business. I will not have time to escort you around, to see that you are taken care of. If all goes well, I will take you and the children—and your mother, too, if she wishes it—next year."

Next year! Next year they could all be dead! She wanted to go with him now—oh, it was not fair that he could go about the world as he pleased and she was condemned to stay at home!

She did not speak to him for three days. And while Jed was sincerely troubled by her anger, her silent reproachful weeping, he did not relent.

At last she made up her mind to take a journey of her own. The day after Jed set sail, she called on the man who once had courted her in Jed's place, Master Thomas Knollys.

4. THE TOTEM OF THE WOLF

1

In January 1675 the body of John Sassamon was found beneath the ice of Assawompsett Pond near Plymouth. His hat and his gun lay on the frozen surface nearby.

John Sassamon had lived between the two worlds of white man and red. He had been the first Indian student at Harvard College, and a disciple of the great preacher to the Indians, John Eliot; he had helped Eliot translate the Bible into Algonquian—the *Up-Biblium God*—and had taught his fellows at the praying village at Natick. He had served with the English during the Pequot War forty years before. If any savage in North America could be thought of as a friend to the white man, it was John Sassamon.

And yet he had remained close to his people, for he had also served the Wampanoags: he had been scribe and interpreter to the sachem Metacomet, the younger son of the great friend of the Pilgrims, Massasoit.

The English called Metacomet "King Philip."

Some weeks after John Sassamon's death the magistrates at Plymouth discovered an eyewitness. Three Indians had killed John Sassamon, he said: Tobias and his son Wampapaquan, and another called Mattashunnamo. Their motive was clear: a few days before his death, John Sassamon had gone to Plymouth with a warning—King Philip plans a general rising of the tribes against you, he said; he wants to exterminate you.

The English had feared this thing since they first set foot on the shores of the New World. Nothing struck greater terror into a white man's heart than the thought of extermination of the settlers at the hands of the Indians. Thus very quickly it had become a crime punishable by fines and whipping to give or sell a gun to an Indian—a stricture that did nothing to prevent the wily French, in Canada, from trading guns to the savages as much as they pleased.

And while the missionary efforts of Eliot and others were generally approved, many whites thought that you could never trust a savage no matter how many psalms he sang.

The three accused were tried for John Sassamon's murder, and on June 8 they were hanged. Word of the execution spread quickly through the forest: roving bands of Indians began to attack outlying settlements, burning houses, shooting arrows—or bullets—into whites as they worked the fields. In late June a party of militiamen came upon a grisly scene at Swansea, not far from Plymouth: the settlement deserted and partly burned, ten white heads stuck on poles. Clearly, the whirlwind was about to descend on the Massachusetts Bay. Night and day could be heard the throbbing of the drums, spreading the message: attack!

John Sassamon had told the truth about King Philip. When Massasoit died, Philip had agreed to keep the Wampanoags' treaty of peace with the white man; but as the years passed, and more and more whites came in, Philip began to nurture a dislike for them. White men tricked him into signing away his lands, and he put his mark to many pieces of parchment: 𝓟. They forced Philip's people to abide by the white man's law—a mysterious code that held harsh punishments for transgression. Worst of all, they tried to foist their own strange God upon the tribes. Once, angered, Philip had confronted the great Eliot himself. He took one of Eliot's coat buttons between his two fingers and pulled at it, saying, "I care no more for your God than that!"

Then Philip's elder brother, Wamsutta—called Alexander by the English—had died after harsh questioning in Plymouth: were the tribes planning an uprising? Was Alexander at the head of a conspiracy? He had denied it, and so they had let him go—so weak and sick that he could hardly walk. Two days later he was dead. Philip always believed that his brother had been poisoned by the English; nothing could shake his conviction. Added to all his other grievances, it blossomed into an all-consuming hatred for the interlopers.

By July the English had mobilized a force to pursue King Philip and his warriors. Captain Thomas Savage led an expedition into the Pocasset Swamp where, he believed, King Philip lay hiding.

The white men, who had faithfully trained for years in military trainbands, marching smartly back and forth in precise formation preparing for just such an emergency as this, were helpless in the great cedar swamp where every bush that swayed in the wind seemed a savage ready to attack. Their muskets were tangled in vines, a thousand stinging insects crawled underneath their armor, their heavy boots caught in the roots of trees, they blundered into snake-infested pools. Worst of all, they made such a racket as they moved that they could be heard a mile away. No Indian would be surprised by that noisy gang.

In the end, King Philip and his braves got away: the English never saw him. Now he went to the tribes—to the Nipmucks, to the Massachusetts—and they believed him when he said that they must unite against the white man;

and sachems who until now had been reluctant to war against the English, possessors of the terrible hot-mouthed weapons, could see for themselves that war had come at last and the tribes must put away their quarrels and unite against the common enemy. The only good white man was a dead white man: Make war!

In the towns near Plymouth, that summer and fall, and near the Rhode Island border, people left their farms and crowded into garrison houses where, night after night, they listened to the drums in the forest drumming out the message of their death. The farms were left to nature; crops choked in weeds, livestock strayed or were stolen by the Indians; many houses and barns were burned.

Almost worse than the attack was waiting for it. Through the long hours of darkness, crowded into their shelters, men and women and children lay awake listening for the first bloodcurdling war whoop. The Indians could move through the forest as silent as a bird in the sky. Not until they were upon you did you know they were there. And then they made noise enough, God knew, yelling and hollering as they fired the house over your head and sank a hatchet into your skull as you ran out to save yourself. Many whites thought that such a death was a mercy, for tales of torture abounded, indescribable agonies at the hands of these savages who were, surely, the Devil's own.

And now King Philip had escaped to fight again another day.

2

Thomas Knollys had long since married; nevertheless, he still thought Catherine Revell, née Mayhew, the finest-looking woman in the Bay Colony, and he was always glad to see her. When she told him what she wanted, he was quick to oblige.

"I know a fellow who's leaving next week," he said. "He's a fur trader, not very civilized, but a good man in the wilderness. He generally makes up a party when he goes back and forth, to earn a little extra. He'll take you along."

When Catherine's little daughter, Lydia, heard that she was to make a journey, she was ecstatic. She had never gone anywhere except to the farm at Muddy River, and that hardly counted. Even at six she knew that there was a great world beyond the narrow confines of the little town of Boston; she had no idea what it might be like, but she was eager to see it. And to visit her Aunt Mary, whom she had not seen but twice, whose face she could not even remember—Lydia thought she would burst with excitement.

On a morning in late May Catherine kissed her sons good-bye, and her mother, and her father and mother-in-law; she gave a final warning to the servants about the running of the house; and she and Lydia and the black slave, Missy, set forth in the little caravan: the fur trader; a young man who had recently been hired as schoolteacher to the town of Groton; a family going out to settle; and Catherine and her two charges. Catherine rode a glossy bay mare, with Missy riding pillion behind; Lydia rode her own little pony. It was a fine summer day, a sunshining day, the breeze blowing fat, puffy clouds across the bright blue sky. Lydia's heart was beating fast as the little convoy made its way across the great bridge and past the College and onto the Western Way. Soon all signs of civilization were behind them: they rode through the forest where trees grew so thick that the light was dim. Here and there dappled sun shone through, and once, to Lydia's delight, she saw a doe and her fawn, startled into immobility by the sight and smell of humans. Birds twittered in the treetops; squirrels clattered along the branches. Once they passed a clearing, and on the far side they saw a bear; it stood on its hind legs for a moment, then dropped to all fours and lumbered into the trees. Lydia was enchanted at this wilderness world: she was a child of the town, she had never imagined that so vast a forest existed.

In the late afternoon they came to Concord, where they spent the night in the house of a settler. It was a rude place, rough pine furniture and no light save dim rush lamps. The men slept on the floor, and the children of the host family were turned out of their bed to let the visiting women take their places—although the mattress, stuffed with moldy grass, was so uncomfortable that Lydia almost would have preferred the floor. Concord was swampy; all night mosquitoes whined in her ears and bit her mercilessly. Lydia began to be a little less happy then, but her mother assured her that there were no mosquitoes in Lancaster, and so she cheered up again.

At last, at the end of the second day, they came to Lancaster, a wilderness settlement of a dozen houses and barns scattered over the countryside, a large garrison house, a crude little church, and the minister's house.

And then what a happy reunion! Catherine, stiff from the long journey, hungry and thirsty, forgot all her discomfort as she jumped down and ran to embrace her sister. A year and more since they had met—and how tired Mary looked, how thin!

The company bade farewell to the fur trapper, who was continuing on foot, and to the settling family and the schoolmaster, and Catherine and Missy and Lydia followed Mary into her house. Like the house they had visited at Concord, this was a frontier place with few amenities. Rough pine boards served as the floor; a crude loft was the sleeping place for the children. Meals were served on woodenware; the only objects of beauty to be seen were two pewter plates and a silver cup, made by Jed, on the pine chest. The windows were very small, covered with oiled paper, so that even with the shutters turned back, the house was dark. Catherine's heart sank. This was her first visit to Lancaster; if she had known it was so bleak here, would she have come?

But then, looking around, she saw that Lydia was happily engaged in feeding a litter of puppies who had just learned to drink on their own; her cousins said she could name the smallest one. And Mary was so happy to see her—ah, yes, she had been right to come, she would stay a good long time.

Her heart sank even more when she looked at her older sister. Mary had never been a beauty, but now she was so worn down by work and loneliness that she seemed like a woman of fifty. She was not, though; she was still young enough to breed, for only three months before she had given birth—in this wilderness!—to her eleventh child; six children lived. It was a boy: big and healthy, almost sure to survive.

Mary's husband was a tall, silent man who found eloquence, it seemed, only when he was preaching. When he took the pulpit, he seemed to be given a voice from God; the people in the settlement were grateful to have him. But otherwise he said little. He tilled his land and cared for his livestock from dawn to dusk and never spoke ten words at a time. In the evenings he took a precious candle and sat by the fire reading his Bible long after everyone else had gone to bed—which they generally did right after supper, for all of them worked hard, and none harder than Mary.

After a day or two Catherine realized that Mary did not want to hear the news of Boston; she was not interested in the latest gossip, in news of the latest fashions, or word from England. She had grown narrow and dull, uncaring of the world beyond this small settlement in the wilderness. Catherine had brought her three books—a great treat, she thought, particularly *Paradise Lost*, but they lay untouched; Mary had no interest in reading.

The summer passed and autumn came; the forest was aflame with color, red and gold and coppery brown glowing in the sun. The settlers were busier than ever now, getting in the harvest to store for the winter; a great mound of pumpkins glowed by the doorstep, and the back shed was sweet with herbs hung to dry. One day John and several of the men went hunting and returned with a deer. Catherine thought she would be ill, watching them disembowel it and cut its meat to cure, blood glistening over the slippery intestines, Mary covered with gore as she worked alongside the men; but Lydia was fascinated.

No word came from Jed. The brilliant leaves dropped from the trees; the wind blew hard from the north: November. Catherine grew uneasy. She could imagine life here when winter came. Sometimes, Mary told her, they did not leave the house for weeks: where would they go, with the countryside buried waist deep in snow?

At last one day toward the middle of the month Catherine said that she must go home. She hated the thought of living in Boston without Jed; more, she wanted him to return from England to find her gone, and beg her to come home. And she hated to leave Mary alone (for so she thought of her) to face yet another long winter—but even more, she did not want to spend a winter here herself. Surely, she thought, I will go mad if I have to stay cooped up here until spring. And if she were to go, she must go now, before the snows came. No one could travel to and from the frontier towns in the winter—no English person, that is; the Indians, children of the forest, could come and go as they pleased on their snowshoes.

She and Lydia and Missy could not make the trip by themselves, of course, and so it had been arranged that Talbot and one of the other men would travel with them. She hated to take Mary's husband from her. "Does he need to go?" she said. "We would be all right with someone else."

But Talbot did need to go, although he did not tell the women why. All through the autumn the settlement had been plagued by theft: not from one of their own, but—he was sure—from Indians. A goat and two sheep had been stolen only the week before, and before that, some tools and a bag of seed corn. Despite the garrison house, the settlers were poorly defended, at the mercy of an Indian attack. Talbot had made up his mind to go to Boston to ask the authorities for help: for more families to settle, and perhaps for a few militia as well. Only the day before, a lone white man on horseback passing through to Deerfield had given a warning: the Indians were hostile, he had heard that they planned an attack. He did not know exactly where. There had been fighting near Rhode Island, some whites killed—best be prepared for trouble.

And so the sisters spent one last evening together shadowed by the knowledge that in the morning they must part. Catherine made Mary promise that in the spring, after mudtime, she would come to Boston.

Mary's face showed no pleasure at the thought. "Yes," she said, "I will come. But it is hard to leave. I have all the more work when I get back, and I—"

She broke off, holding up her hand as a warning to Catherine to be silent.

They listened: they heard nothing save the hiss and crackle of the fire, John's soft snoring in the bed in the corner, the night wind gusting against the stout wooden walls of the little house.

"What is it?" said Catherine softly.

Mary shook her head. "I thought I heard— There! There it is!"

The sound of a drum: not the tattoo of an English military drum, but the deeper, ominous sound of deerskin stretched over a hollow log.

Mary's hand flew to her throat.

"The savages!" she said. And in the next instant she had shaken her husband awake. "John! Drums!"

At once he was on his feet; he had slept in his clothes these past days because he had feared this very thing. He motioned them to silence and went to the window; unbarring the shutter, he put his head close to the oiled-paper panes. Yes: there it was, a little louder now. Some white men—Roger Williams, for one—would have been able to interpret those sounds as easily as speech; John Talbot could not do that, but even so, the message was clear enough. Savages did not drum at night in the forest for no purpose.

He fastened the shutter again and turned to the two frightened women. "We must get to the garrison house. I am going to rouse the others."

"John—no! Not at night!" The houses were widely scattered; he would need his horse, he would be an easy target. But not so easy as in daylight, he thought.

"Perhaps they will come in on their own," said Catherine. "They must hear it, too. John, do not go—please!"

At last he assented. They would watch all night, he said, and at dawn he would fire the warning that all the settlers knew, the summons to the garrison house: three shots, three seconds of silence, then three shots again.

He took down his flintlock from where it hung near the door, and a stock of bullets and powder, and sat by the fire to load it. The women watched him, hardly believing what they saw. Catherine thought that she must be having a nightmare. Surely this could not be happening! Not to her—not to Mistress Jedediah Revell, wife of one of the richest merchants of Boston, a woman of good breeding who had every luxury that the Colony could offer, who lived in comfort and security— No!

Although she sat close to the fire, her hands were icy cold; her heart beat so fast that she thought she could not breathe. She strained her ears; she could hear nothing but the sounds of John working on his gun.

He looked up at the two women watching him and said, "Catherine, can you handle a weapon like this?"

Foolish question: whyever would she know a thing like that? "No," she said; her voice was a whisper, her throat dry and aching. Guns were men's business—his business, not hers. But then she understood the reason for his question: if he were killed, or badly wounded, it would be her job, and Mary's, to fight the savages, to protect the children.

"Well, it is no time now for you to learn," he said. "Mary, do you remember what I showed you?"

From his flask he poured powder into a hollow turkey bone to get the right measure. He emptied the powder into the barrel, dropped in the ball, and tapped in a wad of paper with the ramrod. Then he half cocked the gun, pushed the steel forward to uncover the pan, poured in a bit of powder to prime, and pulled the steel back into place.

Mary nodded. The flintlock was heavy; she had never be able to hold it well enough to aim.

"Good," he said. He lifted his head, listening. They all heard: the drums again, and now, too, what sounded like faint cries, whooping and yelling.

"We will pray now," he said. The three of them went on their knees: three vulnerable souls in the midst of the wilderness.

"Merciful Lord, we beseech Thee to deliver us from harm at the hands of the savages. . . ."

His voice was quiet, steady; he prayed so often that he talked to God as easily as he did to his fellow human beings—perhaps more so. He did not sound frightened at all, Catherine thought: he sounded as if he had every confidence that God heard him and would do as he asked.

She wanted to say a prayer, too, but she could not find the proper words. *Do not let us be killed*—but she could not say such a thing, she pushed the thought out of her mind and tried to listen to John: ". . . give us strength to bear what torment we must . . ."

She shuddered; she reached for Mary's hand. It was as cold as her own.

All night they sat by the fire, watching, waiting. From time to time they heard the drums again. Although Catherine was exhausted, she was not sleepy; her eyes stayed wide, her ears alert, her stomach churning with fear.

But at some point she dozed. She awakened to horror—savage voices roaring like hellhounds, and then small thuds as burning brands landed on the roof; instantly the wooden shingles caught fire. The children, terrified, came tumbling down; Missy clutched Lydia to her breast, crying and moaning, while the baby screamed and the other children huddled in the corner, too terrified to move.

"Get behind me!" John cried as he seized his gun. "We will have to run for it—make for the garrison!"

Over their heads the roof was aflame. John opened a shutter. The Indians made a terrible noise, yelling and hollering, but over the sounds of their voices could be heard the sounds of gunfire, and for a moment Catherine thought that the others in the settlement, aroused, had come to their aid.

Then a bullet came through the window, straight into John's head. He fell, his gun clattering to the floor beside him.

Now everyone was struck dumb save the baby, who wailed loudly in his cradle. Mary was the first to recover. Snatching up the infant, she looked to Heaven. She saw only her house burning over her head.

"Come!" she cried. Holding the baby in one arm, she pulled back the door bar and threw open the door. It was just dawn: a pale gray light. The instant the door opened, a hail of bullets struck the house like a clatter of stones. Miraculously, Mary was not hit, but as she stepped out, a savage struck her on the head with his hatchet and split open her skull. She fell still clutching the baby. In a moment Catherine dashed out, despite the Indian standing nearby, and snatched the infant from Mary's arms. Mary lay on the ground, a bloody mess, her brains spilling out, her eyes still wide with terror. The savage who killed her raised his hatchet to kill Catherine as well, but then a bullet struck him and he dropped.

Catherine did not stop to think who had fired the shot; she knew only that they must get to the garrison house, which lay a hundred yards off. But as she looked behind her to find the children, the savages were upon her. A tall brave tore the baby from her arms and, holding it by the feet, dashed its head against a tree. She felt a blow to her thigh, and then searing pain. She tried to grab Lydia's hand, but one of the savages was too quick; he seized her and pulled her away, moving quickly, dragging her behind him. "No!" she screamed. "No!" She cast a despairing look backward.

The house was in flames, the children—including Lydia—seized one by one. She could not see Missy. The eldest boy, attempting to fight with a knife, was overpowered: a savage easily wrested the knife away and plunged it into the child's chest. When the boy fell, the Indian stripped him and then—ah, God!— cut his scalp from the crown of his head. The sounds of gunfire came from everywhere: impossible to tell whose guns, whites' or Indians'. Clouds of smoke rose into the still morning air where the settlers' houses burned.

The savage marched Catherine along a forest path; and now she was aware that others came, too, and each one with a captive. "Please—" she gasped, "please—my child—"

He paid no attention. She tried to look behind, but the trees were too thick, she could see no one, although she could hear them well enough, the children crying, the shouts and grunts of their captors.

The attack had come so suddenly that she could hardly believe that it had happened: how had she come to be here, marched through the forest by a savage? She was disoriented, hardly aware of anything save having to walk—too fast—and keep her footing. Her wound throbbed; her shoe was filled with blood. The savage was a fearsome sight: red and black and yellow war paint on his face, a bone necklace around his neck, leather breeches—and a gun.

On and on they went. Catherine thought of nothing save putting one foot ahead of the other. Her mind seemed to have turned off: she could not have said where she was, or why, or with whom—not even her own name could she have said. The pain from her wound spread through her body from head to toe; waves of blackness overcame her, so that she walked unconscious; when she came to she was always in the same place, stumbling through the wilderness, led by a savage. From time to time she heard a voice—her own?—sobbing and gasping; the savage never answered, never looked at her.

At last they stopped. They were in a clearing where some squaws were butchering sheep and pigs stolen from settlers, since Indians did not keep livestock. A great bonfire had been set, and Catherine sank down near it and felt the wonderful warmth of the flames. Then she fainted. When she came to, she was where she had fallen; only now she was surrounded by savages squatting and eating roasted meat.

She sat up. She was very thirsty. They took no notice of her until she tried to stand, at which point, just as she was collapsing again, they spoke angrily to her and a squaw reached up and pulled her down. In that brief moment she had seen the children—a miracle! They were in a little group not far off, their faces illuminated by the light of the flames, for now it was growing dark. Beyond the fire stretched the limitless wilderness, the forest filled with savages and wild beasts.

As weak as she was, and in great pain, Catherine tried to stand again. She must get to Lydia. She must let the child see that she was alive. Her leg throbbed: it was not a leg, it was simply a great searing torment. The blood that had run down from her wound was drying, so that her foot was glued to her shoe. One of the squaws spoke to her sharply. Then a brave came; she could not tell if he was her captor who had marched her through the woods. He held out something to her: a huge hunk of meat dripping blood, only half roasted. She was not hungry, but she did not want to offend him and so she took it. She was thirsty, however. She tried to mime drinking. Someone put a horn cup into her hand, but it was not water, it was strong liquor. She took a sip and choked, and they laughed to see her. "Please," she said when she could speak again, "please bring my child to me." She lifted her arm—how heavy it was!—and pointed to the children.

One of them must have understood her, for a boy went to the children and took Lydia's hand and began to pull her away from the group. She began to scream in terror. Catherine cried out to her to be quiet, but her voice hardly made a sound in the general din—Indians yelling and singing and whooping, the child screaming, the boy shouting at her. When Lydia was beside her at last, Catherine reached up and pulled her down beside her, cradled Lydia in her arms and sang a little soothing song to her. "There, there, all right, now, you are with me, all right, all right . . ." Gradually the child quieted. She sat very still. She said nothing; and now Catherine was too weak to try to talk to her.

The feasting done, the Indians danced for a while around the fire. Their dark forms looked like the imps of Hell. Then the fire burned down; around the embers the Indians slept, leaving a few to stand guard. It began to snow. Catherine huddled with her child. From time to time she put a handful of snow into her mouth to quench her thirst. When morning came she could not move.

The savages broke camp. One of the children had died in the night, Catherine could not tell which, and two Indians took it away. Catherine had forgotten who those children were; she did not realize that it was her own niece or nephew who had died, she did not remember that her sister and her brother-in-law had been killed the previous day. When her captor told her to get up, she could not. To her surprise he was not angry with her; he went away and came back with a horse, and when she could not mount it, he and another lifted her onto it and put Lydia into her arms. Fortunately the child clung to her, for Catherine had no strength to hold her.

They set off: a line of savages on the forest trail, their captives strung out between. At mid-morning the snow stopped. The forest was white and still, the animals burrowed in for the winter, here and there a bright flash of color as a cardinal or a bluejay took wing.

The horse had no saddle. Soon they came to a steep descent; Catherine could not hold on, and she and Lydia both tumbled over the horse's head. How the Indians laughed at that! But then when she could not get up, her captor came and stood over her. He looked very angry; the unintelligible words that he spoke were angry also. He pulled his knife out of its sheath and held it menacingly above her; its sharp blade glittered in the sun just now appearing. Catherine's eyes clung to the shining metal of the blade—as bright and shining as a new-made silver cup, she thought. She had often seen such silver—where? She passed in and out of consciousness. The Indian crouched over her; he held his knife ready to plunge into her breast.

O Lord deliver me; give me strength. She heard the words inside her head: her voice begging the Lord for help.

And she had her answer, for somehow she found the strength to rise; she stumbled up, pulling Lydia up beside her. She stood swaying, ready to fall again, but then her captor hailed a squaw and the woman mounted the horse and they put Catherine and Lydia up, too, and the march began again.

That night they came to a camp. Many more Indians were there, and many wigwams. They put Catherine and Lydia into one and gave them a blanket.

After a time the flap lifted and a man came in. Catherine had fallen into a feverish sleep, but she came awake when she realized that he was a white man.

He introduced himself as Peter Mason; he had been captured at Northfield. Captive though he was, when he heard that a white woman was being brought in, he had asked to see her. There was another white woman in the camp taken three weeks ago, he said; she was in a bad way, very near her time.

"You are wounded, mistress? An arrow wound?"

"No. A bullet." He was a rough-looking fellow, but to Catherine he was the most wonderful-looking man she had ever seen.

"That's better than an arrowhead. I was wounded myself. I had help from a plaster of oak leaves; it drew out the infection. I'll bring you some. Have you had food?"

"No."

"I'll see if they'll give me some for you. They're watching us close, they don't want us talking together." He put out his hand and rested it on Lydia's head. "What's your name, little one?"

But Lydia could not speak; she buried her head in her mother's side and would not look at him.

In a short while he was back with a fistful of oak leaves damp from the snow, and a bit of samp—cornmush. "I can't stay," he said. "But listen, mistress. If you can find it in your heart to go to Mistress Joslin, she'd thank you for it." And without further word he ducked out.

They ate the mush—coarse, half-ground stuff—and Catherine pressed the oak leaves against her wound. Cold and wet, they felt good against her burning flesh. From without they heard the Indians yelling and singing, but no one came to bother them, and after a while they slept.

The next morning Catherine's leg felt a little better; the swelling had gone down, the pain was less. Stiff with cold and still very weak, she hobbled to the entrance of the wigwam and looked out. The ground was trampled into mud around the big fire in the center of the camp; twenty or so wigwams stood close together, and beyond, through the trees, she could see a palisade of sharpened tree trunks. Indian men, women and children went back and forth; many of the women were working at one thing or another, dressing meat, grinding grain, pounding animal skins between two rocks.

Taking Lydia by the hand, Catherine hobbled out. She approached one of the squaws; as she tried to speak to her, others gathered around. They stared at her, and then they began to talk amongst themselves, still staring. Then one of them reached out and lifted a strand of Catherine's hair. Her cap had fallen off long since, and her hair was down; it fell like a golden waterfall over her shoulders and nearly to her waist. Catherine willed herself to be still. The squaw held the lock of hair in one hand—how bright it looked against that dark skin!—and stroked it with the other, talking to her companions all the while. Then she gave a sharp little tug, nearly throwing Catherine off balance, and they all laughed uproariously. Then another squaw took a strand of Lydia's hair and held it up for comparison; it was the same color as Catherine's.

"Please," said Catherine, "I want to see Mistress Joslin." They let go her hair; they stood and stared at her, not seeming to understand. She tried again, moving her hands in front of her to indicate a belly swollen with pregnancy. "I-want-to-see-Mistress-Joslin."

An old woman said something; then one of the younger ones, nodding, beckoned to Catherine. She led the way to a wigwam across the camp; Lydia trailed along beside, clutching her mother's hand. As they drew near, Catherine could hear a woman weeping and crying out.

The squaw motioned; Catherine and Lydia went in. In the dim light they saw a white woman, great with child, lying on the ground. Her dress was in tatters, her hair tangled and matted with leaves and twigs, her face filthy and smeared with her tears. When she saw Catherine she stared as if Catherine were a ghost.

"Mistress Joslin?"

"Yes. O Lord, Lord—who are you?"

Because of the pain in her leg Catherine could not crouch, and so she let herself down heavily beside Mistress Joslin and took her hand. "I am Catherine Revell. This is my daughter Lydia. We were taken at Lancaster. Three days ago, I think—I have lost track."

Mistress Joslin, who had briefly stopped crying, began again. "Oh my poor babe—I am near my time, and my poor poor babe will be born into this wilderness, and they will kill it, I know they will kill it, and I will die, too!"

Catherine soothed her as best she could, although in truth she thought that what the woman said was true. Mistress Joslin's voice rose louder and louder; she seemed beside herself, mad with fear, and nothing that Catherine could do or say comforted her.

After a moment a dark head peered in, uttered angry words, and withdrew. Then Peter Mason, accompanied by a guard, came into the wigwam. He was gravely worried; he had been a captive for some months, and he understood a little of the Algonquian tongue.

"Can you quiet her, mistress?" he said to Catherine. "They say she makes too much noise, they are tired of listening to her."

Mistress Joslin's voice rose louder and louder: "Save me! Save me! They will kill me, they will kill my babe! Save me!"

A brave and two squaws came in, so that now the interior of the wigwam was quite crowded. They were angry; they spoke harshly to Mistress Joslin, but she did not seem to hear them, and of course she could not have understood them in any case. Then one of the squaws struck out in a swift, vicious movement and hit Mistress Joslin across the face. Stunned, the woman lay wide-eyed for a moment; Catherine wondered that she had not been knocked unconscious.

But then Mistress Joslin began moaning and crying again, as loud as before, and the Indians turned abruptly and went out.

Peter Mason shook his head. "You got to do something, mistress. They're angry with her. There's no telling what they'll do."

"What did they say?" said Catherine.

He hesitated; then: "I don't like to repeat it, mistress. They're savages all right—bloody heathen! Do as I say and get her quiet, or we'll all be sorry."

His guard pulled him away then, and out of the wigwam, and Catherine and Lydia were left with Mistress Joslin.

But not for long, for soon Catherine's captor came to get her. As he ordered her out, she spoke one last time to Mistress Joslin: "Be of good cheer! I will help you when your time comes, and we will keep the babe safe!"

There was no reply; Mistress Joslin wept unhearing, unmindful of anyone. She was so far gone in her terror, Catherine thought, that it seemed no one could reach her to bring her back to her senses.

She glanced at the brave as he hustled her away. His dark face was stern—as grim as the face of any Puritan father; and his dark eyes were fathomless, she could get no message from them. She had never seen such a pitiless face, and as she stumbled back to her own place of captivity, her leg throbbing, her head reeling, she felt a tremor of fear beyond any fear she had yet known. What would they do to Mistress Joslin to make her be still?

Soon enough she found out. As she and Lydia lay in the wigwam, huddled together under their blanket—and lucky enough they were to have even that, Catherine thought—they heard a great commotion outside, the savages raising their voices in song and shout—for what? Some heathen ceremony to their heathen gods? After a few moments, when the noise did not abate, she struggled up and went to open the flap.

What she saw made her blood run cold, and she thought that perhaps she had been taken by fever again. Dear merciful God!

A large bonfire had been set—but not lit—in the center of the camp, with a stake in the middle of the heaped wood. Across the way two squaws held Mistress Joslin up by her arms, for she seemed to be in a faint. Even as Catherine watched, two more squaws stripped the rags from Mistress Joslin's swollen body until she was naked. There was a good deal of noise, every savage yelling and singing, but now, for once, Mistress Joslin was quiet. When they were done stripping her, they dragged her to the pile of wood and twigs.

Dear merciful Lord! Catherine looked frantically for Peter Mason. He must help—must speak to the savages and make them understand that they must not—could not—do this! She searched every face and form in the crowd, but she could not see him. There were perhaps a hundred savages gathered now, perhaps two hundred, she could not tell. They milled around, jabbering amongst themselves, gesticulating toward Mistress Joslin, who, mercifully unconscious as she seemed to be, was now being lashed to the stake.

This cannot be happening, thought Catherine. Her eyes were filled with tears, making it difficult for her to see, but she brushed them away and staggered out, Lydia in tow, searching for Mason.

She could not find him. And in a moment her search was done, for her captor seized her and held her fast; she tried to struggle free but she was too weak, his hand was like iron where he grabbed her arm. He said a harsh word to her, which she could not understand, and pulled her through the crowd around the woodpile until she stood next to it.

Merciful God! Mistress Joslin's eyes were still closed, she was still unconscious—

A savage put a torch to the wood.

Mistress Joslin's eyes opened.

And now, as she saw her fate, her mouth opened but no cry came forth. Flames shot up around her. She made one futile attempt to wrest her arms free from where they were bound to the stake, and then she went limp.

The flames reached her legs.

The savages chanted, a low thrumming that rose to a barbaric sound, higher and higher with the fire whipped by the winter wind, a shriek from the depths of Hell.

Catherine stood transfixed. Black, acrid smoke made her throat raw; little cinders floated down and landed in her hair, on her clothes, and she brushed them away. Lydia stood with her head buried in her mother's skirts, and Catherine put her arms around the child to keep her from turning to see the horror before them.

Mistress Joslin was lost in the flames now, her body burning with an overpowering stench—and still she made no sound. Her face was a white death's-head through the ruddy fire, her legs and swollen torso blackened and bursting with her lifeblood.

And then she screamed—a cry of agony that seared Catherine's soul.

The Indians' chant rose higher and higher, drowning out Mistress Joslin's screams. They were beside themselves, dancing around the fire, brandishing their weapons, caught up in a hideous ecstasy.

Catherine's captor released her and joined in. She saw him go; she had a last glimpse of what was once a white woman like herself, the all-consuming fire, a scene from Hell— Merciful Lord!

She fainted.

When she came to it was dark. She was in a wigwam, covered by a blanket. Slowly, painfully, she sat up. Her head was aching; her leg throbbed. Automatically she reached for her child.

She felt nothing: Lydia was not with her.

And now Catherine came fully awake with a start. Where was the child?

She got herself upright and opened the flap. She saw the embers of a great fire; in the center were the remains of a stake. Like a blow across the face, the memory of what that fire had consumed struck her, hard, so that she almost collapsed. All the breath went out of her and she nearly fell—but then, remembering why she had arisen, she gathered her strength and went out to find her child.

No one was about; the camp might have been deserted, but she knew it was not.

The savages were there, hiding in their shelters even as they hid in the forests waiting to attack—unseen, deadly, ferocious.

Where was Lydia?

This place was Hell. She must get out.

A little snow had fallen; in the cold white moonlight she saw that it was unmarked by footprints, and so it had fallen since—since what had happened. She was glad that she could think so clearly, for she would need her wits about her if she and Lydia were to make their escape. And they must—they must! Something had happened that must not happen to them.

She stumbled over a snow-covered mound. It might have been a log, or a bundle of animal skins. But it was not: it was a body. She bent over it; she brushed the snow away from it.

Peter Mason's white, rigid face and unseeing eyes stared up at the heavens.

Her mind registered the fact of his death and then turned back to her problem: where was Lydia?

She tried calling, very soft: "Lydia?"

No answer save the night wind soughing in the trees. She was very cold, but no matter. She moved on, cautious and stealthy, an intruding spirit in this place of death. "Lydia?"

She came to a wigwam. As if guided by some greater strength than her own, her hand lifted the flap.

All dark within, darkness filled with the stench of their bodies, bear grease in their hair and blood on their hands—

Someone seized her. She heard a cry escape her lips. *No!*

Someone was speaking to her, dragging her away. *"Lydia—"*

A blow to her head, and all was darkness again.

Cold dawn when she awakened. She lay in a wigwam with several savages. Dark and close—faugh, what a stench! When she tried to sit up she realized that her hands were bound. She tried to think. What had happened? The woman burned—Lydia gone—

Horror pressed in on her. She heard a sob: her own. At once, at the sound, one of the savages sprang up: a squaw. She came close, peered into Catherine's face. She chattered a few words. Then she unbound the leather thong around Catherine's wrists, turned away for a moment, and came back with a handful of grain and water and fat made into a paste. When Catherine did not move to take it, the squaw put it into her hand.

"My child," said Catherine. Her throat was raw, it hurt her to speak. "Where is my child?"

The squaw spoke again. Her face was broad, expressionless.

The voices had aroused one of the men—her captor, Catherine saw. He came close and looked at her intently.

"My child," she said. "I want my child."

He frowned and shook his head. Catherine had been trying to stay in control, but his gesture panicked her. She knew that she must not rave and weep. Mistress Joslin had done so, and they had punished her cruelly for it. But somehow she must make them understand that she wanted her child, she would not rest until she had her.

The squaw motioned for her to eat. Obediently she put a little of the paste into her mouth, but she choked when she tried to swallow. They brought her water in a horn cup, and she drank. That, at least, tasted good. She was aware of a dull pain in her leg, but it was not as bad as before. The oak leaves were healing it, then. Oak leaves made her think of Peter Mason. Somehow—she did not know how—she knew that he was dead.

Dead. Mason was dead, and Mistress Joslin—

She fought down her panic. She must not think of the dead. She must think of Lydia, and how to get to her.

She was aware of activity around her. The other inhabitants were awake and moving about, packing up their blankets and their other possessions, going in and out. Through the open flap she saw that the camp was astir: everyone busy, horses loaded with heavy packs, children fetching and carrying—

They were leaving.

Not without Lydia!

"Please—" But when she turned to her captor, he was not there, he had vanished. Only the women were with her now, and they ignored her.

"Please . . ." She wiped her sticky hands on her filthy skirt, she pushed her hair out of her eyes. She touched one squaw on the arm, but the woman ignored her.

She turned to another, and another. They paid no attention to her; she might not have existed.

But when she moved to go out, they held her back. They spoke to her; she did not understand. "My child," she said. She heard her voice cracking and filled with fear. "Please, where is my child?"

Her captor looked in and spoke to the women. They took Catherine by the arm and led her outside. A horse stood waiting. Before she could protest, she was lifted onto it. "Wait—wait—no!" But they ignored her. The horse began to walk. She tried to slide off, but her captor pushed her back on. Then she did slide off— or fell, more accurately—and her captor stood above her, yelling at her, his knife glittering as it had before, and her heart quailed at the sight of it. She heard her voice, far back in her mind: *Stay alive and find your child. If you die now you will not see her this side of Heaven. Do what you must, but stay alive.*

Before they left, they fired their wigwams; tall columns of smoke rose into the winter sky as they set out. Not many hours later a party of English soldiers arrived at the deserted camp; the wigwams were still smoldering, but the Indians were gone, having once again eluded their pursuers.

All day the Indians traveled through the forest. At night they camped by a river not yet frozen over; they did not erect any shelters, but slept on the snowy ground wrapped in their blankets, some with a bearskin or wolf skin thrown over them. For nourishment they boiled pieces of a deer's legs, skin, hooves, and all. They gave Catherine a little of the broth. It scalded her throat, and she drank no more than a sip.

The next day they traveled, and the next. They forded a stream by a beaver dam; since she could not keep her seat without a saddle, they made her dismount and climb up and down a valley on foot. Once they came into a thick swamp where the branches of trees grew so low that she must dismount again and walk on ice that broke, so that she walked in water up to her knees.

Only one thought sustained her: stay alive to see the child again. Sometimes she thought that she was dead. Sometimes she thought that she was dreaming. She had forgotten who she was. If you had said, "You are Mistress Jedediah Revell, a wealthy lady of Boston," she would not have known of whom you spoke. She was no one: only a body barely surviving, fallen into the midst of the savages of Hell.

Why?

Searching for reasons was beyond her.

At the end of the third day they came to a large Indian camp. Many men and women came to greet them. Many stared at Catherine, and some examined her more closely, pushing their faces into hers, lifting her hair, touching the fabric of her dress. They put her into a wigwam where sat a squaw, legs crossed, head held high, a proud and severe look to her. Her face was painted black, her hair powdered, jewels in her ears, bracelets up to her elbows, necklaces adorning the fine soft doeskin of her dress. Around her waist was a heavy belt of wampum made in a design: the totem of the wolf. They forced Catherine down onto her knees; by their gestures they gave her to understand that this was to be her mistress; she was to be a slave.

And so began her life in the service of the Princess Weetammo, which meant, in Algonquian, "sweet heart."

Sweet heart! Never was a name worse chosen. This was a squaw sachem— a powerful woman, once wife to King Philip's brother, Alexander. Weetammo nursed a hatred against the English for Alexander's death; and, like Philip, she was angered by the relentless English encroachment of the Indians' lands. And so she was a harsh mistress, and had no mercy for her captive. She gave Catherine so little food that Catherine had to beg from other savages for a bit of samp or a piece of venison to sustain her; she kicked Catherine, and hit her, for the slightest reason—or none at all.

Only one thing saved Catherine from worse treatment: she knew how to sew and knit. One day Princess Weetammo handed her a length of kersey and with signs and gestures made Catherine understand that she was to sew a shirt from it for Weetammo's papoose. And when Catherine had done that satisfactorily, she was told to make a shirt for a brave; then to unravel a pair of stockings and knit them over again, for they had been badly made by someone else.

The winter came on. Snow lay deep in the forest beyond the Indian camp, and Catherine realized that even if she could escape—an unlikely event—it would be impossible to get to any English settlement.

And so she waited, and kept count of the days as best she could. Surely Jed must have returned by now; surely Boston must have had word about the attack on Lancaster. He must think that she was dead. Had he sent a search party, or perhaps come out into the wilderness himself with a few of the militia, looking for her? The Indians were expert at eluding their pursuers; he could never find her in all this vast wilderness.

At such times she lost heart and wept—but only in secret, for if Weetammo found her weeping, she beat her.

One day toward the end of the winter—in late February, she thought—there was a great commotion in the camp, and soon she saw why: King Philip was coming in.

He was a tall, imposing man; she could not tell his age, but he was not old: perhaps forty. He wore a suit of fine deerskin and a wide wampum belt; around his neck hung a necklace of bones—whether human or animal, it was impossible to tell. His face was painted red and black, his head shaved save for a cockscomb of shiny black hair stiffened with bear grease.

They feasted King Philip that night with venison and bear meat and wild turkey, and a stew of corn and beans and ground nuts. Even Catherine was given a little; it had been so long since she had had a full meal that her stomach could hardly accept so much.

After the meal one of the Indians who had come in with Philip came to Catherine and squatted next to her.

"So, mistress," he said. He wore no bone or wampum decoration; he had an English woolen shirt over his deerskin breeches, and on his finger she saw a silver ring.

She stared at him.

"Do not fear," he said. "I am James Printer."

She had heard that an Indian had helped in the setting of type for Eliot's *Up-Biblium God.* "Are you a praying Indian, then?" she said.

"For a time I was. Now I serve Metacomet—Philip, as the English know him."

She was astonished. Here was a man—a savage—who had lived and worked at the printery at Harvard College; he had walked the streets of Cambridge, perhaps he had visited Boston. For a moment she felt as though she had met a friend—a fellow countryman: this man knew, as the other Indians did not, the sights and sounds of home.

"Now listen, mistress. The English are looking for you. They want to buy you back. Princess Weetammo wants to sell you to Albany for gunpowder, but Metacomet thinks he can get more for you from the English. He knows that your husband is rich. He wants to know what your husband will pay for you."

Catherine needed a moment to understand: they were talking about her freedom!

She gazed across the crowded camp to where King Philip sat; boys and girls attended him, fetching and carrying, and on either side of him sat his braves.

"I—I don't know," she said. She stifled a sudden impulse to laugh. Jed—and his father, and her dear father, too—had made their fortunes by bargaining: trading this for that and always at a profit. Now she was to bargain for her life, and she had no experience at it.

James Printer watched her speculatively. "Metacomet wants to talk to you," he said. "You should have some price ready to give him, so that he can decide what to do. Come."

He stood up, and she, also. Her leg had healed over the winter, but still she walked with a limp.

James Printer said a word to Philip, and then he acted as translator as Philip spoke to Catherine.

"Metacomet says that he must have a high price for you. What will your husband pay?"

"He will pay nothing if we cannot have our child."

James Printer did not translate this at once. He gestured to a boy of perhaps nine who crouched beside Philip: a bright, good-looking boy. "That is Philip's son," said James Printer. "He loves him more than he loves his own life."

"Then tell him," said Catherine, "that I feel the same about my daughter. I want her back."

"And your husband will pay double?"

"Yes—I am sure he will."

James Printer and Philip spoke back and forth, and then again. Catherine could tell nothing from their expressionless faces.

"Will he pay twenty pounds for you? And twenty for your daughter?" James Printer asked.

So they knew where Lydia was! "Yes. He will pay that." She knew better, by now, than to beg them to tell her where they kept the child. They had Lydia alive, they would be willing to ransom her—that was the important thing.

Philip spoke again.

"Very well," said James Printer. "I will carry the message to the English in the morning."

Catherine longed to ask if the English were near, but she dared not. This was enough: soon she would be free, and Lydia with her!

All night she lay awake, too excited to sleep. Free! It seemed a miracle. Over and over again she prayed her thanks to God: He had not forsaken them after all, He would deliver them out of their captivity.

But the next day, after James Printer had left the camp, a runner came with an alarm: the English army was coming, they had been sighted not ten miles away and they were looking for Philip, they had promised to kill him.

Instantly all was in turmoil. In no more than an hour the Indians had broken camp, packed up their goods, set their wigwams on fire, and started through the forest again.

Catherine was shattered. Dear God—so close, and now it was not to happen after all. She stood desolate, stunned, unable to comprehend this new turn of events; when Princess Weetammo ordered her to move and she did not move quickly enough, the squaw sachem seized a hatchet and would have struck her with it had not someone intervened.

All day they traveled, and the day after that. Catherine had long since lost any sense of direction, but it seemed to her that since the first day of her captivity, months ago, they had traveled deeper and deeper into the wilderness, always farther from civilization. Now they seemed to be going north, on a well-used trail where the snow was packed down.

On the third day some of the Indians separated and went in different directions, little groups of ten or twenty. Philip and Weetammo were among these; when darkness came, Catherine found herself with a dozen Indians whom she did not know. Then that group, too, separated; with a brave and three squaws she made camp that night. They gave her a blanket, and a wolf skin to sleep on, and a bit of pemmican to eat. When morning came they were all covered with three inches of snow. They shook themselves off, packed up, and set off again. Catherine had lost the horse when she separated from the main group; now, limping, she was hard put to keep up.

At mid-morning they came upon two braves, a squaw with a papoose—and a white boy. He and Catherine dared not speak to each other, but their eyes met, and Catherine thought that she read a message: courage!

That night the Indians shared a pot of rum amongst themselves, and for the first time Catherine saw a drunken savage. Soon after dark the Indians lay snoring around the little fire; and only then did the white boy creep to her side and speak to her in cautious whispers.

"My name is Joseph Bingham. I was taken at Deerfield. They killed all my family, my father and mother and six brothers and sisters. They scalped them before my eyes."

"Have they offered to ransom you?"

"No. Have they you?"

She told him her own story then, and the two of them were silent for a moment in a prayer for the dead.

Then: "They are taking us far to the north," Joseph said. "I think they may sell us to the French."

Catherine smothered a cry. The French would force papism on them, and they would go to Hell! Better, she thought, to die here and now.

"Listen," said Joseph. "I think we should try to escape. Will you help me?"

"How can we do that? And how would we get back to Boston?"

"I have learned much from them. I can travel in the forest now almost as well as any savage. We will walk. That will not be hard." Catherine thought of her leg, but she said nothing. "The hard part," he went on, "will be getting away. But I think we can do it, if you will help. But we must work quickly—now, tonight."

After he told her his plan, she was silent for a time. Her thoughts seemed very heavy; she did not want to think about what he said, and yet she must.

At last she turned to him. She took his hand—a hard, rough hand—and she looked into his face. He was no extraordinary boy: just a lad of fifteen or so, but already so hardened by what his life had been that he seemed like a man of forty. He was right; she knew he was right, and she trusted his good honest face.

And yet ... For one last moment she hesitated. She closed her eyes; she asked God to speak to her. She heard only the night wind and then—terrible sound!—the howl of a wolf. Her heart quailed at what she must do; and yet—she must do it, and now at last it seemed to her that God wanted her to do it: it was, she thought, His will.

"All right," she whispered.

Instantly Joseph was on his feet; as silently as any savage, he darted to his master's pack, took out a hatchet, took another from where it stood against a tree trunk, handed one to Catherine—and then, at the last moment, gripped her wrist so hard that she nearly cried out.

She saw his eyes glittering in the starlight; she saw his face—a mask of hate. "Do not fail," he said. "Remember that they kill English as if we were dogs."

Catherine remembered her sister; and Mistress Joslin; and poor Missy, where was she?—and her child, her precious little Lydia whom they had taken from her. She felt a rush of fury such as she had never felt before. She had not thought she was capable of such a feeling: suddenly she was consumed with a lust for vengeance against these heathen savages, she wanted to harm them in whatever way she could for the harm they had done to her, to all whites.

She gripped the handle; she saw the blade's faint gleam. Joseph motioned to where the savages lay sleeping in two rows, one on either side of the fire.

"Now," he whispered.

She was aware that she watched herself as she moved to do his bidding. She saw herself lift the weapon above her head—and how light it was, how easy to raise!—and she watched as she brought it down onto the dark head lying on the ground: a grunt, a spurt of blood, and it was done and she moved on to the next, and the next—up and down the weapon went, doing its terrible business, and it was she, Catherine Revell, who wielded that weapon, it was she who sank the blade deep into the savages' skulls, over and over, and Joseph, too, was doing the same—a bloody massacre deep in the forest far from civilization, no witness, no one to stop them—ah, now! And now! Her sister's face burned in her brain—poor Mary, and the infant dashed against a tree, its brains splattered on the ground, and her own dear child, lost to her forever— Now again! And again!

She stood shuddering, gasping—she did not know where she was, or who—what had happened?

Joseph gripped her arm. "Quick now—we must get away. No—drop it, leave it, I have this one. Hurry! We have till morning to travel."

But then he paused; and then he turned back to do one last terrible task. She stood near fainting, braced against a tree; she watched herself watching him as he moved quickly up and down working swiftly and efficiently—eight scalps he got, and then they were away, hastening through the dark forest; but the night was clear, he could plot their course by the stars.

Two days later they stumbled into an English camp, militia still searching for King Philip. At first the soldiers could not believe their tale; then Joseph showed them the scalps.

3

Inevitably King Philip was defeated. The English outnumbered him, and try as he might, he could not escape them forever.

His end came in a swamp at Mount Hope in Rhode Island. It was during Sunday worship service that Captain Benjamin Church, one of the principal English military men, received word that Philip had been cornered. Heedless of the prohibition against any activity on the Lord's Day, Captain Church leaped up, summoned his men, and hurried to the scene.

And then once again, but only momentarily, Philip eluded them; but his wife and his son—that fine nine-year-old boy—were captured. Heated debate ensued: should these two be executed? The clergy were consulted. Some favored killing them at once; others pleaded for mercy. In the end mercy won, and Philip's wife and son were sold into slavery to the Barbados.

Meanwhile Philip remained at large. But the English smelled his blood now, and they were hot on his trail. Before they caught him they found Princess Weetammo, her body cast up on the banks of the Taunton River where she had drowned trying to flee across in a makeshift raft.

Then they got Philip.

The authorities offered a bounty for Indian heads: thirty shillings apiece. Many heads were brought in and redeemed. Philip's head went for the same price. Plymouth got his head, Boston his hands; his body was quartered and thrown to the wolves. The great Cotton Mather himself, who was at that time a boy of twelve or thirteen and not yet great, separated Philip's jaw from his skull.

It had been a hard war; it would prove to be the most devastating war in Massachusetts' history: fourteen towns destroyed, ten percent of her army killed, millions of pounds of property damage. Hard on the Indians, too: Eliot's praying Indians from several towns—Natick, Wamesit, Nashoba—had been interned and nearly starved to death on Deer Island in Boston Harbor. Philip's dream of a great confederacy was shattered; the remnants of the tribes, hungry and demoralized, sought refuge with formerly hostile tribes to the north and west. They were the lucky ones, for many Indians who fell into the hands of the English were shot or hanged. Boston Common was a favored place of execution, and soon it was littered with dark corpses. Other Indians were pressed into slavery in New England; still others were sold into the slave markets of the West Indies, or Spain, or Tangiers.

King Philip's War did not end the threat to white settlement; for decades settlers on the frontier—the Connecticut Valley and beyond—suffered Indian raids. But as frightening as these were, they were isolated incidents, not a general uprising of the tribes. The tribes were done for; the land belonged to the white man.

4

On a bright mild day in early spring, Catherine Revell came home, riding pillion behind Captain Thomas Savage. Jedediah waited for her in the midst of a crowd in the marketplace by the Town House. He had wanted to greet her in private—he feared that she would be sick, or fainting, or mad, perhaps—but word had gotten out that she was coming in, and the people had assembled to see her, for she was living proof of God's grace.

From down the Neck came the cry: they are coming! Outriders galloped ahead, setting the crowd to a fever pitch of excitement. Every head craned to see, avid eyes and eager wagging tongues—all aflame with curiosity.

Captain Savage kept his mount at a walk; he nodded to the people lining the way, but he ordered them to stand back, not to block his path. He could feel Catherine holding onto him, and so he knew that she had not fainted; from time to time he spoke to her kindly: "All right, mistress?"

And always he had her answer in a clear, firm voice: "Yes. All right."

They came to the marketplace. Captain Savage pulled up his horse. Jedediah stood at the front of the crowd; he wiped tears from his eyes and then he stepped forward. Never had Captain Savage seen such an expression—grief and joy and a kind of stunned disbelief. Jedediah put up his arms; gently, gently, and yet with urgency and passion, he lifted down his beloved. She had come home to him again; he could hardly believe it. After the first shock of the news from Lancaster, the first desperate days when he thought she was dead, and then—not sure, but hoping, hoping against all hope—learning that she was not dead after all, but alive somewhere with the savages in the wilderness, a prey to every torment that man and beast could devise—at those times he had sometimes gone nearly mad with worry. His business had suffered, and his father had had to step in and take matters in hand before Jed lost everything. For hours at a time through the winter he sat by the fire, brooding, sunk into desolation. And then one day the news had come that miraculously she had walked into an English camp. He could not at first believe it. They did not tell him the details. Captain Savage was a gentleman—and a decent, kindly man for all that he was a fierce Indian fighter. Better to let the woman tell what she chose, he thought; and he had cautioned his men to silence.

She was thin—so thin! Jed looked at her for a long moment before he enfolded her in his arms. He knew very well that there was a law against embracing in public; if any man tried to put him into the stocks for embracing his wife now, he thought, he would kill him. But no one objected; this was an event too extraordinary to be judged by the usual rules.

She stood with his arms holding her tight, and she wondered where she was. It all seemed so strange: all these people, all these white faces and not a savage among them. Buildings and fenced-in garden plots, the Town House and the meeting house, the smell of the sea just there, lapping at the wharves . . . Why, she was home!

She looked up; Jed was gazing down at her. Never had she seen him look so. Why, he looked as if he were going to cry! What was there, here, to cry about? No: it was in the wilderness that one wept—captive among the savages, watching innocent women and children done to death with such cruelty—

She shuddered, and with an enormous effort of will she pushed those thoughts into a corner of her mind and slammed the door shut on them. She was home; she was safe.

She lifted her arms in their poor tattered covering and put them around his neck. He was not a dream. This place was not a dream. The other—the wilderness, the savages—that was a dream. Now she had awakened; she had come back.

Jed took her home. The family was there to greet her, those who had not gone to the marketplace. Her mother took one look at her, gave a great cry and fainted. Bartle took her poor, worn, thin hands into his own and, his voice choked with tears, said, "Welcome, daughter-in-law. We gave you up for dead."

They put her to bed; they took off her filthy, tattered dress and undergarments and washed her and clothed her in a fine white nightdress. The doctor came to look at her wound and said that he could do nothing; it had healed badly, she would always bear the scar and probably would always limp, but it had healed, after all, that was the main thing.

Her hair was beyond salvation, matted with twigs and leaves and grease and encrusted with some dark stuff that was as hard as stone. They tried for hours to clean it, to comb it smooth. In the end they gave up and cut it off. When it grew in again, it was nearly white.

She ate; she slept; she awakened with a terrible cry, imploring Princess Weetammo not to cut off her head.

They ran to her, they comforted her: you are here, you are safe.

She seemed in such delicate health that no one dared broach the subject of the child. But at last, a week after her return, when she sat up in the great bed and hungrily finished a bowl of clam chowder, Jed sat beside her and took her hand and gazed into her lovely eyes—those eyes that had seen horrors he knew not what.

He choked, so that for a moment he could not speak. Then, recovering himself, he put to her—gently, gently—the question that had hung between them every moment since her return: did she know the fate of their child?

The house was quiet; the fire crackled in the hearth, the cold April wind buffeted the diamond-paned windows.

She had felt better, but now, as he spoke, she felt as if he had dealt her a death blow. Before his eyes she seemed to shrink and cower—as if he had accused her of some great crime, as if he had pronounced a sentence of execution upon her.

Tears welled up in her eyes and spilled down over her pale, thin cheeks. She made no sound.

Jed did not want to hurt her—God knew he did not—but he wanted her to understand that he was organizing a search party for the child, and Catherine could help them greatly if she could give them some notion of where she had been when the child had been taken away from her, or perhaps the names of the savages who had taken her . . . ?

Slowly, as if it was a great effort, Catherine turned her head from side to side: No. She did not know—she could not tell. They had marched this way and that, day after day in the wilderness—ah, he did not know what she had suffered, he would never know!

And now at last she gave way; she threw herself on his breast and sobbed as if her heart would break, as indeed it did, thinking of her poor lost little one, the child she feared never to see again, abandoned to the savages far away— and who knew what her fate was?

She tried to explain to him that it had been impossible to find the child— to learn where they had taken her. If she had questioned them or demanded Lydia's return, they might have killed her even as they killed Mistress Joslin. She had survived, had refrained from taking her own life, only because she clung to the belief that she would see Lydia again; that was all that kept her alive, that was why she had killed—

She heard a warning voice in her mind: say no more. She pulled back; she met his eyes. She saw that he understood, that he would not press her to tell what she could not tell—not now, perhaps not ever.

Gently he laid her back upon the pillows, gave her a drink of Madeira to soothe her, and went out to see the men whom he was sending to search for his daughter. He could tell them nothing; they must do the best they could. He equipped them with money and goods to trade for information; against all law, against all sense of right and wrong, he included rum and guns in the supply. If it took a gun or two given to a savage to get his daughter back, so be it; let those who would punish him for it put themselves in his place.

The spring advanced; Catherine mended. Her sons, Isaac and William, gave her much joy: to see their bright, happy faces, to hold them close and know that they would not be torn from her—ah, that was happiness such as she had never imagined! When she had nightmares, Jed awakened and held her close, comforting her, cherishing her. He never tried to exercise his marital rights; he never asked her if the savages had violated her. He had heard that they did not do so, for it was against their code. It was enough to have her back; he would not ask for more.

Naturally the people of Boston were curious to see her, to hear talk of her adventures. Day after day, at first, they called on her, and when they were turned away, they understood: she needed time to recover. But as the weeks passed they became annoyed. Why could she not talk to them? Did she think that she was so high and mighty that she was too good for them? They led lives of toil and drudgery, with little to amuse them—no theater, no music save psalm singing, no bear baiting or cockfights. Why could they not at least hear an exciting story or two from Mistress Revell?

The authorities, too, wanted to hear what she had to say: they wanted to question her to learn if she could give them some helpful information about the tribes: numbers of braves, what supplies they had, where their camps were.

Jed forbade it. You will talk to her when she is ready and not before, he said; and they saw that he would not be moved, and so they gave it up.

Oddly enough, as Catherine recovered, she began to think more about her captivity rather than less. Every day new memories flooded in on her. Rather than receding, the events of that awful time seemed to be gathering force in her mind; her thoughts would not let her rest, would not let her recover.

At last, one warm day when she sat in the shade of the peach trees in the little orchard next to the house, she asked a servant to bring her pen and paper. She felt an overpowering urge to tell her story—not to eager, gaping townsfolk, but secretly, privately, on page after page filled with her delicate script.

All the rest of the summer she wrote, and into the fall. Now that she had started, it seemed that she would never be done, there was so much to tell.

And yet she did not tell everything: she did not tell about the murders she had done, for they were like a darkness in her mind; at first she remembered them, and yet she could not admit to herself that she had done them, and so after a while the memory went away.

When she finished she had a stack of pages two inches high. Jed was astonished; he had not realized that she was writing so much. A few lines, he thought, that he could take to the authorities to shut them up—but this! This was a book! It must be published!

Catherine did not care. She had accomplished her purpose, she had eased her mind and told her story, and now she was done with it.

Jed went to the licensing board to get a permit to have it printed: *A Narrative of the Captivity and Redemption of Catherine Revell*. Then he took it to John Foster, who had recently started up the second printery in the Colony. Foster was a clever man; he suggested that he make an engraving, perhaps of the raid on Lancaster. It would add greatly to the appeal of the book, he said.

Jed told Foster to do as he pleased. When the book was offered for sale, the first edition of five hundred copies went in a week. Foster had never seen such a run on a book; most books were sermons or scientific treatises with little popular appeal. Mistress Bradstreet's poems sold well, of course, but nothing like this. He printed five hundred more, and then a thousand.

Eventually, in the decades that followed, Catherine's tale and others like it came to form a little subsection of Puritan and Colonial literature known as "captivity narratives." Their significance to later generations was that they were a valuable source of information about the Indians, who of course never got to tell their side of the story. Their significance for their contemporaries was that through the accounts of these survivors, God was telling the colonists that He would help them to triumph over the wilderness. True, many whites were killed battling the Indians; but the fact that some survived to tell their tale was taken as a sign of God's mercy. People read them eagerly: Catherine's, and Mary Rowlandson's, and Cotton Mather's account of Hannah Dustin, and John Williams's—all of these and more were immensely popular, people could not get enough of them, for they confirmed, over and over again, that the land truly was the white man's now, that through his suffering, once and for all, he claimed it as his own.

5

Jed's men could not find Lydia. They came back with nothing; they had traded all the goods, had spent all the money, and always for what they thought was good information, but in the end they failed. One Indian said that he had heard that a little white child with golden hair had been murdered in the north; another said that a little white child with golden hair had been taken to Canada; another said that a little white child with golden hair was living not far from Hadley, on the Connecticut River. The men went; they found a deserted Indian camp, the ashes of wigwams. No Lydia.

The following year Jed sent out another expedition. They failed also.

He put the word out that he would pay a prize of £100 to anyone who could give him information that led to the return of his child. He got a considerable amount of news, but none of it helpful.

As the years passed there were days and even weeks at a time when he did not think of Lydia. His life—and Catherine's, too—went on, events crowding in upon them; the memory of the little lost daughter receded, surfacing only now and then.

And then one day in 1689 a man came to Jed's shop, and this man did not want to buy a silver tankard or a pair of candlesticks. This man had information—good, hard information, or so at least it seemed at first.

He had had dealings with a half-breed fur trapper who worked in the far north. The trapper had heard, off and on, the tale of a white squaw; she had golden hair and blue eyes, and yet she was, as far as anyone could tell, an Indian, for she spoke their language and lived their life. She was the squaw of a sachem, she had two or three living children, she was greatly beloved by the Indians because they thought she had been sent from the sun god to live among them and keep them safe.

Jed's knees gave way and he sat down, hard, on a wooden crate. Then: "Will you see this man again—this fur trapper?"

"Yes. If he don't get himself killed."

"Tell him to come to me."

"He don't like towns. Mayhap you could go to him—in one of the frontier settlements?"

Jed made up a story to tell Catherine: he had to go to Salem to deal with one of his captains, he said; he would be gone about a week.

The fur trapper was a smelly, grizzled fellow who was happy to do what he could—for a price. Jed gave him £10 and a message: find this white squaw. Question her: what did she remember? Did she know that she was Lydia Revell, and that her family awaited her in Boston?

For he was sure that this was his daughter. It had to be!

Months passed. Every day he looked for the trapper, who had consented, just this once, to come to Boston when he had news.

At last, almost a year later, the man came into the shop. "Yes, sir. I seen her with my own eyes." He peered at Jed. "She favors you, I'd say. She's a real squaw, all right—except she's white, of course. When I told her what you said, she got confused. She didn't know what to make of it. I stayed for a week, talking to her. And after a few days it seemed she could remember, after all— she remembered this shop, an' all the silver. An' she remembered you, an' her mother. But it wasn't real, if you know what I mean. It was like she was rememberin' a dream. She didn't talk like it was somethin' she could come back to, that's what I'm sayin'. She's happy where she is. She loves her children. An' she's a real princess, like. They treat her good—as good as they treat any squaw. She works hard, but she's happy enough. Her man is good to her. She looks healthy an' strong."

"Does she—does she speak any English?" said Jed.

"Naw. I tried English on her. She couldn't make it out."

The trapper pulled a piece of white, parchmentlike birchbark from his pack. On it was a mark made with the tip of a burned stick.

"She made her mark here to let you know I seen her an' made her an offer to come back, an' she turned it down."

Jed stared at it: the mark that Lydia had seen many times on his silver: ⓡ . He was crying; he did not care that the trapper saw him do so. After a while he dried his eyes and thanked the man, and gave him £50 for his trouble. He put the birchbark into his locked box.

He never told Catherine—or anyone else—about the white squaw sachem, greatly beloved of the Indians, the daughter of the sun god sent to them to keep them from harm.

5. THE SCHOOL OF THE PROPHETS

1

"Me taedet laborem consumere his in studiis molestis," said Isaac. *"Desire, desiderium meum, utinam nunc mihi coram adesses!*—I am tired of this drudgery. I would be with my fair Desire!"

"Quippe tuae nervos confirmat ... mentis?" said William—"Because she invigorates your ... brain?"

The two brothers sat in their little room at Harvard College, blankets over their knees, their books spread out before them. It was late of a bitter day in January. Ever since returning from their classes, they had huddled by the small fire in their study in Harvard Hall, but only William had any interest in his books. Isaac, at twenty the elder by three years, had spent the last hour in the composition of a lyric to Desire, the daughter of Matthew Bradish, the local tavern keeper. This damsel had red lips and an enticing smile and a bosom that promised ecstasy—or so Isaac thought.

He smiled now in a knowing way—the condescending superiority of the elder brother. "It is not my brain that she invigorates," he said. The fact that he spoke in English instead of the prescribed Latin gave William to understand that the day's study was done; he would have no peace, now, until Isaac decided to sleep that night—or to visit Goodman Bradish's tavern, which was strictly against the College rules and therefore a great enticement, even without the charms of the fair Desire.

Isaac stood up, letting his blanket drop to the floor. In his heavy clothing he looked weightier than he was; he stood just over six feet, with a strong slender body and the family look—dark blond hair, thin face, prominent nose, deep-set eyes. There was a sensuous curve to his mouth; for years he had been tormented by his body's demands, and recently those torments had reached a near fever pitch, aroused by the coquettish glances of the tavern keeper's daughter. There were plenty of hideaways in her father's establishment for a young man to explore the delights of Desire Bradish; all he had to do was get her to tell him where, and when, and he would move Heaven and earth to be there. As yet, she had not spoken.

He paced up and down the freezing chamber, trying to subdue his erect, unruly instrument of Nature. William, only seventeen, knew in general what was troubling Isaac, but since his own body—shorter, thinner, less strong—gave him no trouble, he lacked any real understanding.

"Let's go find Sir Jepson," said Isaac, "and take him along to supper." Anything, he thought—anything to get out of this little room where he could not study, but only think of Desire's breasts.

As always, William acquiesced. He was fond of studying; he had been the most brilliant pupil that Ezekiel Cheever had ever taught at the Latin School. But he did not like to be alone in their little room. More and more often, alone, he became melancholy. He was extremely religious; he worried very much about his eternal soul, and about Isaac's, too, and the souls of his parents, and all his little cousins—and particularly of his sister Lydia, who had not come back from her captivity. Brooding, he would become afraid that all of them, but particularly himself, would go to Hell; for all of them, like all humanity, had been born sinful. In his time at the College he hoped to learn the path to salvation, which he would then preach to some congregation for the rest of his life.

When his mother had returned from the savages, William had been not quite nine years old but even so young, he had understood: God had shown them, and particularly his mother, great mercy. If he, William, lived to be a hundred, he could never give thanks enough to God for saving his mother— that much he understood well enough. He was almost certain that his mother was destined for Heaven. As for Lydia—ah, Lydia was the mystery. He did not understand God's intentions in Lydia's case; perhaps some day, if he studied enough, if he became learned enough, he would.

Together the brothers went out into the freezing dusk. The air smelled of wood smoke and cow dung. The red-brick Indian College stood dark and deserted in the middle of the Yard. Only a few Indians had ever come to study, and even those had not lasted; "nasty salvages," President Chauncy had called them once. They had taken sick with hectick fevers or, like James Printer, drifted for a while into another, more suitable occupation before returning to their original state.

The brothers found Sir Jepson, their tutor, peering through the College telescope. It was nearly dark now, the sky clear. They approached on tiptoe; Sir Jepson did not hear them until Isaac cried, "Ho!"—and then the poor young man gave a great start and nearly lost his balance.

"Come on, Jep—come to supper with us and leave your stargazing," said Isaac. He rather liked the dark, sallow little tutor, for Sir Jepson was more interested in his own work at the telescope than he was in the boys' perfectly prepared arguments in Logic, or perfectly translated passages from the Hebrew.

William had heard the College president, the Reverend Increase Mather, say that all Harvard boys needed to be fluent in Hebrew, for that was the language of Heaven; William had never dared question how all those who did not know Hebrew would converse with the Lord—Indians, and women, and all men who did not have a university education.

Sir Jepson, who was called "Sir" because he had a Bachelor of Arts degree, shook his head and turned back to the telescope. "I can't come now," he said. "I am watching the Dog Star. Do you want to see it?"—for Jepson had the soul of a born teacher; he was always happy, in the most gentle and generous way, to teach anybody anything.

"No comets tonight?" Isaac asked.

"No comets," said Jepson. He stifled a sigh. He had missed seeing the Great Comet a few years ago. Both Mathers had seen it, Increase and his son Cotton, and the merchant Thomas Brattle, who was an avid amateur scientist. Sir Jepson had no idea when another comet would come, but he prayed that it would be in his lifetime.

"Well, then," said Isaac. "Come and have your supper with us, and come back to look again later. You'll see better on a full stomach."

But Jepson said that he was not hungry, and so Isaac and William went to supper without him.

The dining hall was crowded and, despite regulations, heavy with the smoke of innumerable tobacco pipes. Long ago the authorities had given up trying to enforce the rules against drinking tobacco; only with a doctor's prescription or parental permission might a boy do so, they said, but the boys ignored them and smoked—or "drank"—as much as they liked. The campaign against long hair had little success either; Harvard boys were, by and large, the sons of the upper class: they did as they pleased, and many pleased to wear long hair.

Confronted with his food—codfish cakes and corn bread and a tankard of beer brewed in the College brewhouse—Isaac found that he was not hungry, after all. The face and figure of Desire Bradish had taken away his appetite. Chewing a particularly bony mouthful, he took a sip of beer to wash it down and with an angry exclamation spat out the whole thing. "This beer is sour—again!" he shouted.

At once his fellows joined the protest. They began to beat their tankards against the oak table while in rhythmic unison they shouted, "Sour beer! Sour beer!" Soon someone threw a piece of bread; someone else an apple; yet another sailed his plate of uneaten cod cakes across the room. The steward, always on the alert for trouble, dashed in to try to restore order, but he failed: the rowdy boys, their natural animal spirits chafing against the curbs of the long winter and longer curriculum, had worked themselves up to a high pitch of excitement, and they would not be stopped until they got it out of their systems. The butler and two of his assistants came rushing in, but they were worse than useless: the boys, seeing them, simply used them as targets.

In ten minutes it was over; there was no more food to throw, no more beer to pour on your neighbor's head. They knew that they were in for a lecture from President Increase Mather, but they did not care; he lived in Boston, refusing to reside in the president's house in Cambridge, and it would be the better part of a week before he spoke to them, by which time everyone would have forgotten the incident.

Afterward there was nothing to do except return to their rooms and study some more, for there were few amusements at Harvard College.

William went back alone, however, for Isaac had made up his mind: tonight he would have his Desire, and there was no place for a younger brother in his plans.

2

The Puritan Fathers had made arrangements for a college almost as soon as they got off their respective boats. In 1636 the General Court passed a resolution to establish a "School of the Prophets"; its location, its name, its president—all were left undetermined, but no matter: their intention was what counted. They wanted a college as good as Emmanuel at Cambridge in Old England, which many of them had attended, or, failing that, as good as any college at Oxford. Its purpose was to provide ministers for the New Jerusalem, for this wilderness Israel, but it was not a theological school. Rather, it was to provide a good Liberal Arts education; and so, in the manner of its day, it did—after a few early false starts.

The first decision was where to put it. A good piece of land, more than three hundred acres with ocean frontage, had been offered by Salem, but the court chose to locate the college instead on an acre in Newtowne near the cow yards, possibly because Newtowne was closer to Boston than Salem—a more central location—and yet untainted by the Hutchinsonian heresy which was then roiling the Colony.

The next decision was what to call it. Around this time a young graduate of Emmanuel, the Reverend John Harvard, had taken a post in Charlestown. He had come over in 1637, and by the fall of 1638 he was dead of tuberculosis. Shortly before he died, he made a will in which he left half his estate to the proposed college—some £1700 and a library of four hundred books. So they named the college after him, and they changed Newtowne to Cambridge in memory of that town in Old England on the banks of the River Cam.

Next, they needed to find a man to run it. They chose Nathaniel Eaton, a friend of John Harvard from their college days who had afterward studied with the Reverend William Ames, a noted Puritan exiled into the Netherlands.

Eaton lasted little more than a year. He had a violent streak to him, and he often beat the students severely. Most schoolmasters did the same, but not so hard. Finally, one day when he beat his assistant with a length of walnut—a hard wood—that was described as big enough to kill a horse, he was prosecuted for assault. On this unhappy occasion the court heard not only tales of

Eaton's beatings, but—almost worse—of his wife's sluttishness and general bad management of the domestic tasks of the College. She admitted to her bad cooking—sour bread and no beef—but she denied serving ungutted mackerel or allowing goat's dung to get into the hasty pudding. She acknowledged a shortage of beer. She was sorry for it, she said; it would not happen again. And as for the blackamoor sleeping in a student's bed while the student was at class—he would be whipped for it, and not allowed near a student's room thereafter.

To no avail did the Eatons plead against dismissal. Soon they were gone, and the College shut down. Later it was discovered that Master Eaton had taken a good part of John Harvard's legacy with him—several hundred pounds, at least.

In 1640 a man of a milder temper was chosen president: the Reverend Henry Dunster. He worked out very well—for a while. Most people liked him; he taught all the classes, and the students had no complaints. Briskly and efficiently he led them through the Liberal Arts, the Three Philosophies, the Learned Tongues; proudly he officiated at the first commencement in 1642 when nine young men delivered orations in Latin and Greek, and some of them framed disputations, and fifty men sat down to dinner in the new College building.

Each of these young graduates had paid a tuition of £1 6s. 8d. per year; if they wanted to eat, they paid extra. Since hard cash was scarce, country pay was sent in: wheat, corn, butter, eggs, cattle on the hoof—which of course needed to be fed—cloth, lumber, and sundry odds and ends. Even wampum came in, much of it such bad quality that it was worthless; President Dunster picked it over himself and had to throw a good many fathoms away.

All through the hard times of the forties President Dunster persevered, and the College managed to survive and even to grow a little. The "first flower of their wilderness" was taking root, and they were sure that it would flourish under so wise and good a man as Henry Dunster. Why, he even bested Satan himself! One time, visiting in Concord, Dunster was summoned back to the College for an emergency: the students, it seemed, had raised the Devil in Harvard Yard. Dunster hurried to Cambridge, rushed to the scene, and blew the Devil out.

But then, in 1654, President Dunster suffered a revelation from God, and all was lost—at least for him.

He was, he said, an antipaedobaptist.

An antipaedobaptist!

People were shocked—horrified. He might as well have said that he was the Devil himself.

Antipaedobaptist!

That meant that he opposed infant baptism.

If he opposed infant baptism, who knew what other heresy he might espouse?

They hauled him before the General Court and attempted to reason with him. He stood firm. He thought that no infant should be baptized: such a proceeding was "unscriptural," he said. He had had three of his own children baptized as infants before his conversion; now he refused to allow it for his fourth, and he even disrupted a public ceremony of baptism for someone else's infant.

It was forbidden by law in Massachusetts to oppose infant baptism. Tirelessly they labored with him: repent!

But President Dunster kept on saying that he was an antipaedobaptist. They could not quiet him; he insisted upon saying it as loud and as often as he could.

And so they dismissed him. A little gathering of Baptists in Scituate took pity on him and gave him shelter, and there, in 1659, unrepentant, he died.

His successors quarreled about baptism also. When the fight threatened to tear the infant college apart once again, they agreed to compromise: one would sprinkle, and one would immerse, each following his own conscience.

3

In the fetid little attic room of Matthew Bradish's tavern, Isaac Revell found a heaven very different from his brother William's. He did not need to speak Hebrew, for one thing. And as for sinning—well, he would worry about sinning some other time.

Desire Bradish was not completely naked in his arms, but near enough. Her bodice was off, her skirts were pulled up. How sweet her flesh was, warm and luscious! He had never felt anything like it. He was beside himself—out of his mind to get himself inside her, to that warmest, sweetest place of all—ah!

Shuddering, heaving, he mounted her and plunged in. Expertly she accommodated him. He was not the first Harvard lad she had taken, nor would he be the last. Fornication was against the law, but she did not care. The law, often enough, was for someone else, not for her. She made good money off these sons of the rich; let the law pay her as much to abstain and she would turn them away.

He was panting, sweating—he could hardly speak. He muttered a few words and she shushed him; despite the noise from the barroom below, her father might discover them, and then he would beat her. It was her father she feared, not the law.

Isaac gave one final, violent thrust and, groaning, lay still. He was heavy; she shifted to ease his weight. As she did so, he raised himself again and began hungrily to worry at her breasts. She didn't mind; she was used to it. Soon he was ready to start rocking and lunging again. These college boys were insatiable; it was all the brainwork they did, she thought, that made them so excitable.

When he finally rolled off her, some time later, he must have fallen asleep— or fainted—because it was very late when he left: the Dog Star had set, the moon was just rising. It was very cold. He shoved his hands into his pockets.

He was not the son of a leading merchant of Boston for nothing: as soon as he did so, he realized that there were fewer coins there than before. He stopped; he counted them with his fingertips.

After a moment he walked on, across the road and toward Harvard Hall. So he had paid for her, after all! He had thought that she was fond of him, that she had given in to him out of a lust to match his own. On the contrary, it now seemed to have been a business transaction in which she took a fee for her service. Well: perhaps that was not so bad. Business was business: despite the lyric that he had attempted to write for her, he was not in love with her. He was as hard-headed as either his father or grandfather; he could acknowledge a truth when it rose up and hit him in the face. If Desire Bradish had done business with him once, probably she would do so again. And by Heaven, she delivered good value, no matter what her price!

The bell was just tolling eleven when he whistled to his friend the butler's assistant, who unlocked the door and let him in. This lad had his price, too, and it was much lower than Desire Bradish's.

And so, this way and that, Isaac Revell got his education at Harvard College. In later life, when people asked him about his college years—about reading Greek and Hebrew, about the arts of Logic and Rhetoric—he would smile and tell them what they wanted to hear: yes, it had been an exciting time, a wonderful education every bit as good, he was sure, as Oxford or the college in that other Cambridge.

But what he remembered most vividly—what brought a flush to his cheek and light to his dark blue eyes—was the memory of Desire's warm flesh, and his own youthful passion for it.

4

In 1686, when Isaac and William Revell were graduated from Harvard College, the Crown revoked the Massachusetts Bay Charter—Winthrop's precious charter—and appointed Sir Edmund Andros governor of the newly created Dominion of New England. The King wanted to assert, once and for all, his control over this lot of stiff-necked Puritans; he also wanted to profit as much as he might from the thriving trade out of the Bay, much of which was smuggled. Further, he wanted to strengthen his defenses against the French, whose presence in Canada was a continuing threat to the English in the Massachusetts Bay and elsewhere. Finally—and not least—he wanted to punish the religious fanatics (for so he thought them) who not only killed Quakers and banished other dissenters, but also harbored the regicides, William Goffe and Edmund Whalley, who had pronounced sentence on the King's father, Charles I. Vengeance aplenty had already been taken on the Crown's Puritan opponents: the dashing Sir Harry Vane's head had rolled in Charing Cross, and the Reverend Hugh Peter's as well—he who had wanted to put Harvard College in Salem. They quartered Hugh Peter; those who watched the execution said that he did not die bravely.

So much bloodshed: and now the Crown wanted its colony docile. The year after Andros came, new taxes were imposed on trade. Truly, the citizens of the Bay felt themselves badly used. Ever since the Restoration in 1660, when the first Navigation Acts had been passed by Parliament (and promptly ignored by the merchants of Boston), the Crown had lusted after revenge on this, her most obstreperous colony. In 1664 the first royal ships sailed into Boston Harbor bearing four of the King's "observers" and four hundred troops. They were soon gone, chilled by the reception they received; but in the next decade, recovered from the plague and fire that had devastated London, Parliament set new tariffs. Again the merchants of Boston more or less ignored them.

Finally, in 1676, just when the Bay was struggling to recover from King Philip's War, Edward Randolph arrived to personally ensure that Charles II was getting his share of the Colony's profits. The merchants of Boston thought to placate the King, to appeal to his sunny nature, by sending him a present of cod and cranberries. It is not recorded whether the King enjoyed these delicacies, but in any case he did not relent: taxes must be paid! The merchants pointed out that they were not represented in Parliament, but this seemed an irrelevance to the King.

The merchants of Boston hated Randolph on sight. They accused him of setting the great fire of 1676, which he emphatically denied, and they came near to lynching him when, in 1680, he began to seize their goods. He marched in, as bold as brass, and impounded them—warehouses of salt cod, and hogsheads of grain, and barrels of rum—for the King!

The ministers prayed to God for deliverance, and ordered a Fast Day. The merchants fumed and thumbed their noses at the King. If they needed to smuggle goods in and out to survive, so be it. A pox on the King—and on Edward Randolph as well!

5

In all the Massachusetts Bay Colony, people said, there was not a more respected man than Bartholomew Revell. When in 1688 his family celebrated his eightieth birthday, the old man sat in his chair, his faithful Susannah at one side, his daughter-in-law Catherine at the other, and received his well-wishers. Half the town was there, it seemed—not only his children and grandchildren, but his neighbors and fellow merchants, all the people who had done business with him over the years.

He still had all his hair and most of his teeth. It was the fashion now for some men to wear great wigs—the "horrid busshe of vanity," as Samuel Sewall called them—but Bartle had no vanity of that kind.

One by one they came: the Shrimptons, and the Vassalls, and now Sam

Sewall himself, a little roly-poly fellow with sharp eyes that took in everything. Sewall's eyes shifted after a moment to Catherine. He had an insatiable curiosity about her: a woman who had survived the unspeakable rigors of captivity, and who had spoken nevertheless—written, rather, for everyone to read. And yet he wondered if she had told everything. He would have liked to speak to her now and perhaps get a word or two from her to put into his diary, which he kept faithfully, but the press of people behind him was too great and he was forced to move on.

Bartle reached for Catherine's hand. "All right, daughter-in-law?"

"Yes, Father." She smiled at him as their eyes met. She had drunk a cup of sackposset and it had given her strength to survive this crush, for she did not like crowds.

But then he felt her grip tighten reflexively, and he turned to face his next well-wisher.

"The L-L-L-Lord be w-w-w-with you, M-M-M-Master R-R-Revell." At twenty-five, Cotton Mather was already a famous preacher despite his stammer. Bartle did not like him, or his father Increase, either. The Mathers were a busy bunch, quick to cry Hell fire and very jealous of their position as the most famous ministers in the Colony. But there was something sinister about them in spite of their well-advertised godliness.

Bartle pressed Catherine's hand to give her courage.

"You know my daughter-in-law," he said.

Mather smiled unctuously. "Who does not?"

Strengthened by the sackposset, Catherine met his gaze. He sounded as if she wore the scarlet A on her bosom, she thought: he gives a nasty insinuation even to his most innocuous words.

And then, in a sudden burst of courage that surprised them all, she said, "And how do your little afflicted girls, Mr. Mather?"

He heard the tone of her voice: it was not respectful. Instantly he was on the alert, for here was a woman who had lived with the Devil's spawn—the savages—and who no doubt had been bewitched herself.

He warned himself to be cautious with her, for the Devil lay all about, waiting to snatch him, and the Devil could assume Catherine Revell's shape as well as any.

"They s-s-s-suffer, m-m-m-mistress, and I s-s-s-suffer with them."

The room was dim despite the several lamps. The Reverend Mather peered at Catherine. His jaw dropped. There! He blinked and peered again. Just for a moment he thought he saw the Devil sitting on her shoulder in the Shape of a great black crow. Yes: he was sure of it. He was being jostled by people crowding in behind, wanting to pay their respects to Bartle, but he felt as though he stood rooted to the floor; he could not move, the Devil would not let him.

He blinked again. Mistress Revell stood calm and quiet, looking at him strangely. No bird sat on her shoulder.

But he knew what he had seen: the Evil One. Beware! Trembling, shaken, he moved on.

William Revell, earnest and devout, had taken both his Bachelor of Arts and his Master of Arts degrees at Harvard College, and was waiting now to be called to a parish. He thought that Cotton Mather was the most brilliant man he had ever met. And even better, Mather was a young man, and so William felt close to him as he did not to older men. To William, Cotton Mather was everything that a minister should be: eloquent, passionate, learned—and wise enough to admit that the Devil lurked everywhere, that all men, but particularly men of the cloth, needed constantly to be on the alert to fight the fiends of Satan wherever they might show themselves.

On the night of his grandfather's eightieth birthday celebration, William stood outside with the guests waiting to go in, or who had already paid their respects. He did this partly because he was a member of the host family, and he was helping to attend to the guests; but he also wanted a word with Mr. Mather in private. And so now when the minister came out, still shaken by his experience with the Devil—should he report it? Should he record it in his diary? Should he pray and fast?—William fell into step with Mather as he made his way toward his house on Copp's Hill.

"Mr. Mather, I wanted to ask, would you allow me to observe Martha Goodwin?"

Mather glanced at the younger man. The narrow street was dark; there was no moon. "I would," he said, "if you can bear it. She is a pitiful sight—a terrible sight."

"Yes, I am sure she is. But I would see her. To know what the Devil does. If I am to be a minister, I should know my enemy."

"C-C-C-come tomorrow after dinner, then," said Mather. He sighed to himself. He never had enough time to read and write, and for weeks past in all his waking hours, and often in his sleep as well, he had been preoccupied with a case of witchcraft such as Boston had never seen.

It had begun with an Irish washerwoman named Goody Glover. She had had a disagreement with Martha, the eldest daughter of John Goodwin, a girl of thirteen or so, about the price charged for laundry. Soon the girl fell into fits, and she claimed that Goody Glover had bewitched her. Goody Glover denied it. She was arrested, examined for witch marks on her body—two were found—and thrown into prison. When her room was searched, two or three little puppets were turned up—sure evidence that she was bewitching someone. So they tried her and found her guilty of witchcraft.

And there the case rested now: Goody Glover in prison, Martha Goodwin and her two younger sisters and younger brother bewitched, falling into fits, suffering the torments of Hell. Mather had taken Martha into his own house to try to cure her—but also, if the truth be told, to observe at firsthand the workings of the Devil; for he planned to write about the case and like all born writers—for such he was—he was relentless in his quest for good material. The fact that Martha Goodwin's presence in his household was extremely upsetting to his wife mattered not a bit.

The following afternoon William Revell presented himself at Mather's door. Even before he had a chance to knock, he heard a commotion within: a sharp staccato scream that hardly sounded human, followed by loud thumps, as if someone was falling down a flight of stairs.

The door opened, startling him. Mrs. Mather, looking nearly bewitched herself, let him in. Whatever word of greeting she gave to him was drowned in the noise which continued unabated, and now William saw its source: a young girl racing up the narrow staircase and then descending it by jumping, hard, with both feet, on each step down. Her brown hair tumbled about her face; the neck of her bodice was unbuttoned; from her throat came the eerie cry that William had heard from outside: *"Eeee—eeee—eeee—eeee!"*—a high-pitched screech unlike anything he had ever heard.

She thumped down to the bottom. Tossing her head so that for a moment her hair was out of her eyes, she spotted him. A strange expression came over her: cunning, ravenous—a most unchildlike expression.

She hopped over to him and, craning her neck in an exaggerated way, peered up into his face.

"Who are you?"—a deep voice now like a croaking bullfrog.

William did not want to upset her further, and so, as calmly as he could, he said, "My name is William—"

"You lie! Your name is Beelzebub! And that—ah, that is your familiar! Watch! *Watch!*" With a violent movement she kicked at something that he could not see, something beside his foot, apparently: she kicked and kicked at it, but seemingly it would not budge, for she turned suddenly away from him as if in terror and ran up the stairs again, where she turned and once more began her thumping descent.

From upstairs a door slammed; the Reverend Mather came out of his study. He stood at the top of the stairs and with a kind of gloating curiosity watched as the girl landed in a heap at the bottom. Then he nodded to William. "G-G-G-Good day, M-M-M-Master Revell. C-C-Come upstairs if you w-w-w-will."

William sidestepped the girl and went up. But before he had a chance to enter the minister's study, he heard swift, light steps behind him, running upstairs, and then before he knew what was happening, the girl leaped on him from behind. Her arms went tight around his throat, nearly strangling him; her legs wrapped around his waist. He staggered and nearly fell, as much from astonishment as from her weight. Then he tried to get her off, because he could not breathe, her arms were like iron bars, choking him—*the Devil!*

After a moment during which Mather seemed to be watching the proceedings, he came to William's rescue. He gripped the girl's wrists and pried apart her arms, freeing William's neck and forcing her to drop her feet to the floor. William shook himself together and turned to her. She seemed to be fainting; Mather held her in his arms. Then, with a word thrown over his shoulder to

William—"I must put her to bed, she will stay fainting for a while"—he half carried, half dragged her along the little corridor to a bedroom. William followed. Mather had laid her on the bed; now he was undressing her. He stroked her stomach, his hands caressing her skin over and over as he watched her face. She seemed to be smiling.

After a while he stopped. The girl lay quiet, her eyes closed. He cautioned William to be silent as he led the way out of the room.

"She will sleep for a t-t-t-time," he said when they were back in his study. "Her bewitchment follows a pattern, you see. It has very nearly become p-p-p-predictable."

"You mean, the Devil comes and goes on schedule?" said William. He did not mean to sound flippant; he believed in the Devil just as he believed in God.

"On schedule—yes, you c-c-c-could say that." Mather thought for a moment. He looked tired, as well he might with such a battle under his roof: he and the Devil fighting for the soul of Martha Goodwin. "I confess to you that I do not know what to do for her," he said. "I have tried everything I know—praying, fasting, the laying on of hands such as you have just seen. I have worn out my knees here on this very floor, begging God for revelation in this case." William noticed that as the minister warmed to his topic, his stutter disappeared. "And now," Mather went on, "I know of only one thing to do more. The court has judged that the Irishwoman is a witch. She must be executed to break her power over Martha Goodwin."

At this, William felt a little twinge of horror ripple down his spine, but he thought that Mather was probably right: as the Word of God said, "Ye shall not suffer a witch to live."

A week later the witch Glover was hanged at the gallows by the town gate on the Neck; her body was thrown into the common grave for criminals. She had jabbered a good deal as the time of her execution drew near, but since she spoke only Gaelic, no one knew what she said. The interpreter who had assisted at her trial had himself fallen ill—an ominous sign, people said; the sooner she hanged, the better.

William watched the execution, along with many others. He saw the woman's body swing from the rope. At that moment he would not have been surprised to hear a thunderclap, or to see a bolt of lightning—some evidence of the Devil's displeasure. But nothing happened; it was a mild gray day in October, and not even a breath of wind stirred the body as it hung.

Afterward he went around to the Reverend Mather's. And there he had a terrible shock, for no sooner had he been admitted to the house than he heard violent screams from upstairs—shrieks and groans—someone thumping on the floor over his head—strange hissing noises.

Martha Goodwin ran down the stairs and through the downstairs rooms. She flapped her arms as she went, scattering candlesticks and dishes and upsetting the spinning wheel, knocking away anything in her path. From her mouth came a honking noise like the cry of a goose; around and around she swooshed until William wondered why Mrs. Mather, who stood by with a martyred air, did not open the door and let her fly away. Now came Mather himself; he caught her, pinioned her, held her tight. Suddenly she went rigid in his arms. "Oh—Oh—Oh—I am in chains! I cannot move—I am held fast!"

Mather lifted one hand and with a short, chopping motion he brought it down—ah! With God's help, the chains were broken! He was sure that he felt the cold metal links break under his blow; he was sure that he heard them clatter to the floor.

William had to admit to himself that he had heard nothing, but then he was not so experienced in these matters as Cotton Mather.

For many days after Goody Glover's hanging the Goodwin children, and particularly Martha, were further tortured by the Devil and his late servant, the witch Glover.

Alone in his study, in his rare moments of tranquility, Mather tried to understand: why were they still possessed? Were other witches tormenting them?

He wrote a little treatise on the Goodwin affair. He was sure that in doing this work, he was carrying out God's will. Many people read it, and took note of its message: keep vigilance, for there are witches among us!

Witches could come in anywhere, he said; *even into a minister's family*. No one was safe!

These things happened in 1688 and 1689. A few years later the world saw that Cotton Mather spoke the truth.

6

That winter, Bartle took a chill that lingered into the spring. Day by day the old man grew weaker; he coughed until his body was worn thin by it, his eyes grew bright with fever. His beloved Susannah nursed him faithfully, never leaving his side. She made a posset of saffron in wine; she prepared a syrup of elecampane; she called the barber-surgeon in to bleed him.

Nothing worked. The winter passed, April came. The first soft breezes of spring began to melt the ice and snow so that the streets of Boston were thick with mud. The buds of the apple trees in the little orchard next to Bartle's house began to swell with sap, and the hawthorn tree by the door took on a veil of green as its leaves began to show.

And all through Boston Town the word went out: old Bartholomew Revell is dying. People could not believe it. Like the beacon on Beacon Hill, Bartholomew Revell had always been with them; he was their link to their beginnings.

On a day in early April, Jedediah was polishing a silver tankard in his shop when he heard a commotion on the wharf outside his door. Telling his clerk to wait, he stepped out. A crowd surrounded a tall, well-dressed man who had just disembarked. Grim-faced, he strode purposefully up the wharf toward King Street.

Jedediah recognized him: he was John Winslow, a grandson of one of the

Plymouth founders. He had been on a mission to England; obviously he had brought back important news.

With a word to his clerk to send for him if he were needed at his father's bedside, Jed pulled on his coat and took his hat from the peg and followed in Winslow's wake. He was headed for the Town House, where the General Court sat.

The crowd swelled in the short distance to the Town House; as Winslow went inside, the people stayed by, muttering. All sorts of rumors had come in over the winter, every ship that landed brought new word: King James was dead; the Queen had had a son who had died; the Queen had had a son who had lived and who would be reared a Catholic like his father—but now here was John Winslow, a trusted emissary, and he would tell them the truth.

And so he did: King James II, a Catholic, had been overthrown by his son-in-law, William of Orange, a Protestant (and a Dutchman). John Winthrop's precious charter—the charter that had allowed the Massachusetts Bay Colony to exist for nearly sixty years—was null and void.

As Jed stood talking with his fellow merchants, digesting the news, speculating on its consequences, he saw his clerk making his way through the crush. He was wanted at his father's—hurry!

The day had clouded over; cold rain spat at him as he hurried toward Bartle's house. So King James was gone! And his chief man in the Bay, Edmund Andros, would no doubt be gone soon, as well. Jed hoped that his father was conscious, for this was news that the old man would love to hear.

All the family was gathered; Jed thought that this was not a bad way to die, surrounded by one's family, safe and warm at home instead of dead in an Indian raid, or drowned in a storm at sea.

"Father?"

Bartle lay still, his eyes closed; but then, at the sound of his eldest son's voice, he looked up and made a small nod of recognition.

"Father, there is great news. William of Orange has overthrown King James."

Jed heard a few shocked whispers from the others, but Bartle, for a moment, made no response. Then slowly he nodded; a faint smile came to his lips.

"Protestant," he said.

"Yes."

"Andros will go."

"Probably."

Susannah had been holding her husband's hand: now he looked around the circle of faces bending over him until he found Catherine, and he nodded to her. She came forward; she leaned down to kiss him. She understood, he thought. Since her captivity they had grown close; in these past few months she had tended him as faithfully as his wife. He was aware that his breath was coming hard. He did not want to die, but if his time had come, he was ready. He was aware that the room was full. He and Susannah had produced a fine big family. He had never been a man to waste words, but now, when he was about to go away, he wished that he could speak. He wanted to tell them to keep on, he wanted to tell them that they had made a good start here, and that no matter what the Mother Country did, they would survive and prosper. They had all this vast land at their doorstep, they had all its riches to trade in their ships—what else could they do but prosper? This struggle upcoming would be nothing; they would get their charter back, or they would get a new one. England was too far away to rule them tightly; the most she could do was try to get a little profit out of them, while they themselves got rich. They could not fail; failure was impossible.

All this he wanted to say; perhaps he thought he did say it. But he was very weak; he could not have spoken so much. He gave them one last look—his children, his grandchildren, his dear wife—and then his soul left his body and he was gone.

They buried him in the new cemetery at the Granary, next to the Common. His slate gravestone was carved with a winged skull at the top bordered by a motif of trumpeting angels and the imps of Death; around the skull ran the motto *fugit hora*.

The funeral was very grand—too grand, some said; they believed the new fashion of elaborate burials far too extravagant and worldly a way to send a soul to its Maker. But the Revells could well afford it, and so they had a procession of black horses, each wearing a small escutcheon on its forehead, a portrait of Bartle in an oval frame. The horses' hooves were muffled, the black-draped coffin was borne on a carriage, and hundreds of mourners followed in procession as the drums rolled the death march. Jed made six gold rings for the coffin bearers; all the mourners received scarves, and family members and close friends got a pair of gloves as well. Afterward there was a great feast; Bartle's good Canary sack flowed freely, and everyone said what a splendid family they were, for they knew how to do things right.

The next day came revolution. The country people, stirred by the weeks of rumors about the King's overthrow, had been streaming into town for days; the captain of the warship HMS *Rose*, at anchor in the harbor, was seized so that he could not order his gunners to fire upon the town. The drums beat the alarm; more and more men came in from the countryside, most of them armed and ready to fight; tempers were high on both sides.

Governor Andros and his henchmen were taken prisoner: revolution in the old country, revolution in the new. The Bostonians put a pistol to Andros's head and demanded that he surrender the garrisons at Fort Hill and at Castle William in the harbor.

Andros refused. He had had no such orders from London, he said.

The pistol was cocked; he felt its cold steel against his temple.

"Surrender!"

He gave in. They put him in chains and ferried him out to lie in the dungeon at the Castle.

Meanwhile a declaration had been drawn up: the "Declaration of the Gentlemen, Merchants, and Inhabitants of Boston and the Country Adjacent." It was read aloud from the Town House to the expectant crowd in the streets. It stated that New Englanders were loyal subjects of the Mother Country; nevertheless, they had certain grievances that they wanted the new monarch to hear—most prominently, the threat of Catholic rule, the revocation of land titles, and excessive taxation.

Then they bundled Andros and his men onto the *Rose* and sent them back to England.

This country was theirs: let the King, whoever he was, remember it!

6. THE DEVIL
IN MASSACHUSETTS

1

In a clearing in the forest a few miles from Salem stood a rude cabin with a wattle-and-daub chimney. Before it lay a large, handsome garden planted in circles and squares, knots and oblongs and neat borders—a physician's garden, it seemed, for it contained a pharmacopoeia: Saint Johnswort and feverfew, wormwood and poppy, hellebore and elecampane, basil and dittany and rue— and, in a far corner, a few plants of the deadly poisonous monkshood.

On a summer's day in the year of our Lord 1690, a woman stood in the cabin by the fireplace, but she was not preparing a meal. She smoked her pipe as she stirred the evil-smelling stuff in the kettle; from long experience she would know when it was ready. She was a tall woman, heavyset; once she had been handsome, but now, in middle age, her looks had gone. She was forty-two. Her dark hair was more than half white; today it was coiled on top of her head—she wore no modest cap—but some days it fell down around her face, giving her a wild, fearsome look. She hummed to herself as she worked: a strange, tuneless sound which some people would have thought a charm—or a curse.

Her ears were sharp; she looked up now as she heard a sound in the distance, the faint snap of a human foot treading on a branch. Not her son's foot: a lighter step than his.

At once she removed the kettle from the iron crane and set it on the hearthstone. She stepped outside, pulling the crude door shut behind her. One of its leather hinges was rotting and would need to be replaced before winter. Waiting for what she knew she would see—a supplicant—she stood with folded arms, her pipe clenched between her teeth, a figure of strength and dignity despite her worn, stained dress which bore on its bosom the marks of a sewn patch, now torn off, in the shape of the letter A.

From out of the forest came the visitor: a young woman, plainly but richly dressed, a white linen coif under a high-crowned hat, a brown linen skirt and bodice, a white scarf draped around her shoulders and across her bosom. Her face was pretty, but just now it was drawn with worry and fear.

When she reached the far edge of the garden she stopped. Then, taking a deep breath: "Rebecca Sparhawk?"

The tall woman nodded, removing her pipe from her mouth before she spoke. "And you are Joanna Craddock."

Mistress Craddock paled a little. "How did you know my name?"

Rebecca watched her. "I knew it, never mind how."

The younger woman advanced along the neat path between the plantings. When she reached Rebecca she stared up at her with a gaze that was both pleading and defiant. "And do you know why I come to you?"

"Perhaps."

No one ever came to pay a friendly call upon Rebecca Sparhawk; everyone who came wanted something of her, and Joanna Craddock was no different.

The sun was high. The young woman was perspiring from her three-miles walk from Salem, but when Rebecca offered her a drink of water, she declined. A woman like Rebecca could poison even clear, fresh water.

Rebecca led her visitor to a fallen log at the edge of the forest, and the two women sat—not close—while Mistress Craddock explained what she wanted. She did not look at Rebecca as she spoke; she stared at the ground and twisted the ends of her scarf, her face flushing and then going pale again, her words halting and painful.

"I have been married to Captain Craddock for two years this past May. He is not a young man, but he—he is a good husband, he is strong and virile. And he is disappointed in me because he wants a child, and I—I have not given him one. I have not even conceived. I think I must be barren. And now he is growing impatient. He wants a son before his old age."

"Is he at home now?"

"No. He has gone on a voyage to Maine. He will be back in two or three weeks."

"When did he leave?"

"Yesterday. And he said that if I did not conceive by the end of the summer, he will—he will get a bastard if he must." Mistress Craddock turned away; under the brim of her beaver hat Rebecca saw her crimson cheek. "He is angry with me. He beats me—he says it is my fault. Oh, Goody Sparhawk—"

Suddenly she whirled to face Rebecca; she leaned toward her beseechingly, both little fists pounding the rough bark of the log. Her pretty face was wet with tears. "I must get a child—even a girl, although a boy is what he wants. Help me! I will pay you anything you ask. You have helped others, I know you have. Make me a potion—enchant me—I will do anything you say, but I must have a child!"

Rebecca was silent, staring at her; she seemed to have gone into a trance. From the forest came the sound of birdsong, clear and sweet; crickets thrummed hypnotically in the garden. It was possible to drowse here in the warm sun, to fall into a kind of dream . . .

But Rebecca was not dreaming. She was thinking that this young woman was pretty—and quite desperate. Good: so much the better for what must be done.

"All right, mistress," she said. "Five pounds now, and five pounds when the child is born. And if it is a boy—six pounds. In gold. I don't take country pay."

"Five—ten, eleven pounds!" Mistress Craddock stared at her in shock. "I cannot pay so much—where will I get it?"

Rebecca shrugged. "That is up to you. Perhaps you do not want a child, after all."

Mistress Craddock struggled with herself. How she hated this woman—hated coming here, having to beg for help.

She rose with what dignity she could muster; Rebecca made no move to stop her. Then Mistress Craddock thought of her husband's angry face, his hurtful blows upon her shoulders. She paused.

"Very well," she said, and now her voice was not pleading, now she spoke with dislike—but not too strong, for she needed Rebecca's help, after all. "Very well, you shall have it." Fortunately she had brought a number of *dolars* with her—more than five pounds' worth, although she did not say so to Rebecca. She counted them out. As she handed them over, she could not help staring at the outline of the A on Rebecca's bosom. Shuddering, she looked away.

Rebecca went into her hut; in a moment she came out with a packet: the root of the dogstone plant ground into powder. "Tonight—not before sundown—mix this with a tankard of your best Canary wine. Heat it, and drink it quickly. Tell me how you live. Are you alone?"

"Yes."

"Good. As soon as you drink the wine, get into bed. Say no prayers. No—do not argue with me. You must not pray tonight. Get into bed and concentrate on the vision of a child—a newborn babe. You must think of nothing else or the spell will be broken."

Mistress Craddock's pretty little mouth dropped open as she listened to Rebecca's instructions. They were not so bad: she had feared worse. Slipping the precious packet into her bosom, she hurried away.

Rebecca watched her go. Then, when Mistress Craddock had been out of sight for some minutes, she gave a long, low whistle. Soon a boy appeared from the forest. He was tall, dark-haired; he very much resembled her, for he was her son.

She told him what she wanted him to do: go to Salem, find a certain young man who lived by the harbor, give the young man certain directions. At once the boy was off at a run; he was as hardy and strong as any denizen of the forest, for that was where he spent much of his time. He was ten years old and had never seen the inside of a schoolhouse, had never learned to read and write. And yet he knew many things: how to snare a wild turkey, how to skin a deer, even how to make a few simple recipes, for his mother had begun to teach him. He knew the name of every herb in her garden, and how to nurture it; he knew when to harvest the plants, how to dry them, how to distill their essence.

When he had gone, she stood for a while at her doorstep puffing on her pipe; she enjoyed the warmth of the sun on her weatherbeaten face, she loved the sharp smell of the herbs mingling with the piny scent of the forest. In her rather difficult life she had learned to take pleasure when she found it, even so simple a pleasure as this.

But even as she sunned herself she felt a small worry niggling at her heart. Her boy was known in Salem, and by and large people treated him kindly enough; even so, whenever she had to send him in, she did not rest easy until he returned. Accidents could happen; he did not know how to swim, and more than one boy had drowned at the harbor. And sooner or later, no matter how often she warned him, someone would entice him into a tavern, some slattern would offer herself.

Rebecca sighed. For some time now she had known that her boy would not be content to live in the forest forever. One day she would have to get him into the world beyond this little clearing which had been their haven for so many years, ever since he was born. Not to Salem, of course—Salem was the last place she could live. And not to Boston, either, for both Salem and Boston were under jurisdiction of the Bay. She knew that there was a world beyond; they would go to New York, perhaps, or to the Swedes in Delaware. Already she had begun to prepare for their escape. Mistress Craddock's *dolars* were part of her plan; when she had saved enough, they would leave. The boy would learn a trade. And she—well, she would do what she must.

2

Everyone in Salem knew Rebecca Sparhawk and her bastard son, for if she no longer lived among them, she was a presence in the town nonetheless. Many people of Salem visited her in her little hut in the woods; sometimes she was even called into town to deal with some particularly difficult case, for she was a skilled midwife with an excellent knowledge of herbs. Some people muttered that Rebecca's skill had more to do with charms and magic potions—with dealing with the Devil—than with medical skill, but no matter. They were reluctant to cross her; they did not want her to put the evil eye on them. And everyone admitted that she harmed no one and often did much good, particularly in matters of pregnancy and childbirth.

Once, years ago, she had been the wife of William Sparhawk, who kept the Blue Whale tavern near Salem Harbor. She hadn't seen much of him. He was forever pulling up and taking passage with one vessel or another, leaving his business in the capable hands of his wife; he had itchy feet, and no one—

certainly not Rebecca—could keep him at home. And he did not do badly in his wanderings: he worked for his keep and a share of the voyages' profits, and over the years he had, as he said, made more than he would have made with his feet planted behind the bar of the Blue Whale. And besides, Rebecca ran the tavern well; she had two husky young brothers to help her whenever a customer got rowdy, as many did, and she never complained of her husband's long absences.

She never complained, because that was not her way. But she did get lonesome; not for him particularly, for she hardly loved him after ten years of marriage and half a dozen stillbirths or miscarriages. She thought his seed was bad, although she never told him that; in recent years he had taken his pleasure with whores and, to her relief, left her alone to run the business. And if she was lonely—well, there were worse things for a woman than loneliness. He never beat her, never demanded all her money.

And then one night a new lad came in; he kept his eye on her all evening. He was overgrown, his matted hair and beard filthy-looking, his rough leather doublet and trousers reeking with bear grease—or worse. He never said a word to her, just drank his rum and watched her. Every time she turned around, his eye was on her. Three times he signaled for more drink with only a nod; then, as she was closing up, he went out and never a glance back.

As soon as he was gone she forgot about him; but the next night he was back, and the next. And always the same: staring at her until she felt queer all over. Rebecca was a hearty, handsome young woman; she liked to joke and laugh with her customers, always knowing that her brothers could get rid of any troublemakers. More than once the court had had to put one of her customers into the stocks for drunkenness, but that was in the nature of the trade. The court would have liked to close her down completely, she supposed, and short of that they made rules: no gaming, no shovel-board, no dancing, no cardplaying—in short, they made it impossible to do anything but drink, and so what did they expect except drunkenness?

At last one night when she was closing up, the staring fellow—for so she thought of him—turned to her as he was leaving. "What's your name?" he said, so muttered and abrupt that she hardly understood him.

The question startled her after his long silence, and to cover her slight confusion she laughed. "Goodwife Sparhawk," she said.

"No. Your own name, I mean."

Not quite impertinent, but oddly intimate all the same. She hesitated. He stared at her; and now, for the first time, he smiled. Many men smiled at her; she was used to that. But this one was different, somehow. "Why d'you want to know?" she said.

"Because I'm going away and I want to remember it."

She felt a little stab of disappointment, and she chided herself. She didn't care one whit if he went away; certainly she did not. Very well, then . . .

"Rebecca," she said.

He stood by the door. It was a bad night, cold heavy rain. He nodded at her. "I'll remember," he said. He was gone before she could reply—before she could ask his name in return. She pressed her lips in irritation. Men!

A week or so later she had sad news. Her husband had been lost at sea with the ship and all its contents. For a long time, all during the winter, she asked for further word—for often such reports were mistaken, and men had been known to reappear months after they were supposedly drowned. No such word came; he was gone. The tavern was hers. Very well, she thought; she had lived without him most of the time, she would go on in the same way.

3

Phineas Griffin—for so the young man was named—left Salem the following morning. His destination was a place far to the west, beyond the Connecticut River to a camp where waited his partner, a half-breed trapper called Black Joe. For the past ten years Phineas had spent every winter in the forest trapping beaver. He had been born a London wharf rat, abandoned on the docks, sold to a carpenter who took him to Boston. The carpenter was a brutal man who beat the boy and starved him; one day, Phineas had run away. With Black Joe's help, he had become a skilled trapper.

The two men needed to travel farther inland, for the rich beaver meadows nearer the coast had long since been depleted by the voracious demand for skins. Everyone in England—everyone in Europe, it seemed—wanted a fine beaver hat. Millions of beaver pelts had been sent to London since the first white men settled New England, but still the demand ran high, and Phineas and his partner knew that they could sell whatever they caught.

After some days they came to territory that had not been hunted out. Here the forest was not so dense; for many miles were lakes and ponds and streams—rich beaver country. They set up camp, for they would stay here as long as the supply of beaver held out—weeks, perhaps.

The beaver is a nocturnal creature who works by night and sleeps during the day. The next morning, therefore, the two men walked a little distance to a pond where a beaver lodge rose from the center of the ice like a rustic castle. At the edge of the pond Joe held up his hand: listen. An eerie sound: the chatter of the beaver family from within their lodge. Phineas had heard it before, but he had never gotten used to it.

Joe took a step onto the ice: one foot, then two, treading carefully toward the lodge. The ice held. With a movement of his head, he bade Phineas follow him. As silent as Indians, they moved toward the beavers' house; and yet the creatures must have known their presence, for the chatter stopped. Another step, and then another—

Suddenly Joe raised his hatchet, and with a tremendous thrust he brought it down onto the roof of the lodge. Another, and another—the place lay in ruins, the clumsy creatures within scrambling to save themselves down the little passageways that led to the waters of the pond beneath the ice.

But they were aquatic creatures; they could not move well out of water. Phineas speared the largest, and Joe got another big one with his harpoon. Several escaped, and as the men lugged their catch to shore, they watched for signs of a beaver at an air hole, or for the telltale trail of air bubbles beneath the surface of the ice.

In this way they spotted and killed three more of the family; two kits drowned, and one adult managed to lumber away into the forest where, if it did not find a beaver family to take it in, it would die.

The icy surface of the pond was crimson with blood: a good morning's work.

They stayed at the camp for the better part of a month, and then one morning they moved on. All that day it snowed, and into the night. They slept in the open, keeping their fire going by turns. In the late afternoon of their second day traveling they heard a crashing sound in the forest ahead, and Joe held up his hand: wait. In a moment they saw a huge black bear, the biggest they had ever seen. It had been coming toward them, but now, about fifty feet away across a little clearing, it stopped. It reared up. It was eight feet tall at least. It lifted its snout, sniffing their rank, human smell. Then it dropped to all fours and charged them, so quick they had no time to load their guns; they hardly had time to pull their knives. And now, as it came, Phineas could see protruding from its side a broken arrow shaft.

Phineas scrambled up the nearest tree, dropping his gun as he did so. Black Joe was not so fortunate. Even as he ran, the bear got him and with a powerful swipe of its paw knocked him down. Before Joe could get up, the bear was on him. Joe screamed. He wrestled with the bear in a hideous dance—a dance of death. The bear's talons raked Joe's face and took off one side of it from forehead to chin. Further maddened by the smell and taste of blood, the animal sank its teeth into Joe's throat and began to gnaw on that tough flesh. When it hit the jugular, Joe's blood spurted out onto the snow in a crimson stream. He stopped struggling and lay still. The bear worried at him for a little while, and then pulled back. Phineas, in his perch, knew that he was not safe, for a bear could climb a tree quicker than a man. This time he was lucky. The bear shook itself all over in a tremendous shudder. Then it lumbered into the darkening forest.

Phineas looked down. In the middle of a patch of trampled, bloodied snow lay a thing that had once been a man. Phineas felt his head spin, but he managed to keep his grip. It was almost dark. Soon the forest predators would come; he dared not be on the ground then, for he and Black Joe carried the same human smell, and the predators would make no distinction between them. He could see his gun lying in the snow, but he dared not try to fetch it.

He heard a wolf howl, and then another. They were very close. Soon he saw their dark shapes slinking out of the trees into the little clearing. Their eyes glittered like cats' eyes. There were five of them. They snarled softly as they feasted. A long time they were there. Then they went away. After a while Phineas could see other, smaller shapes approach the mess in the snow. They poked at it; then they left, too.

Phineas concentrated on holding on. He moved a little all the time, shifting his body so that he would not freeze. He talked to himself. He thought of the woman in the Blue Whale tavern; over and over he said her name: Rebecca. He made up conversations with her. He tried to imagine coupling with her. He grew a little excited at that, and more wakeful.

By and by the night passed. The sky was clear; well before sunrising he could see as much as he needed to.

He let himself down as silently as he could. Two or three small animals were scrambling over what had been Black Joe, but Phineas did not look at them. He picked up his gun; swiftly, in the half-running gait that the Indians used, he got away.

He lived with the Indians that winter, the remains of a tribe that had been decimated in Philip's War. They suffered him to live with them; they hated the white man, but they knew he was not like other whites, and he could be useful to them, particularly if they needed a translator. And they let him trap as much as he liked; no man owned the forest, any man could take what he found there.

When spring came he portaged his load of skins to a trading station. Then he began to walk toward the coast. Something beckoned to him there; he was not a thoughtful man, or a man who hoped for much, but now he had a thought, he had a hope, and he meant to act on it.

4

He sat in a corner of the Blue Whale, watching her. She had seen him come in, but her brother had served him; she was aware, however, that he kept his eye on her, and so she was not surprised when, at closing, he came to her and said her name.

"Yes," she said. "So you remembered."

He did not know what else to say. He was hardly civilized: he had had little to do with townfolk.

"Well?" she said. "What is it? We're closing."

"I'll walk with you," he said at last; and he was startled when she laughed at him.

"Walk with me! In the middle of the night! And where would we walk?"

"Home," he said. He was confused; his wits were addled. He could see her breasts beneath her green bodice; a strange miasma was overtaking him, his hands were trembling and his tongue was thick in his mouth. He had had very little rum, so he knew he was not drunk.

She pointed to the low ceiling blackened with the smoke of innumerable tobacco pipes. "Home is up there," she said. "Would you see me up the stairs?"

"Yes," he said. "I would."

Of course she knew what he wanted. All men wanted it, and no matter how the preachers thundered their warnings, no preacher could take away a man's desires.

Women, of course, had their desires as well. It had been a long time since Rebecca's husband had taken her to bed; and now he was at the bottom of the sea and she would never have him again. No matter: he had been an indifferent bedmate; even with no one else to compare him to, she had known that.

The tavern was deserted except for the two of them. Through the open door came the warm, soft breeze of the May night, fragrant with the smell of the sea and the blooming trees, the world growing green again.

Suddenly he moved toward her, but she put out her hand and he stopped. "Tell me your name," she said.

He did.

"Well, Phineas Griffin, you are a rare prize." She couldn't help laughing at him again. She realized now that he was quite young, and that, perhaps, explained his behavior. "I wouldn't let you in, where I live—not as you are. Have you never had a bath?"

"In the river."

"Well, I don't have a river handy. But you need a proper scrubbing—and a razor, too."

Like a dumb animal he stared at her. At last, with a sigh that was not entirely exasperated, she relented. "Out back," she said. He followed her like a docile dog; she led him into the kitchen in the lean-to and stoked up the fire. She emptied hot water from the kettle into the big wooden tub and started another kettleful heating.

But before she did anything she made sure that all the outside doors were locked; she wanted no surprise visitors, and the authorities were not shy about butting in even in the middle of the night if they suspected any irregularity.

"All right," she said, scooping a handful of soap from the soapbox. "I'll leave you to it. Mind you get clean. I'm going upstairs to find you a razor."

Which she did: an old, rusty one that she stropped halfway sharp. When she returned, the kitchen door was half open; she peered in.

He was sitting in the washtub, his knees under his chin. The sight of his naked body made her heart give a sudden wrench, but not with lust. He looked like a little boy—the child she had never had. He was, she judged, about ten years younger than she: about twenty.

She shook her head, irritated with herself, and marched in. He didn't seem to mind that she saw him so. "Now," she said with mock severity, waving the razor at him. "We'll see if you know how to manage this, and then we'll see what kind of a face you have under all that growth."

He grinned at her. He was perfectly happy. No one had ever taken care of him before. Soon she was scrubbing him as if he were in fact a child, laughing at him when he winced at her rough handling of his ears and neck.

She gave him a length of coarse cloth to wrap himself in; she sat him on a

stool and shaved him and made only a few nicks here and there. He could see
how happy she was, and he let her do what she would. At last she stepped back
and studied him, pleased with her handiwork.

"Well now, Phineas Griffin," she said. "You're a fine-looking fellow underneath all that. I have a glass you can look in, upstairs."

They took his clothes with them so that the scullery girl would not find
them in the morning, and before they left the kitchen Rebecca emptied the tub
out the back. Then she led him to her room above the tavern. It was small,
with a low, sloping ceiling and a dormer window. When she handed him her
small looking glass, he studied himself curiously for a moment and then handed
it back to her. Dark hair, a lean, homely face, a lump on his nose where it had
been broken once—he did not care how he looked, as long as she found him
attractive.

He was used to seeing Indian female flesh, but he had never seen a white
woman's skin save face and hands. When she moved to put out the candle, he
stopped her. He was hungry to see her—hungry to take her, too, and soon they
were tumbling in her big feather bed. He was a revelation to her, as well: she
had never imagined that a man could perform so lustily. She was not nearly
satisfied when he was done, and so after a little while she took him again, and
again, until at last, toward dawn, they were both worn out, and they slept.

After that, he came to her every night. She warned him to be careful, for
there were many prying eyes in Salem, and nosy neighbors were not reluctant
to report misdeeds. And she knew that she needed to be careful in other ways,
too, and so she went to Goody Whipple and got a potion of juniper berries
from her to make her monthly flow come on time.

They didn't talk much, those nights in her bed, but once in a while she
told him a little about herself, and she got from him what little he knew about
his own life. He tried to tell her about Black Joe and the bear, but he could
not convey to her—and she saw that he could not—the horror of that day.

And then one night he told her that he would be leaving soon—the next
day, in fact—to go back to the forest. Beavers were best caught in winter, but
there were many other skins to get: mink and fox and deer. But he would come
back, he said; it never occurred to him that he might not be welcome.

Rebecca was surprised at how saddened she was at his news. And yet, how
could she entice him to stay? Could she marry him? She wasn't sure she wanted
to: marriage was a holy thing—and besides, she had already been married and
she had not liked it. She would lose all her property if she married—the tavern,
and a good amount of acreage in the forest outside the town.

And so she bade him good-bye as cheerfully as she could; and when he had
gone, she paid another visit to Goody Whipple. Something must have gone
wrong, however, for she missed her monthly flow once, and then again. She
went to Goody Whipple one last time, and got from her a pessary of black
hellebore root.

Still she had no welcome sign of blood; still she vomited in the mornings and felt her breasts grow sore and tender; and soon she began to swell with Phineas Griffin's leavings.

5

He headed north this time, far up into Maine. As much as he had enjoyed Rebecca's bed, he had begun to feel stifled in the town; he was glad to be away. By the middle of June he was almost into Canada. With his skin burned dark by the sun, and his new growth of dark hair, he could have passed for a bearded Indian, if such existed. One day, emerging from the forest at the shore of a great lake, he came upon an Indian camp; they spoke a variation of the Algonquian tongue, and so he was able to communicate with them: he would accept their hospitality.

But later, as he was settling down to sleep in the chief's tent, he heard men's voices—angry voices—outside, and by catching a word here and there, he understood that not everyone in the camp was happy to have him as a guest. Even so far north the tribes had been partisans in Philip's War, and ever since that defeat, many Indians hated every white man, no matter how friendly he seemed.

So the next morning he pushed on. He thought that they were not sorry to see him go.

As attuned as he was to the forest, he had not been born a child of the wilderness. Small sounds occurred that he did not hear; a smell wafted on the breeze that he did not catch. By the time he realized he was being followed, they were close behind him. He turned to see two braves. When he greeted them, they did not respond; they stared at him in a hostile way. Then one of them spoke. He accused Phineas of being a spy for the white chiefs in the Bay.

Phineas denied it. As he spoke he calculated his situation: he could not outrun them, and if he made a move to lift his gun, they would attack him before he could load and aim. He stood on a narrow path; the forest grew thick all around, hard going if he tried to escape that way.

So he tried to bargain with them; he offered them good pay for any skins they could bring to him.

They did not reply. They stared at him sullenly; their hatred for him—for any white man—seemed a palpable thing, so strong he felt it like a blow.

Suddenly they jumped him. Phineas tried to grab his knife, but they were too quick. They wrestled him down; he saw their dark hate-filled faces silhouetted against the treetops, and then the flashing blade came down and buried itself in his skull.

6

By October Rebecca could no longer hide her condition, and she knew that it was only a matter of time before the authorities came to deal with her.

They sent for her one mild, Indian summer day; they hauled her before the court and charged her with her crime. Two witnesses appeared to testify that they had seen a man leaving her place near dawn.

"What say you, Rebecca Sparhawk?" they demanded.

But of course there was nothing that she could say. She had not been impregnated by the Holy Ghost; some mortal man obviously had sinned with her. He was not to be found, and so Rebecca must take the punishment by herself. They ordered that she be fined £5, and that henceforth she wear the scarlet letter A upon her bosom. They debated whether the letter should be A or F. They decided upon A because her crime was adultery; her husband was said to have been lost at sea, but no man was legally dead for seven years, and William Sparhawk had been missing for far less than that.

She felt the eyes of the community burning through to her soul as she stood before them branded as an adulteress. She held her head high; other women had done the same, or worse—her only crime was being caught.

And in truth she might have been punished more severely: she might have been put into the stocks, or whipped, or even hanged. She had seen a woman die of a flogging, once, and she shuddered now as she remembered the scene: the jeering crowd, the woman's skin flayed from her back, the blood spattering on the dusty town square. No: the scarlet letter she could bear. And no one would see it in any case, for she knew that she must go away, she knew that she must leave her tavern to her brothers, for no one would patronize it now if she still ran it.

She knew where she would go: to her property beyond the town limits. Her brothers helped her to build a hut there; and when her time came, Goody Whipple helped her through it.

She bore a boy, and she named him Remonstrance.

7

Remonstrance returned at dusk. He had done what she told him to do, he said: the message had been delivered.

Good: and tonight, Rebecca thought, Mistress Craddock, drowsy and giddy with wine and the contents of the packet she had been given, would receive a visitor. Perhaps, in the morning, she would not remember him; or perhaps she would think him the fragment of a dream brought on by Rebecca's potion.

Over the winter, Rebecca was called into town once or twice; on these visits she heard that Mistress Craddock was expecting a child. She gave no reaction to this news; she merely nodded and said that she wished Mistress Craddock well. In the spring when the child was born, she was not called upon to assist at the birth, but she heard that the baby was a fine big boy, and that Captain and Mistress Craddock were overjoyed that at last God had favored them with a son.

Rebecca waited a while, a month, two months, and when summer came and Mistress Craddock still had not paid the £6 she owed, Rebecca went to see her.

Mistress Craddock opened the door herself, her babe in her arms. When she saw Rebecca she tried to slam shut the door, but Rebecca was too quick for her; she held the door open while she spoke.

"I've come for my money," she said.

Mistress Craddock stared at her coldly. "I don't know what you mean."

"Yes you do. You owe me six pounds." Rebecca did not trouble to lower her voice, and there must have been someone else in the house, for Mistress Craddock came out and shut the door behind her—although this was hardly a solution to the problem of eavesdroppers, for the house was in the center of town, and neighbors were close on all sides, all too willing to stretch their ears.

"Now you listen to me," said Mistress Craddock. "I owe you nothing. I don't know you. I don't know why you came here. But if you don't leave at once, I'll call the constable on you and he'll have you in the stocks."

"For what offense?" said Rebecca. She felt her temper rising at this foolish woman. "I've done nothing wrong."

Mistress Craddock reached out and pulled at the edge of Rebecca's shabby cape. "There!" she said. "You've taken off your scarlet letter! They will put you into the stocks for that, I'll warrant."

Mistress Craddock was afraid of Rebecca, but she could not afford to show her fear. She could not afford to pay what she owed, either: she had nowhere near £6, and nowhere to get it. And if her husband found out what she had done—! She must get rid of this woman, once and for all.

"Go away," she hissed. Her teeth were clenched, her eyes bright with hatred and fear.

"And what if I choose to stay and talk?" said Rebecca.

"You will not stay! You have nothing to say to anyone!"

"Haven't I? You know different, mistress! I have a tale that will make them prick up their ears, indeed, and you know very well what it is!"

Rebecca saw the fear on the woman's face—fear, and a sudden vindictiveness. She did not care; she had enemies enough, and one more would not make any difference.

"I will deny whatever you say—and they will believe me before they believe you! Get away!"

Before Rebecca could reply, Mistress Craddock turned and fled into the house; Rebecca heard the scrape of the bar being thrown into place across the door. And so she went away; she would bide her time, and somehow she would get her money. She muttered to herself as she walked down the street, and people turned to stare at her. She was a forbidding figure, tall and wild-looking in her tattered clothing, a strange, distant look in her eyes.

After a time she realized that she stood in front of the Blue Whale; the carved, painted sign hung above her head, swinging in the breeze from the harbor.

The Blue Whale! She had almost forgotten its existence.

And her brothers—how long had it been since she had seen them? After they helped her to build her hut in the forest, years ago, they had not come to visit her, they had not wanted to be associated with the notorious Rebecca Sparhawk. Now, on a sudden whim, she thought that she wouldn't mind looking in on them.

She went in. It was midday, not a busy time; a few men sat at the tables, and behind the bar was a neat-looking blond woman who stared at Rebecca in an unfriendly way.

"Get out!" she snapped. "No beggars here!"

"I was looking for Eleazar Deane," said Rebecca.

"Don't know him."

"He used to—he used to run this place."

"Never saw him. My husband and I own it now, never heard of no Eleazar Deane—be off!"

And so they had gone—without a word of farewell to her. She supposed she could ask for them up and down the streets, but she had lost her sudden impulse, she wanted now only to get home to her boy. He had been conceived beneath this very roof, but she was not a sentimental woman and she did not think of that time now.

One evening the following year, when Goody Whipple called her in to assist at a difficult birth, Rebecca was stopped in the street by none other than Captain Craddock himself. He said that he wanted to talk a little business with her.

What kind of business? Rebecca wanted to know. Surely not his wife's debt, she thought.

"I understand that you own some land," he said.

Like many of his brethren, Captain Craddock wanted a good safe place to put his profits, and there was no place safer than land. The town was expanding; Rebecca's property stood in the way of that expansion. He would offer her a fine high price, he said.

"I live there," she replied. "I don't want to sell." Not just yet, she thought. Soon, perhaps, but not now. And so no matter how he argued with her, she would not agree, and by and by he gave up—for the moment.

Captain Craddock was not alone in wanting Rebecca's property. Over the next few months she had two more offers; again, she turned them down, but she began to think more seriously about leaving. Her son was growing up; perhaps now it was time to move on.

She did not visit the town again for several months, and so when Captain

Craddock's little son suddenly sickened and died, she did not hear of it right away.

But then, at a lying-in, Goody Whipple told her—and told her, too, that Mistress Craddock, half mad with grief, had put it about that the child had been bewitched. Perfectly healthy one day, dying in agony the next—who but the Evil One could cause such a thing?

And then one day Rebecca sent Remonstrance to Salem for some tobacco—for she dearly loved her pipe—and he came back bearing a strange and chilling tale. Some of the girls in the village, the Reverend Parris's daughter and niece among them, had apparently been afflicted by witchcraft, and one by one they were naming those who had harmed them. Several witches had been arrested already, and had undergone a preliminary examination at Deacon Ingersoll's ordinary; their trial would be held soon. All the village was agog with tales of witchcraft; a delegation of ministers had traveled up from Boston to investigate.

She stared at him, struck dumb for a moment by the implications of what he said. How tall and strong he was, how quick he learned whatever she taught him, how steady and dependable he was at whatever task she gave him!

And yet he was a boy still, only twelve years old, and if for any reason she were to be taken from him, she doubted that he could survive on his own.

At once she made up her mind: she would seek out Captain Craddock, or one of the other men who had spoken to her, and she would sell her property, and she and Remonstrance would go.

For Rebecca Sparhawk, remembering Mistress Craddock's grudge against her, had no doubt that if witches were being discovered in Salem, she would be one of them.

"What is it?" said Remonstrance. "Why do you look so?"

"Never mind," she said. She gave him his supper and sent him to bed; she herself stayed awake half the night, making her plans, putting by her few possessions, plotting their escape—for she knew that they had to go, and quickly. They would live in the forest if necessary, but they could not stay here.

But she was too late: the next morning the authorities came to arrest her.

8

Truly, the Devil had Salem Village fast in his grip that year of 1692: everywhere you turned, you saw him or his minions—always cleverly disguised, of course.

There! See him run, that sleek gray cat who disappears silently around the corner—do you not see? That was the Devil!

And there! Even into the meeting house he comes! A black bird on the rafter—do you not see it? Look—now he flies away!

And there! The frog that peers from beneath the leaves in the swampy meadow grass, his great unblinking eyes fastening the chains of Hell upon you—can you not see that, at least?

It was whispered among the townspeople that the Devil held his witches' Sabbath in the Reverend Parris's meadow. At midnight his horn would sound, and from all across the countryside witches and wizards would mount their broomsticks and fly in. There they would hold their hellish communion, drinking blood and making their fiendish compact with the Old Deluder.

Has your cow died? Your child sickened? Your milk turned sour? Have you lost your silver spoon? Did a blight strike your orchard?

People clucked and nodded: Satan's work, all of it!

And the afflicted girls—the girls who with every passing day were naming more and more witches—why, you could not look upon them writhing in their agonies and not believe that they told the truth about what their trouble was. They were bewitched! Falling into fits! And as soon as the authorities arrested the person they named, they would be afflicted again, and name someone else!

It began, some said, with Tituba: the Reverend Parris's black slave. She had amused the Parris children with tales of her native Barbados. But the tales became something else: they became charms and spells, voodoo and mumbo-jumbo. All the long New England winter, bleak and cold and dreary, Tituba spun her enchanted web; and now, at the beginning of spring, they were all caught in it.

Everyone knew that witches existed, and that they must be got rid of: else why would the Bible say, "Ye shall not suffer a witch to live"?

Poor frightened ignorants! They did not know that King James I, that wretched misogynist, had inserted that sentence himself into the translation of the scriptures that bore his name.

Scriptures or no, for centuries witches had been hunted down and tortured to death in the old country—in England and Scotland, in Germany and France and Sweden. Even here in the New World, many witches had been caught and executed. But never in any New World colony had anything been seen like this: witches everywhere! Under the beds—in the meeting house—flying in and out the window—what did it mean? Why was God allowing Satan this triumph?

They stiffened their backbones; they hardened their hearts. Every witch must be caught; not one must escape.

9

They took Rebecca to jail and there three women appointed to the task examined her body for witch marks. They handled her roughly, stripping off her faded garments, poking and prying beyond all decency. On her stomach they found their proof: a little black mole. They pricked it with a pin and it oozed a yellowish fluid. Then, satisfied, they contemptuously thrust her clothing back at her, chained her, and left her with the others—Goody Parker, and Mistress Martin, and Goody Cloyce, and several whose names she did not know.

Her fellow prisoners told her that the executions had begun: not a week since, three women had been hanged on Gallows Hill. And so now there was nothing to keep the authorities from hanging more. Three witches or a hundred, what did it matter? They were doing God's work, they must keep on doing it until their task was done, until no one cried out that he or she was afflicted by witchcraft.

Then the women fell silent, save for one who prayed aloud, over and over again, for God to save her. Another wept. Most simply sat in their chains in stunned silence, unable to comprehend what was happening to them.

The little square of sky visible through the high window grew dark, and the night cold penetrated the dank cell. After a while the jailer thrust a kettle of porridge through the door, and some of the women helped themselves. Rebecca did not. All night she sat with her back against the wall, trying to think of ways to defend herself.

For days they kept her in the jail. Many more accused were brought in, until the place was so crowded that Rebecca felt that she could not breathe in the fetid air. Some men were being arrested, too, they heard; they were kept in another part of the prison.

One morning the jailers came to call Goody Parker and Mistress Martin to their trial. A hush fell over the crowded cell: would these two be judged guilty, or by some miracle would they be found innocent?

All day the prisoners waited, anxious and trembling, to learn the fate of the two women. In the late afternoon they learned it: guilty. The two would be hanged in the morning. They came back weeping, fainting, pleading for mercy; all night the jail rang with their cries: "I am innocent! I have done no wrong!"

At dawn the constable came to get them. Mistress Martin went docilely, but Goody Parker shrieked and struggled as they put her into the witch cart to take her to the scaffold. For a long time after they left, the women remaining sat in a kind of stupor, unable to speak, numb with fright—for this would be their own fate, they could not escape it.

Days passed. Rebecca grew thin; her matted hair hung down around her face, her eyes sank into dark sockets in her skull. Even though the others spoke to her from time to time, they were shy of her: she was a strange woman at best, and now, in her hour of trouble, she seemed stranger still. All of the women in the jail were sure of their own innocence; but Rebecca Sparhawk— ah, there might be a witch indeed! None of them wanted to contaminate herself by seeming too friendly with Goody Sparhawk.

Often she thought about Remonstrance. She was glad that he had not tried to visit her, that he was lying low in the woods—or gone away, perhaps, which would be the safest thing. She wondered if she would ever see him again.

At last one morning the constable came to fetch her to her trial. She emerged into the bright day blinking at the unaccustomed sunlight; she walked awkwardly because her hands and feet were chained, but even as she came so slow, so halting, she saw the watching crowd shrink back at her approach. Here is a witch indeed—just look at her!

Three judges sat before her in the courtroom. Their names were Hathorne, Saltonstall, and Sewall, but she did not know that. They were stern-faced men, weighted down with the burden of their monstrous task.

"Rebecca Sparhawk, you stand accused of the foul crime of witchcraft. How plead you?"

"Not guilty!" She was glad that her voice was steady; she would have been ashamed to show fear before these men.

"Oh!" The cry came from a girl sitting in the front row of spectators. Everyone stared at her as she craned her neck, twisted her head, watched with wide eyes—what? Something that only she could see, flitting about the room.

"There!" she cried. "See—there it flies—a snake with two heads! It is flying—ah!—watch—there! It twines itself about Goody Sparhawk's body—see—now it slithers on the floor!"

Everyone shrank back in horror lest the monster touch them—women cried out their fear of it—the girl screamed and screamed—the judges called for order—there! The thing was gone—out the window!

The girl fainted. Rebecca stood stolid and grim. The spectators fell into a deathly hush.

"Let Mistress Craddock come forth," called the clerk.

The captain's wife emerged from the throng and took her stand not ten feet from Rebecca.

"What say you, mistress? Has this woman bewitched you?"

"My babe," said Mistress Craddock. "She put a spell on my babe."

"He died, did he not?"

"Yes."

"Do you know the cause?"

"No. I mean—yes. He was bewitched. He was healthy—" And here her voice broke; after a moment she went on: "He was healthy when I put him to bed. In the night he awoke. He was in a fit—screaming. He seemed to be in great pain. Before morning, he was dead."

"And why do you say Goody Sparhawk bewitched him?"

"Because—" She seemed near fainting, but then she gathered her strength. "I saw her Shape."

A few spectators moaned; a few let out sharp exclamations: this was what they had come to hear!

"How did you see it? Where?"

"She was hovering over him—floating in the air. When I came, she flew out the window."

Just as they thought: the same spectral evidence that they had heard from the Reverend Parris's girls. Shapes, and demons, and familiars; death and illness, damage to crops, mysterious comings and goings in the night—all of it the Devil's work!

"What say you, Rebecca Sparhawk?"

"I say that Mistress Craddock lies, and she knows why she lies. Ask her how she got her son."

A gasp from the crowd; what did the woman mean?

Mistress Craddock held her head high, but she would not look at Rebecca.

"Explain yourself, Goody Sparhawk," said the examining judge; he was a lean, gray-haired man with a long thin nose, a long thin mouth, and two specks of granite where his eyes should have been.

"I have nothing to explain. It is she who must do the explaining."

The judge frowned. He disliked impertinence, particularly from women—particularly from women accused of witchcraft.

"Well, Mistress Craddock?"

"I do not know what she is talking about!"

Rebecca was angry now. "She came to me!" she cried. "She asked me for—" But it was no good; she was admitting her own guilt if she told them of the potion she had sold to the woman, the magic potion that gave her her child. And as for the young man who might testify to his part in the matter, he had gone away, months ago, and had not returned.

Suddenly Mistress Craddock began to tremble. She shook and shivered, she cried out, she held up her hands as if to ward off—what? Something flying at her, something trying to bite her, to peck at her—"No! No! Do not! Help! Help me! It is the Devil!"

She fell into a heap on the floor. No one moved to assist her; how could they? They dared not, for then the Devil might attack them. Everyone stared at her, fascinated. Then one of the girls sitting in the front row began to moan and twitch. She raised her arms as if she were wrestling with—what? Her eyes were closed. Her cries came sharper and sharper. The people on either side of her drew away. She leaped up and began a dreadful, jerking, spastic dance—just as if, people thought, someone were forcing her to dance, just as if she were fighting off one who would make her dance against her will—ah! There! Another girl jumped up, and she, too, began the dance—a dance with the Devil, for certain! Then another cried out, and another, jumping up, whirling, writhing—pandemonium!

The judges called for order. Half the audience was caterwauling now, waving their arms, jumping up and falling back, stamping their feet, warding off blows from the powerful presence that was loose in their midst.

Again and again the judges tried to quiet them; no one paid any attention, everyone was caught up in the madness.

Everyone, that is, except the accused: Rebecca stood silent while the room erupted around her—and for that, too, she was suspect. Why was she not afflicted like all the others?

Because—of course!—she was the cause of their affliction! She was the Devil's tool, his willing handmaid!

The judges pounded for order. At last the crowd quieted. The jury withdrew to consider its verdict, but of course everyone knew how it would come out: the evidence had been compelling, much more so than in other cases where a guilty verdict was returned.

Soon enough they were back. The foreman spoke to the chief judge; and he in turn spoke to Rebecca. He stared at her as he spoke; his eyes bored through her as if he would see into her soul, as if he was trying to see the Devil in her.

"Rebecca Sparhawk, you are found guilty of the crime of witchcraft."

Palpable relief could be felt washing over the spectators: guilty! One more witch done away with!

He went on, his voice dry and harsh: "In accordance with this finding, the court now pronounces sentence upon you, which is that you are to hang by the neck until you are dead."

Rebecca had stood quietly waiting all this time. She felt curiously detached, as if she were a spectator, too, instead of the center of attention. But now the judge's words registered, and she felt a sudden panic sweep over her. Somehow she must try to save herself. When the constable put his hand on her arm—brave man, to touch a witch!—she pulled away from him, she stepped toward the judges so sturdily that she nearly frightened them, and they stared at her, shocked.

"No!" she cried. "I am not guilty! I never bewitched anyone—I never harmed Mistress Craddock's child! You condemn me wrongly, and God will punish you!"

At this, a man in the crowd cried out: what right had a condemned witch to speak of God?

"Be quiet, woman!" said the granite-eyed judge.

"No! I will not! You have no right to hang me! You cannot prove that I killed the child—you cannot prove that I ever harmed anyone! These accusations are groundless, and if there is a God in Heaven He will punish you for what you do! If you must arrest evildoers, arrest them!" She pointed her long, dirty finger at the girls who sat cowering in the front row of spectators. One of them, she was sure, was trying to stifle laughter.

"Out!" roared the judge. "Take her out!"—and the constable seized her and hustled her away.

But her outburst troubled them. Not that they feared God's wrath, for they knew that they did God's work, but they feared Rebecca Sparhawk and her dark powers, her covenant with Hell. Who knew what harm she could do, even from jail?

Best to hang her at once, in the morning, and put her vengeful spirit to rest.

As Rebecca passed out of the court, she met Mistress Craddock's eyes. For a long moment Rebecca stared at her accuser, and in the end it was Mistress Craddock who looked away.

10

In the jail that night, for the first time since her nightmare began, Rebecca felt tears come to her eyes and spill down her cheeks, cold in the little breeze from the window. Her life had not been much, but just now, when she was about to lose it, it seemed very sweet. She had not lived without sin—who had?—but she had never meant to harm anyone, and she had given good value to those who called on her for help.

Someone was at the window. He had come so silently that he startled her now when he spoke a low word. But then she recognized him: Remonstrance.

She dragged herself close to the small barred square. In the pale light of the stars she could not see his expression, but she heard his voice and she was grateful for this one last chance to talk to him.

"Here," he said. "I brought your pipe. And a bottle of rum." He thrust them through the bars; she took them, and then she clasped his hands. Dear God, she would never see him again!

She gritted her teeth in an effort to steady her voice. "They will whip you if they find you here," she said.

"They will have to catch me first."

"Listen to me," she said. "You must leave Salem. And you must have some money." And she told him where to find her little hoard, hidden in the stones of their fireplace. He must go out of the Bay, she said; to New York, perhaps, or even to England. And there was something else—something she had never told him, but which, now, he was entitled to know: who his father was. "His name was Phineas Griffin," she said; in truth, she knew little else to say about him, for she did not know if he was alive or dead, she did not know why he had never come back to her. "And you must take that name. You must be Remonstrance Griffin now."

She had thought of calling him to testify. He would say that Mistress Craddock had, indeed, come to her for a potion; that he had gone to Salem to deliver a message to a young man, which message was to go to Mistress Craddock in the night—ah, but what was the use? They would say that he lied to protect her. Perhaps—and it was this that terrified her more than anything—perhaps they would accuse him of witchcraft, too. Already they had a five-year-old girl in jail, little Dorcas Good, whose mother was accused as well. Would they hang a five-year-old child? Or a twelve-year-old boy? Men were as vulnerable as women; wizards were as dangerous as witches, and already the authorities had arrested Goodman Cory and John Alden (son of the Pilgrim Father), and Philip English and his wife—there was no end of the Devil's work, it seemed. Even now, tonight, it was being whispered through the jail that the governor's wife herself, Mistress Phips, was cried out on—the governor's wife!

Rebecca knew that Mistress Phips would not be tried for witchcraft, much less hanged. She had powerful friends who would help her to escape, if it came to that. Some of the accused had already fled, traveling to New York where the sane and sturdy Dutch would have no truck with witchcraft.

All night Remonstrance stayed by her, heedless of the danger, and in the dark morning when they came to take her away, he joined the crowd that followed the procession of the condemned. Under the clouded sky the drummer drummed them to the top of Gallows Hill, three women in chains in the witch cart, the jailers walking at their sides. Several ministers accompanied them in case one of them wanted to make a last-minute plea to God for forgiveness. None of them did.

When they reached the top, where the gallows stood, Rebecca suddenly went a little mad, or so it seemed. She began to shout at them; violently she wrestled with her chains until her wrists were red with her blood. Two jailers held her fast; they hustled her up the scaffold where the hooded hangman waited.

"No!" shouted Rebecca. "I am innocent! I have done no wrong!"

She lifted her face to the sky as she shouted, as if she were crying out to God; and now the expectant crowd looked up, too, and what they saw was remembered in Salem as long as the witchcraft itself. The clouds had parted, and yet the sky was growing dark; all over the land came the shadow of night—the shadow of Death, they thought—for now, in midday, the sun was obscured as if by the hand of God Himself. The sun was dark—half black—ah! God was angry with them for allowing these Devil's whelps to live even one moment more!

The faceless hangman stepped forward. He put the noose around Rebecca's neck. At his signal, the platform dropped. She swung. To the awe-filled crowd, moaning in terror, quaking at the wrath of God, she looked like a witch's puppet—a little lifeless thing. In a moment the other two swung beside her. In the eerie noonday twilight the crowd waited, afraid to speak, to move—ah, God have mercy upon us!

At last, after long, agonizing moments, the sun came back and the day was bright. It was a sign from God. They were sure of it: God approved what they did, ridding the land of witches.

Some few in the crowd recognized the tall boy standing apart from them, stony-faced, deathly pale, his hands clenching and unclenching. In the ordinary way, had his mother died of consumption, say, or of an infected wound, they would have gone to him to offer sympathy and help. But they did not dare to speak to the son of a convicted witch: what if he had inherited her deviltry?

But then, after all, someone did approach him: a kindly looking man accompanied by a female child. The man said nothing; he put his arm around Remonstrance's shoulders, and Remonstrance could feel the man shuddering with repressed sobs; the girl's face was red and swollen from crying.

These two had good reason to weep, for one of the other women hanged that day was the man's wife, the child's mother: Jane Tyler, accused of killing a neighbor's cow by witchcraft, and of causing another's dog to go mad, and sundry other things—strange things, inexplicable things.

As the little trio moved away, the crowd, fearful of contagion, parted to make way for them.

The bodies hung until nightfall; then the constable and his men dug a shallow grave and dumped the women into it.

Edmund Tyler owned a shipyard in Salem. For a while, after his wife's execution, his business suffered; but as the old year passed into the new and the witch craze subsided, he began to prosper again. He never thought of leaving; he knew that an injustice had been done, not only to his wife, but to all the condemned—old Goody Nurse, and the Reverend George Burroughs (Judge Samuel Sewall's classmate at Harvard), and all the others—all of them wrongly condemned, all of them needing to have their names cleared.

That first night, when he took Remonstrance home with him, he said little; he fed the boy and gave him a place to sleep. In the morning he told Remonstrance to stay as long as he liked. He felt a terrible guilt that he had not been able to save his wife; by offering help to Remonstrance he felt in some way that he was atoning for that guilt.

Remonstrance stayed because he did not know what else to do. A curious lethargy had come over him; he felt so tired that he could hardly lift his head, he could hardly put one foot in front of the other to walk across the room.

All day he lay in bed, not sleeping, but lacking strength to rise. He ate hardly anything. Then, after a week or so, he got up and went outdoors. He was surprised to see that the world went on. People went in and out of the shops; ships came in and out of the harbor; children sat in the schoolhouse learning their lessons, and on Sunday and Lecture Day everyone went to church.

Tyler had told him to come to the shipyard. It was a busy place, men working hard to fashion the ketches and schooners and barques that were making rich the merchants of Massachusetts. The smell of pine pitch and fresh-sawn wood filled the air; the din of hammers and saws rang in his ears in a pleasant way.

"I'll put you to work if you want," said Tyler, "and give you room and board and a little pay besides. Can you read and write?"

"No, sir."

"You'll have to learn, if you stay with me—and figure sums, too."

"Yes, sir."

He did not mind; he lacked the will to decide anything for himself, and so, for a time, he was content to let this man guide him.

11

That summer and into the fall of 1692 the Court of Oyer and Terminor condemned thirteen women and seven men to die for the crime of witchcraft. All of these save one were hanged; old Giles Cory, a stubborn and cantankerous man, was pressed to death with stones because he would not enter a plea to the court, and without pleading, no one could be tried.

They laid him on the ground outside the jail and they put a heavy rock on his chest; and then they asked him: "Will you plead, Giles Cory—guilty or not?"

To which he replied—stubborn man!—"More weight."

They put another rock on top of the first, and they asked him again: "How plead you, Giles Cory?"

His breath was coming hard now, his crushed ribs collapsing into his lungs; but still he managed to get out: "More weight."

They brought up a third rock, so heavy that it took three men to lift it. Before they laid it on him, they asked him one last time: "How plead you, Giles Cory?"

He was still conscious. His face was black, his eyes bulged out of his head, a stream of blood flowed from his mouth. And even so—did the Devil give him strength?—he whispered his reply: "More weight."

And so—what choice did they have?—they put the third rock on him, and soon he was dead.

In October Governor Phips dissolved the court. The judges were left to ponder what they had done. There were still more than a hundred accused witches in the jails of Salem and Boston, but even those who had been tried and condemned would not die now, for the frenzy was abating; people felt as though they were awakening from a long illness—a terrifying plague spread out of control. Surely not even the Devil himself could enlist so many helpers in one small corner of the world.

Doubt grew to open argument: no more trials, people said, no more hangings. A letter came from some ministers in New York: they doubted the existence of witches, they said, and they begged their compatriots in the Bay to go cautiously in their condemnations.

At last the terrible questions began to be asked aloud: What if the judges and juries had been mistaken? What if the accusers had erred? What if their evidence—tales of Shapes, allegations of midnight covens—had been only the fantasies of their distracted minds?

The governor ordered the release of those lying in jail; even those who had been tried and condemned, he said, must be set free. No more innocent blood must be shed; and by now, it was agreed, innocent blood undoubtedly had been shed, and for that they must all look to their own consciences.

Some of the judges were unrepentant; they would go to their graves believing that they had carried out God's will.

Samuel Sewall—that inveterate diarist who embodied in his plump corpus much of the best and some of the worst in the Puritan character, and who teetered on the cusp between Puritan and Yankee—was not so sure. Doubt nagged at him; the open criticism of men like Thomas Brattle and Robert Calef cast his mind into a pit of horror: had he done wrong? Had he and his fellow judges sent innocent people to their deaths—and, worse, excommunicated them so that they might never know the glories of God's Heaven if in fact they were not witches at all, but among the Elect?

On Christmas Eve in 1696—not a holiday celebrated in Puritan Massachusetts—Sewall sat coaching his son, young Sam, in the mysteries of Latin so that the boy might gain admission to the College. Laboriously, Sam Jr. read aloud from Matthew 12, 7: *Quod si nossetis quid sit, misericordiam volo, et non sacrificium, non condemnassetis inculpabiles*—"If ye had known what this meaneth, 'I will have mercy and not sacrifice,' ye would not have condemned the guiltless."

"Ye would not have condemned—"

The elder Sewall sat dumbfounded. God had spoken to him. To him, who had condemned—how many? They had seemed guilty at the time, but now God was sending His word: *guiltless.*

Guiltless?

Three weeks later, on a general Fast Day in penance for the witchcraft ordered by the governor in the midst of the coldest winter in memory, Samuel Sewall wrote out his confession and gave it to his minister, Mr. Willard, to read while he, Sewall, stood before the congregation.

Cotton Mather never repented; he believed in witches always, and he published a detailed, credulous work about the Salem affair: *Wonders of the Invisible World.* In 1693 he even found another case of witchcraft, a young Boston girl horribly afflicted. Mather had to visit her as she lay in bed—an episode that gave the doubters much glee. Robert Calef had the temerity to write a response to Mather's book on witchcraft. He called it, mockingly, *More Wonders of the Invisible World.* Cotton Mather was in a fair way to becoming a laughingstock, for many people read that book, even though his father, Increase Mather, the President of the College, burned it in Harvard Yard.

Robert Calef was a *tailor.*

Cotton Mather was—well, he was a *Mather.*

And was it not the Devil's work that in this new world, after the Glorious Revolution, after the revocation of the old charter and the institution of the new, a common tailor could hold a Mather up to ridicule—and get away with it?

12

In 1699 Remonstrance turned nineteen. He was a tall, good-looking boy who resembled his mother. He had served his years of apprenticeship with Edmund Tyler; he had been like a member of the family ever since that terrible day when they had met.

He had never returned to his mother's hut in the woods, he had never retrieved the money she told him about. He didn't need the money; he couldn't bring himself to go back to that place where he had lived with her. He did not know what had become of her property, nor did he care—Captain Craddock got it, very cheaply, but he never got a son to inherit it, and so it did him little good.

In the first winter after Rebecca's death, Remonstrance did as she had told him and took his father's name: he was Remonstrance Griffin now. He felt a vague sense of disloyalty to her, but he understood why she had instructed him so, and he obeyed.

One summer night, when he had worked late at the yard to finish a fine new sloop in the allotted time, he returned to the Tylers' house. The family had all gone to an evening lecture at the meeting house—all except Charity, who waited there for him to give him his supper. Tyler had remarried, and Charity did not like her stepmother; she was glad to be away from her this little while, and even more pleased to have this chance to do for Remonstrance.

She was a small girl, sixteen now, with brown hair and a pretty, round-cheeked face. She had about her a hesitant air; she was easily frightened, and even now she was not fully recovered from the horror of the witchcraft, seeing her mother hanged, living through the fearful days when no one in the town would speak to them, when no one stepped forth to offer friendship and support. Gradually life had returned to normal, but even now, sometimes, she had nightmares; she felt as if she could trust no one except her father and her brothers and sisters, for in the witch time they had had only themselves to look to for support.

And Remonstrance, of course: he had been one of them, he had suffered what she suffered, seeing his mother condemned and hanged, and not a soul to take her part. Charity felt that she and Remonstrance had a special bond between them because of that; no one else in the world could understand what they had suffered, he was the only one outside her family who knew her grief, her terrible anguish.

She bade him sit down while she served up his supper: baked beans and a side dish of pumpkin stew. She poured him a glass of beer to wash it down, and sliced some brown bread that she had baked herself that day. Her stepmother was an indifferent cook, and was hampered in her housekeeping by the steady arrival of babies, one every year.

Remonstrance smiled at her; he was fond of her. She sat with him while he ate, busy at her knitting but ready at any moment to fetch him anything more he wanted; and when he had finished, she put a plate of blueberry slump before him, and glowed when he complimented her on her cooking.

He felt good: well fed, content with her company. When he suggested that they walk in the garden—for the kitchen was always stuffy, winter and summer—she happily put by her knitting and went out with him.

A big yellow August moon hung over the treetops. They could not smell the sea tonight, for the wind was from the southwest; for a moment the smell of flowers and herbs blooming all around them reminded Remonstrance of his mother—of their home in the forest, and the garden she had nurtured there. Sometimes, for days at a time, he did not think of her; and then all of a sudden, catching him unawares, she was with him, and he felt his agony again, his helplessness, and grief washed over him and left him desolate.

Charity stood beside him, the top of her head barely reaching his shoulder. She was a good, sweet girl, he thought; and she had, deep within her, that secret sorrow just like his own, that sorrow that no one else in the world could understand.

A week or so before, Tyler had mentioned that he would be taking on a new apprentice. The boy would live with them, as apprentices did. Unspoken, but understood, was the next thought: Remonstrance would probably want to go rather than share his bed with the new boy.

Now, standing with Charity in the warm, fragrant garden, Remonstrance realized that the worst part of leaving would be leaving her.

Awkwardly, clumsily, he put his arm about her. She leaned toward him, resting her head against his chest. She was warm and soft in his embrace, and yet there was a kind of tension about her; she was not a passive thing, she worked hard, and she knew very well how to manage a household.

He bent his head to hers; he kissed her. He felt her respond. She put her arms around him and held him fast. His head spun; all his carefully held emotions broke loose, and he kissed her as if he could never stop. Suddenly he realized what he must do: when he left the Tylers' household, he must take Charity with him.

And so they had their banns read, and before the winter they were married.

13

No Revell was ever accused of witchcraft, although Cotton Mather continued to have his doubts about Catherine. After Jed took Isaac into the family business (trade—the boy was not interested in silversmithing), Isaac's brother William was called to the pulpit on the northern frontier, at Haverhill.

As the years passed, William spent a good deal of time preaching to the Indians. In this way, he thought he was following God's plan: these heathen savages, who had captured his mother and who still held, perhaps, his little sister—these savages were fertile ground for William's strong missionary impulse. He felt that they came to accept him as their friend; he learned a little of their language, he read to them from Eliot's Bible, he even went to live with them from time to time.

And in the end it was, perhaps, God's mercy that William never knew what hit him—a bullet from out of the forest, a hostile Indian on the warpath once again. William fell dead all in an instant, his faith in his work undisturbed. Two weeks after the family buried him in the Granary Burying Ground, Jed keeled over in his shop, a half-formed caudle cup dropping from his hands. And so the running of the family business was left to Isaac; and because he was his father's son, he handled it well and made an excellent marriage, too—to Elizabeth, one of the Chauncy girls, who brought with her a handsome dowry.

On the day before his wedding, when Isaac was distracted by a thousand details—the final touches to be put by the tailor on his wedding suit, the final instructions to his servants fitting out his grand new house in North Square—he was distracted further by a commotion at the waterfront.

"They're bringing him in!" cried his clerk, and so Isaac, as curious as anyone else to see a celebrated man, dropped everything and went to view the spectacle: the notorious Captain William Kidd, a prisoner on orders of the governor, the Earl of Bellomont. Kidd had had a spectacular career these past few years, starting out as a privateer with letters-of-marque, and ending up as a full-fledged pirate; but now they had got him, and he would never command a ship again. He was a tall, fierce-looking fellow, wrapped in chains from head to toe and escorted up the wharf by a passel of militia; they threw him into the gaol, and there he rotted for six months until they sent him back to London to be hanged the following year.

By that time, 1701, Elizabeth had given Isaac a son; they named him Benjamin Chauncy Revell.

PART II

REVOLUTION

THE REVELLS

Benjamin
(1701–1792)

m.

Hannah Pemberton
(1704–1755)

Ebenezer   Seven infants die
(1735–1799)

m.

Griffin   1.   Emilie Griffin
Revells   (1741–1762)

Thomas   Nathaniel
(1761–1805)   (1762–1846)

m.

Jackson   2.   Mercy Jackson
Revells   (1740—1767)

James   Samuel
(1766–1848)   (1766–1851)

m.

Abbott   3.   Abigail Abbott
Revells   (1741–1818)

Hannah   Philip   female   Roger
(1770–1810)   (1772–1846)   (1773–1773)   (1774–1852)

Elizabeth   Francis   Elias   Mariah
(1775–1775)   (1777–1850)   (1779–1862)   (1780–1854)

This province began it. I might say this town, for here the arch-rebels formed their scheme long ago.

General Thomas Gage
Letter to Lord Dartmouth
July 24, 1775

1. THE MOST DANGEROUS GAME

1

June 1768. A mild, tranquil night when the moon hung low over Boston Harbor and the soft sound of ships' bells mingled with the *slap-slap* of water against the wharf pilings. Through the dark, narrow streets of Boston Town a silent shadow sped its way, avoiding the watch, darting from doorway to doorway, alley to alley, until it reached its destination: the merchant Benjamin Revell's mansion house in the North End.

"Master Revell!" The shadow materialized into the form of a young man. He threw a few pebbles against the window at the second floor and called softly again: "Master Revell!"

After a moment the old man's head appeared, nightcap and all. "Who goes? Is't you, Davey?" In the moonlight he thought he recognized a lad who had worked for the Revell firm for two years now, a good, dependable boy.

"Yes, sir. Master Ebenezer sent me. The Customs'v'boarded th'*Emilie*, sir, an' Master Ebenezer's locked up th'officer! He says y're t'come right away!"

Damn and blast! Benjamin had warned his son only a week ago: sooner or later you're going to be caught smuggling; why run the risk any longer?

To which Ebenezer had replied: "There is a greater risk, Father, letting them tax us to death. If we do not smuggle our goods in, the House of Revell will not survive. It is as simple as that."

And now, sooner rather than later, the trouble had come. The old man called softly: "Tell Master Ebenezer I will come straightaway. Go on—don't wait for me."

A hurried toilette, shrugging on his clothes, his white silk stockings and black breeches and dark blue coat, not bothering to tie his stock properly, his hair messily clubbed—damned young fool! Consorting with the troublemakers,

165

Samuel Adams and young Hancock, deliberately tweaking the nose of the British lion!

Down the stairs, no danger of rousing the housekeeper, who always slept soundly; and no one else to rouse, for his wife was long dead. Ebenezer, his only offspring, was a widower himself twice over; he lived in his own place on lower Beacon Street with his four children.

Carefully Ben opened the heavy front door and went out, closing it again behind him. Every house was dark, for it had just gone midnight. Dark and silent streets: no matter how lightly he stepped, his heavy shoes sounded like a soldier's tramp. But there was no help for it: he had to answer his son's call. If the watch stopped him, he'd buy his way free with a shilling or two.

In all the town of Boston—in all the Province of Massachusetts Bay—only the Hancocks had amassed a greater fortune than Benjamin Revell and his son Ebenezer. Most of it came from the Golden Triangle: rum from New England distilleries taken to Africa and traded for slaves; slaves taken to the West Indies and traded for molasses; molasses brought home to be made into more rum. A hundred percent profit on each leg of the voyage—how could a man help but grow rich? And they traded miscellaneous goods as well, dry goods and hardware and wine and paper and glass brought in, grain and meat and clapboards taken out. Revells had been trading since the Massachusetts Bay Colony was founded: first old Bartle, the founder of the line; then his son Jedediah, silversmith as well as merchant; then during the early years of the present century, Ben's father Isaac, who had tripled the number of ships going out and transformed the Family from one that was fairly well-off to one that was rich.

Rich! What good was all their money if the British Parliament was bent on taxing them to death? In recent years it had seemed that the Mother Country, making up for decades of benign neglect, had begun to tax the Colonies with a vengeance, and not only to demand outrageous levies on goods brought in, but to intrude on people's liberties as well. There was a new instrument called a Writ of Assistance: a document that allowed the Crown officers to break into any man's house or warehouse and confiscate whatever they found. The King's officers used it indiscriminately, breaking in at all hours, seizing goods at will, arrogant and vindictive.

Consequently, the merchants of Boston had resorted to large-scale smuggling, bringing their cargoes in under cover of darkness and dispersing the contents of their ships' holds into hiding places in the hinterlands before the Royal Customs Agents could slap on their levies. But sometimes—tonight, for instance—the Customs officers had the good fortune to stumble into such an operation before it was completed. And then there was trouble.

Ben turned onto King Street and headed toward the harbor and Revell Wharf. Still quiet. What had happened? *Clomp-clomp, clomp-clomp.* His footsteps sounded loud enough to wake the dead, but no one challenged him; he might have been alone in a deserted city.

And now in the moonlight he could see the wagon and its team of oxen waiting on the wharf, and at anchor next to it the dark shape of the brig *Emilie*, newly come in that very afternoon. Beyond, a score of other trading vessels anchored in the inner harbor; beyond them, the dark hulk of the *Romney*, a ship of the line, the British Navy's finest, a fifty-gun man-o'-war recently come down from Halifax.

Ben hurried down the wharf, leaped onto the *Emilie*'s deck, and with a quiet word to the guard, went below. He found Ebenezer in the hold with their captain, supervising the unloading of a cargo of wine from Madeira and molasses from Barbados. Swiftly and silently—as silently as possible—

"Who was it?" said Ben. "And where did you put him?"

"Jabez Pratt," said Ebenezer. "And three of his tidesmen. They came to serve a writ on me."

"And—"

"I had Pratt locked into the small cabin. His lackeys ran away."

He turned to give an order to the seaman operating the winch, by means of which the heavy hogsheads were being lifted out of the hold and onto the wagon. He was tall—taller than Ben, who was over six feet—and powerfully built. His hair was the color of burnished gold, and in the light of the hanging lantern his deep-set eyes shone darker than their customary dark blue. His features, like his physique, were large and strong, his nose pronounced, his brow high—not exactly a handsome man, the ladies said of him, but intriguing.

"Was it necessary?" said Ben. "To lock him up?"

"Yes, Father. It was."

"And what will you do with him?"

"I will keep him safely out of the way until we are done, and then I will warn him to keep his mouth shut, and let him go. I wanted you here in case they sent reinforcements and arrested me. Then you would have to assume responsibility for the cargo."

"In the old days," said Ben, "they were happy to take your money and never say a word about what you brought in."

"The old days are gone," said Ebenezer. "We can't waste time regretting them."

From the cubbyhole where he had been put, Jabez Pratt heard thuds and thumps, the whine and scrape of the tackle. In vain he pounded on the door, on the bulkheads. "Revell! In the name of the King, set me loose! You are in violation of the Acts of Parliament! Ho! Listen to me!"

But no one paid him any attention. Time passed: he could not tell how many hours. He was cold, he was stiff, the damp had entered his bones—when would that scoundrel set him free?

At last, toward daybreak, Captain Brant came to open the door. Pratt stumbled out. As cold and stiff as he was, more than anything else, he was angry—furious!

"Where are your masters?" he snarled.

"Awaiting you in my quarters."

Without a further word Pratt stomped ahead. Ebenezer gave him a glass of rum and a friendly smile; Ben stared with a grim face. Father and son looked much alike, but their demeanor was very different.

"Good morning, Mr. Pratt," said Ebenezer. "And a fine day it looks to be. Did you sleep well?"

Pratt glowered up at him; without a word of greeting he fished in his pocket for the writ, pulled it out, and thrust it under Ebenezer's nose. "I'll have you in irons for this," he growled. "I serve you now with this writ, and I'll have your ship impounded! I know what you did last night! Yes! And manhandling me and my men in the bargain! You Yankees think you can do as you please, but I am going to teach you a lesson! Just you wait—"

To Pratt's astonishment, and Ben's as well, Ebenezer accepted the writ. He held it for a moment between finger and thumb, as if the sheet of parchment held some dangerous infection—smallpox, perhaps. Then he moved to the heavy oaken table bolted to the middle of the deck; a candle burned there in its pewter candlestick. He held the parchment to the flame and smiled as he watched the heavy paper catch fire.

"There, sir, is your writ," he said. "It burns pretty, don't it?"

"What are you doing?" squawked Pratt. "You can't do that! That is a Writ of Assistance!"

"And now you listen to me, you puking little clerk," Ebenezer went on. He was still smiling. "This flame that you see now is nothing—nothing!—compared to what will come if you and your men don't leave us alone. Do you understand me? Nothing! You will see flames far brighter, far more terrible than this, if your damned Parliament and your damned King don't let us trade in peace." The parchment had nearly burned now, and so he stepped to the small high port, open to catch the morning breeze, and dropped the blackened, cindery sheet into the waters of Boston Harbor.

Pratt was so astonished that for a moment he stood speechless.

"Now," Ebenezer went on. "Your men were sent on their way some time ago with the same warning that I give to you. You are to mention this affair to no one. Do you understand? No one. You were not here last night. Tell that to your wife, and see that she understands as well. You slept in your bed all night. You did not know that the *Emilie* came in. This morning you will come down with your men to inspect her, and I will pay duty on the few miserable pipes of wine that I have been able to bring in."

Few miserable pipes! Pratt gnawed his lip in fury. The man had unloaded a fortune in goods all through the night! Hundreds of pounds' worth, and not a shilling of duty paid on any of it!

Ebenezer stepped close; he seized Pratt's neckcloth and pulled him up so that the smaller man's feet no longer touched the floor.

"And as for your threats—I will overlook them this time. But now I will make a threat in return. Listen to me, and listen well, Jabez Pratt. If you or any of your men speak one word of this night's work, so that my father or I or any of our men are called to account, you will ride the wooden horse in a fine suit of feathers, and I promise you that it will be a journey that may well be your last. Do you hear me?"

Pratt was strangling; he could not speak. But after a moment he nodded, weakly, and felt himself being lowered to the floor. He shook himself together with as much dignity as he could muster, but catching sight of the look on Ebenezer's face, he forbore to give any further reply.

"Then you may go," said Ebenezer pleasantly. "And I will see you here again this morning—say, about nine o'clock?"

But when a Customs man came to inspect the *Emilie* that morning, it was not Jabez Pratt, and this new man seemed not at all interested in anything but getting through with his business as quickly as possible and retreating again to the safety of the Customs House.

"You burned it?" said Samuel Adams. "Hmmm. An interesting tactic." He sat nursing a cup of grog at his table at the Green Dragon Tavern in Union Street, a place that served as his office and recruiting station and home away from home, all in one.

"I wasn't thinking of tactics, Mr. Adams." Ebenezer smiled at the older man. "And I admit to you now that perhaps it was ill-advised. But I was so angry—he shoved it into my face, and I wanted to knock him senseless. Burning the writ was the less violent act."

Adams nodded slowly, thinking, gazing at Ebenezer in a contemplative way. "Tell me again what you said. Something about the wooden horse?"

"I warned him of that, yes. Perhaps I spoke too freely."

"No. No. I think it was, ah, not an unwise thing to say. Scare him a bit. Of course, as to whether we would actually do such a thing . . ."

Adams's blue eyes—or were they gray?—gazed at his companion across the table. He might have been calculating a sum in his head, but instead of molasses and tea, Adams's business was politics; he tended to it as assiduously as the Revells did to their trade.

"All right," he said. "You've warned him. Now we wait."

"For what?"

A little smile hovered over Adams's dour face. "Why, for their next misstep. You can be sure it will come, sooner rather than later."

When it did come, after a week or so, it was a dandy.

Ben and Ebenezer were taking inventory in one of their warehouses on their wharf one muggy, threatening morning when two constables and a Customs officer named Smoot marched in and arrested Ebenezer for smuggling. Then they impounded the *Emilie*, placing her under the King's broad arrow, and ordered her lines cut so that she could be towed to the *Romney*.

Ben was furious; Ebenezer seemed to take a kind of grim satisfaction at the incident.

"Don't worry, Father," he said. "Just send for Mr. Adams, tell him that I am enjoying the Crown's hospitality, and say that I would like to see him."

"This is insupportable!" raged Ben, raising his fist as if he would strike Smoot. "Get off my property, you lackey!"

But they paid no attention to him. As they made their way back down the wharf, Ebenezer in tow, a crowd thronged around them, hooting and catcalling—"Hey, let him go! Get out, go back where you came from! We don't want you here!"

"So your friend Pratt told his tale, after all," said Samuel Adams when, shortly, he paid a visit to Ebenezer at the jail. "Better get Cousin John to defend you. He's a skillful lawyer, and he doesn't charge too much, either."

Ebenezer spent only one night in the lockup; the next morning John Adams arranged for his bail, and a fine high price it was: £3000.

Later that day Jabez Pratt tried to seize a cargo of tea and ironware that the merchant Anthony Trowbridge was bringing in, bold as brass, right up onto Long Wharf. But before Pratt could impound a single crate, the cobbler Mackintosh and a gang of ruffians appeared as if from nowhere, hauled Pratt away, and paraded him up toward the Common. The crowd grew by the minute until it filled the streets for a quarter of a mile around, jeering and hooting. Someone brought up a wooden horse—a fence rail; none too gently, they put Pratt on it.

Ebenezer had gone to John Hancock's house to report on his jailing and release. He had been closeted with half a dozen men for the better part of an hour when the meeting was interrupted by the angry shouts from without.

Ebenezer, Samuel Adams, Dr. Warren, and the others hurried to the terrace. They watched as the tree-studded greensward of the Common rapidly filled with the crowd: now people parted to make way, and their shouts rose to a great roar as half a dozen rough-looking fellows brought up a man riding a rail, his arms tied behind, his feet lashed together, men holding him upright.

"Well, Mr. Revell, here is your Customs officer getting his comeuppance at last," said Dr. Warren.

"Pratt—?"

He remembered his threat against the man. Had he meant it? Too late now to wonder; the mob had him, and it would do its work whether he, Ebenezer Revell, approved or not.

In the center of the Common was a great bubbling vat of tar; on this hot day its acrid stench drifted up the hill to where they stood. Eb shuddered. To have that boiling, sticky stuff painted on one's flesh!

He turned to Adams. "It is no more than he deserves, I agree," he said, "but it is very cruel. Could we not intervene? He's had his scare."

His voice trailed off in the cool glare of Adams's eyes. "Would you go down into that mob, sir, and try to turn it around? They are determined to do their work. No one can stop them now."

"Except—Mackintosh, perhaps?"

Over the sea of heads Ebenezer saw the towering figure of the hulking Scot who ran the mob for those men who, like Ebenezer Revell, could not or would not run it themselves. He wore a red knitted cap and he carried a cudgel which he brandished in Pratt's face. His hoarse voice came to them over the noise of the mob.

"Now, Jabez Pratt, do you renounce your place as His Majesty's Customs officer?"

Pratt mumbled an inaudible reply.

"What? Speak up, man, that we all can hear!"

"Yes!" cried Pratt. His voice broke with fear, and his reply was drowned in the roar of the crowd.

"Silence!" bellowed Mackintosh. They obeyed him. "Fall back!" They obeyed him again. The vat of tar was suspended on a crane over a hot-burning fire; there was a little space around it because of the heat. Now Mackintosh advanced and, with his cudgel, reached into the boiling cauldron and stirred it.

Pratt seemed to have fainted.

Ebenezer and his companions stood at the edge of Hancock's terrace gazing down on the scene. "This is an ugly thing, I grant you," said Adams. "But most men survive a tarring and feathering. And even if he does not, I think that one death is preferable to many. And there will be many deaths if we do not manage to convince Parliament that we are sincere in what we say."

The men supporting Pratt on the rail brought him next to the barrel of tar. He had come to; he made a violent wrench, as if to free himself, but of course he could not. The crowd's excitement grew higher and higher; they yelled and shouted, they could not contain themselves. "Give it to him! Put on his coat! A fine new suit of clothes!" Ebenezer had never seen a bear baiting, but he imagined that it must be like this: the blood lust of it, the excitement of seeing some poor creature's pain.

And now Mackintosh gave the signal, and they set to work. At the first lathering of the boiling tar on his skin, Pratt let out a shriek of agony—"*Aaaieee!*"—and by the time they had half covered him, he had fainted again.

Quickly and efficiently they worked, coating his flesh with the tar and then cutting open half a dozen feather pillows and emptying them over his head until he looked like a huge, grotesque fowl. Then, with a ferocious yell, they moved on, carrying him on the rail. All through the town they went, to the Liberty Tree, the marketplace, the Town Dock. Ebenezer heard their roar, and he wondered what tale Pratt would tell London—if, indeed, he lived to tell anything.

The next day all the Customs officers and their families took refuge on Castle Island, and there they nursed Jabez Pratt back to health. When he had fully recovered, in the winter, he sent a package to London containing pieces of his skin with the tar and feathers still sticking to it. On this evidence of his devotion to the Crown, he was awarded a pension of £200.

2

"A bluestocking, by God!" roared Ben. He stared at his son as if Ebenezer had suddenly sprouted another head. "I don't believe it! That won't do! Won't do at all! Bluestockings don't have female parts, everyone knows that! Have you gone mad? What are you thinking of? Abigail *who*?"

Ebenezer was so convulsed with silent laughter that he could hardly speak. "Abigail Abbott, Father. And she is completely female, I assure you."

"Now how do you know that?" Ben replied, not a bit reassured. "Don't tell me you've bedded her! My God, you'll have a bastard before you know it! Why do you choose her? You're a prize catch for every scheming female—and her mother—in the Province of Massachusetts! You could take your pick!"

"Even with four young children to give to my bride as a wedding present?"

"What of it? They are splendid children, every one of 'em—splendid! Any woman would be proud—happy, I say, proud and happy—to take them over! Bring 'em up! Yessir! But now you say you've taken up with this scribbling female—they're dangerous, lad! Very dangerous! Why, my friend Talcott told me about a bluestocking he knew in London—"

"Father! Listen to me! She is *not* a bluestocking. She writes poetry in her spare time, that is all. And she has little enough of that, I might add. She runs a dame school in Summer Street. Thomas and Nathaniel go to it. She is a widow. She is also the mother of an eight-year-old boy. So we know that she is, ah, completely a female, do we not?"

Ben was not placated. A widow with money to bring to the marriage was one thing; an impoverished schoolteacher was quite something else. "Is she beautiful, at least?" he said. "Pretty face? Good shape?"

And now Ebenezer could not contain his laughter. "Don't worry, Father!" He clapped the old man on the shoulder as he took his leave. "She is not beautiful at all. But she *is* an absolute delight!"

Ebenezer was right: she was not beautiful. Her face was long, her chin pronounced, her nose equally so, her eyes blue and deep-set but rather small. Her hair had once been blond; now that she was approaching middle age—she was twenty-seven—it had gone a pale brown. Her best feature was her mouth: wide and full-lipped, it had character—as did her face—but no prettiness; it was not what the fashion demanded, a sweet little rosebud of a mouth. She was further out of fashion in that she was tall and rather thin; and so despite the fact that she had obviously persuaded Ebenezer to fall in love with her—through some kind of feminine wile, some witchery, perhaps—when Benjamin met her at last, he was prepared to dislike her.

Ebenezer brought her to dinner one afternoon not long after the incident with Jabez Pratt—brought her to his own house, that is, and invited his father, too. Ben was late: legitimately late, having been detained by a problem with one of his employees suspected of stealing. He hadn't arrived until two-thirty.

When he finally did, he followed the Negro butler into the parlor and beheld a pretty scene: his son and a female standing by the fireplace, facing each other, Ebenezer holding both her hands in his.

"Mr. Benjamin, sir."

"Ah! Father!" With a delighted smile Ebenezer came across the room and put his arm around Ben's shoulders and ushered him in.

"Abigail—my father, Benjamin Revell—Mrs. Abigail Abbott, Father—"

"How do you do, sir?" she said.

Ben was aware of a little sensation in the region of his heart, no telling what it was, but he thought she wasn't so bad-looking after all, she had good teeth and a pleasant smile, and a confident, forthright way of speaking; she was not some simpering little fool.

What she had, and what Ben discovered almost immediately, was that most precious quality, better than beauty, better even than a great fortune: what she had was charm.

She knew it, of course. She watched now as he began to thaw under her attentions. Crusty old man! She didn't blame him. Ebenezer was a great prize for some fortune-hunting female. From what he'd told her, he'd been lucky in his first two marriages. Well, she would see to it that people said the same of his third.

She began to talk to him, or, rather, to ask him questions, nothing too bold, but enough to let him know that she longed to hear whatever he had to say, tales of his adventures at sea, his accounts of his grandchildren, splendid little fellows every one—Thomas and Nathaniel, whom she knew, of course, and the two-year-old twins, Samuel and James. They were napping now, he thought; she could meet them later—or the next time she came.

By the time they went into the dining room to take their meal, he was completely taken with her. From above the mantel twin portraits gazed down upon them—the portraits that Ben had ordered at Ebenezer's first marriage. Mr. Copley had been the artist, a man of rare talent whose pictures made his subjects look positively alive. There was a quality about those pictures, Ben could not have said what it was, that made you think that the person there—that handsome young man—was about to speak to you.

"Fine, aren't they?" he said to Abigail. He couldn't quite make out the expression on her face. Not envy—certainly not that—but a kind of wistful longing. She was somewhat shortsighted; he thought her little squint was as charming as everything else about her. He followed her glance to Emilie's smiling face. He remembered when it was being painted, and he'd stopped in at the sitting. He was paying for the pictures, damned if he didn't have the right to see how they progressed. Copley had not been pleased to see him. Emilie had laughed and lost her pose and had needed some little time to get it back again.

And now there she was for all time, the first Mrs. Ebenezer Revell: a golden beauty in a gown of pink silk narrowly trimmed in black velvet; much of her bosom was exposed, her flesh fair and unblemished. Her hair was dressed high over horsehair cushions and decorated with black feathers and pearl combs; her pretty red lips were parted, her face alight, as if she were about to tell some delicious secret to the viewer.

Ebenezer's portrait was an excellent likeness as well, for the artist had captured something of the young man's ruthless vigor. He was posed standing at a table before a window, through which could be seen a bit of the Family wharf and a ship at anchor. One hand rested on his hip; the other rested palm down, fingers splayed, on a map on the table. He looked straight at the viewer; his expression seemed to say: "My ships sail the world spread here before me; all of this territory is mine from which to extract my riches." In the fashion of the day he wore a turban of wrapped silk and a loose brocade robe, but the womanish dress did not hide his strength, his air of determination.

Ben caught her eye; for a moment he saw the expression of hunger—or was it simply love?—that crossed her face.

"He's got the Family look, all right," Ben said. "He looks like me when I was young. A bit taller, he is. And I take after my father."

"Indeed?" Abigail was all attention again, and she threw him a charming little glance of gratitude as he held her chair for her.

"That's right. And my father's mother—now there was a woman! She was quite famous in her day. Catherine Mayhew Revell, her name was. She was captured by Indians and wrote a memoir of it. She had a daughter with her who was never found."

Abigail nodded sympathetically; she seemed to hang on every word. "How dreadful."

"Oh, yes. Times were hard then, I can tell you," Ben went on. "Let's see— we're in 1768—almost a hundred years ago, now, when she was taken. I have her portrait at my house. You can come around and see it any time. 'Course it's nothing like these"—he gestured at the portraits—"but it's a handsome thing all the same. It was her husband, Jedediah, who made these candelabra." He gestured to the silver candlesticks on the shining mahogany table. "He was as much an artist in his own way as Mr. Copley there. And Jedediah—well, he was the son of the first one of us who came over. Bartholomew. Came with the Pilgrims down at Plymouth. Later he came to Boston. Started the business right up from nothing. Yes, indeed. We've gotten soft in these modern times. Those people had backbone, let me tell you. Those first settlers. Soft as custard, we are, compared to them." Suddenly he caught his son's eye. Ebenezer was smiling at him—at both of them. Condescending pup! Ben cleared his throat rather more noisily than necessary and said, "Now, madam, what about you? Can you tell me a little about yourself?"

"My history is not so dramatic, I fear."

"Not many are. But never mind. What about it? You were born in Boston?"

"Yes. My father died soon afterward, and my mother remarried a gentleman from Roxbury. She moved there and left me to be brought up by her sister, who died not long after my own marriage."

"And your mother is gone as well?"

"Yes. I have a half sister and two half brothers, but I seldom see them. In fact one brother sailed for London last month and announced that he would not return. So I am a widow, I live with my son John, and I keep my little school."

"Where my two older grandsons are enrolled, as I understand it?"

"Thomas and Nathaniel, yes."

"Right smart little lads, aren't they? Emilie Griffin here was their mother."

If there was one thing in the world that Abigail understood, it was parental pride—or, in this case, grandparental.

"We have the twins comin' along, y'know, James and Samuel. They're the Jackson Revells, their mother was Mercy Jackson. Both she and Emilie died of childbed fever. Those two boys of hers are a regular handful. Good thing for all of us they don't look alike. Ha! We'd never know who was who if they were identical!"

Suddenly he leaned in toward her, ignoring the Negro footman who stood at his elbow holding a platter of roast fowl sauced with cranberries. "Now you listen to me, my dear. I'll play straight with you. Honesty's the best policy, no doubt about it. I trade sharp but I trade fair. Anyone who's done business with me will tell you that. Now what I want is a half a dozen more grandchildren. I had only this one boy here, I have to make up for it. Half a dozen more— that's what I want. And I intend to have them."

"Father—" Ebenezer saw a flush rise to Abigail's face, and he thought that his father had gone too far, embarrassing her.

"What? You think I'm being too bold? Nonsense. Abigail understands, don't you, my dear? You're a great reader, aren't you? Yes? There you are. People who read a great deal are people who understand their fellow human beings. What's the matter, Ebenezer? You seem to be choking on your wine."

3

The trouble was, she loved him.

The trouble was, she could no longer imagine living without him.

She sat before her glass late at night, a tall spermaceti candle throwing its gentle glow upon her face, her slim white throat rising from the lace-trimmed ruffle of her nightdress. Because she was shortsighted she needed to lean in as she stared into her own wide blue eyes, like a seeress searching for a vision. She spoke in her mind to that image, she spoke to herself as she would have hoped a sister would have spoken, or her mother were her mother alive, or a dear friend.

You are a poor widowed schoolmistress, proprietress of a dame school. Why do you think he has chosen you?

Because he tells me that I please him.

But perhaps he is only playing you for a fool.

Would he ask me to marry him, then, as he has done?

He is leading you on. He will abandon you. He will never marry you.

He swears that he will.

He will find someone who has a fair face and a fortune to match.

He does not need a fortune, he has his own. And as for my face—he tells me that he can see into my heart, and what he sees there is more pleasing to him than any beauty's face.

Take care, my dear! Else he will break that heart, and leave you to recover by yourself, still with your boy to look after, a widow woman alone in the world— take care!

A breeze shivered the flame. Her image wavered in the glass. She stared at herself. Did she know that woman just there? No beauty, to be sure, but clever and quick, a woman with a mind that could be useful to a man like Ebenezer Revell, a man of affairs, a man of the world, busy always and in need of a woman who could understand him.

Ah, yes! She loved him well; and if he would marry her, she would happily be his wife.

4

Meanwhile the merchants of Boston waited to see what retaliation Pratt's tarring and feathering would bring. The Customs officials dared not set foot in Boston—not for the moment, at least. Everyone knew that they would come back, but when? And with what new authority to break the stiff-necked merchants of Boston?

At last, in September, they had their answer: eight British warships sailed into Boston Harbor and landed twelve hundred troops of the 14th and 29th Regiments.

Down the gangplanks they came, their scarlet uniforms and glittering sabers shining in the autumn sun. Here was a spectacle! Fifes shrilled, drums beat the martial cadence, as the troops marched in perfect step up King Street. Row upon row of redcoats, on and on they came, haughty, arrogant—let the people of Boston try to oppose *us*, their hard eyes seemed to say: we will keep order here and the mob be damned!

The people of Boston, sullen and resentful, watched them pass. Then the Sons of Liberty spread the word: any Bostonian caught helping these interlopers, or cooperating with them in any way—by agreeing to work for them to build barracks, say—will wear a suit of feathers at our expense.

All in all, the troops were a most unsavory bunch. Within a week of their arrival twenty-four incidents had been complained of by civilians: a soldier jostling an old man out of the way, a soldier stealing tobacco from a shop, a soldier beating up a boy who had taunted him. "Lobsterback!" the children called, rude little urchins that they were. "Lobsters for sale!" The Bostonians hated these gorgeous interlopers—and hated them all the more when they learned that the Quartering Act held that they had to house these men, as well as put up with them in the streets.

"Give them room!" exclaimed Abigail. "Do we have to?"

"I don't know," said Ebenezer. "We must wait and see."

Some years before, on the occasion of his marriage to Mercy Jackson, Ebenezer had built a fine mansion house made of whitewashed brick in Georgian design; it sat amid a terraced garden on the rise of lower Beacon Street, a few doors up from King's Chapel and not far from the old Faneuil mansion. Neither he nor Abigail wished to have it ruined by a plague of soldiers.

They were to be married in November. Sometimes she felt as though the wedding day would never come. Sometimes she felt as though it would come too soon, and she would not be ready for it—although there was little enough to do, since it was a second marriage for her, the third for him. For that reason, and because of the difficult political climate, they would have only a small celebration.

He put his arms around her and kissed her neck. He could feel her pulse there, throbbing and strong, her sweet warm flesh—and she responded to him, she lifted her arms and pulled his face to hers and kissed him. Always she had the sense of wonder that he truly loved her, that he wanted her to be his wife— ah, yes, she was lucky indeed, the impecunious young widow with her son to support, and now she was marrying Ebenezer Revell.

It was very late. She had waited up for him, for his nightly visit, despite the fact that she had to rise early in the morning to open her little school. Ebenezer's older boys, Thomas and Nathaniel, attended it; thus he and Mistress Abigail Abbott had met. She would have to give it up, of course; the wife of one of the wealthiest merchants in Boston could not keep a dame school.

Now she felt a draft: the door into the hall had opened a crack. She pulled away from Ebenezer, almost as if she had been caught doing something wrong. That child!

"John? Is that you?"

No answer.

"It is all right. You may come in."

Still no answer, and so she went to the door and opened it. Her son stood there: a boy eight years old, sturdy little frame, brown hair, brown eyes, a fine sprinkling of freckles.

"What now! You will freeze yourself! Did you want to say good night again?"

He was shy; he said nothing, but sidled in and edged toward the fire to warm himself. In his white nightgown he looked like a sprite from one of Mother Goose's rhymes.

Thank heaven, she thought, that Ebenezer has four boys of his own and knows about children, for now he stooped so that his eyes were level with John's, and he spoke softly, smiling, to put the boy at ease. They had met, of course, but as yet John had given her no hint of whether he would accept this big, imposing, even rather intimidating man as his new father.

Ebenezer held out his hand, and after a moment John responded, offering his own small one.

"Do you know what we have at the house?" said Ebenezer. "We have a mynah bird. Have you ever seen one? No, of course you haven't. It is a big black bird. One of my captains brought it in last week, he thought my boys would like to try to teach it to talk. So far, they haven't had any success. Will you come tomorrow and have a try? And then when you come to live with us, you and the bird will be somewhat acquainted, so to speak. Thomas has no patience with it, he says it is impossible that that bird will ever say anything. Nathaniel is better with it, but I think he could use some help. Will you come?"

Still without a word, John nodded.

"Will you really? Yes? Good! Now we'll shake hands on that, and you must go back to bed so that you can be as clever and as stubborn as that great black bird. Off you go, now!"

Solemnly, John returned Ebenezer's handshake; then, still grave but looking somewhat reassured, he allowed himself to be ushered back to bed by Abigail.

She was laughing when she came back to the parlor. "How wonderful you are with him," she said, returning to his embrace as if they had never been interrupted. "I think he is going to worship you. Do you really have such a bird?"

"Yes. Caesar built a cage for him. We will have to have him in the house for the winter, I am afraid. So we will quarter the bird, if not the British."

"A troop of lobsterbacks in the house! I can't believe that they would simply move in on us. Have we no rights at all?"

"At the moment it is a request only," he said. "I'll grant you, I don't relish the thought myself, even though we'd probably get an officer rather than enlisted men. The fellow's table manners would probably be acceptable—but no, you are right. We don't want any Britisher under our roof. I'll refuse this first request, and we'll see what happens."

What happened was that Governor Bernard gave the soldiers Faneuil Hall to use as a barracks. This large, red-brick structure by the Town Dock had been given to the people of Boston by the wealthy merchant, Peter Faneuil, in 1742. It held a marketplace below, and meeting rooms above; its arched windows alternating with brick pilasters, the building was topped by a copper grasshopper weathervane made by Deacon Shem Drowne in imitation of the weathervane atop the Royal Exchange in London—the family symbol of Sir Thomas Gresham, Chancellor of the Exchequer.

In 1761 Faneuil Hall burned down. It was rebuilt by Onesiphorus Tileston; to raise the money, the town fathers instituted a lottery. Bostonians were fond of Faneuil Hall; as their troubles with the Mother Country increased, they gathered there so often to hear the orations of Samuel Adams and James Otis and other patriots that it became known as the "Cradle of Liberty." Many people thought that putting British troops there was a deliberate slap in the face to the people of Boston.

The less fortunate troops stayed in tents on Boston Common. As winter drew on, the children of Boston made their sport by throwing snowballs at those beautiful targets, the bright red uniforms of the British Army. And not only snowballs, but snow packed around razor-edged clamshells, little missiles that could give a nasty cut on the side of the face. Every night half a dozen soldiers got into a brawl at a tavern; many nights someone was beaten up. Soldiers were pushed into the water; women were accosted and insulted if they were lucky, raped if they were not. An occupying army, this was, without a declaration of war. The citizens of Boston felt abused, singled out for punishment. No other town in America had to suffer what Boston suffered. Why were they being picked on?

5

They were being picked on because for years they had offered the stiffest resistance of all the colonies to what they considered the outrages of the Crown. For years they had rioted and protested and printed scandalous propaganda in their newspapers; they had flouted Parliament's decrees; they had organized bitter opposition to the King's men. In short, they had behaved like the cantankerous Yankees that they were.

It had begun, most men agreed, in 1764 when Parliament, far away in London, had decided to raise revenues by passing a new tax on "foreign sugar"— molasses. This was in fact a lower tax than before, but now it was to be strictly enforced: 3 *d.* a gallon.

The Colonial merchants had always disregarded the Crown's customs duties, and many men, the Revells among them, smuggled in more than they brought in legally. The price of smuggling a gallon of molasses into the Port of Boston was 1½ *d.*, paid as a bribe to the Customs collector. And why not? the merchants said. Their lives were hard, their undertakings extremely difficult. They deserved every penny they earned, legal or not.

Parliament was obdurate. The Mother Country had taken a fresh look at the profits to be made from her North American colonies; the tax on sugar must be paid!

At the annual town meeting of Boston in May that year, James Otis thundered his opposition: "No taxation without representation!"—for while the colonies had agents in London, they had no standing in Parliament. The colonies must unite, raged Otis; we must protest this Sugar Act or we will be taxed to our very deaths!

Most merchants agreed. In August, at the urging of that clever, stubborn man, Samuel Adams, the Bostonians decided on a boycott until the Sugar Act was repealed. "Nonimportation" was the key: the colonies provided an endless market for the British manufacturing towns, and once the Americans refused to buy British goods, the nature of the growing emergency would be made clear to Parliament by its own people.

Parliament was not, for the moment, impressed; the Lords of Trade refused to take the colonists' agitation seriously.

In March of '65, therefore, Parliament passed new acts: the Quartering Act, which required the colonists to house British troops; and, far worse, the Stamp Act, which required every piece of paper used in the colonies—bills of lading, newspapers, wills, court papers—to carry the embossed seal: the "stamp" of the Crown.

Here was a pretty mess! Those stamped papers would have to be paid for! This tax would eat into the very heart of the colony's affairs. No man went a day without dealing with paper, all kinds of paper. And every one to bear this stamp—?

Outrageous! Not to be borne!

News of the Stamp Act reached Boston in May. In June the Massachusetts General Court called for a meeting of the several colonies to consider how to proceed; further, the court recommended that a circular letter be sent from colony to colony so that the chief men in each might keep abreast of events in all the others.

But some men in Boston took more immediate action, among them Ebenezer Revell.

One balmy night in early June, walking cautiously to avoid the watch, Ebenezer made his way through the silent, deserted streets to Chase & Speakman's distillery on Hanover Square. He found the door locked, as he had expected; the man who admitted him held up a candle to inspect him first.

He went upstairs to a small room which by day served as the distillery's office; now it had a less orthodox purpose. The others were already assembled, among them Thomas Chase, whose place this was; the printer Benjamin Edes; John Avery, like Ebenezer a Harvard graduate, and now, like Chase, a distiller. The distillers had suffered particularly hard under the sugar tax; now they were among the most ardent advocates of doing away with the stamp tax as well.

The men who met that night soon would refer to themselves as the Loyal Nine. Their loyalty was not to King George III but rather to themselves and, as they thought of it, to their country—this new country, so different from the old. Week after week they met that summer, always in secret, always at the distillery, thrashing out the ways in which they could successfully oppose Parliament's growing tyranny.

One night when Ebenezer climbed the stairs to the little meeting room under the roof, he was surprised to see a newcomer. He had never met him, but he knew who he was: one Mackintosh, a hulking Scot, a shoemaker who led the South End mob in its annual battle with the North Enders on November 5: Pope's Day.

For a moment Ebenezer felt sick. He had no idea how many years Mackintosh had fought in the Pope's Day battles—those annual celebrations of the

capture of Guy Fawkes, a Catholic who in 1605 had tried to blow up the
Protestant Parliament in the infamous Gunpowder Plot, and had been tortured
to death for his pains. As a boy, Ebenezer had been forbidden to leave the
house on November 5, for the mobs raged back and forth, ransacking and
fighting, and no man's life was safe if he got in their way; on Pope's Day all
prudent citizens barred their doors and waited out the storm, praying that their
property would be spared. But one time, when Ebenezer was ten years old, and
his father unavoidably detained on business in Newburyport, and his mother
languishing ill in bed as she so often did, a careless servant had allowed him
out. He had been accompanied by his little slave, Scipio. Together they had
gone to watch the procession: a huge wagon carrying the figure of the Pope
attended by various imps and devils, the mob roaring along, drums beating,
whistles sounding, the men's drunken faces illuminated in the torchlight as if
they themselves were so many Hellish demons. Watch! Step aside! Do not get
caught, for every man had his club, swinging indiscriminately, heads knocked
and split open, bodies trampled underfoot—a wild time, an orgy of hate for the
Catholics climaxing when the two mobs, North and South, met in pitched
battle: which Pope would win?

He would never forget it: the rum-sodden man who chased them, his own
escape—but Scipio, a cheerful little fellow despite the fact that he was lame,
unable to run fast enough. They had caught him. Ebenezer had screamed and
screamed, he could not speak for days afterward, but no one had come to help.

The room above the distillery was very warm, but although Ebenezer was
sweating so that his shirt was soaked, he was trembling, too, as if he was freezing to death. Mackintosh was saying something, and now John Avery answered:
"We do not want a Pope's Day. Pope's Day is finished. It is a waste of time. If
you are going to run a mob, run it with a purpose—for us, and with a specific
target. We no longer have the luxury of tearing through the streets like a pack
of mad dogs; whatever we do now must be done deliberately. You have the
power to inspire terror in the hearts of men, Mackintosh. We will tell you
whom you shall terrorize—and when."

Not long after, Mackintosh began to earn his pay. On a fine August morning he led his mob to a grand old elm tree down at Deacon Elliot's house, and
there they hanged an effigy of Andrew Oliver, the Stamp Master. Forever after,
that elm was known as the Liberty Tree.

Next, Mackintosh and his men marched on the Town House; then they
proceeded to the waterfront, where they destroyed Oliver's warehouse and his
dwelling house both. Oliver had fled at the first word of the unrest, for he
understood Boston people very well. At the moment the mob burst into his
house, he was in a longboat headed for the safety of Castle William in the
harbor. And so while they tore out his wainscoting and smashed his mirrors
and plundered his extensive wine cellar, the hapless Stamp Master could only
imagine the damage being done—and could give thanks to God that He had
saved his life. As darkness fell he stood at the parapet of the Castle and looked
across the harbor. From the town he could hear, drifting across the water, the

cries of those who would have killed him; then, on Fort Hill, he saw a light which shortly became a bonfire—a great blaze to the heavens, signaling even as the old fire on Beacon Hill had signaled: trouble coming!

Less than two weeks later Mackintosh called out his followers again. This time they went after Judge Storey, of the Admiralty Court, and Benjamin Hallowell, the Comptroller of Customs. Both men's houses were attacked and severely damaged—furniture wrecked, paneling ripped away, doors and windows torn out. In the light of flaring torches the faces of the men who did this work looked like animals' faces, avid and rapacious, insatiable in their hatred of these pillars of the Crown.

And then they confirmed the doubts of some of their masters, for they were not yet satisfied: the night is still young, let us find new prey!

About nine o'clock that night old Benjamin was sitting in his great chair, reading the latest issue of Edes's *Gazette*, when he heard a noise like—what? Like a great waterfall, he thought: a roaring in the distance—but no, not a waterfall, for this sound rose and fell, rose and fell and rose again to a great, deep-throated chant.

In an instant he was at his door, and as he flung it open he saw the first of them coming into North Square, shouting, whistling, their heavy boots beating on the cobblestones. One man held a flag with the image of a snake cut into pieces; some brandished torches, others clubs and hatchets.

At once Ben knew: they headed for the nearby house of the lieutenant governor, Thomas Hutchinson.

No man in Massachusetts was hated more. Here was a native-born American, a descendant of the persecuted Ann Hutchinson, a man who should have been their fastest friend, and yet he was a tool of the Crown, a despicable lackey who only recently had been exposed for what he was. Benjamin Franklin himself, the chief American agent in London, had sent to Samuel Adams a packet of letters that Hutchinson had written to his English masters—letters in which he gave frankly his opinion of his fellow Bostonians. A wretched crew, he said, plotting revolution. We must keep them under our heel lest they throw us over.

And so now, tonight, the mob would finish its work at the home of Thomas Hutchinson. The damage to Hallowell's and Storey's was nothing compared to what they would do here. A great beast, indeed—a thousand hands, a thousand voices, the beast rampaging!

Mackintosh's hoarse cry echoed through the square: "Come out, Thomas Hutchinson! Let us see your damned face!"

A moment of silence while the beast waited.

No reply: the house was dark, deserted. Hutchinson had been warned, he had fled only moments before.

"Now!" Mackintosh brought down his arm like a general commanding his troops.

They obeyed him; they leaped to the attack. Fueled by wine from Hallowell's cellar, they swarmed over Hutchinson's house, they battered in the doors and windows, they destroyed every piece of furniture, every glass and dish, they stripped off the wainscoting, they found Hutchinson's papers—his precious manuscript which was to be a history of this very place, this Massachusetts—and threw them out the windows, trampling them in the dirt. They stole his money—£900 he had, in cash!—and so they were even paid for their night's work, and they stole his silver, his cherished tea set and his silver candlesticks, and they ripped his fine portraits to shreds, and slashed his mattresses and emptied them into the square in a blizzard of feathers.

They had even begun to tear the slates from his roof when at last, for what reason will never be known, Mackintosh called them off.

But the point had been made, indelibly: "No tax! No stamped paper!"

After that night the authorities called out the militia to patrol the town—a symbolic gesture only, for if the mob had decided to take on the militia, no one had any doubt who would win.

And so now they waited: the bundles of stamped paper were to arrive any day, and on November 1 every man in the colony would have to use those stamped papers to transact his business.

Unless they decided not to.

6

"Are you out of your mind?" said Ben. He stood facing Ebenezer in the Revell warehouse on the Revell wharf. It was a bright, cool day, the first hint of autumn in the air. The harbor sparkled in the sun, crowded with ships, some of which were their own.

But at this moment Ben was not thinking of his business. "Loyal Nine—Sons of Liberty—I don't care what you call yourselves! London will call you traitors!"

Ebenezer met his father's angry gaze with a steadfast stare. "We are no traitors, Father. We have our rights, and we cannot let London take them away."

"Rights? What rights? The right to sack and burn like a band of savages? The right to murder—oh, yes, don't tell me that Thomas Hutchinson would not have been murdered if they had caught him! I saw that mob—*your* mob—running into North Square! I know what they could have done! And then what? Am I to watch you hang? Is that what I have worked for, to see my only son become a killer, and then see him die for it?"

"No one is talking of killing, Father." Ebenezer bit his lip; in truth, men might yet die, by accident if in no other way. But the issue was not killing: it was survival. "Do you not see that if we let them tax us now, they will tax us forever, greater and greater—we will be taxed to death, *we* will be killed, for there will be no more profit in our trade, it will all go into London's coffers for the King!"

A shout interrupted them just then, and they looked out to see a boy running down the wharf. "Here!" he cried. "They've come!"

"The stamped papers!" said Ebenezer. He hurried out, leaving his father behind. At the dock was a lighter; a crowd of merchants gathered around the man who had just disembarked. "Yes," he was saying, "they're here. They're at Castle Island—bundles and bundles of them. Under guard, they are—and so they had better stay, or we'll make a fine bonfire with 'em."

And there they did stay. No stamped paper ever found its way into a Boston merchant's office, or into any court of justice, or into any newspaper printer's shop. The people of Boston simply refused to use them. The merchants engaged in a flurry of business in October, procuring papers for their voyages before November 1; but when the deadline came and went, and ships lay idle in the harbor, still they refused to use the papers that Parliament had authorized, and the stamped documents remained where they were, safe at Castle William.

After a few weeks, business got under way again. The merchants of Boston went on in their usual fashion; they pretended that every cargo they brought in and out was perfectly legal, just as it had always been. No one was going to let his fortune disappear for a sheet of paper. A bill of lading? Right here—you see, no stamp necessary, we can carry on just as we have always done.

No stamps! No tyranny! No taxation without representation!

7

The following spring came the news that Parliament, in its wisdom, had heard the message from its obstreperous colony, and had repealed the Stamp Act.

The town of Boston held a great celebration. The Liberty Tree was hung with banners and flags; every church bell pealed with glad news. Drums and fifes sounded through the streets. People thronged out of doors; no one worked that day. Ships' cannon in the harbor fired salutes; even on Castle Island the cannon sounded. Rejoice! No stamps!

The silversmith Paul Revere put up an enormous obelisk of oiled paper, decorated with the strange insignia of the Freemasons, a group to which he belonged, and with political cartoons, and the eagle of Liberty. Three hundred lamps inside it illuminated its designs. More light came from the Liberty Tree, for as darkness fell, the people of the town hung lanterns from every bough, and then they paraded the streets with more lanterns, till all the town was alight. Huzzah! No stamps!

In his mansion house on Beacon Hill, John Hancock held open house for his fellow merchants, and he sent down pipes of wine for the townspeople thronging the Common.

The rooms were crowded, with the usual smell of sweat and pomade and food and wine all mingled together. From the Common came the sound of revelry, the townspeople singing their praises to Hancock and his wine. Samuel Adams stood by an open window. Here among the wealthy folks' finery he looked out of place, for he was a poor man, a failure in the family distillery, a failure at everything except politics; and politics did not pay, not at least for honest men.

He nodded at Ebenezer. "Your father could be a great help to us, Mr. Revell. Do you think we could persuade him to, ah, join our side?"

Ben was talking very animatedly to Hancock; unlike most of the guests, he looked angry.

"My father has been a devoted subject of the Crown all his life," said Ebenezer.

"As we all are," interjected Adams.

"Indeed. But since he is older than we, he has been loyal that much longer. I think that he is not a fool, however, and in time—"

"In time, yes. In time the merchants of Boston will see their profits taxed to nothing. I would hope that well before then you would be able to persuade him to, ah, see the light." Adams smiled. Every man in the room was rich, while he was poor; and yet it was Samuel Adams who would save their fortunes for them in the end, while he himself stayed poor.

"I heard an interesting rumor the other day," Adams went on. "Do you know what it was? The Crown wants to offer me a sinecure—a well-paid post. To shut me up! Can you imagine it?" He chuckled in his somber way, and Ebenezer laughed out loud.

"You should become Commissioner of Customs, sir. Then we could pay our bribes direct to you, and you would accept them peaceably, and everyone could go about his business."

Adams nodded, still smiling. "Tell that to your father, Mr. Revell. Tell him that if he does not come over soon, he will be responsible for my corruption!"

Someone else came to talk to him then, for Samuel Adams knew everyone in Boston and, more important, everyone knew him. Ebenezer passed through the brilliantly lighted rooms and out to the terrace to look down over the Common where lanterns glowed in the darkness. Then a cry went up and everyone rushed out, for the fireworks had begun; now they flared up, dazzling streaks of light, and at the end a huge pyramid flowering high in the night sky.

And so Boston celebrated the repeal of the Stamp Act. Ben was man enough to congratulate his son: "All right this time, m'boy. You won your point, I'll admit. Saw you talking to Samuel Adams. You'll never build your fortune associating with the likes of him, believe me. And now what happens next time? You don't think they'll leave us alone, do you? What then? More mobs? More destruction? Where will it end?"

It was a question for which Ebenezer had no answer. Nor, he thought, did Samuel Adams.

But he knew that his father was right: Parliament had done a great deal of damage to the merchants of Boston, and constantly looked for ways to do more.

It came, not long after, in the Townshend Acts—new duties on glass, paper, paint, lead, and tea. The Boston men renewed their resistance: if Parliament was determined to tax goods coming in to American ports, then by God no goods would come in! Or not openly, at least: for by adopting this plan, the merchants did not intend to ruin themselves, but merely to outwit the King's men.

Their success in getting the hated Stamp Act repealed had given them a sense of their own power, and the Sugar Act, too, had been modified so that its terms were not quite so onerous. But now, they said, we are faced with the worst taxes of all—intolerable taxes!—and with the writs of assistance, as well: those unlimited search warrants that gave the King's men the right to break in anywhere, any time, to search for contraband. So—officially, at least—we will import nothing, and so we will have no goods for the King to tax; and what we do in the dark of night in Boston Harbor, or in quiet bays and inlets up and down the coast, is our own damned business, thank you very much, and keep your bloody noses out of it!

Oh, they were stiff-necked and arrogant, those merchants of Boston, with their fine mansion houses, their silks and satins, their slaves and their carriages! And their street mobs constantly threatening to riot, jeering and rock throwing at the King's men, wrecking the King's property, tarring and feathering!

The Royal Customs officers dug in their heels. Taxes would be paid! Ships would be searched—and warehouses and dwelling houses, any place a shipment of wine or tea, iron goods or woolen goods, might be hidden.

In the Spring of 1768 the Massachusetts Legislature voted to send to the other colonies a circular letter telling what had happened in Boston and what the Boston men were doing about it.

Governor Francis Bernard demanded that the letter be rescinded, since it was nothing but treason from first to last. Samuel Adams refused. The governor insisted. The matter was put to vote, and after considerable argument, the Legislature voted 92 to 17 not to rescind. Ebenezer Revell, who had only just been elected, voted with the majority. A triumph!

With several other Sons of Liberty, he commissioned the silversmith Revere to make a commemorative bowl, forever after known as the Liberty Bowl: silver, of one-gallon capacity, it was engraved with all manner of insignia and an ode to the nonrescinders.

Ben had not been pleased at Ebenezer's election—much less at his now open defiance of the governor.

"You'll ruin the business altogether if you take up politics. Look at Samuel Adams. He hasn't a penny!"

To which Ebenezer replied that since their business was so far curtailed already, thanks to Parliament, he saw no harm in using his time in what might turn out to be a profitable way: forcing Parliament to leave the merchants of Boston alone so that they could return to improving their fortunes.

The old man was not placated, but he said nothing more. His son was his own master—a Revell, for sure, and Ben could not but admit that he held a grudging respect for those of his fellow Bostonians who were standing up to the King's men.

"You got clear last month when Pratt came with his writ," he said. "But next time, what then? You're a marked man now. Everyone knows you're with Adams and Hancock. They'll watch you every minute."

Ebenezer did not smile, but he gave his father a look that said, "Let them do their worst. They are few; we are many."

"When the next crisis comes—we will be ready!"

8

In early November that year, Ebenezer Revell, merchant, and the Widow Abigail Abbott, schoolmistress, were united in marriage. Afterward they had about fifty people to the reception—a small affair, one befitting the troubled times they lived in.

Abigail wore a dress of pale blue and a silver ring that had belonged to Ebenezer's mother. "My great-grandfather Jedediah made it," he told her. "You see his mark? It is appropriate, is it not? An R in a heart. He was the one whose wife was captured by the Indians—Catherine Mayhew Revell."

Abigail shuddered. "How horrible that must have been. I could not have survived it."

He watched her. He loved her very much—enough so that he understood that his judgment of her might be skewed. "We survive what we must," he said. "I imagine that we will have times that are as hard as those, if in a different way."

She turned her face up to his, and he saw there her love for him, her absolute trust in him, but also a glimpse of something harder—strength of mind, strength of character, that she might well need in the days ahead. "I imagine that you are right," she said. She looked away from him; she gazed at the family cat, whose whiskers twitched as it slept by the fire. In her shortsighted way she squinted a little. He smiled to himself. Already that had become one of the things about her that he loved: that nearsighted squint, her way of focusing intently on what she was trying to see. It gave her an air of decisiveness that he found appealing.

And what he had said to her had been true enough: there were hard times coming, harder than any they had yet had. He wanted no simpering, silly female at his side in those times coming; no flirt, no empty-headed, untested lass. He wanted a woman like Abigail, someone who had survived hard times and survived them well. The test of her womanhood, of making a living for herself and her son, indicated that he could count on her; and although he did not know exactly how, he had the sense that he would need to count on her many times when the British lion had had his beard tweaked once too often and the colonists were finally called to account for their behavior.

When the wedding festivities were over and the guests had gone home, Grandfather Benjamin took the servants and all the children, including Abigail's John, to stay with him in his house in North Square. Ebenezer and Abigail stayed on Beacon Street. Food had been brought in and prepared so that no domestic duties should disturb the couple for the first day or two of their union—a time which, as Ben devoutly hoped, would begin the production of yet another grandchild.

9

And so the Town of Boston was an occupied town, a garrison town, and her citizens suffered month after month of insult and outrage, the yoke of British oppression heavy and chafing on their necks. *How long, O Lord . . . ?*

"The important thing," said Ebenezer, "is to keep the people's anger directed toward the soldiers—and toward Parliament, of course."

"Instead of toward yourselves, you and Adams and Hancock and your friends, who have made all the trouble," Ben replied.

"Call it what you will," said Ebenezer. He stretched his long legs toward the cheerful blaze in the hearth; it was a cold, snowy night in January 1770, well into the second year of Boston's occupation by British troops. Ben had joined his son and daughter-in-law for dinner and had stayed on into the evening to wait out the storm; now, given the weather and the danger of being abroad at night, he would sleep at his son's house and return home in the morning.

"Mind, I don't say you're wrong," Ben went on. "Not any more, I don't say it. But listen to me, my boy. If real trouble comes—"

" 'Real trouble'?"

"If war comes—"

Odd, thought Ebenezer. Only last week he had used that word, war, in talking to Samuel Adams. The older man had given him one of his quick, sharp looks, but he had not denied it, had not assured Ebenezer that war was unthinkable, that it would not come.

"If war comes," Ben went on, "you must think of your family." Instinctively he raised his eyes; above them slept Abigail and all the children, and now at last Abigail was expecting a child, the first of her marriage to Ebenezer. It was due in March.

"Of course I think of them," said Ebenezer.

"But if you are—" Ben struggled with it; such things were hard for him to say. "I am an old man. Of course I will do what I can for them. But if you are called away, if you must fight, if you should—if anything should happen to you . . ." He could not say it: could not tempt Death by mentioning his name.

10

Not six weeks later, on Friday, March 2, 1770, a soldier named Kilroy, looking to earn extra money, applied for work at Gray's ropewalk. He was rudely turned away—"No lobsters wanted here—unless you want to clean the shithouse!" He and his companions began to fight the fellows at Gray's, and considerable damage was done on both sides. His commander filed a complaint with Governor Hutchinson, but neither the governor nor his council took any action.

In the next two days news of the affair got around town quickly; a thousand resentments simmered on both sides, a thousand grudges waited for redress. It needed only a little thing like this—one more small encounter—to explode.

Monday, March 5, passed without incident. A deep snow covered the ground; as darkness fell, a new moon rose. As usual, the soldiers on patrol that night had to contend with catcalls and abuse from the citizens of Boston. Unbeknownst to any of them, on that very day, far away in London, Parliament had repealed the hated Townshend Acts; only the tax on tea remained. But even if that news had been flashed to Boston with the speed of light, it would not have done any good: matters were too far along, citizens and soldiers alike too entrenched in their hatred for each other.

Around nine o'clock a lone sentry stood guard at the Customs House at the head of King Street, opposite the State House. Not far away, in Dock Square by Faneuil Hall, a crowd gathered. Some of them exchanged blows with passing soldiers, but officers hustled the men away before a major battle broke out. Soon a man said a few words to the crowd. He was tall, and dressed in the white wig and flowing red robes worn by judges of the court. No one recorded what he said; no one knew who he was.

Meanwhile, in King Street, a similar crowd gathered before the sentry. They shouted insults at him; then they began to throw stones, and snowballs filled with clamshells. The guard was no fool; he shouted for help. Captain Preston, a sergeant, and six men, all of the 29th, came at once.

Then, around quarter past nine, all the bells in the town began to ring; no one knew who ordered them. At this familiar alarm, the warning of crisis, the people of Boston ran to see what the trouble was: "Town-born turn out! Town-born turn out!"

In his house in lower Beacon Street, Ebenezer Revell and his father kept a vigil: Abigail was in labor, and neither Dr. Goldthwait nor the midwife could say when the child might be born.

When the bells began to ring, the coachman's son ran to see what the matter was. After a few moments, when he had not returned, Ben said, "Go on, Ebenezer. Go and see for yourself. You can do no good for her here."

The bells were still ringing as Eb went out. In the cold, clear night he could hear, over the sound of the bells, the sound of men's voices rising to the full-throated cry of the mob—that equally familiar sound in Boston Town, and always, like the bells, a warning of trouble: "Town-born turn out! Town-born turn out!"

He hurried down School Street and turned into Cornhill. On the southerly side of the State House was a crowd of several hundred, at least. In the light of flaring torches their faces were contorted with hate. Already some of them were fighting with the soldiers.

Then a shot rang out. A tall black man fell dead. Crispus Attucks, his name was—a former slave from Framingham lately employed as a dockhand. The crowd roared, and roared again. It surged toward the redcoats.

Another shot—and another, and another—

The mob bellowed as if from one throat. Two—five—eight—no one knew how many civilians had been hit.

"Murderers! Murderers! Kill them all! Kill the lobsters!"

Oh, these damned interlopers! These damned hated redcoats! Get them, kill them!

Suddenly a voice cried out from the State House balcony: "Citizens of Boston! I beg you to hear me!"

It was Governor Hutchinson. To Ebenezer's amazement—and perhaps to Hutchinson's as well—the crowd obeyed him. They quieted; they listened to what he had to say. He promised justice—a full inquiry. The perpetrators would be brought to trial—which perpetrators, British or American, he did not say.

In the trampled, bloodied snow lay sixteen men. Three had died on the spot; two more would die within the next day. And now the citizens of Boston, perhaps fully realizing for the first time what had happened here, bent to retrieve their dead and wounded and carry them away. The soldiers retreated to their barracks. The crowd went home. The moon rose, shining on the little town huddled at the edge of the sea, on the narrow, crooked, snow-covered streets, the small wooden houses crowded together, the merchants' fine mansions, the soldiers encamped on the Common.

The silversmith Revere had only the month before bought a century-old house for himself and his family in North Square. Whether or not he was entirely settled by the first week in March, he set to work at once to make an engraving of the affair, which he called "the late horrid Massacre."

Hadn't it been that—a massacre? Bloody redcoats murdering peaceful citizens?

He got it all wrong: he showed the redcoats in strict formation, as if in battle, firing on command, and it had not been like that at all—but no matter. His purpose was not authenticity—and certainly it was not art: it was propaganda.

What a gift to the Sons of Liberty! To the Whigs! To all New Englanders, indeed to all Americans—a vile, bloody massacre of innocent citizens by murderous soldiers of the Crown!

Ebenezer returned home that night to learn that in his absence, Abigail had given birth to a girl. They would name her Hannah, for Eb's mother. He went to them at once, leaned down and gently kissed Abigail's soft, warm cheek. "All's well, my dear. She is a beautiful child. How happy you have made me, to give me a daughter at last!"

When old Ben saw the baby, his eyes misted over; he was beside himself with joy. A granddaughter at last! A three-branched trunk, they were now—Griffin Revells, Jackson Revells, and now Abbott Revells. The next child that Abigail produced would be a boy, for sure. He took a sheet of parchment and began to sketch a family tree; it was flourishing nicely, thank you, and—God willing—we've many more sprouts to come!

11

By 1772 the brief and peaceful lull between the Mother Country and her obstreperous colony was drawing to a close. In the fall of that year, Samuel Adams set up the committees of Correspondence, whereby the colonies from Massachusetts to Georgia could keep each other informed; when his friends questioned his actions, he shook his head and said, "It is true that we forced the withdrawal of the troops after the Massacre. But we are not done yet with interference from London. And when the time comes, we will need each other's support; we are powerless alone."

Well: not exactly. Many of the Boston men were merely waiting for an excuse to tweak Parliament's nose again.

The following year it came when, in a fit of incomprehensible stupidity, Parliament passed the Tea Act. This was done at the behest of the East India Company, which was nearly bankrupt. The company had forty million pounds of tea, sitting in London warehouses. A captive population, many of whom were very fond of tea, sat across the water in America. Therefore: call a monopoly on tea for the East India Company, tax it in London, ship it to designated tea consignees in the colonies, forbid any other merchants the tea trade, sell it cheap—and there you are! Bankruptcy averted; everyone happy.

When Samuel Adams heard about the Tea Act, he was delighted: the very thing he had been waiting for, the spark to dry tinder!

A monopoly on tea? he cried. Then why not a monopoly on ironware, or glass, or paper, or cloth, or anything else? Give them this monopoly, my fellow citizens, and you will suffer a monopoly on every necessity of life!

And the consignees? Who are they who are designated to grow rich? Governor Hutchinson's sons? They are rich already—and arrogant beyond endurance! Stupidity piles on stupidity! The fools in Parliament could not have chosen a better pair to arouse the anger of the colonists. Hutchinson's sons! Let me tell you this, my dear Bostonians: from this moment we will drink not another drop of tea. We will refuse it as if it were poison. We will let it rot in London, we will let the Hutchinson boys sell not an ounce! No tea will come into the Port of Boston; no tea will be drunk in Massachusetts—or in any other colony.

And so the innocuous tea leaf became the symbol of British oppression. Tea was a mildly stimulating beverage, not nearly so stimulating as coffee; in fact many people found it quite soothing.

Properly cultivated, shaded by mulberry trees, the tea shrub, *Camellia Sinensis*, grew about two feet high. The shiny, saw-tooth leaves could be harvested as often as four times a year. Some were fermented: those were the black varieties. Some were steamed: those were green.

The Chinese called tea "the brew of the immortals—liquid jade": smoky Lapsong Souchong, or fine, delicate Hyson, robust Keemun—English breakfast tea—or the lighter South China Congou.

It was the Dutch who introduced tea into Europe around 1640; not long after, they brought it to the New World, to their colony at New Amsterdam. For a long time Westerners did not know how to drink tea, or even how to prepare it. Ladies from Salem or Boston well drilled in the niceties of behavior would brew a pot of Bohea, throw out the liquid, and eat the leaves with butter and salt. Even when they began to drink the tea, for a long time they drank it black and bitter, without milk or sugar.

But eventually they learned better; they grew inordinately fond of it, they loved it better than anything.

Now Parliament was trying to exploit their liking of tea by dictating the terms of its consumption.

Intolerable!

Already the first tea ships were on their way. And the Sons of Liberty were planning their reception.

12

"Halloo! She's coming in—the *Dartmouth*! She's sighted down the Roads!"

A day in late November 1773: the day they had all been waiting for, when the first tea ship would arrive.

Now, with a word to his clerk, Ebenezer hurried out. The news had spread quickly, and as he went down the wharf, he saw little knots of men, heads together, muttering, their faces somber. For weeks the town had been in a ferment, meetings day and night. The Hutchinson boys had been summoned to the Liberty Tree to publicly resign their commissions. They had refused. Afraid of the mob, they had fled to the Castle and the protection of the British garrison.

At the Bunch of Grapes tavern he found Samuel Adams, Josiah Quincy, and Thomas Crafts surrounded by a dozen other men. They were composing a broadside: "Friends! Brethren! Countrymen! . . ." By morning it would be printed by Ben Edes at the *Gazette* and posted all over town. "A meeting at Faneuil Hall," said Adams.

"For what purpose? What can we do?" said Ebenezer.

"For the moment—nothing." Adams's voice was calm, but his eyes burned. "Except that we will warn Mr. Rotch"—a Nantucket man who owned the ship—"not to unload her. But of course he knows that; he cannot do it. And then—we wait."

But not for long: the *Eleanor* and the *Beaver* came in a few days later. By Massachusetts law an incoming ship had to unload within twenty days, and no ship could leave the harbor without unloading. The people of Boston were determined that the tea should not be taken off the ships. Only Governor Hutchinson could countermand the law and issue the order that would allow the tea ships to sail back to England still carrying their hated cargo. This he refused to do; more, he double-shotted the cannon at Castle William and put two warships on the alert to prevent the tea ships' unauthorized departure.

On December 16, when the *Dartmouth* had been in port for eighteen days, Samuel Adams called a mass meeting at Old South Church because Faneuil Hall was not large enough to hold the hundreds who streamed in, not only from Boston, but from all the surrounding countryside. It was not a town meeting; it was much larger than that. They called it "the Body." Most who attended, including women and children, could not vote, but no matter: they roared their approval when called upon to do so, and no man stood by to check them off on a list of legal voters.

As he left his house that day, Ebenezer embraced his wife and chucked the latest Revell, little Philip, under the chin. Just over a year old, Philip was the second child born to Abigail and Ebenezer.

"When will you be home?" Abigail asked a question asked by wives since the beginning of time, but particularly urgent now. She stood in his arms, cradling his face in her hands.

He kissed her again. She was heavy with their third child, and so all the more precious to him. "I don't know," he said. "Before dawn, I should think."

Dawn! It was now mid-morning. Abigail stood at the portico and watched as Ebenezer went down the walk to Beacon Street, his black tricorn atop his neatly clubbed golden hair. In his fine brown coat and breeches and gray cloak, he looked like a merchant of Boston—which he was—rather than a political conspirator. Which he was also.

All that day speaker after speaker kept the crowd at fever pitch while they waited for word from Governor Hutchinson: would the tea ships be allowed to leave still carrying their cargo, or would they not? Hutchinson was at his country seat in Milton, where Rotch had gone to confer with him.

Darkness came; candles were lit, reflecting in the tall windows. Suddenly a stir at the door, and Rotch, breathing heavily from his long ride, came hurrying in. Before he said one word, they knew from his face what the governor's answer had been: the ships must be unloaded.

Rotch spoke briefly to Samuel Adams; then Adams stood and faced the crowd. He was silent for a moment; then, abruptly, he called out the prearranged signal: "This meeting can do nothing more to save the country!"

The crowd exploded, war whoops and hoarse voices: "Boston Harbor a teapot tonight!" They streamed out; they raced to the dock. From the North End, from the South End, came the sound of shrill whistles and the old familiar cry, "Town-born turn out! Town-born turn out!"

Ebenezer Revell was among them, for Adams insisted that some of the leaders go along to keep order: this night more than any other, the mob must be disciplined.

A rough blanket thrown over the fine broadcloth coat and satin waistcoat, a smear of red paint and lampblack over the face, a tuft of feathers in the hair, a sturdy hatchet—a tomahawk—in hand: "Town-born! Town-born!"

In the cold night air Ebenezer ran with the crowd to the dock where the three tea ships lay at anchor. Raising his arm as a signal, he led thirty men to the *Beaver*, took the keys from the frightened ship's mate, and led the way down to the hold. In the light of a lantern he saw the rows and rows of tea chests, black lettering on the wooden slats: CHINA BLACK TEA.

"All right," he said. "Start here." The men hauled out the crates, and heavy they were, lined with lead and weighing 360 pounds each. Before many minutes had passed, the "Indians" had worked up a fine healthy sweat, hoisting up each chest by block and tackle onto the deck, and there, before the eyes of the ship's crew, splitting her open and over the side with a *splash*! The crowd on the wharf watched in silence while from the other ships came the same sounds: splintering wood, then the broken crates falling into the water. The tea floated out; at the next tide, a crust of tea leaves bordered the shore all the way down to Dorchester.

For hours they worked, those grim, silent Mohawks; they destroyed 342 chests of tea worth £10,000. When they finished, they marched off the ship and down King Street to the State House, where they disbanded, some to sleep, some to work, some, like Paul Revere, on urgent business—for Revere would ride to New York with the news of what was done in Boston that night.

Toward midnight Ebenezer arrived home. Treading as silently as an Indian, he went upstairs; Abigail was in bed but wide awake, the room alight. He had forgotten how he must look; now her startled eyes reminded him, and he ducked to peer into her glass. A wildly painted face looked back at him, the red and black smeared across his cheeks and forehead, his queue undone and his hair disheveled, his stock hanging around his neck, several feathers caught in his clothing.

"What—?" She had been half frantic with worry; now, greeted by this apparition, she didn't know whether to laugh or give way to her fear.

He bent to embrace her, and as always he felt the tug at his heart, the conflict between his private life and his public. And now, for the first time, he realized what he had done, and he began to laugh.

"What is it?" she said. She saw nothing funny in his escapade, whatever it had been. "What has happened?"

"A little tea party, my dear." He heard a sound at the door: James and Samuel, trailing their nightshirts, their eyes wide with wonder at the sight of him. John, Thomas, and Nathaniel stood behind them, staring.

"Good evening, children!" he cried. "Is your father not a sight to behold? I have been to a tea party—the biggest, grandest tea party you ever saw! And not a drop was drunk the whole night, not one sip of tea!"

And with the attitude of a man who had not a care in the world, he jumped up, whooped his way across the room, and caught the twins up into his arms—their tall, handsome papa, a dignified merchant of Boston, dancing a war dance in the middle of the night.

13

The Boston Tea Party was a master stroke: it caught people's imagination as nothing else had done, and not only people in the Province of Massachusetts Bay, but in all the colonies. Those Boston men know how to tweak the royal nose, people said; they're tough, they are. A tea party!

Parliament heard of it in January. They were stunned; they were outraged. Dumping the damned tea!

At once they promised revenge. We will show those Boston men who rules! And if we catch Samuel Adams, we will bring him here for trial, and his fellow conspirators with him, and then we will see who calls the tune in Boston!

He won't drink tea? Throws it into the harbor? By God, we will pour tea down him till he floats!

Lacking Samuel Adams, they did what they could: they closed the Port of Boston, they passed a new Quartering Act, they promised toleration to Catholics in Quebec (a danger signal to the descendants of the Massachusetts Bay Puritans), they forbade more than one Town Meeting per year. Worst of all, they recalled Governor Hutchinson.

Ebenezer Revell had always thought that he would be glad to see Hutchinson go; but now he realized his mistake, for the governor's replacement was a military man, General Thomas Gage. The troops had been recalled after the massacre; now, with half a dozen regiments, Gage arrived in May of 1774 to enforce military rule once again on the Town of Boston.

Brazen and smartly marching, the redcoats marched up King Street as their predecessors had done six years before. They bivouacked on the Common until quarters could be found—and how were hundreds and hundreds of new troops to find quarters in the crowded little town with its hostile inhabitants refusing to give them a bed, refusing even to labor for them to build barracks? Any man who worked for General Gage was subject to a tarring and feathering from his fellows; no man dared to risk building British barracks, not even for the high wages the general promised.

Five days later the last trading ship cleared the port. The harbor was empty save for the British troop ships, the wharves and warehouses quiet and deserted. The merchants of Boston—with no trade!

The troops settled in, with much animosity on both sides, and the people of Boston began to look about to see how they would survive as summer came.

14

"Yes, mistress," said Mrs. Brimstead. "It's all I could get, and lucky to have it we are. They've got nothing now, down at the market, no matter how much money you wave in their faces."

Abigail knew that the housekeeper was right: since the port closed, the people of Boston had been dependent on what could be carted in across the Neck—not nearly enough to feed a population of nearly seventeen thousand and several thousand troops. She looked at Mrs. Brimstead's basket: a small sack of cornmeal and half a dozen eggs.

"It is not too late to plant," Abigail said to Ebenezer later that day. "We could send to Brookline for seed. And your father has the cow."

Ebenezer repressed a smile. Ben's friends had often twitted him about his old-fashioned ways, keeping a cow in this modern day and age. Ben didn't mind; the creature reminded him of his youth, when everyone had at least one cow in the barn, and when some people still pastured them on the Common. No cows on the Common now, of course: just bloodybacks with their stinking latrines and their even fouler language.

"I believe he is selling her milk, and his housekeeper is making butter and cheese," he said (for Benjamin Revell was a merchant born and bred, and if he could not sell shiploads of tea or molasses, he would sell a firkin of butter—and for a good price, too).

That afternoon Ebenezer took Thomas and Nathaniel fishing. They sat on the wharf, their lines dangling, and were delighted when they got their first bites. After a couple of hours they had a pailful of fine fat mackerel—not Abigail's favorite dish, but better than nothing.

Bostonians were in fact in danger of starving, had it not been for the kindness of the country people who came in with provisions every day over the Neck. But so famous was Boston's little rebellion the previous December, that people from all the other colonies as well were moved to help her. People everywhere sent in food and clothing and money—although what that money was to buy, no one knew, since the market stood empty, and no ships came in laden with manufactures. Some planters in South Carolina even sent in a load of rice, carried by sea to Salem and entered at the Customs House there before being taken overland to Boston.

By the end of June Ebenezer and his servants had taken up most of the garden with its plantings of roses and phlox and lilies; they laid out neat rows of peas and beans and squash, and Ebenezer ordered Caesar, the black slave coachman, to weed and water them.

At this, Caesar's dark face clouded over; he had a fine black coat and a pair of handsome leather shoes which he kept well-polished; he did not want to work in the garden like a common indenture. "Yass, sir," he said in a mournful voice.

"Only for a few months," said Ebenezer, "only until the fall. You understand we are on hard times, now, Caesar, and we all must do what we can. Next year, with any luck, we will be back to normal."

Next year! It did no good to think of next year, for by then they might all have starved to death.

Not long afterward, Abigail gave birth to a son, whom they named Roger. He was a small baby, rather thin, and he did not gain weight as rapidly as Dr. Goldthwait would have liked. The doctor ordered a special diet for Abigail. "Feed her up," he said to Ebenezer. "I know it's hard to get food, but you must do your best. And milk—she must drink plenty of milk. The child needs the nourishment."

Abigail refused to have a wet nurse; she was perfectly capable of suckling her own child, she said, and besides . . . she turned away so that Ebenezer could not see her tears. The baby who had lived for only a few days, last year, haunted her still. She was determined that this one would survive.

So the next day Ebenezer and Caesar went into the countryside to forage for food; and Ben's cow came to Beacon Street to share the barn with the horses.

15

In early September General Gage, mindful of the colonials' unrest, sent an expedition to Charlestown to retrieve two cannon and a quantity of gunpowder stored at the arsenal there. He got them, but only in the nick of time: word went out through the towns that the British were on the march, and not an hour after the redcoats departed with their booty, three thousand angry Minutemen converged on the spot—members of local militia who were able to respond to an alarm "in a minute."

When Gage heard of the colonials' response, he was shaken. So great a mustering for so small a thing—a little seizure of armament which in any case rightfully belonged to him? *Three thousand armed men?*

But he was sure they would not fight. The British army was the greatest army the world had ever seen. No ragtag and bobtail band of country people could take it on. They would be massacred—destroyed in half an hour. Surely they must know that.

16

The baby, Roger, lived. By the new year he was chubby and strong, a bright little thing with a head of pale, silky hair and a sweet, shy smile.

Ben came nearly every day to see his grandchildren. Hannah, nearly five, was the only girl, and she delighted in that special status. She sat on Ben's lap and recited the *Primer* to him as smart as you please, and begged him to take her riding on his big black horse, as he used to do. But he did not like to ride now; it was no pleasure for him to traverse the town and see squads of redcoats at every turn, strolling up and down the Mall by the Common, filling the taverns, shouldering citizens out of the way in the narrow streets.

In February Ebenezer departed for Concord, where the General Court was sitting. It was no longer a colonial legislature, for it had recomposed itself, under Samuel Adams's direction, into a self-governing body with no allegiance to London.

Abigail bade him good-bye with a heavy heart. When would he return? And how? In chains, under military arrest? For the Provincial Congress sat in defiance of Parliament, and its leaders knew that if the Attorney General in London pronounced them traitors, Gage could arrest them and send them to London to be tried for treason—a capital crime. And if Hancock and Adams could be arrested, so could they all, including Ebenezer Revell.

To her surprise, he returned not three weeks later. He came bounding into the house, bringing a gust of cold air with him, throwing off his great blue cape, calling for her. She had been with the younger children in the nursery. Now, hearing him, she hurried down the stairs and into his arms—oh, how good to feel his embrace again! He held her tight, he kissed her as if he had been gone a year.

"Why have you come back?" she demanded, laughing, when she had caught her breath. "I thought you said two months, at least."

"And so I did. I was not certain that we could come in today, and so I said nothing about it. We decided to come all together, a show of force, if you will. It is the anniversary of the Massacre. Dr. Warren is to give the oration. Come—dress yourself while I get a bite to eat. There will be a big turnout, and we want to get a place."

He was right: Old South was jammed. A cadre of redcoats loitered at the back. Samuel Adams, who could, if the occasion demanded, behave as arrogantly as any Britisher, bade them seat themselves down front, directly beneath the pulpit.

"Why did he do that?" whispered Abigail as the soldiers clumped down the aisle, nasty smiles on their faces. Oh, how hateful they were! "Those are the best seats—why not leave them for the townspeople?"

"Because he wants to keep an eye on them," Ebenezer replied. "There have been rumors that someone may try to assassinate Dr. Warren—and Mr. Adams, for that matter."

"Assassinate!" Instinctively she clung to his arm, feeling his strength through the heavy broadcloth of his dark green coat. That word brought home to her, for the first time, the reality of those political events which, outside her own domain of domesticity, had never seemed entirely real to her, not even when they had called her husband away to Concord. *Assassinate!*

If they could kill Dr. Warren, or Mr. Adams, surely, then, they could kill anyone, including her husband, Ebenezer Revell.

Now Mr. Adams was speaking, introducing Dr. Warren. This day, March 5, had become a kind of secular saints' day—not that good Yankee Congregationalists celebrated saints' days. It was a day of infamy, a day that would live forever in the hearts of men, and now here was their dear friend, Dr. Joseph Warren, to address them. Adams turned expectantly.

But Dr. Warren did not appear. The crowd began to shift uneasily: had some harm come to him? The room was packed from wall to wall, the aisles jammed, people hanging over the gallery. A few of the redcoats, lacking space in front where they had been bidden, sat on the steps leading to the pulpit.

Still Warren did not come. Adams looked worried: had he been arrested? Harmed in some way?

Suddenly a little stir at the front: the window behind the pulpit slid open and in climbed Dr. Warren, with the aid of a ladder. He was dressed for the occasion in a white, flowing toga; he presented his profile to the crowd, and a true Roman profile it was.

The crowd fell silent. Warren began to speak. He reminded them of their heritage as free men; he portrayed their future, which might call for armed struggle to maintain that freedom. The redcoats began to heckle him; they hissed and booed, mocking his words. He paid them no attention. For the better part of an hour he held the crowd with his eloquence, his heartfelt patriotism.

At last, when he was done, Samuel Adams stood to remind the crowd that they would celebrate this day again next year—this day of bloody massacre.

"Bloody," in England, was a curse.

"Fie!" cried the soldiers. "Fie! Fie!"

Bostonians were notorious for dropping their r's. People thought the cry was "Fire!" Pandemonium! Get out! People jumped from the gallery, raced for the door—"Fire! Fire!" For a wonder, no one was trampled to death. In the street a regiment was marching by, fife and drums drowning the cries. The street was narrow, the crowd panicked, the redcoats determined to keep their formation. A few blows were exchanged, but by some miracle another massacre was averted.

And not one of the provincial leaders was arrested.

Ebenezer slept in his own bed that night, safe in his wife's arms. She was heavy with child; he had not the heart to tell her that he would not be with her when that child came.

The next morning Ebenezer returned to Concord. Before he left, he had a word with the three older boys. John, Abigail's son, was just fifteen, and his own Thomas and Nathaniel were due to turn fourteen and thirteen, respectively.

"Yes, sir?" They stood before him, fine-looking lads all, well-scrubbed faces, clean fingernails, but more important, they were decent-looking boys, with clear, honest eyes to look at you straight and never flinch or waver.

"I want you to promise me that you will care for the Family and the property while I must be away. For the younger children, for Mrs. Revell of course, for the servants, the garden, the horses—everything."

"Yes, sir." They understood the seriousness of what their father said; they were attentive and grave, and he could see that as they promised, they would do all that they could to keep the Family safe. From what, he could not tell them.

"Sir?" It was John who spoke; of course he did not resemble the Revells, but he was a good-looking boy, just beginning to fill out, his voice deepening, no whiskers yet, but they would come soon enough. He had brown hair and brown eyes, a thin face; lacking his own father, he had been devoted to Ebenezer from the time he came to live with the Revells, more than six years ago now. Fortunately, Thomas and Nathaniel had welcomed John into the Family, and the three of them had become good friends.

"Yes, John?"

"Will there be war, sir?"

"It is possible, yes."

"Will you fight in it, sir?"

"Probably."

"I would like to fight beside you, sir."

"Ah, John, no. You are just fifteen, we don't want to take lads so young." And, seeing the boy's disappointment: "I will tell you this. If there is a war, it will probably last for some time. So next year or the year after—why, then you can come along and fight with us and we will be glad to see you."

John said nothing more than "Yes, sir." Like many boys—and men, too, for that matter, thought Ebenezer—he had a completely inaccurate picture in his mind of what war actually was. Well, he'd probably find out, sooner or later.

Ebenezer was grateful to Abigail for not asking when he would come home again. He had no idea; the only answer he could have given her was, "When General Gage is gone."

And when that happy day would come, and under what circumstances, no one could say.

The lowering sky mirrored his mood as he rode out across the Neck. A body hung at the town gallows by the gate. The guards at the fort, watching him with insolent grins, checked his pass and allowed him to proceed. They knew that before long he might well be tried for treason; then he would dangle like this poor wretch.

Long after he left them he felt their eyes following him: he was a marked man, a traitor to his king. Any day now he and his fellows would need to find a safer haven than Concord, distant though it was.

And if real trouble came, he would need to rely on others—on Ben, on the boys, on strangers, even—to protect his beloved Abigail and their family.

2. ONE IF BY LAND . . .

1

A week later Abigail was sitting by the fire reading *Tom Jones*, when through the tall front windows she saw a little Negro boy in an elaborate footman's costume coming up the walk. He rang; Caesar answered; and in a moment Caesar came in bearing a card on a silver tray. Abigail read: Mrs. Joshua Loring.

Betsey! Abigail's half sister, who lived in Roxbury, and whom she had not seen since she married Ebenezer.

"Of course—show her in at once!"

In a moment Betsey Loring swept into the room in a cloud of heavy scent. Although she and Abigail had had the same mother, the two women looked nothing alike; only their coloring was similar, and as Abigail now saw, it was obvious that Betsey had begun to improve on Nature, for her cheeks were quite startlingly pink, her lips very red. Abigail squinted to make sure: yes, absolutely. The lively blue eyes, however, were the same as Abigail remembered, and the plump, pretty figure as well.

"Abigail! Dearest! I had no idea you were expecting! Your *fifth*? No, no, don't get up." Betsey embraced Abigail briefly and then straightened, casting an appraising eye around the handsome Revell parlor. Then she sat down opposite Abigail, just by the fire, for it was a bitter cold day, the wind rattling the panes and sending little showers of sparks down the chimney. "My dear, you have no idea what we've been through," Betsey went on. "I cannot begin to tell you what it is like in Roxbury—and, I suppose, in all the countryside. Last week a mob surrounded our house one night and stoned it! We were asleep, and we awakened to find bricks sailing through the windows! It is a miracle that we were not killed." Betsey shuddered, remembering; then she continued. "When we sent word we were coming in to town, the quartermaster gave us a house in Water Street. It is not bad—not as large as our house in Roxbury, but

then we don't have all our servants, either. I brought along two Negroes and
my cook, and I'll hire others here, if I can. Oh, Abigail, what a time we have
had! The country people are nothing better than a pack of dogs. They set on
anyone they don't like. No one loyal to the King is safe."

Abigail felt the smile freeze on her face. Loyalists! The Lorings were Loyalists! She might have known.

"You needn't look so shocked, my dear," Betsey said. "What's wrong with
being loyal to the King?"

"The King does not deserve loyalty."

"Indeed! And I suppose Mr. Adams does, with his mobs and his tea parties!
I'm surprised that you would follow that rabble. You come from decent stock,
after all. Mother always said—"

"I don't want to hear what my—what our mother said." Abigail's old
wound festered still; her mother had left her behind when she remarried and
moved to Roxbury to start a new family: Betsey and two sons, all of whom
had lived in comfort, while she, Abigail, had lived on sufferance in an aunt's
house in Boston. "The point is," Abigail went on, "that we are treated as the
enemy, we are made to suffer an occupying army—"

"Oh, come, now, do you really suffer?" Betsey gave a sudden smile, a quick
parting of her red lips to show her glistening little white teeth. "I will tell you
frankly, I look forward to meeting some of those handsome gentlemen. Aren't
their uniforms splendid? Of course, in your present condition you can hardly—
But never mind that. Here. I've brought you a present." And she reached into
her muff and took out a small packet.

Abigail put out her hand automatically to take it; but when she realized
what it was, she tried to give it back. When Betsey would not have it, Abigail
dropped it onto a side table; only with difficulty did she refrain from wiping
her hands on her skirts. It was tea!

"Oh, come now," Betsey said. "What harm can it do? To drink a cup of
tea, I mean. On a bitter cold day like this, to warm yourself—and you know
what a delicious effect it has. Whenever I am low, and broody—as I have been
for weeks, I don't mind telling you—why, then, I simply drink a cup or two,
and I am right with the world again. Isn't it too bad that they've taken even
that small pleasure away?"

Of course the Revells were staunch supporters of the boycott on tea; they
drank "Liberty Tea," a dreadful substitute made from raspberry leaves.

"It is the principle of the thing," Abigail said; her voice sounded stiff and
cold.

"Principle!" Betsey laughed. "Let me tell you about principle, my dear
sister. Principle is what men fight over—die over, if necessary. And when they
are done dying, what remains? Principle? You can starve on that—freeze to
death on it. Now tell me honestly: isn't it silly to fight a war over tea? For that
is what it will come to, isn't it? War! We had a letter from London only last
week, from Joshua's cousin there. He says that Mr. Adams's Congress—where
is it sitting now? At Concord?—well, Mr. Adams's little group is committing

treason. The Attorney General gave the opinion in December. Treason, Abby! They could be hanged for what they do. Think about it. If they continue down this path to Hell, we all will suffer."

Abigail knew that what Betsey said was true enough: probably there would be war, probably they would all suffer. But how could she go against her husband? Especially when, as she firmly believed, her husband was right.

"Ah, well." Betsey shrugged. "Suit yourself." She reached out and retrieved the little packet of tea. "I'm sorry that you are so stubborn. I had hoped to find a friend here. But for me at any rate it is difficult to have a friend who does not drink tea."

"I can offer you coffee—"

"No, I cannot drink it, it upsets my stomach."

Abigail was tempted to make some rude reply, but she held her tongue. She did not, after all, want to quarrel with her half sister, who had been kind enough to take the trouble to come to see her, a thoughtful thing to do, and all the more so because thoughtfulness was not part of Betsey's nature; she had always been selfish, rarely thinking of anyone else. On the few occasions when Abigail had seen her over the years, she had never really liked her, for in Betsey's world there was room for only one person, and that was Betsey herself.

And so why, after all, had Betsey come to see her today? To renew sisterly ties broken through circumstance—or, more like it, never forged in the first place? For they had never been close, had never even really known each other. She realized that Betsey was still talking: ". . . wanted to ask, how is that good-looking husband of yours? Ebenezer Revell certainly seemed like a splendid catch for you. I've heard that the Revells are very rich. And, indeed, his father put on a good spread at your wedding, didn't he?"

There was a brief silence. Then Abigail finally managed to say, "Ebenezer is well, thank you."

"His business has suffered, I assume."

"Perhaps, somewhat."

"And where is he today? I would like to say hello to him."

"He is—attending to his affairs." Abigail felt a slow flush rise over her face.

Betsey gave her a peculiar look, but made no comment; soon she rose to take her leave. "I know you don't go out now, so near your time," she said, "but as soon as you are recovered, you must meet Mrs. Gage. She is a charming woman."

"I don't think—"

"Oh, Abigail, really you must. Mrs. Gage is no more responsible for her husband's activities than any of us. And she is an American, she is from New Jersey. She'll be delighted to know you, I'm sure. You'll see!"

2

"And so, gentlemen, I move that this Congress be in session until April fifteenth, and that we then adjourn until May tenth. Mr. Hancock and I will not be with you in May, since our presence is required at the Continental Congress in Philadelphia." Samuel Adams's voice shook with the palsy that had always afflicted him, but that now came worse than ever. Nevertheless, his authority was such that every man in the room assented; no man in the Provincial Congress, at this late stage, would have dreamed of opposing Samuel Adams—not publicly, at least.

As Ebenezer stood, stretching his long legs, he glanced out the small-paned windows of the tavern that was their meeting place. The late afternoon sun slanted across the new-ploughed fields. Springtime: planting time. But not if war came; not if—

A hand touched his elbow. He turned to see Dr. Benjamin Church. If war came, Dr. Church would be in charge of the wounded. He was a skilled surgeon and an able administrator.

"He's cutting it a bit fine, isn't he?" said Church, motioning his head toward Adams. "Why don't we adjourn now? Give us a chance to disperse before the bloodybacks come looking for us."

"No one ever said that Samuel Adams is not a brave man," Ebenezer responded.

"Bravery has nothing to do with it, dear fellow." Church tapped his forehead meaningfully. "It's good old-fashioned common sense that I'm talking about."

"Surely if General Gage means to arrest Mr. Adams—or any of us, or all of us, for that matter—surely we will be warned. He will have to send a detachment. They will have to march through the countryside. A squadron of redcoats cannot hide; people will see them, they will warn us."

"And we will saddle up and ride like the wind to escape them!" Church smiled. Ebenezer felt the hairs rise on the back of his neck. There was something about this man that he did not like; he could not have said what it was.

They walked out with the others, glad of the fresh air after the stuffy, smoke-filled room. Golden light illuminated the landscape. The trees were just coming into leaf, the bright new green of early spring; the air was sweet with the smell of earth, of country life. The small white houses strung out around the green Common sparkled as if they were freshly painted; in the distance cattle lowed, waiting to be taken home. A peaceful scene: a landscape of spare, pristine beauty. Out here in the country, away from the tensions of Boston, their deeds seemed more possible of success. This was their land; by God, they would govern it without London's interference.

And yet even here the grim prospect of failure intruded on all that they said and did. Every day wagonloads of provisions and ammunition were carted to safe hiding places against the day of a British attack, and only last week two suspicious strangers had passed through, two men posing as innocent travelers. They had been unable to disguise their accents, however—so different from the nasal Yankee twang—and everyone had simply assumed that they were British spies and had given them false information accordingly.

Ebenezer slept fitfully that night, his thoughts keeping him wakeful, chasing around and around. They had all come too far to turn back; if the Mother Country would not let them go peacefully, they would simply have to fight. That was the point of all this stockpiling, wasn't it? And all this plotting—and all the while trying to save their skins, for no one of them had any illusions about what would happen to him if he were captured. A swift ship to England, a show trial, and very probably a show hanging.

Restlessly he tossed and turned; toward dawn, exhausted, he got up. He would saddle his horse and ride out awhile, he thought, before the day's deliberations began; the exercise would relax him, and clear his head.

He took the road to the river and, beyond, to Barrett's farm, where considerable provisions were stored. In the first light of the sun the countryside glistened with dew; birdsong sounded cheerfully in his ears, and the river splashed and gurgled around the pilings of the bridge as the mare's hooves rumbled across the arched wooden flooring.

And yet—not fifteen miles away was the enemy who would see them hanged, who undoubtedly had set spies throughout the countryside. This same sweet springtime landscape harbored danger, harbored unseen eyes, someone who watched him, who watched them all, sent back reports to General Gage.

Barrett's farm lay about a quarter of a mile up ahead. He could get breakfast there, he thought.

He saw a figure coming toward him on the road, a boy of eighteen or so, familiar-looking—yes. He was the stableboy at the tavern.

And what was he doing along this road early in the morning?

Probably nothing; probably he had some perfectly good reason to be here, and yet . . .

Ebenezer trotted on; and now the boy stopped, staring at him, getting a good look at him—and then, to Ebenezer's surprise, the boy took off across the fields, running like an imp out of Hell, heedless of how his heavy shoes tore up the newly ploughed and seeded furrows.

Instantly Ebenezer turned his horse and went after him. But the horse balked at a stone wall, and so Ebenezer dismounted, swiftly tethered her to a sapling, and scrambled over the wall in pursuit. Perhaps fifty yards ahead he could see the boy running; he was headed for the river.

Ebenezer ran. Across a meadow, across another field—and then they were at the river, and the boy seemed to have disappeared.

Ebenezer was panting, his heart racing. He scanned the shore, which was littered with great boulders and small clumps of trees and bushes, any one of which might provide a good cover. He saw no sign of his quarry, but he would keep on until he got him. The lad was up to no good, that much was certain, else why would he have run away?

The sun was well up now, the day growing warm. Ebenezer heard no sound save the pounding of his heart and, over it, the murmur of the water and, in the distance, cattle lowing; he saw no movement save the flutter of birds' wings. But then—yes! Some way down the shore the lad was making a run for the bridge.

Ebenezer chased after him. For a few moments it seemed as though the lad would get away, but then he tripped and fell. As Ebenezer caught up, he saw the boy lying face down, not moving.

He bent and turned over the body. Around the lad's neck he saw a rawhide thong; pulling at it, he drew from beneath the coarse wool shirt a small leather pouch. He opened it and pulled out a folded sheet of parchment which bore an unreadable message—a cipher, certainly—and some numbers.

The boy's eyes opened. For an instant he stared calmly at Ebenezer, as if he had no idea of their circumstances. Then suddenly his memory returned, and with a frightened, half-strangled cry he leapt to his feet.

"Not so quick—" Ebenezer grabbed at him—caught him, but his grip was not firm enough and the lad wrestled away. He was panicked, his eyes starting from his head. Before Ebenezer could catch him again he ran to the bank of the river and plunged in. He thrashed his arms about until he was well toward the middle; nevertheless, he hardly seemed to be a good swimmer, and, in fact, even as he allowed himself to be carried downstream by the current, he thrashed with less and less success until at last, just before the bridge, he disappeared beneath the surface of the water.

"And so we have a spy in our midst," said Samuel Adams. "Not that wretched lad—of course not—but someone who employed him as a courier."

He looked once again at the ciphered message that Ebenezer had brought to him. It was early still; the Congress had not yet begun the day's deliberations. And now, thought Ebenezer, Samuel Adams needed to stand up in front of them all and tell them that this message had been discovered, that some one of them had written it—

"You spoke to Barrett?" said Adams.

"Yes. He said that they had seen no one, but that the dogs had set up a howl shortly after dawn."

"Hhmm. Yes. I am assuming—and it is only an assumption, mind you— that the boy did not write this message himself. Probably he was illiterate, and this bit of writing, undecipherable as it is, was done by an educated man. The letters are well formed and so on. So. What do we have? We have an illiterate stableboy carrying a message. We have him in the vicinity of Barrett's farm, either on his way back here to Concord or—more likely—to Boston. Now we might assume that this has nothing to do with us—that he was carrying a coded love letter, say. Hhmm? What do you think of that?"

Ebenezer allowed himself a small smile. "Not much. Given our circumstances, I think we must assume that this is information about us, about our stockpiles, intended for General Gage."

Adams nodded. "I agree. Mind you, we have not a shred of evidence to point to, ah, one of us as the writer."

"No, sir."

"But I think—given the particular information that Gage wants—that it must be so." He stared at Ebenezer for a moment; then he gave a grim little chuckle. "Of course, General Gage is not the only man who employs spies. And *my* spies tell me that any day now he expects a letter from the Attorney General in London. It will contain explicit instructions to arrest us and send us back for trial. He could have come for us long before now, but he is a cautious man, General Gage. He would never take upon himself that responsibility. He waits for his orders. When they arrive—so does he."

Ebenezer thought of his conversation the day before with Dr. Church, who had complained of Adams's lack of caution in not fleeing long ago. But he said nothing. Dr. Church was a high Son of Liberty, one of their staunchest men. It was inconceivable that he would betray them.

"And as for the boy's disappearance," Adams went on, "I think that we should say nothing. An inquiry will undoubtedly be raised, but he will not be the first stableboy to have run away from his master, nor will he be the last. And so if anyone should happen to ask—why, of course we know nothing."

The following Sunday—Easter Sunday, April 16—they had a visit from Paul Revere, who rode out from Boston to alert them to two developments: the grenadiers and the light infantry had been put on the alert, relieved of their regular duties and told to stand by for special assignment; and, more important, General Gage's orders had finally arrived. Any time now, any hour, he would order a contingent of his men to march out to Concord—or to Lexington, where some of the delegates had gone for the weekend—to arrest the conspirators.

Revere stood in the warm spring sunshine, a short, dark, determined-looking man of about forty. He was their best rider, their best courier when a horseman had to ride quickly to New York or Philadelphia to get their news out. Now he was telling them his plan: "I will wait until I see how they proceed—what route they take, whether across the Charles or out the Neck and through Brookline. I have arranged a signal that will be seen on the Charlestown shore. That way, if I cannot get out myself to bring you warning, someone will see it and will come ahead."

"What signal, Mr. Revere?" said Adams.

"Lanterns. They will be shown in the steeple of Christ Church on Salem Street."

"And the message?"

"One if by land; two if by sea."

3

Old Benjamin Revell had never been a social creature. All his life he had tended to his business; he had had little time and even less inclination to frequent the coffee houses, or to join the Freemasons whose lodges had come to Boston some years ago.

Now, however, lacking business to keep him occupied, and—more important—wanting to assure himself of his son's safety, he began, at the age of seventy-odd, to cultivate acquaintances. Mornings he visited the stores and warehouses of his fellow merchants; then he stopped at his own place for a word with the Revell assistant, Seth Larkin; then he made his way up King Street to stop at the Royal Exchange Coffee House, where he assumed the unaccustomed position of Wise Old Man: a veritable sage who could remember farther back than anyone, and, in so doing, bring forth little bits of age-old wisdom that might, somehow, help them through this present crisis. Why, people said, old Ben Revell can remember Cotton Mather! He can remember the funeral of Wait Still Winthrop, the old governor's great-grandson—the grandest funeral ever seen in Boston, it was. Ask him—he'll tell you about it! And Peter Faneuil, and the fight they had to put up Faneuil Hall!

Ben was glad enough to reminisce, but he preferred to listen. Like a back-fence gossip, he avidly sought information—any kind of information: what new orders had arrived from London for General Gage? How many new troops were coming in? What provisions had been made to house the country people and the wealthy Loyalists who were coming in now at such a great rate?

Once in a while he strolled past Province House, an imposing mansion built a hundred years before by Peter Sergeant and used since 1716 as the residence of the royal governors. On the day after Easter he saw considerable activity there: uniformed men hurrying in and out through the tall iron gate with its guards; then an officer spurring his horse away down toward the Neck. Ben hastened to the Royal Exchange. There he heard news that froze his heart: Gage's orders had come. He was to seize the stores at Concord and arrest Samuel Adams and John Hancock—and undoubtedly others as well.

"Are you sure?" Ben leaned across the table, nearly upsetting his coffee. His blue eyes blazed in the dim light; his hand, when it gripped the arm of his informant, was as strong as a man's half his age.

"As sure as I can be." Peleg Frost, before the death of the Bostonians' trade, had been a middling successful trader, hardly in a league with the Revells or the Hancocks. He had been pleased, in recent weeks, to become the acquaintance of old Benjamin Revell, who in easier times would not have noticed his existence.

"Who told you?"

"My daughter."

"Your daughter! And where did she get it?"

Frost nodded confidently. "From her maid. Who is, I may say, as honest as the day is long."

"Honesty counts for nothing when the information is false. Where did the maid get it?"

Frost smiled triumphantly. "From the horse's mouth, my friend. That girl's sister is"—and here he lowered his voice to a whisper—"Mrs. Gage's personal attendant. Nothing goes on in Province House that that young lady don't know. I'm telling you the absolute truth. The ship came in on Saturday. The letter with the orders was taken to the general at once. Sunday morning the girl had permission to go to church. She stopped to pick up her sister—my daughter's girl. S'true as I'm sittin' here. You know what Gage is like. He wouldn't make a move till he got the orders. But now—"

Yes—now. Now he would move with a vengeance. Now he would send his men—

"What we got to watch for is anything different in their routine," Frost went on. "F'r instance, the light infantry and the grenadiers have been taken off garrison duty as of Saturday. Now why is that, eh? Somethin's up."

Ben felt that he could no longer tolerate the hot, crowded room. He wanted to get out—to walk, to think. What could he do? Something—anything!

With a word to his companion, he hurried out. It was midday, the bells just going. For all that the town had become crowded with refugees over the winter, the streets seemed oddly quiet. Those people who were abroad looked guarded and tense, as if they were waiting for some calamity. But the calamity would come in Concord, not in Boston, thought Ben. He walked aimlessly for a while, up and down the crooked streets of this city he knew so well. He had lived here all his life, save for his time as supercargo on one of the Revell ships. Where else in the world would a man live, if he had the choice? With the innocent pride of the true provincial, Ben thought that Boston was the best place on earth—and if not Boston, then any town in Massachusetts. Now it seemed a strange place to him—a town in the grip of an occupying army. But the army was not foreign: it was sent by the Mother Country, to chastise her errant offspring. None of it made any sense. And the most senseless thing of all was that Ebenezer—his only child, his beloved son—might well be killed by that very army, or at the very least arrested for treason—treason!—and taken in chains to London, where undoubtedly they would hang him.

Bitter thoughts for an old man—ah, what sense did any of it make?

Damned interlopers!

With a weary sigh he turned his steps toward home.

4

The next day was Ben's seventy-fourth birthday. He would have dinner with Abigail and the children; to the best of his ability he would say nothing to alarm her, for she was very near her time.

Accordingly, he went around to Beacon Street with a smile on his face and a bag of sweetmeats for the children, and he managed to get through the meal—a tough piece of goat and a dried-apple pie washed down with a little of their precious Madeira—without hinting at what he knew. But he could not refrain from glancing, more often than he realized, at the portrait of his son that hung over the mantel. He hardly looked at its mate, the lovely Emilie, but time and again his eyes went to the handsome face, the shrewd eyes, the commanding figure that was his son. Damn Copley for his talent! Ben thought that a less skillful representation would not pain him so much—for here before him, so lifelike that he seemed about to speak, was the son whom he might never see again.

The day was fading, and now the servant came in to light the candles. When she had gone, Abigail made up her mind to speak. She had no idea what her father-in-law knew, if anything.

"We must trust him, Father-in-law."

Ben had been lost in thought; now he started at the sound of her voice. "Oh, I trust him all right," he said. "It's Gage I don't trust. And his men, who are trained killers."

"He will not let himself be caught. And the country people will protect him. The Minute companies will respond to an alarm—"

Caesar knocked just then, and came in bearing a letter on a small silver tray. He presented it to Abigail.

"Who brought this, Caesar?"

"Boy brought it, missus."

"Do you know who he was?"

"No, missus."

Of course she recognized the handwriting. With an elated glance at Ben, she broke the seal—Ebenezer's own, from the sealing ring she had seen a thousand times. In an instant she scanned the few brief lines; then, to Ben's amazement, she started to laugh.

"What is funny, daughter-in-law?"

Without a word, still laughing, she handed the letter to him.

> Dear Niece Abigail:
> I write to tell you that Henry
> has married the Waterson's daughter.
> Since you are so fond of him
> I was sure you would want to know the
> happy news.

I trust that you and the children are
well.

Your loving uncle,
John Carter

"What is this?" said Ben, bewildered. "It is Ebenezer's handwriting, but—"

"Sympathetic ink!" said Abigail. "Wait—I will show you!" And she ran to the kitchen and had already demanded what she needed before she realized that they probably did not have it: a lemon.

"A lemon!" said Ben, hard on her heels. Where in the embargoed port of Boston would they find such a thing—in Boston, where lemons used to come in on every ship, as common as apples?

As luck would have it, he had had a gift not a week ago, lemons and limes from a friend, a merchant in Newburyport who thought he might like to mix up a little toddy. He sent a servant to his house with a note, and in twenty minutes they had it. Abigail squeezed it into a bowl; then she brushed the letter with it and held the sheet of paper over a lighted candle. And as if by magic new words appeared:

We will leave here at a moment's notice.
We will have warning to make our escape.
My thoughts are with you.

With a cry of joy she threw her arms around the old man's neck. Ebenezer was safe!

Ben left soon after. He wanted to savor his son's welcome message in solitude. Safe! And by God, he would continue so!

In the April darkness he walked up Beacon Street to Hancock's house, dark and deserted now save for a few servants. From this vantage he could look down over the Common where the soldiers' campfires gleamed like the red eyes of predatory beasts in the forest. He shivered, although the night was not cold; he walked on down the hill toward the shore where flowed the tidal basin of the Charles. A little crowd of townspeople had gathered; more to the point, he saw lines of troops standing at attention, and, in the water, a fleet of transport boats ready to receive them.

At once his brief happiness disappeared. So they were going out, after all. He had not believed it until this moment. And they would find not only weapons and supplies, but conspirators ripe for the gallows.

He walked through the crowd; he heard muttered snatches of conversation:

". . . going to Concord . . ."

". . . they'll not get what they want . . ."

". . . what is that?"

". . . the cannon!"

"... and Mr. Adams, too! They'll not get him! Nor Hancock, nor Revell ...!"

If Gage's aim was a surprise attack, he had certainly failed, thought Ben; everyone in the crowd, and probably everyone in Boston, seemed to know of this expedition into the countryside.

And long before these troops could march the fifteen miles or so to Concord, a fast horseman could cry the warning, could save the cannon and powder and foodstuffs—and save the necks of the men who had stockpiled them.

He watched for a while and then turned away. Restlessly he walked: back across the Common, past King's Chapel, past Faneuil Hall and through Dock Square toward his home in the North End. The town was dark but hardly quiet; the darkness seemed alive, shadowy figures hurrying back and forth, heedless of the British patrols, bent on secret errands. At length Ben found himself in Salem Street near Christ Church. Scanning the dark with a mariner's eye, he looked up to its tall steeple, which, like every other in the town, would be dark, only a shadow against the starry sky.

But this steeple was not dark. Ben shook his head. Was he imagining it, or did he see—yes, there! Two lantern lights gleamed out, two steady golden beams, clearly visible to him—and to who else? Someone watching on the Charlestown shore could see those lights very clearly. Could see them—could understand their message, and clamber onto a fast horse and ride like the wind—

Suddenly they were gone. Ben blinked; had he imagined them? The steeple was dark again, like any other—and yet he knew he was not mistaken. Those lights had been there—a warning, a signal, and whatever their message had been, he was sure that it would help to save his son's life.

5

All night he sat by his fire, too keyed up to try to sleep. He felt that he should be dressed and ready, but for what emergency he did not know. When light came he drank the cup of coffee that his housekeeper prepared for him. His thoughts were far away; in his mind's eye he saw the scarlet-clad troops disembarked from their transport boats and marching into the countryside—to find their quarry, to seize the stores and the rebels both.

No! He shook his head, trying to clear it. He wanted to have some work to do, but there was nothing—no trade, no buying and selling which had occupied him all his life. Still, he was too restless to stay at home, and so shortly he went out to search for news: what had happened?

Treamont Street was blocked, filled from wall to wall with troops. The line of men stretched down past the Common: Lord Percy's brigade massed in brilliant scarlet formation, standing perfectly at attention.

Ben had been briefly cheered by his son's message, and by the sight of the signal lanterns in Christ Church. Now, however, at this stunning array—hundreds of crack troops, their gallant leader at their head—his heart sank once again. The British army was the finest on earth. They would decimate the Massachusetts men in half an hour.

A light breeze fluttered the regimental flag; the sun rose, hotter and hotter: a fine spring day. Not a man moved a muscle. Little knots of citizens had begun to gather, to gawk at this glittering display of military might; but for a wonder no one cried a rude epithet, no small boys threw mudballs at the inviting targets.

Why were they waiting? For a signal—a message?

The minutes crawled by. Ben grew restless again. At last he moved away; he headed toward the Royal Exchange, hoping to find news.

None of his acquaintances were there, no one to tell him what was happening. He walked out and passed Province House. The guards stood at attention, but the house was closed and quiet. Ben paused to gaze at the Royal Arms over the portico. The lion and the unicorn, the same as decorated the State House: the symbols of the Crown. A copper Indian weathervane rose incongruously above the cupola, a reminder of the place the Crown governed. Ben had never thought that the day would come when he was not a British subject. It had been a comfort, somehow, even with all the troubles over taxes, to know that he was a citizen of the greatest power on earth. Ebenezer had talked of freedom, but Ben did not feel free now: he felt cut adrift—lost.

Suddenly he heard the sound of martial music—fife and drums. He went at a trot to School Street and back up to Treamont. The troops were moving out at last, Major Percy at their head—a long, scarlet ribbon of men winding down toward the Neck. The fifers played that favorite, mocking tune, "Yankee Doodle."

Ben felt cold fear constrict his heart. They would march to Concord. They would capture the stores—and the men they called traitor. Maddeningly, his brain made up a little verse to go with the jaunty tune:

> Major Percy went to catch
> Ebenezer Re-vell,
> And when they got him, he would hang
> To save the King some trouble. . . .

He turned away. Someone in the crowd spoke to him by name, but he brushed past without answering.

If the signal lanterns had not been seen—if the messenger had not reached his destination—if the patrols followed and found their quarry—

Tears blinded him. He stumbled and nearly fell. Poor old man, people said; but when they moved to help him, he pushed them away.

He started to walk again. By and by he found himself at Dr. Warren's house in Hanover Street. He knocked. Someone peered at him from behind the shutters; then a maid opened the door.

"Is Dr. Warren at home?"

"No, sir."

"Where is he?"

"I—I don't know, sir."

"Gone for good, is he?"

"I—I think so, sir."

"Very well." Abruptly he turned away. If Warren had left, then indeed the crisis was upon them, for he was devoted to his patients, he would not leave until the last, most desperate moment.

At midday Ben went to Abigail. She was pale but calm. He told her what he had seen: the troops embarking in the boats, the lantern signal in the steeple, Major Percy's column—now departed at last—drawn up by the Common that morning. She grew paler still, but she remained calm.

"Soon enough, we will hear," she said. In a way, his news was almost a relief after the long days of waiting.

"Yes." Or we will see him, he thought: we will see him under arrest, or we will see his body brought in. . . .

After he left, having refused anything to eat or drink, Abigail went to lie down. The younger children were in the nursery, the two oldest boys, Thomas and Nathaniel, playing in the garden, with strict orders not to leave the property. School had been canceled, the schoolmaster—a Loyalist—busy, no doubt, with more important matters.

After half an hour she got up again. She was exhausted by her pregnancy but she could not sleep. She wished that she could walk out through the city, as her father-in-law did, but in her present condition that was impossible.

Two o'clock came and went; then she heard the clock strike three.

What was happening? When would they hear?

She walked heavily around her room; she splashed water on her face. A hot day. She felt so drained that she could hardly move, and yet she must find something to do or her thoughts would drive her mad.

Where was he?

Was he safe?

Or bleeding to death, or captured, or dead?

Wearing only her loose dressing gown, she went downstairs and stepped out into the back garden. The servants had planted vegetables again; along the neat rows she saw the first green shoots. In the summerhouse the boys were laughing, playing with Nathaniel's pet squirrel. The silversmith, Revere, had made a chain for it; the boys were taking turns leading it around and around on the wooden floor, training it as if it were a dog. The sound of their voices, laughing and chattering, was a comfort to her: a homely, familiar thing, children's voices.

But then she heard something new: a faint sound like the sound of thunder, coming from the west. She turned her face to the sky: it was cloudless and serene, no sign of a storm. But still, she knew the weather here was always unpredictable. A storm could blow up in no time.

She sat on the bench under the hawthorn tree, just now coming into bloom—the most luxuriant bloom she had ever seen, a full, white shroud of fragrant blossoms, an exuberant welcome to the springtime. The boys returned to the house; she had the garden to herself. She closed her eyes, glad of the little breeze that had sprung up. A hot day, so early—

There it was again: a sound like thunder, only this time there was another sound, too: a sharp *pop-pop*, a staccato counterpoint to the heavy boom. It was not thunder. Not thunder, not hailstones rattling down—"Caesar!" She heard the shrill note of fear in her voice, and in the moment before he came running, she heard the sound again. It was the sound of cannon and muskets, she was sure—all the more ominous, all the more terrifying, because it was so far away.

"Go and fetch Mr. Benjamin," she said.

"Yes, ma'am."

"And—wait—if he is not there, leave word with his housekeeper that he is to come at once when he returns."

But Ben arrived on his own not two minutes after Caesar left; he had been at the Royal Exchange again, looking for news. He had found none.

"Listen!" said Abigail. In the fading light of the golden April day they stood in the garden and heard, even louder, the sounds of war.

"Give me a bite to eat," he said, "and then I will go to the ferry slip. When word comes, it will come there."

A short time later he stood at the ferry dock at Houlton's Point. Across the water he could see the scarlet uniforms of the British army moving across the Charlestown peninsula. A crowd had gathered on the Boston side, and now he saw Peleg Frost, his gossipy acquaintance from the Royal Exchange. "What news?" said Ben.

Frost nodded glumly. "Heavy fightin'. Nobody knows how many dead."

How many dead!

Torches flared now in the growing darkness, and Ben gazed around at the anxious faces of the citizens of Boston as they waited for news. Like the crowd earlier in the day that had watched Major Percy's brigade, this one was unwontedly silent. Bostonians were known for their sharp tongues, their ready insults, particularly to the British; but now these people stood as if in shock, silent, watchful, too stunned to speak.

"Look—here they come . . ." A whisper shuddered through the crowd as all eyes turned to the water. They saw a transport boat; but now, instead of a load of proud, beautifully turned out soldiers, it carried a dozen—two dozen— wounded, bloody casualties. As the boat bumped against the dock, the injured passengers were lifted out. Some moaned; some screamed in agony as their bodies were jostled onto wagons; some lay unconscious—or dead. Their gleaming white breeches were dark with blood and dirt; the scarlet coats were undone, the tall black headpieces of the grenadiers abandoned. One of them, who seemed younger than the rest, was openly sobbing. One after another they were lifted out and loaded onto wagons. Torches made shining paths across the water, illuminating the scene with a hellish light.

What had happened?

And then, like a poisonous mist, word of the day's events began to filter through the waiting throng, carried across with the soldiers like plague. Whispered from one to another, spread through the streets of the town by swift messengers, circulated at the coffee houses and taverns, passed from servant to master, from maid to mistress, the terrible news got out.

A battle had taken place—and not only a set battle, an orderly battle with one side ranged against the other, but first an initial skirmish at Lexington Green, and then a real fight at Concord. The British had cut and run. And then, all day long, the nightmare retreat as the redcoats, the finest fighting force the world had ever seen, were harried and hounded through the countryside like a pack of livestock attacked by marauding wild dogs. Yes, sir! A pack of bleeding cattle, they were! Marching along the road, as neat as you please, and some damned farmer pops up behind the stone wall and takes a shot, and before the soldier can aim his piece the Yankee's gone, ducked down and running till he finds a tree to shelter him, and out he pops again!

Bloody cowards, the British said; their hearts were filled with hate for these country bumpkins who had humiliated them—disgraced them.

The Americans snickered behind their hands: bloody fools, the British were, to march out a thousand bright red targets and not expect the Minutemen to take a shot at them.

All through the long, hot day they had come, those haughty troops, hounded and persecuted back from Concord through Lexington, back through Menotomy, through Cambridge, stumbling at last through Charlestown half mad with anger and fear—who would have thought that the farmers would dare to fight? And they had got so angry as they came, hotter, thirstier, ever more frantic, that they had committed certain outrages along the way, certain killings of civilians that no honorable soldier would ordinarily commit—but the damned Americans had asked for it! They got no better than they deserved, damn them to hell!

If Major Percy's relief column had not appeared, the slaughter would have been considerably worse—the slaughter of the British, that is. As it was, they suffered seventy-three dead and two hundred wounded or captured out of a force of fifteen hundred—a near twenty percent casualty rate against a band of cowards who would not come into the open and fight like men, who skulked in the underbrush like a band of savages.

General Gage was appalled. He heard Colonel Smith and Major Percy make their reports; when they had gone he took a drink of French brandy to steady himself.

Then he wrote an account of the day's events for his superiors in London. It was three in the morning when he finished, but when his wife came in to speak to him, he saw that she was fully dressed. She smiled at him; in her eyes he saw a peculiar gleam that looked like joy.

6

In the days after the battle of Lexington and Concord the citizens of Boston, panicked, began to stream out of town, across the Neck, seeking safety in the countryside. Meanwhile, the country people loyal to the Crown, who had been trickling in to Boston for months to escape the persecutions of their patriot neighbors, now came in by the hundreds, seeking the protection of the army in Boston.

The selectmen made a bargain with General Gage: every Boston man must surrender his weapons; he could go out and take his family with him, but he must leave everything behind—money, provisions, valuables—everything. He could take £5 to live on.

"Can you travel?" said Ben. He looked doubtfully at Abigail's swollen abdomen; she would not wish to bear her child by the side of the road, or in some crowded pesthouse of a country tavern! On the other hand, Boston would undoubtedly be in flames before long. The Americans had drawn up their siege lines; a company of militia guarded the Neck beyond the British fort, and soon—if they had any sense—the Americans would surround the town on every side from Dorchester Heights and Roxbury to the south through Brookline and Cambridge and out to the Charlestown peninsula on the north. Then they would attack.

"I can, if I must," she said; but where would they go? "Perhaps you should leave, Father-in-law, and I will stay."

Ben snorted. "I am not of a mind to leave my property to the mercies of General Gage. Those fellows got a licking out there, and they're in a nasty mood. They'll ruin any house that's empty. They can't understand what happened. Two hundred wounded! They've taken the Manufactory House for a hospital, and they need every doctor left in Boston. They were bad enough before, but now they'll be murderous."

He gnawed his lip in frustration. What to do? If they fled, they had no assurance of a place to stay, nothing to live on; if they remained, they were part of the tempting target that was Boston. Probably the town would be destroyed, and its inhabitants along with it. Most of those, now, were Loyalist; far more were British troops.

"All right," he said at last. "Let us wait until the—until you have had your confinement. Not more than a week or so now, eh? Then, when you have recovered, we will see what the situation is. It will be a month at least before the Americans are ready to attack, and by then we can be well away, and the baby with us." As always at the thought of a new Revell in the world, he felt a flush of pride—of pure joy. He could hear over their heads the sounds of the younger children romping in the nursery. Yes! He must do everything in his power to keep them safe, now that their father was unable to protect them. He was an old man, but the demands on him now made him feel young again. He would stay to protect Ebenezer's family, and to keep his own property safe, and his son's as well. Damned British!

For the older childrens' edification he drew a map. He asked Abigail for a sheet of precious paper from her little Winthrop desk, not caring if he wasted it; if they were all to be destroyed, why save paper? Dipping a quill into the inkwell, he began to draw what looked like a giant tadpole. From its lower left side he drew what might have been an umbilical cord. A little to the right of its center he put an X.

"Here we are," he said. "And here"—marking it—"is Charlestown to the north; across the harbor to the south is Dorchester Heights, with Roxbury, Brookline, and Cambridge between."

"Will they attack us, Grandfather?" asked Thomas.

"Attack us! They cannot do that! Which way would General Gage direct his troops? The Americans can outrun them. They would simply retreat into the countryside; Gage could never catch them. And even if he did, they would simply do what they did before: harry him from the cover of the country."

"You are a regular military strategist, Grandfather," said Nathaniel.

"It is not strategy. It is simply common sense," Ben replied.

They had no word from Ebenezer, and in truth they hardly expected any. "We will hear soon enough, if he's been captured," said Ben. "So we must assume he's safe. Listen, my girl, if those Britishers had got Ebenezer, or Mr. Adams, or Johnny Hancock, they'd parade 'em down Treamont Street in chains. So don't you worry about him. He's all right!"

Unless he had been in the fighting. Unless he had been wounded, or— No. Best not to think of that. He was alive; Ben was sure of it.

Three days later the baby came: a girl. She was a good-sized infant, but oddly weak; she did not suckle vigorously. Abigail's labor had been more painful than any of her previous ones, but mercifully quick, not more than four or five hours. She bled a great deal, however, and she did not recover quickly. Her neighbor, Mrs. Bowdoin, and a midwife had attended the birth; no doctor in Boston had time now for a childbirth, what with two hundred wounded soldiers to attend to in the Manufactory House.

Ben put his gnarled, mottled hand on the baby's tiny throbbing skull and felt the warmth of her life. Another Revell! Now, he said, as soon as Abigail was stronger they could leave.

The next morning Abigail was sitting up in bed nursing the baby, who would be named Elizabeth, when she heard a tap at her door.

"Come!"

It was Thomas, looking very frightened.

"What is it, Thomas?"

"I found this, ma'am."

As he approached, she drew her shawl over the baby so as not to embarrass

Thomas, or herself, for that matter. He carried a folded note, which now he held out to her.

She read:

Dear Mother,

    I have gone to join your husband, who is to me like my own father, and I would be with him when he takes up arms against the enemy.

Your loving son,
John

She felt suddenly weak, and not from childbirth. John—gone!

"Did you know about this, Thomas?"

"No, ma'am."

"When did you see John last?"

"When we went to sleep last night, ma'am."

"You never heard him get up in the night?"

"No, ma'am."

Somehow John had managed to slip out so quietly that no one heard him: toward dawn, probably, so as not to have to wait too long for the watch to go off duty.

And now, hours later, he was beyond recall. Had he been stopped by the guards at the Neck? Or had he gotten across to Charlestown in a boat? Or had he perhaps been shot by some tense, angry Britisher, shot dead, or wounded, or taken prisoner?

"Go to your grandfather," she said. She was alarmed at how her voice trembled. "Tell him what has happened. Tell him that if he has any advice, I would be pleased to hear it."

But Ben would have no advice. What could he say? What could he do? Go to General Gage's headquarters at Province House to inquire whether a lad named John Abbott, son of Mrs. Ebenezer Revell, had been taken prisoner?

Weak from her ordeal, frightened, beginning to despair, she began to weep; her bitter tears fell onto the tiny upturned face of her newborn daughter, and she thought of the day that her son had been born, had been a helpless, cherished infant like this new one, her dearly beloved boy, gone from her now and perhaps gone forever.

Ah, Ebenezer!

They were going to have a war, for sure: and she would have to fight it—or endure it—on her own.

3. THE SIEGE OF BOSTON

1

In the first confusing days after the British retreat from Concord, people had gone in and out of the town of Boston in a haphazard way, stopping only to be searched for weapons at the guardhouse at the Neck. Now, however, General Gage attempted to put some order into the business of evacuation. Every citizen of Boston who wished to leave must get a pass from the authorities, he said.

Accordingly, Benjamin Revell presented himself at Province House one morning and applied for a pass for himself, for Abigail, the children, and several servants.

The town major stared him up and down. Ben willed himself to be calm. He could not remember ever having to ask for anything in his adult life; and to have to appeal to this—this foreigner (for so he was, now)—was gall and wormwood to the proud old man.

"Denied," said the town major.

Denied! "Why?" said Ben, more sharply than he had intended.

"Passes only for the person applying. Missus, ah, Revell must come herself. She may apply for her children and servants if she wants."

Ben was too disturbed to speak delicately. "She has just had a child. It is too far for her to come here."

"If it's too far to come here, then it's too far to go to the country, isn't it?"

"She will have a carriage. It is our business to take care of her, we will get her out well enough."

Impatient, the town major tapped the stack of pasteboard cards. "Do you want a pass for yourself or not?" There was a long line behind Ben, and no time to argue.

Ben shook his head. Impossible to go alone and leave her here with the children. He leaned in; he took a doubloon from his waistband pocket and held it under the town major's nose. "I could make it worth your while," he said, "to write a pass for her." He had bribed Customs officers often enough; this man, too, had his price, he was sure of it.

The town major looked thoughtfully at the gold coin. "I didn't see that," he said. "But I'd remind you, bribery is a crime."

"Since when? You people were always happy enough to take our money before. Why not now?"

"Enough, Mr. Revell. You know the rules. Now move aside."

Defeated, if only for a moment, Ben stepped away; he walked out. Damned lackey! Who would have thought they'd find honest men to serve the Crown at this late date?

Never mind: in another two weeks or so Abigail would be well enough to apply in person, and they would leave then. And as for his property . . . well, he would lose some of it if he must.

As he walked out he felt the first splatter of rain: a raw day, more like March than May. He passed through the tall iron gates and then paused. He did not want to go directly to Abigail with his bad news, she was still weak from childbirth, and fretting and grieving over her son's disappearance. So he turned toward home instead. Now that he knew that he was to leave, he wanted to try to hide as much as he could: gold coins, silver plate, some of his late wife's jewelry.

He had no sooner arrived than he was disturbed by a knock at the door. He heard the servant answer; then she came to announce the caller. "A Mr. Dawes, sir."

He did not know any Dawes, but no matter. "All right," he said.

A young man came in. He was poorly dressed—shabby, in fact, like the poorest farmer. And like such a man, he knew better than to offer to shake hands. He simply nodded, fished in his pocket, and pulled out a folded scrap of paper which he handed to Ben.

"What—?" It was only a line or two, and straightforward, no nonsense this time:

I am safe at Watertown. John is with me. Bring the family.

E.

For a moment he went weak with relief, and he put his hand on a table to steady himself. Safe! By God, his Ebenezer was safe! And Abigail's John as well!

"Who are you?" he said to his visitor. "Dawes? I don't know you. Where are you from?"

"From Boston, sir. I was—well, I went out to Concord to give the alarm."

"To Concord? How did you get there?"

"On my horse, sir."

Ben saw a gleam of mirth in the young man's eyes, and he decided that this was a clever fellow, sure enough. A member of one of their secret clubs, no doubt. He remembered his rage when he learned that Eb had joined such a group. But members of secret clubs were staunchly loyal to one another. This handwriting was Eb's; he had entrusted it to this Dawes, and if Eb trusted Dawes, Ben could do no less.

"I am to bring out any message you may have, sir." A small smile brightened Dawes's thin face.

"Message? You mean you come and go as you please?"

Dawes shrugged. "The guards at the Neck take me for a drunken farmer. They are letting farmers in to bring in food. I've been back and forth three times now, so they know me. And of course I'm careful to bring a good load of food along every time. Better not give me a piece of paper. Just tell me and I'll repeat it."

"He is at Watertown. Is the Provincial Congress there as well?"

"Yes, sir. And Mr. Revere, and Mr. Edes and his printing press. They'll be printing money now. Mr. Adams and Mr. Hancock have gone to Philadelphia."

"You have seen my son?"

"Yes, sir."

"He is not harmed?"

"No, sir."

"Very well. Tell him that he has a new daughter." Again he saw the small gleam, the half smile. "Say that as soon as Mrs. Revell can travel, we will come out. We will have very little with us in the way of money or provisions, but no matter. We will come to Watertown and join him there at the earliest possible moment. Two or three weeks at most."

Dawes nodded. "Very well, sir. And good day to you."

"Wait!" An awkward moment; Ben did not quite know what to do. He opened the drawer of his desk, fished in the little money box. "Here—for your trouble." He held out a piece of eight. Dawes hesitated; then he took it. "No trouble, sir. But thanks all the same."

Stuffing the precious slip of paper into his waistband, Ben went at once to Abigail. Now he could give her the bad news—the denial of her pass—because his good news was so much more important.

"Safe!" he cried. "Both of 'em!" He pulled out the scrap of paper to show to her. "And we will be with them! How are you today, eh? Stronger?"

"Yes. I am much better. Oh, Father-in-law—what wonderful news! Thank you!"

This day, for the first time since her confinement, she had risen from her bed and dressed herself. She sat in a chair beside the window. He peered at her. Yes: she was recovering. And as for the baby . . .

He stepped to the cradle to peer down at the tiny creature lying so quiet, so pale. Still, the journey need not harm her; she could lie sleeping in her mother's arms, it would be a day's travel, no more.

"On Monday," he said. "We will go together for your pass."

But before Monday came, the town was set on its ear—and General Gage's nose put out of joint—by the arrival of three Important Personages: Major

General Sir Henry Clinton, Major General Sir William Howe, and Major General John ("Gentleman Johnny") Burgoyne. A crowd gathered to see them disembark and, attended by their retinue, make a grand progress up King Street to Province House.

The generals were not happy to be there. Boston was an awkward place to defend, and, more important, it was militarily unnecessary. If a war was to be fought, it would be fought to the south. New York was the place to be. How had Gage managed to get himself into this mess? the generals wanted to know. Chased back to safety by a gaggle of country bumpkins, was he? Well, we'll soon show them!

2

On the following Monday morning Abigail and Ben presented themselves to the officer in charge of passes—a new man, Ben noted.

"Names?"

"Benjamin Revell. This is my daughter-in-law, Mrs. Ebenezer Revell. We will also need passes for—"

"Just a minute."

The officer picked up a list of names and studied it. Then he looked up, staring hard at Abigail.

"Your husband is Ebenezer Revell, merchant?"

The room was crowded: several soldiers standing guard, a throng of citizens awaiting passes, talking amongst themselves. When they heard the note of accusation in the officer's voice, they quieted.

"Well?"

"Yes," she said.

The officer shook his head. She thought she saw a fleeting expression of malice pass over his face. "Denied," he said.

"Denied! On what grounds?" said Ben.

"Couldn't say." The man moved his head impatiently. "Next!"

But Ben would not move, nor would he waste his time trying a bribe. "I want to see your superior."

The man behind them was trying to push up to the desk. Ben held his ground. The officer shook his head. "Not permitted," he said.

"Out of the way, mister." The man shoved Ben; Ben shoved back. "Now see here, mister," the man said, "you've had your turn. Give us a chance."

Ben ignored him and turned back to the officer. "I said I want to see your superior. I have a right to know why Mrs. Revell's pass is denied."

Wrong, thought Abigail. We are under military occupation; we have no rights at all. She pulled at Ben's sleeve, wanting him to come away. They could do no good here, they would only bring trouble.

But then, to her surprise, the officer hailed one of the guards. "See if Captain Baker is in," he said.

The guard obeyed, and in a moment he was back, beckoning them to follow him. Captain Baker had an office down the hall. He was slightly more intelligent-looking than the man handling the passes, but no less hostile.

"Well?"

"My daughter-in-law has been denied a pass to leave the city," said Ben. "I want to know why."

"Name?"

"Mrs. Ebenezer Revell."

And now they saw that this man, too, had a list. He glanced at it and put it aside. He was seated behind his desk; he stared up at them from beneath heavy brows. "Certain persons cannot be allowed to leave. Mrs. Revell is one of them."

"Why?"

"That is confidential."

"Damn you!" Ben brought his fist crashing down on the polished surface of the desk. The captain started and jumped to his feet; for a moment Abigail thought that everything was lost, that they would arrest Ben on the spot. For losing his temper? It didn't matter; these men were little despots, they could arrest anyone they chose, for any reason.

"I demand to know why she has been denied!" Ben was shouting now, heedless of the need to remain calm.

"She has been denied because her husband is Ebenezer Revell."

"Yes? Go on!"

"That is all."

"For that? And nothing else?"

"For that, yes."

They could get nothing more out of him. Ben demanded to see someone higher up, but he could not. At last, since Abigail was looking very weak, he gave up and took her home. He fumed all the way. "Damned military men. Let me tell you about the military mind, my dear. It sees nothing—nothing! Nose to the ground, can't think for itself! We'll get you a pass if I have to—have to—" What? He had no idea. "They're making a hostage out of you," he said. "D'you understand? A hostage! They're afraid the Americans will attack. Gage was wrong to let so many go out. Now they see his mistake. They think if they keep you here, if they keep the relatives of men like Hancock and Adams—and Ebenezer, too—and people like Mr. Rowe and Mr. Andrews, the chief men of the city—and me, for that matter, although apparently my name wasn't on their damned list—then the Americans'll think twice about burning the place to the ground. Which is what they ought to do, by God. They ought to! We'd survive it somehow."

But Abigail shuddered at his words. Burn the town! They would never escape. How could they, with eight children, one of them newborn?

But now in any case they would be imprisoned here for weeks—months!

For that was what they were: imprisoned. The town was nothing more than a huge garrison; troops were everywhere, eleven thousand of them; and she and a few hundred others were their only shield from an attack. How long could the siege last? How long—oh, how long before she saw her son and her husband again?

3

General William Howe had been in Boston for less than forty-eight hours when he met Betsey Loring. With his eyes riveted on her abundant bosom, he bent his handsome head and kissed the plump little hand that she held out to him, and then kissed it again.

At once she decided to have him—that is, to make a conquest of him. And why not? she thought. Her husband was a dolt; she couldn't bear him. He thought of nothing but money; he was—thank God!—indifferent to her physical charms; his breath stank; he had a nasty temper.

But General Howe—ah, now there was a prize indeed, a handsome, dashing figure of a man! And what fun he was—he liked to drink, he liked to gamble, and above all he liked her. He was, in fact, quite enchanted by her, blowsy golden beauty that she was. The very first night they met he invited her into his bed. But Betsey was no fool; she kept him waiting for three whole days and nights before she relented, so that by the time the general finally got her, he was so besotted with lust that he kept her awake all night.

After that, they were inseparable. Howe took her into his quarters and paid off her husband with a fat plum: the Commissioner of Prisons, Joshua Loring was, and he had all the pickings that went with the office. His wife? Damn and bother his wife! Let her do as she pleased. He was going to get rich off this war!

In his sober moments Howe acknowledged that he was in Boston to make war, not love. According to his informants, American militiamen were flocking to Cambridge, where old General Artemas Ward was in charge, but they were as yet hardly a trained army: a few thousand farmers armed with whatever weapons came to hand, probably short of powder and ammunition, certainly not capable of withstanding a British assault.

Accordingly something must be done—some strategic territory must be taken to break out of this humiliating siege. Dorchester Heights was the most logical place: control of the heights would mean control of the entire town and harbor. And since that point must be obvious to the Americans as well, the British generals agreed that soon—any day now—they must move to secure Dorchester Heights before the Americans did so. Yes, said Howe: tomorrow we make the move. Or the day after, at the latest. He sipped his rum; he thought longingly of Betsey Loring's soft skin. By God, she knew how to pleasure a man!

On June 13 the Americans had news from their informants that the British planned to seize Dorchester Heights. They knew that they must prevent such a move at all costs: they must provide some diversion. Accordingly, on the evening of June 16 they gathered two hundred volunteers onto the Cambridge Common and there, in the last of the cool bright day, they had a prayer from the Reverend Samuel Langdon, president of the College. Then they moved off in silent formation toward the Charlestown peninsula, to a place called Bunker's Hill.

4

Abigail slept restlessly that night, awakened by troubled dreams in which John was running away, down to the docks, and she called to him but he would not answer. She could hear her voice in her ears, calling, calling—*John!* And then at last, just before he leaped onto the deck of a waiting ship (but it was foggy, a thick white mist, and so how could they sail?), he called back to her: "Not yet!"

At first light she arose, troubled, remembering her dream, and went downstairs and out into the garden. The sky was pale toward the east; dew lay heavy on the grass and shrubbery, on the new green sprouts of the vegetable garden. She heard sweet, trilling birdsong and the call of a mourning dove; from some distant place in the town came the cry of a rooster welcoming the day. She sat on the bench under the hawthorn tree, its blossoms gone now. Even so early the day was warm. She would ask her father-in-law to take the older boys fishing, she thought: the catch would be useful, and they would be cooler by the water. And later, perhaps, she would—

Dear God! What was that sound? She felt her heart stop; for a moment she went weak. Cannon—the sound of cannon somewhere not far off, deep booming salvos, coming and coming. The American attack on the town at last!

She stood up; when she was sure that her legs would carry her, she ran into the house. Get dressed—quickly—send for Ben—they must get out, they could not stay here and let themselves be slaughtered, burned to death—

"Caesar! Caesar, wake up! Go fetch Mr. Benjamin!" She pounded on the door of his little room behind the kitchen and heard his reassuring response; then she went to awaken Mrs. Brimstead, but no need, she was awake already, and now the children were awake, too, the youngest ones crying, for only the dead over in the Burying Ground could sleep through such a racket, *boom* and *boom* and *boom*—hurry!

No time to be laced into a corset, no time to do up her hair—hurry! Speak to the children, reassure them—"Yes, yes, it is all right, we will be safe, no one is coming with a gun—"

"Abigail!"

She ran to the balustrade. Ben was just coming in, running up the stairs.

She greeted him with a cry of relief. "We can take our carriage, and Caesar can take the boys in yours—"

"No! No! We cannot! They will not let anyone past the Neck, but it is all right, they are not attacking Boston. Those cannon are firing on Breed's Hill, behind Charlestown."

"Breed's Hill! Why?"

"The Americans have fortified it. Overnight! It seems they are trying to draw out the redcoats—lure them into an attack. The Americans will be slaughtered, of course, but it is a shrewd move all the same. Make martyrs of those men—like the Massacre! Afterward, Samuel Adams will have no trouble getting support for his rebellion from here to Georgia!"

Martyrs! "Do you—is Ebenezer with them, do you think?"

"I trust not. He was not in the militia."

John had wanted to fight. Pray God that he stayed with Ebenezer, stayed safe.

"It's a foolish thing," Ben went on, "to sacrifice those men, but if it had to be done, it's as well it is done here."

She stared at him, appalled. How could he talk so blithely about death— about any man's death? She knew that he had always dreaded war, dreaded losing Ebenezer. Now it was as if he wanted a war, or wanted this war, at any rate. Even to the point of sacrificing his own son.

And hers.

"Get a bite to eat. I'll have something, too. Then we'll go around to Converse's house. He lives in the North End, near the old graveyard up on Hull Street. We can watch from his roof. Something to tell your grand-children!"

Abigail did, in fact, tell the story of the Battle of Bunker Hill to her grand-children; how, early that morning, she and Ben and the four oldest boys hurried to the North End and up Copp's Hill, the streets filled with anxious throngs, for both Loyalist and Whig had relatives and friends in the battle; many of the women and children were the family of British soldiers, and many of the Americans had family in the outlying towns—in Ipswich and Acton and Billerica and Bedford—whose menfolk would have come to fight today.

The noise was deafening, unrelenting. General Gage had ordered three small cannon atop Copp's Hill, and down in the waters of the Charles that surrounded the Charlestown peninsula were the warships: HMS *Lively*, the *Falcon*, the *Somerset*, the *Glasgow*—all guns blazing, round after round directed at what the thousands of spectators could clearly see: newly dug trenches and breastworks on top of the easternmost hill on the peninsula, which was Breed's. Ben had brought his glass, and they took turns peering through it: in the magnified circle they could see a tall thin man striding atop the works, seemingly heedless of the shells and cannonballs falling all around him. It was not Ebenezer.

Nearby, in the steeple of Christ Church where two months ago a pair of lanterns had been hung, General Gage saw the same man. He inquired of his companion, a Loyalist, whether he recognized the American. "Yes," replied the Loyalist, "he is my brother-in-law, Colonel William Prescott."

"Will he fight?" said Gage.

"Until his last breath."

Not many nights before, General Howe had first enjoyed the favors of the delightful Betsey Loring. Now, in this warm June morning, he was summoned from her arms by the emergency. Reluctantly he left her; then, with a sense of rapidly increasing urgency, he dressed and ordered out his troops. They stood at attention on Boston Common. As always when he saw them, his heart filled with pride: stout fellows, none better! And they would easily carry the day, for the Americans had played their hand very stupidly, they would cut and run at the first assault wave. A frontal attack, he decreed: straight up the hill and over the top. We'll win in half an hour. General Clinton studied his maps; then he offered his advice: go in behind the hill and cut off the Americans from their reinforcements in Cambridge.

General Gage demurred. The first rule of military strategy was never to allow your men to be trapped between two enemy armies. Howe was correct, he said. Straight up the hill, lines of men marching to the drumbeat, scare the buggers to death before we shoot 'em.

Word spread through the watching throngs: the troops are marching down King Street, they are loading onto the barges at Long Wharf, and at the North Battery as well. By now it was midday. Soon the spectators saw the troops standing at attention in the boats as they were rowed across to land at Morton's Point on the Charlestown side. The sun blazed from a clear blue sky, it glittered on the men's bayonets, it made their scarlet coats glow like fire. Barge after barge, in perfect formation—nearly two thousand men set to vanquish the fool-hardy Americans.

Someone in the crowd on Cosgrove's roof had brought food and drink. Abigail was not hungry. Even though she was not tightly laced, her stomach was heaving up, she could taste the bile in her throat. *John was on that hill!* She knew it: knew it as sure as sure. She was about to see the battle that might kill him. Or it might kill her husband. Or—God forbid—both of them. And she must stand and watch and pray . . .

Ben put a mug of cider into her hand. She took a few sips but she could not eat the bite of bread that he handed her. She squinted, trying to see better; her wide-brimmed straw hat did little to shield her eyes from the glare of the sun. She saw a mass of color: the redcoats standing in formation on the Charles-town side of the water. "What are they waiting for?" she said. "Why don't they attack?"

"When Howe is good and ready," said Ben. "He'll get— Nathaniel! Stand back!" He caught the boy's shirt and gave him a shake. "No more than three feet from the edge! You can't stay otherwise. We don't want any American casualties on this side of the water!"

And now a little cry went through the crowd: There they go! In perfect formation the lines of tiny, scarlet figures had begun to move up the hill. The watchers could hear the beat of the drum through the noise of the cannon: in precisely timed steps, eighty steps to the minute, the Britishers went up, went up—stopped to fire their muskets—went up again—

In the redoubt at the top of the hill Ebenezer Revell and his stepson John waited with the others for Prescott's command to fire. The sun blazed down, making the breast-high excavation a blazing pit for the men who occupied it. John had practiced with one of the militiamen, but Ebenezer knew that he was far from being a competent shot; on the other hand, the line of redcoats made an easy target.

"All right, boy?" said Ebenezer.

"Yes, sir."

And indeed John had the confidence of youth: he gazed at Ebenezer with clear, determined eyes and a quick, assured grin. "We'll beat 'em, see if we don't!"

Each man held his rifle loaded and ready, and now, as the scarlet-clad figures advanced, as cannonballs crashed around them and the drumbeat sounded louder and louder, each man tensed, listening for the command. Colonel Prescott knew that they needed to save ammunition, and so he had given the order: "Don't fire till you see the whites of their eyes!"

Now the soldiers were very close, their faces sweaty under their headpieces, their Brown Bess muskets raised—closer, closer, till Ebenezer saw a boy's wide dark eyes staring straight at him.

"Fire!"

The boy went down.

The watchers in Boston saw a line of flame explode from the redoubt. Many of the scarlet figures dropped to the ground. After a moment those in the rear went on, stepping over the bodies of their companions.

Again the flame of rifle fire from the Americans; again the dreadful toll, redcoats dropping—ah, look!

They could not believe their eyes: the British were retreating! Falling back! But not in defeat, surely—only to regroup. And yet they were running down the hill, as if they were frightened.

And then another burst of cannon fire, and an anguished cry: "Charlestown's burning! They're burning Charlestown!" The savages! Deliberately setting fire to the place, firing artillery shells loaded with incendiaries!

In only a few moments the entire town was ablaze. Heavy clouds of smoke drifted to the west. Those on the Boston side could feel the heat of the flames. Every house, every church and public building in the old town was burning, burning—damn the British, making war on civilians!

And now the troops were arrayed for a second assault.

In the redoubt, Ebenezer rammed home the paper wad on the ball and powder in the muzzle of his gun. He had little powder left. John worked steadily at his side. Down the line he saw Dr. Joseph Warren. They had no time to speak, but their eyes met and Warren nodded, as if to say, "Good luck to you." Neither man had much in the way of military training; Ebenezer assumed that like himself, Dr. Warren had come onto the hill today to satisfy some inner need, more than from a desire to be of practical help to Colonel Prescott.

When the order had come from headquarters in Cambridge—"Fortify Bunker's Hill!"—Ebenezer had volunteered. He had not done so lightly. He had understood that this day might be his last: this was war, not a sporting expedition. He might never see his family again—his beloved Abigail, his dear children, the new daughter who had been born in his absence.

But all the same he needed to be here—to be with these men, brave and perhaps foolhardy, who made this stand against the enemy. John had felt the same. In the end Ebenezer had not had the heart to order the lad to stay behind. "Come then, if you must," he had said, "and if worse comes to worst, your dear mother will have to bear a woman's grieving, as women always do in war."

Now once again the scarlet line went up in perfect formation, and once again the watchers held their breath—now! Now! And then it came, that blaze of gunfire from the hilltop, the long rifles sending out their bullets with deadly aim. Didn't the British know that the Americans used their guns to hunt? Hunters needed better aim than soldiers, and in any case, the British were armed with muskets—the Brown Bess, they were called, an inaccurate weapon—and they were trained simply to fire in the general direction of the enemy, not to take aim like a hunter bringing down a deer.

Once again scarlet figures dropped; once again their officers—those who remained—ordered the survivors to go on as they had been trained to do: advance in a line, stop to fire; advance again. And then:

"Look!" cried Ben. His eyes were shining, his face pink with excitement. "They're falling back again! Twice, by God! Huzzah!"

It seemed impossible, and yet—they were. Defeated again!

It was late afternoon: about four o'clock. Abigail felt as though she had been watching for days, instead of only since that morning.

"Ah!" cried a man next to them. "Now we'll see—Clinton is landing with reinforcements!"

Howe's men had regrouped. And now, with General Clinton's fresh troops, the British made their third assault. Ben peered through his glass. "They've finally smartened up," he announced. "They've let those poor lads remove their packs. Must've weighed a hundred pounds each. Now we'll see 'em run up!"

And, indeed, the British troops completed their assault this time, and as they neared the redoubt, the spectators saw rocks flying through the air, and they understood: the Americans had run out of powder and ammunition, they had only stones to fight with. As the redcoats swarmed over the fortifications, a few cheers went up from their supporters, but most of the crowd was silent.

Everyone was astonished at the day's events. Three assaults—and many, many casualties.

"Aye, they've won," said Ben. The guns were silent now, the burning town across the water belching smoke and ashes, the sun descending in the west. "But at what price, eh?" He stared around at the stunned, exhausted faces of their companions. "Too costly a victory, I'd say. Too costly by half. Did y'see the way those boys cut 'em down? Gage can't afford many more victories like this!"

When Abigail returned home that evening she took leave of her father-in-law without even a hint of a smile, of putting up a brave front.

"All right, my dear," Ben said. "Try to get some rest. We'll find what news we can, as soon as we can."

But she could not rest: she was far too distraught to rest, or even to engage in her customary solace, reading. Her eyes burned from hours of straining to see the battle: her head throbbed, her heart pounded in her breast, pounded, pounded—like the pounding of the drum that sped the men to battle, to their death.

John was dead.

Ebenezer was dead.

Or they were badly wounded.

And she had no way to learn their fate. She must stay here and wait and worry, fighting off her panic, trying to stay calm, trying to convince herself that they were safe.

She needed to do something, to take some positive action, so after a while she led Thomas and Nathaniel into the garden. "We must find a safe place to dig," she said. "A hiding place."

"Why?" said Thomas. "What are we hiding?"

"Valuables. If they burn the town, or if—"

Seeing the expression on their faces, she stopped. No point in frightening them more than they were frightened already—although they did not seem so; they gazed at her solemnly, ready to do her bidding. She must do all that she could to protect them.

At last they decided on the summerhouse. They could lift two or three of the floorboards and dig underneath. The boys set to work, and soon they had a good-sized space, large enough to hold the candlesticks that Great-Great-Grandfather Jedediah had made, and the sugar box, too, and some tankards and cups of a later date, a box of gold and silver coins, some plate and three beakers. It was only a small portion of what they had, but it would be enough to help them survive if they lost everything else.

They wrapped the pieces in coarse cotton and laid them in the earth. Then they filled in the dirt, replaced the floorboards, and went to the well to wash their grubby hands.

Abigail stayed in the garden after the boys went indoors. It was a warm night, a little breeze blowing off the water; it still contained the smell of gunpowder and burning wood. The sky, overcast, reflected a faint ruddy glow from the embers across the river, all that remained of Charlestown.

Had Ebenezer fought in the battle? Had John? Were they wounded, lying in the dirt along the road to Cambridge, unable to get to safety?

Or were they there on the hill, gazing sightless at those same red-tinged clouds: a sky stained with blood, she thought.

Wearily, as if she was once again picking up an enormous burden, she stood and walked back to the house.

5

All that night and into the next day the barges brought the dead and wounded into Boston. As they had done two months before, after the battle of Lexington and Concord, anxious townspeople crowded around the ferry slip to search for familiar faces. But this time the carnage was much worse: out of a force of two thousand, the British had sustained a fifty-percent casualty rate. Two hundred and eighty-seven dead, more than eight hundred wounded! Every man on General Howe's staff had been either killed or wounded; the general himself, miraculously, had escaped harm. As the carts lumbered through the streets carrying the injured men, their moans and shrieks of agony mingled with the cries and wailing from those in the crowd who recognized them. Of the dead, only the officers were brought for burial; ordinary soldiers were buried in mass graves where they fell on the slope of Breed's Hill.

Among those brought over were thirty-one American prisoners, men who had been too badly wounded to escape the onrushing British. These were put, not into the hospital in the Manufactory House, but into the town jail; the cuckold Joshua Loring had charge of them.

Three days after the battle, the Americans in Boston were horrified to see a British soldier hawking a coat taken from the body of one of the American casualties at Breed's Hill. They were even more horrified when they learned whose coat it was: it had belonged to Dr. Joseph Warren. Dr. Warren! The truest patriot, the finest doctor, the best friend the Sons of Liberty ever had— a gentleman beyond compare, the flower of American manhood, cut down at the age of thirty-four by a dirty Britisher.

The coat was sold for eight dollars. The men who had stripped Dr. Warren's body in the redoubt had found some papers in the pocket of the coat. These they delivered to General Gage. One of them contained the names of certain patriots in Boston, or families of patriots—men to call on in time of need.

Benjamin Revell was just sitting down to dinner when he heard the pounding on his door. His housekeeper answered. The callers pushed past her and into the dining room; they were officers of the Crown, come to arrest him on a charge of treason. They would not tell him more. Rights? He had no rights. This land was in a state of rebellion; the King had so declared it. No one here had any rights.

The housekeeper ran at once to Abigail. "Right away from his dinner they took him, missus. Didn't even let him finish his meal!"

"To where? Where did they take him?" said Abigail.

"I don't know, missus. They didn't say. Just marched him off. Oh, missus, what will become of him?"

Of all of us, thought Abigail; but she said nothing more, thanking the housekeeper for bringing the news so promptly. "Go home," she said, "and if anyone tries to commandeer the house, let me know at once. I will inquire, I will see what we can do."

Her heart sank. She thought of the hostile officers who had refused her a pass. How much more hostile would they be now? For after their costly victory on the seventeenth of June, the British had turned nastier than ever: they kicked civilians out of the way in the streets, they pummeled anyone who let slip a remark they deemed offensive, they ransacked vacant property without so much as a by-your-leave.

Who could help her find Benjamin—and, more, help her get him released?

The merchant John Rowe was a particular friend of her father-in-law's, and although he was a patriot, he had many friends among the British. Yes: she would go to him. Accordingly she put on her gray silk dress—a handsome costume, but modest—and, summoning Caesar, set out for Rowe's house.

"My dear!" Mr. Rowe was kind, concerned for his friend. "I remember you very well—and your husband. How is he?"

"He is—I don't know." If she said one word about Ebenezer she would cry, and she did not want to do that—not now, not here. She longed to say that he was alive, but she could not; she did not know, nor did she know about her son, alive or dead, she could not say.

"Hm. Yes. Well. To the business at hand. Arrested Benjamin, did they? What a mess! All the same people, all the same good English stock—and here we are fighting each other. Doesn't seem right, does it? Very bad for business, I'll tell you. Very bad indeed. Well, come along with me. I know Captain Linzee, he married my niece. We'll see what he has to say."

Captain Linzee was cool, even to his uncle-in-law. He would look into it, he said. Come back—tomorrow? No. Day after, at the earliest. Good day.

Rowe was disconcerted at their treatment. His plump face was pink with indignation, his jowls trembled, and Abigail thought she saw tears glistening in his eyes.

After a moment he recovered himself. He gave her a speculative look; then: "Let's just walk around to Queen Street. I'd not ordinarily take a lady to see the jail, but these aren't ordinary times, are they? Let's just have a look."

The jail was a gloomy place, a stone fortress with barred windows and a stench that penetrated to the street. The guard gave them short shrift, and threatened to arrest them if they did not leave at once. From within they could hear cries and shouting from the prisoners. Abigail shuddered. Benjamin Revell locked up with common criminals!

At home the younger children were fractious. The baby was sleeping. Abigail stared down at her still little form. Then at last her tears came, and she wept.

All the next day she waited, and the next. No news came of Ebenezer or John, nor did word come from Mr. Rowe, whose nephew-in-law was obviously not disposed to help.

From time to time as the hours passed she tried to distract herself by reading, by composing a poem, but she could not concentrate. She picked up a piece of embroidery, but her hands were trembling and she pricked her finger till it bled, spotting the square of linen.

She grew more and more frantic. Where was Ben? What did they want from him? Did a prisoner in a town under military rule have the right to a trial? Or were such men simply executed, hauled before a firing squad?

Oh, Ebenezer, come home to me!

The next morning she summoned Caesar, and with her head held high she marched down the hill to Province House. "I want to see General Gage, please," she announced to the guard. He looked her up and down, not bothering to reply.

"I said I want to see General Gage," she said again, louder this time. She was standing at the gate; passersby turned to stare at her, but she did not care.

No answer.

"I said, I want to see General Gage!"

"Say, Billy, here's a fishwife for you!" Two officers were coming down the walk from Province House. They stopped to see the commotion: an American lady—for obviously she was a lady—shouting at the poor lad on guard duty.

The officer who had spoken was tall, dark, slender, about twenty-five or -six. His bright dark eyes gleamed in his thin, fine-boned face; his teeth were white against his sunburned skin. As he and his companion came up to the gate, the guard opened it and they passed through. The officer took Abigail in at a glance, even as he made a little bow to her. He was laughing; his bow was not meant as a gesture of respect.

"What a temper!" he said. "Don't they teach you any manners over here? No proper young English lady would shout like that, eh, Billy?"

His companion, an officer also, was blond, thick-set; he chuckled and nodded, staring boldly at Abigail. She remembered her aunt's stricture, years ago: If you want to be treated like a lady, you must act like one.

But that was long ago—a different time, in a town that was not this sad, terrifying place.

"What's the matter?" said the first officer. "If you want to flirt with General Gage, you've picked the wrong man. His wife is right here beside him."

How hateful they were—how arrogant! She felt a small, hot burst of anger far in the back of her brain. It gave her sudden strength. Her fear had made her frantic; now this new sensation calmed her.

She pulled herself up to her full height, which was not much less than his.

"I must see the general," she said. "It is a matter of the greatest importance."

"Oh?" He smiled again, mockingly. "To you, perhaps. Not to him."

"Perhaps to him as well."

"Indeed? And what could you possibly have to say to General Gage that he would consider important?"

This was not the way she had planned it, but no matter. Fate played strange tricks, and if there were a chance in a thousand that this man could help her, as offensive as he was . . .

"My father-in-law has been arrested. I must know where he is."

"Father-in-law arrested!" Again the mocking, up-and-down gaze. "You do not look as though you come from a family of criminals, but of course you can never tell about an American. And why should the general consider that to be important?" He spoke with a curious kind of drawl; she had heard a southerner speak once, but this was different, less musical.

"Because he is—" She was aware that their conversation had attracted a little crowd; a dozen people were eavesdropping.

The officer sensed her reluctance to speak. Dismissing his comrade, he offered her his arm. "I smell an intrigue," he said. "You have aroused my, ah, curiosity. Come and take a cup of coffee with me and tell me about it."

Abigail had only a glimpse of Caesar's astonished, outraged face before she found herself propelled along the street, past the State House and into King Street and into the Royal Exchange Coffee House. Caesar followed close behind; now he waited for her at the door. She had never been in a coffee house; ladies did not frequent them. She saw a few women, most of them with men in uniform; they were not ladies.

"Now," said the officer when they were settled at a table. "Allow me first to introduce myself. I am Major Richard Southwait, Thirty-eighth Regiment. And you are—?"

The waiter came just then, and in the moment it took for her companion to order coffee—"You do not drink tea, I imagine? No"—she wondered whether to give a false name. But that would destroy the means of getting help from him if he could.

"I am Abigail Revell," she said. She saw a flicker of recognition on his face before his smooth, polite, slightly sardonic expression returned.

"Related to Ebenezer Revell?"

"I am his wife." And proud she was to say it. Yes—Ebenezer Revell, who by the grace of God is still alive.

"Ah." His smile was a bit more strained. "Lately wanted for treason, I believe? With Mr. Adams and Mr. Hancock? And, ah, Mr. Robert Treat Paine?"

But treason she would not admit to. The coffee arrived, bitter, black, hot. She sipped a little although it burned her mouth and tongue.

"And what would the wife of Ebenezer Revell want to say to General Gage? What is the, ah, important message you wanted to give to him?"

"What I told you before. They have arrested my father-in-law. My husband's father," she added unnecessarily.

"I know what a father-in-law is. I had one once myself. Go on."

"We don't know why he was arrested. We don't know where he is. He is an old man, he cannot harm you—"

At this, Southwait's eyebrows shot up. "Can he not? You would not believe—or perhaps you would—what these people can do. But no matter. Go on. You want to learn his fate. You want to make sure that he is not badly treated. When he will be released, and so on."

"Yes—yes. All of that. He has done nothing, he committed no crime!"

"No crime—that you know of." He held up his hand to ward off her objections. "I mean no disrespect. But you understand—this is war. What happened the other day at Charlestown was sheer luck. We should have had an easy victory. And the next time, we will. This time next year Massachusetts and all the other royal provinces will be happily back where they belong, under the King's rule. The Americans cannot win. I only hope, for your sake, that they realize that fact sooner rather than later. But meanwhile, as long as they so stubbornly persist, we must deal with them as best we know how. No doubt you think we are monsters. We are not. We have a job to do, and we intend to do it. As simple as that. Part of that job is to see that our plans—our situation, our numbers of men, our supplies—are not betrayed to the enemy. Who, unfortunately for you, is your husband. And no doubt his father as well."

He is lecturing me as if I were a bumpkin, she thought. The small bright flame of anger at the back of her brain flared up again. She pushed back her chair, but before she could rise he seized her hand. "Wait—do not go." He smiled at her: a pleasant, friendly smile. "Where do you live?"

"That is no affair of yours, Major."

"Never mind. I can find out easily enough. You are a brave woman, Mrs. Revell. I admire that. In time of war, women need to be brave, as well as men. And until the next battle comes, we might as well enjoy ourselves, eh? If I were to call on you—tomorrow afternoon, say—we might think of some amusement, you and I, that would make the time pass more pleasantly."

His grip loosened momentarily, and she snatched her hand away. She stood up; with as much dignity as she could muster she said, "Good day, Major Southwait." She saw his look of disappointment; before she went three steps, he caught up with her.

"Where are you going?"

"Some place—anyplace—away from here." She paused; then: "But I will say this one last thing before I go. If my father-in-law dies, or if any of the other arrested civilians die, you will pay penance. I do not know what it will be. But you will pay it."

She swept through the doors of the coffee house, nearly colliding with a slatternly-looking woman coming in, and beckoned Caesar to follow her. Stupid, stupid! To think that a British officer would help her! Tears blinded her so that she nearly stumbled; from across the street she heard a couple of privates hoot at her and make nasty, sucking sounds.

"Come on, missus," muttered Caesar. "You be doin' no good here."

All the way home she upbraided herself for her momentary weakness in allowing Major Southwait to—to what? Make her tell her story to him? So that he could tell it to his fellow officers in their barracks, and laugh at the stupid American woman who thought she could get help from the enemy? Even Caesar, a black slave, knew better than that.

Exhausted, she arrived home and threw herself down on her bed. And in an hour, when she awakened, she knew exactly what she must do.

6

Late the following afternoon Abigail ordered Caesar to bring around the carriage. He was delighted to do so: it had been weeks since he sat in the coachman's seat, and so now he hurried to hitch up the handsome matched bays and present himself ready to take her to her destination.

"To Fort Hill, Caesar," she said. She bade good-bye to the boys, to little Hannah and Roger and Philip, entrusted the baby to the housekeeper's care, and they set off.

It was the end of a brilliant day in late June; the red-brick buildings of the town glowed in the warm sunlight, and the leaves of the trees shone bright green, washed by rain the night before.

Abigail tried to settle herself on the carriage cushions as the vehicle jolted over the cobblestones. All day she had been battling second thoughts as she prepared herself for this expedition, as she dressed herself and enlisted Mrs. Brimstead's help to arrange her hair over thick heddus rolls so that it rose fashionably high. Already her scalp itched, but she did not dare to try to scratch it. She wore a gown of rose silk trimmed in Brussels lace. She had had it made before Hannah's birth, so that now it was extremely tight, and, she thought, far too exposed in the bosom.

At length they came to Fort Hill. General William Howe was billeted there. Betsey Loring openly shared his quarters. Most people, thought Abigail, were not aware that Betsey was her half sister. And just as well for both sides: certainly Betsey, in her newfound glory as Howe's mistress, would not want her connection to a leading patriot like Ebenezer Revell, however tenuous, to be widely known.

The grade up the hill was steep, difficult for the horses. They stopped at number 36: a handsome bow-front red-brick house, at the end of a row and therefore having a small side garden. A scarlet-clad guard stood at the door. The windows were open; as Abigail descended from the carriage she could hear from within the sound of raucous laughter.

Inside, the large double parlor to the right was filled with people—Britishers in their gorgeous uniforms, civilian gentlemen clad in dark coats, a number of well-dressed women. Abigail was glad that she had taken trouble with her appearance; she would not want to look drab in this company.

The air was thick with tobacco smoke, and the noise of laughter and rapid-fire repartee grew louder as Abigail made her way into the crowd. She could not at first see Betsey; at one of the card tables toward the back she saw a handsome man in the uniform of a high-ranking officer who might, she thought, be General Howe. Then she saw Betsey sitting beside him, plump, blond, and pretty, and she knew she had guessed right.

"They say she's a demon for gambling," said a man's voice at Abigail's side. "I wonder if the general will pay her debts?"

Abigail's heart dropped like a stone as she turned to see Major Southwait. He bowed slightly and smiled at her.

"And if I may say so, madam, you are looking exceptionally fine this afternoon. Be careful that General Howe does not take notice of you, or Mrs. Loring will scratch your eyes out! Here . . ." He took a cup from a tray offered by a waiter. "Have some punch. It is quite strong, it will relax you."

Automatically she took a sip. It burned her throat and she choked a little, her eyes watering. Her coiffure felt unsteady, and her scalp itched fearfully.

"Have you changed sides," the major said, smiling at her, "or are you a spy?"

"You know why I am here."

"To rescue your, ah, father-in-law."

"Or at least to get permission to see him, to take food—"

"What do you plan to do? Plead your case here, in front of half the British officer corps?"

"Of course not. I will ask for a word, a minute of General Howe's time—"

Southwait snorted. "The general has a short leash, from what I hear. Mrs. Loring is quite possessive; I doubt she'd let you be alone with him. You may have to go into the bedroom and encounter him in his nightshirt, eh? There, they have finished their game, for the moment, at least. Come along. I will introduce you."

"No, wait—" This would not work, not at all.

But he paid no attention to her protests; seizing her elbow, he led her through the packed room to where the general sat with Betsey Loring. They were laughing uproariously; his hand gripped her knee under the pearl-colored satin of her dress, while his eyes were fastened on her bosoms, which seemed likely to spill out of her bodice at any moment.

Southwait stood courteously by until she recognized him. "Major. How delightful to see you." Her shrewd eyes traveled to Abigail, who had positioned herself behind Southwait and who now, very deliberately, turned her head from side to side in a gesture that meant: "No." Miraculously, Betsey seemed to understand. "And who is this lady, whom I have not had the pleasure—"

"Mrs. Loring. General Howe." A casual salute, and then before he could present Abigail, she blurted: "Mrs. Danforth."

Shrewd eyes: and what did they see? Abigail felt suddenly stripped naked under Betsey's stare, but it was too late now, she must continue her charade.

"I thought I knew everyone," said Mrs. Loring. "Why do I not know you?"

"I—I have been confined."

"Ah. I trust it went well?"

"Yes."

"A boy?"

"No."

Mrs. Loring shrugged. "Better luck next time. Come, join us for a round." She waved her hand at the two officers who sat opposite, and at once they rose to make room for Abigail and Major Southwait.

"I don't think—"

"I insist. Yes, General? This delightful lady and Major Southwait must play with us."

Howe giggled. He seemed very drunk. "Play with us. Yes. Whatever you want." Suddenly he keeled over so that his head fell into her lap.

With a great shriek of laughter she clapped her hands to his ears, lifted his head, and suffered him to nuzzle at her breasts. "Oh, General, General—we are a pretty sight! General!" He pressed himself upon her so hard that her chair toppled backward and they fell into a heap upon the floor. They were laughing uncontrollably, and all around, the spectators were laughing, too.

At once a dozen men leaped to help them up; they supported Howe as he shook his head, trying to clear it. "Bed," he mumbled, lurching at her.

"Ah, General, you are a caution! Just one more round?"

"Bed!" He reached out, grabbed her arm.

"Very well. My apologies, Major—Missus, ah—the general is very tired, you must excuse us." And with a little nod she beckoned the men to follow her with the sodden form of her lover as she led the way out.

The room fell silent as they departed; then the hum of conversation rose again. "Congratulations," murmured Southwait into Abigail's ear. "You carried that off very well."

Not half so well as Betsey Loring did, Abigail thought. "I only hope she remembers me."

"She will. I've never seen a woman who could hold her liquor like Betsey Loring. And now, Missus, ah, Danforth, since you apparently cannot accomplish your business with General Howe, perhaps you will allow yourself a little pleasure." He smiled at her, his warm brown eyes dancing with merriment. "For instance, just now at sundown there is a particularly pleasant view over the harbor. If you will accompany me into the garden, I can show it to you."

She knew that she should go home; but home meant dealing with the children, and coping with the endless demands of running the household, and trying to fend off her growing loneliness, which always seemed worst just around this time, around sunset, and not even her father-in-law, now, to stop by to cheer her up. Yes, she was brave, she would continue to be brave, but every now and then she felt her strength begin to waver.

She realized that he was watching her with a curious expression: sympathy, kindness perhaps—not the expression that one expected to see on an officer of the occupying army.

"All right," she said. Madness! But for the moment, for a while at least, she did not want to go home. Not just yet.

They walked through the hall and out the door that gave onto the garden. The setting sun cast a golden-rose glow over the waters of the harbor. The sky was opalescent blue, rosy at the west. A little breeze stirred. Southwait was silent for a time; then, abruptly, he said, "I hope you do not misinterpret what you saw just now."

"Misinterpret—what?"

"General Howe's, ah, condition. When General Gage is recalled, as he may well be, General Howe will take command. If you should happen to speak to any of your, ah, American acquaintances, you should take care not to report that Howe is a drunken fool. He may be drunk tonight, but he is never drunk on the battlefield—and certainly he is no fool."

Abigail thought differently, but she kept her opinion to herself. And before she could manufacture a tactful reply, they were interrupted by a servant hurrying out from the house.

"If you please, madam," she said, "Mrs. Loring wants you to attend her upstairs. I am to bring you to her, at once, she said."

Southwait arched an eyebrow. "You will have your wish, after all," he said. "What are you waiting for? Go! The mistress of the house—if I may so describe her—has summoned you, and from what I understand, she does not like to be kept waiting. By anyone."

To Abigail's relief, Betsey was alone in a little sitting room at the top of the stairs. She held a glass of amber liquid in one hand and a little ivory pipe in the other.

"Well, sister!" she greeted Abigail. "I certainly give you points for gall. I could be seriously compromised if it were known that my half sister is the wife of the notorious traitor Ebenezer Revell. I had hoped you'd keep your distance. Fortunately General Howe is, ah, indisposed." She nodded her head toward a closed door that presumably led to a bedchamber. "Now tell me why you are here. Not for the pleasure of my company, I wager."

Without Betsey's invitation, Abigail eased herself down onto a little gilt chair. She swallowed hard, trying to remember the speech she had prepared. "Betsey, I do not want to cause you trouble, but I am desperate. My husband— who is no traitor, believe me—has been unable to communicate with me for weeks. I do not know if he fought in the battle on June seventeenth. My son" —and here her voice wavered—"may have fought in it also. I do not know if they are alive or dead. I do not know— Well. I am not here on their behalf. I am here to plead for my father-in-law."

An expression of satisfaction passed over Betsey's face. She had heard of the fabled Frenchwoman, Madame du Barry, who was a woman of tremendous power because she shared the King's bed. Anyone who wanted a favor from the King needed to seek du Barry's help. Betsey fancied herself in a similar position: and if Boston was not Versailles—well, no matter. True, William Howe did not yet have all the reins of power, he was not yet the military governor, but he would be, soon enough. Gage had failed; he was on his way out.

"More points for gall!" Her smile had a nasty edge to it. "You ask me to help a traitor!"

"No! He is not that!"

"Has he disavowed his son? Has he openly declared his allegiance to the King? No! Then he is a traitor along with all the rest of them."

"He is an old man. They have arrested him—taken him away—I don't know where he is, I don't know if he has food or drink. If you could just get me a pass to go to see him . . ."

Betsey thought for a moment. Then: "And what do you offer me in exchange for what you ask?"

"Offer?" She didn't know; she hadn't thought about it. What did she have that this woman might want?

Betsey shook her head, as if Abigail were a naughty child. "You can't expect people to— Well, never mind. The reasoning of a stiff-necked Whig is beyond me, I confess. Our mother was a woman of great common sense, and I must say I think she gave all of it to me. You are all of you fools, but if you want to suffer defeat, that is no concern of mine. Now here is what I have to say to you. It is free advice, I ask nothing in return. We are under siege here. God knows how long the siege will last. If it goes into the winter, it could be very difficult. I don't have to tell you what winter is, in New England. There will be no food, there will be no fuel, no means to survive. For you, I mean. For us—well, the Americans will prey on our shipping, but still some will get through. We will be supplied from London. We may not live in luxury, but we will survive. I cannot say the same for you. And so my advice to you is, let the men fight this war as they will, and you do what you must to survive. You have children, do you not? Yes. How will you feed them, come winter? How will you keep them warm? You might do well for yourself, if . . ."

She paused; she contemplated Abigail. "If you wanted to, ah, be of service."

For a moment Abigail misunderstood; she felt her face go red, then drain of blood until she was sure she looked like a specter.

"Oh, no!" Betsey burst out laughing. "I didn't mean that! Great heaven! I didn't mean that at all!" She laughed and laughed. "With all due respect, my dear, you aren't the type to, ah, take your place in some officer's bed. I can tell, just by looking at you, that you are one of those women who will be faithful to her husband always. So dull—but never mind, it leaves the field clear for the rest of us. No, no, no, I didn't mean that!"

But what she did mean was even more disagreeable: "I am simply saying, my dear, that if you should happen to hear of any little bit of news—any word of what plans might be hatching, some hint of conditions in the American camp, some inkling of what they propose to do— Yes, I know that what I say is unpleasant. But war is unpleasant, is it not? Very unpleasant indeed. And while the generals and their men pile up their honors, it is we women who

suffer the results of their folly. And if your husband should try to communicate
with you, if he should by chance give you some tiny scrap of information—
why, then, I might be able to help you to turn that information into something
of value to yourself. And to your children, of course. We all want to survive,
do we not? And why not survive as comfortably as possible? That's my motto.
I'd advise you to take it for yours."

For a moment Abigail was too stunned to reply. Betsey wanted her to
betray Ebenezer—to betray the American cause! She wanted Abigail to sell her
husband's honor for a peck of flour and a bundle of firewood!

No, thought Abigail. I do not know if he is dead or alive, but either way,
I will keep faith with him.

Betsey was the first to speak. "I see," she said. "Well, I was only trying to
help you. This situation we find ourself in is going to get worse—much worse—
before it gets better, I am afraid."

There was a noise at the door, the sound of female voices in the hall. Three
young women came in, none of whom Abigail recognized. They greeted Betsey
with little shrieks of joy; they did not seem to notice Abigail.

But Betsey did, for one moment more. "So kind of you to call, Missus,
ah . . ." She smiled; she waved her hand; and Abigail, her defeat rising like bile
in her throat, understood that she was dismissed.

7

The summer advanced, June to July, the days hotter and hotter, tensions rising
in the crowded little town. Rumors flew constantly: the Americans were preparing to shell the town; they were preparing to withdraw their siege; they
were going to stay put and raise and train an army—the Army of the United
Colonies—under the newly elected commander, General Washington. Even now
he was making his way north; and on July third he was known to have taken
command in Cambridge—a moving and heartfelt ceremony under the Great
Elm on Cambridge Common. Even the Americans trapped in Boston knew it:
the colonial forces were preparing to fight a long war. Washington settled in
on "Tory Row," not far from Harvard, in the former home of a Loyalist. Here
he held daily meetings with his generals: Artemus Ward, Israel Putnam, and
Charles Lee. The College had been forced into the countryside, its dormitories
used for barracks, its kitchen feeding hundreds of men who in their old age
would joke about having been Harvard men—"Terrible food, it was! Terrible!"

One morning in the second week in July, while Abigail was nursing the baby
in her room upstairs, she heard a commotion at the front door: men's voices,
the housekeeper's tones growing more and more shrill, the men's voices harder,
louder, and over it all the fierce barking of the dog, Agamemnon, an elderly

Labrador. Dear God, what now? Were they all to be put under arrest? Caesar had taken Thomas and Nathaniel to look for food at the market; one of the maids was minding the younger children in the garden. Abigail stood up; the baby had given up suckling some few minutes ago, and now she lay very quiet, her eyes closed. I should burp her, thought Abigail, but she hardly ever cries, pray God she will not cry now. Although perhaps it would be better if she did; even the damned British might not want to take a squalling infant into jail.

Hurriedly she put the baby in the cradle and straightened her nursing gown. It was hardly decent, more like a nightdress, really, but ordinary conventions had long since disappeared. She did not care if they saw her so.

But before she could leave her room the housekeeper burst in. "Oh, ma'am—it's soldiers, ma'am!"

"What do they want?"

"They're comin' here, ma'am!"

"What do you mean?"

"They're billetin', ma'am. Quarterin' on us!"

Abigail rushed out of her room. In the hall below stood several officers. *Damned British!* One of them, at the door, was directing a man bringing in baggage, gesturing toward the upper floors. The baggage handler started up the wide, curving staircase. Arms outstretched, Abigail stood at the top to block his way. The man stopped. He was so surprised that he nearly tumbled backward.

"Get out!"

The officers, hearing her voice, looked up at her; one of them smiled and bowed. "Missus, ah, Revell. Good morning."

She did not reply. Major Southwait started up the stairs. "I should have sent word that we were coming, but it has been a busy morning. Several Americans were taking potshots at our fortifications on the Neck, and we had to send a party to deal with them. Now, madam, if you would be so kind as to let my man pass, we will settle in." He brushed past her and went down the hall, pushing open doors and peering into the rooms. "Yes, very good, and there is a third floor as well? Yes." She had followed him, too outraged, too horrified to speak. *How dare they?*

Suddenly he stopped and turned to her. His face was grave, his demeanor cool and businesslike. She remembered his kindness, his flirtatious manner. Perhaps in front of his men he did not want to seem too friendly, she thought.

"You have how many servants?" he said.

"My servants are my concern—"

"Never mind. They can sleep in the barn if necessary. Now, I must ask you to take whatever personal effects you wish, and retire to the third floor."

"Mama! Mama!"

A small firestorm, a little tornado of a boy, came tearing up the stairs. It was Samuel, age eight. His face was red, his features contorted with anger. "They kicked Aggie! He's hurt! They kicked him hard!" He rushed to her side, pulled at her hand. "Make them go away!"

"All right, Samuel. I will see to him. Don't cry." That was the important thing, she thought: don't cry, don't show any weakness. She took a deep breath and met Major Southwait's eyes. "You have no right to take this house," she said.

"The Quartering Act says that I have."

"Then the Quartering Act is wrong."

Suddenly Southwait stepped close to her. His men were bustling in and out, up and down stairs, carrying in their equipment and supplies; Southwait spoke in a low voice so as not to be overheard.

"You remember what I said to you the first time we met," he said. "We are at war here—and war is not child's play. I have taken this chance to quarter on you to prevent someone else from coming in—someone who might be far less, ah, congenial. We have a good many officers who look for the chance to do harm to Americans, and I did not want you to suffer with one of them. I will try to inconvenience you as little as possible, but I have been authorized to take this house, and take it I will. You could do far worse."

Before she could reply, he returned to his duties; when rooms were assigned, he took hers and Ebenezer's for his own.

8

And so Abigail Revell became a prisoner in her own house. She and the children stayed upstairs and out of the way. Her biggest problem, aside from getting enough to eat, was keeping the children occupied. Through the long, hot days she passed the endless hours with games and stories, reading aloud Mother Goose (a Boston woman, long since dead) and *Robinson Crusoe*, making up little challenges—"Hannah, if you can say the alphabet, you may look out the window." Such things, she began to understand, helped prisoners to survive: a shaft of sunlight on the floor was an exciting thing for a prisoner, or the sound of mice's feet scrabbling behind the walls.

The worst times were when the little ones asked about their father. The oldest, Thomas and Nathaniel, never did: it was as if they understood that some things, because they were too painful, must not be mentioned. But the little ones, Hannah and James and Samuel and Philip, often asked for him and for John as well, and each time was like a stab in her heart.

"Soon," she would say; "soon they will be here again." Satisfied for the moment, they would cease their questions, but inevitably they would ask again.

Every morning and evening Abigail and the children crept down the back stairs to the kitchen, where Mrs. Brimstead gave them what she could from her slim supplies. She had taken Caesar's little closet behind the kitchen, and Caesar had moved to the barn.

As prisoners will, Abigail lost track of time. She thought only of the present: she had no heart to think of the future, and she could not bear to remember the past. As difficult as the past had been, at times, it seemed like heaven compared to her life now. Get through the day, she told herself; get through the night; let tomorrow take care of itself.

Sometimes, at night, she heard them downstairs laughing and shouting, drinking, no doubt—for Ebenezer had had a large store of wine and brandy in the cellar and certainly they had discovered it. Those were the times when her situation seemed most unreal: I am Abigail Revell, wife of Ebenezer Revell, I am in my house on lower Beacon Street in the town of Boston, Province of Massachusetts Bay. It is the year of our Lord seventeen hundred and seventy-five. Enemy soldiers are encamped in this house and have made captives of me and my children. And she would long to fall asleep so that she might awaken into her former life: Ebenezer and her boy would be home again, and the war would not exist, the British would be gone.

One stifling day, as they sat sweltering in their little room under the roof, the children lying half dressed on their pallets, dazed from the heat, a knock came at the door. With a great effort Abigail went to open it.

"The major asks you to come downstairs, ma'am." A young aide, hardly more than twenty from the looks of him.

"Why?"

"Don't know, ma'am."

"All right." Anything, she thought, to get out of this stifling room. After splashing a little water on her perspiring face, she went out. The second floor, she thought, was at least twenty degrees cooler than the third. Damned British—they could allow the family to sleep downstairs, at least!

Southwait was in the front hall. He suggested that they walk in the garden—"There is a little breeze there, I think." In his uniform, he looked as uncomfortable as she felt in her soggy dress and petticoats.

He was silent for a time as they walked toward the summerhouse; then, after they were seated on its narrow benches, and after they were both refreshed by the cool air blowing up from the harbor, he said, "I wanted to make sure that you are all right—and the children, too. We may be enemies, but that does not mean that we cannot also be, ah, friends. If I can be of any service to you, any help—"

"I have already appealed to you for help, Major. You did not give it."

"I could not."

"You did not. Not even to an old man who never harmed you, not even to a helpless woman."

"I ask you to understand my position. I cannot help you by committing an act that would have me court-martialed. Even so, while we are here in your house, I would be honored if you would consider me a friend."

He reached to take her hand; she snatched it away. If Ebenezer or John were dead or wounded, they might have been hit by a bullet fired by this man sitting before her—this man asking for her friendship.

Friendship! With the enemy—never!

She drew herself up; she heard her voice, cold and hostile: "Your eyesight is failing, Major Southwait. You mistake me for someone else. My name is Abigail Revell—not Betsey Loring!"

For a moment more he looked at her: impossible to read his expression. Then he stood and, with a little bow, he turned and walked down the path toward the house.

9

Late that afternoon, after Southwait and his men had had their dinner and gone out, Abigail went down to the kitchen to get something to eat. As she passed through the house she noted the damage that was being done, the shining floors scarred by heavy boots, the stain on the painted paper on the wall where someone seemed to have thrown a glass of red wine, the chipped paint and muddy carpets.

Mrs. Brimstead was just setting out Abigail's ration of boiled salt fish and corn cakes. She had had the same the day before, and the day before that. She did not believe that she could swallow it again today.

"Major Southwait brought you lamb to cook for him," said Abigail. She tried not to sound accusing; their circumstances were not the housekeeper's fault, after all.

"Yes, ma'am, he did." Mrs. Brimstead was a sturdy, gray-haired woman of about forty.

"I don't suppose there is any left over?"

"No, ma'am."

Abigail sat at the table and listlessly picked at the unappetizing food. When she had had her share, she needed to take a portion to the children awaiting her upstairs. She thought that she would take it all, for she could not eat. On the other hand, she needed to keep up her strength for the infant she nursed, baby Elizabeth. Suddenly, undoubtedly because she was so tired, exhausted from the tension of living like a prisoner, she felt tears well up and spill down her cheeks. She turned away; she did not want Mrs. Brimstead to see her so. But of course the housekeeper knew perfectly well that her mistress was crying; Mrs. Brimstead didn't blame her.

"Here, now," she said, her rough voice softened in sympathy. "I'll just nip in and see if I can get you a bit of their wine. Do you good." She was back in a moment with a full wineglass which she handed to Abigail. It was strong stuff, and Abigail, who had not had liquor in weeks, choked a bit as she drank it. Almost at once she felt the warmth of it flow inside her and a welcome relaxation overtake her.

"If only I could see Mr. Revell's father," said Abigail. "Old Mr. Benjamin. How can they be so cruel, to keep him locked up—and for no reason."

"I heard yesterday that there's a lot of gentlemen locked up," the housekeeper said. "Altogether, a lot of ladies are lookin' for their menfolk."

Abigail was drinking the last of the wine—Ebenezer's stock, undoubtedly, which now she was forbidden to drink, just as she was forbidden the use of her own house, or decent food, or permission to see her father-in-law ...

She swallowed the last sip and stared at Mrs. Brimstead. The housekeeper's words lingered in the air. "All together," Abigail repeated slowly. "Why, of course! That is exactly what we must do, Mrs. Brimstead! We must all go together, there is always strength in numbers, and we will present ourselves as a delegation and demand to see our men. Tell me, where did you get that bit of news? In the market?"

"Yes, ma'am."

"And from whom did you hear it?"

"From Mrs. Buckle's cook, ma'am."

"Ah! Mrs. Buckle!" Abigail thought for a moment. She knew the lady: a sharp-tongued, elderly widow, an outspoken Whig who had loudly refused to evacuate the town and abandon her property to the British.

"Mrs. Brimstead, I have had an idea." Abigail felt herself smile: a strange sensation.

"Yes, ma'am?"

"I am going to send a note to Mrs. Buckle. Do you think you could deliver it?"

"Yes, ma'am."

"Good. And I want you to wait for a reply."

Not two hours later, the response came: the lady herself, puffing up the rise of Beacon Street. As befitted their situation, Abigail received her in the kitchen.

"What do you think, Mrs. Buckle? Could we go all together in a delegation to demand of General Gage that he allow us to see our men?"

White-haired, bright-eyed, Mrs. Jeremiah Buckle hid a generous heart under her sharp tongue. "He'd better! Or we'll have our own revolt, right at Province House! My son was taken, too, you know. But now tell me how you do, Mrs. Revell. We heard that you had been quartered on. How are they? Civil, at least?"

"No more than that." Abigail smiled at the spry little woman. "They restrict my movements. I am not allowed to go out. But if you will tell me when to come to you, I will make some excuse and get away."

Mrs. Buckle thought for a moment. "I want to make sure that I get as many women as possible to join us, and that may take time," she said. "How about—ten o'clock in the morning, three days hence. That is Thursday. Yes? And we will show General Gage a thing or two! Mrs. Winthrop Sears told me that she had the very same experience you did, rudeness beyond belief, and Miss Sally Clark the same when she went to inquire of her brother—oh, they are very foolish, those Britishers, very foolish indeed. Well! I must be off! I know twenty women at least to whom I can send a note, and even if only half of them join us, we will have a good-sized delegation."

So saying, she took her leave into the summer twilight, leaving Abigail with the first optimistic thoughts she'd had in days. Perhaps—just perhaps—she would soon see Ben, after all.

On the Thursday morning, with a word to Thomas and Nathaniel to mind the younger children, Abigail went downstairs. The dining room door was closed; from behind the smooth white panels she could hear men's voices. Some military business, she thought. Good: she could slip out unnoticed. Agamemnon, who had been lying in the hall, limped up to greet her; as she bent to pat him, the dining room door opened and Major Southwait stood staring at her.

"What are you doing here?" he said.

"I was just—"

"Eavesdropping? You have orders to remain upstairs."

If Southwait learned that Mrs. Buckle awaited her, he could prevent her from going. Therefore: "My father-in-law's housekeeper is ill. I am going to see her."

"And bring back the pox, no doubt." He thought for a moment. "Very well. This once you may go."

Outside, it was a warm day, but she felt a breeze from off the water and she breathed it in gratefully. Fresh salt air! She was so glad to be free, even for only an hour, that she did not even mind the occasional rude remark thrown her way by the passing soldiers—for the town was thick with soldiers, all of them bored out of their wits by the long weeks of enforced inactivity. Everyone is a prisoner here, she thought, soldiers and civilians alike.

Mrs. Buckle lived in Long Lane. She greeted Abigail warmly and motioned her to a brocade settee. There were a dozen ladies in the room, most of whom Abigail knew at least in passing.

"Now here we are," said Mrs. Buckle, "all of us ladies whose menfolk are in gaol. Each of us individually, I believe—yes?—has tried to visit there, and each has been refused. I must say, General Gage is unwise to treat us so. Mrs. Revell has had the idea of going to see him as a petticoat army, and we are going to encamp on the steps of Province House until he gives us permission to go in with food, and spruce beer for the scurvy, and medicine and clean clothing and whatever else our men may need." She waved her hand toward the sideboard, which held eight or ten baskets filled with provisions. Where had all that come from? wondered Abigail, but she did not ask. Mrs. Buckle nodded briskly. "The general will not throw *us* into jail, I can assure you!"

Then she gave the signal, and the group rose as one and marched out of the house and up Milk Street. Soldiers in the street stared at them, small boys hooted at them—no matter. Mrs. Buckle had her umbrillo, and she used it as a sword, making her way for them. Let Gage turn them away at his peril!

The guard at Province House was so astonished at the sight of them, Mrs. Buckle at their head, umbrillo upraised, that he opened the gate at once at her command. Up the walk they marched, through the door—

"We demand to see the general!" announced Mrs. Buckle to the officer there.

"He is not here."

"Yes, he is! Ladies!" And in they went through the doors of the front parlor, the general's office. Several officers sat in scattered chairs; Gage was behind a large table.

"General!" harumphed Mrs. Buckle. "We are American ladies of the town of Boston. We demand to see our men in the gaol. You have had some of them prisoner since June seventeenth, and you have arrested others since that time. We are their womenfolk, we have been patient long enough, and we demand to see them! Now, sir! Today!"

Abigail noted one of Gage's aides struggling to control his laughter. The general himself was so taken aback that he was speechless. He seemed a decent enough man, she thought, if not terribly bright. But even the dullest brain in the world could understand that here was trouble: no general wanted a delegation of angry women—Amazons!—to complicate his affairs.

And yet he had to save face. "It is against regulations, madam—"

"Hang your regulations! We have heard that conditions there are very bad—abominable! If those men die in your jail, your regulations will not save you from General Washington's fury!"

"Madam, I assure you that the men are being cared for—"

"And I assure *you*, General, that they are not! Have you visited them?"

"No, I saw no need—"

"Then you cannot possibly know what you are talking about! We have our informants, General, and they tell us that you have a disaster in the making at that jail. We have come to save you from it."

Gage raised his eyes to the heavens as if seeking divine guidance; then, with a resigned shrug and an apologetic glance around at his men, he took a sheet of paper, scribbled a note, and handed it to one of his aides. "Sergeant Enright will escort you," he said.

"Thank you, General!" said Mrs. Buckle; and, with a triumphant wave of her umbrillo, she led them out.

Down the walk, through the tall iron gates, along to Queen Street to the jail. Brandishing her pass from the general in the astonished guard's face, Mrs. Buckle swept them in. They had done it!

But now their momentary triumph vanished, and as the women began to circulate through the prison, each searching for her loved one, the terrible truth of the rumors they had heard hit them with force of a blow. Men wounded at the battle who had lain for days and days without medical attention, without even food or drink; men picked up after the battle, arrested and thrown into jail without a hearing, without trial; everywhere they looked they saw misery, and more than one woman at the jail that day found no one waiting for her, for many men had died for lack of care.

Abigail found Ben in a cell on the first floor. Here the common criminals were housed, while the wounded had been put into a dormitorylike room upstairs. To her enormous relief, he was safe—thin and hungry and dirty, but not sick, not dying of some foul disease. She set down her basket of food and threw her arms around him. For a long wordless moment they embraced; then, pulling back, she stared at him.

"Ebenezer?" he said. "Have you had word?"

"No." She turned away so that he would not see her tears.

"Nor John, either?"

"No."

"They're alive," said Ben. "I'm sure of it. If they'd been killed or captured we'd have heard, one way or the other. All right, now—all right." He patted her arm; then he gave a cheerful smile and reached for the basket she had brought. "You put in a bottle or two of spruce beer, I hope? Yes. We've a lot of scurvy here. After a lifetime of lookin' after my crews, I don't want to come down with it myself!"

He took out the spruce beer, and after a long pull at the bottle, he set to work on a fat turkey leg.

"No, dearest girl, they didn't hurt me," he said between mouthfuls. "Kept me in irons for a few days, that's all. Nothing very bad. But upstairs—" He gestured toward the low ceiling. "Upstairs they put some of the men from the battle. Only yesterday Asa Miller died, a bullet in his leg, and not once did they have a doctor for him. His leg swelled up this big"—and he held his hands a foot apart—"and he went delirious. The men called and called for a doctor, I'm surprised you didn't hear it up on Beacon Street." Ben's face was dark, a grimace of hate. "You know who has the prison concession. Yes—Joshua Loring. Husband to that sister of yours—there, daughter-in-law, don't worry, I don't hold it against you."

For Abigail's face had gone crimson and tears filled her eyes. Dear heaven, it wasn't her fault that Betsey Loring was her half sister!

"Just keep it quiet," Ben went on. "You don't want it gettin' about that you have any connection to those—those *collaborators*. It's Loring who's responsible for these men dying. Wounded men coming in from a battle—and no medical care! Nothing! Listen, my dear, it's wonderful to talk to you, but as you see, I am well enough. But you must—if you can—go to those men upstairs. And when you leave here, you must tell everyone you can about what the damned British have done to us. Such treatment of wounded men is against all the rules of civilized warfare. You must—ah, well, I don't want you to get into trouble. I was going to say, you must somehow get word to the Congress at Watertown about conditions here. But someone else will do that, I am sure. Wait—before you go. Let me look at you again. Is it the light, or— You seem pale. Are you well?"

She hadn't intended to tell him about the men quartered on her, but now, seeing him and realizing how much she missed his doughty strength, she gave him her bad news: "They came—I don't know—two weeks ago."

"Are the children safe?" he said.

"Yes."

Ben nodded. "They are quartered on my house, as well. Oh yes—we've an efficient grapevine here, off and on. I didn't hear about your situation, but still. Now go, this is no place for you, even though I'm very glad you came. What a world, when ladies must traipse through prisons! But upstairs before you go, eh? You must see for yourself what they've done. And mind! Talk about it to everyone you see!"

With a sinking heart she ascended the narrow stone stairs to the big room on the second floor. It was filled with American wounded. The stench was beyond belief. She choked, covered her mouth and nose with a silk handkerchief, and pressed on. The floor was covered with bodies; some of them moved, some did not. Here and there the women who had come in were ministering to someone; off to one side a woman wept uncontrollably, undoubtedly because she had discovered that her man—son, husband, brother—had died. The men lay as they had been deposited, covered with muddy, blood-soaked clothing; their moaning filled the air: "A little water! Can you give me a little water? And a bite of bread—we've had nothing for days. Aaahhhh! Don't touch the leg, the bullet went in there!" She saw a hideously bloated arm, a shattered hand.

Suddenly she thought of who was responsible for this Hell: Betsey Loring's husband. Tarring and feathering was too good for such a man; if the Americans ever got him, they would draw and quarter him, and charge admission to see the show.

As she left the prison that day, she had just one happy thought: wherever Ebenezer was, on earth or in Heaven, she was grateful that he was not here.

10

A week later, with no explanation, Ben was released. He appeared one day as bright as a new shilling, asking to see her.

"Well, daughter-in-law! Come and walk out with me this fine day!"

Major Southwait and his men were just clattering down the stairs, getting a late start after a night out. Ever courteous, Southwait extended his hand. Ben drew himself up to his full height—taller than the major—and lifted his chin. Even at seventy-four he was a fine figure of a man, his full head of white hair neatly queued, his linen brilliantly white, his gray broadcloth coat trimmed with gold buttons, the silver buckles on his shoes newly polished.

After a long moment as their eyes met and held, and Ben made no move to respond, Major Southwait, flushed with annoyance, dropped his hand and with a curt word to his men went on out.

"Shake his hand!" muttered Ben. "Damned if I will!"

There had been a time, Abigail knew, and not so long ago, when he would gladly have responded to Major Southwait's gesture. But not now: not after his experience in jail watching the American prisoners die, while Joshua Loring stole the provisions allotted them and made his profit.

She put her arm in Ben's and they walked out: down Treamont Street toward the Common. It was a brilliant August day, a sky so blue that it was nearly indigo, the trees on the Mall newly washed bright green by a little rain in the night.

"No," said Ben, "I don't know why they let us go. Everyone's out—'cept them who died, of course. And those poor devils weren't like us anyways. We were political prisoners. The damned lobsterbacks made me promise not to leave town. Ha! Fat chance!"

As they approached the Common they heard music, and soon they saw a regimental band gathered under the trees. A few people were promenading along the Mall; among them Abigail saw an elegant figure whom she knew to be Hugh, Earl Percy; the other, Ben told her, was Johnny ("Gentleman Johnny") Burgoyne. "He fancies himself quite a wit—writes plays, I'm told. Plays!" Ben snorted. These gentlemen each had a lady on his arm, and Abigail gasped when she realized who they were: the Byles girls! Even Betsey Loring had more sense than to go parading in broad daylight with General Howe. These were the daughters of the Reverend Mather Byles, the minister of the Hollis Street Church in the South End; he was a notorious Tory and a self-styled wit—"An old toad's bladder filled with hot air," as Ben described him. The Byles girls simpered and tittered, each hanging onto her Britisher. "Their father ought to lock 'em up," fumed Ben. "Little hussies! They've got a good case of scarlet fever, for sure, an' they disgrace themselves and every decent American woman while they suffer it!"

Then, as they walked on, Ben got down to serious business: "I wanted to talk to you away from the house. I know you trust your servants, but who you trust in peacetime and who in war are two different things. I've got two officers and a Loyalist family from Milton quartered on me. They get plenty of food from the quartermaster, and from ships coming in—the ones that get past our privateers out of Salem and Newburyport. Don't I wish I had a share in that business! But never mind. The point is, I can get supplies for you. There's no point in you and the children starvin' to death."

Abigail pictured Mrs. Brimstead cooking up special meals in which the officers would not share. "I don't think—"

"No never mind, young lady! And don't ask me how I'm payin' for it, either. My father taught me—well, he showed me how to put in all kinds of special places to fox the Customs men, places to hide what we don't want 'em to see. I've got goods to trade—an' money, too, for that matter. So don't you go hungry while those damned British stuff themselves!"

That evening, as Mrs. Brimstead worked in the kitchen, she saw a figure dart past the window. She went to the back door and opened it cautiously. She saw no one. Then, before she could retreat, a boy appeared, thrust a folded paper into her hand, and vanished.

At once she tucked the small square into her apron and withdrew, locking the door. She realized that her heart was beating fast, her hands were trembling. She could not read, but even had she been able to, she would not have wanted to know what was in this message. Trouble for sure, she thought.

But when she took it to her mistress, secretly, waiting to creep up the stairs until the interlopers were well along in their evening's occupation, their wits dulled by drink—then she realized that it was not trouble at all, but the greatest good news in the world.

Two words:

Both safe.
E.

Abigail laughed and cried, hardly caring if the Britishers heard her, and she lay awake all night with the joy of it, and sent Thomas and Nathaniel running in the morning to fetch old Ben so that she could tell him, too—safe! By God, safe and sound!

Ben's release brought a new freedom to Abigail, for despite the old man's rudeness to Major Southwait, the Britisher seemed willing to allow her to walk out whenever Ben called. Abigail thought she saw a curious kind of respect in Southwait's eyes whenever he looked at her father-in-law. As if, she thought, the major would have behaved the same in Ben's place.

Dreary day followed dreary day, and the summer drew to a close. The weather was still warm, but every now and then they felt a chilly breeze, and they were reminded of what lay ahead of them: the New England winter, bitter cold and snow, the town shut up inside itself with thirteen thousand British troops and a few thousand civilians, all of them on the knife edge of tension as each army, American and British, waited for the other to move.

11

The baby sickened. She had never been strong, and now, in the waning days of summer, she lay still and pale in her cradle and hardly had the strength to suck. Abigail sent for the doctor, a new man, come in with the Loyalists in the spring. He gave the infant a cursory look, scribbled a note to the apothecary, and demanded his payment. Abigail had not thought about payment; she had nothing to give him, so she sent him to Ben. And she sent Nathaniel to the apothecary—"Tell him that grandfather will pay him, too—but hurry!"

The medicine, a brown, bitter liquid, did no good. The baby could not swallow it; she choked and cried and then fell silent again. All night Abigail sat up with her. Ben had been with her earlier, but because of the curfew, he needed to leave before dark. He promised to return in the morning.

The house was quiet. Major Southwait and his men were there, but for once she heard no noise from them, no sounds of drinking and laughter. Nathaniel and Thomas and the twins, and her own three little ones, were asleep. In the flickering light of the candle she could see them crowded onto the mattress, the little ones very fair, the older boys a darker blond—all these Revell children, all these hostages of war.

Ah, Ebenezer! Abigail's tears dropped onto the light cotton wrap that enfolded the baby. The tiny skull covered with golden down, the closed eyes with the miniature golden lashes, quite distinct, the sweet little face that somehow had never had the look of a child that would live—always, she had seemed not quite alive, somehow, as if she had known that God did not intend to allow her to stay.

Please let her live, thought Abigail. Her throat ached so that she could not even whisper the words, and so she prayed silently, the words burned across her mind: Please let her live, let my sweet little girl live!

Back and forth, back and forth she rocked, as if the motion would put the spark of life into her child, back and forth, back and forth, her tears falling faster and faster. Please let her live, please dear God let her live—

All of a sudden she stopped. She blinked, trying to clear her eyes. Dear God! The tiny fist was cold, tight-clenched; the tiny heart quiet, no breath, no life—

And then she gave a great shriek that shocked the sleeping children awake, not knowing, not caring who heard. In a moment heavy boots thundered up the stairs, the door flew open, and Major Southwait stood appalled, staring at her.

When she saw him, she fixed on him as the sole author of all her pain and grief, and she raged at him—"Get out! You murderer! You killed my child! You bastard, all of you are bastards, get out! Get out! Leave us alone, you have no right, *get out*!"

The smaller children were crying now, terrified of this virago whom they did not recognize as their mother, the older boys horribly embarrassed and not a little frightened, too, and now she staggered up, still clutching her dead baby, and with her free arm she was beating on Major Southwait's scarlet chest, her hair tumbling down, her face splotched with tears. He was helpless to calm her; he had no idea what to do, he tried to take the baby from her and this brought forth new rage, new imprecations—"Don't touch her! Get away! She is mine, she is mine and you killed her! Murderer! *Murderer!*"

How long she went on they none of them knew. At last he was able to quiet her somewhat, so that while she would not give up her child to him, she at least allowed him to lead her downstairs—into her own dining room—and give her a glass of good French brandy; in doing so he was not only acting as a good officer must, to keep order, but from the kindness of his heart, as well. He was not a monster: far from it. He had flirted with her as he flirted with all women who were not positively deformed, but that was at another level of human intercourse. This domestic crisis—for that is what it was, to him—was a very different thing. He sympathized with her; his gallant heart went out to her. As difficult as her behavior was, it was entirely to be expected. He reached out and refilled her glass. She sat before him, disheveled, disoriented, clutching the corpse of her infant. Poor woman! And soon, no doubt, she would be even worse off, when the Americans shelled the town and the inhabitants, Loyalist and Whig alike, exterminated in the process. She would be lucky indeed, he thought, to get out of it with even one or two of her children alive, not to mention herself; and viewed from that perspective, perhaps this infant's death tonight was a blessing.

She could not stop crying. The brandy was false courage; it left her weaker than before. She sobbed and sobbed; once one of Major Southwait's men looked in and the major motioned him away. For a while, at least, he would defer his business and try to help this anguished woman.

And at last, when nothing he could say seemed to help her, he gathered her to his splendid scarlet bosom and put his arms around her—gently, gently, as if she were a wounded child, as indeed in a way she was, and he let her cry as if her heart would break, as indeed it had.

The next day they put baby Elizabeth into the family plot in the Granary Burying Ground. As the tiny coffin was lowered into the ground, the little circle of mourners heard distant shouting, and then the tolling of a bell—many bells. Some new emergency; some new affright. Abigail did not care about it; she did not care about anything. When the earth was shoveled in, she turned and let Ben lead her the short distance home. She went upstairs through the silent house; she threw herself onto her makeshift bed; at once she was asleep.

The noise that day came from the far end of the Common, down by Frog Lane. The soldiers, bored and restless, looking for amusement, had decided to chop down the Liberty Tree. A few sullen, angry Americans gathered to watch them, but no one dared to protest. And so the soldiers went at it with their hatchets, working industriously, *thwack! thwack!*—but the day was not all amusement, for one private who had clambered up into the tree to crow their little victory lost his grip and fell down dead, and so when the grand old tree came crashing down a few minutes later it was not the triumph the British had hoped for.

So tell that to His Majesty, people said. That fat German farmer! Probably he can't even understand English!

12

September came and went, and with it General Thomas Gage—that dim, ordinary man caught up in the extraordinary situation that was the siege of Boston. His masters in London said that they wanted him to return for consultation only, but everyone knew that when he sailed out of Boston Harbor on a day in early October, he left America behind for good. Into his place stepped General William Howe, a dedicated gambler who was confronted, now, with the highest stakes of his career: to attack—and if so, where?—or to hole in for the winter and wait for the reinforcements that would surely come in the spring? Every day his spies sent news of the growing strength of the American army ringed in redoubts around the city; but they sent, too, the news that the American soldiers were enlisted for a short time only. At the end of December their time would be up, and, farmers that they were, undoubtedly they would all go home, leaving General Washington sitting in his confiscated Tory mansion house over in Cambridge with no one but a little band of part-time officers. So what Howe needed to know was: would Washington get a new army?

In early October, around the time that Gage left, Howe lost one of his most valuable informants when Dr. Benjamin Church, the surgeon-general of the Army of the United Colonies, and a high Son of Liberty, was unmasked as a British spy.

He was undone by his sometime mistress, a woman who had bungled the transmission of one of his messages to General Howe. Washington had her in for questioning, and after many hours of interrogation, she broke. Who was her master? Why, Dr. Benjamin Church, she said.

The Americans were astounded. Washington had put two teams of men to deciphering the letter she carried; both came up with an identical wording. Church had attempted to transmit detailed information about the strength of the American lines, the extent of their supplies, the state of their morale, and other important tidbits.

Immediately Church was arrested. A few weeks later he was tried by the General Court in Watertown. They found him guilty, and sent him away to prison in Connecticut, where, it was thought, he could do no more harm.

Howe sent out new spies. Unfortunately for the British, none of them was as productive as Dr. Church. Howe desperately needed to know: what was Washington going to do?

General Washington, for his part, did not know what he would do; but he needed to know Howe's plans. Was he going to attack the American fortifications ringed around the city, or would he lie quiet until the spring?

13

"She was a beautiful woman, was she not?" said Major Southwait. "Your, ah, predecessor."

Abigail made no reply. Squinting a little, she stared up at the Copley portrait of Emilie Griffin Revell—a magnificent thing, all pink and gold and white—and thought bitterly that no one would ever say of her that she had grown old and ugly through the horrors of war, no one would ever say of her that she was not strong enough to withstand the siege of Boston.

". . . to meet your husband someday," Southwait was saying. "When all this, ah, unpleasantness is over. We are the same people, after all. There is no reason why we should not be friends."

Abigail's gaze shifted to her husband's portrait. A younger Ebenezer, a man she had never known. He had a familiar look to him, though, she thought: a certain arrogance, a light in his eye, completely captured by the artist, that said: "I am my own man, free and independent; do not coerce me." But after a moment she looked away. She could not bear to look at him; she knew that the sight of his face ought to remind her of her obligation to be strong, but it did not. It only made her realize all over again how she missed him, how she feared that she would never see him again.

It was a cold, blustery morning in late October. Abigail had been rooting in the vegetable patch, gathering the last of the pumpkins and squash before the hard frosts. Now she sat in the dining room, an unwilling guest in her own home; she was still cold from her time outdoors, her hair was windblown, her hands grubby—what did Southwait want with her?

Since the baby's death, since the night she had sobbed her grief in his arms, she had tried to avoid seeing him. His schedule was more or less the same every day, and she had come to know the times of his coming and going; those times, she stayed upstairs, coming down to the kitchen only when he was out of the house, and never going near the front rooms. She was not embarrassed at her show of grief—why should she be?—but now she shied away from any further sympathy from him. It would have been more fitting, somehow, if he had mocked her—berated her, perhaps, for weakness—more in character with the monsters that the British were supposed to be. No matter what happened, she thought, she would not give him such a chance again.

But this morning he had seen her in the garden and had ordered her in. She did not trust him, not for a minute, and so now she sat, stiff and uncomfortable, not wanting to converse, not wanting even to be polite to him. It was because of him that she had been in the vegetable patch in the first place. She avoided his eye; she looked around. Mrs. Brimstead was an unwilling servant to these men, and so now the remains of last night's meal still covered the table; the bones of a fowl lying in congealed grease, half-empty wineglasses— Ebenezer's wine!—stubs of candles in the candlesticks, the shining surface of the mahogany table covered with little burns from carelessly smoked pipes, and with spilled food and liquor—pigs!

Southwait went to the sideboard, to the silver tray bearing a teapot and several cups. He lifted the lid and in a rather exaggerated gesture inhaled the aroma of the steeping tea.

"It is a cold day to work outdoors," he said. "Won't you join me in a cup of this delicious brew?"

Damned Britisher! Saw her working, but didn't move to help! And as for his offer of tea, it was a deliberate insult, as he knew perfectly well.

"I'd as soon drink poison," she said. She heard her voice, strong and clear. Ebenezer watched her from his place over the mantel: Ebenezer, and that other one, the beautiful one. In some strange way she felt that she must not let them see her behave politely toward the enemy.

Southwait remained calm and smiling, and this, too, irritated her. He gave a slight shrug of his shoulders, poured himself a cup, and sat down at the table. "Tell me," he said, "doesn't it bother you that out in the country—in the towns, in Cambridge and Salem and Roxbury—people are living their lives more or less free, while you are cooped up here under military rule, deprived of your, ah, liberty? That's the great thing for you people, isn't it? Liberty?"

She watched him. What was he getting at?

"It seems unfair," he went on. "Why should you suffer, when no one else must do so?"

It was a question that she had asked herself more than once, but she did not intend to answer it, now, for him.

He sipped his tea. "Really, this is excellent stuff," he said. "Won't you try just a little? No one will know; certainly I will never betray you. Just a half cup, to warm yourself."

Oh, what she would give for a cup of tea! She was salivating from the desire for it—hot and fragrant, warming all the way down and then working its magic on her brain, sharpening her wits, stimulating her whole being!

He jumped up; he poured a half cup and set it in front of her and then sat by her again. She clenched her hands in her lap to keep from lifting the cup to her mouth.

"Stubborn," he said. "That's what all you Americans are: stubborn. Pity. All this quarrel for nothing. You know"—and he leaned toward her, his elbows on his knees—"if General Washington does not attack—and we have no reason to believe that he will—we are going to have a long, cold winter here. I would imagine that you will be far more uncomfortable in January even than you are now. But I could make your life much easier. There is no reason, for instance, why you and the children have to stay upstairs. I could easily shift some of my men up there, and you could come down to your own rooms. And there is really no reason why you have to take your meals in the kitchen, like a servant. Wouldn't you like to eat here, with us?"

No, she thought, I would not.

He reached out, took her hand. For a moment she resisted; then she let him take it, and she even went so far as to place it, quite deliberately, upon his knee, which was covered by the sparkling white cloth of his breeches. When, after a moment, she took it away and saw the muddy smudge she had left, she was pleased with herself. They took enormous pride, she knew, in their spit and polish.

She saw a small flame of annoyance behind his smiling eyes. "You surprise me," he said. "You are an intelligent woman, I can see that you are. No one would criticize you for, ah, cooperating. War is men's affair. Women must survive it, that is all. And if not for yourself, then for your children—"

For one dreadful moment she thought that he was going to mention the baby who had died, and she knew that she would not be able to bear it. She stood up, startling him. "Major Southwait," she said, "you must do as you are ordered, even when it means making war—as you do—on women and children. It is your war; you started it. Yes—you did."

"We only acted—"

"You forced your taxes on us, you quartered your army on us, you murdered innocent civilians, you tried to ruin our shipping, you took away our right—our birthright—to govern ourselves—"

He was smiling at her; she could see that he did not take her seriously. Nothing was more infuriating.

He stood; again he reached for her hand, and when she pulled it away, he took her arms and tried to draw her to him. "The Goddess of Liberty," he murmured, "come to life in a traitor's dining room."

"He is not a traitor!" She stepped back, nearly stumbling over the chair. "It is you who are the traitor! You who will not stop meddling in our affairs!"

She was more than angry: she was afraid. For one moment she had heard the voice of treason in her mind, and it had said, "Why not? Why not let him make your life easier? Why not let him protect you when the attack comes, as surely it will, now or next spring? It is his place—any man's place—to protect a woman; and since your husband has abandoned you . . ."

He sensed her hesitation. Swiftly he caught her up in his arms and held her so close that she could smell his strong male scents of tobacco and leather polish and soap. Ah, how long had it been since Ebenezer had held her so!

"Sweet goddess," murmured Southwait.

He pressed his mouth on hers, gently at first . . . Ah, Ebenezer, my husband, save me! For one long second that seemed an eternity, she responded: she did not embrace him, she did not press her body to his, but she returned his kiss for one damning second before her reason returned to her and she pushed him violently away, staring at him with wide eyes, horrified—what had she done? And the worst of it was that Ebenezer had seen her, had been watching her as she shamed herself. I didn't mean it, she thought—it was a mistake, I never meant—

Frightened, mortified, she ran from the room, ran up the broad curving stairs to the second floor, up the narrower stairs to the third, and thus when she came into the room where the children were, she did not mind that they saw her panting and out of breath, she had good reason to be breathless after such a run.

She calmed herself; she told herself that the incident was not important, that she had not behaved badly, that he would forget about it, as she would, in a day or two. She washed her face and hands and settled down with Thomas and Nathaniel to hear them read a passage from the Bible. She could not tutor them in Latin and Greek, she could not help them with mathematics and theology, but she could have a reading every day, and from the twins as well, from whatever books were at hand, and she could oversee lessons in penmanship.

After a short while she heard the front door slam shut and Southwait call for his servant, and she breathed a little sigh of relief. No harm done, she told herself. It meant nothing.

In the afternoon the men did not return for dinner. No matter; certainly she did not care. Shortly after three Ben appeared and asked her to walk out with him. It was a cold, cloudy day still, but he insisted that she needed to get out of her confinement—as indeed she did—and as long as it was not pouring rain, he urged her to come out with him.

"How goes it?" he said as they walked down Beacon Street toward Treamont. "They're not givin' you any more trouble than usual?"

Just then a horse chair passed them in the street, and for a moment Abigail had a glimpse of the passenger: a flash of golden hair, a pretty, plump face—Betsey! General Howe's whore, the despicable harlot who warmed the enemy's bed.

"Who's that?" said Ben. "Ah—I see." He spat a spectacular distance, hitting the back of the horse chair as it went on down the street. "Good thing not many people know she's related to you. No offense, m'dear. You understand. I don't recollect any woman's bein' tarred and feathered, but I'd say that one's got a good chance of it. If she don't get away in time."

Abigail shuddered. Yes—a fit punishment for a woman who behaved as Betsey did. She turned to smile at her father-in-law. "We are all right," she said in answer to his question. "They don't bother us, we don't bother them."

"Good. Just keep out of their way, that's all, an' you'll come through safe and sound. He's not, ah, pesterin' you, is he?"

"Pestering me? No. Not at all."

"That's right. Just let him keep his distance. I hear stories all the time about women who—well, never mind. They aren't Abigail Abbott Revell, now, are they?" And he smiled at her with his warm, family pride glowing on his face; no Revell woman would disgrace herself as Betsey Loring did.

As they approached the Granary Burying Ground, Ben slowed his usual brisk step; glancing at her, he said, "How would you feel about, ah, goin' in here for a minute? If it'd bother you too much, you can wait. I just want to see—well, I want to see my father's name. And his father's, too—and even *his* father's. All of 'em. I had such a dream last night, so strange—I dreamt that the damned British were havin' a great muster on Boston Common. All thirteen thousand of 'em, standin' at attention. And we were standin' on a platform along the Mall—all us Revells, all the way back to old Bartholomew. And the women were there, too. My dear wife, and my mother—my wife was a Pemberton, and my mother was a Chauncy—and my grandmother—ah, now there's a tale! Have you ever read her book? Yes! Her very own book that she wrote after she was delivered from captivity with the savages. Oh, she was a remarkable woman I can tell you. I remember her very well. I was always a bit afraid of her when I was a child, not that she wasn't pleasant, but there was somethin' about her— You'll come? Good. It isn't bad to see the stones, y'know. It lets you know you're part of somethin' that's—well, bigger than you are. A continuation, y'know. You're part of that long line that goes all the way back—when did you say your people came over?"

"My mother says that it was just after the Restoration. Sixteen sixty-two, I think."

"Ah. Yes. That was Catherine Mayhew's year, too. She's the one who was captured. 'Sixty-two. Not bad. Any time before the turn of the century is all right, I always say."

They went in through the gate and stepped carefully among the gravestones. At last, toward the back, they came to the Revell plot. Abigail looked at the tiny, freshly carved stone that covered baby Elizabeth's grave. She did not mind that Ben had brought her here; she was even glad of it. It comforted her to see that small stone among all these other Revells; even such a very young Revell had a place among the family, and Abigail was certain that in Heaven, where they all undoubtedly were, some Revell woman was looking after her.

Ben stood before his father's stone: Isaac Mayhew Revell, 1664–1729. And

Jedediah Revell, Isaac's father, whose wife had been the famous Catherine. She had lived to a fantastic old age—1642-1741.

"We brought Ebenezer to her not long after he was born," Ben said. His eyes were bright with remembering. "Ebenezer's mother had—well, she'd lost many babies. Five, six, seven—I've forgotten. And so when Ebenezer came, and lived, he was like a miracle to us. And of course his mother wanted to protect him too much. She was so afraid of losing him, you see. And overprotection can be very bad for a boy. No son of mine was going to grow up to be a sissy! But in any case, she was afraid to let us take him to see his great-grandmother. It was cold weather, y'see. But of course we had to. She was so old, but clear as a bell. And how delighted she was to see him! It was the connection, you know. She knew that she had to die soon, and she wasn't sorry about it. Her time had come. But it comforted her to see that a little bit of her would live on. That's the important thing. We none of us can stay forever, but all of us live on, the family gets bigger and bigger, and we'll branch out—wait till this war is over! You'll see—there's land to the west that's there for the taking, we'll get rich on it, and we'll expand our shipping—why, we'll start shipping to the East Indies before you know it! You don't believe me? Wait and see—and it will be our ships that go there, Revell ships! Did Thomas tell you I took him down to the wharf last week? Yes! And I told him exactly what I expected him to do: he must ship out as a supercargo, I said, to learn the business. Meet the agents, not only in London, I don't think we'll be doing much business with London for a while. But in the West Indies—and in the East Indies, too, I said. Go out there! No Massachusetts man has put into those ports, you be the first! And if I'm not here to see it, come back and tell me about it, I said—come right here to the Granary Burying Ground and stand in front of my stone and tell me about it! And what profit you made, I said! What cargo? Who's your captain? Wherever I am, I want to know!"

14

That night Abigail went to sleep when the children did, as soon as they had finished their supper. Sometimes she sat reading by candlelight long after they had drifted off, but this night she was exhausted. Some time later, she did not know how long, she was awakened by a tap on the door. She dragged herself up and went to answer. It was Mrs. Brimstead.

"I'm sorry to disturb you, missus, but the major wants you downstairs."

"What for?"

"I don't know, missus."

From below she could hear the men's voices, loud laughter. Mrs. Brimstead held a candle; in its little light her eyes met Abigail's. Both of them understood that a request from Major Southwait was not a request but an order. Nevertheless . . .

"Tell the major that I am indisposed," said Abigail.

A faint, grim smile crossed Mrs. Brimstead's face. "Yes, ma'am."

Abigail went back to bed and fell asleep again. Her sleep was heavy, dreamless—as if her brain was responding to the tension of her conscious life by allowing her this respite. The night passed, the bells tolled the hours. And then suddenly she was awake again, and she heard the last of the bells, but what hour it was she did not know. In the sudden silence after they ceased she heard the sounds of revelry from below—here, in her house. Heavy, booted feet stamping on the floor, the crash and splinter of glass, men's voices lifted in drunken song—and female voices, too, coarse and raucous, high-pitched female voices laughing, laughing—

Abigail felt her heart stop and then begin again. Females! She had no doubt what kind of women these were: the whole back side of Beacon Hill was infested with loose women, so that the area was known as "Mount Whoredom." Caught like everyone else in the siege, they suffered less than decent citizens because the army gave them so much business. The entire north slope of the Hill was one vast brothel—a necessary evil, perhaps, but one that was at least kept out of sight. But to have these creatures brought into a decent house, under her very nose!

She had half risen, but now she lay back. She could not go down and protest; they would only laugh at her, they would shame her in front of their whores. Despite Hannah's warm little body next to her, she was very cold. The sounds of Major Southwait and his men and his whores drifted up. She had never felt more alone. She lay in the cold, in the dark, and bit her fist to keep from sobbing. Where would it end? How would they all survive? For a long time she listened; then she fell asleep again—and again awakened, but this time to silence. What hour? The dead of night: no bells rang, no sound came from below. She came fully awake, straining to hear—what?

Nothing.

And yet—something nagged at her. The sounds of drunken revelry had alarmed her, but this silence alarmed her more. Were they all lying drunk and unconscious, perhaps, a candle overturned and catching fire to the carpet, blazing up the curtains?

She slipped out of bed. The cold hit her with the force of a blow; she was shivering so much that she could hardly draw her woolen wrapper around her. In the dark she felt with her feet for her warm sheepskin slippers; shuffling them on, she crept to the door and opened it. The house was dark and silent. Cautiously she began to go down the stairs; as she neared the second floor she heard deep snoring, and she smelled the stench of cheap, heavy perfume. In one of those rooms—one of the beautiful, spacious family rooms—slept a drunken British officer and a denizen of Mount Whoredom.

No use searching them out, she could do nothing about them, and they were not the problem in any case. No: the problem lay downstairs. She went on, step by cautious step, down the broad, curving stairs. A faint, wavering light emanated from the dining room, whose pocket doors stood open. Still no sound. Down and down . . .

She came to the bottom of the stairs. From where she stood she could see into the dining room: one of her fine Chippendale chairs overturned, a piece of cutlery on the carpet. She stepped into the open doorway. In the dim, flickering light of a single candle guttering in the old pewter candelabra—and thank Heaven she had hidden her best silver—she saw, all down the length of the table, the remnants of a magnificent feast: plates of half-eaten food, half-empty bottles of wine, brandy, port; the carcass of a roasted turkey with bits of meat still clinging to it; a piece of apple pie; a bit of cheese. Across the table lay an unsheathed sword and, beside it, a pistol. Above it all, from their safety over the fireplace, were Emilie Griffin Revell and the man who once had been Emilie's husband. In the near darkness their eyes seemed to gather what little light there was; their bodies, their clothing, even their faces were dim, but their eyes were curiously alive.

Abigail looked back to the table. These brutes, gorging themselves while she and her children went hungry!—for even with her father-in-law's help, they had little but salt fish and salt pork and small rations of baked beans. She saw a plate holding a few pastries, and a little tray of sweetmeats, and suddenly, fully awake, she was hungry—starving. How long had it been since she had seen such a feast? Feeling like a thief in her own house, she reached out and took a little cake. How long since she had tasted sugar, and how delicious it was, the icing melting on her tongue! She turned to the carcass, and now she began to strip it, shoving the morsels into her mouth as fast as she could chew. And wine—ah, Ebenezer, you laid in a good cellar! She lifted the bottle and took one sip and then another; it was wonderful stuff, far better to warm her than the forbidden tea. If only—

"Well, well, well!"

The voice startled her so that she nearly choked. In the doorway stood a man she had never seen before, his scarlet coat unbuttoned, his linen stained with wine. He seemed very drunk; he swayed as he stood grinning at her, and even from a little distance she could smell the liquor stinking on his breath.

"Stealing?" he said. He came into the room and braced himself against the back of one of the chairs.

Once, when she was a girl, she had attended a dancing party at which a young man had drunk too much rum punch. For a little while, before he was ejected, he had made himself obnoxious to the young ladies. The best way to deal with inebriation, they had all agreed, was to ignore it if possible, but at all costs maintain your dignity: never allow yourself to be flustered or thrown off guard.

And so she said nothing, simply stood her ground and tried to stare him down. She was aware that within her reach lay the sword; if she could seize it and somehow intimidate him—

He came toward her, holding onto the backs of the chairs as he advanced. In her nightdress and her loose woolen wrapper, without the comforting security of her corset and hoop, her hair undone and falling about her shoulders, she felt naked under his glance. Even as drunk as he was, he must realize that she was in a state of undress.

He was nearly upon her now. She shot out her hand to grab the sword, but he was too quick for her. He seized her wrist and twisted it so hard that she cried out in pain.

"Want a little bite of somethin', do you?" he said. Roughly he pulled her to him, his free hand grappling with her nightclothes. She pushed at his ugly face and felt her nails dig into his skin.

He was surprised at her ferocity, and in that moment when he hesitated, she scrabbled desperately in the clutter on the table and felt her hand hit on the butt of the pistol. And now she seized it and put its mouth into his neck; it was heavy, she did not know if she could pull the trigger, she did not even know if it would fire.

"Why, you damned little whore—"

He grabbed her wrist and pulled the pistol away just as she squeezed the trigger. In the quiet night the sound of the explosion was deafening. She thought that she must have killed him, and she was surprised to see that he remained upright, he did not drop to the floor with a bloody hole in his head.

"Thompson!"

Her attacker froze. Major Southwait stood in the doorway. His tunic, too, was unbuttoned, his hair uncombed, but he seemed sober, at least, she thought. She had never thought she would be glad to see him, but certainly she was glad now. With a rough little shove her attacker let her go and she collapsed into a chair. The pistol fell from her hand.

"Get out," said Southwait; he stood in the doorway, his eyes fixed on the other man.

"I was just—"

"She is the mistress of this house. The whores are all upstairs. Go up there if you want one. No—do not. Get out. You are not quartered here, you have no business here—get out!"

For a moment Thompson hesitated. He was taller than Southwait, and much heavier, and Abigail thought that if they came to hand-to-hand combat, Thompson, whoever he was, must surely win.

The smell of gunpowder hung in the air. The sword glittered on the table. A church bell chimed: one, two, three. Thompson gave in. With a muttered oath and a look of hate at them, he lumbered out of the room; in a moment he was gone from the house, slamming the front door, letting in a brief gust of freezing night wind.

Southwait took two fresh candles from the box, inserted them into the candelabra, and lit them with a spill from the embers in the hearth. He stirred up the fire and threw on a scoop of sea coal; he looked about him for a clean glass, and when he could not find one, he took a teacup from the cupboard and poured a tot of brandy into it.

"Here," he said, offering it to her. "You will not object to drinking this, surely."

She took it and sipped. It burned all the way down, and she choked a little. Still, it was bracing; at once she felt stronger. "Who—who was he?" she said.

"A captain from the Twenty-ninth. We, ah, entertained a number of officers here tonight."

She felt stronger still; she remembered the sounds she had heard. "Yes," she said. "You made a good deal of noise."

"I trust we did not—"

"You brought—" She could not say the word. "You brought women into my house."

"Some of my men did, yes."

Stronger and stronger— "That is despicable. I should report you."

"To whom, dear lady?" He could not help laughing. "I apologize for disturbing you, but I must give some diversion to my men, they are growing restless and we are hardly at the beginning of the winter. In the barrack in the Hollis Street Church the enlisted men gamble and complain, and they wonder when this interminable siege will end. We had word today that General Washington is raising a new army. My men long to fight, they are sick of being cooped up here, as sick as you are to have them, I assure you. But unless Washington decides to attack— which he may well do, but I doubt it—we must wait till spring to have our battle. And meanwhile—" He shrugged; he shook his head at her. "We must endure."

He was right; she knew that he was, but she hated to agree with him on anything. She shifted a little in her chair, moving her arms and legs to make sure that she had not been injured by her attacker. Then she tried to stand up, and to her surprise she was able to.

"You're not going?"

She saw his look of genuine disappointment. For some reason it struck her funny: that he should care about anything she did!

He put out his hand to detain her, but he did not touch her. "Let me tell you that I am very sorry indeed for—for what happened. He will not come into this house again—not, at least, as long as I am in charge."

She swallowed the last of her brandy. She felt very courageous indeed now, strong and confident.

"If my husband were here," she said, "he would kill you—all of you. I am sorry that I cannot do it for him." For an instant her eyes flicked to Ebenezer's portrait; then to Emilie's; then back to Major Southwait.

Something had not quite registered; something was not right—

"Mrs. Revell, I assure you—"

Her eyes had returned to Emilie's portrait. She squinted, trying to see it more clearly. Southwait saw the expression of astonishment on her face, and he turned to look at it also.

And then he burst out laughing; but she did not. She did not think it funny at all.

When she had fired off the pistol, she had put a bullet straight through Emilie Griffin Revell's heart.

4. MASQUERADE

1

By mid-December smallpox raged in the British camp, and Howe ordered a general inoculation. Nothing terrified people more than smallpox—festering sores, and hideous, scarring pocks, and hemorrhages, and rotting flesh, delirium, blindness, insanity—ah, God keep us safe!

"You've had the inoculation before?" Ben asked Abigail. "Yes? Good. I remember when I had one, it was during the great epidemic. Seventeen twenty-one, that was. I was just twenty, just out of Harvard, ready to see the world. Of course everyone was terrified when the smallpox came—off a ship from the Salt Tortugas, some filthy French sailor brought it in. We'd heard of a new procedure in England, brought there from the Turks. Lady Mary Wortley Montagu had her daughter inoculated, and the royal princesses had it done, too. So a few of us thought there was something to it, you understand. And around the same time, Mr. Cotton Mather had the story from one of his slaves—how the Africans did it. In those days we protected the cut with half a walnut shell, although Mr. Mather held that warm cabbage leaves worked better. But nobody really believed in it. No doctor in Boston would do the procedure save Dr. Boylston. He called for volunteers, and I thought I'd give it a try. Most people were terrified of it—deliberately give someone the infection? Feelings ran so high that one time they threw a bomb into Mather's house. Would've killed him, except that the fuse fell off."

With the coming of cold weather, the troops remaining on Bunker Hill were ordered into barracks in Boston. Snow fell, and fell again; the streets, narrow and clogged at the best of times, became well nigh impassable; people huddled in their houses—or in their confiscated properties—and kept close to their fires.

But some people had no fire, for wood was scarce, and little sea coal came in on the few supply ships that managed to get past the American privateers who patrolled the waters beyond Boston Harbor.

The soldiers in their barracks grumbled with discontent: nothing to do, not even any makework, just sit and freeze to death.

Some of them began to steal firewood where they could: a fence, a cowshed, a rotting shallop lying on the shore. When they began to tear down abandoned houses, General Howe issued strict orders: any man caught stealing wood was to be whipped. As the winter wore on, the penalty increased: one hundred lashes, five hundred, a thousand—but no man could withstand a thousand lashes, such a sentence was the equivalent of execution, and some men suffered it.

But some taking of firewood was approved by the general, and so that winter the black and ancient house of Governor John Winthrop, hard by South Church in Marlborough Street, a stone's throw from the State House, was sacrificed to keep the soldiers warm. The North Church was torn down, too, thereby creating a confusion that dogged historians ever after. Some have assumed that this was the church from which the famous lanterns were hung on the night of Paul Revere's ride, but it was not: that church was Christ Church in Salem Street, an Episcopal church frequented by the British. After the original North Church was dismantled for firewood, Christ Church became known as Old North, but it was not so called in Revere's day.

To add insult to the considerable injury that they did to the proud little town, the British took the South Church for a riding school. They tore out the pews, they scattered gravel on the floor, and all winter they exercised their horses, round and round over the bars. And so the walls that had echoed to the stirring phrases of the patriots, Warren and Adams and Hancock, now heard the sounds of galloping hoofs; the place reeked of dung, and loose women in the galleries screamed profanely to the men below.

The heavy snow that winter meant good sledding, and those boys who remained in the town wanted to have their usual sport. School Street, from the corner of King's Chapel down to Marlborough Street, was short and steep, a favorite sledding place. One bright day a group of boys, the nine-year-old Revell twins among them, took their sleds and started coasting down it. At once a sentry barred their way, and when they would not desist, he ordered that ashes be strewn so that the boys' sleds would not slide.

The boys were angry. Bloodybacks! Damned lobsters! Some of them started to make snowballs, saying that if they could not have one kind of sport, they would have another. But others, remembering tales of the Boston Massacre, refused to engage in a battle with the soldiers. Best go home, they said, and not make trouble.

The Revell twins, Samuel and James, disagreed. They were prisoners in their own house; for months, now, they had needed to skulk and hide and keep out of the way of their oppressors; for an even longer time they had not seen their father, did not even know if their father was alive or dead, and all because of these same scarlet soldiers who were camped on the town in a cruel occupation, who had perhaps murdered their father. And now they and their comrades were prevented even from sledding! Throwing snowballs would do no good; we will go and demand our rights, they said. Now! Together!

They stood at the center of the little group of boys. Even at nine they were quite tall, and their dark blond hair and dark blue eyes marked them as their father's sons: they both had the Revell look, and it was not a matter of appearance only, but the way they carried themselves, the tilt to the chin, the arrogant look in the eye. This was their town—theirs and their father's and their grandfather's, too! Ben had taken them to the Granary Burying Ground, had walked them up and down the Revell Wharf. This is our place in the world, Ben had said; never forget it. And so now they were not going to let a pack of stupid soldiers deny them their birthright—sledding down School Street!

"Come on!" they cried. All the boys ran with them, around to the tall iron gates of Province House. Of course the guard would not let them in, but then they had a bit of luck, for a contingent of officers was just going in, and before the guard knew what was happening, the boys had slipped in along with them and scampered up the walk and into the lion's den.

At once a guard seized Samuel, and he began to make a frightful noise— "Help! Help! Murder!"—and the others took their cue and began to holler along with him, until in no more than a minute the quiet hall of the great mansion house rang with the cries of these miniature rebels, and the grown men who had hold of them began to feel shame. Attacking children was not in the order book.

General Howe, hearing the disturbance, sent an aide to enquire; and when he learned what the trouble was, he puffed in astonishment. A gang of boys sent to attack? Surely not. Send them in to me!

The guard had Samuel by the ear, and he was none too gentle as he dragged him in to the general's presence. Samuel just caught himself from falling as he was thrust in front of Howe; it all happened too quickly for him to be afraid, and in any case he had James and all his friends to back him up. The boys stood in a group before the might and power of the British Empire, and to their credit, every single one of them held his head high and uttered not a whimper of fear, even in the presence of this monster—for so Howe seemed to them—this most fearsome bloodyback of all.

Howe put on a stern face. "Well? What is this?"

Samuel stepped forward and James stepped with him. "If you please, we have come to claim our rights." He paused. "Sir," he added.

Howe's lips twitched but he continued stern: "Your rights, boy? And what would they be?"

"Our rights to School Street," said James.

"School Street? You'd better explain."

"It's where we sled," said Samuel. "The sergeant forbade us."

"We have always sledded on School Street," said James. "It is our own place, every winter."

The general shook his head; he covered his mouth with his hand lest these little rapscallions see him smile. He was a pretty good general, and not a bad human being; certainly he had never thought to land in such a mess as this siege, and truth to tell, he was growing sick of it.

"You two look like brothers."

"We are twins," they said in unison.

"Indeed? And what are your names?"

"I am Samuel Jackson Revell," said Samuel.

"And I am James Jackson Revell," said James.

At this, the general perked up his ears. "Ebenezer Revell's sons?"

"Yes, sir."

"Your father is a traitor. What do you say to that?"

"I say, no, sir, he is a patriot." Samuel had not intended to get into a discussion about his father; he never wanted to talk about his father, because he did not know if his father was alive or dead, and the subject, therefore, was entirely too painful. But if this monster sitting in front of him wanted to talk about Ebenezer, he, Samuel, would grit his teeth and talk back to him.

Howe shook his head, exasperated; he turned to an aide. "What are we to do with these people, Wilson? Even their babes defy us—look at this bunch of infants, come to spout their little speeches! They have sucked in treason with their mothers' milk!"

"They are Boston boys, sir. What else can we expect from them?"

"That's right, Wilson. Boston boys! Little chips off the old block! As stubborn and defiant as their fathers! Well, Samuel Jackson Revell—and James, too"—and he swung around to face them again—"you are bold as brass, and by rights I ought to clap you in irons. But I am very busy today, I have no time to waste on a troop of little troublemakers. So off you be, and have your sledding on School Street if it means so much to you. But mind! No trouble with the sentries!"

After the boys had gone, hardly able to believe their good fortune, Howe sat for a moment thinking about the incident just past. A group of little boys, come to defy him! And it was at that moment, perhaps, that he understood the seriousness of the situation confronting him: these people were so imbued with the idea of what they called "Liberty," that even their children spouted it. And if the idea of Liberty was so deeply ingrained in the American character, then he and his troops could fight forever and they would never win: they were a foreign army here, sent across the ocean to subdue a clever and tenacious people fighting for their homeland. He and his men were doomed.

Bleakly, he turned to the next delegation come to consult with him.

The twins were exultant. Victory! With a wild yell they led their little troop back to School Street, and there they sledded all the rest of the day.

And it was not till sometime later, when they were relating the story to their grandfather, that they realized what Howe had said: "He said, 'Your father is a traitor,' Grandfather! That means he's safe!"

Ben was laughing so hard that he had a pain in his side. What a story! What a wonderful, absolutely splendid story! And what wonderful boys! His grandsons—bearding the lion in his den! And getting away with it!

And of course they were right: Howe had intelligence all the time. He would know at once if a high Son of Liberty like Ebenezer Revell had died.

And so—he was alive!

2

Every night, that winter, Howe and his men amused themselves with card parties and balls and even theatricals held in Peter Faneuil's Hall. On the night of January 8, 1776, General Howe, General Clinton, Earl Percy, and a number of other officers—including Major Southwait—some of them accompanied by their female companions, were enjoying a performance of "Gentleman Johnny" Burgoyne's farce, "The Blockade of Boston." The author of this delightful piece was not in attendance, having departed a few weeks previously, and that was a pity, for it was with this single performance of his work that he gained his greatest fame as a dramatist.

A ridiculous, periwigged figure strutted and staggered onstage, all stuttering and bombast: General Washington. The audience howled: a true picture, the very like! Several other characters came on: caricatures of the patriots. What genius, what a cunning satire! Rude bumpkins, slobbering sly Yankees—

Suddenly another figure dashed onstage. "The Americans are attacking!" he shouted.

The audience laughed and laughed. What fun, what indescribable hilarity!

But the actors were confused: this line was not in the script. The actor, if such he was, cried his news again: "The Yankees are attacking! At Charlestown!" He came down to the front of the stage and shouted at the assembled officers. "They have set fire! They are raiding supplies!"

And now at last his message penetrated, and the officers leaped up and made for the doors. The audience panicked and stampeded, racing to get out, some of them leaping down from the galleries, a terrible crush at the exits—it was a wonder that no one was trampled to death, everyone screaming and beating down his neighbor to get away. The Yankees attacking! In the dead of winter, when no sane military man made a move!

General Howe ordered a reconnaissance party across the Charles to investigate, but they were too late: the Americans had taken what little was left in the few remaining houses of the town that had been mostly burned on the day of Bunker Hill, and they carried away five British soldiers as prisoners. And so it had not been an attack on Boston, after all, but merely a warning: we are here, all around you, strengthening our fortifications every day. You cannot withstand us: we can besiege you for years, if necessary. Surrender!

3

Abigail had taken to going down to the market every Wednesday and Saturday to buy what she could. Mrs. Brimstead offered to go in her place, but Abigail said no, she wanted to go herself. She no longer minded the rude words flung at her from passing soldiers, she was no longer afraid to walk alone—in daylight, at least. The incident with the drunken attacker under her own roof had shown her that there was no real safety anywhere, and she was doing no good staying cooped up in two small attic rooms. She had not thought that the twins' adventure with General Howe was as funny as Ben had, but she understood their instinct: they must stop cowering in their houses, they must show a brave face to these interlopers. Even a woman of delicate birth, supposedly frail and helpless, could lift her chin and sustain herself on her good American pride.

And so she trudged down through the filthy snow to the market at Peter Faneuil's Hall and haggled like any farmer's wife over a few turnips or a bit of high-priced fresh beef, and she felt that by doing so she had struck her own little blow for freedom.

This day, which was cold and overcast, she made her way through the crowd—soldiers, civilians, many coarse-looking women who were attached to the troops, legally or otherwise—and at the stalls she managed to buy a pound of flour. She was just turning away from the farmer's cart when a heavy countrywoman jostled her.

"Beggin' your pardon, ma'am."

Abigail nodded: no harm done, no need to apologize.

Then she realized that the woman—and what a strange, deep voice she had!—had seized her hand. Instinctively Abigail recoiled—no telling what pigsty the woman had been cleaning—and then she realized that the woman had given her something.

It was a small packet of paper: a letter, folded and sealed, but not marked by any seal ring.

Before she could say a word, the woman had vanished: very quick on her feet for such a one.

The marketplace was crowded; Abigail was afraid to look around for fear that she would meet someone's eyes—someone who was watching, perhaps; someone who had seen—

A letter! She had a pocket at her waist, but she could not get to it through the heavy folds of her cloak. So she clutched the little folded square and headed rapidly for home. She was frantic to reach the quiet of her room, to read the precious message.

She had refused, months ago, to use the back door of her house; she would come and go as she always had, she said, through the front—a small point, more important to her than to Major Southwait. And so now she trudged up the front walk, up the granite steps kept neatly shoveled by Caesar, and opened the door—to Bedlam.

In the middle of the entrance hall sat Roger, eighteen months, and Philip, three and a half. They were bawling, their little faces red with fury, screeching at the top of their lungs. Hovering over them were Mrs. Brimstead and Lieutenant Mason, one of Southwait's aides. Mrs. Brimstead looked up with relief as Abigail came in. "Oh, missus, I'm glad you are here, an' I'm sorry for this—"

"What is it?" said Abigail. Thrusting the bag of flour into Mrs. Brimstead's hands, she bent to pick up Roger. He did not want to be picked up, not even by his beloved mama. He kicked and screamed, his little limbs rigid with fury.

"They was sleepin'," Mrs. Brimstead went on. "I thought they were good for an hour more. Master Thomas and Master Nathaniel went out with the twins an' said the little ones'd be all right, but they must'v'woke up, an' came down on their own, 'course they don't know they aren't allowed"—this with a hostile glance at the lieutenant—"an' they was callin' for you, lookin' for you, they were."

As tightly as Abigail was clutching Roger, she was holding the folded bit of paper in her fist just as hard. Suddenly she felt the lieutenant grasp her hand, and before she realized what was happening, he had pried it open. He lifted away the letter; with a suspicious glance at her, he broke the seal.

"No—"

She made an instinctive move to grab it back from him, but he evaded her. Roger continued to scream. Lieutenant Mason moved into the parlor as he scanned the single sheet of handwriting.

Abigail stood in the hall and held her child and felt as though her very life had been snatched away from her.

In a moment the lieutenant was back; without a word to her he bounded up the stairs.

"Give me my letter!" cried Abigail. She was too angry to be afraid; she went right up after him. He knocked on Major Southwait's door; at Southwait's order he went in, closing it in her face. *That is my room—!*

She threw open the door and went in.

Southwait sat at her little desk by the window; he seemed to have been writing a letter of his own. Now he held hers; he glanced up at her but he went on reading it.

"I demand that you give me that letter!" she said.

No answer. Lieutenant Mason stared at her in an unpleasant way. Roger continued to cry, but not so loud; exhausted by his temper, he lay on her bosom, sobbing, hiccupping.

At last Southwait finished; still holding the sheet of paper, he spoke to her in a tone more severe than she had ever heard from him.

"It seems harmless enough, but of course it is a communication from the enemy and I must show it to my superiors." He paused; he glanced at Mason. "Dismissed, Lieutenant."

"Yes, sir." Mason's face betrayed no surprise, no suspicion; he turned and left the room, closing the door behind him. Southwait waited a moment before he spoke again; they heard Mason's footsteps going down the hall and down the stairs.

Southwait came close and spoke quietly. "It is against all rules for me to allow you to read this," he said. "But I will do so if you will promise me that you will read it here, in front of me, and that you will immediately give it back."

"Yes," said Abigail; she knew that she should have refused such a humiliating bargain, but she was too weak; she must read it. She was certain that it was from Ebenezer.

Southwait would not allow her to hold it; he sat her down at the little desk and put it in front of her. Roger lay quiet in her lap as she read.

31 January 1776
Watertown

My Dearest Friend:

Every day, every hour, you and my beloved children are in my thoughts. Even now as I write, I feel that you are with me. I know that you suffer. I long to be with you, to help you through this bad time, but I cannot, as you understand.

I would not ask of you this sacrifice if I did not believe that we will prevail, and that in the end we will free ourselves and our children from the heel of the oppressor. We *must* be free. If we are not free—if we are not willing to die to secure freedom for our children, if not for ourselves—we are nothing. A man who will not fight for his Liberty is no better than a slave.

I pray that this perilous experiment will succeed, and that soon I will embrace you again and see your dear face, dearer to me than any other.

Be strong; kiss the children for me; and believe me to be—

Your loving husband,
Ebenezer Revell

This is the fourth letter I have written to you since Breed's Hill, but only one brief message could be carried. I fought and escaped without injury, as did John. He is with me.

She sat quiet for a moment, absorbing the message—they were safe!—but also trying to think how to keep it from Major Southwait—or, at least, to destroy it so that he would not carry it to headquarters. This was hers; they would not have it!

He had been standing by, watching her, but now some noise from the street distracted him and he moved to the window to look out. In that moment she seized the letter, jumped up, and ran to the fireplace where burned a little seacoal fire. But he was too quick for her. In the blink of an eye he seized her hand, forced open her fingers, and had the letter from her grasp.

"You impose on my good will too far, madam. What were you going to do? Burn it? I would have had it out of the fire before it even caught. But now with your action, you have as much as admitted that there is something more here, perhaps, than meets the eye. What is it? A message in code?"

"No."

"Then why try to burn it? Don't you realize that now you have incriminated yourself?"

She did not realize it; she had not thought about it. She had simply wanted to put it beyond his reach.

He folded it as if to slip it into the front of his tunic. "We know that information about our forces goes out of the city every day. And I cannot deny that we have information coming in to us, as well, about the American lines. You have received a message from the enemy. How are we to know what he may have intended to communicate? And even more, how do we know what you may intend to communicate back to him? Oh, yes—it would be very easy for you to send out intelligence. Even the smallest detail—something that might seem quite unimportant to you—might have great significance to General Washington. I have allowed you to go out whenever you wish, you are free to go about, to look at our fortifications, at the men's encampments. I daresay you could get a good deal of information if you put your mind to it. And how do I know that you have not, eh? But in any case, that is not what concerns me now. This"—and he shook the letter at her, as if to taunt her with it—"this concerns me. Is it what it seems? Or does it tell you something else?"

"What could my husband possibly want to tell me of a—a military nature?" It was too absurd; surely he must know that.

"That, madam, remains to be seen." He glanced at Roger, now half asleep on her shoulder. "For the moment I will not order your arrest—"

Arrest!

"—but I will order you to remain within this house until you have my permission to leave. Now—upstairs, if you please."

And without a further word he ushered her out.

As soon as he had gone, undoubtedly to headquarters, she sent for Caesar and told him to fetch her father-in-law. Half an hour later, from her rooms at the top of the house, she heard a pounding on the front door and the sounds of an argument. Even as she hurried downstairs she knew what the trouble was: they would not let Ben in to see her, and Ben, in true Revell fashion, was fighting back.

"Out of my way, you—you—damned whelp!" The old man was pink with anger as he shouldered his way past the fuzzy-faced little private. Benjamin Revell cared about only two things in the world: his family and his business. He would fight to the death for either—and, in fact, Abigail went to him in some alarm, for he looked likely to drop of a stroke.

"Well, daughter-in-law? What is it?"

But of course she could not talk to him there, and so he needed to wait until they had climbed the two flights upstairs. When she told him, he growled with pleasure—at least until he considered the consequence of headquarters' perusal of Ebenezer's message.

"Safe! That's the main thing! And of course he wasn't sending in a military message. Do you know any codes? No. Of course you don't. Ridiculous. Well, let them see what they make of it. In any case, what would he be sending in? News of General Washington's plans? Not likely. Sympathetic ink? Well, now, what about that? No chance to wash it, eh?"

When she thought about it, she had to admit that it was not inconceivable that Ebenezer might try to warn her if the Americans planned an attack—might try to provide some way for her and the children to escape, across to Lechmere's Point, perhaps.

But he would not do so in code, for although she knew how to reveal sympathetic ink, she knew no code. He was a clever man; he would find some other way to rescue her.

And so now his letter was at Province House, providing a little puzzle for the officers. Well, they were welcome to make what they could of it. They would get no military secrets from Ebenezer Revell.

The next morning Southwait summoned her to the parlor, which served as his office.

"I am ordered to escort you to headquarters," he said.

"When?"

"Now."

"I cannot leave now. Mrs. Brimstead has gone to market, Philip has a fever, and I cannot leave him with the children." Not even with Thomas and Nathaniel, she thought, dependable as they were.

"I am afraid you will have to."

"No. I will wait until they awaken, and then I will bring them with me if necessary, but I will not leave them here alone."

She had the upper hand, and they both knew it. He could have had her taken to headquarters by force, but of course he would not do that, he was a civilized man. He scribbled a note and handed it to one of his men to take to Province House. Later, he said; Mrs. Revell would come—later.

But General Howe was not so considerate. No sooner did Southwait's message arrive at Province House than the general sent a guard to fetch her—at once.

"I cannot," she said.

The guard retreated. In a moment Southwait came up. He seemed embarrassed. "The general wants you now," he said. "I am sorry."

"It is not your fault that the general is a stupid man," she said. "Tell him again: I will come when I can. What does he think I am going to do? Swim away?"

Which had been done by more than one man, across the Charles to Lechmere's Point. But not in winter and not by a woman.

"I am afraid that you must come now," said Southwait. "It is the general's order."

Suddenly all the anger, all the frustrations of the past months, blazed up in Abigail, and she shouted at him, "To hell with the general's order! I cannot leave my children—I will not! I will come when I can! Can't you understand English?"

Southwait was offended. According to his lights, he had treated Abigail very fairly. Now she was not doing the same for him. It would reflect badly on him if he could not deliver her—a woman, with no standing at all to defy anyone!—upon the general's order. Obviously she did not understand the military mind.

He cleared his throat and tried again. "Mrs. Revell, General Howe has ordered you to appear. He has not requested it. He has *ordered* it. He is the military governor of this province. We are under military rule here—not just those of us who serve in the army, but everyone, civilian and military alike. General Howe can order anyone to do anything. He is like the captain of a ship: he has absolute authority."

Abigail stared at him defiantly, her chin high, her eyes steady. "Then let him use his authority," she said, "to carry me to him. I will not walk—not now."

Southwait gave a little shrug. "As you wish."

He left her then; shortly he sent up two guards to escort her away to General Howe. She thought briefly of carrying out her threat, but she decided against: they might trip and fall, carrying her down the stairs; and in any case she did not want their hands—as they surely would be—on her body.

And so, with a word to the older boys, she suffered the guards to lead her by the arms downstairs. Thank heaven Mrs. Brimstead was just coming in; her face went blank with astonishment, but she nodded when Abigail told her to tend to Philip.

"Yes, missus, I'll give him a bit of cordial. Don't you worry."

In the street and all the way down the hill to Province House people gawked at Abigail as she walked between her guards; some of them recognized her, and someone ran to fetch Ben.

As the guards hustled Abigail up the steps she remembered the last time she had been there, and she wondered if General Howe remembered the petticoat army that had forced its way in to General Gage last summer. And, remembering it, if he would recall one of those females in particular—or, more recently, the small, determined Revell twins, demanding their rights.

It was a dark day, threatening snow; General Howe and his officers were in a room illuminated with many candles. The general sat behind his table; the others stood by his side, or in little knots of men around the room. Their desultory conversation ceased as the guards, one holding each arm, led Abigail in. The hood of her cloak had fallen back, and they had not freed her hand so that she could put it up again, so now she was very cold, and somewhat windblown, and as they deposited her before the general, she tried to wrench her hand free to push back strands of hair that had blown loose. They wouldn't let her, at first; but then the general nodded at them, and said a word, and they released her.

General Howe, as everyone knew, was very fond of women, but only when they behaved as women should, and not like petticoated men. This one, he decided, had shown an alarming amount of recalcitrance; but she was a lady, after all, and perhaps, at first, he should proceed gently. And so while he did not smile at her, he spoke in a moderate tone, an almost fatherly tone, as he tried to get from her what he needed to know.

"I am sorry to trouble you, Mrs. Revell, by ordering you to come in. But we have had this message—"

And now she saw that Ebenezer's letter lay on the table before him. It was badly smudged; they must have washed it to look for sympathetic ink.

"What did your husband say to you, madam?"

"Nothing."

"Nothing? He wrote a whole page."

"Nothing—of interest to you."

Howe grunted. He picked up the letter. "Will you, ah, translate this for us, madam?"

"There is nothing to translate. It says what it says. No more."

"I do not believe you."

She shrugged. "That is your affair." An insolent reply, one that overstepped the narrow bounds of ladyhood.

General Howe's handsome, sensuous face settled into hard lines of disapproval. Only the previous day he had had some unsettling intelligence: cannon were coming in to the Americans from the west. No confirmation yet, but still. "No, madam. It is your affair. I want you to tell me what this letter says—what it really says."

"It says that he is well."

"And?"

"That he longs to see his family."

"Including those insolent boys, no doubt. *And?*"

"That he survived the fighting on Breed's Hill."

Howe's face darkened; he did not like to be reminded of what had been the worst day of his career.

"Come, come, Mrs. Revell. We know that the Assembly is at Watertown. We could, if we wanted, send out a party to take them all, and question them as much as we please."

This was untrue, and Abigail knew it as well as he. The British did not dare to do that, for they would be annihilated the moment they left the safety of their fortifications at the Neck.

Howe continued: "Let me ask you again, madam. Will you decipher this letter?"

"I cannot. It is not a cipher."

Howe glared at her. His stomach rumbled. It was past noon, nearly time for dinner. He wanted to eat; he wanted to drink; he wanted a good game of cards and a tumble with his mistress. Now this stubborn traitor's wife was disrupting his schedule. He tried again, a different tack: if she cooperated, he would guarantee her safety and that of her children in the event the Americans attacked.

But this was nonsense, and even Abigail knew it. When the Americans attacked, Boston would go up in flames, and no one's safety would be guaranteed; it would be every man, woman, and child for itself.

Then he tried threats: "I can have you whipped, Mrs. Revell, for any number of reasons. I beg you not to force me to such a desperate measure."

The red whipping post stood in front of the Town House; many times over the winter it had anchored some poor wretch being flogged for far less than trafficking with the enemy. Women were whipped as well as men—for breaking and entering, for stealing, for selling stolen goods.

Abigail refused to think about whipping. She kept her eyes on his and concentrated on keeping her voice steady. She would never beg him for mercy—never!

Howe glared at her. Then he started all over again: how did the cipher work, what was the coded message, what were the plans of the American forces, why was her husband communicating with her just then—on and on, over and over. The room grew warm; Abigail was very tired of standing.

And General Howe was growing tired of this unrewarding game. He wanted his dinner. Stubborn woman!

"Put her upstairs," he said to the guards; and in the next moment Abigail found herself hustled out and up the stairs to a room on the third floor furnished with a narrow bed, a table by the small window, a chamber pot, and a half-burned candle in a pewter candlestick. Without a word the guard shoved her in; she heard the rasp of the key in the lock.

She sank down onto the bed; dazed and exhausted, she was too disoriented even to cry. Imprisoned—and for how long? This place was better than the jail, she thought, but on the other hand, in jail she would not have been so isolated. How long could he keep her here? As long as he pleased, she supposed, until the city was destroyed in the battle that seemed inevitable.

Darkness came; she had no way to light the candle. She heard the sounds of the men below: feet pounding up and down the stairs, loud masculine voices. At some point she heard laughter and singing; the officers had parties every night, she knew. She wondered if Betsey Loring was about. She wondered if other prisoners were kept in other rooms here. By now her father-in-law must have had the news. He would come at once, she knew, demanding to see General Howe, demanding that she be set free. He would be fortunate if they did not imprison him, too. You could not demand anything of these people; you could only endure until they went away.

Until the war was over.

She was cold. She lay curled up on the bed in her cloak and tried to think of happier times. She was determined to keep her fear at bay. She felt it in the back of her mind, waiting to overpower her, but she must be strong; she must not give way to it.

The night passed; she slept; morning came. Some time after sunrising, she had no idea how long, a guard came to unlock the door. He carried in a tray. It held a teapot, a cup and saucer, a wedge of coarse bread, and an orange. She inhaled the pungent odor of the steeping tea. No, she would not drink it! But the orange and the bread—yes, those were safe to eat, and she devoured them greedily, feeling her strength return to her as her belly filled.

Hours passed. She stayed by the window, looking out, but she could see only the snow-covered back garden and the muddy stableyard. A strange calm descended on her: she was powerless to act, worrying would do no good, and so she simply waited, suspended in time.

The day came to an end. Sometime after dark the door opened again and a guard brought in a bowl of boiled fish and a lighted candle. She was too proud to question him, and he volunteered not a word. She slept fitfully that night; she heard the bells go two and three and four; then she slept until light, awakened when the guard came again with her breakfast.

At midday, just after the bells tolled twelve, a guard came to fetch her into the general's presence. He sat as before, his aides surrounding him—but this time Mrs. Loring was there as well. She gazed at Abigail with no hint of recognition; elaborately coiffed, dressed in blue silk, she sat at the general's right hand and seemed perfectly at ease in this masculine, military company.

"Now, Mrs. Revell, what do you have to tell us today?" Howe's face was stern; the table before him was bare save for the smudged sheet that was Ebenezer's letter.

"Nothing." They must have been busy, she thought, still trying to decipher Ebenezer's message.

"I would remind you, madam, of your precarious position here. I am offering you this one last chance to save yourself. I assure you that I will not hesitate to have you whipped. Concealing information is a capital crime, and I ought by rights to have you hanged."

Abigail lifted her chin, pulled back her shoulders and looked slowly, steadily around the room; she met every man's eyes, sending a silent message to them all: *shame! War is men's business! Why do you make war on me?*

One of the men was Major Southwait. His face was expressionless, his eyes blank. She wondered if he realized his error in having her arrested—for it was an error, she was not concealing information, and surely they all must realize that now. Even their own skilled cipherers could make nothing of Ebenezer's letter, because it contained nothing beyond its surface message.

"Well?" Howe's voice barked out suddenly, startling her.

"I can tell you nothing, General, beyond what I have already said."

"You swear it?"

"Yes."

"I do not believe you." He stared at her, hostile, and suddenly her anger, which she had kept banked in a low fire at the back of her mind, flared up again. She was Abigail Abbott Revell of Boston, an honest woman—and this interloper did not believe her, not even when she swore to him!

Damn him! "But even if I knew the message, I would never tell you, not even if you ordered a thousand lashes on me!"

A look of fury descended on the general's face. She understood: by defying him, she had humiliated him in front of his men. He was so taken aback that for a moment he could not speak. Then he collected himself, smashed his fist against the table and roared: "One hundred! By God, woman, you have condemned yourself! One hundred lashes—now! At once!"

But then, just as two guards moved to hustle her out, she heard Mrs. Loring's voice: "Wait! Perhaps we could settle this another way!"

As she leaned over to speak into Howe's ear, he held up his hand; the guards kept their grip on Abigail, but they did not try to take her out of the room.

Mrs. Loring whispered for a moment more. Howe drew back and stared at her as if she had lost her wits. She smiled brilliantly at him, leaned in, and whispered again. The anger disappeared from Howe's face; then he, too, began to smile. At last, when Mrs. Loring had finished, he let out a chuckle.

"By God, Mrs. Loring! That is the most amusing thing I've heard this month!" He laughed out loud. "I like it! Indeed I do! A game of cards! Ha, ha! Very well—we'll do it!" He pushed back his chair and stood up.

"Mrs. Revell, we are going to have a round of whist. Mrs. Loring and I will play you and—where is he? Yes! Major Southwait! Come along, the tables are in the parlor!" He gave an expansive wave of his arm. "Everyone come! We want an audience! You understand, Mrs. Revell, you are playing for high stakes! You must hope that Major Southwait is as fine a whist player as he is an officer. If you win, you are free!"

And if I lose? thought Abigail. But of course she would lose: she had learned the rudiments of the game years ago, but she had never liked it, had never played much. General Howe and Betsey Loring, on the other hand, were past masters of whist. Even with Southwait's help, she thought, she hardly had a chance against them.

She followed Howe, Mrs. Loring, and Major Southwait across the hall and into the parlor; half a dozen officers came along. The four players seated themselves, and then the general announced the rules of the game. As he spoke, Mrs. Loring, incapable of sitting still, picked up the pack of cards lying on the table. Swiftly and expertly her plump, beringed hands shuffled them.

"We shall play a single game of five points only," said Howe. And, with a stern look at Abigail: "You understand, Mrs. Revell. One point scored for every trick taken over six in each hand played. To eliminate the element of luck, we will not count points for high-card honors in each deal."

The first deal fell to Southwait. Mrs. Loring cut the cards for him after Howe shuffled. Over the soft slap-slap of the cards falling onto the polished mahogany surface of the table, the only sounds were the spatter of sleet against the windows, the murmur of the sea-coal fire in the hearth.

Southwait turned over the last card dealt—to himself—to establish trumps. It was the ace of hearts. He paused for a moment and glanced at Mrs. Loring. Abigail could not read the look on his face—thoughtful, quizzical, she did not know what.

In rapid little flurries they tossed their cards onto the table to play their tricks. In the course of the play, Abigail heard the general, obviously annoyed, make a small clucking sound, but the game was too swift and confusing for her to understand why.

At the end of the hand Major Southwait had seven tricks—the first point. As the general dealt the next round he admonished Mrs. Loring: "Second hand low, Betsey! Second hand low!"

"Ah, General, did I make a mistake?" Even seated at the card table, Mrs. Loring seemed constantly in motion: her hands fluttered, her head bobbed back and forth, a stream of ejaculations and giggles issued from her mouth. And yet, thought Abigail, she cannot be the fool she seems, for her eyes behind those swooping lashes were hard and observant, and her mouth had a cruel twist that no fool's mouth ever displayed.

"If you hadn't, my dear, the score would have been reversed."

"Oh, my dear general—don't *carp*!"

Abigail glanced at Major Southwait. His gaze was fixed upon Mrs. Loring.

They played another hand, and then another. The room was warm. Abigail felt faint. Several times she tossed out a card almost without thinking. Her fate dangled by this thread—the luck of the draw—and she felt powerless to change it. This is a double punishment, she thought, simply delaying her inevitable journey to the whipping post.

All this while, Mrs. Loring kept up her ceaseless chatter until at last, exasperated, Howe admonished her to silence: "Whist, Betsey! Whist!"

She widened her eyes at him and pursed up her lips into a little moue. "He is always so serious about his cards," she said to Southwait. "I cannot keep quiet, it is not in my nature. Ah, General—come, now, we will win! Was I not right? Isn't this more exciting than playing for money? See—we are ahead, four to three! Now we will finish it!"

Southwait dealt: spades were trumps. Abigail's heart sank. Her hand was very bad, with only four low trumps and one court card, the king of clubs, guarded by the two.

Southwait looked grim as he examined his hand; Howe, on the contrary, seemed very pleased with his. "Perhaps we should have counted honors, after all," he said as he rapidly led out the ace, king, and queen of spades, collecting all but the seven—did he have it?—and Abigail's eight.

Mrs. Loring, for a wonder, had fallen silent. The officers ringed the table, watching intently; if one or another of them was signaling, Abigail could not spot it.

Howe led a small club. Abigail faltered, nearly paralyzed by indecision. Her hand held little possibility for tricks, except for the eight of trumps. Impulsively, already feeling the lash upon her back, she threw down her king of clubs.

"Second hand low, Mrs. Revell," murmured Howe; he was smiling.

Too late, she realized her mistake, but then to her astonishment it was not a mistake after all. Her king won the trick: Mrs. Loring had no clubs.

Abigail did not know what to play next, and so she played her eight of trumps—the highest card remaining in her hand and her only sure trick; then at last she played her one small club.

Southwait took the trick with his ace.

Then he played his queen. The general played one of his two remaining clubs.

Abigail, having no more clubs, played a diamond. Mrs. Loring played a heart.

The trick was Southwait's.

Instantly Howe exploded. He jumped up, toppling his chair; he threw his remaining cards onto the table. His face suddenly flushed with anger, he roared, "You are free, Mrs. Revell!"

As he stalked out, his aides in his wake, Mrs. Loring rose, an unreadable expression on her face. "Excuse me," she murmured, and she, too, hurried away—to soothe the general's anger, perhaps, with a game more intimate than cards.

The denouement of the little drama had happened so quickly that Abigail was confused, hardly knowing how she had escaped Howe's sentence. She glanced at Southwait, who was looking at her thoughtfully.

"Why did General Howe throw in his cards?" she said.

"Because he realized that I held all the remaining clubs, and that therefore I would make our eight tricks—and the game. Remarkable, really, since neither you nor I held a single honor except in clubs."

Abigail tried to remember something that had happened at the beginning of the game. "The ace of hearts in the first hand—was that important?"

Southwick allowed himself a faint smile. "I think, rather, that it was a case of second hand high."

He made a little bow to her as he excused himself, and then he was gone.

And so to her surprise, all of a sudden, she was free. They did not even send a guard with her as she went home; they simply hustled her out of Province House and slammed the door behind her.

Free! She was trembling as she pulled her cloak around her against the raw wind. No lash upon her back, no searing pain. Down the walk, through the tall iron gate, down Marlborough Street toward School. Free!

A fine, stinging snow had begun to fall; after the oppressive warmth of General Howe's chambers, the flakes felt cool and soothing on her face. Few people were about; the town had the air of a place without life, without the usual hustle and bustle of a city. They were all waiting for Death, she thought, in whatever way he chose to come.

The snow thickened rapidly, so that by the time she reached the corner of Beacon Street, at King's Chapel, she could hardly see ten feet in front of her. A cadaverous horse pulled a cart; half a dozen soldiers trudged down the opposite side; otherwise she was alone. She was cold now, and not so much hungry as faint from lack of food: she had had only a mess of dried peas for breakfast, and that seemed many hours ago.

As she entered her house she heard men's voices from behind the closed doors of the dining room. She was glad that they were at their meal, that she would not have to face any of them. She went to the kitchen. At least, she thought, she could have a cup of hot water to drink, with a little lemon juice, perhaps.

Mrs. Brimstead greeted her with a cry of relief. "Oh, missus, I thought you was gone for good! Here, sit down, I was just bakin' with the flour you got, we'll have lovely bread out of it, I got a little yeast from Mr. Bowdoin's cook, I hope them bloodybacks don't take it all for themselves—"

"How is Philip?"

"He's better, missus. No fever today. I told him you'd be home soon, and that cheered him up. Have a bite, he's sleeping now, and then you'll feel better when you see him."

Abigail had just sat down at the large, scrubbed oak table in the center of the room when the door to the back garden opened and in came Nathaniel, covered with snow, his cheeks reddened with cold and his eyes red, too, she saw, as if he had been crying. Despite her having been gone for three days, he did not greet her. He stood just inside the door, his face a study in misery; then he advanced into the room and put what he carried onto the table.

It was a little heap of gray fur. Nathaniel bit his lips to keep in his sobs, but then his sorrow overcame him and he turned away, weeping.

"Oh, Nathaniel—" Instantly Abigail forgot her own difficulties; she went to him, she put her arms around him and held him fast as he wept.

"I didn't have anything for him to eat," said Nathaniel. "Just a few sweepings of hay from the barn. And he wouldn't eat those. And he was starving! I didn't have any acorns, or anything, and I couldn't stand to see him so hungry. And he wouldn't mind if we—if we—"

He could not say it—could not put into words what General Groundnut's fate was to be. But that evening, when Mrs. Brimstead served up squirrel pie for the family, Nathaniel did not eat one bite.

When Ben heard what Nathaniel had done, he gave the boy an approving clap on the shoulder. " 'Course it was hard," he said. "And you were a brave lad, a good lad to give 'em a meal. These are hard times, boy. An' your father'll be proud of you when I tell him what you did. It was the right thing. Well! Save the chain, an' I'll get you a monkey for it with the first ship I send out."

But while he put on a brave face for his grandson's sake, in private the old man was less sanguine. They were still only in the beginning of February; the winter had at least another six weeks to go. Food was scarcer than ever; the American privateers were doing a splendid job of intercepting British supply ships bound for Boston Harbor, but in that success lay hardship for the besieged town. And if there was little food for humans, there was almost none for animals. The next morning Ben went to the officer in charge of his house and asked him for the loan of a pistol. This, of course, the officer refused, as he was bound to do, but he did agree to send a man out the barn with Ben, and do as he asked; and so Ben said good-bye to his horses, poor starved creatures that they were, and stood by while the officer put a bullet through their eyes. The three carcasses were butchered and taken to the kitchen, and the household ate the horsemeat, tough and stringy, for the next four weeks.

The next day, Ben went to Abigail and suggested the same: keep the cow, he said, but tell an officer to kill your horses. They will starve before the siege is lifted; you might as well have the benefit of them now.

4

Before the siege is lifted . . . The old man had spoken confidently, out of his faith in his son and, by extension, in the American forces. He had no hard intelligence; he had no notion that even as he spoke, even as he steeled himself to endure one more day of occupation, of hunger and cold and constant worry—even then, help was coming.

Until the previous year, young Henry Knox had been the proprietor of the London Book Store near the South Church. He was a tall, fat young man, a great student of military strategy; he was fond of discussing military affairs with the British troops who patronized his store, but he was a patriot at heart. His wife was the daughter of a prominent Loyalist; she gave up a fortune to marry Henry, and the two of them escaped from Boston at the last possible moment, just after the Battle of Concord and Lexington, leaving everything behind including Henry's splendid uniform, designed by himself. His wife carried out his sword in her petticoats.

When the Vermonter Ethan Allan and his Green Mountain Boys captured the British cannon at Fort Ticonderoga, Knox went to General Washington with a daring proposal: I will take a company of men and bring those cannon to Boston, he said. They can do no good to us at Lake George; but in Boston they will help us drive out the enemy.

Washington did not believe that the thing could be done: tons of cannon dragged on sleds across hundreds of miles of wilderness in deep snow, the dead of winter—an unlikely prospect. But, having nothing to lose, he sent Knox on his way; and now Knox was coming. Already he and his men had crossed the Hudson, and had come a good part of the way into Massachusetts. The latest intelligence put him at Springfield. In every town along his way people cheered him: he was a great hero. Any day now he would arrive—an unbelievable feat of daring and skill and determination.

General Howe had news of Knox's progress, but the civilian population of

Boston did not. Every day a new rumor sprang up: Washington had signed the order to fire the town; Howe's reinforcements were on the high seas and would come in at any moment; the British had decided to fight their way out and burn the town behind them. Gaunt and hungry, frantic with worry and fear, the citizens of Boston, patriot and Loyalist alike, lived from day to day with the knowledge that as spring inexorably approached, their day of reckoning drew nearer; the end, when it came, would be harder than anything that had gone before.

5

One night Abigail dreamed that she and Ebenezer stood in a crowd on the Common, watching a celebration. An ox was roasting; people were laughing, singing, the war was over, the enemy vanquished. Heavy clouds of smoke drifted up, stinging her eyes. She moved away, but the smoke followed her. She felt as though she would smother. She began to run, but she could not escape.

She came awake. She smelled the smoke, not in her dream, but here in the quiet night.

She leaped out of bed, calling to the children. "Hurry—Thomas! Nathaniel! Get up! Fire!"

Fire was the most dreaded thing of all. Time and again fire had devastated the crowded little city of wooden houses, sweeping from rooftop to rooftop, destroying everything in its wake—"Philip! Get up!"

The night was bitter cold, the boys protesting. She scooped Roger up into her arms and made the others go out ahead of her, down the narrow stairs to the second floor. Thick smoke, choking, blinding—"Cover your nose and mouth!" she cried. "Hurry!" Down and down she went. She could not tell where the blaze had started, but then—yes—she saw as they came out into the second floor hall that below, the parlor doors were shut, and from beneath them came a steady stream of smoke. Just as she had always feared—drunken soldiers, an overturned candle, a spark from the fire—

Down the main staircase she went, shepherding Philip and Hannah, the older boys racing ahead. She heard the crackling of the flames from behind the doors, felt the heat— Hurry!

And now one of the men emerged from a room on the second floor. He came out rubbing his eyes, dazed from drink; then, as he realized what was happening, he raced to awaken the others. "Bingham! Townsend! Major South-wait! Come out—fire! *Fire!*"

Down and down—through the hall—out into the freezing night—Abigail had been so intent on getting out that she had not thought to try to save any of the family's possessions. Now, seeing that the children were all safe, she stood by the gate and looked back at the house. The windows at one side of the first floor were ablaze, and now the rooms above it, too, were belching flame. Everything would be lost—every family treasure. She heard one of the men order another to run to the fire company, but even if they arrived in an instant, they would be too late.

Suddenly, impulsively, Abigail thrust Roger into Thomas's arms. "Stay here!" she commanded. "Don't move from this spot!" She was aware that the neighbors were awake, the soldiers quartered on them running out, calling orders for a bucket brigade from the well. A bucket brigade would do little good; the fire was too far advanced.

Abigail ran up the snowy path to the house. She nearly collided with Major Southwait. He was trying to account for all his men, shouting out their names— "Bingham! Where is Bingham?"

She pushed past him and into the house. The fire had spread rapidly through the structure, so that now the ceiling of the dining room had caught, but the room itself was not yet ablaze. She caught at the arm of an officer just coming down, racing for the door. "Help me!" she cried. He paused and stared at her as if she had lost her wits, but she would not let him protest, she recruited him to help. "In here!" she cried. "Hurry!"

She pulled a chair to the mantel and, hoisting her nightdress, clambered up. The frame was heavy, the wire caught on the hook. Given strength by her desperation, she wrestled with it. At last it came free: Emilie Griffin Revell. "Take it out and come back," she cried. "I must get them both"—for how could she leave Ebenezer here to burn?

Panting and gasping, hardly able to breathe, she struggled with Ebenezer's portrait and got it down. Then she climbed down and began dragging it to the door. Major Southwait was in the hall. He stared at her as if she were a ghost, but then quickly he took the portrait from her and carried it out into the night.

The ceiling looked about to collapse. What else—what else could she save? She ran to the sideboard, flung open the doors, grabbed two pieces of heavy silver, and with one in each hand ran out just as the first burning timber collapsed into the room.

On the porch, Major Southwait was hurrying back into the house. He looked frantic—wild with fear. In the distance she heard the first clanging of the fire bells, and, from within, a crash as some portion of the house collapsed. The major grabbed her arm, pulled her down the steps. "You fool! What were you doing?" he yelled. No use to answer: she hardly knew herself.

The children huddled by the gate. Propped against the stone wall were the portraits, their images clearly visible in the light of the flames which now consumed the house from top to bottom—a roaring conflagration, impossible to halt.

In less than an hour the house was in ashes. Fortunately there was no wind, and so while cinders fell on neighboring structures, no other house caught fire. Abigail and the children spent the rest of the night at the Bowdoins', next door, and in the morning Ben came around at once. "I've had three more officers put on me in just this last week," he said, "but come along anyway. At least we'll all be together."

He walked to the window and peered out across the frozen garden, now littered with black ash and cinders, and peered at the still-smoking ruin of his son's house. A total loss. Too bad!—but there, it was not so bad after all. They had got out with their lives, that was the important thing. The house and everything in it could be replaced, not old Jedediah's silver, to be sure, but the walls and the roof, the clothing and the furniture—all of that would come again. When the war was over, when trade picked up, they'd make their fortune again. They had the boys and the boys would grow up in the Revell trade and make their fortune ten times over.

And—clever girl!—Abigail had saved the portraits!

6

By February 15 the last of Henry Knox's men had arrived in Cambridge with their ox-drawn carts carrying the captured cannon.

The next day General Washington met with his council of war and announced his plan. He stood before them, tall, stern, the very picture of what a commander-in-chief should be. He had visited Lechmere's Point, he said—a place in East Cambridge with only a narrow strip of water between it and the North End of Boston. The ice was frozen thick, a foot deep, at least. His generals knew that he had authority from Congress in Philadelphia to attack the city whenever he thought it expedient. Now, he said, now while we have the ice, we will march across from Lechmere's Point and take the besieged town before the thaw. General Howe has fortified the Neck so as to make it impassable, but over the ice, we will succeed. A stroke well aimed at this critical juncture might put a final end to the war.

His generals vetoed his plan unanimously. Too risky, they said. We would be slaughtered if we tried to attack from that direction.

Far better, they said, to deploy the cannon at our redoubts around Boston. We have intelligence that Howe will wait for his supply ships to come—not before April, and possibly May. A more daring commander would have taken Dorchester Heights long since, for to command the heights is to command the city and the harbor as well. But he will not do that; and now that we have the cannon, we can wait him out.

7

"The question is," said Ben, "why hasn't General Howe broken out? Why has he not taken Dorchester Heights, at least?"

"Perhaps he is waiting to be resupplied," said Abigail.

"Perhaps. Perhaps. But it doesn't make sense to me. No sense at all."

A bitter cold day, mid-February. Ben and Abigail had finished their meager dinner with the children, and now the two adults sat draped in blankets by the last of the dwindling fire, one slim log for the children's sake, now nearly gone.

The old man peered at her. Although the house was at this hour empty of its hated tenants, out of habit they spoke softly. Now he said, very quiet: "How's that sister of yours?"

She felt the sudden rush of embarrassment that always came when Betsey Loring was mentioned.

"I don't know."

"Haven't seen her since, ah, your little card game?"

"No."

"You know that General Howe is giving a masquerade ball tomorrow night?"

"Yes."

All of Boston knew it. To those citizens faithful to the American cause, such a thing was an insult. For months, all during the siege, they had watched as, every night, Howe engaged in card parties and plays, dances and concerts. Really, people said, the man is as frivolous as any woman! He was sent to wage war—on us, to be sure—and he does nothing but entertain himself.

"Strange, isn't it? The way he carries on? An experienced military man like that letting himself be bottled up here for all this time? You know"—and Ben leaned in closer and lowered his voice even more, although there was no one to hear them save his housekeeper, faithful servant for fifteen years, who would probably, if asked, have laid down her life for him—"you know, Abby, they say that young Knox has brought in the cannon from Ticonderoga. Hard to believe, isn't it? But if it's true! Now here's what I think. I think that if General Washington had been given his wish, he'd have wished just what happened: a good long time to get his army in shape. No movement by General Howe. A chance to bring in those cannon, eh?"

"What do you mean?" said Abigail. She knew that he was thinking out loud, trying to sort something out.

"I mean, there's been a lot of nasty talk about Mrs. Loring. No offense, y'understand. It's not your fault you are related to her. But perhaps we've been looking at her through the wrong end of the glass. Up close, I mean. But step back a little, turn the glass around, and what do you see?"

Abigail shook her head. What was he getting at?

"Why—you see a woman who has sacrificed her good name to do General Washington's work for him, that's what you see! Howe has done exactly what benefits the Americans the most—he has sat tight here, besotted with Mrs. Loring, not making a move, while Washington pulls the American forces together, gets his cannon—"

Abigail stared at him, too astonished to reply.

"Yes—think about it!" Ben laughed, delighted with his solution to the mystery of General Howe's passivity. "Now listen, m'dear. Here's what I'm going to do. I am going to get you an invite to that masquerade ball. Never mind how. Yes! And when you get there, I want you to have a word with your dear sister. Let's just see if she has one last thing to do f'r us. You go up to her and you say something like, 'Thank you.' See what she says in reply. See if she doesn't have some bit of information to give you. Abby, I'm convinced of it! Betsey Loring is working for the American side! And she's done a damned good job!"

8

The lights of Province House blazed from every window, and the sounds of music and laughter filtered out into the bitter February night as Abigail arrived at General William Howe's masquerade ball shortly after nine. Already the great mansion house was crowded with a glittering company: where, in these days of deprivation, had people gotten up such costumes? Abigail saw a Roman lady in a toga, and a red-haired Queen Elizabeth wearing a huge white ruff, and any number of would-be counts and countesses, dukes and duchesses, none identifiable as to their models, but all showing a fine display of distant, ancient, extravagant nobility.

General Howe himself, like many of his officers, wore the costume that he always wore: splendid scarlet coat, gleaming white breeches, a fine satin sash, and half a dozen medals. All the officers wore half masks like Abigail's, and many of the women did as well, so she did not feel out of place; a patriot woman, after all, did not carry a telltale birthmark, she did not wear horns. Abigail moved freely among the company, glad of her mask, at ease as she would not have been had every guest been identifiable. Even so, she thought she recognized a number of faces: people she had seen for years in Boston, people she had seen over the winter among the influx of Loyalists from the countryside.

The regimental band played with verve, pretty much in tune, and soon an officer asked her to dance. It had been a long time since she stood in the line of a reel; she was glad that she remembered the steps. In and out—change partners and curtsey—in and out again—why, this was fun! She had not had fun in a long time, an eternity, it seemed, and so when the music came to an end and another officer came to claim her, she was not sorry to accept. No one bothered with introductions; this was a masquerade, after all, and dancing with strangers was part of the excitement of such an affair.

She danced until she was ready to drop. Most of the guests did the same;

they had a fevered gaiety, as if they were dancing in the face of Death, to defy him. Even General Howe danced, once or twice; his partner was always a small, plump woman in an elaborately embroidered brocade dress and a white wig; her white jeweled half mask did nothing to hide her identity.

After a time Abigail retreated to the sidelines to catch her breath, but she kept on watching Betsey Loring. Certainly Howe doted on her; he never left her side, and the two were quite shameless in their fondling of each other, their open display of affection.

What if Ben had been right? What if Betsey Loring's purpose was something other than her own advancement? What if—

"Good evening, Mrs. Revell." An officer stood before her, a half mask covering the upper portion of his face—but of course she recognized him: Major Southwait. She had not seen him since the night of the fire.

"To what do we owe your presence here this evening?" he said. "Don't tell me you have switched sides?"

Laughing at her! She lifted her chin. "Whatever I do, it is none of your affair."

"Perhaps not. Nevertheless, I am glad to have this chance to say that—"

The band struck up again, and he leaned in to put his mouth close to her ear. "To say that I wish we had met in a different place. A different time, perhaps. I wish we had not met as enemies; I wish that you had not been married, and particularly to—"

Involuntarily she shook her head; she did not want to hear this.

He drew back; then without a further word he took her hand and led her out to the dance. She went along: no point in arguing with him now, not when he—when all of them—might be dead within the month.

Major Southwait left her after that one dance. He took her hand, lifted it to his lips, bowed over it as he kissed it—and then he went away, and she was astonished at the fact that she was sorry to see him go. He was the enemy personified, he had made her a prisoner, he had had her arrested and hauled in for questioning; and yet now that he was gone, she wished that she had said some gracious thing to him. Not a word of affection, for she had affection—love—only for her husband: but something, she did not know what—she could not sort it out.

An officer called for silence then, and General Howe made a little speech to thank them all for coming. Then prizes were given for the best costume. Queen Elizabeth won, and a man in full armor, and the winner of the lottery was given a bottle of French brandy. Supper was served: a bountiful feast, and where did they get the turkeys, and the roast of lamb, and the flour for baking all those pastries? Abigail had not seen such a spread since she couldn't remember when; she ate her fill and washed down her food with several cups of punch.

At last it was time to go; but she could not go, not yet, not until she had spoken to Betsey Loring. She looked around, afraid that she had missed her, that Mrs. Loring had taken the general off to bed; and then she saw her, deep in conversation with a man in civilian clothes.

She approached; she caught Mrs. Loring's eye. Suddenly she was afraid: surely this was unwise? But it was too late; Mrs. Loring had disengaged herself, had turned with a slightly tipsy smile to Abigail, whom she recognized at once.

"How lovely you look tonight, dear Abigail," she said. "No, don't worry. I will not betray you. Have you enjoyed yourself? I saw you dancing with Major Southwait. Such a handsome man. Well? What is it? If you want to bid me good-bye you had better do it now, for God only knows—" She broke off; then, always nimble-footed, she recovered at once. "I won't kiss you farewell. We don't want to draw attention to ourselves, now do we? So I hope that you survive, and perhaps we shall see each other again. If not in this world, then in the next."

"Wait!" For Mrs. Loring had turned away, and Abigail put a hand on her arm to detain her. "I wanted—I have a message for you."

"A message? What is it? From whom?"

"He is—an admirer. He believes that you are a true friend. He said, 'Thank you for your help.' "

Mrs. Loring's bright blue eyes stared out from her domino. They were steady, unblinking; Abigail could not read their expression.

"I will not ask you who he is," said Mrs. Loring, "but I have a good idea. He is an American, is he not?"

"Yes."

"So am I." Mrs. Loring's voice was light, pleasant—entirely impersonal. "You may tell him that I have always had one rule in life, and that is to enjoy myself." The exquisite lips curved into a little smile. "And if I can serve some higher purpose at the same time—all the better! So my advice to him is this: he must look to the heights." She had taken Abigail's hand, and now she held it in her own and squeezed it so hard that Abigail had to press her lips together to keep from crying out. "Did you hear that?" hissed Mrs. Loring. "He must look to the heights! That is what I have to tell you. The heights!"

9

"The heights!" said Ben. In the light of the wavering candle that she had carried to his cubbyhole to awaken him with her news, his lined, weatherbeaten face glowed with sudden understanding. "I knew it! That's what it is, dear girl, that's what it is! Howe isn't waiting for the supply ships! He's goin' to fortify Dorchester Heights! And that splendid sister of yours gave us the word so that we can get it out to General Washington, and he can get there first! By cracky, she's one fine woman, she is!"

First thing the next morning, after the quartered troops departed for their day's duty, Ben set off. "I know someone who can get this word out, he's been back an' forth all winter bringing in goods for market. 'Course I won't tell him where I got it. But he'll pass it along, for certain."

Abigail watched him go, a tall, thin old man only slightly bent with age, not watching his step on the ice, slipping, righting himself before he fell, so obviously in a hurry on an important errand that the patrol might stop him just for that—for hurrying.

In half an hour he was back, and before he could say a word, she could see that he was crestfallen—defeated.

"Gone!" he said, slumping into the single chair in the room that she shared with the children. They huddled on the bed, listening, all save Thomas and Nathaniel, the big boys, who sat on the floor. Everyone was shivering, for they had no fire.

Ben was so downcast that he spoke freely, not minding that the children overheard. "His wife hasn't seen him in a week, not since the last time he went out. He never came back."

"Is there no one else?" said Abigail.

"Probably there is. I've got to find him, that's all. And that might take time. And time is what we don't have. Unless I miss my guess, General Washington will want to have that information you got, and he'll want it right away. No time to lose! Especially now! This has been the threat all winter, d'y'see? That Howe would move to take the heights—that he would move to do *something* instead of just sittin' here warm an' cozy. And now we know. We know for sure. And we've got to get the word out so th'Americans can move before he does. If Washington gets beat here, he's beaten for good. Well, let me think. There's bound to be someone who can be trusted, who can get out without raising suspicion."

But later that day, when he went to find a man who had been recommended to him, he discovered that the British had stopped all traffic back and forth across the Neck. "Completely!" he said to Abigail. It was a raw February dusk, just candlelight. Weary and discouraged, Ben sat at the kitchen table with Abigail and the two older boys. From the dining room they heard the raucous laughter of their hated boarders. "So there it is," Ben went on. "I found someone who ordinarily might be able to get through with no questions asked—and who might be trusted. But as of today, the damned lobsters have shut us down. That means Mrs. Loring's information was correct, if y'ask me. Something's up. Damn! If only we could get out the word!"

"Grandfather." It was Thomas who spoke: a rangy lad of fourteen with the Family looks, high forehead and long jaw and prominent nose, deep-set eyes. "I can go, Grandfather."

"What?" The old man thought that he must not have heard correctly. "What did you say, Thomas?"

"I said, I can go."

"What? To General Washington?" Ben snorted in annoyance. "Now how could you get through the guards and the fortifications down on the Neck, if the regular travelers who know the ropes can't get through? I'm telling you, they've shut us down. Tight as a drum, we are. They're not even letting in food nor livestock. We'll all be starving soon, if it keeps up."

"I wouldn't go by the Neck."

"Oh? And how would you go, pray? You couldn't swim in this cold, and besides, everything's froze solid—"

"That's right," said Thomas. He had spoken almost without thinking, but now as he considered the prospect, his voice quickened with excitement. "Everything *is* frozen, Grandfather. And that means—remember the ice skates Mr. MacLeish brought you from Edinburgh two years ago? I learned to skate pretty well that first winter we had them. I could get across somewhere."

There was a brief silence while Ben digested his proposal. Then: "No. Absolutely not. No grandson of mine is going to risk his life—"

"Grandfather! Listen to me! You said yourself that this is vital information for General Washington! You have spent all day trying to find someone to take it out! Well, I will do it! I can get out! I know I can! And wherever I get to, I will just ask them to take me to Father. He is in Watertown with the Legislature, is he not? And if Father vouches for me, they will know I am telling the truth."

Abigail felt her heart beating heavily. No, she thought. Not another child put in danger of his life!

"No!" For a moment Ben forgot where he was; his voice sounded very loud in the sudden silence, and his fist came pounding down on the tabletop like an artillery shell.

Without a word Thomas got up and went out before either adult could stop him. After a moment Nathaniel followed him.

"Damned young fool!" said Ben. "That's what I get for blabbing in front of him. Never thought he'd want to try it himself, but I should have known. D'you want to know where he's gone? He's gone to get those skates, that's what. He knows just where I keep 'em. But he won't find 'em this time, because I hid 'em to keep the lobsters from finding them!"

And he moved to stand up himself, wincing at his creaky knees. "Well, well. Never thought I'd see the day—"

"What are you going to do, Father-in-Law?"

"Do? Why, what can I do with a lad as stubborn as that? I'm going to sharpen those skates, that's what! They haven't been used since I don't know when. And I'll have to be quiet about it, won't I? So as not to disturb our house guests. And tomorrow we'll make our move."

10

The next afternoon Ben and Thomas made their way through the narrow streets and alleyways and back gardens of the town, evading the patrols. Ben wore his battered tricorn hat and his old dark blue woollen cloak, beneath which he carried the freshly sharpened skates and his telescope. The day was cloudy and cold, bitter cold as it had been for days.

"Not far now," said Ben as they emerged onto Essex Street. He glanced at the thin, drawn face of the lad beside him. Thomas was nearly as tall as the old man, and not through growing yet. "Are y'all right?"

"Yes, Grandfather."

"Warm enough?"

"Yes."

"If you change your mind, no harm done. This is a man's job, and no one'll think the worse of you if you don't want to do it."

"I will not change my mind, Grandfather."

They came to Beach Street, at the far end of the shallow bay beyond Windmill Point. They saw a band of redcoats passing, and they sheltered behind a shed until the way was clear. Then, freezing, they made for the house of the carpenter Israel Jones, where Mrs. Jones let them in and gave them a cup of hot flip and a chance to warm a bit by the fire.

"Thanks, mistress," said Ben. "Your man's working?"

Mrs. Jones shrugged. "He's out, Master Revell. He don't tell me where he goes, and it's just as well. These days, a body can know too much."

Ben nodded. "Indeed. Now we'll be off for a bit, and then we'll be back. We'll take a bite of something later if you have it about, thank you kindly." Jones had worked for the Revells for years, when there was work to be had, and Ben did not doubt either his loyalty or his wife's—to the Revells, not to the King.

He and Thomas went out again, the day colder than ever, a biting, withering, breath-taking cold that gripped a man and would not let him go. With a careful glance to make sure that no troops were about, they slipped across the road and made their way down to the frozen marsh along the shore. To be less conspicuous against the skyline, they sat beside a large boulder while Ben gave his grandson the lay of the land—and of the frozen expanse across which he would have to make his way.

"Here, Thomas. Take the telescope." Ben handed it over after squinting a look. "You see the place you're heading for? You can see it with the naked eye, but I wanted you to see it clearer in the glass. That's the Shirley-Eustis house. William Shirley was the governor, 'way back, and he built it. Then Eustis came into it, and he's a Loyalist, so the Americans commandeered it. They're using it as a barracks. You just get there and ask for your father, and you'll be right as rain.

"Now here's how you go. You set off here and you move easy along the shore, no need to rush. Go slow and go quiet. Stay bent over as much as you can. The old Gibbons shipyard is just down there on your right, you'll be heading due south and it'll be southwest. When you get past that wharf, you'll see the fortifications on the Neck and you'll have to go left, get out into the middle of the bay. Gallows Bay, we call it—ha! Get out into the middle and straighten up and go as fast as you can. If they're going to get you, it'll be at that point. Two things can happen: either they'll chase you on foot, in which case you'll get away easy, or they'll start shooting. If they do that, you start to weave—eight or nine strides one way, eight or nine the other. They won't hit you, not a chance in a thousand. Y'see Nook's Hill there opposite, keep it on your left, on your port side, and as you get down the bay it'll fall behind you. All right? It's only a little over a mile, and I'll be watching you all the way. Mind the brook that enters the bay just there at the far end, there may be open water near it."

"And when I get to the Americans—"

"Just ask for your father, lad! And tell him that General Howe's going to move on the heights. That's the message: General Howe is going to the heights! They'll know what it means."

Thomas nodded. "All right."

Suddenly Ben turned and gripped the boy by the arm. "Are you sure, Thomas?"

"Yes, sir."

"All right." Ben looked deep into the boy's eyes for a moment, and then clapped him on the shoulder. "Now let's go back to Mrs. Jones's and warm ourselves and get a bit of food into us. We'll come back when it's well dark and they're near the end of their watch out there on the Neck. They'll be tired and cold, not as sharp as they should be."

At ten o'clock that night, having eaten and warmed themselves and rested awhile, Ben and Thomas crept down to the shore again. Ben peered at the landscape while Thomas strapped on the freshly sharpened skates. When he had finished, he touched Ben's arm.

"What is it, Thomas?"

"What will happen to you, Grandfather? It is after curfew. How will you get home?"

"Don't worry about me. I know this town like the back of my hand. I'll sneak back easy enough. I know a dozen secret ways if I have to use 'em. If I have trouble, it'll be at my own front door."

Reassured, Thomas got to his feet and took a moment to balance himself; he had not skated in over a year. Then suddenly, impulsively, he and the old man embraced; when they drew apart, Ben was unable to see for a moment through his tears.

"Good-bye, Grandfather!" whispered Thomas; and then he was gone, swooping silently across the frozen surface, frozen at least a foot thick in this bitter winter, no danger of falling through, and Ben wiped his eyes and took up the glass to follow Thomas's progress. Damned if that boy wasn't the bravest boy in Christendom, he thought—with pride, with an apprehension that he had not let Thomas see.

He stood on the shore, watching, watching, muttering a silent continuous prayer to God to keep the boy safe, to keep him alive. Yes, there he was, that dark skimming shadow moving easily and quietly—ah!

He saw the flash from the shore, heard the report. They had seen him! Had fired at him! Ah, dear God, what had he done, sending this precious boy on this errand; he should have locked him up in the attic—and there it was again, the deadly flash, the report—

His knees went weak, his hands were trembling so that he could hardly hold the telescope. Firing at the boy! But hadn't got him—a dark night, a cloudy night, far safer than bright moonlight but hard to see—ah, there he was! The shape nearly flying now, faster and faster, weaving back and forth—good boy! He wanted to shout, he wanted to yell as loud as he could—hurry! Hurry! But of course he could not. And so he bit his lips in an agony of fear and peered through his glass, searched the white wasteland of ice, damn he'd lost him, but at least the bloodybacks had lost him, too, no more shots came—yes, there he was, far down the bay now, a small moving dark spot, well away from danger. He would do it; he was safe.

11

Saturday, March 2. Ben and Abigail were gathered that night in the kitchen with the children, to take their meager supper. It was bitter cold; all of them were shivering, and the twins had the sniffles and a bad cough. Thomas had been gone for nearly two weeks. Ben was telling them stories to cheer them up, talking of his youth.

"Oh, yes, I had my run-ins with pirates. Why, I remember one time we were just a day out of St. Kitts—"

CRASH!

A thunderous explosion, close by—"The attack!" cried Ben. He held up his hand, but he hardly needed to motion them to silence, for they were stunned by that first tremendous explosion and then, in rapid succession, by a barrage of artillery shells coming fast and thick.

"What is it, Grandfather?" said Nathaniel, raising his voice to be heard.

"It's the Americans! They've begun the attack at last! *There!*" And they jumped, startled as a shell landed close, nearly on the house by the sound of it. The earth shook, the crockery rattled on the shelves—

There—and *there*—and *there*— Nathaniel and the twins hurried to the windows; they could see the night sky alight with fires, and now amid the din they could hear the warning sound of fire bells, men shouting, women screaming.

Abigail met the old man's eyes. "You were right," she said. "Thomas got through, just as you said."

"He certainly did!" cried Ben. "Bless him! Safe and sound, told 'em what they needed to know!"

Little Roger, frightened, had started to cry, and Philip clung to his mother's skirts in terror. Hannah and the twins sat cowed, eyes wide, watching the grown-ups for direction. If we panic, thought Abigail, so will they; she tried to throw them a reassuring smile, but the sound of shattering glass not far away wiped it from her face.

"And now?" she said to Ben.

"And now—I'd wager it's just a matter of time before we see the real battle begin!"

The British returned fire that night, but General Howe did not order an attack. On both sides guns went on firing. At dawn, out of respect for the Sabbath, they stopped. When darkness came they began again.

That night, Sunday night, Howe sat at cards with Betsey Loring and two of his officers. At other tables around the room sat other couples, equally gay, equally drunk. They were all very noisy. Still, they heard the guns, they heard the crash and explosion in the streets as the shells slammed into the town.

Howe was determined to ignore the noise outside; his officers, therefore, ignored it also. Gamely they played on.

12

The following night two thousand American troops walked silently out onto Dorchester Neck and up onto the fog-shrouded heights. Behind them came ox-drawn carts bearing picks and shovels, and fascines—bundles of sticks—and gabions—wicker baskets filled with earth and stones—and the larger, cumbersome chandeliers, wooden frameworks in which to stack the fascines.

Major General Richard Gridley, the senior engineer of the American forces, commanded the expedition. As the first men arrived, he directed them where to dig. The ground was frozen, but the men set to work with a will. Any noise they made was covered by unrelenting cannon thunder. Soon the outlines of the entrenchment began to take shape.

Toward midnight they had a trench line two hundred feet long; they began to fortify it on the Boston side with the chandeliers which they covered with earth that soon froze into a solid wall.

Occasionally they could see a streak of flame that marked the path of a bursting shell; otherwise they worked in a thick white blanket of fog. They were grateful for it; they thought that it had been sent by God to protect them from being spotted by the British.

General Gridley stayed with them all night; even as some of the exhausted men were sent out and fresh troops came in, he stood by, overseeing them, encouraging them: "Good lads, you'll have a surprise for 'em in the morning, sure enough!"

At dawn the next day—March 5, 1776, the sixth anniversary of the Boston Massacre—a British sentry looked out across the Dorchester Flats. A strong wind had blown away the previous night's fog, and now he saw what had not been there the day before: an entrenchment more than two hundred feet long across the top of Dorchester Heights.

Word was sent at once to General Howe. Still groggy as he was every morning, he got up from Betsey Loring's embrace, threw on his clothes and went to see for himself.

Damme!

An enormous fortification, the work of many thousands of men. How had they done it?

And now at last he was forced to do what many people said he should have done months before: he ordered an attack, for if he did not, if he sat tight, the Americans would destroy him and all his troops, and his name would go down as one of the most bungling, one of the most cowardly commanders in the history of the British army.

He ordered Major Percy to take two thousand men in transport boats to Castle William and from there to land an attack force on the heights.

Major Percy set out. But the wind was blowing hard, rain pelted down, and his boats were nearly swamped. The men could not land at the Castle, much less get across to Dorchester.

Howe called off the attack. They would try again the next morning.

But the next morning the storm increased: a veritable hurricane, it was, even so early in the year. Gales of wind, torrents of rain—never in memory had there been such a storm.

The Americans in their trenches waited and prayed. God had sent the fog to help them; now He was sending this storm. While they prayed, they worked, fortifying their position. By the third day, when the storm began to die down, they were so firmly entrenched that Howe knew he was beaten. He remembered Bunker Hill; he knew that he could never take the heights now.

And so he sent out a different order instead: prepare to evacuate.

13

"You're not going to try to see her?" said Ben.

"No."

"She may never come back."

"I understand that. But she will be frantic, trying to get ready to leave on such short notice. Even if I went to her, she would probably turn me away." Abigail started as a shell landed nearby with a terrific thump. For days now the cannons had been firing, but still she flinched every time a strike came near, she couldn't help it.

They spoke, of course, of her half sister Betsey—the notorious Mrs. Loring whose name by this time, after a winter of openly living with General Howe, was the byword among all the patriots in America for traitorous debauchery. People despised her; worse, they mocked her—and the general as well:

> Sir William, he, snug as a flea
> Lay all this time a-snoring
> Nor dreamed of harm as he lay warm
> In bed with Mrs.——

Now it was at an end: the long bitter winter, the scandal, the siege. The hated interlopers were leaving, and whether they or their unwilling hosts were more relieved, no one could have said.

Since the moment Howe gave the order to evacuate, the town had been crawling with looters. Every soldier wanted a souvenir of Boston, it seemed, and now in the rising panic to flee, no one watched very closely as houses were broken into, warehouses ransacked, goods carried away into the ships that would take them—where? Halifax, people said; we are going to Halifax.

Halifax?

No one wanted to go there. A few Anglophiles wanted to go to London; a few people wanted New York. No one wanted Halifax.

Ben had promised to look after the property of some merchant friends who had left the city when it was still possible to do so. Now those houses and warehouses were in danger: furniture, silver, paintings, clothing, pipes of wine, stocks of cloth and spices and ironware stored by the docks—everything was in danger of being taken. Ben had hired men to guard each place, offering to pay them the outrageous sum of two dollars a day. "But they're not dependable," he said. "They'll take a bribe in a minute and look the other way while some lobster steals what he pleases."

General Howe issued an order forbidding looting, but no one paid any attention. He issued a new order, therefore, announcing that anyone caught in the act of stealing would be hanged on the spot. As usual, he was too late to prevent a good deal of the damage; one warship loaded with stolen goods actually set out for Halifax, but to the delight of the Americans whose possessions she carried, she was captured by an American privateer and returned to Boston.

One day Ben and Abigail and the older children walked down to watch the Loyalists board the ships awaiting at anchor in the harbor. It was a gray day, raw with the promise of snow. In an attempt to keep order in the face of the rising panic, General Howe had ordered a number of troops into the streets. They stood at attention, their faces expressionless as they watched the citizens of Boston loyal to the King scurrying to make ready to depart. For the first time, Abigail realized that soon the soldiers would be gone. She had grown so used to seeing the hated bloodybacks that she could hardly imagine Boston without them.

They came to Long Wharf, where a number of people waited to clamber into one of the skiffs that were ferrying passengers to the ships; their voices were sharp with panic as they called to each other to hurry.

Standing nearby but a little apart from the others was a woman in a dark gray hooded cloak; with her was an enlisted man trying to load several trunks into a small boat. She turned to give him an order, and Abigail, squinting, saw

who she was: Mrs. Loring. Neither woman spoke. Then Betsey lifted her chin—
a prideful gesture, even arrogant; after a long moment she turned away. The soldier
attending her handed her down into the boat amidst her luggage—far more than
the ordinary allotment—and the oarsmen began to row her to the *Minerva*.

Ben followed Abigail's gaze. "Ah, yes," he said. "She's making sure she
gets away safe. She'd better!" He saw a tear spill down Abigail's face, and then
another. She fished for her handkerchief and wiped them away.

"Don't cry, Abby," he said. "She'll be a great success in London—if she
ever gets there!"

14

On the morning of Sunday, March 17—St. Patrick's Day—the last British troops
stood at attention on Long Wharf prepared to board their transports. A few
citizens of Boston gathered to watch them; the crowd was quiet, and for once
no one catcalled or threw snowballs. But then, as the last scarlet uniform climbed
into the last boat, a ragged little cheer went up. Huzzah! The back of them, at
last! The soldiers stayed impassive, as happy to leave as the Bostonians were to
get rid of them.

The fleet dropped down to the Nantasket Roads, but then it went no farther. The Americans grew worried: what were the British waiting for? Did
Howe have some trick up his sleeve?

No matter. The town of Boston was free—delivered from the enemy. As
the American troops rode in over the Neck, they saw the way littered with
caltrops—vicious iron things, balls with spikes all around so that no matter
which way they lay, a spike protruded to pierce the foot of man or beast
unlucky enough to step on it. And on Bunker Hill the British left straw men—
uniformed dummies propped up to look like real soldiers, to fool the Americans
into thinking that some troops remained.

On March 20, while the fleet still lay off the coast, Washington and his
men came into the town. In the days that followed, those Americans who had
fled, or those who had been trapped outside even as others were trapped within,
began to come back. They walked the streets as they would have walked a
battlefield, looking for casualties: so much damage done, houses torn down,
possessions looted, animals starved or butchered—and South Church desecrated!
The Liberty Tree gone! The Common torn to pieces!

Permission was given to take whatever was needed—or wanted—from abandoned Loyalist property, and so now the looting went the other way, and many
Americans made up for what they had lost as they helped themselves to good
pickings.

Shortly before noon on a bright, mild day not long after, Abigail was in the kitchen with Mrs. Brimstead when she heard the front door open and slam shut. For one bad moment she thought that she was back in the winter, and that a British soldier had just come in. But then she remembered that the British had gone. Then who?

She heard a step in the hall—a familiar step, even though she had not heard it for so long. Hurriedly she wiped her hands and went out. All in a moment— and then her heart gave a great leap, and she flew to him, she rushed into his arms. His face was alight with joy, and he felt tears sting his eyes as he enfolded her. Laughing, crying—

"Ah, my dearest, my dearest—you are safe! Thank God, thank God!"

She could say nothing. She held him fast, her face buried in his neck, and felt his strong arms holding her as she had so often imagined over the last terrible months. Home! She could not believe it. And safe!

She pulled back; she held his face between her hands and stared and stared at him. Safe—but how tired he looked, how much older, silver in his hair, his face lined as it had not been when she saw him last, a year ago now—an age.

"John did not come," he said, answering her question before she could ask it. "General Washington allowed only those people who have had the smallpox, or who have been inoculated. But John is safe and well at Watertown. You will see him soon, and Thomas as well. What splendid boys they are!"

And then he embraced her again, and then the children came running, and old Benjamin, too; and when Thomas and John came in together at the beginning of April, no family in Boston had a happier reunion than the family of Abigail and Ebenezer Revell.

Thomas carried with him a letter that was to be his most treasured possession; when he showed it to them, old Ben glowed with pride. "You see! We were right! Here, Ebenezer, see for yourself!"

And Ebenezer took the neatly written sheet and read:

Cambridge, 31st March 1776

Dear Sir

I could not depart this Camp without paying you the Tribute of a Letter. My thanks are due, and sincerely offered to you, for the infinite Service rendered to your Country. Your Enterprizing & daring feat accomplished on the night of 20th Ulto brought information of great Import for our Army & hastened in a timely Fashion our preparations for taking possession of Dorchester Heights and Nook's Hill, so as to anticipate a similar Action by the Enemy.

Your Virtuous effort in the cause of Liberty brings Honour to yourself and to your father Ebenezer Revell & to the Town of Boston.

That the Almighty may preserve & prosper you and your family is the sincere & fervent wish of Dr Sir Yr Most Obedt & Affecte H: Servt

Go: Washington

15

And so, all of a sudden, the British were gone—from Boston, at least. Eventually the French came in on the American side, thanks in large part to the efforts of Benjamin Franklin, a native son of Boston who had left her long ago. On a bright September day in 1778 the French fleet sailed into Boston Harbor. No one knew what to expect. For a hundred and fifty years New Englanders had been taught to hate and fear the French, but now, it seemed, the French were valued allies. The Bostonians gaped and gawked at them as they marched through the streets in their splendid uniforms, more splendid even than the British. Some people believed that all Catholics had horns; some believed that the footfall of even one French boot would contaminate the pure Massachusetts soil. The people of Boston were amazed: such elegant gentlemen, such charm—and they were even gentlemen enough not to laugh when the Bostonians tried to get their tongues around those strange French sounds.

Naturally the French brought their own chefs, their own bakers. The Bostonians hadn't seen good white bread in an age; they were starving for it. The French set up a bakery—for themselves. Some Bostonians tried to buy some of the long, fragrant loaves coming out of the bakers' oven. *Non—non, messieurs, mesdames!*

The Bostonians, notoriously cantankerous, insisted: sell us your bread! *Mais non—c'est impossible!*

In time-honored fashion, the Bostonians started a riot—right there in front of the bakery. To the horror of all concerned, a Frenchman was killed: the Chevalier de Saint-Sauveur, a son of the nobility.

The affair was hushed up: no one wanted a breach in the new alliance simply because some Bostonians lacked the good manners of the French. In the dead of night a little party accompanied the body into the catacombs of King's Chapel, and there a Franciscan monk said the burial mass—the first mass ever said in Massachusetts.

In an effort to repair relations, the merchant Benjamin Revell invited the admiral, Count d'Estaing, and some of his officers to dinner. The old man had observed the French closely in their brief time in Boston; he was sure he knew what they liked, and he intended to give it to them. But he kept the menu a secret between himself and his cook; not even his daughter-in-law knew what was to be served. As the company seated themselves at Ben's table, the soup tureen was brought in. Abigail watched as Ben began to ladle the soup into bowls which were handed around. He looked very pleased with himself, she thought; he was proud that an American could offer a good meal to those notorious high livers, the French.

The admiral put his spoon into his soup to taste it. Something moved. The admiral put down his spoon, peered closely at what was in front of him, and then, ever so delicately, put thumb and forefinger into his soup plate and pulled out—a frog! *Mon dieu!* By now the other guests had been served, and they, too, examined their plates. One by one each person reached in, found his *gren-ouille*, and held it up. The admiral started to laugh; everyone joined in, even Abigail. She couldn't help it. Frogs! How delicious! They laughed and laughed until their sides ached, until they could not have swallowed a mouthful of—frog soup!

Ben was bewildered. What were they laughing at? He had seen the Frenchmen lurking around the Frog Pond on the Common with a greedy look in their eyes. He had wanted his guests to have the delicacy they prized most highly, and so that very morning he had sent his servants at dawn into the marshes of Cambridge to catch better frogs than lived on Boston Common. What was so funny about that?

Damned foreigners!

16

When Ebenezer returned that day in March 1776, he stayed just long enough to help his father fit out two privateers with good, dependable captains, obtain their letters-of-marque, and send them on their way. Trade was impossible, what with the British blockade, and so the merchants of Boston and Salem and Newburyport—and every other American port, for that matter—survived as best they could by preying on enemy shipping.

Then he was gone again—to the south, where the war was. War was bad for business: let us fight this one—and win it, certainly—and get on with our trade! From time to time he managed to get home again, sometimes to welcome a new member of the family, a new infant: Abigail bore six more children to him, and three of them lived.

And so he missed those famous Frenchmen, and he missed, too, the day when Colonel Thomas Crafts stepped onto the little balcony of the State House and read to an expectant throng the Declaration of Independence just arrived from Philadelphia. John Hancock had signed it with an outrageously large signature—"So His Majesty can read it!" he said. But that was Hancock for you: if ever a man had a high opinion of himself, it was John Hancock of Beacon Hill. When General Washington came to Boston in 1789—President Washington then, he was—John Hancock, the governor of Massachusetts, refused to call on him. It was a matter of seniority, he said. Washington should call on me. But his advisors persuaded him that he really must defer to the President, and so, later in the day, Hancock had himself carried in to Washington's presence with a red cloth wrapped around his leg: his gout, he said, prevented his walking. He was sure that Washington would understand.

Washington cast a cold eye on him. Everyone knew that Bostonians lacked manners, that they were sharp-trading Yankees with no notion of how to live the gracious life enjoyed by southerners.

Nevertheless, the two men settled their differences and reminisced a bit about the old days, when Washington had been camped in Cambridge and General Clinton had "protected" Hancock's mansion. And after all, Hancock had done his bit—more than that—to persuade Massachusetts to ratify the Constitution.

They had had a scare a few years before, when a farmer in the Connecticut Valley, Daniel Shays, deeply distressed by debt, asked the new government to forgive his obligations—and, indeed, those of all farmers. Further, he wanted to halt all foreclosures on farmers, he wanted paper money instead of hard coin, and he demanded the abolition of imprisonment for debt. He was a veteran of the late war, he said, and so he deserved special treatment. To make his point, he and a band of followers seized the arsenal at Springfield.

Old Ben was outraged. "Veteran! Lots of folks are veterans, my son Ebenezer among 'em! His trade was ruined by the war! What about that, eh?"

The militia put down Shays' Rebellion, but the episode lingered in the minds of the wealthy classes who lived mostly along the seacoast. Every man of them had risked his life, his fortune, and his sacred honor to engage in the struggle against the British. Now were they to be threatened by an upcountry rabble demanding their so-called "rights"? And in any case, who had the idea of giving such men the vote? Better watch out, or they will take over the state some day!

They needed a strong federal Constitution. The Federation of the United Colonies could not work.

And so when the Convention at Philadelphia sent up just such a document, Ben and Ebenezer argued mightily in favor of it. The farmers—the men from the western towns, Shays' men—were suspicious of any agreement so strongly supported by the wealthy classes, and so they argued against it.

In Boston, all that winter of 1788, men gathered every night at hospitable houses to continue the ratifying debates begun during the day. Many gravitated to Ebenezer Revell's house, where a blazing hearthfire and a seemingly bottomless punch bowl filled with hot flip awaited them.

"Ratify?" said Ebenezer. "Of course we must ratify. We must make a new country. We are not that—not yet. Why did we fight the war if we didn't intend to have a new nation—our own country, not some monarch's province!"

"No," said a grizzled, weatherbeaten man from Amherst. "I can't vote for it, sir. It gives the national Congress the power to tax, and as we very well know, the power to tax is the power to destroy. We can't let the national Congress set our taxes."

"And a six-year term for senator?" said another westerner. "Why, they will forget whom they serve. They will grow fat with power, and forget that they derive that power from the consent of the people—from us!"

All around the table men nodded slowly as they considered this point. Yes: it was a good one. They would be exchanging one tyranny for another.

At last, day after day, night after night, the men in favor of ratification saw that if they wanted the farmers and country men to vote aye, some reassurance would have to be given them that the power of the new government would be at least somewhat restricted. And so those two old revolutionaries, John Hancock and Samuel Adams, decided to offer certain amendments, not to the document before them, but points to be considered by the first Congress.

For instance: an amendment to guarantee the free exercise of religion.

And a free press.

And the right to bear arms.

And freedom from unreasonable search and seizure. Remember the Writs of Assistance? The farmers might not remember, but the merchants of Boston and Salem certainly did—the knock on the door at midnight, the forced entry, no protection from the King's lackeys save one's own strength and ingenuity.

The delegates nodded agreement; the westerners approved of what Samuel Adams said, and the Boston men marveled once again, as they had in the old days, at his mastery of the art of politics—a mastery which now as always served them so well.

And so they voted to approve; and because Massachusetts voted aye, New York and Virginia did also. And their votes meant that other states followed, and the document was adopted, and the United States of America was born.

Any person who was male, and white, and over twenty-one, and had a certain amount of property, could be an enfranchised citizen. Even some black men were citizens, legally free now that a court had abolished slavery in Massachusetts.

Mrs. John Adams had a thought about the new Constitution which she communicated to her husband: "Remember the ladies, for all men would be tyrants if they could."

He thought it was a ridiculous suggestion, and so he ignored it.

17

"Thomas? To China?" said Abigail. "But how can he do that?"

"In the *Columbia*, of course," said Ebenezer: a grand new ship built on the North River at Scituate. He lifted his glass in a toast to Abigail and to the *Columbia* as well, swallowed the last of his Madeira—a good shipment, it had been, and about time, too—and pushed his chair back from the table. It was four o'clock of a brilliant August afternoon; he had plenty of time yet for a brisk walk down to the wharf. He had spent the morning there, but now he wanted to visit the ship again, to have a chat with her master. Soon the *Columbia* would make the voyage of a lifetime, and she fascinated him; he could not keep away from her.

In the decade since the war for independence was won, the Revells, like every other merchant in the new republic, had seen their shipping revive only very slowly. All British ports were off limits; on the other hand, European wars made commerce with the combatants profitable—when the ships were not captured; and the Barbary pirates in the Mediterranean were an increasing menace, capturing American crews and selling them into slavery in Tunis and Algiers.

So canny merchants hungry for profits had had to look elsewhere to trade, and now they had found their place: the East. For centuries the riches of the Indies, of Cathay, had glittered in white man's dreams, and in fact the Dutch, the English, the Portuguese had for decades traded there with immense profit. And so now, since trade with Europe was so difficult, the Americans wanted a part of that business. The *Empress of China* had gone out from New York in 1785 with a Boston man, Samuel Shaw, as her supercargo; more recently Elias Hasket Derby of Salem had sent two or three ships of his own. And now it was time for the merchants of Boston to begin: the *Columbia* would round the Horn, trade with the Indians of the Northwest coast for furs—seal and otter—and then across the Pacific to China to trade the furs for a cargo of tea and silk and porcelain.

On a bright September day all the Revells went down to the wharf to bid good-bye to Thomas, who would sail on the *Columbia* as supercargo: the business manager of the voyage, the man responsible for their trade. Ebenezer envied him; even as he embraced him and wished him Godspeed, he wished that he himself could make this voyage. To China—the ends of the earth!

But of course he could not go: he was too old. So he was sending his eldest son instead, a shrewd, solid trader who would bargain skillfully and bring back a cargo richer than any they had yet seen.

Thomas embraced his brothers and sisters, he said a last word to Abigail, gave his father one final handshake—and then he was gone. The ship's master called the orders; the anchor rattled up; the great white sails were hauled up the masts, where the wind caught them and they billowed in the fair breeze. And then at last, bearing all their hopes, carrying their future within her, the ship turned and headed out of the inner harbor, the proud female figurehead pointing toward the sea.

PART III

TRUNK &
BRANCHES

GRIFFIN REVELLS

Thomas
(1761–1805)

Nathaniel
(1762–1846)

m.

Emma Rollins
(1780–1833)

Artemas	Caroline	Hamilton
(1804–1873)	(1805–1890)	(1809–1886)

JACKSON REVELLS

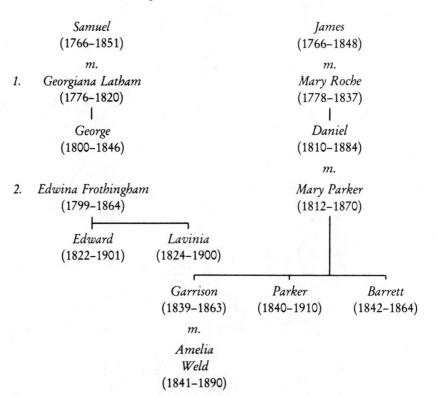

Samuel
(1766–1851)

m.

1. Georgiana Latham
(1776–1820)

George
(1800–1846)

2. Edwina Frothingham
(1799–1864)

Edward   Lavinia
(1822–1901)   (1824–1900)

James
(1766–1848)

m.

Mary Roche
(1778–1837)

Daniel
(1810–1884)

m.

Mary Parker
(1812–1870)

Garrison   Parker   Barrett
(1839–1863)   (1840–1910)   (1842–1864)

m.

Amelia
Weld
(1841–1890)

ABBOTT REVELLS

Hannah	Philip	Roger	Francis
(1770–1810)	(1772–1846)	(1774–1852)	(1777–1850)
m.		m.	m.
Malachi Martin		Mary Winthrop	Rachel Motley
(1765–1812)		(1799–1867)	(1781–1840)
		William	Francis Jr.
		(1825–1902)	(1806–1881)

Elias
(1779–1862)

m.

Dolly Kendall
(1787–?)

Washington
(1811–1875)

Mariah
(1780–1854)

Consider the subtleness of the sea; how its most dreaded creatures glide under water, unapparent for the most part, and treacherously hidden beneath the loveliest tints of azure. Consider also the devilish brilliance and beauty of many of its most remorseless tribes, as the dainty embellished shape of many species of sharks. Consider, once more, the universal cannibalism of the sea; all whose creatures prey upon each other, carrying on eternal war since the world began.

Consider all this; and then turn to this green, gentle, and most docile earth; consider them both, the sea and the land; and do you not find a strange analogy to something in yourself? For as this appalling ocean surrounds the verdant land, so in the soul of man there lies one insular Tahiti, full of peace and joy, but encompassed by all the horrors of the half known life. God keep thee! Push not off from that isle, thou canst never return!

Moby-Dick
Herman Melville

1. FAN-KWAE

1

On a bright November day in 1799, James Jackson Revell stepped onto Revell Wharf in Boston and into the arms of the tremendous crowd, several hundred people at least, that had gathered to greet him. He had been away for nearly two years, and in that time he had become famous. People were thrilled to see him; ecstatic, they shoved and shouted, reaching out to shake his hand. "There he is, safe and sound! A pox on the Bashaw! We'll show him, we will! Welcome home, Mr. Revell! And God bless you!"

With some difficulty James made his way through the crowd to where his twin brother Samuel stood at the door of the Revell warehouse. People who had known him before he left thought that he looked very thin—haggard, even, as if he had endured some very bad times, as indeed he had: more than a year before, serving as supercargo on one of the family ships, he had been captured by the Barbary pirates who preyed on American seamen in the Mediterranean. His ship was taken; he and his men were sold into slavery. The Bashaw of Tripoli, Yusuf Karamanli, realizing that he had acquired a rich prize, had sent a message to the House of Revell: pay a ransom of $10,000 and your captain and his men will be returned. Ebenezer, outraged, had paid it—and had let President John Adams know in no uncertain terms that the new nation, weak and vulnerable though she was, had better begin to fight back or she would be destroyed before she ever had a chance to prove herself. The despots of the Mediterranean kingdoms—Tripoli, Algiers, Tunis: tiny dots on the map compared to the United States of America—had captured hundreds of Americans in the past decade, selling them into slavery, demanding ransom for their release.

"Well, James. Welcome home."

"Brother—" And he was suddenly overcome, he could say no more for the tears that choked him.

They embraced, not caring that they showed their feelings so plainly. What man would not embrace his brother, and his twin at that—one who had survived such horrors, and was now by the grace of God and their father's fortune so mercifully returned to them?

Ebenezer stood a little apart from his sons, struggling to choke back his own tears while Nathaniel, Ebenezer's eldest at home, stood at his side. And now in this moment of high emotion, Nathaniel had a thought for his own brother Thomas, not a year older, so that he and Nathaniel were almost like twins themselves. Thomas had gone out to China some years ago, and had been a skilled, reliable agent for the firm. He sent back cargo after cargo of goods that sold very well, tea and silk and porcelain and ivory. Nathaniel was glad to see his half brother James; he would have liked even more to see Thomas.

And now Nathaniel watched as his father embraced James—this son whom he had given up for dead. The old man seemed deeply moved, more than Nathaniel had ever seen him.

Home again!—and now it was his own turn, the greeting, the embrace, and he felt how thin James was, worn away to nothing. Then they got James into the waiting carriage and took him to their fine new house on the Tontine Crescent, to greet his stepmother Abigail, and those of her offspring who were at home.

In the years since independence, the Revells had prospered as much as any merchant family in Massachusetts, and more than most. Ebenezer was lucky, people said, to have such a fine lot of sons to join him in the business, just as old Benjamin, seven years dead now, had always longed for. And Ben had been right, clever old man! Thomas in China, and Nathaniel and Samuel here in Boston, and now James as well; and Philip and Francis and Elias of the Abbott Revells, Abigail's sons. Only Roger, whose infant temper tantrum had led to his mother's arrest by the British, was not in business. He had chosen to continue his studies of Latin and Greek, and wanted eventually to teach at the College. John, Abigail's son by her first marriage, had died of pneumonia two years ago: a heavy loss, for he had been a steady, dependable partner, and Ebenezer had thought of him as his own son. They had shared a special bond, too, having fought together at Bunker Hill; yes, Ebenezer had mourned John deeply.

Of all Ebenezer's offspring, only his daughter Hannah, Abigail's firstborn, had married; she and her husband lived in Salem. But now it was to be Nathaniel's turn at last, for only the previous week he had asked Miss Georgiana Latham's father for her hand. Mr. Latham was agreeable—very much so. Both he and his pretty, brown-eyed daughter were as enticed by Nathaniel's fortune as by his steady, hardworking self: he was a splendid catch, no doubt about it.

The Lathams gave a reception a month or so later to celebrate the couple's engagement. At the last minute, only an hour before the appointed time, Nathaniel had word that one of the Revell ships had come in with only half her crew and a badly damaged cargo. There had been, it seemed, an attempted mutiny.

This was an emergency that could not wait, not even for his prospective in-laws. In great haste, Nathaniel went down to the wharf; the Lathams held their party without him.

Georgiana, that night, was a vision in pale green silk trimmed in lace, a matching turban trimmed with egret feathers covering most of her hair, her mother's pearls at her throat. Naturally she was disappointed that her fiancé could not attend, but perhaps she could find someone else to amuse her—for that evening only, of course.

"We haven't met." The young man's eyes swept over her as if he was appraising a cargo up for auction, she thought; and when he took her hand and lifted it to his lips, he held it there far too long. "I am, ah, your future brother-in-law. Half-brother-in-law, that is. Samuel Jackson Revell."

Of course Georgiana knew by now that the Revells were not one family but three, offspring of her prospective father-in-law's three wives. This was one of the middle family, the Jacksons. His twin brother James, who had not come to the party, had just been ransomed from the Barbary pirates. Odd, she thought, how they all looked alike, and yet so different. This young man had the Revell height, the dark blond hair and piercing blue eyes, but aside from that, he was as different from Nathaniel as chalk from cheese.

All through the evening Georgiana was conscious of Samuel Revell's eyes upon her. She became unnerved; her heart fluttered, her hands shook. She wished that Nathaniel would come. He did not. The guests took their leave; Samuel was one of the last to go. He took her hand again and murmured, so soft she could hardly hear, "What a fool he is, to leave you alone."

He did not go home that night; instead, he went to a gambling club in Ship Street in the North End. He was glad of the walk, which helped him think. He understood what was happening to him; he was no fool, he knew his own nature very well. He had always been restless—uncomfortable in the narrow confines of his life and yet unwilling to strike out on his own, to leave the solid, secure House of Revell.

Awaiting him were his best friends, companions from his time at the College. Samuel had been a reluctant scholar, barely managing to graduate, but he had enjoyed his time in Cambridge nevertheless. With a group of kindred souls he had managed to leave a greater imprint on Harvard than many a brilliant Latinist. They had formed themselves into a little club, very exclusive, to which they admitted young men from only the best families—young men like themselves. Each time they met, in a form of reverse tribute to the terrible food at the College, they dined on roast pig. When the time came to choose a name for themselves, they accepted at once Samuel's suggestion: "The Porcellian Club." Jolly fun! And the best of it was, they knew that they always had a place of refuge, safe from the unwanted company that, even at Harvard, might intrude at any moment: farmers' sons, or poor schoolmasters' sons, or outlanders from New York or the South. At the Porcellian you could behave as you pleased and no one would ever tell tales; you could depend on your chums because they were like you: Boston boys, Massachusetts boys, sons of the rich, the best fellows on earth. Samuel thought that his membership in the Porcellian was the most important thing that had ever happened to him.

The next morning Georgiana had a note from Nathaniel saying that he needed to go to Salem; he hoped to return by the beginning of the week, four days away.

Georgiana was desolate. Her happiness had turned to dust. What good was it to be engaged if her young man had taken flight?

All day she sat by the window in her bedroom, watching the snow fall—an early blizzard, eight inches before midnight, when it stopped. Her mother was alarmed at her dejection; Georgiana refused to eat, refused to join the family downstairs. All that night she lay awake, tormented by her thoughts: was Nathaniel Revell the right young man for her? Of course she loved him; of course she wanted to be his wife—but not if this was to be her fate, desertion at any moment in favor of his business.

The next afternoon, after dinner, Samuel called. The weather had cleared; now, at sunset, a full moon was rising over the snowy landscape. On such nights the young folks of Boston often went for a sleigh ride over the Neck. Would Georgiana like to come? They were getting up a party, they would all ride out and have a late supper at the Globe Tavern in Roxbury.

With her parents' permission, Georgiana assented. Samuel helped her into the sleigh, tucked the fur robe around her, and clucked the horse into a trot. They went around to Pond Street to pick up the other members of the party, only to find that some mistake had occurred: no one was at home.

Samuel smiled at her. "Will you trust your reputation with me?"

They both knew the protocol: no young woman engaged to one man went driving alone with another, not even if he was her fiancé's brother. Georgiana knew that she should say no; she knew that she should ask him to take her home at once. But she was unhappy; she was extremely annoyed with Nathaniel; she was even in the grip of a demon not unlike Samuel's. When he put his arm around her she did not protest. It was as if she watched herself as she teetered on the precipice of ruin, but no warning voice cried out to her: "Beware!"

Not long after, she found herself in a little room at the top of the tavern. She was giddy, but not from the wine she had drunk; had Samuel not held her so tightly, she would have fallen. She had stopped watching herself; she no longer knew what she did, she was no longer aware of the danger before her. Urgently, ferociously, he kissed her. She let him. For a little while she did not return his embrace, but then, as if her demon—and his—had suddenly energized her, she did. And only at the end—only when he managed to disrobe her, to lay her sweet flesh open to his—only then did she utter one feeble protest, a word only, and so quickly did he ravish her that it was as if she had never spoken.

2

"You what?" said Nathaniel. He stared at Samuel as if he was a stranger—as, indeed, he now was. "What are you talking about?

"About Georgiana, of course. She cannot marry you."

"I don't understand. What in heaven's name has happened?"

Samuel shrugged; he turned away to pour himself another tot of brandy. The brothers were in the parlor of the Revell home in the Tontine Crescent.

Samuel may have been a rake—indeed he was—but he was not a heartless one; and he had a considerable measure of family feeling. He had not, therefore, burdened Nathaniel with the details of his seduction of Georgiana. Nevertheless Nathaniel understood perfectly, as Samuel had known he would.

Now he watched as Nathaniel struggled to control himself. His face had gone from pink to white to pink again; deeper and deeper came his color as he digested Samuel's news.

Betrayed! By his blood brother!

Nathaniel's acquisition of Georgiana had been like all his other acquisitions: she was a good bargain, choice goods at a fair price. Now Samuel was telling him that he had made a bad bargain: he had been misled, the goods were shoddy—and, now, worthless.

He had never known rage until this moment. But now it surged up in him; he felt its red mist cloud his brain. Blindly he swung his fist at Samuel; the younger man ducked, easily avoiding it, and seized Nathaniel's wrist.

"Wait—no! Believe me, I understand what you—I respect your honor. Yes! And I know that you want to—to defend it. Very well! But not here, not where Father can see. Nathaniel—listen to me—" For Nathaniel tried to wrest himself free, he wanted desperately to hit, to smash Samuel's handsome face into a pulp. Ruined her! Ruined his own Georgiana!

"Pistols," said Samuel. He thought fast. Their father was at the wharf, due home at any moment, and Samuel did not want him to come in to find this battle. "Tomorrow morning," he said. "We can go to William Langmore's"— the home of a fellow Porcellian, a large, secluded estate near Salem; Langmore Jr. had in fact fought a duel there himself only last spring. Fortunately he had only wounded the fellow, a shot in the thigh; they had spirited him away on a ship to the West Indies, for dueling was illegal.

Somehow Ebenezer learned of their plan. Nathaniel swore he had not divulged it, but Samuel never believed him.

Samuel spent the night at the Langmore home. Before dawn he arose and, with Langmore Jr. as his second, trudged out into the snowy woods. Shortly they heard the sounds of hoofbeats on the hard-packed snow of the road, and Nathaniel and his second appeared.

The brothers shook hands; then they paced off fifty paces. As they turned and took aim, they heard someone else approaching: Ebenezer, he and his horse both badly winded, a look on his face such as neither son had ever seen.

"Stop!" Ebenezer's voice was a cry of terror, anguish—

Too late. In that instant they fired. The sound of their pistols in the quiet black-and-white landscape was like an earthquake; it echoed and reechoed through the trees until they thought that it must be heard all the way to Boston—to Georgiana's bedroom where she would be peacefully sleeping; or perhaps not, perhaps she lay awake, tormented, struggling with the scandal about to erupt on her. In any case, she did not know what they did here this morning.

Both of them missed. Ebenezer had flung himself from his horse, and now he stood immobilized between them, furious, terrified—appalled at this folly, this undreamed-of breach in the family's solidarity. No one spoke. Their breath puffed in the air like little puffs of gun smoke. Nathaniel was trembling so violently that he nearly collapsed; Samuel was steady enough, but sorry that their father had witnessed the affair.

Without a word Ebenezer turned his back on them, mounted his horse, and got her away at a trot. He had no idea where she went; he was distraught as he had never been in his life, more even than when Nathaniel's mother died.

He looked with unseeing eyes at the landscape. His sons! Dueling! Trying to kill each other! He could not believe it—could not bear it. His own two boys! Murderers!

He felt a sharp pain in his chest, as if someone had thrust a knife into him. His left arm seemed to go numb. He couldn't breathe. In a moment more he toppled from his seat, dead before he hit the ground.

For weeks afterward all Boston—all eastern Massachusetts—chewed over the delicious scandal, masticating it until it was dry cud: Nathaniel's engagement to Miss Latham canceled, the two brothers dueling, Ebenezer dead of the shock—and then Miss Latham marrying a Revell after all, but not the one she had originally chosen. It was the biggest sensation to hit Boston in years—bigger even than the Crowninshield stunt when, a few years before, Jacob Crowninshield of Salem had brought to Boston an Elephant. It had caused an enormous uproar: no one had ever imagined that such a creature existed on earth. Huge, rough-skinned monstrous beast, his trunk ready to snatch you up, his enormous legs and feet ready to trample you, his wise little eyes peering down at the crowd who, for a quarter of a dollar—ninepence for children—thronged to see him.

That Elephant had been so successful that in time, Crowninshield, who had paid four hundred dollars for him, had sold him for ten thousand.

But even the Elephant could not compare to the Revell affair. *Samuel*—the bridegroom? And Ebenezer dead—?

Eventually, of course, the talk died down. What remained was the breach between Nathaniel, a Griffin Revell, and Samuel and James, the Jackson Revells—for while James did not approve of his twin's conduct, he felt a blood loyalty to him. The two sides did not speak; they did not acknowledge one another's existence. Hostesses learned not to invite Nathaniel to an evening's entertainment if they invited James or Samuel. Nathaniel left the Brattle Street Church, the Family church, and joined Trinity Church—an action that let people know the depth of his anger, for Trinity was an Episcopalian church, anathema to patriots like the Revells a generation before.

In time this condition of hostility came to be accepted as normal; no one thought anything of it.

When in the summer of 1803 Nathaniel married Miss Emma Rollins, talk picked up a little as people reminisced about the scandal, but that was the season that a well-known lawyer was caught in flagrante with a client's wife, so the Revells, for once, got short shrift.

3

In August of 1806 Nathaniel received a letter brought by the *Mary*, Captain Wilson, a Revell ship out of Canton and around the Horn.

> Canton
> December 24, 1805

Mr. Nathaniel Revell
Revell & Co.
Revell Wharf
Boston U.S.A.

My dear sir:

It is my sad duty to inform you that your brother Thomas died last night after a most unfortunate accident. He was bitten by a cobra—a highly poisonous snake that infests this region. After three days of intense suffering, which he bore with great courage and dignity, and which neither the native physician nor the excellent doctor from Edinburgh attached to the British compound was able to alleviate, he expired. As he requested, he was buried at sea.

Captain Wilson brings Mr. Revell's personal effects with him.

Please accept my deepest sympathy for your loss. Mr. Revell was a pillar of our community here, and he will be sorely missed.

I am, sir, most sincerely,

> Samuel Shaw
> American Consul

The words blurred. Nathaniel blinked, and then took out his red silk handkerchief and wiped his eyes. It was a hot day. Still holding the letter, he stepped to the open door of the warehouse to get a breath of air. Bulfinch's new wharf met his eyes—India Wharf, it was called, a huge granite monument to their commerce, lined with granite warehouses, good Quincy granite, the best in the world. As he gazed out at the busy life of the harbor, a scene familiar to him since his earliest childhood, he tried to imagine the place where Thomas had died. China! He had heard descriptions of it time and again, had even seen little pictures of it painted on porcelain pitchers and punch bowls, and still he had no image of it in his mind. It seemed to Nathaniel the worst thing in the world to die so far from home, and yet Thomas had wanted to stay there, he had turned down the chance to come back only the year before.

This year, he, Nathaniel, would turn forty-three. Thomas had been just a year older; the two of them were the sons of their father's first wife, the beautiful Emilie Griffin Revell, immortalized by the magnificent Copley portrait, and perhaps even more by the bullet fired into the canvas one desperate night by their stepmother, Abigail, during the siege of Boston. He and Thomas had often reminisced about those days, and Thomas had entrusted to him his most valuable possession, the letter from General Washington praising Thomas's heroism when he took to his skates to deliver to the American forces the crucial information about General Howe's plans to take Dorchester Heights. How proud of Thomas their grandfather, old Benjamin, had been! Benjamin had died in 1792; then their father, Ebenezer (best not to remember the bitter circumstances of *that* death!); and now Thomas.

There was no help for it: someone would have to go out to China to replace him. Not a Jackson Revell, of course—the Jackson Revells, Samuel and James, had formed their own trading house with a passel of jumped-up folks from New York. No: an Abbott Revell would go, one of his stepmother Abigail's boys. Not Roger, for Roger was an odd duck, no liking for trade, a teacher at the College, Latin and Greek, very odd indeed; and Francis was newly married, certainly not willing to go off to the other side of the world; Elias was a steady enough man but he had already announced that he did not want to live anywhere but Massachusetts.

No: Philip was the one. The eldest of the Abbott Revells, a good sound man of business and, as luck would have it, recently bereaved, his new young wife dead in childbirth, and the infant with her. Probably he would be glad to have a change of scene.

Stuffing the letter into his coat pocket, Nathaniel took his hat from the peg and set off to call on Philip and, not incidentally, to inspect the progress of his own new house going up on Beacon Street across from the Common, not far from the old Hancock mansion and the site where he had lived as a child, now occupied by Bulfinch's new Statehouse. He'd got Alexander Parris to design this new place for him, since Bulfinch was so busy: half the price, and damned if the fellow wasn't equally talented.

Philip seemed to welcome Nathaniel's request. He had been deep in melancholy for the past six months, since his wife and child had died; he was glad of the chance to make a new life for himself, an intelligent man, sensible of the challenge that his half brother put before him. He grasped Nathaniel's hand.

"I'll do my best for you," he said. "For us—for the Family. I know that Thomas was a good agent. I will try to be the same."

"I have no doubt that you will," said Nathaniel, and he meant it.

Some weeks later Philip embarked as supercargo for the House of Revell, Boston USA; he sailed on the *Star of the Sea* bound for Canton.

4

Not long after, in the face of increasing foreign depredations on American shipping, President Thomas Jefferson, that radical Republican and a southerner to boot, declared an Embargo on all trade: no ships allowed in or out, he said. Such a policy is our only hope of survival, for if we continue to offer targets to the French and the British, at war with each other on the Continent, we will be ruined.

The New England merchants were appalled.

Embargo? No ships in or out?

Jefferson has made war on *us*, they said—he treats *us* like the enemy! An Embargo will destroy us!

Frantically they scurried to clear their vessels before the embargo went into effect; surreptitiously they made their plans to keep their vessels trading from foreign port to foreign port, never coming home to idle at the wharves.

And so once again Boston Harbor was closed and guarded by watchful ships enforcing the law—but now the ships were American, and the law came from their own government, the nation they and their fathers had fought for and died for, stopping their trade as effectively as the British had ever done.

Impossible! Outrageous!

As in Revolutionary days, the merchants sought loopholes—ways to get around the law. The Massachusetts governor, John Sullivan—a Scots-Irishman, a Protestant like themselves—was empowered to issue a few certificates allowing "necessary" trade. They went for high prices on the open market.

Many merchants could not get these valuable pieces of paper, and so they took a more direct action. Like a strange replay of what had seemed ancient history, Boston's Customs officers were once again in danger of their lives. Mobs threatened them if they did not issue clearance papers to allow ships to leave the port; bribes crossed their palms, huge amounts of money that no man could refuse.

As the months dragged by, the town stiffened its opposition to President Jefferson. The merchants of Boston had won a previous struggle with an unfriendly government; they would win this one, as well. The town meeting passed a resolution refusing to aid the Embargo; the General Court—the Legislature—passed a resolution stating that the Embargo was not binding on citizens of Massachusetts.

Many merchants took up their pens to become political propagandists. Samuel Jackson Revell was among them. In the space of less than a year, he produced fifteen pamphlets which he printed and distributed at his own expense, all urging stout opposition to Jefferson's folly. Embargo spelled backward, he said, was "O Grab Me"—and wasn't that what Jefferson was doing? Grabbing them and squeezing the life out of them?

Resist the tyrant!

But in fact resistance was difficult, and many merchants, particularly in the smaller ports, were ruined. And even the most prosperous men, like the Perkinses and the Amorys and the Crowninshields and the Revells—even those men had to depend on smuggling to stay free of bankruptcy.

5

"Aye, Mr. Revell, ye'll be a 'fan-kwae' now," said Captain Sampson.

"A foreign devil," said Philip, smiling. "Yes—I feel like one already."

They stood at the rail of the *Star of the Sea*. At Macao they had received their "chop"—their official permit to proceed—and had taken on a pilot, a small, skillful Chinese who guided them now up the Pearl River toward Whampoa, the port for Canton.

They glided past the Bogue Forts, Portuguese gun emplacements on the red sandstone bluffs on either shore. Then they came to the great bend in the river, and rounded it, and saw, stretching before them, Whampoa Reach.

Philip was speechless. He had never seen such a sight—had never imagined it: for two miles and more stood a line of foreign ships, the flag of every nation, it seemed. They were not allowed to sail beyond Whampoa; traders had to go to Canton itself in a Chinese "fast boat," while their ships anchored here.

The pilot guided them in. As they neared the wharf a little cry went up from those on shore, and now Philip saw a procession approaching: a small Chinese boy, not more than eight or nine, carrying a lacquer box, followed by three officials attired in handsome brocade robes, little pillbox hats atop their shaven heads, with only a pigtail down the back remainder of their hair. The one in the lead had a long, wispy beard; despite his strange, high-soled shoes, he moved with some agility. He could have been any age, thirty or sixty.

"Here he is," muttered Sampson. "He's what they call a mandarin. He'll give us the permits to go upriver to Canton, but first he'll want his cumshaw—gifts, to put it politely. And we'll have to take tea with him, and make nicee-nicee."

The official in the lead, who seemed to be the chief mandarin, kept his arms crossed over his stomach, his hands thrust into his wide sleeves. He smiled; he spoke a few words in Chinese. Philip and Captain Sampson bowed to him, and greeted him in English. At a nod from his master, the boy set the lacquer box on the table, opened it, and took out a small teapot, a packet of tea, and three small, handleless cups. From the rear one of the retainers brought forward a wicker basket, which, opened, was seen to contain a repast of blood-red oranges—mandarin oranges—and lichee nuts and small, doughy pies that Sampson called "dragon pasties."

The captain called for the cook's boy to bring boiling water. The Chinese boy prepared the tea and poured it into the cups. They all drank. The Chinese boy handed around the pastries and fruit. Then, swallowing the last of his tea, the chief mandarin looked expectantly at Captain Sampson.

"Now he wants his cumshaw," the captain muttered. He went to his seaman's chest and took out a few sheets of paper, a cheap pocket watch, and a small music box. With a broad smile that Philip, at least, could tell was patently fake, he handed these to the mandarin.

The Chinese examined them, held the watch to his ear to see that it ticked, wound the music box to hear a few notes. Then he smiled and nodded: everything satisfactory. He barked an order to one of his underlings, whereupon the man whipped out a piece of parchment already covered with Chinese characters and handed it to Sampson. The delegation left the cabin, and within seconds a "fast boat" appeared at the side of the ship; this, Sampson said, would take them to Canton, where their real business would begin.

And now, as the great line of European and American vessels fell behind, they proceeded upriver. The water was crowded with traffic: great salt junks and ships of the Java trade, six hundred tons and more, towered over tiny sampans crowded with entire families, cooking fires on deck, baskets of live fowl hanging over the sides, children playing, their safety secured by wooden buoys around their necks. River junks with paddlewheels operated by naked coolies jostled "mandarin boats" with bright flags, red and white, fluttering in the breeze, and red sashes wrapped around the muzzle of their cannons. Some of the larger vessels had huge eyes painted on their bows—"to watch for sea devils," said Sampson. Still other boats were decorated with ornately carved wood and colored glass; these, Sampson informed Philip, were "flower boats"— floating brothels patronized by the mandarins.

Voices crying the incomprehensible Chinese tongue echoed across the water; the smell of strange cooking odors drifted from the little boats, overlaid by the pungent odor of sandalwood joss sticks burned to propitiate the river gods. Here and there Philip saw an individual face, pale yellow, black-haired, staring at him even as he stared at it, and he realized all over again how far from home he was, how vulnerable to the goodwill of these people. He felt as though he had been picked up and set down on another planet; not even the long voyage across the Pacific, interrupted for several months as they traded for furs with the Indians of the Northwest coast of America, had prepared him for the strangeness of this exotic port. Even the water and the sky seemed different here, and the green hills beyond the rooftops of Canton seemed unlike any he had ever seen—as indeed they were, for they grew tea bushes.

Twilight came. Philip saw a pagoda silhouetted against the rosy, sunset sky; a thousand lanterns blossomed over the water. He heard the sound of a gong, and then faint strains of music—weird, atonal, unlike any music he had ever heard.

Their boat bumped against the wharf. They were at Jackass Point, the barbarians' dockage at Canton.

Philip stepped onto Chinese soil.

When in 1742 the Ch'ien Lung Emperor, the Son of Heaven and ruler of the Celestial Empire, decided in his mercy to allow the barbarians to trade with his people, he decreed that they could do so at one port only: Canton. The foreign devils, with their loathsome white skin and their huge, ugly feet and their disgusting dietary habits and incomprehensible languages, would be restricted to a small part of the city, less than half a mile of "factories"— warehouses and apartments—strung along the riverfront; no barbarian was allowed elsewhere save by invitation. Moreover, no barbarian was allowed to learn Chinese, and any Chinese caught teaching the language was subject to execution; no barbarian could have his wife or family with him; no white man could stay at Canton beyond the trading season, the autumn and early winter, but must remove himself to Whampoa or, better yet, to Portuguese Macao. The white men could trade only with the thirteen officially designated merchants, or "hoppos," each of whom wore his button of office, each of whom was responsible for the behavior not only of the particular foreign devil with whom he dealt, but for that man's crew downriver at Whampoa.

These and a hundred other restrictions the Son of Heaven decreed, because he was, in truth, not very interested in trading with the barbarians. They had nothing that any Chinese wanted—save the aphrodisiacal ginseng root (the "dose of immortality"); and the rich dark skins of the sea otter from the Northwest coast of America; and specie—hard coin. Later, the barbarians learned that the Chinese also wanted certain exotic items that could be picked up on the voyage out: sandalwood; and birds' nests to make soup with; and the delicious bêche-de-mer—the sea slug.

The white men were willing to put up with the restrictions because the market for Chinese goods—tea and silk and porcelain—was so vast; they suffered the contempt and insults of their reluctant hosts, they obeyed the rules set down by the Son of Heaven, and they got rich.

Trade relations were one thing, however; diplomatic relations quite another. When in 1793 Lord Macartney, sent out as British ambassador, journeyed to Peking to present his credentials to the Emperor, the presents that he took from George III had to carry the motto "Ambassador bearing tribute from the country of England." This was insult enough, but worse was to come: the Chinese court officials said that Lord Macartney must perform the ceremony of the "kowtow" before the Emperor. This was an exercise that involved kneeling, then prostrating oneself before the Emperor and beating one's head on the ground three times—three prostrations, nine beatings of the head. Lord Macartney refused to do it. The Chinese officials insisted. At length Lord Macartney made an awkward nick of his knees, a kind of little curtsey. The court flunkies hastened to explain to the Emperor, who gazed in astonishment at the foreign devil's ridiculous and inadequate performance, that this was in fact the English version of the kowtow.

Until the colonies revolted, Americans had got their Chinese goods via London; afterward, when for a time Britain would not trade with her former colonies, American merchants went to China on their own. The most aggressive and successful were from Massachusetts. Before long the Chinese called all Americans "Bostonians." When a Chinese drew a map of North America, the entire area east of the Mississippi was labeled SALEM.

"Here, y'see, is where you'll be," said Sampson. He waved his hand to indicate a little plaza surrounded by buildings—the hongs, or warehouses, where Philip, as representative of the House of Revell, would carry on his trading. "You'll live upstairs while you're here," said Sampson. "At the American Hong. Then when the wind shifts, and the ships leave, and the trading season's over, you can go back to Whampoa—or even to Macao, if you want."

In the apartment over the American Hong, Philip was greeted by Ethan Pritchard of New York, like Philip an agent for his family's firm. "We keep tight quarters here, Mr. Revell, but we're here for only a few months, until the winter, so we don't mind. I expect you'd like a wash, and then they'll be bringing dinner."

Philip ate little that first night—bird's nest soup and several platters heaped with spiced, mysterious chunks—and, of course, all the steamed rice he wanted, washed down with cups of tea. He liked the tea, at any rate: wonderful stuff, this was, strong and full-bodied, with a smoky overlay that he had never tasted before. He wondered if here, at the place where the tea was grown, cured, and sold, the Chinese merchants had ever heard the story of the Boston men dumping tea into Boston Harbor—and, if they had heard it, if they understood it.

Pritchard's parting words before turning in for the night were: "Mind your netting's secure."

Philip smiled. "I'm a pretty sound sleeper. Flies don't bother me."

Pritchard snorted. "It's not flies you need to worry about. Scorpions, more likely—and lizards, although they're harmless enough; they'll eat the flies for you if you let 'em. But the scorpions are nasty—and the snakes . . ." He paused, embarrassed; both men remembered Thomas's death, and Pritchard had witnessed it.

The next morning Pritchard showed Philip the compound where he would spend the next few months putting together the cargo for Captain Sampson to take home. The foreigners' district was bounded by Thirteen Factory Street. Here were shops of every description: a tea shop, and a shop selling colorful birds, several of whom "talked"; he saw a shop for silk goods, for incense, for fireworks, for painted porcelainware. Fans, umbrellas, jewelry made of ivory and of iridescent birds' feathers—every exotic thing in the world was for sale

here. The only Chinese he saw were the shopkeepers; all the customers were
European, mostly sailors spending their pay, bored with waiting for their ships
to get a full cargo.

After the noon meal Pritchard announced that they were to have a visit from
the Co-hong merchant who would be responsible for the *Star of the Sea* until
it departed. If any part of the incoming cargo was unsatisfactory, if any of the
seamen committed any crime, this man would be held accountable; further, he
must arrange for the outgoing cargo and bargain with Philip for a fair price.

His name was Houqua. Like all merchants in China, he was of only middling status: the Chinese did not look on merchants with any great favor. He
was of medium height, slim, with a high domed forehead, his skull bald on top
but with a longtail down his back. His eyes were deep-set, his small, delicate
face rather long for a Chinese. His skin was the color of old parchment. His
manners were exquisite. He wore a dark red silk robe over brocade trousers;
around his neck were several ropes of jade and ivory beads, and on his chest he
wore his button of office. He moved easily, balanced on his small shoes with
platform soles and turned-up toes. His nails were long, buffed to a high shine.
He looked, thought Philip, as if he were Confucius himself—filled with ancient
wisdom leavened by a faint hint of humor, as if he were laughing, not at Philip,
but at some larger, cosmic joke. Philip liked him.

At length, after many days, and with the aid of an interpreter, Philip and
Houqua began to bargain. The interpreter was called a "linguist"—surely a
misnomer, Philip thought, for the man spoke only pidgin English (a corruption
of "business English").

"You makee first chop tea, chow-chow for boat," the linguist said, bobbing
his head, smiling.

Very well, thought Philip. He thought of Nathaniel, eagerly awaiting the
return of the ship; then, giving himself over to the Chinese, for the moment at
least, he followed his mentor into the hongs.

Over the next few weeks, with infinite tact, Houqua offered to Philip a
choice of goods for shipment to Boston. First came the selection of teas. Together with the linguist they went to the tea warehouse, where Philip tasted
cups of tea made from the various kinds: black (or unfermented) Bohea; green
Hyson; Pekoe; and Imperial ("large pearls"). After his fifth sample, Philip felt
that he could no longer distinguish between them. He rolled the flavor in his
mouth and tried to imagine the Boston ladies of his acquaintance sipping of an
afternoon any one of these: which would they like best?

In the end he settled on fifteen hundred piculs of the black, four hundred
piculs of the green, and four hundred of oolong, or mixed.

By that time his life as the Canton agent of Revell & Co. had settled into
a routine: he rose early, drank the tea that the servant brought, and called for
the barber. When he was dressed he went out for a walk; then, around mid-
morning, Houqua arrived and the two men spent three or four hours arranging
for the disposition of Philip's cargo or visiting the hongs to make up his new
one. Then came dinner, which he took with his fellow Americans. Then he visited

Europeans in the compound; or read one of the trunkful of books he had brought out; or wrote accounts to Nathaniel that would be carried back on the ship.

One day toward the middle of November he received a card. It was about ten inches by four; at the top was a Chinese character whose meaning he did not know but which, he learned, meant "Kwang"—"to shed luster upon." Underneath was the message:

> On the 7th day the wine cups will be prepared.
>
> On the 10th day they will be filled, when your presence is expected. To what dignity will it aid us to rise! In the evening at 8 the tables will be prepared.
>
> To the Eminent in Learning, Le-vell, Venerable first-born. Hing-Fung, born in the evening, bows to the ground and worships.

"Congratulations," said Pritchard, waving his own card. "It's a real honor. It means Houqua gave you a good report."

The merchant Hing-Fung was rumored to have grown rich in the opium trade. On the night of his dinner party for the fan-kwae, he sent coolies to carry Philip, Pritchard, and a few gentlemen from the British Hong in sedan chairs to his estate, which lay outside the city boundary. Passing through a tall wooden gate in a high brick wall, the visitors found themselves in a parklike garden so large that they could see only the curving roof of the house through the treetops. On every side pots of flowers were grouped about the lawns, chrysanthemums and carnations and camellias; fruit trees bordered the walks, which were paved in pebbles fashioned into designs of birds or fish. Small stone bridges crossed lagoons where floated giant lily pads; goldfish swam among them, sparkling in the sunlight. Across the lawns strode bright-feathered ducks—mandarin ducks, they were called—and storks, and gorgeous peacocks flaunting their huge fantails.

The house itself was not one building, as in Boston USA, but rather a series of rooms, one or two stories, separated and connected by courtyards, bounded by colonnades and verandas. The guests entered a door guarded by twin devil dogs, and at last their host welcomed them, smiling and bowing. He led them through one room and then another. Never had Philip seen such a magnificent place; it made his own home, which was the height of elegance in Massachusetts, seem like a hovel. Here were marble floors, pink and white and pale brown, covered with silk and velvet carpets woven in an intricate Chinese pattern; delicate, lacquered furniture and heavier pieces carved of ebony; porcelain vases of every size; bronze statues; carved open-work screens of teak and mahogany. A heavy odor of incense hung in the air; from the courtyards came the sound of tiny bells and wind chimes wafting in the breeze.

In the dining salon—too elaborate to be called merely a room—a small number of tables were set about, so that the guests were seated in groups of four. Not one woman was in attendance, and in fact Philip had not seen a female since he entered the gate; the Chinese, he knew, did not permit their wives and daughters to meet outsiders. The tables were decorated with flowers;

small silver and porcelain cups were set out for tea. No knives or forks were provided: only ivory chopsticks and curiously-shaped spoons.

The meal began with birds'-nest soup with bêche-de-mer; then sharks' fins and roasted snails and plovers' eggs; then a series of steaming dishes, vegetables and chopped-up meat.

Philip was hungry. Clumsily he tried to grasp his food with his chopsticks, but he dropped more than he managed to get into his mouth. Toward the middle of the meal the host, a portly, smiling man, began to make his way around the room followed by a servant carrying a pot of wine—the fierce Chinese rice wine called Samshoo. He stopped at each table, chatted merrily and for the most part incomprehensibly with his pale-skinned guests, poured wine into their cups, and went on.

"Of course you must drink it," said Pritchard. "It would be hideously bad manners to refuse."

Philip took a sip. His throat seemed to have caught fire. He could not breathe. He felt as though he were going to faint. He managed to grasp his teacup, sipped a bit, and was able to breathe again.

At the end of the meal the servants handed around trays of oddly shaped "cookies." Philip saw that his fellow diners did not eat these at once; rather, they broke them open and extracted from them little slips of paper printed with a few Chinese characters. And now Hing-Fung was going around the room again, translating. Philip broke open his own and took out the slip of paper. Hing-Fung came to his table; a genial smile enlivened his face. He took Philip's paper. "This is you fo'tune now. Yes? Let me see. Ah—good. Here it is. 'The wind goes where the feet cannot.' Ah, that is good, good! You unnastan'? The wind brot you to us. You feet, no. Good! Good!"

By the first of December Philip had been at Canton for three months. The tea harvest was over; the barbarians' ships would leave within the next few weeks. The foreigners who formed the little exile colony at Canton would withdraw to the lovely old Portuguese settlement at Macao to wait out the winter.

For Philip the initial strangeness of Canton had worn off. He felt as though he had lived in the Celestial Empire half his life. The sights and sounds of home—of Boston USA—were growing ever more dim in his memory. The crowded, noisy, odiferous Orient had taken him over; he had only begun to make its acquaintance, but he felt increasingly drawn to it, as if in some strange way Fate had intended him to come here, as if this, and not his birthplace, was meant to be his home—as if, in some previous life, perhaps, he had been a Chinese.

These somewhat metaphysical speculations preoccupied him one evening as he walked out with Pritchard. At the river they leaned against the stone parapet and gazed at the water, so crowded with junks and houseboats and sampans that the surface was hardly visible. Behind them, across the little square, stretched the row of thirteen foreign hongs; beyond those lay the city of Canton, where they were not permitted to go on their own. And beyond that . . . ? Suddenly Philip felt nearly overwhelmed. China had been an ancient civilization, he knew, when his own Revell ancestors had been pagans in the forests of England and the Continent. No wonder the Chinese called white men "barbarians"! No wonder they looked with amused contempt upon the colony's missionary, Dr. Morrison, an earnest Scot bent on preaching his Presbyterian homilies.

Philip lacked a religious temperament. He had accepted his upbringing in New England Orthodoxy as he accepted his place in the little world of Boston; never had he questioned it. The Orthodox God was not an immediate presence in his life; every Sunday he had listened to the minister's sermons because that was what he had been brought up to do, because not to have listened would have been impolite.

Now, however, as he gazed upon the myriad lanterns on the bobbing riverboats, as he heard the soft jumble of sound made by the voices of all those Chinese living there, as he thought about the millions of other Chinese who lived on the vast continent at his back, he had a sudden epiphany. Perhaps New England Orthodoxy was not the way to Heaven, after all; perhaps Confucius—blasphemous thought!—had had more wisdom than Christ. There were, after all, many more Confucians than there were New England Orthodox.

Hesitantly, as if he were afraid of being accused of some capital crime, he ventured this thought to his companion. Pritchard smiled and nodded.

"That's right. They outnumber us Christians ten to one—a hundred to one, I don't know how many. They have a sensible view of religion, I think. They don't mind what a man believes, as long as he pays his taxes and doesn't make trouble. Why, they even have a mosque here, I'm told, although I've never seen it. Think of that! The Mohammedans've been here before Dr. Morrison!"

Because he had been educated at Harvard, Philip knew a little history. "I wonder how the Emperor, whoever he was, would have taken the Crusades."

"The Church militant? Not very well, I think. Each man to his own conscience, that's the Chinese way. And as for some flaming missionary coming in and trying to convert every coolie to the teachings of St. Paul—why, they'd just have slapped a tax on him, and after a while they'd do what they do to everyone. They'd just absorb him. No one can conquer China. Not with an army—and not with an idea, either."

The next day Philip fell ill with what he thought was a minor stomach complaint. He grew worse, however, and the day after, weakened by diarrhea and fever, he consented to see Dr. Morrison, who doubled as the colony's physician.

"Ach, man, y've got a touch o'th'Emperor's Revenge," said the Scot. "I'll just send the boy up with th'pipe and you let him show you how to use it, and you'll be better in no time."

Philip was too weak to protest, and too miserable to refuse anything that might make him well. The *Star of the Sea* was to sail within days, and he must be up and about to supervise her final loading—his first undertaking for the family firm, a job that must be accomplished satisfactorily.

In no more than five minutes one of the servants appeared bearing a small silver tray. On it were a fantastically carved pipe in the shape of a dragon, and a small chinaware bowl containing a bit of dark, sticky stuff.

Smiling, bobbing his head in respect, the servant spoke in Chinese, and at the same time, with elaborate gestures, demonstrated how to use the pipe. Then, having lit it, he handed it to Philip, whose hands shook so that he could hardly hold it. He inhaled once, and then again. The servant stood by, watching, his hands folded over his stomach, his black eyes expressionless. Philip felt a wonderful peace begin to overtake him. The pain in his belly lessened. The world seemed suffused in a golden light. A sense of ineffable well-being buoyed him on a cloud of contentment.

After a while, when the servant departed, Philip did not notice.

A week later the *Star of the Sea* set sail for Boston. Philip, recovered from his illness, spent the last day before her departure writing a detailed account for Nathaniel of all the transactions he had made for the Revell firm. Then, after dinner, he went to the shops on Thirteen Factory Street to select a few pieces for his own account—items that he asked Nathaniel to hold for him. Nathaniel, or any other of his brothers or sisters, could use them, or display them if they wished; they were, in a way, a family gift from Philip. He chose a miniature pagoda carved from ivory, a large porcelain punch bowl decorated with a scene of Canton, an ivory chess set, several lengths of silk, a dozen fans, and a tea service for twelve. The next year he ordered a Chinaware dinner set of 160 pieces with a "family crest" that he designed himself. Word came back that a number of other Boston families wanted to order similar sets; Nathaniel forwarded their requests, each with a drawing of a family crest. They were all the rage, he said—and the firm made a two hundred percent profit on them as well.

Philip was surprised to see that one order for dinnerware came from his brother Elias Abbott Revell, who had been married. Philip could not help smiling. Elias had always been marked as a bachelor, a confirmed, lifelong bachelor, by everyone who knew him. Now, it seemed, some female had caught him: Miss Dolly Kendall, whom Philip did not know, but whose elder brother he had met at the College.

With a fleeting regret for the wife and child of his own whom he had lost, he sat down at once to write a note of congratulation to Elias, to wish him every happiness in his marriage. Dolly, he said, was a charming name, and he was certain that the young lady was equally so.

6

With great care, Dolly opened the door of her bedroom a crack and listened. No sound: she might have been alone in the house, but she knew she was not. They were there—in the kitchen, probably: the housekeeper, Mrs. Vetch, and her husband, the coachman and general handyman. And no doubt the maid, Bethiah, as well—their daughter, she was sure, although they would not say so.

Pulling her cloak more firmly about her shoulders, Dolly stepped out into the hall. Cautiously she started down the wide, curving stairs that led to the foyer. At the bottom she paused. Still no sound. She glanced around; she felt that from some hidden corner, from behind a door, perhaps, they were watching her. They did that, she knew; Elias had instructed them to do it, and they obeyed him. They would not obey her, although she was mistress of this place; all their obedience, such as it was, went to him.

Swiftly, silently, she crossed to the front door. It was heavy; and because the wood swelled in the damp, it often stuck. With a hard little tug she got it open. Pulling it shut behind her, she stood on the steps under the portico. She was surrounded by whiteness, fog so thick that she could not see to where the drive entered the allée of elm trees which led to a tall iron gate a quarter mile away.

She descended the steps and hurried along the path that led around through the garden to the back terrace. From there, on a clear day, you could see down the lawn stretching to the bluff and, beyond, the ocean. But now the fog enveloped everything; soon her cloak and her hair were dripping with beads of water, and her dainty little morocco shoes were soaked. She did not care. She needed to get out—away from that great white house with its empty, echoing rooms, all furnished in exquisite taste: Hepplewhite and Sheraton, rosewood and mahogany, satiny brocade, gilt-trimmed woodwork, the most expensive painted paper smuggled in from France. But empty all the same: no voice but her own and the servants', for trade had picked up and Elias was often in Boston for days at a time.

Worse: to punish her, he would not allow her to be with him. He had sold their house on Pearl Street, where they had begun their married life, to one of the Perkinses; he had built this place near Salem instead, during the Embargo, when workmen could be had cheap. The architect Samuel McIntyre, who was to Salem what Bulfinch was to Boston, had designed it: a four-square Georgian mansion house of white-painted wood topped by a widow's walk which Dolly had never seen because she was afraid of heights. She would have told Elias that if he'd asked her, but of course he did not.

She had known from their first meeting that Elias Abbott Revell wanted her— hungered for her in a desperate way, so unlike the enjoyable flirtations she had with younger men. He was ten years older than she, very serious, very businesslike—even about marriage. Perhaps especially about marriage. He had stared and stared at her till she had grown uncomfortable; she was used to men's stares, but still.

She knew that she was a beauty; everyone told her so. Her face, underneath her crown of golden curls, was a perfect oval, her skin alabaster touched with pink, her blue-green eyes fringed with dark lashes, her mouth a moist red Cupid's bow. Equally enchanting were her plump white shoulders, her bosom half revealed by the fashions of the day—high-waisted silk slips of dresses which made perfectly clear that she wore no old-fashioned stays or petticoats underneath—nothing at all, it seemed. The Empress Josephine had set that fashion, and young ladies everywhere (and some not so young) rushed to imitate her.

A few days after she and Elias met, he had spied her father on the Merchants' Exchange and took him aside and had a word with him.

And not long after that, Miss Dolly Kendall became Mrs. Elias Abbott Revell.

The morning after her wedding night, she felt like a sometime madwoman who, after months of folly, had all of a sudden—too late!—regained her sanity.

Steadily she walked across the lawn to the edge, to where the land dropped away. In such a fog as this, one might easily misstep and go hurtling down to where the sea pounded the jagged rocks below. If they were watching her from the house, she thought, they would have lost her by now; she could see nothing beyond a few feet, although she could hear well enough the relentless pounding of the surf. So they would not see her fall.

One step, she thought, and it would be done. She tried to imagine it: falling, her body crushed on the sharp edges of the rocks, the sea washing her away . . . No. She could not do it. She stepped back. If she was to die, it would be in some different way.

But she was not going to die. She drew a deep breath, the cold salt air stinging her throat. *She was not going to die.* There was life beyond Revell Hall, and she meant to have it.

I built it for you, Elias had said. She had been shocked—appalled. She had not wanted it, had not wanted to live here, miles from anyone, isolated, no one but the hateful servants for company day after day.

She had wept and wept until she thought her eyes would fall out. Her face was so swollen and distorted that she could not see anyone for days. She had pleaded with him, raged at him. Nothing swayed him. He was one of the wealthiest merchants in Massachusetts, he had a right to build himself a fine country house in one of the most picturesque spots of all—the magnificent coastline north of Boston, fronting on the sea which had, as he reminded her, brought them all their wealth. Any proper wife would be delighted to have such a place, he said.

She was not deceived. She knew why he brought her here. He was angry with her; he wanted to punish her. He did not approve of her behavior. She had always flirted with every man in sight, and simply because she was Mrs. Elias Revell, she had seen no reason to stop doing so. Wasn't that why men were here—to flirt with, to dance attendance on pretty young women like her?

His patience came to an end on the night when Calvin Rowe, a Porcellian like Elias, but only twenty-one or so, only recently graduated, had given every indication of being seriously in love with Dolly, dancing with her all evening, monopolizing her, even, once, trying to snatch a kiss.

In love—with Elias's wife!

And she had not discouraged the scamp—had led him on, in fact, laughing and teasing, until the guests had begun to comment openly about her behavior to Elias himself.

It was after that night, and after the terrible scene they had gone through afterward, that he had summoned McIntyre.

Even Dolly's mother had turned against her. When Dolly had gone to her, to ask her for help in persuading Elias not to do this, her mother had refused. He is your husband, she said; you can hardly complain of his cruelty when he wants to spend a small fortune building you the most magnificent house outside of Boston. Many women would be glad of such a place.

Once, in the summer, she had ordered Vetch to bring around the chaise. She was going for a drive, she said—by herself. He had refused. He had not spoken to her politely, as a servant should; he had simply sneered at her. Orders from the master, he said: she was not to be allowed either the chaise or the carriage—not even a horse.

She had been so furious that she had started off down the drive on foot. When she reached the gate she was exhausted, her ankle throbbing where she had turned it. And in any case the gate had been locked—again, no doubt, on Elias's orders.

So there was no doubt about his intentions: he meant to imprison her here, safely away from all the young men of Boston who danced attendance on her, married though she was.

And now was to come the worst imprisonment of all, for in the last month she had become sure that she was with child. She had told no one; certainly she would not tell Elias. He wanted a child more than anything—more than he wanted her. Well, he would have it on her terms or not at all.

She lifted her pretty little chin. The solid wall of white around her made her feel dizzy. Or, more likely, it was her condition that made her feel as if she were going to faint. She turned away and headed back toward the house. She knew what she had to do: something nearly as bad as throwing herself off the cliff. Somehow she would find the strength to do it. Once, when she had been a student at a fashionable boarding school in Cambridge, she had heard one of the girls tell an appalling tale; Dolly did not remember many of the details—if, indeed, they had ever been mentioned—but she knew well enough the main thing she had to do.

As she approached the house, looming large and white, whiter than the fog, she heard the rattle of a carriage from the drive at the front. For a moment her heart lifted: company! Even if it was only someone from Salem, she didn't care; she was so lonely that she would have been glad to see the dullest, the most countrified lady.

Her step quickening, she hurried around to the drive. The coachman was proceeding to the stables. Her heart sank as she recognized Elias's carriage. Why was he here—in the middle of the day, in mid-week?

She hesitated. Perhaps she would not go in, after all. But then, feeling the cold damp penetrating the thin soles of her shoes, feeling the sodden cloak over her shoulders, she reminded herself that this was her house, just as Elias had said; she had every right to be here.

She went in. Elias was in the parlor, just touching a light to the fire. He turned to greet her; his expression was blank, unreadable.

"What?" he said. "Out in all this damp? You'll catch your death."

"I was . . . restless." She moved to the fire to warm herself; she was glad that he did not try to embrace her. "What is wrong?" she said. "Why have you come?"

He gave a short, forced laugh. "Why have I come? This is my home. You are my wife. I had a little respite; I thought it could do no harm to visit."

She made no reply. She stood facing the fire, feeling the warmth of it spread through her body. After a moment Elias lifted the cloak from her shoulders and tossed it onto a little brocade sofa. It was damp, she thought, it would make a mark; but she said nothing. She did not care about the sofa; she did not care about anything in this house.

She remembered that she had planned to ask him for something; she had thought to have more time to prepare her little speech. No matter. She would say what she had to say now, and get it over with. It was a way, she thought, of making him earn the child he wanted: she would make him bargain for it, but without telling him so.

As if she was remembering lessons learned years ago, as indeed she was, she turned to face him. Her realization of what was at stake—her future, her very life—gave to her face an animation, a lovely spark that Elias had not seen there for a long time. He wanted suddenly to take her in his arms, but he restrained himself. If he had learned anything, it was that he must not give way to her whims, her girlish willfulness.

Still, the sight of her just now gave him new hope. She was at last getting over her homesickness, she had come to accept her life here, just as he had known she would, given enough time.

He took her hands and cradled them against his white shirtfront. "What?" he said. "I can see you have something to tell me."

She heard the gentle note in his voice. It gave her courage.

"Yes," she said. "Yes, I do. I must—Elias, listen to me. I know that you have been . . . very generous—" The words choked her, so that for a moment she could not go on. "I know that you thought to please me by building this house. And I thank you for it." Again she paused; if flirting was second nature to her, lying was not. "But Elias, listen to me. I have tried to live here. I have tried to be content. All these months—oh, I know that you do not think so, but I have tried. And I cannot do it. I am not happy here, I will never be happy here. I want to go back to Boston. I want to be with my parents, and my brothers, and my friends—oh, Elias, do not keep me from them! If I angered you by my behavior, I swear to you that I will not behave so in the future. I will not go to any parties—no, not any! I will stay home if that is what you want, I will keep busy with charity work, I will sew for the poor—Elias, listen to me! I cannot live here! I will go mad if I have to spend the winter here! It is not in my nature to live like this, isolated, longing for company—but I will forswear company if only you will let me live in Boston."

At her first words his happiness faded. He let go her hands. For a moment she thought he was going to walk out of the room, but he only went to pull shut the pocket doors so that their conversation would not be overheard by the ever-present servants.

"I had hoped that you would come to like it here," he said.

"Oh, Elias, it isn't the house itself that I dislike! If this house were in the middle of Boston, I would be perfectly content. It is this—" She gestured toward the tall windows which, this day, showed no pleasant view but only the thick white fog that enveloped the landscape, pressing against the glass. "It is this place," she went on, "so far away from everything—from everyone. I cannot bear to live here any longer. I—I hate it." Her voice broke; sobbing, she sank onto a delicate shield-back chair, one of a set of six especially made for the house.

Suddenly Elias became angry. Always he had tried to control himself, but now, more roughly than he had intended, he pulled her to her feet. From the frightened look on her face he knew that he was in danger of losing control, but he felt his anger flowering in him like some poisonous tropical plant, and he could not check its growth.

"Never let me hear you say that again." He heard his voice, cold and hard; he did not want to behave so, but his duty compelled him. She was his wife: she must obey him! "Do you hear me? Never! This is your home. It will be your home always! You will live here because I tell you to!"

Her knees gave way, and he held her to keep her from falling. "Do you hear me? You will always live here! Answer me!"

Sobbing and sobbing, she choked, "Yes! Let me go— Yes!"

She writhed, she tried to pull his hands away, but he would not set her free. Then suddenly he felt his disgust rise up within him—for her, for himself— and with a little shove he thrust her back onto the chair so that she lay sprawling, half falling off. In an instant she sprang up; before he could touch her again, she ran from the room. Her wild cries echoed behind her like those of some animal, he thought: hardly a human sound. He heard her feet pounding up the stairs, and then the sound of the bedroom door slamming shut.

Then silence.

He took a deep breath and went to the cupboard where he kept his brandy. What with the Embargo, he had needed to ration it, but now he poured a generous amount into a tumbler and sipped it greedily, as if its burning warmth would banish the chill that had settled into his heart.

Foolish Dolly! He could hardly remember how much he had loved her. She had been a great disappointment to him. But he would persevere; in time she would accept the life he decreed for her.

A child would help, he thought. He would have his dinner; he would give her time to sleep a little. Then he would go to her; he would soothe her, and lie with her. Surely, some time soon, he thought, he would get her with child. Then she would be docile; then she would see what her life was supposed to be and she would accept it.

After his solitary dinner he smoked a pipe. The house was quiet. He heard the wind rising; when he went to the front door and stepped out, he saw that the fog had lifted, and here and there in the cloudy night sky a star peeped through.

He took the clearing weather as an omen. Returning to the house, he ascended the stairs two at a time and stopped at the bedroom door. He listened: no sound. He knocked lightly. No response. She was sleeping, then, as he had known she would be.

He felt a spasm of tenderness for her. She was young, she had a good deal to learn—but she was not hopeless, she was not stupid and petty like the wives of some of his friends.

He put his hand on the latch and pushed open the door. The room was dark. A few embers burned in the fireplace; he touched a spill to them and lit the candelabra on the mantle. Then he looked for her, as if he expected her to have been sitting in the dark waiting for him.

He saw her lying on the bed. She seemed to be asleep. Quietly he stepped to her side. Her eyes were closed. She was still fully dressed. Softly he spoke her name.

No reply. He would wake her, he thought, and help her to undress. He touched her cheek. It was cold; she did not respond. Then he took her hand. "Dolly?"

Her eyes fluttered open. In the dim light of the candles he could not tell if she was fully awake; he thought that she did not recognize him.

"Are you feeling better?" he said. "Here, let me help you, you cannot lie like this all night."

At first he could not find her other hand to pull her up, to help her.

Then he realized that she grasped something in a grip as tight as death. And then he realized that her skirts were disheveled, and she seemed to have spilled something.

She whispered to him, but he did not catch her words.

The bedclothes were soaked with it, whatever it was—some dark, sticky stuff. He felt suddenly sick—so weak that he had to sit on the edge of the bed. She was whispering again, and he leaned in to her.

"You would have had a child, Elias. If you had let me go home. But not now."

His head was swimming, the room rocking back and forth. Some pit of horror yawned before him, her words had opened it at his feet and now he was stumbling into it, falling into Hell—

And now all of a sudden he understood, and like a fog more smothering than any he had ever seen, a red mist of rage overcame him.

"You—" He could not believe it—not even when the truth of it lay here before him, the blood-soaked bed, the woman dying—for she was dying, he was sure of it—*damned stupid woman!*

With a cry of rage he seized her by the throat and pulled her up so that her face was not an inch from his own. "What have you done? What in God's name have you done?" His hands tightened, he felt her flesh, her throat give way as he pressed, harder and harder.

"Ah, God—what have you done?"

For a moment her eyes remained open; she saw that he understood, and a faint, fleeting expression—of triumph? of joy?—came over her; then, still in his grip, she fainted.

7

Inevitably war came again. It was so unpopular that people called it "Mr. Madison's war" after the President who declared it. He declared it against Great Britain. Since all war was bad for trade, the merchants of New England did not want it, and most particularly they did not want war against England. France was the enemy, they said—that Corsican bandit, Napoleon. They cheered England's victories against him; they said they would not fight. They were as vehement against this war as they had been against Jefferson's Embargo. They pamphleteered, they speechified, they agitated—to no avail. The infant country was at war, and that was that. Once again British warships guarded Boston Harbor, and once again American privateers roamed the high seas. Those ships unfortunate enough to have been bottled up lay at anchor up and down the coast adorned with "Madison's nightcaps"—upended tar barrels on their mainmasts. And any merchant unfortunate enough to have too many such ships went bankrupt.

But this time, unlike the War for Independence, the Americans had a navy. It was only a small one, to be sure—half a dozen frigates against the British navy's hundreds. Still: they were grand ships, and none better than the USS *Constitution* out of Boston. People loved that ship, right from her beginnings—ah, she was a beauty, with her proud Hercules figurehead symbolizing her strength, and her masts raked, her sails set to catch the wind!

Colonel George Claghorn of New Bedford had supervised her building at Hartt's shipyard in the North End. Her frames were made of live oak from the sea islands off Georgia; her masts were tall white pine from Maine. Her decks were white oak from Massachusetts; her sails were made of flax, an acre of sails woven in the attic of the Granary building next to the cemetery, the only place in Boston big enough to hold such a spread. Paul Revere manufactured her hardware, and the copper sheathing for her bottom; and of course he made her bell—a grand 242-pounder. When it came time to put up her rigging, the rope-makers carried the miles of cable from the ropewalks at Barton's Point, near the mill dam; they marched through the city to fife and drum, cheered along the way by the proud populace who understood all too well what this splendid ship with her forty-four guns would do for them—declare their independence every bit as much as that sheet of paper covered with lofty words. What good were words, what good was old Governor Hancock's signature, if the new nation had no power? The USS *Constitution* would give them that power: she'd fight the French and the British and the Algerians and anyone else who tried to defeat them, for certain she would!

Not long after her launch, she had proved her worth when she shelled the Bashaw's palace at Tripoli. After that, the Bashaw had come onto her decks to sign a treaty of peace, and all the other Barbary pirates had ceased their depredations.

Now she was to engage in a larger fight, closer to home.

In mid-July 1812, not long after the war began, against all odds and with great skill and cunning, the USS *Constitution* escaped a squadron of five British warships off the New Jersey coast, among them a frigate called *Guerriere.*

She proceeded to Boston for new orders, but the orders were late. Her captain, Isaac Hull, decided to leave Boston to avoid being trapped in port.

On August 19, at three-thirty P.M., the *Constitution* encountered the *Guerriere* six hundred miles east of Boston. As the *Guerriere* waited, the *Constitution* closed. At five, at a distance of one mile, the *Guerriere* opened fire—most of which fell short.

At six, within pistol range, the *Constitution* fired broadside at her opponent. The *Guerriere* fired back. The Britisher suffered enormous damage: her mizzen sails and rigging were destroyed, her hull was shattered—and then her bowsprit caught in the *Constitution*'s rigging. The Americans were amazed at how their own ship had escaped serious injury. One gunner, whose name has been lost to history, watched as the balls flew at the *Constitution* and bounced off her stout oak timbers, and he cried, "Hurrah, men! Her sides are made of iron!"

Because the seas were heavy, the Americans could not board the *Guerriere*, and so the ships pulled apart. Almost at once the *Guerriere*'s foremast and mainmast fell. She was a wreck, helpless, foundering in the sea. After her men were taken as prisoners onto the *Constitution*, Captain Hull ordered her set afire; when she had burned to the waterline, her powder exploded and she sank.

On August 30 the *Constitution* returned to Boston with 297 prisoners of war and a new name: "Old Ironsides."

The men of Essex County, north of Boston, were particularly vocal in their opposition to Mr. Madison's war. Elias Abbott Revell was among them. They called themselves the "Essex Junto." They went so far as to advocate secession from the national government. In the fall of 1814 the Massachusetts Legislature issued a call for a convention to be held at Hartford, in Connecticut, to consider the matter. Elias Abbott Revell attended, as did Samuel Jackson Revell. Nathaniel Griffin Revell would have gone, but when he heard that Samuel would be there, he declined. The wrong that Samuel had done him—fifteen years ago, now—hurt him still. Stealing Georgiana—ruining her!

And in the quirky manner in which Fate deals out life's twists and turns, it was a good thing, in the end, that Nathaniel stayed home.

On the mild and hazy autumn day that New England's firebrands met in Hartford to talk about splitting up the union their fathers had fought and died to bring into existence, Nathaniel had a visit in his counting house from one of his acquaintances, Jacob Browning.

"I'm driving out to Waltham," Browning announced. "Mr. Lowell's got somethin' goin' on there I want to see. A factory, it is. Come along—the drive'll do you good, get out into the country."

Nathaniel sniffed. Factories were of no interest to him—filthy dirty places running on little better than slave labor. England had factories aplenty, and from what he'd heard of them, Manchester and Liverpool and Birmingham, no decent American would want to bring them here.

Nevertheless he was at loose ends, looking for ways to occupy his time. What with the war and its consequent depression, the town lay under a spell, it seemed. India Wharf, which Bulfinch had designed as a kind of great granite monument to the source of all their wealth, lay as quiet and deserted as all the other wharves, Long Wharf, and Revell's, and Rowe's, and all the wharves of Salem and Newburyport and Gloucester—every wharf in Massachusetts was deathly still, ships rotting at anchor, no goods in or out. Beacon Hill had been cut partway down some years ago to make fill for the grand new city arising, but now building had ceased, grass grew in the streets, and house lots went begging because no one could afford to build.

"All right," he said at last; he sent a note to say that he would not be home for dinner, and he and Browning set off. While they jogged along in the carriage, Browning told what he knew of Lowell's experiment:

"People call it Lowell's Folly, but I think he's on to somethin'. He's a delicate man, a high-strung man. And a few years ago he went abroad for his health. Well, he has a very active mind, y'know. He's a real mathematical one, and he can't stand doin' nothin' for long. So while his wife was traipsin' around seein' the sights—they were in England at the time—he took himself to visit the factories. What gave him that idea? I don't know. His mother's people were Cabots, y'know, and they had some small cotton factories up around Beverly. Nothin' much. They finally went bankrupt, I believe. And what with th'Embargo, an' all the trouble we've always had dependin' on England and the Continent for manufactured goods, I suppose he thought of startin' somethin' here. And the English, y'know, have the best machinery in the world. Oh, yes. But they don't allow it out, y'see. It's a crime to take out a piece of machinery from an English factory—or even a plan. Not a single drawin' of a loom or a spinnin' jenny can you take out. So Mr. Lowell just went around, lookin' at everythin', watchin' what they did, askin' questions all innocent like, as if he was merely passin' the time of day. And all the while he was memorizin' the bloody things—the looms an' the jennys an' the cardin' machines, every blasted one of 'em—an' he smuggled 'em out in his head! No Customs officer could arrest him, because he didn't have anythin' to declare. It was all stored up there in that brain of his, an' when he got back to Boston he hired a mechanic, an' they set up in a machine shop down in Broad Street, an' they fiddled an' tinkered an' tried this an' tried that, all accordin' to Mr. Lowell's rememberin', an' one day they had it all, right there—spinners and power looms an' I don't know what all. An' now they've set it up in a factory out here to get the waterpower of the Charles, an' they'll be lookin' for investors soon enough, if I don't miss my guess." Browning winked at Nathaniel. "Get in early, I say. We've all got capital to invest, and if we can't put it into ships' cargoes, we'll put it elsewhere. This war's a lesson to us: we're too dependent on England for manufactures."

At Lowell's factory, that day, Nathaniel watched as the waterpowered mill wheel drove the looms that wove a coarse cotton cloth. In another room a dozen spinners tended their bobbins; their machines, too, were powered by the river. It was all very efficient: raw cotton in at one end of the building, finished goods out at the other.

Impressive, he said. Even promising. But if the thing were to be undertaken on a large scale, more waterpower was needed, yes? The flow of the Charles here at Waltham is not great enough to power an enterprise to rival England's.

Lowell and his assistant nodded; first things first, they said. We will run this place as a kind of laboratory experiment; when we see that it works, we will look to expand.

2. LEVIATHAN

1

"Papa! Papa! I want to see the monster!"

Little Washington Abbott Revell, age six, came hurtling down the stairs and out the door. He threw himself into his father's arms and gave a great hug and a great kiss to match Elias's for him. Then, as Elias set him on the ground, he resumed his plea: "Papa! They say it is a hundred feet long, and it rises straight out of the sea—so high—can we go to see it, Papa?"

"Yes, yes! Give me a moment to catch my breath!" laughed Elias. As the coach boy took the horse and chaise around to the stable, Elias brushed the dust of the road from his coat and followed his son into the house. He would have a little refreshment, and then—yes, of course, they could go for a drive along the coastline and look for the creature that had excited so much interest since it was first seen the previous year. A real sea monster, it was, a serpent of enormous size, and now it had come again, right in Gloucester Harbor. Reliable sea captains had seen it, and sober merchants like Thomas Handasyd Perkins—no, this was not a hallucination, this was real.

Accordingly, not long after, the two of them were bowling along the coast road. Wash prattled happily. He adored his father; Elias's weekly visits from Boston were the high points of his existence. The rest of the time, he lived with his nanny, Miss Millbank, and the servants. From time to time he was permitted to visit relatives in Boston—his father's kin, and, less often, relatives of his mother's.

He had never known his mother, had never seen a portrait or a drawing of her. He knew that her Christian name had been Dolly, but he knew very little else about her. She had died, his father said. As young as he was, Wash knew that his father did not like to speak about her, and so he never questioned too much. From time to time, as if simply seeking reassurance, he would say, "Where is my mama?"

"Dead, child."

And that was that, until the next time.

The harbor shore was thronged with people on the watch for the sea serpent—*Scoliophis Atlanticus*, as the members of the Linnaean Society named him. Spyglasses were passed from hand to hand; every now and then a false alarm would be called and people would rush from one side to the other, peering at the water.

Elias boosted Washington onto his shoulders. People glanced at them and smiled to see how much they looked alike, father and son. And so well dressed—better than most people in Gloucester, for this was not a wealthy China port like Boston or Salem, but a fishing port, which it had been from its beginnings, back in Pilgrim times.

At last, after an hour of watching, peering through Elias's glass, enduring several false alarms, they gave up. They would come back another day, Elias promised.

They set off for home. Wash, refusing to give up hope, kept his eye on the sea every time it appeared around a curve in the road.

Suddenly he gave a great shout. "There! There he is! Stop!"

Elias pulled the chaise off the road; they scrambled down and ran to the edge of the low headland. There—no need even for the glass to see him: a huge, snakelike thing rising straight up from the water. Elias judged the height to be ten feet at least, and he could see five times that length in the water, curved and humped just like a sea monster in an old Scandinavian drawing he had once seen: a Norway Kraken. Cautioning the child to be quiet, he looked through the glass: an ugly head, oddly equine, atop a sinuous neck, rough skin, a dark brownish-gray color. He handed the glass to Wash, helping him to hold it steady.

"Can you see it?"

"Yes, Papa! Oh, how ugly it is! It's opening its mouth! It has teeth! It's a real monster, Papa!"

For a long time—twenty minutes, perhaps—they watched the creature; then with surprising swiftness, all in an instant, it vanished into the water. The surface of the summer sea was smooth again, unbroken.

Washington turned his shining eyes upon his father. At six, he did not have the vocabulary to express what he felt just then; all he could say, over and over, was, "We saw it! We saw it!"

When they returned home, he tried to describe it to his nanny. He did a pretty good job. She was mightily impressed; she laughed and screamed and held her hands up to her face in what seemed like real terror—"Oh, I'm glad I didn't see it, that I am! No, don't say any more! You'll frighten me too much!"

———

Washington was the light of his father's life. He was born in the spring of 1811, more than a year and a half after his mother had aborted her first pregnancy.

All winter after that unhappy event, Dolly's life had hung in the balance. At last, in the spring, she had recovered, in body if not in spirit. She had lost the sparkle in her eyes, the sweet flirtation of her smile that had attracted Elias in the beginning; now she was like a sleepwalker, pacing through her days, hardly aware of her surroundings.

Elias clung to the belief that if only she had a child, she would be content. One night in the summer following her recovery he had made love to her as gently as he knew how—gently, tenderly, he loved her as a man loves his wife; and he could not but believe that such gentle passion would bear fruit. He was relieved that she submitted to him; she had recovered from her temporary madness, he thought, and now at last she would become a proper wife to him.

When she became pregnant again, he made sure that some female relative was always with her—her mother, or his sister Mariah, or one of Dolly's sisters-in-law.

He need not have worried. She had suffered too greatly to try another operation on herself. As her time drew near, and she needed to look beyond it to the day when she would be herself again, her thoughts turned over and over in her mind. What should she do? How should she live? She did not know—not yet.

When the baby was born, Elias decided that they should name him Washington. Many people thought the merchants of Boston no better than traitors for their opposition to the Embargo; well, he was not a traitor, no Revell was a traitor, and by God, he would prove it. He would name his son for the father of their country.

In the months following Washington's birth, Dolly recovered well. Her strength returned; she got her waistline back; at her insistence Elias hired a wet nurse so that she need not suffer months of milking—like a cow, she thought.

The baby thrived, too. He was a beautiful little thing, with a head of blond ringlets and dark blue eyes. He had a sunny nature, hardly ever fussing; from the moment he opened his eyes and looked around to see what kind of world he had come into, he had a charm about him that caused everyone to adore him, even more than the usual adoration accorded to infants.

Everyone, that is, except his mother. She accepted him well enough, but she hardly adored him. Nevertheless, Elias was so happy with this wonderful gift she had given him that he relaxed his monitoring; Dolly no longer needed to be watched night and day, he thought, and he even, once or twice, allowed her to be driven to Salem.

One fine summer day the coachman, having been appointed to meet Dolly at a certain hour in Salem to drive her home, waited and waited to no avail until nearly dark, at which time he returned to Revell Hall by himself to send a message to Elias in Boston that the mistress had somehow, he did not know how, turned up missing.

At the very hour that the coachman waited fruitlessly for her to appear, Dolly was safe on a sloop bound for Newport. As land dropped out of sight, she stood on the deck, a cashmere shawl wrapped around her shoulders against the cool evening sea breeze. She felt reborn: a new woman. Vaguely she missed her child, but not enough to have stayed. She knew that a life in Revell Hall would have been death for her, one way or another. Someday, she thought, she would try to see her son; for now, she must leave.

When Elias had the news of his wife's abandonment, he realized that he was not so surprised as he might have been. To preserve appearances, he instituted a modest search for her; he put an announcement in the papers; he made a few inquiries. He learned nothing. He consulted a lawyer friend; and eventually he began proceedings for a divorce.

In the autumn after he saw the sea monster, Washington began to attend a dame school in Salem. In time, Elias thought, he would bring the boy to Boston during the winters so that he could attend the Latin School. But Revell Hall was Washington's home; he was happy living there, and so for the time being he would stay.

He was a handsome child, tall and straight and fair, with a boundless curiosity about the world—his world, sea and forest and meadow, curious plants growing in the kitchen garden, a passel of baby rabbits born in the woods, strange and beautiful shells gathered on the shore. His nanny was hard put to keep up with him, questions day and night, expeditions hither and yon.

Very soon after he began to read and write, he started to put little stories down on paper. His favorite was the story of a boy who saw a sea monster. He wrote it over and over again, until by the time he was ten he had a dozen different versions of it, each more rich in description than the last, some of the later ones having a little plot.

Because he was so charming in an artless way, and because he wanted to hear about everything both in the world and out of it, he spent long hours in the kitchen with the housekeeper—a new one; not the one who had guarded his mother before he was born. This lady, plump and jolly, was a native of Salem; she knew everyone and everything that was to be known about the town and its inhabitants. Moreover, she had a steady stream of visitors, tradesmen, and relatives, and who-knew-all; with them, she gossiped for hours in her kitchen—her domain—and often little Wash sat by, listening. Thus he heard the story of the Widow Enright, who stalked her widow's walk for years—and who eventually died on that narrow walkway—waiting for the husband who never returned from his last voyage; from time to time she might still be seen, pacing back and forth, weeping and wailing, calling for her husband.

And he heard the story of the pirate who buried his treasure in the woods outside Salem Town, back in the days of King George I, a hundred years ago now; he put a curse on it, saying that whoever tried to rob him of it would die a terrible death. And sure enough, ten, twelve, fifteen men had tried over the years to find that hoard, and all of them had died before their time, in strange and sometimes terrible ways—dropping down dead on the road in the light of a full moon, falling into the sea from the deck of a ship, one man torn to pieces by his own mastiff.

One of Wash's friends at school was a lad named Abraham Griffin. His family were merchants and shipbuilders, comfortably well off, if hardly the equal of the Revells, and well-known and -respected in Salem. They lived in a big house on Chestnut Street. From time to time Wash visited them. When Abraham's mother first heard Wash's name, she smacked her lips in surprise. If she was not mistaken, her husband's grandfather's sister had married a Boston Revell, 'way back, before the Revolution. Emilie Griffin, her name had been; folks said she'd had a beautiful picture painted of her. In the manner of many Massachusetts folks, Mrs. Griffin was devoted to genealogy, to family connection; she would have liked Washington Revell in any case, such a charming lad he was, but this happy connection made her all the more partial to him.

Quite by accident one day, as if she was speaking of some perfectly ordinary thing, Mrs. Griffin happened to mention that her husband's ancestress—not the lady who had married Ebenezer, but someone long before that—had been hung for a witch.

Instantly Washington's ears perked up. He was almost descended from a witch! He begged her to tell him about it. And so she did, as much as she knew, which was not much. Many people were hanged in the witchcraft, she said; those old times were very superstitious, people were ignorant beyond belief.

All the way home, the next day, Wash felt something brimming in him—an excitement, a fever, he didn't know what. He went directly to his room; he took out his paper and pen. He was almost eleven, and he could write a clear, easy hand; he began a tale about a boy who lived in Salem in the present day, whose ancestress had been hanged for a witch, and who now saw her ghost and was haunted by it, until one dark night . . . what?

He couldn't think of an ending.

No matter. He liked what he'd written so far; even so young, he trusted his instinct, he knew that sooner or later an ending would come to him.

That night the wind rose, the trees surrounding the house lashed their branches against the windows, and from beyond the bluff Wash could hear the heavy pounding of the surf on the rocky shore. He huddled under his warm, lamb's wool coverlets, imagining himself back in time to the crowd on Gallows Hill so long ago. In his mind's eye he saw the scaffold bearing its awful fruit; he heard the shrieks of the condemned, the wail of the crowd.

And then he was asleep.

The storm rose; the house creaked and moaned, the wind buffeted the corners and whistled down the chimney.

Suddenly Wash came awake. Dark night, the thrashing storm—and something else.

Not since he was a little fellow had he wanted a night light; always his room was dark, and he never minded it. Now, however, he was afraid.

Something was there in the darkness with him. Just there, by the fireplace. He could sense it, he could see it—he could even smell it, an acrid, bitter smell that was, he imagined, very like the smell of brimstone.

It was a tall thing, a woman's shape, a shape of glowing pale stuff that shimmered in the darkness, that emanated a terrible cold, the coldness of death, the coldness of the grave. And he knew that if he touched it, he would die too.

He *knew*—

She had a reason for coming to him. She wanted to speak to him, perhaps: wanted, after a century and more, to protest her killing, to say that she was innocent of witchcraft.

He did not remember calling for help, did not remember how quickly his father, there for a few days' visit, came running into his room.

But what he did remember—what he never forgot all his life—was the sense of that apparition, and the certainty of who it was.

She had come to him.

She had come.

To *him*—why?

2

A few weeks later, on a cold, bright November day, Nathaniel Griffin Revell of Beacon Hill, a wealthy merchant and, at fifty-nine, the eldest member of the Revell family, climbed into his carriage, ordered the coachman to proceed, and went around to collect a few of his most trusted business associates. Then he took them into the wilderness, which is to say, East Chelmsford, a farming community thirty miles northwest of Boston near the New Hampshire border. When they arrived at their destination they alighted, stretched their cramped legs, and began to perambulate the snow-covered fields adjacent to the subject of their investigations: the Pawtucket Falls of the Merrimack River.

"I say, Revell, not so fast." Kirk Boott came puffing up behind Nathaniel, his face red with exertion. Nathaniel hardly heard him; he forged ahead until he reached the riverbank. Then he glanced back, nodded, and returned his attention to the spectacle before him: the enormous falls, the water rushing down from the mountains of New Hampshire, gathering force, swelling, swelling, until here at the falls the swollen rapids went over in a mighty drop, a thirty-foot fall, roaring down, spray blowing in their faces, a sound like constant thunder—waterpower! Yes, here—here in this wilderness—they would make Lowell's dream come alive! Lowell was dead and buried these four years now, but he had had the genius to foresee what could be done, if the proper place was found. He had died never knowing of this place, this magnificent gift of Nature in her wildest aspect. A thirty-foot drop! They would buy it, and harness it—dig their canals, put in place their waterwheels—why, they would build a city here, a New World manufacturing Paradise! And it must have Lowell's name, to make him immortal.

"And who will tend those machines, eh?" said Boott. "You don't mean to have factory slaves like England's, do you?"

"Of course not." Nathaniel sniffed, thinking about it. No one wanted a permanent factory population. "Farmers' daughters will come to work for a year or two before they marry. They'll be glad of a chance to earn a little money."

Which was true enough, but first, the Boston Associates needed to buy the land, and good frugal Yankees that they were, they needed to buy it cheap. If the farmers who owned it learned what it was to be used for, they would jack up the price to an unconscionable level. Therefore:

"Mr. Fletcher? My name is Nathaniel Revell. How'd'y'do. Ah, I was just up looking at your pasture by the river—field, is it? Yes. Well. Ah, my friends and I live in Boston. We're looking for a place, not too far, where we can hunt waterfowl. Just a little recreational shooting, you understand. Yes. Well. Ah, what would you say to a dollar an acre?"

The farmer hid his smile. They were talking about a hundred acres, perhaps more. If these fools wanted to pay such a price for the pleasure of duck hunting, it was certainly agreeable to him. Easiest money he ever earned—far easier than wresting a crop from the poor, thin, rocky New England soil.

But it was Nathaniel who had the last laugh. Within six months Hugh Cummiskey and his gang of Irish canal cutters had walked from Charlestown to dig the canals and lay the foundations of the first cotton mill—thereby increasing the value of the land a thousandfold.

That night, returning from his expedition, Nathaniel entertained some of his friends for dinner; he told them about his hopes for the new enterprise. He invited them to subscribe to the factory which would, if all went well, be in operation within a year. It would be only the first of many, he thought, but he kept that rash speculation to himself.

His friends were skeptical, but like Nathaniel, they had profits from the China Trade, flourishing once again since Madison's War; they had profits from European trade, from whaling, from shipbuilding, from the northern fisheries—profit, profit, and where to put it? Where to invest it?

Very well, they said; they felt a strong loyalty to him, he was one of them, they would stand by him. Five thousand dollars each, they would put in—just as an experiment. Five thousand—not a penny more, mind! We might as well kiss it good-bye, for we do not expect this experiment to work. No one can manufacture cotton cloth on a large scale except the British.

Nathaniel was satisfied. He was sure that the experiment would succeed. And if it did not—well, each one of them could afford a loss of five thousand. Five thousand was a small sum compared to the profits that awaited them.

They sat in the dining room finishing the last of their meal—just the gentlemen, for Nathaniel's sons were away at school, Artemas at Harvard, Hamilton at Phillips Andover. His wife was asleep, as she often was; his only daughter, Caroline, was presumably reading in her bedroom—a pastime in which she engaged with increasing frequency.

As always when he thought of his sons, Nathaniel felt a little ripple of pride. They were good boys, splendid boys. They would carry the Family along very well. He glanced up to where the portraits of his father and mother hung above the fireplace: Ebenezer and Emilie Griffin Revell. Some day, he told himself, he should have the bullet hole just below her bosom repaired. On the other hand, the portrait had been known for years as the "Bullet Revell," so perhaps he should leave it alone. How beautiful his mother had been; how he wished that he had known her! His gaze shifted to his father: a stern, handsome man, a serious-looking man, and yet Nathaniel could remember, as if it had happened yesterday, the night of the Tea Party, when Ebenezer had come home disguised as an Indian and danced around the room.

He shook his head; he came back to the warm, convivial present, his friends all around him, supportive even though they doubted him. A good day—a good evening. He was not unaware that he was a fortunate man. At length, having had their fill of his Madeira and his good food, the company rose and said good night. Nathaniel stood on his doorstep watching the last of them make their way up Beacon Street or down across the Common. It was snowing again: they would have a hard winter, from the looks of it. No matter. As long as trade kept up, he did not care what the weather was.

He came inside and shut and locked the door and went upstairs, up the broad, beautifully curved staircase that spiraled up and up to the top, where it ended in a cupola. He loved to go there and look down across the crowded little city to the wharves, to his own wharf where stood his own warehouses, where his own ships lay at anchor. Those wharves and warehouses and ships had brought him and all the Revells great wealth; and now, he was sure, this new enterprise would bring him even more.

He saw a light under Caroline's door. He ought to put a stop to her reading so much, but he did not like to upset her—an edict against reading would certainly do that. He did not understand her; did not understand any woman. He had the vague feeling that women were not meant to be understood—that God had intended them to be mysterious always, with their humors and their fainting spells and their tiny little brains, so delicate, so liable to be corrupted.

He passed on, past his wife's room—no light there—and into his own. Women!

But as he undressed he thought of a piece of news he had had only last week, and in fairness—for he always thought of himself as a fair man—he had to admit that sometimes men could behave strangely, too. One of the Abbott Revells, Elias's brother Roger, who had shown his difference early on by electing to remain at the College as a teacher of Greek and Latin instead of going into business like the rest of them, had announced that he was going to join

Dr. Samuel Gridley Howe, a prominent Boston man, an eminent humanitarian, and go to Greece to help her in her fight for independence against the Turks.

Really! Had anyone ever heard an odder thing?

Greece!

Nathaniel couldn't understand such behavior. The Abbott Revells were his half siblings; their mother, Abigail Abbott, had married his father Ebenezer in 1768. Nathaniel had been six years old then, and so Abigail, for all practical purposes, had been the only mother he'd ever had. And a very good one, too—level-headed, reliable, sensible, a wonderful woman whom they'd all loved very much. So how had one of her sons turned out to be a radical—a man who picked up and went off to fight for some foreign cause?

Of course Roger taught Greek, and no doubt he wanted to see the country—but to take part in some silly war? War was bad: bad for business, bad for men who got themselves killed. Fortunately Roger was not married, so at least he would not leave behind a grieving widow and orphans for the rest of the Family—Nathaniel, most likely—to look after.

He could not imagine what Greece might be like, any more than he could imagine China, where Philip had served so well all these years. Only the previous month he had had a letter from Philip stating that the season's shipment would be leaving in mid-December. Good, dependable man! Nathaniel reminded himself to put Philip down for a share in the new factory.

3

Samuel Jackson Revell was not a very religious man, but he did not discount the existence of God altogether, and in fact from time to time he even thought that perhaps God did exist, and perhaps that God was punishing him for the wrong he did, years ago, to his half brother Nathaniel. He had seduced Nathaniel's fiancée—a wicked thing, and he had never really understood why he had behaved so. An impulsive act, it had been—one of those reckless acts that changed the course of one's life.

The result of it had been his marriage to the young lady, followed by the premature birth of their only child, named for her, adored by her, spoiled to death by her, their son George.

Samuel had heard the boy—although at twenty-four he was no longer a boy—stumble in last night very late, past midnight. Bad company—bad behavior! George couldn't continue like this, thought Samuel, for he'd ruin his health. Or get himself expelled—and certainly that would be a shame, for at twenty-four he was far too old as it was, still to be an undergraduate. Samuel resolved to have a frank talk with him after dinner—threaten him, perhaps; put a good scare into him.

And so, filled with good resolves, he went out and walked down to his countinghouse.

Meanwhile that bright summer morning, that same young man, George Jackson Revell, awakened in his own bed in his own room in his father's house on Colonnade Row, across from Boston Common, and he did not know where he was.

The iron bands of a severe headache tightened around his temples. His eyeballs twitched with pain when he opened his eyes, and so he kept them shut. He felt as if he were going to vomit.

God! What a night! All the Porcellian fellows, of whom he was one, had hosted all the Hasty Pudding fellows at a dinner, the last of the year. Afterward they had played cards until quite late. They had gotten very drunk. They had—yes, he was sure of it—visited a brothel. He couldn't remember anything more.

Gingerly he moved his splitting head slightly on his pillow, trying to find a comfortable position. Before he succeeded, he heard a knock at his door. He did not have even enough strength to groan. Go away, he thought. Instead the knock came again, and then he heard the door open. He peered through half-open eyes. Dear God, how the light hurt them!

It was one of the maids, bearing a letter on a small silver tray.

" 'Mornin', Mr. George." Her voice ripped through his head like a saw rasping through wood. He had not the strength to reply. "He says it's important, sir. He's waitin'."

"Who?" muttered George. His head was going to crack open, he knew that it was, any moment now.

"Him as brought this. He wanted you to have it right away."

George groaned. He could hardly see, let alone read. He held out his hand and the girl put the letter into it. With trembling fingers he broke the seal and unfolded the single page.

To the bearer:
One thousand four hundred thirty-three dollars on demand.

He groaned again. The maid's expression did not change; Mr. George was known to the household help as a wild one, and so his condition this morning was not surprising.

He tried to think. He knew who the caller was. He needed to deal with the fellow somehow; his father must not see him. Neither must his stepmother. His stepmother disliked him; already she had borne his father a boy, the start of a second family, and now she was expecting again. George's mother, Georgiana, had adored him—worshiped him. Since her death, and his stepmother's arrival, he had felt out of place here, an intruder in his own home.

"All right," he said. His voice sounded strange in his ears. "Tell him I'll be down directly."

With an enormous effort he stood up, splashed water on his face from the basin, and pulled on his clothes. Treading very carefully so as not to jar his curdling brain, he went downstairs.

The fellow who awaited him was not a Porcellian but a Hasty Puddingite. And certainly not a gentleman.

He'd come for his money, he said.

"You'll have it," said George.

"Now. I want it now."

"I said, you'll have it." Cur! Dog! Wasn't a man's word good enough?

"When?"

George couldn't help putting his hands to his head, one on each temple, pressing hard, because if he did not, his head was going to split open, his brains were going to spill out onto the new Chinese carpet that his hateful stepmother had insisted on having because the old one wasn't good enough for her.

Next week, he said—the week after, for sure.

The fellow didn't believe him. If I don't have it by then, he said, I'm going to your father. Then he went away.

You weren't supposed to press a fellow for gambling debts. George knew of cases where a man had paid his debts run up in College ten, even twenty years later, when he'd had a chance to make his way in the world. No proper gentleman pressed a young fellow for money. This person was a fool if he thought George had ready access to all that cash. It was one of the disadvantages of being a Revell: people thought you had money coming out of your ears. What they didn't realize was that very often the richest men, of whom his father was one, were the most penurious, and particularly with their sons. There was a certain Yankee way of looking at the world which held that it was good to keep a rich man's son on a short rein. During his time at the College, George had learned, to his chagrin, that his allowance was less than that of many boys from far more modest circumstances.

He went back upstairs. He lay down. He passed out. When he awoke, it was mid-afternoon. From downstairs he heard his father's voice. The odor of food drifted up: they had started dinner without him. No matter: in his present condition, he couldn't have eaten anything.

After a while the maid came again, this time with a summons to his father. George pulled himself together, tied a remarkably neat twist to his cravat, and went down.

Samuel awaited him in his study. In his late fifties, he was as straight and trim as he had been at his son's age. At his son's age he had been graduated from the College; at his son's age he had already started in the Family business. He looked now on this younger version of himself, so alike physically and yet—how had it happened?—so different. Samuel held a letter—a most unhappy, discouraging letter—from President Kirkland: that good man, reluctant to offend one of the First Families of Boston, had taken it upon himself to break the news, as gently as possible, that George Jackson Revell, class of '25, had been dismissed from the College not only for failing grades, but for severely intemperate behavior.

"What is the meaning of this?" said Samuel.

He handed over the letter. George's eyes could hardly focus, but seeing the signature, he knew well enough what it said.

"I said, what is the meaning of this?" Samuel Jackson Revell was known as a hard trader, an honest man but a very sharp one, a cold man, rather grim—not your hail-fellow-well-met. Many people did not like him much, including his eldest son.

"I don't—"

"You are a Porcellian," said Samuel, putting first things first. "And a student at my alma mater. Now I see that you have disgraced me. You have been dismissed from the College. Dismissed! Explain yourself!"

George wanted very much to sit down, but he could not: he did not have permission, and even if he had, sitting would have been a sign of weakness.

He gritted his teeth because he thought that he was going to throw up. The room tilted; he felt sweat on his face but he had neglected to provide himself with a handkerchief.

"Well?"

"Yes, sir. It isn't—I mean—"

The door opened a crack: the second Mrs. Revell, looking in. Nosy thing: really, he couldn't stand her. His own dear mother, dead these four years now, had been the sweetest, most loving mother in the world. He didn't understand how his father could have taken this shrew as her replacement. Soon there would be a passel of little shrews all over the house. George felt a tear come to his eye, and he sniffled.

"I said, explain yourself!"

The door shut.

George swallowed hard. His knees were growing weaker by the minute; he did not know how long he would be able to stand. One thousand, four hundred and thirty-three dollars. It might as well have been a million.

And as for flunking out—well, admittedly that had been a mistake. He hadn't intended that. Like all the other Porcellians, George had aimed to get no more than passing grades. A good, solid "pass" was a gentleman's grade. Anything higher was a sign that you were pushy, or so insecure about your place in the world that you needed the reassurance of a high mark. No Porcellian was insecure. They all got gentleman's grades.

"Yes, sir." He had forgotten the question. He needed to lie down.

"Damn it!" roared Samuel. His thin, pale Revell face was growing pink with anger. This weak reed, this spoiled sodden child—was this the son he had aimed to produce? The Revells were tough, had always been tough. This nearly effete young man looked like a—like a Frenchman!

George was not afraid of his father's rage—he had seen it before—but he was very very tired. He swayed on his feet, trying to stay upright.

"Listen to me!" shouted Samuel. He seized his son by the cravat and pulled him up; they were nearly of a height, but next to his father, George looked like a little boy.

"You are a disgrace! Do you hear me? And don't think I don't know about your debts! People tell me things. I get about. I don't know the exact amount, and I don't want to know—but that you are in debt—yes!" With an angry little shake, Samuel let go, so suddenly that his son staggered back and only just caught himself against a delicate mahogany table.

"Don't you know," said Samuel, his voice dripping contempt, "that Revells do not go into debt? Don't you understand that? We do not go into debt! We do not owe money! And if we do, it is not owed for gambling!"

George did not reply; he concentrated on not vomiting.

"In the morning," Samuel went on, "you look for work. But not with us. Not with my firm. You may go anywhere you please, but not to us. You need to learn a little about the meaning of life. Do you know that? Do you know what the meaning of life is? Eh? The meaning of life is"—and he held up his hand to tick off the points on his fingers—"hard work, honest dealing, and profit! That's all! Just those three things! And now you're going to have to learn all of it on your own! Look at you! What's the matter? You drank too much? Disgusting! No gentleman drinks too much, not ever! Go on—go back to bed if you're too sick to stand. But I don't want to see you again until you're gainfully employed, do you understand? No more college for you! Porcellian? You aren't fit to be a Porcellian!"

With that, he flung himself out of the room. He needed to walk a bit, needed to work the bile out of his system. Damned whelp!

With his long, purposeful stride, as distinctive a Revell Family trait as the color of the hair, the particular blue of the eyes, Samuel strode out of his house and across Tremont Street and onto the Common. It was June: the trees were leafed out, the grass was growing nicely, its bright green a pleasant contrast to Bulfinch's red-brick Statehouse and, more recent, the Park Street Church that had replaced the old Granary building.

Before he knew it, he had reached the top of the Common, the mall that paralleled Beacon Street. Over the low bank and through the iron railings of the fence at its top he could see the house of his half brother Nathaniel. The glass in the windows was purple. He stared at it for a moment. Ugly stuff, inferior quality; it had turned when the sun first struck it. Why didn't Nathaniel have the sense to replace it? Samuel was as frugal as any man, but to spend a small fortune on a house—and Nathaniel's house had certainly cost that—and then to skimp on such a thing as window glass made no sense; it was bad business.

Bad business: that was his and Nathaniel's story. Bad, bad business. Who had challenged whom? He couldn't even remember. Silly, stupid—to carve up the Family that way, over a young woman. Who had turned out to be a perfectly acceptable wife, but still—

Just then the door opened and Nathaniel came out with a group of gentlemen, half a dozen or so. Samuel stepped back; he did not want to be seen. They seemed in high spirits; they laughed and clapped each other on the back and shook hands all around before each one went his own way.

Nathaniel went inside and closed the door. Samuel turned and walked down the path toward Tremont Street, catching up after a moment with two men who had been at Nathaniel's. He didn't know them; he overtook them and went on. As he passed them he heard one say, "A profit of fourteen percent! Every year!"

The next morning, just after first light and well before anyone save the scullery maid and the cook were about, well before Samuel would awake, his errant son, George Jackson Revell, threw a few clothes into a satchel, let himself out of the house, and went to the Exchange Coffee House, where, he knew, he could catch a stage for New Bedford. By nightfall he was walking up Johnny-cake Hill looking for an inexpensive room. What he found was a place in a bed already occupied by a foul-smelling seaman who informed George that he was about to sign on for a whaling voyage that would, he said, probably last two years at least—"If we make it home, lad! They don't like us, y'know—the great whales! Don't like us at all, an' they try to get away if they can, and stove us if they can't!"

In the dim light of the whale-oil lamp he peered at George, a grin spreading on his stubbled face. "Yer lookin' to sign on, too? A mite tender, ain't ye? Whalin's the hardest job there is—harder than any job before the mast, harder than the navy, harder than the China Trade. You got to have all yer wits an' all yer strength t'earn yer share. Now I know Cap'n Macy, he's a Nantucket man, an' if y'like I'll put in a word f'r ye. Y'look honest enough—an' as f'r the work, he'll beat it out of ye if he must. He's a Quaker. All the best whalin' cap'ns'r'Quakers, but they're mean as mean, they're hard hard men, an' don't say I didn't warn ye."

With that, he turned over and went to sleep, leaving George to ponder his words and decide if indeed he really wanted to ship out on a whaling voyage under the fearsome Captain Macy. He decided that he did.

4

At Macao: late winter. The gardens washed with rain, the cloying odor of incense permeating the house.

Philip stood at the window looking out, but he did not see the gravel walks, the stone benches, and the small goldfish pond. He was waiting for a visitor to his apartments; soon he would hear her little bound feet hurrying along the passage to his door—his "small-footed woman," his "Golden Lily," far more beautiful than the two such who had been taken to London not long ago and presented to George IV, much to the outrage of proper English society.

Late—late— Where was she? He was unable to tolerate frustration, he hated to have to wait for anything. Tall and thin, he had grown (it seemed) taller and more gaunt with each passing year, more than twenty, now, since he had come out. And despite his physical differences with the small, yellow-skinned, black-haired people here, he had in fact become more Chinese than Western. During the many months that he spent each year here at Macao, he had been allowed to study the language—a great help, of course, in transacting business, but also important in understanding the people, the country. No white man could hope to comprehend more than a fraction of the vast, mysterious land that was the Celestial Empire, but at least, Philip thought, he had made a beginning.

He turned away from the dreary view; he went to his small lacquered desk and opened one of its drawers. He took out a small pipe carved into the shape of a monster fish, and a box from which he extracted a dab of opium paste. Since his first opium pipe those many years ago, when he was suffering from an intestinal illness, he had become extraordinarily fond of the drug. It soothed him and lulled him into a haze of contentment; it took away all his worries, all his desires. When he had opium in him, he was the calmest man on earth: nothing worried him, nothing bothered him, he entered a golden trance of indifference to the world and its cares, and there he stayed, happily floating above the fray.

He lit up and took a few puffs. Pritchard had warned him to give it up, but Pritchard was wrong. And dead—he had died last year, dropping dead of a stroke. Probably, thought Philip, because he had not allowed himself the soothing pleasures of opium.

He heard a light tap-tap at the door. He was too tired to get up and open it, so he called out for her to come in.

He peered at her; his vision was a little cloudy now, but still he could see her well enough. She was an exquisite thing, hair like black lacquer, skin like a ripe peach, her tiny feet tortured into a shape that Westerners found grotesque, but that was, for the Chinese, erotic in the extreme. Nothing aroused a Chinese male more than the sight of a woman's bound feet.

The pungent odor of the drug assaulted her nostrils as she came in, but she made no reaction; she came to him, knelt before him and felt his hand on her perfectly arranged hair. Then, raising her face to him, she smiled at him—a bold gesture, but one that she knew she could safely make. He would not object.

She looked directly into his eyes. His pupils were pinpoints. He tried to speak to her, but he could not; he could only smile at her, nodding, content that she was with him. In her exquisite, silent beauty she embodied everything that he loved about the Orient, for he did love this place, he thought of it now as his home. Always there had been certain whites who fell in love with the East—who, when they went there, understood that that was where they were meant to be. Philip was one of those: hopelessly in love with his real mistress, the Celestial Empire itself, he accepted the ministrations of her surrogate, the small-footed woman with him now.

5

By the time the factories at Lowell had been in operation for ten years, Nathaniel Revell and his associates understood that not only had they been successful in their gamble, but they had fomented a revolution that was no less than the one their fathers had begun at Lexington and Concord: an Industrial Revolution, a new way of organizing the country's getting and spending.

There were many factories at Lowell now, insatiable in their demand for raw cotton, productive and profitable beyond the wildest dreams of their corporate owners.

The cotton goods were sold to ready markets: to China, where the ginseng root was not so popular as it had been, and so American merchants, including the Revells, needed new goods to trade. And to the South, to clothe the black slaves who grew and harvested the raw cotton. Raw cotton to Lowell to be made into cheap calico to clothe the slaves who grew more raw cotton . . . you could call it a modern version of the Golden Triangle.

Or you could call it a covenant with Hell, which is what that intrepid native of Newburyport, William Lloyd Garrison, called the slave system. Garrison was a professional Abolitionist—a new breed of man on the American side of the water, although England had a few such.

The cotton manufacturers paid no attention to Garrison at first. He started his little newspaper, *The Liberator*, and he came down to Boston and gave his first speech at Park Street Church, which had been built at the corner of the Common on the site of the Old Granary.

Garrison's message was simple enough: immediate emancipation for the slave. In the first issue of *The Liberator*, he stated his credo: "I am in earnest— I will not equivocate—I will not excuse—I will not retreat a single inch—AND I WILL BE HEARD."

Obviously such a man was a fanatic. Fanatics were excitable creatures; they lacked good breeding. No person of social standing—no Porcellian, no member of one of Boston's first families—became excited over a cause, particularly so unpopular a one.

Unless that person happened to be James Jackson Revell, in which case— why, yes, he was an Abolitionist, and proud of it. He'd been a slave himself, once, a captive of the Barbary pirates. So he knew what slavery was, better than anyone.

He was proud to be a Jackson Revell, too, twin to Samuel, as rich as Samuel—nearly as rich as Nathaniel, he thought with grim satisfaction, although Nathaniel would never acknowledge it. James was proud of his son, as well: Daniel Jackson Revell, who only recently had joined with Garrison in what both young men thought of as their holy mission.

As James saw it, his son Daniel was upholding the best traditions of the Revell Family: acting on his conscience. Hadn't their father, Ebenezer, done exactly that when he joined Samuel Adams and the other patriots to fight the

Revolution? "Go ahead," he told Daniel, "do your work with Mr. Garrison, and I will see to it that you get a full share of our profits"—for there was no point in impoverishing the lad simply because he followed his own calling.

Garrison found subscribers for his paper, enough to support it, and with the help of a few like-minded disciples, he started the American Anti-Slavery Association and the Massachusetts Anti-Slavery Society and—worst of all—the Boston Female Anti-Slavery Society.

The cotton manufacturers looked around; some small thing, like a mosquito, was annoying them. *The Liberator*? Garrison? Swat it—shoo him away. He will annoy our southern brethren. Do not forget that our success depends on their goodwill. They can cut us off—they can choose to sell only to England, whose Manchesters and Birminghams have ten times our capacity. And then where would we be?

A mosquito's sting: or the first faint tremor before the earthquake strikes. So they swatted him away, and then they tried to ignore him. He was nothing: a nobody. He had no fortune, no social position, no Family. He was a nonentity—a fanatic. He must be silenced! He will cause us to lose money!

In the summer of 1835 a proslavery group—businessmen, churchmen, leading politicians including Mayor Theodore Lyman and the former mayor, Harrison Gray Otis, and the well-known merchant and manufacturer, Nathaniel Griffin Revell—held a public meeting in Faneuil Hall. While these men harangued against the Abolitionist, Garrison was hanged in effigy outside. Public sentiment was whipped to a frenzy. Down with the Abolitionists! Down with Garrison! Catch him! Tar and feather him! Hang him if necessary—but silence him! Silence him! He is bad for business!

This incident, said Garrison, showed that the grand old hall was no longer "the Cradle of Liberty." Now, he said, it was "the Coffin of Liberty."

A few weeks later the Boston Female Anti-Slavery Society announced its anniversary meeting in the society's rooms at No. 48 Washington Street, next to the *Liberator* office.

6

"Lloyd? Are you ready?" said Daniel. "Here they come—Miss Seymour and the others." He turned from the window to glance at the man seated at a desk behind him, rapidly filling a sheet of paper with ink-blotted scribbling.

The writer looked up, squinting his eyes through his spectacles. He was a young man, not quite thirty, but already he had begun to go bald. His face was oddly gentle for a man with so fearsome a reputation: to many people in Boston, he was the Devil personified.

"Yes," he said. "One moment . . ." He added a few more words, blotted the sheet, and, getting up, pulled on his worn black frock coat.

They heard footsteps on the narrow stairs. Coming out of their little office, they saw the first arrivals—a group of half a dozen or so women, four white and two colored—and, following on their heels, several men.

"We have Wheeler and Ashby coming," murmured the bespectacled man to Daniel, "but I want you to sit in front until they do. Then use your best judgment."

Daniel understood: these men just arriving were so-called gentlemen, but they were as capable of violence as any ruffian. They trooped in now, faster than the women, and stood at the back of the narrow hall, nasty smirks on their faces; as the women filed in and took their seats, they catcalled insults which the ladies pretended not to hear.

Miss Seymour, the association's president, stood at the lectern; pale and trembling, she asked that the meeting come to order.

"Shame!" called the men. "Sit down! No woman should speak in public!"

Miss Seymour persevered. "We are honored to have as our speaker this afternoon Mr. William Lloyd Garrison."

"Shame! Shame! He is a traitor! Damn him—he will not speak!"

Miss Seymour flushed. She seemed close to tears. No one had ever told her that when her tender heart went out to the plight of the black slave, and when she resolved to act to help him, she would be subjected to such abuse. Bad enough to have to speak to women—but to men! And rude, rowdy men!

Garrison stood up. The unwelcome visitors at the back roared a stream of jeers and hisses. Daniel stood also, looking to see that no one had a gun. He knew many of these men: he saw them at social gatherings, he knew their families, one of them had attended Harvard with him. They were as uncivilized, he thought, as the working-class Protestants who had burned the Ursuline Convent in Charlestown the year before.

Garrison stepped behind the lectern. The little room reverberated with the shouts and catcalls of the intruders. "Ladies and gentlemen," he began, "we are here today to celebrate the anniversary of the Boston"—he raised his voice—"Female Anti-Slavery Society"—shouting now—"which was founded two years ago"—pandemonium—useless to continue. Feet stomping, fists pounding on the wall, voices yelling the cruel taunt, "Sam-bo! Sam-bo!"

Daniel saw Mayor Lyman come in. He took one look at the scene and pushed his way toward the front where Garrison was still trying to make himself heard and Miss Seymour stood openly weeping. Lyman seized Garrison by the arm and hustled him aside. "Quick, man—get away! They are waiting for you in the street, they are going to lynch you!" And, to Daniel: "Mr. Revell, I know your father. I appeal to your good judgment. Do not allow your friend to be made a martyr for your cause, I beg you. The city of Boston would never recover from the shame of it. No! Stand back!" For some of the men had pushed their way to the front, and now they tried to seize Garrison. In an instant he got away, across the hall and into his office, Daniel at his heels, and slammed shut the door and locked it.

Garrison was pale, breathing hard, and yet he had a light in his eye, a triumphant look about him that Daniel understood. Garrison would fight to save his own life just as any man would, but in the end, unlike many men, he would welcome martyrdom.

At the urging of the mayor, the ladies had begun to exit. They went two by two, black and white side by side. This spectacle further enraged the mob which waited for them in the street—hundreds of men, most of them "gentlemen." The women lifted their heads, stiffened their spines already held ramrod straight by their corsets, and ducked as their wooden sign came crashing down, to be splintered by the mob.

Inside, the men pounded on Garrison's door. In a moment a few of them put their shoulders to it. Just as they broke it down, Garrison went out the window, onto the roof of a shed, and down to an alley which led to the place of a friend—a carpenter's shop. Daniel went after him, but as he landed in the alley he turned his ankle so sharply that he thought he must have broken it. The sudden agonizing pain took the breath out of him; in the precious moments that he lost trying to recover, he heard the mob roar in at the carpenter's. Shivering with pain, Daniel limped around to the front of the shop. Over the heads of the jeering, yelling, ferocious crowd of well-dressed men, he saw Garrison being led out, a rope around his neck.

They will hang him!

Desperately Daniel looked around for help. He saw another Abolitionist, Adam Wheeler, a big, brawny man, trying to push his way through to Garrison, but he could not. The mob had begun to tear at Garrison's clothing. They ripped off his coat and his shirt: his trousers hung in shreds. Like animals they tore at him, like wolves in the forest. They pulled him along to the head of State Street, to the south door of City Hall—the old State House, the very spot, as it happened, of the Boston Massacre. A dozen hands held him, a hundred voices reviled him, they pulled and hauled him as if they would tear him limb from limb.

Suddenly Mayor Lyman and two constables appeared.

"Quick—get in—" They threw open the door, they hustled Garrison inside. The mob roared its fury. Daniel stood in the shelter of a building across the way; he did not personally fear these men, for they were not after him, but he was appalled, reeling at this display of human ferocity. Without question they would have killed Garrison just now had the mayor not rescued him.

Inside, Mayor Lyman scurried around and managed to come up with a few articles of clothing for his nearly naked "prisoner." After Garrison had put them on, Lyman announced his plan: "Mr. Garrison, I cannot guarantee your safety. Therefore I am going to put you into jail. It is the only place where the mob cannot reach you."

The mayor ordered a carriage to take Garrison to the Leverett Street jail. With some difficulty its driver got through to the door. When Garrison came out, the mob did not recognize him at first, and they let him get in; but then, as the horses started off, they realized their mistake and in a great wave they fell upon the rig, they tried to upset the carriage—roaring and roaring, until Garrison and the two constables inside who guarded him were certain that they were done for.

The driver lashed the mob with his whip and tried to beat the horses into a gallop. He could not go the direct route; he went down one street and up another, and still remnants of the mob caught up with him and tried to grab the reins, to pull the horses up. Again and again he lashed at them until many of them were cut and bleeding, and still they came.

At last they reached the jail. The constables hustled their prisoner out of the carriage, through the doors and into a cell, fighting off the men who had managed to keep up with them. Locked up and safe, Garrison threw himself down on the hard wooden cot and listened to the roar from the street. He was sure that he had done right in escaping: his wife was pregnant, he wanted to see his child—and he wanted to see slavery's end! By God, he would live to see it!

In the evening Daniel went to him. With the Quaker poet John Greenleaf Whittier, he stood in the street outside; they spoke to Garrison through the barred window.

"Thee is very brave," said Whittier, "but braver, perhaps, is thy wife. Does she know thee is safe?"

"I believe that Daniel—"

"Yes," said Daniel. "I took a message to her just after—well, after I knew that you were safe here."

They stood for a while longer in the chill October night, and then, promising to meet in the morning, they went away.

Alone once more, Garrison did what men and women in prison have always done: he left a message on the wall of his cell:

> William Lloyd Garrison was put into this cell on Wednesday afternoon, Oct. 21, 1835, to save him from the violence of a "respectable" and influential mob, who sought to destroy him for preaching the abominable and dangerous doctrine that "all men are created equal," and that all oppression is odious in the sight of God.

7

Caroline Griffin Revell, Nathaniel's daughter, was not beautiful, but given what she stood to inherit, people said, her looks hardly mattered.

Undeniably she was a Revell: tall, long-boned, a long chin and high cheekbones, prominent nose, deep-set blue eyes—the spitting image of her father and indeed she resembled him perhaps even more than his two sons did. Further, she had about her a restlessness, a forcefulness, that reminded Nathaniel of himself when he was young, and so perhaps it was the quality of her character that kept her single, that made people look after her as she walked down Park Street: "She's a Revell, for sure!"

Caroline passed her twenty-fifth birthday, and then her thirtieth, but no suitors appeared. Her mother died heartbroken that Caroline remained unchosen. She began to develop a number of rather eccentric habits: she refused to eat meat; she talked to herself; she read everything she could get her hands on, and insisted on buying a ticket to the Athenaeum, a private library housed in William Scollay's building on Tremont Street whose membership was almost entirely male.

Most eccentric of all, every Fourth of July since her twenty-first birthday, she read—aloud—the Declaration of Independence. Like most families, the Revells always celebrated a traditional Fourth: salmon and peas, ice cream, going to watch the parade and the fireworks. It was hard, that first time, to find a convenient half hour to indulge Caroline in her wish. Then, when she finished reading and asked why the document did not apply to women as well as men, they were sorry they had accommodated her. Aunt Mariah Abbott Revell, still coy and flirtatious at fifty-odd, still hoping to find what she called her "Prince," did not hesitate to criticize Caroline in the strongest possible terms. "Come to your senses, niece Caroline! What are you thinking of? Women—equal to men? My dear! We are *superior* to the male race! Why would we want to be equal?"

One year toward the end of the thirties, the family was attending Fourth of July services at the Park Street Church. They had just finished singing a new patriotic hymn written (to the tune of "God Save the King") by a student at the Andover Theological Seminary: "America," he called it. Caroline was an enthusiastic singer. She had just uttered the last stirring phrase and was trying to catch her breath—a hot day, her corset tight—when, quite by accident, her glance met that of a man sitting across the aisle.

Of course she looked away at once. As she did so, however, she was aware that he did not; his gaze was still on her. She looked down to her lap, where her hands in their crocheted mitts lay tightly clenched. She looked up. The minister was speaking. Without turning her head, she flicked her gaze to the right. Just beyond the straw brim of her bonnet she saw him—staring at her.

As strong-minded as she was, as intelligent and resourceful, at that moment she felt confused. Perhaps he mistook her for someone else. But no, that was not possible. She was too distinctive a figure, no one would ever do that.

The minister was still talking. Then another hymn was sung. Caroline, after a moment, joined in; but she sang softly, absentmindedly; her heart was not in it.

When the service was over and the congregation filing out, Caroline was surprised to see the man speaking to her brother Artemas. At length they went to her father, and Artemas introduced them. The Family began to walk slowly up the hill toward Beacon Street and home, where dinner awaited them. Caroline walked with her sister-in-law, Artemas's wife Elizabeth. As soon as she reached the house, Artemas introduced her: "Caro, this is Richard Morris. He was my classmate at the College." (Not a fellow Porcellian, but no need to add that detail just now. This young man—and not so very young, either—was poor, his father a farmer in the western part of the state. The Porcellian would never have admitted him.)

Mr. Morris stayed to dinner that day, and when it came time for Caroline to read the Declaration, she discovered that, for the first time, she was oddly reluctant to do so. And all the while she was trying to get out the words without stumbling, she was intensely aware of Mr. Morris's eyes upon her, and his ready smile on the single occasion that she looked at him.

Afterward he told her how much he had enjoyed it. He seemed sincere: he took her hand, he gazed at her with tender regard.

Caroline felt her heart beating so sharply that she glanced down to see if the lace-trimmed bodice of her dress did not tremble and flutter from the disturbance within. And when he asked if he might call the next day, she could hardly speak for nervousness. Nevertheless she managed to say yes.

The next day he called again, and the next. Aunt Mariah was beside herself when she heard the news.

"Three days in a row? But my dear—that is unmistakably, ah, a bull's-eye! He is Artemas's classmate? That means he is, ah, thirty-seven or -eight? But since you yourself are, ah, past thirty, that is an ideal age, is it not? And he is—what? An inventor? Yes, indeed! Splendid!"

Since Aunt Mariah had never given up husband hunting, people said that it was very generous of her to be so pleased about Caroline's suitor—for that, it quickly became apparent, was what he was.

He was a charming man, a good-looking man despite his rather weak chin. Caroline could hardly believe her good fortune. Only a few days after meeting him, she decided that she was deeply in love with him. She was sure that he was going to ask her father for permission to marry her. Her eyes glowed at the thought; her skin grew warm, her heart beat fiercely in her bosom. She would be married! Nothing mattered more, for a woman, than to find a husband.

Nathaniel came upon the couple in the garden one evening at dusk. Mr. Morris had just put Caroline's hand to his lips. Caroline was so flustered, still so unaccustomed to such attentions, that she did not hear her father approach. He startled her terribly when he gave a loud "Harumph!"

Not five minutes later Mr. Morris was closeted with Nathaniel in the library; and after half an hour of extremely unpleasant conversation, the younger man, without a word to Caroline, went away.

Suspecting the worst, she had waited in the warm, fragrant garden, her hands turned to ice, her heart sinking with dread. She had known her father for thirty-three years; she knew when he was angry.

And he was angry—furious. The nerve of this fellow! The impudence! A nobody—wanting to marry Caroline Griffin Revell!

No, he said: out of the question. No impoverished inventor from the back of beyond was going to marry his daughter. The man was a fortune hunter, pure and simple.

And so Caroline's suitor was gone—ushered out by the butler, given fair warning never to return. Nathaniel took a small snifter of brandy to reward himself for a difficult job well done. Smarmy twit! Looking to cut himself in on the House of Revell!

Very late, when Caroline still had not come in from the damp night air, Nathaniel went to fetch her. He found her sitting on the marble bench under the Chinese maple that Philip had sent twenty years ago; like Philip, it had flourished in exotic soil.

Caroline looked like marble herself: hard and cold and white. She did not answer when he spoke to her.

"Caroline. Come in now. It is late, you will catch a chill." Never in her life had he spoken to her in this way, gentle and concerned. But he was uneasy about her: he had never seen her so deadly quiet, so removed from him.

She would not respond to him—would not look at him, would not acknowledge his presence in any way. He put his hand under her elbow and tried to ease her up. She responded then—pulled away and cast him a glance that even in that pale moonlight he knew to be filled with anguish. She put her hands over her eyes as if to blot out the sight of him, bowed her head and turned from him in a gesture of such complete renunciation that he felt the pain of it in his heart for days afterward.

He left her and went to his library to listen for her, to keep her vigil with her. Very late, past two, he heard her come in. She went upstairs. He stepped out into the hall to listen. He heard her open the door of her room and shut it behind her.

For a week she lay in bed with a sick headache. Then, with a face perhaps slightly more rigid than before, the little vertical line of tension between her eyebrows slightly more pronounced, she got up, ordered her maid to lace her into her corset, put on her petticoats, her hoop skirt, and her usual thirty or forty pounds of clothing, and went again into the narrow corner of the world that unmarried Boston ladies were allowed to inhabit.

When Aunt Mariah learned of Mr. Morris's abrupt departure, she shook her head until the finger curls on either side of her long, thin, Revell face bounced violently.

"I told Caroline," she said. "I *told* her, that if she wanted to catch a husband, she must never, never, never mention the word 'equal'!"

8

"Eh? What? Going out on such a day?" Nathaniel peered at his daughter, squinting to sharpen his sight. Like the rest of him, his eyes were not what they once were. He thought that at the moment, they might be deceiving him. Was this really Caroline?—dressed to go out on such a foul day, sleet and a raw east wind, a bleak December day when any sensible woman kept to her fireside and tended to her needlework.

"Yes, Father." She wore her plainest bonnet and brown broadcloth cape; no jewelry adorned her neck or earlobes, no rings sparkled on her fingers.

"Where?"

He had a right to ask, but still, recently, she had come to resent such questions. "To Mrs. Smibert's, Father. She is one of the committee's cases. She has just, ah, lain-in." Caroline flushed slightly; even to one's father—perhaps especially to one's father—one did not mention indelicate matters like childbirth, particularly if one were a maiden lady.

Nathaniel sniffed. He felt rebuffed—abandoned. His sons, Artemas and Hamilton, were married and well started on their own families. Now Caroline, too, was running off to care for someone else and leaving him alone.

"Mind you're back before dinner," he said. "I want you to read to me. I can't see the print in the newspapers any more, and I want to know what's going on in the world."

"Yes, Father. No, don't see me out. I can manage with Ellen"—the parlor maid, polishing windows in the front entryway. The butler was running errands; he did not ordinarily go on duty at the door until noon.

With a sense of escape, Caroline stepped out onto the porticoed steps and, mindful of her lacing, took a few breaths of the cold, damp air. The sour salt smell of the sea was very strong today, as it so often was.

The tall clock on the landing had struck ten some little while ago: already she was late. She hurried down the steps and up Beacon Street toward Bowdoin. She had lied to her father—a deed so unworthy of a good Christian woman (for such she was) that she could not bear to think about it. So she put it out of her mind, and she thought instead of the errand ahead of her, which had nothing to do with Mrs. Smibert's lying-in.

In moments she had passed the Statehouse and arrived at a boardinghouse on Bowdoin Street, where Miss Dix awaited her impatiently. "You are late," she said; "I cannot tolerate lateness; I have too much to do."

Like many humanitarians, Miss Dorothea Dix was not a pleasant person. She was not interested in being pleasant; she was interested in accomplishing what she had come to think of as her work. Now she hastened down the steps of her boardinghouse and motioned Caroline to the closed carriage awaiting them at the curb. "You understand," said Miss Dix as she settled her skirts around her, "Mr. Forrest will use any excuse to keep me—to keep us—out. And that includes lateness. If he said ten-thirty and we arrive at eleven, that will be enough to prevent us from going in."

Miss Dix was a small, plain woman about Caroline's age but seeming much older; her face had a determined look seen on only the most dedicated reformers—Horace Mann, for example, or the fanatic, Garrison; her voice was low, her words carefully enunciated; her dress was dark and plain, so that she looked like a Quakeress, although she was not.

As the carriage rumbled over the bridge to East Cambridge, Miss Dix tried

to prepare Caroline for what she would see: "They are hostile, some of them—
or terribly withdrawn. If you speak to them and they do not answer, try again.
It is not a personal thing, it has nothing to do with you. If at the second try
you still have no answer, go on to the next. Sometimes you get the opposite
reaction: they beg you to stay, they seize your hand and will not let you go."

Caroline had met Miss Dix at the Mt. Vernon Street home of Dr. William
Ellery Channing, the noted Unitarian preacher. Nathaniel did not approve of
Dr. Channing, who was an Abolitionist; but Channing was after all a minister
of the gospel, and so Nathaniel could not forbid Caroline absolutely to associate
with him. Dr. Channing was a man of wide interests; two or three times every
week he welcomed conversational groups into his parlor. At one of these, Miss
Dix had told the company about her experiences at the East Cambridge jail.
Without knowing what had prompted her to do so, Caroline had asked if she
could accompany Miss Dix on her next visit.

Miss Dix had said no. She knew instinctively that she was just now, near
middle age, finding her mission in life. She did not want to be hampered by a
bored and wealthy woman who was, no doubt, simply looking for new amusement.

But Caroline had persisted, and so now, on this dreary morning, she told
a lie to her father in order to get out of the house—for Nathaniel would have
preferred to see his only daughter dead in her grave in Old Granary rather than
doing what she was doing now. This afternoon, when she returned, she would
tell another lie if he asked her how her charitable visit went. She did not care.
She had the sense that this was an important day in her life—a red-letter day, a
day that she would always use thereafter as a reference point: "Before I began
to work with Miss Dix," she would say; or, "It was about six months after my
first visit with Miss Dix."

They drew up at the jail. They alighted and walked up the granite steps.
Caroline was frightened; she had a sudden sense of unreality; what was Caroline
Griffin Revell, the daughter of one of the wealthiest men in Boston, the daughter of one of the most prominent Families in Massachusetts—what was she
doing here, about to enter the East Cambridge jail?

A shiftless-looking man sat behind a desk in the lobby; to one side was a
door marked "Superintendent." When Miss Dix asked to see Mr. Forrest, the
man did not at once respond; he simply stared her up and down, and then
Caroline, too, in an insolent manner such as Caroline had never seen. But even
so, she understood it well enough: this was no place for ladies. Therefore these
two women, by their very presence here, established the fact that they were
not ladies, and so did not deserve to be treated as such.

But at last the man extricated himself from his chair and sauntered over to
the door, which he opened without knocking. After a moment the superintendent appeared. He nodded curtly at Miss Dix and acknowledged Caroline's
presence. "Come along, then," he said. "They've been pretty quiet today, you
won't have no trouble."

He led them down a corridor to a locked door; taking a key from the ring at his waist, he unlocked it, ushered them through, and locked it behind them. Caroline was aware of a heavy, musty odor, as if this place had never been dry and clean. From somewhere overhead she heard a steady drip-drip; once, twice, she heard a human voice, but what it cried she could not make out. Their footsteps echoed on the damp stone floor; the stone walls on either side oozed moisture; and even though they were indoors, it seemed colder here than the raw, cold day outside. Soon they came to another locked door; as their guide unlocked it and pulled it open, they were met by a cacophony that seemed, at first, to come from the depths of Hell.

They were in a large room. About forty or fifty women inhabited it. They were filthy, dressed in rags, many of them, their hair straggling in greasy hanks, their eyes staring vacantly, seeing . . . what? Not Miss Dix and Miss Revell, certainly. Others focused their gaze on the two visitors—they did not seem to notice the superintendent—and at once approached them, reaching out their filthy hands so that Caroline, half fearful, half ashamed, cringed and stepped back. Other women cried out a greeting—some coherent, some not—but could not come forward because they were chained to the wall. Caroline did not at first realize this; when she did, she had to stifle her exclamation of disgust. No human being should be chained, she thought—not a convict, not a black slave— not even a lunatic, which was what these poor creatures were.

Miss Dix turned to the superintendent. She was obviously angry, but she spoke quietly, in a dignified way, as she always did.

"Mr. Forrest, I thought I understood you to say that you would try to get a stove for these women. They are obviously cold. We are in December now, with the winter ahead of us. Can you not keep them warm, at least?"

The superintendent shrugged. "I couldn't get no money for a stove. But like I told you, you don't want to worry about that. These people are all crazy. An' crazy people don't feel the cold like you and me. Everybody knows that."

"Then why are they shivering?" said Miss Dix.

"Dunno. Puttin' on a show for you, maybe."

Smothering an exclamation of annoyance, Miss Dix began to walk among the inhabitants. With some uncanny sixth sense they seemed to recognize her as a friend; they kept on reaching out to her, but at the same time they made way for her, they let her move freely among them. After a moment, gathering up her courage, Caroline followed. She saw them close up, these poor creatures trapped in madness: women of sixty, and girls hardly into their teens; a lass of twenty or so nursing a newborn babe; a strong, raven-haired Amazon, mouthing gibberish, who wept like a child when Miss Dix touched her hair.

For more than an hour Miss Dix made her slow circuit of the room—that part of the jail where the insane females were kept. As she said to Caroline later, no insane person should be put into a jail. "Insanity is an illness, just like consumption. And the insane can be cured. I am convinced of it. But I cannot do this work alone. I must have the help of the Legislature. They must appro- priate the money for decent treatment for these people. And to persuade them to do that, I must amass more evidence. As bad as the jail is, I must know more, I must have more facts."

The two women had returned to Miss Dix's boardinghouse. They sat together in the dining room, deserted now at midday, and tried to warm themselves with cups of steaming tea—although Caroline, for one, thought that she would never be warm again, after her time in the freezing cold of the jail.

Miss Dix reached across the table and put her hand on Caroline's. "You did very well. Are you all right now? You looked faint when you were in the carriage coming back."

Caroline laughed a bit to cover her embarrassment. She had, in fact, thought that she would faint. The cold, the degradation, the misery—the utter hopelessness of the poor creatures they had visited had thrown her badly off balance. But the tea had revived her, and she realized that she now felt better than she had in a long time. An odd reaction, surely, to such a difficult morning, but it was so. She felt invigorated, filled with a sense of purpose such as she had never known.

"Yes," she said. "I am perfectly all right. Miss Dix—" She struggled to control the excitement building in her. "Miss Dix, I want to help you. What can I contribute? I don't mean money, I have very little money of my own. But my time, my energies—what can I do? What are you going to do?"

Miss Dix contemplated her. She nodded; she pressed her lips together with that determined look that would, one day, make strong men wither.

"I am going to investigate," she said. "You know—or perhaps you do not—that in every village and town in Massachusetts—and elsewhere, too, of course—there are pauper insane who are put out to the lowest bidder. I have seen a few of these poor unfortunates, but I have never made a systematic study of them. Now I must. That is the way I must proceed. I must travel—everywhere. I must gather my facts. I must poke my nose where I am not wanted. I must make a pest of myself. I must throw light on what many men would prefer to keep in darkness."

"And I?" said Caroline. She thought she saw a look of pity on her companion's face.

"You have a—well, a certain social position to maintain," replied Miss Dix. "I am not sure that your father would approve, if he knew—"

"That is true. He would not approve. But I want so much to help you. There must be something that I can do!"

And of course there was. For the next two years, working late at night after the household had retired, or during the days when Nathaniel was out of the house on business, Caroline transcribed the voluminous notes that Miss Dix made while she investigated the pauper insane and the conditions in which they lived in the Commonwealth of Massachusetts in the fourth and fifth decades of the nineteenth century, in a Christian country, in a nation dedicated to the proposition that all men are created equal.

Miss Dix found, chained in outhouses, pauper insane who had been chained there for years, summer and winter, with barely enough clothing to cover their bodies, and only scraps to eat; she found pauper insane who had their hands and feet cut off because they were frostbitten; she found men and women lying in their own filth, their bodies covered with festering sores; she found them beaten and abused, baited the way a bear or a bull is baited, for entertainment; she found one man in a cage, where the neighborhood boys made their sport by tormenting him, throwing rocks and dung at him, and poking him with sharp sticks.

All of these things she saw, and more. She made her notes at night in country inns in bad light when she was so tired that she could hardly see; and she gave the notes to Caroline Griffin Revell to write up.

9

"What's this?" Elias looked up from his newspaper at his son Wash, smiling expectantly before him.

"My book, Father. It's just out. They've sent two copies."

"Damned generous of 'em." Elias put out his hand to take the slim volume bound in dark red: *Salem Tales* by Washington Abbott Revell.

Wash had not expected his father to offer effusive praise, for that was not the old man's style. But from the way Elias handled the book, opening it carefully to read the title page, leafing through, Wash knew he was pleased. Like all his kind, Elias valued the arts. He did not value them as much, perhaps, as a cargo of tea and porcelain from Canton, or a million yards of calico from the mills at Lowell, but he had a fair regard for them all the same. And by now he was reconciled to the fact that his only offspring, his beloved Washington, would not enter the Family business, but would spend his time instead writing stories and even books.

Even books: there was the problem. He had had this little success, but even he, neophyte that he was, understood that nothing was more evanescent, more insubstantial, than one's first little bubble of popularity. Here today, gone tomorrow—yes, if he wanted to make his place secure, he needed to come up with something new, something striking.

Elias nodded and cast an approving glance at his son. In his spare, dry, chilly Yankee way, he loved him very much. And Elias was no fool: he understood a good deal about life. He understood, for instance, that his son was not cut out to be a merchant or a cotton manufacturer. Washington was a handsome, charming young man with a little talent. With luck, and a certain amount of effort, he could have a successful career as a writer. Few Americans, in 1841, had that: the new nation had had to get itself under way, it had to grow past its infancy and into—at least—its adolescence. Elias was a faithful alumnus of the College. Several years ago he had attended the graduation ceremonies and there had heard a really quite remarkable speech, a call for American scholarship and letters, by a sometime minister from Concord, Mr. Emerson. Elias was perfectly happy to think that Wash might be some small part of this New World flowering of the arts.

"What will you do next?" he said. "Another one?"

"Ah—well, I'm not sure." Wash flushed slightly. With the canny instinct born of years of sharp trading, Elias had hit on his problem. What next?

"You should do another one right away." Elias puffed at his meerschaum pipe; the air here in his library at Revell Hall was thick and blue, for he was a great reader, and while he read, he smoked. "How about a longer one? A novel, isn't that what y'call them?"

A new—"novel"—form, practiced with great success abroad for nearly a century now, Fielding and Smollett, Scott and Dickens. As yet, only Fenimore Cooper, Susannah Rowson, and Charles Brockden Brown this side of the water had written anything substantial in the form.

"Your Uncle Nathaniel can tell you considerable about the Revolution," said Elias. "That's your subject, y'know. The Revolution! Why, it's in your blood. We made that fight, we did—your grandfather Ebenezer was right there at the Tea Party, he fought at Bunker Hill, and his stepson John was with him, he was your grandmother Abigail's boy. She was my mother: she lived through the siege, and Nathaniel was with her the whole time. Go and talk to him! You'll get a dozen books out of it!"

And so Washington journeyed down to Boston. Nathaniel & Family were delighted to see him. He was a charming young man, really an astonishing young man—so handsome, so flushed with this first literary success, and yet unspoiled, a sweet-tempered, kind, sympathetic soul whom everyone liked very much.

And, yes, Nathaniel had a fund of good stories about the old days, the days of General Howe and the siege: the one about the time Grandfather Benjamin served frog soup to the visiting Frenchmen; and how Benjamin and Abigail and the boys had watched the Battle of Bunker Hill from the rooftops of the North End; and—most thrilling of all—how Nathaniel's older brother Thomas, dead out in China these many long years, had risked his life one night to take a crucial bit of information to the Americans outside the city. A real hero, he'd been: General Washington had sent him a letter of thanks. It was right here in Nathaniel's library; after dinner they could have a look at it. Yes, indeed, Nathaniel was pleased to tell these tales to such a receptive listener as his nephew Washington.

But it was Nathaniel's daughter Caroline who gave her cousin a hint of the best story of all.

"I don't know the details," she said, "but haven't you ever wondered why the Griffin Revells don't speak to the Jackson Revells, Samuel and James and their families? Of course James is an Abolitionist, so naturally Father would never allow him into the house. But there's more to it than that."

Washington liked his cousin Caroline. She was a few years older than he, the perfect type of New England maiden lady. On bright, brisk autumn afternoons the two cousins strolled the Common; in the rosy twilight they sipped tea in the Revell parlor and looked out at the deepening dusk, deeper and more purple than it really was because of Nathaniel's tinted glass. Washington had never met a woman like Caroline: frank, forthright, not a coy bone in her tall, angular body. She was, he thought, thirty-six or -seven.

One day at dinner Nathaniel announced that within the next week he would take a delegation of visitors to see the works at Lowell. Graciously, like the gentleman he was, he inclined his head toward his nephew. "You're welcome to come along if you wish, young sir. Picturesque—yes! If you're looking for material, you need go no further than Lowell, Massachusetts. Material! Ha!" And he chuckled, alone, at his little pun.

"I believe the young ladies at Lowell are as picturesque as anything in the world, sir," Wash replied. "Is that not so? I would like very much to see them, indeed I would."

Nathaniel nodded affably; then he saw the look that passed between Washington and Caroline, and he was not surprised when, later, Wash approached him with a request.

"I think she'd like to come along, sir. Could we include her in the party?"

"Hm. Most unsuitable. Her mother never wanted to see 'em." His wife had died ten years before; sometimes he missed her.

For two days Caroline waited in suspense. Then Nathaniel delivered his verdict: yes. She could come. But mind—no talking out of turn! No impertinent questions! His business associates would be in the party: he did not want his daughter to embarrass him by forward, unladylike behavior.

10

And so, one day not long after, they boarded the cars for Lowell and settled themselves on the bristly upholstered seats. Nathaniel and Artemas and the visiting gentlemen sat toward the front, Caroline and Washington to the rear. The conductor called the "All aboard!", the engineer rang the bell, and off they went down the tracks in a blaze of smoke and cinders, the coal tender stoking the fire, *clackety-clack, rattle-rattle-chug, watch out, here we come!*

Caroline gripped the arms of her seat until her knuckles went white. Through the clouds of smoke trailing past the windows she saw the bright fall foliage speeding by at an incredible rate. Surely it was against Nature to travel so fast?—the iron dragon, roaring through the peaceful countryside. Every now and then she saw the face of a bystander along the tracks, mouth gaping in amazement; and once she saw a spooked horse rearing up, threatening to upset his owner's cart.

She glanced across the aisle at Washington. He smiled at her and winked; in the noise of the train, speech was impossible, but if he could have spoken, he would have said something like, "This is all part of the New Age—the second Revolution that the Revells have helped to start!"

In little more than an hour after leaving Boston, the train arrived at Lowell. The southern gentlemen in the party declared that they had never seen anything like this railroad; if they saw nothing else during their northern journey, they said, their trip would not have been in vain. The English members of the little group were less astonished: they had seen railroads in their own country, fearsome black dragons hurtling through the countryside at an even greater rate than this, and so now they could only congratulate their American cousins for catching up at last with the wonders of modern technology.

Alighting from the cars, they walked the short distance from the station to the Commonwealth Mill. They passed a row of boarding houses, four stories high, each freshly painted with scrubbed front steps and bright white curtains at the windows. Here, Nathaniel told them, lived the famous mill girls, those Yankee paragons of virtue so unlike—

He caught himself. The three Britishers present would surely not appreciate any unfavorable comparison between American and English mill workers. Everyone knew that the wretches who slaved in the mills of Manchester and Birmingham were a shame and a living testament to the inhumanity of the British factory system. No American—and certainly not Nathaniel Griffin Revell—had wanted to be responsible for bringing such a blight to the American landscape. No degraded, gin-soaked mill hands here, no little children slaving day and night year in and year out (although nine or ten months out of the twelve did not hurt them); no woman dying of bad lungs at twenty-five or -six, illiterate, consumptive, a skeleton dragging herself to her looms.

At the end of the street was a high wall with a stout wooden gate. Nathaniel spoke to the gatekeeper; at once they were admitted.

They stepped into a courtyard surrounded by the high brick walls of the factory buildings. An unpleasant racket assaulted their ears; a steady rumble and thump of machinery that even here, outside the buildings, was much too loud for comfort. It was like the voice of the great god Mammon, thought Wash; overpowering, insistent, drowning out every other sound.

A narrow-gauge railway track bisected the courtyard, and leading off it were doors to the various buildings of the mill complex. Now from one of them came the agent, Mr. Paige. He was a dark, tense man with a prominent bulge in his forehead and an obsequious smile.

He led them into one of the buildings. Instantly the racket assaulted them— a shrieking, pounding, mind-shattering cacophony. They walked down an aisle bounded by rows of clattering metal-toothed carding machines that instantly devoured the seemingly endless supply of fluffy gray-white stuff—raw cotton— being fed into them.

Of course speech was impossible in such a place, but Caroline saw one of the southern gentlemen gesture, waving his hand as he tried to express himself. Instantly the agent caught it and held it, shaking his head, presumably warning the man of the dangers of amputation.

Caroline noticed that even though the women tending these hellish machines needed to pay strict attention to their work, they found time nevertheless to steal glances at Wash. His head of golden curls shone like the sun in the dim, lint-filled air of the carding room; his fresh, handsome male face looked oddly out of place in this so-called paradise of working women.

Wash put his mouth past the brim of Caroline's bonnet and shouted, "Do you want to stay?"

Nathaniel and his party had already vanished up the narrow circular staircase to the spinning room on the second floor. Caroline was uncomfortable in the hot, humid air of the mill, air that was kept warm and moist so that the threads would not break.

"No!" she shouted back to him.

Accordingly, they made their way out again into the courtyard and through the gate and down the boardinghouse row. As they went they heard the noon bell. In no more than a moment they were overtaken by a horde of women rushing to get their dinner at their boardinghouse. Caroline noticed that no one glanced at Washington now; they were all intent on getting fed.

In a moment the street was quiet again. "Even in the worker's paradise, one dare not be late for dinner," said Wash. Under the brim of his high-crowned hat his handsome face smiled gently down at her.

"You don't think well of it here?" she said. She was surprised. For years her father and the other entrepreneurs, the founders of this industrial miracle, had talked of how fortunate the mill girls were: to live at Lowell, to partake of the genteel atmosphere, the opportunities for self-improvement, the lending library, the Lyceum Lectures—and, more important than anything, to have the chance to earn money. No decent woman was able to do that except by teaching school or by dressmaking, neither of which paid even as little as factory work. Sweated labor in the cities—sewing shirts or making artificial flowers—was out of the question for wholesome New England farm girls.

"I think that I will reserve my judgment," he said. "Come, let us investigate the shops. I understand that the young ladies are paid in hard cash instead of scrip, and so they may buy what they please, if they please."

They proceeded down to the main street of the city, a dusty thoroughfare, raw and new like all the rest of the place, with shops lining either side, boardwalks in front, awnings over the entrances. They passed a drygoods shop, a milliner's, a grocer's—and then they came to a stationer's. Wash's book was in the window. Caroline caught the little gleam of triumph on his face before his natural modesty returned.

They went in. A young lady browsed among the two dozen or so titles. Washington, having removed his hat, approached her; his smile was so disarming, his manner so hesitant, that she could not possibly have taken offense.

"Begging your pardon, miss. We are visitors from New York. I am James Streeter, and this is my cousin Miss Margaret Streeter. I wonder, are you employed here?"

"I was. I went home for the summer—that's in Dunstable—and now I'm back. I start again tomorrow."

"And you are—what? A spinner?"

"Weaver."

"Ah. Yes. You like it here? You find the place congenial, the pay sufficient, the other young ladies, ah, suitable companions?"

She was a plain young woman, average height, dark eyes in a round face, a dark dress and straw bonnet: at first glance, nothing at all exceptional. But now she looked at him with undisguised contempt, so blatant that Caroline felt it like a slap across the face.

"It's a way to earn money, mister. If they don't cut us down to nothing on our wages."

"Cut you down?"

"To keep up their dividends. They got to keep 'em up, no matter what happens to us. Some folks got a movement goin' for Ten-Hour last winter, but they all got fired an' blacklisted."

"You mean a ten-hour day instead of—"

"Twelve. Fourteen in summer. If they don't lay you off. Summer is low water, an' they can't run the machinery. So they lay us off. We go home, rest up."

"But even so, it is not a bad life here?"

"Compared to what, mister? We got rules for work, rules in the houses, rules everywhere. We got th' lung, an' hair caught in the machinery, an' problems with our backs from standin' all day, an' pay cuts, an' I don't know what all. But compared to livin' an' dyin' on a farm somewhere up in the hills without seein' another soul from November to May, workin' just as hard an' not a dollar a week to call your own, it ain't so bad here. We ain't free, but what's freedom, for a woman?"

3. A MAJORITY
OF ONE

1

"Say, friend! How do I get to Walden Pond?"

"Easy. Two miles down the Walden Road out of Concord Center. Look for the split boulder on your right. Then follow the path through the woods."

2

In June of 1845 Washington Abbott Revell published his first novel: *The Siege of Boston*. It was a great success with the public, if not with the critics, almost as popular as Herman Melville's South Sea adventures, *Typee* and *Omoo*, and suddenly Wash was semifamous.

More than that: suddenly he was a prize on the marriage market. He had never particularly wanted to marry. He was thirty-four years old, tall and slender, golden-haired in the Revell way but with the difference that his hair was curly (an inheritance from his mother), and his features were so handsome as to be almost beautiful. He was like a Greek statue, people said; it seemed almost indecent for any living man to look so.

And now, with his success, he became much sought-after; and because he was no longer a very young man, and because he had the novelist's understanding of human nature, together with a character trait most unusual in novelists—a refreshing lack of self-importance—he was able to view the sudden upturn in his fortunes with the opposite sex with a certain amount of detached amusement.

Until the day he went to visit friends in Concord, and met Miss Celia Stoddard.

She was short, black-haired, and voluptuous; her face was pretty enough as faces went, but it was often marred by an expression of absolute determination unbecoming in females. Since she was not stupid, she was aware of this one flaw in her otherwise delightful self, and so, having clapped her eyes on Wash and decided that she must get him for her own, she took a moment to relax the muscles of her face and put on a charming smile.

But behind the smile her busy brain was hard at work: he needed a wife to manage his literary career. He needed another fortune—her own—to give him complete financial security. He needed someone to protect him from the clamoring world, someone who could give him the tranquility he needed to compose another masterpiece (for she thought *The Siege* was that, even if the critics did not).

The next day it was proposed (but not by Miss Stoddard) to get up an expedition to visit Walden Pond and its new resident. "Going to see Henry," as someone put it, had become one of Concord's most popular recreations.

Wash was eager to go; and so Miss Stoddard held her tongue, climbed into the wagon with the others, and off they went. Eventually they disembarked and walked through the woods. The sun was warm on this late August day, but under the trees the air was cool. There were eight or nine in the party; as if by mutual agreement, they fell silent as they drew near their destination.

And so as they approached, treading carefully, they heard the sound of a flute, the high sweet notes of some Concordian Pan.

One of the gentlemen nodded approvingly. "Good. He plays his flute when he has finished his work for the day. That means he will have time to talk with us."

It was eleven o'clock in the morning. Wash thought that a man was fortunate indeed who had so little work to do, but then he remembered what someone had told him: Henry Thoreau had said, in his commencement address at Harvard, that he wanted to reverse the biblical injunction, and labor for one day and rest for six. Apparently he had not been joking.

All of a sudden they came to the clearing. Beyond it, Walden Pond sparkled in the sun. Thoreau sat on a stump beside a small cabin perhaps fifty yards from the water. He put down his flute, stood up, and held up his right arm, palm out. "Welcome, Englishmen!" he said; this, apparently, was his attempt at humor. Then, to put them at their ease, he shook the men's hands in a normal way.

Introductions all around; Wash saw—or thought he saw—a flash of recognition when his own name was mentioned, but their host made no comment on *The Siege*, and so he thought he must have been mistaken.

"Warm from your walk?" said Thoreau. He waved his arm toward the pond, whose white sandy bottom was visible through the sparkling clear water. "Plenty to drink, better than anything I could prepare for you."

One of the men walked around the cabin to inspect it. "Good work, Henry," he said. "You plan to stay the winter?"

"Yes."

"What's Waldo charging you for the land?"

"Nothing. I work it out. He bought the land to save it from the developers, and so now I am to clear it of underbrush and plant it with new pine. In return, he let me build this place and live here until I finish my book."

"I hadn't realized you were writing," said Wash. "May I ask what about?"

"Some time back, my brother and I—" Thoreau's voice was suddenly husky; he paused, swallowed, and began again. "My brother and I—he is dead now—went on the Concord and Merrimack Rivers for a week. I wanted to write about it. I thought I would get it done quicker out here than in Concord."

Thoreau was of average height, with dark brown hair, and gray eyes alight with intelligence and curiosity. His most prominent feature was his aquiline nose, which curved down over a firm mouth. Thin body, long arms—a wiry, strong young man who seemed perfectly at home here in the outdoors, with this rude cabin for his home. Wash had heard that Thoreau was a fine classical scholar, fluent in Latin and Greek. But he didn't look like a scholar; he looked like a woodsman.

Because the ladies in the party were soon tired—Thoreau having, as he said, only three chairs (three being his idea of a crowd)—the party soon went away, but not before Wash asked if he could return.

Thoreau did not quite smile as he replied, "Afternoon's best."

Back in Concord, what with his host's wish to keep him entertained, and Miss Stoddard's determination to become Mrs. Washington Abbott Revell at the earliest possible moment, Wash's time was pretty well taken up. It was not until the following week that he made his way back to the shore of Walden Pond, this time alone. It was a hot day, the sharp scent of the pine forest strong in his nostrils, the *caw-caw!* of a family of contentious crows loud in his ears. As he approached, he heard no flute beckoning him on, and he worried for a moment that no one was at home, so to speak.

But then as he came out into the little clearing, he spotted Thoreau on his haunches by the woodpile; he seemed to be intently studying something on the ground in front of him. As Wash's well-shod foot trod on a branch, snapping it, Thoreau made a little movement with his hand, as if to say, Hush! But he did not take his eyes from whatever it was that he was peering at so intently.

Cautiously, Wash came up beside. He looked down to where Thoreau was looking. On a chip of wood, two ants were doing battle: one red, one black. They fought with the intensity of deadly enemies; the black was three times the size of the red, and yet the red seemed more ferocious, more eager to attack, to fasten himself upon the leg of his enemy and gnaw it off. But then the black tore open the red's chest and looked in a fair way to win the battle, except that just then two more reds came over the edge of the chip and threw themselves on him, and he went down before their onslaught.

And now at last Thoreau stood up and held out his hand in greeting. "I took a similar quartet inside last week," he said, "and watched them under a microscope. They battle with all the bravery, all the tenacity, of Spartans and

Athenians during the Peloponnesian War. And who knows but that in their world, equally as much is at stake? Well! Enough of battle. What can I do for you?" And it was odd, thought Wash, that he seemed to understand that that was why people came to him—because he could do something for them.

"I don't know," said Wash truthfully. "I— Well, I admit I am curious about why you have come here to live. But I don't want to pry, I don't want to, ah, intrude."

Thoreau smiled: a lovely smile, clear and honest.

"I will not let you intrude," he said. "And I am glad that you came to ask something *of* me, instead of to do something *for* me. Doing-good is one of the professions which are full. If I knew for a certainty that a man was coming to my house with the conscious design of doing me good, I should run for my life."

Wash could not refrain from laughing outright. It had seemed to him that Thoreau was a fey, eccentric individual, as much a creature of the wild as a deer; to have such solid Yankee bluntness fall from his lips was a relief.

Thoreau moved his head in the direction of the woods. "Let's walk," he said. "I am like Alcott—walking stimulates my mind, and I talk better when my legs are moving."

They went along a forest trail that followed the shore. Sunlight glimmered through the branches; on their left the pond danced in little waves in the cooling breeze. Earlier, thinking over what he wished to say, Wash had thought that perhaps his questions, his observations would seem silly—irrelevant to a man of Henry Thoreau's determined character. But now he felt as though he was with a lifelong friend—a friend to whom he could say anything, who would understand everything.

"Can you tell me exactly why you have chosen to do this?" he said. "To live in Nature, so to speak?"

"All of us live in Nature. Some of us—most of us—do not realize it, and so we cut ourselves off."

"Yes, but—"

"I came here, Mr. Revell, to live, and to confront the essential facts of life—to learn what life has to teach, so that, when I come to die, I will not discover that I have not lived."

A horse chestnut dropped with a little thud at their feet. Thoreau stopped, picked it up, and examined it with the same intensity with which he had watched the war of the ants. From the surface of the pond came a sharp little *plop!* as a fish broke the surface, and for a moment Thoreau turned his gaze there. Then, again with that half smile, he glanced at Wash and said, "For years I have watched my fellow men, some of whom are so unfortunate as to have inherited property—houses, barns, cattle farms—why, they are condemned to worse than the twelve labors of Hercules! They begin digging their graves as soon as they are born! Those Augean stables will never be cleaned. All their lives they live on the limits, trying to get into business, trying to get out of debt, promising to pay, promising to pay. These men are enslaved not by a southern overseer, not by a northern factory boss, but by themselves—they are the slave drivers of themselves!"

They were walking again; Thoreau paused to examine a cluster of pale green berries; then he went on. "Self-emancipation, Mr. Revell, is the important thing. What a man thinks of himself, that is what determines his fate. The mass of men lead lives of quiet desperation. I did not want to do the same."

When in later years Wash remembered that autumn of 1845, what he remembered most vividly was the curious sense of leading a double life, as if he and his soul had been split in two, and each half needed attention.

One half of him was courting Miss Celia Stoddard, and this, too, had a curious air of unreality about it, for it was as if he had suddenly discovered his fate and was now acting it out—without question, without protest. Fate had intended that he court and eventually marry Miss Stoddard; he would do so. She exercised a curious power over him; he understood that her managerial talents were to be practiced on him to the betterment of his career, and he was content with that arrangement.

But the other half of him was in conflict with his courtship of Miss Stoddard: for he had discovered also the company, and the mind, of Henry David Thoreau.

Miss Stoddard did not like Thoreau. He was a mite tetched, she thought, so far from the usual Yankee go-getter type that he seemed almost a different species. Miss Stoddard had lived in Concord all her life; she knew that the town harbored a little coterie of philosophers, called Transcendentalists, who talked a great deal among themselves—and to the public, too—at the Lyceum. Talking! Talking! And full of harebrained schemes: a number of them had gone to West Roxbury a few years before to a Utopian community they called Brook Farm, there to live in harmony with Nature and arrange a more perfect life. When Wash told her that he had lived briefly at Brook Farm, she suffered a moment of doubt about him.

"You! At Brook Farm! But why?"

"I stayed for less than a month," he said. "I was curious."

"Curious! And what did you find?"

He laughed, a little embarrassed. "I found that I do not like shoveling manure. I was so tired, and so hot and dirty, at the end of my daily stint at the manure pile, that I had no energy left for writing."

She nodded briskly. "I could have told you that," she said. "A writer needs time—needs to have his time protected for him, if necessary. Experimental communism won't help someone like you."

Oh, she was itching to manage him into a position of real fame! With the proper handling, she thought, he could be the most famous author this side of the water. Europeans in general, and the British in particular, had nothing but contempt for American letters. They needed someone like Washington Abbott Revell to show them that an American could be as—well, as famous as any Englishman.

And so she plotted—as much as any author, she plotted—and when, around Thanksgiving, Wash asked her to marry him, she was only too happy to say yes.

3

"Thoreau?" said Elias. "Never heard of him. What's he worth?"

"Ah . . . I don't know, Father," Wash replied.

"Well, what's his line of work?"

"He is a surveyor. And his family has a pencil factory. Some while ago, Henry invented a new pencil, hard and black—the best in the world."

"Hhmm. Well, a man can get rich off pencils as well as anything else, I suppose," said Elias. He paused to allow a child rolling a hoop to run across their path. It was a day in October, unusually mild; father and son were strolling across Boston Common. "Does he have any property?" Elias went on.

"He built a cabin on Mr. Emerson's land. In the woods at Walden Pond."

"Built—on someone else's land? That's damned foolish. What'd it cost?"

"He gives it as twenty-eight dollars, twelve and a half cents," said Wash.

Annoyed, Elias glanced at his son. It was unlike Wash to give flippant answers when he knew that only simple facts were wanted.

"What d'y'mean, 'he gives it'? Does he get asked much about his property?"

"Oh, yes. All the time. There's hardly a day goes by that someone doesn't go out to see him, to talk to him."

Elias was sincerely puzzled. "But what does he *do*?"

"Well, he—ah—he studies Nature."

"You mean he makes lists of flora and fauna, and so on?"

"I don't know if he makes lists, exactly, but he, ah—he lives in Nature. He seeks truth in Nature the way other men seek it in religion, or philosophy."

Elias was silent for a moment; then, with the air of a man who is dismissing an unpleasant subject once and for all, he said, "Any man who has reached the age of—what did y'say, near thirty?—and who doesn't have property any more than that, and who goes to live in the woods instead of workin' for a livin' like honest folks do, is never goin' to amount to a hill of beans. When I was that age, I'd been around the Horn, I'd been supercargo for the largest shipload ever brought in to Boston Harbor until that time. And I was worth a good deal more than twenty-eight dollars, I can tell you."

Father and son, that day, were engaged on a visit that Elias, for one, never thought that he would make: they were going to pay a call on Elias's brother Philip, home from China at last. On his return to Boston, Philip had bought a house in West Street, about a block from the Common, and had set about making it into a showplace to rival any mandarin's at Canton. He had refused to accept or to pay any calls until it was ready.

Three weeks ago he had sent out invitations to a reception to be held this day; all the family was invited, including the feuding Griffin Revells and Jackson Revells, and he let it be known that if they wanted to come, they needed to be civil, at least while they were under his roof.

They were greeted by a Chinese manservant in a blue brocade coat and black satin trousers, a pigtail down his back. This individual was already a sensation in Boston. He was not the first Oriental in the city, but he was by far the grandest: as remote, as haughty as his master, he conveyed even in servitude his contempt for all whites everywhere. Now he bowed and ushered them in. A few people had already arrived. The house smelled odd—a cloying yet harsh odor that was, Wash realized, burning incense. He gazed around, nodding at uncles and aunts and cousins. He did not see Caroline. He wanted to tell her about his new friend, for he knew that she would be far more appreciative of Thoreau than was Elias.

They came into the drawing room. A huge porcelain statue of a stout, stylized Chinese, smiling, sitting cross-legged, dominated the rear wall; the floor was covered with a carpet of blue, gold, and white, and the walls were papered to match. Although the day was mild, a fire burned in the fireplace, making the room uncomfortably warm. A few pieces of ebony furniture were scattered about; at the front bow window were two large porcelain jars, and on the mantel a pair of small, blue, very fierce dogs.

There was no sign of Philip.

When the servant seemed convinced that the company had had time to examine the drawing room, he ordered them out into the garden to the rear of the house. Here they saw not a proper New England garden, but a small space enclosed by a wall made of porcelain tile, a place of graveled walks and little pools and tiny bells that swayed in the breeze, and statues here and there, and clumps of chrysanthemums glowing bronze and purple in the autumn sun.

Meanwhile, upstairs, Philip sat in his carved ebony chair and smoked his opium pipe and tried to convince himself that he wanted to go down to greet all these strangers who were, it seemed, his Family.

His servant looked in. Philip waved him away. Fifteen minutes later he came back. As the door opened, Philip heard the rising hum of voices from downstairs. There was no escape: he must go down.

He stood up. The drug had made him light-headed. He stood for a moment regaining his balance; then, slowly, with great dignity, he descended to his guests.

As he came into view a few of the women stifled their startled screams, while Elias went forward to clasp his hand—the brother he had not seen in decades, and would not have recognized in a thousand years.

Then one of the children began to cry—Hamilton's son, little Oliver, just five and already smart as a whip. He was frightened by Philip. They shouldn't have brought a child to an event like this, people said. Of course he was frightened! Look at this apparition in front of him, ancient and wizened and yellow, a face like old parchment, an inscrutable expression—a fan-kwae, right here in Boston USA!

For a season, over the winter of 1845–46, Philip Abbott Revell was the talk of Boston Town, and he suffered his celebrity the way other men—religious men— suffered penance. But he was not happy in Boston; even surrounded as he was by his Oriental possessions, his Chinese manservant, his Chinese chef who cooked the delicacies he had become accustomed to, even with his steady supply of the drug to which he had become addicted—even with all of these things, here in his native land he was a "foreign devil" as much as ever he was in Canton, and he was too old, and too set in his Oriental ways, ever to be a Yankee again.

In his blacker moments, which came often, he brooded about his fate. He had not wanted to leave, but he had had no choice. The British had insisted on trading opium to the Chinese in the face of the Emperor's edict against it. The Emperor, aroused at last to fatal anger by England's refusal to obey his dictate, had cut off trade completely. The British were arrogant and, worse, stupid; because they were the mightiest power on earth, they thought that they could do as they pleased. They had started shooting. Come hell or high water, they wanted to preserve the riches that the opium trade had brought—supplying the drug to a market of millions of desperate opium addicts.

For decades the British had been selling opium to the Chinese. In 1764, and again in 1810, the Emperor had forbidden the opium trade to continue, but no one obeyed him—not the millions of Chinese desperate for their drug, nor the British traders who were getting rich. Eventually the Americans entered the trade as well; they got their opium from Smyrna, in Turkey, because the British held a monopoly on the purer Indian drug. At those times when the Emperor tightened up his edicts with stricter customs inspections, both British and Americans conducted the trade from opium ships anchored at Lintin Island, at the mouth of the Pearl River at Whampoa.

But now at last, once and for all, the Emperor was determined to rid his people of the addiction which was ruining their strength, their industry—which would, he saw, destroy the Celestial Empire as no enemy had ever been able to do in all the centuries of its existence.

And so a war had started. The Emperor had no cannon, no armament; in the face of British warships, he was impotent. The British won. The opium trade continued. But in the course of the hostilities, the trading stations in Canton had been shut down and the House of Revell there, along with a number of others, had failed. Even if Philip had been able to return, there was nothing to return to. Any future trade done by the Revells in China would be done through other houses; Philip's work there was at an end.

When he had told his small-footed woman that he was going away, she had stared at him without a flicker of emotion. Well-trained as she was, she would never argue with him, would never—for instance—beg him to take her along. Such a thing was unthinkable, and they both knew it. But the next day, when he awaited her as he always did in the late afternoon, just before dusk, she did not come; and when he sent for her, his servant returned with the news that she was indisposed. Philip had thought that odd: never before in the many years of their relationship had she been ill. He sent again, and again her maid said that she could not come. And so at last he had gone himself, and he had found her, perhaps as she intended, sleeping in her bed, but sleeping for eternity, no longer breathing, no longer dreaming, her delicate little hands already cold and stiff, her eyes sunk into her skull, sharp lines around her nose and her beautiful mouth. A small porcelain cup on her bedside table held the dregs of the poison she had drunk; already the death's-head had come, already she was a stranger on earth.

So now Philip sat in his splendid house in Boston and suffered the visits of the curious, and waited for Death—the only caller he wanted to see. Occasionally he thought, with grim amusement, that he was a curiosity in more ways than one, for he was living proof that a man could survive without a heart. He had left his own in China; he would never have it again.

One day when Philip was in a particularly black mood, he had a visit from his nephew William, his brother Roger's son, a student at the Medical School.

"Good afternoon, Uncle," said William. "Feeling better today?"

"No. But sit down anyway. Have some tea. Why should I feel better when I'm going to die soon?"

William made no reply, but he watched his uncle, fascinated. He had never heard anyone predict his own death. The interesting thing, he thought, was that the old man was probably right.

"And when I die," Philip went on, "you should perform an autopsy on me. As a matter of fact, I'll give my body to the school. You can do what you want with it. I know you've trouble getting corpses to study anatomy on. Deal with resurrectionists, don't you? Grave robbers? I heard they even dug up a body in the Copp's Hill Burying Ground. Maybe they got old Cotton Mather himself, eh? It's easier this way, save you a lot of trouble."

"Now why do you want to donate your body to science, Uncle?" said William.

Philip smiled with not a little malice; his old face, yellowish, looked positively Oriental. "Because," he said, "I am a medical mystery. I have no heart and yet I live and breathe."

Two months later Philip died. Because he had not put into his will his desire to be autopsied, the female members of the Family, ever alert to the demands of propriety, insisted that he be buried decently. They cared not a whit for the needs of the Harvard Medical School; they simply wanted to avoid scandal, and in this they succeeded. Philip was buried at Mt. Auburn, the new garden cemetery over in Cambridge; and the Medical School, desperate for corpses, had to do without him.

4

"Henry?"

Wash knocked again at the door of Thoreau's cabin. No answer. Disappointment—on the very day he wanted to tell his friend his good news!

Cautiously he pushed open the door and looked in. No Thoreau—of course not, or he would have answered. Nor a note: Thoreau was as much a creature of the wild as any four-legged thing, and no animal would leave a message when it moved on. "Simplicity!" Thoreau had cried once; "simplicity! simplicity!" And here it was: a narrow bed that he had caned himself, a chair, a desk, an armless rocker. On the desk a copy of the *Iliad* in its original language, a small volume titled *Bhagavadgita*, and a stack of manuscript, beside which lay his flute. A lamp; surveyor's tools.

Wash went outside, pulling the door shut behind him. The day was warm, for Indian summer had lingered late this year, and he was a little tired from his walk from Concord. After scooping up a drink from the pond, he sat under a tree, grateful for the thick cushion of leaves and pine needles. The sun brought out the sharp piny scent of the forest; the water lapped softly at the shore. From the branch of a tree a songbird trilled its flutelike song. Wash fell asleep.

He awoke to see Thoreau standing above him, smiling down. A few moments later they sat on the shore of Walden Pond while Wash, suddenly hesitant, told Thoreau not his own news, but about his uncle Philip.

"Ah, yes," said Thoreau. "The China Trade." His voice was dry, flat, with no hint of condemnation, and yet ... "How old did you say he was?"

"Seventy-three or -four," said Wash.

Thoreau nodded. "And all his life, buying and selling, buying and selling—far away over there in that strange, strange land!"

"Have you never wished to travel?" said Wash. "To see the world?"

"Why should I travel, when I am already here?" replied Thoreau.

" 'Here' meaning?"

Thoreau waved his arm, a gesture encompassing the pond, the surrounding forest. "Here—at Walden. Or, when I leave Walden, as I will surely do, for I have other lives to live, then at Concord. These few square miles are my home, the place on earth I was intended to be."

"But you do get away, now and then."

"Oh, yes. Somewhat. I went to Maine last year, and I went down the Concord and on up the Merrimack, as you know. And I would like to see Cape Cod. They say it is worth the trip, and I intend to go there."

"But not to China."

"No. Not to China. There are continents and seas in the moral world to which every man is an isthmus, yet unexplored by him. It is easier to sail many thousand miles through cold and storm and cannibals, than it is to explore the private sea, the Atlantic and Pacific of one's being alone. This pond is my unexplored universe. My own self is the white space on my chart, and by living here, I will fill it in. That is my life work."

Thoreau was silent for a moment. Then: "I have had many occupations, you know. I have been a carpenter, a house painter, a mason. I have manufactured pencils. I have been—and still am—a surveyor. And thanks to my time at Harvard, I have been a teacher. Harvard is a strange place: it gives all the branches of learning and none of the roots. And certainly it did not prepare me for what I was expected to do in teaching. They said I had to flog the boys in my classroom—in the public school, right here in Concord. I refused. Flogging is not the way to educate a boy, I said. They insisted. I resigned." He lifted his shoulders in a little shrug, smiled his fleeting half smile, and gestured toward the pond. "What about a swim?" he said. "Are you warm enough for that?"

In a moment they had stripped and plunged in. The water, warmed all summer, had not yet been touched by freezing temperatures. Wash stood on the white sandy bottom and looked at his feet wavering through the water. Then he splashed out toward the middle, to where Thoreau had already gone.

The naked Thoreau, he thought, was the appropriate one for this place: stripped to his essentials, more than ever a creature of the wilderness, his hairy body like that of an otter or a seal, a sleek creature as much at home in water as on land.

As the sun lost its warmth they came out and dried themselves with their shirts. Then Thoreau cooked supper on an outdoor fire: fish from the pond and turnips from his garden. And it was not until after the meal, when they watched the stars come out in the darkening sky and listened to the hoot owl calling his nightly soliloquy, that Thoreau turned to Wash and said, "Now. What was it you really wanted to tell me?"

Wash was not surprised, as he once might have been, by Thoreau's intuition. And he was happy enough to share his secret. "I am planning to ask Miss Stoddard to marry me," he said.

Thoreau did not reply at once. He was gazing out across the pond, and now, with a slight movement of his head, he said, very soft, "Look."

Down the shore, a doe and her fawn had stepped to the water's edge, and now in the dusky light they bent their heads and delicately drank—two wild creatures accepting the hospitality of their host, as it were, except that Thoreau held an Algonquian view of the wilderness: he believed that no man owned it.

Then Thoreau turned to Wash and said, "You are to be congratulated."

The light was fading fast; was it Wash's imagination, or did he detect a gleam of sympathy in Thoreau's eyes?

"By you, I hope," Wash said. Like all writers, he was a sensitive. He understood that Thoreau's response was not so warm as it might have been, and he thought he understood why. "We cannot all be like you, Henry. We must marry, and live in the world, and rear families—"

Thoreau held up his hand to forestall anything more. "Of course I understand that," he said. "And you understand, I hope, that if a man does not keep pace with his companions, perhaps it is because he hears a different drummer."

"Of course. But when you look at me like that—"

"Like what?" Thoreau was surprised, genuinely curious.

"As if you disapprove. It frightens me to think that you would not approve my marrying."

Thoreau shook his head. "Never talk of being afraid," he said. The last light of day glimmered on the water, and it was reflected in his luminous gray eyes. "Never even think of it. Nothing is so much to be feared as fear itself. Marry her, live with her, rear your family—do as most men do! Not every man can be Henry Thoreau. I would not wish that they were. It is enough that I live this way; you do not have to do likewise."

5

"My God—they've arrested Henry!"

A summer afternoon, late July, and Mr. and Mrs. Washington Abbott Revell—which is to say, Wash and Celia—during a week-long visit to Celia's parents in Concord, had driven out in her father's chaise to pay a call on the Emersons. Wash did not in fact know Mr. Emerson very well, but he had a new novel, written over the winter and about to be published any day, and Celia thought that a little call on one of the Concord literati would not be amiss. There were many such in Concord: not only Emerson and Thoreau, but Hawthorne and Alcott, Margaret Fuller and (not far away) Professor Longfellow. The visit had progressed well enough until this moment, the conversation coming nicely around to Wash's efforts, and Celia was annoyed at this interruption—a boy running to the door with a note, from whom she did not know, to announce that Mr. Thoreau had apparently committed some crime. Celia was not surprised; she had never liked him, shiftless, odd little man that he was, no friend to women, given to speaking in phrases that sounded like parables but were not quite.

Emerson had gone pale. "You must excuse me. I need to go to him. This is most unfortunate, most unfortunate indeed—he threatened, but I never thought that he would actually—"

"Who threatened?" said Wash. "And to do what?"

"Henry. He has refused for the past three years to pay his poll tax. He understood that the authorities would no longer tolerate his rebellion. He saw what happened to Mr. Alcott, jailed two years ago for the same offense. We urged him, this year, to pay. He insisted that he would not—and now they have caught up with him." The little trio stood awkwardly in the front hall; Emerson was too well-mannered to walk out on company, but plainly he wanted very much to leave.

"We will come with you," said Wash, ignoring Celia's dark looks. "Or, better yet, my wife will go home—to her father's, that is, where we are staying—and I will go with you, Mr. Emerson."

And so it was arranged, despite Celia's displeasure, and soon Wash found himself proceeding at a fast clip in Emerson's buggy to the center of town, where the jail was.

A little crowd of onlookers had gathered at the side window, and Wash guessed that that was Thoreau's cell. And sure enough, he saw the familiar face behind the bars, and Thoreau gave him a little nod of recognition. Emerson, having tied his horse, strode through the crowd to address his friend.

"Henry, what are you doing in there?"

And Thoreau replied, "Waldo, what are *you* doing out there?"

Thoreau was a disciple of Emerson's, but his attitude now toward the older man was hardly respectful, Wash thought. He stepped forward and Thoreau nodded a greeting.

"Henry, it is only a poll tax. What does it have to do with—with anything? What is it that you are protesting?"

"I am protesting this government—the American government! A man cannot without disgrace be associated with it!"

"Because?"

"Because we have declared war on Mexico to expand the slave territory! Because I will not pay tax to any government that engages in such a war! Because Massachusetts—my native place—will not condemn this slave system, and if she will not condemn it, then she supports it! As indeed she does by supporting the war!"

"But how does it help the slave for you to go to prison?"

"Prison is the only house in a slave state in which a free man can abide with honor."

"They can keep you there for a long time, Henry. You will grow homesick for Walden."

"Pah! Homesick! They think that my chief desire is to stand on the other side of that stone wall. How industriously they locked the door—on me, on my flesh and blood and bones, but on my meditations also. How foolish they are! My meditations followed them out again without hindrance, and *they* were really all that was dangerous."

"You must pay the tax, Henry," said Emerson.

"I was not born to be forced."

"Nevertheless. You are in a minority, and they can—"

"In this instance, Waldo, they can go to the devil! A minority, you say? Because I oppose slavery? But I am right to oppose it, as you very well know. And any man more right than his neighbors constitutes a majority of one already."

At length the crowd drifted away, and Emerson and Wash went also, promising to return in the morning. Emerson's long, lean Yankee face was drawn with worry as he guided the horse toward home; for all Thoreau's love of the wilderness and his preference for simple, even primitive living conditions, he was subject to bouts of consumption which would only be exacerbated by the damp jail.

But sometime later that day a mysterious thing happened: a veiled woman appeared at the jail (she was Thoreau's aunt) and much to Thoreau's annoyance, paid the tax. Thoreau should have been let out at once, but the jailor had his supper in front of him, his boots off and the prisoners settled for the night, and he could not be troubled to disturb himself. So he freed Thoreau the next day. The erstwhile prisoner promptly went on a huckleberry party with a band of neighborhood children, and not until some months later did he put pen to paper to write his thoughts about his night in jail. When at last he did, he called it "Resistance to Civil Government." It was published in an obscure, short-lived periodical put out by Elizabeth Peabody, one of the most devoted of the Transcendentalists, Nathaniel Hawthorne's sister-in-law. Probably fewer than a hundred people read it. And of those who did, probably none could have imagined the strange and wonderful life it was destined to have.

Wash read it, and thought it a bit extreme.

Caroline read it and thought it splendid.

6

"I say, Revell! Did you hear about Dr. Channing's midwifery demonstration yesterday? Twins, by God! And Bobby Minter fainted!"

A brisk morning in October 1846. The two Harvard medical students hurried down Charles Street toward the Massachusetts General Hospital, where they would climb the narrow stairs to the operating amphitheater in the Bulfinch dome and watch as Dr. John Collins Warren, the nephew of the Revolutionary hero and the most famous physician in America, gave to his students a demonstration-lecture in surgery.

"No," laughed William. "I missed that. How's the mother?"

"Oh . . ." His companion waved his hand dismissively. "I don't know. All right, I suppose, or we'd have heard. But it was the little nippers that were so fascinating. Identical! Amazing! I did hear that the mother yelled a good deal while they were popping out."

It was 9:45. The two students picked up their pace. Dr. Warren was notorious for starting on time; latecomers were barred. Surgery was the most difficult, the most dreaded course that confronted students at the Medical School, and many young men, faced with its bloody reality, dropped out rather than disgrace themselves by becoming ill. But for those who could bear it, Dr. Warren's class was the most fascinating of all, for here the doctor was making full use of his powers, and he was engaged in a struggle such as no other human being ever had to face—invading the body, playing God, as it were, and forcing Nature to heal what might have proved fatal.

The only problem was that to be a surgeon, a man had to have amazing dexterity, superhuman strength, and a technique as disciplined and perfected as that of the finest musician. No operation could last more than a minute or two at most, because no patient could stand the prolonged pain of it. In and out—off with the leg—away with the tumor—hurry! Hurry! Two or three stout boys holding the patient down, whiskey and opium to deaden his senses a bit—but they don't succeed, and he screams and tries to thrash away, shrinking in terror from the cruel surgeon's knife and bone saw. Ah, the horror, the bloody stench of it, the pain, the fear, the nightmare! The filthy sponge, and sawdust on the floor to sop up the dripping blood, and the surgeon's coat all spotted and stained with the blood and pus of a hundred such operations, and his hands filthy, too—why wash up when he will only be fouled again by the next patient? Better to wait until the end of the day, when all the dirty work is done, and then have a good cleanup before going home to dinner.

William and his companion raced up the narrow stairs to the amphitheater, where they would perch on uncomfortably small seats on a sharply rising tier and look down into the well where, with the hospital's two Egyptian mummies observing, Dr. Warren would perform his operation on some poor screaming wretch.

As William emerged, panting a little, into the top tier of the amphitheater and gazed down across the rows of spectators, he saw not only Dr. Warren and his assistants in the well, but several other physicians, professors at the Medical School. Such an assembly was unusual, and he wondered at it.

A stir at the door, and the patient was brought in: a young man in a red plush wheeled chair. The assistants strapped him into it, and then, one on either side, they got a good grip on his arms. Still Dr. Warren waited. What was keeping him? The tension was nearly palpable, William thought: everyone seemed nerved up, and yet so far there was nothing unusual about the scene save the presence of those extra doctors. Warren looked at the door; impatiently he tapped his foot upon the bloodstained floor. Ten minutes past ten; twelve past . . .

Suddenly another stir at the door, and in burst a young man followed by another, slightly older. The younger one looked flustered, nearly distraught; he carried an apparatus made of glass, and a bottle of clear fluid.

Dr. Warren nodded; then he turned to the class and said, "Gentlemen, I have invited Dr. Morton today to give us a demonstration of his method of rendering a patient insensible to pain during a surgical operation."

A low hum of disbelief swept the amphitheater, followed by immediate and total silence as Dr. Warren held up his hand. All eyes fastened upon the little drama that was now being enacted in the well. Dr. Morton poured the fluid into the globe and put the apparatus to the lips of the patient, who began to inhale from it. A minute crawled by; two; three. At last Dr. Morton—who was not a physician but a dentist, and therefore perhaps even more attuned to the need for painless procedure than the doctors at the Medical School—turned to Dr. Warren and said, "Your patient is ready."

Dr. Warren lifted his surgeon's knife, found the spot, and made his cut into the patient's neck, where he would remove a large tumor under the jaw. Blood spurted from the incision—onto him, onto the assistants, dripping down to the floor. The patient did not move; he showed no sign of pain. His eyes were closed, his attitude relaxed. Dr. Morton stood by, but he gave no more of his magical preparation to the patient.

The students stared, transfixed, as Dr. Warren worked with his customary speed; the best surgeon was the quickest, and Dr. Warren was the best of all. But of course now there was not the same desperate need for haste: the patient lay supine, at peace, blissfully unconscious of what might have been his agony.

William could hardly believe what he saw. He knew that what he witnessed was very nearly a miracle—that is, if the patient regained consciousness. If he did not—well, perhaps Dr. Warren and Dr. Morton both would be prosecuted for manslaughter. For centuries doctors had been searching for a way to eliminate pain; could it be that on an ordinary morning in the ordinary routine of surgical demonstration at the Harvard Medical School, at the Massachusetts General Hospital, an unlikely genius in the form of Dr. Morton had produced the solution to this age-old dilemma?

At last Dr. Warren finished. With a final glance at his patient, who was beginning to stir back to consciousness, he handed his bloodstained scalpel to an assistant, turned to face his audience, and said to the hushed throng: "Gentlemen, this is no humbug."

When William arrived home that afternoon, his mother told him that they were to have a guest for dinner: his father's great friend and companion-in-arms years ago in the Greek war for independence, Dr. Samuel Gridley Howe. William was delighted: Dr. Howe was famous as a humanitarian as well as a doctor, and William wanted to tell him of that day's demonstration. As he had anticipated, Dr. Howe listened intently, nodding, and, at the end, smiling a little. "I have thought for some little while now," he said, "that sulfuric ether might be the answer to the problem of pain. But I have had no time to experiment with it myself. I am delighted that this man—what is he, a dentist?—has done so, and has made so useful a contribution. And, yes, I will certainly come to the next demonstration. Meanwhile . . ."

And he returned to his discussion of his work, which was being funded by the China merchant, Thomas Handasyd Perkins. This man, rapacious and hard in his business dealings, which included heavy trafficking in opium, had bestowed upon the people of Boston great philanthropy: large donations to the hospital that William had just left; to the Athenaeum, so that Bostonians might remain the most literate people in America; and, most recently, to an institute named for himself, devoted to the teaching of the blind.

"We are making considerable progress with one of the patients," Dr. Howe said as he finished the last of his meal. "She is young, of course, but remarkably bright. I think we will succeed in the end, although it may take time. And by succeeding, I hope to put to an end, once and for all, the idea that the blind and the deaf are mentally deficient as well." He turned to William. "Would you like to come to observe her?"

Indeed William would. And so, a few days later, he presented himself at the Perkins Institute in Pearl Street; an attendant led him to Dr. Howe's office.

"Ah—good morning, William." Dr. Howe was a stern man, a formal man, extremely handsome, intimidating in his authoritarian majesty. Now he gestured to the other person in the room, a female child about ten years old who sat in a chair in the center of the floor. She sat calmly, quietly; not intimidated at all, thought William. She wore a plain dark dress; her eyes were open but she was obviously sightless. So still, so quiet . . .

"Laura Bridgman is not only blind, she is deaf," said Dr. Howe. "Under my care and instruction, she has made amazing progress in communicating with that world—our world—outside her prison of darkness and eternal silence."

He proceeded to take the child's hand and hold it in his own. Rapidly with his fingers he made a series of movements upon her little palm. After a moment she lifted her face toward Howe's; then, in what seemed to William the most beautiful sight he had ever seen, she smiled. It was like the break of dawn—like the sun's golden rays banishing the clouds. Next the child took Dr. Howe's hand, palm up, and with her fingers spelled a message back to him.

William was fascinated. Dr. Howe had achieved what seemed impossible: communication with this sorely deprived child. Howe seemed to have forgotten that William was in the room; his face as he gazed upon his protégée was joyful, radiant—no man on earth could look happier, thought William.

And of course he understood why. This was the reason—the real reason—to suffer through the difficult curriculum of the Medical School: to acquire this ability to help, if not to heal; to bring some surcease of suffering to one's fellow human beings. Often, one Family member or another had asked him, in a rather puzzled way, why he had gone in for medicine—so exhausting a profession, so much less remunerative than trade or the textile manufacture.

And sometimes William had been caught short for a reply. Henceforth, he thought, he would only need to summon up Dr. Howe's expression of this moment, and he would never lack for explanations.

7

Celia Stoddard Revell bit her lips in irritation, narrowed her gaze, and felt her face fall into lines of determination as she watched her handsome, charming husband once again allow himself to be exploited by a scheming hussy.

This one was an eighteen-year-old with a perfect complexion, a stunning figure, and a determination fully equal to Celia's. Her name was Bella Trask. She claimed to have aspirations as a poetess. In fact, Celia thought, her only aspiration was to monopolize the attentions of the noted author, Washington Abbott Revell. They sat together now, the two of them in a corner. A few sheets of paper were spread on his knee, but they ignored whatever was written there—some of Miss Trask's stupid poetizing, no doubt—as they carried on their conversation, each looking deep into the other's eyes, Wash oblivious to the fact that he was host to a dozen people, all of whom were eager to have a little of his time.

It was not surprising: he was the handsomest man in the world, and more, he had about him a charm, a disarming sympathy that both men and women found irresistible. Celia knew that: she had been unable to resist him herself. She had not bargained on the fact that once she had married him, other women would continue to pursue him, even as Miss Trask pursued him now with her fluttering eyelashes and her trembling lips and her palpitating bosom.

Suddenly, overpoweringly, Celia was homesick for Concord. Why—*why?*— had she insisted that they come here to Stockbridge? All the reasons that she had given to Wash now seemed no reasons at all.

They had visited in the summer. The clear, invigorating Berkshire mountain air, the quiet hills and valleys, the natural beauty, the attitude of the natives—taciturn, uninterested in celebrity hunting—all that inspired Celia to urge her husband to remove to Stockbridge for the winter to finish his latest book. Washington Abbott Revell was a literary lion now, sought after, even hounded, people coming to call at their house in Boston at all hours. Concord was as bad, a little village where everyone knew everyone else. And Revell Hall was no better—was out of the question, in fact, for Wash's father, Elias, had taken a chill last winter and had died there, all alone one night when the woman attending him had gotten drunk, and the butler inexplicably out of the house— in Salem, he claimed. Wash and Celia had been abroad. When they returned, Wash had gone to Revell Hall to spend a night and had returned the next day, shaken, refusing to say what had happened. After that, he would not go back. He had let the place to one of the Griffin Revells for the warm months; now, in the autumn, it stood empty save for a caretaker.

When they had come to Stockbridge last summer, Celia had thought that it was the ideal place for Wash to finish his new book. They had rented a spacious home not far from the town center but set in ample grounds that gave privacy and quiet. Celia had decreed a rigid household schedule: her husband was not to be disturbed between the hours of nine and one, he was then to be given a cup of beef broth and a piece of toast, and he was then to go out on a brisk walk. At three o'clock dinner was served. At first Celia had thought that this meal would be just for the two of them, but unaccountably, Wash had begun to chafe, he had asked for company. So, lacking anyone else, she had begun to invite the locals. When she complained to Wash that they were not so interesting, not so witty or entertaining as people in Boston or Concord, never mind London and Paris, he had smiled indulgently and said, "For me, my dear, they are far better. They are wonderful material—unspoiled, each a true individual in the old Yankee way. In ten or twenty years, what with the railroads coming, and Mr. Morse's telegraph, everyone will visit everywhere and communicate everywhere, and these local types will die out. I must get to know them now, while they still exist."

So much for Celia's plans to protect him from the outside world while he did his great work. He did not want to be protected; he wanted to talk to people. Now winter was coming on—it was mid-November—and she had to face months and months in this house, with Bella Trask imposing on all his time outside his working hours—oh, it was too much to bear!

Ever since she married Wash, she had devoted herself to furthering his career: cultivating people who could help him, sending copies of his books to selected influential somebodies, visiting bookstores to see that Washington Abbott Revell's books were always in plentiful stock and well displayed.

Her efforts had been successful: Wash's tales of old New England Puritan ghosts and witches, and stories of the Revolution, grew increasingly popular as the nation became more mechanized, as the factories multiplied and the railroads spread their tentacles over the land. The pace of change was too swift; people could not adjust to it. So they found escape in Wash's tales of Endicott chasing Thomas Morton from Merrymount, and of Cotton Mather's witches, and of the Battle of Lexington and Concord, and the Siege of Boston, and General Howe's masquerade ball just before the evacuation.

Now, as Celia gazed wearily at her guests, she saw that Miss Trask was being edged aside—thank God!—by Levi Pratt, the owner of a small paper manufactory.

"Mr. Revell! A moment, if you please. There's somethin' I want to give you. Thought you might be able to use it some way." From the pocket of his black frock coat, Pratt took a small volume with a dark blue cover that looked both stained and mildewed. He held it open so that Wash could read the faded brown ink—for this was a handwritten little book:

Journal
George Jackson Revell

Washington's handsome face lighted up in the way that Celia loved to see. "But this is extraordinary! Only yesterday, for no reason at all, I was thinking of this man. He was my cousin, you know—the eldest son of my father's half brother, Samuel. George ran away to sea when he was still at college—some problem with gambling debts, I believe. We never saw him again." He took the little volume and held it carefully, as if by doing so he could pay his cousin some final respect. "How did you come by it?"

"I got it from a bookseller in Cornhill, last time I was in Boston, a month or so ago."

"And he . . . ?"

"He said this man's first mate brought it in. The mate said he tried to give it to the family, and they wouldn't take it."

"Ah. Too bad." Wash shook his head. "Well! This was thoughtful of you—most thoughtful."

When it came time for his guests to depart that evening, Wash realized that Miss Trask seemed reluctant to leave. She sighed; she pouted; shamelessly she fished for an invitation to go driving with him in his chaise.

Wash could almost feel himself pulling back from this dangerous chasm that he seemed to have come upon. He was perfectly happy to be managed by his wife; he wanted no intrigues with the local belles. Miss Trask seemed to have misunderstood his interest in her. For him, she was like everyone in the world: a specimen of humanity, therefore interesting, therefore potentially useful. He had no desire to philander; if he had wanted to do so, he would not have chosen Stockbridge, Massachusetts, as his locale. So . . .

"Good night to you, Miss Trask, and I hope to see you again sometime!"— very brisk, markedly impersonal.

At last they were gone, Celia retired, the door shut against the night, his comfortable chair awaiting him. He began to read the journal of George Jackson Revell. He knew how the story ended. His cousin's fate had been the subject of shocked and horrified discussion among the Family the previous year: George's ship had stopped at the Fiji Islands to pick up water; the islanders for unknown reasons had taken offense at something George and the other crew members had said or done; the natives had murdered the whites, and then had eaten them. One man only, had escaped, the same mate who had returned to Boston.

Now, as he began to read, he succumbed to the vision of the life it presented—to that life so distant, so very nearly unimaginable even to him with his magnificent powers of imagination, and yet here it was:

> The whale ship a speck on the vast Pacific, and the watch, at dawn, seeing the huge white sun rise out of the flat green surface of the water;
>
> and, other times, riding the swells—enormous, watery mountains— sliding down and down and down, waiting in the valley for that breathless moment, waiting for the mountain to crash down on you, then climbing up, climbing up and up and up until you rested high on the top, only to perch there for a moment and then begin the downslide once again;
>
> and peering through the glass, looking for the quarry, looking, looking—until at last, far in the distance, the telltale spout appears, and the cry rings out—"There she blows! She blows! She blows! She bloooows!"
>
> And then the chase is on—the small boats lowered, each with five men working the oars with a mighty vengeance. Fortunately they must sit with their backs to their destination; it is an article of faith among whaling captains and their mates that if the men were able to see the leviathan they headed for, they would panic and refuse to go on rowing—or, worse, abandon their oars altogether and jump overboard, there perhaps to be sucked up in the whale's dinner of plankton and brit, swallowed whole, like Jonah.
>
> The harpooner hurls, and hits his mark. Suddenly the water is red with blood. The whale cries out in pain. She can be heard for miles, and as she calls for help, her family circle in, crying in response, keening, calling, moaning, singing a song of pain and loss and death, powerless to

help, to free her—and liable to be killed themselves if they come too near.

"Stern away!" cries the steersman, and swiftly the men back the dory off so as not to be caught by a fluke as the whale thrashes in her agony.

The harpoon line, two thousand feet of it coiled in its tub, whistles out and around the stern loggerhead so fast that it smokes, and the men must wet it down lest it catch fire. Through the boat it goes, so fast that it cuts a man's palm like a sword, through the forward chocks it plays out, it plays out—and now she goes, surging through the waves, and they will have their Nantucket sleigh ride, thirty knots and more as their quarry speeds through the water, pulling the little dory behind, she goes, she goes!

They keep their hatchets ready, for sooner or later the whale will sound, and if that line fouls, they will sound also and go to their watery graves that very day.

Laboriously they haul in, drawing ever nearer until they come next to her, and at last they take her. The lance drives in and seems to pierce her heart. A fountain of blood spumes up, showering them with her gore.

She is dead.

They tow her back and lash her carcass to the side of the ship until they can chop her blubber for the tryworks. But she cannot stay there long, because sharks will come, and with their razor teeth they will strip her flesh from her bones in a feeding frenzy. The men drive them away with their spades but still they come, some wounded, devouring their own entrails when they cannot get at the whale, snapping at the heels of the harpooner who dangles from the monkey rope to put the blubber hook into her. They peel her and get her blubber into the tryworks as quick as they can, and soon the telltale greasy smoke rises from the furnace as the oil is boiled out. All over the Pacific the sign of a successful voyage is that same thick black column rising from the ship into the vast blue sky.

The tall clock on the landing chimed midnight; then one; then two. Wash kept on reading. The wind rose, lashing the house. Dry leaves scuttled across the porch; a cloud obscured the moon. The household cat, dozing on the cooling hearth, stirred and stretched and miaowed in surprise to find her master still awake.

At last, toward three, he came to the final entry:

Aug. 12, 1846. Arrive Fejee.

All the rest of that night Wash lay awake thinking of what George's life had been. And thinking, too, that he could not use this material, any more than he could use the Lowell mill women, any more than he could use the frightful murder of Dr. Parkman that had convulsed Boston and Cambridge last winter and spring. Real life—contemporary real life—was not his subject. He found his stories in the past; that was what appealed to him, long years ago, decades ago—centuries. His new book was a tale of the Pilgrims. Modern times held little interest for him. Modern times were too grim—too *real*. He shuddered now as he thought of the Webster-Parkman case. His cousin Caroline had urged him to write it up in fictional form. He had been horrified at the suggestion. The disappearance of Dr. Parkman had been a sensation, and his discovery—or, rather, the discovery of parts of his body—even more so. And then to have had a member of the faculty of the Harvard Medical School indicted, tried, convicted, and hanged for the crime—it had been too awful, too distressing. Gruesome details had kept the public on tenterhooks for weeks, and all the while the antidissectionists had rioted, demanding that the Medical School be burned to the ground—for that was where the few remains of Dr. Parkman had been discovered, and the janitor who had found them, people said, was no better than a resurrectionist himself, selling corpses to the medical students at twenty-five dollars each, or parts of bodies for five or ten.

But if Wash could not use his cousin George's journal, he knew someone who could: a man who had a connection to the Webster-Parkman case, in fact, for his father-in-law had been the presiding judge at the trial. But apparently Herman Melville had no more interest in the subject than Wash did, for Melville, living on his farm over in Pittsfield, was known to be working on a very different book.

Hawthorne had said that it concerned a whale.

8

One way or another, people said, those Jackson Revells were trouble. If it wasn't Samuel's son George running away to sea and getting himself killed in the most horrible way, it was Samuel's twin brother James and James's son Daniel, working with the fanatic, Garrison, to abolish slavery. James had died in the winter of '48, but Daniel carried on in the cause. Sooner or later, people said, he was going to run afoul of the law.

"Open! In the name of the law, Daniel Revell, open!"

A thunderous pounding in the quiet of the night, windows popping open as neighbors roused from sleep peered out into the damp spring darkness. And, in the Revell house on West Cedar Street, Beacon Hill, frantic activity as the family rushed to avert disaster.

"Hurry! Take nothing—I will bring what you need tomorrow—but for now, get away!"

In the light of a small oil lamp, and watched by two fugitive slaves, Daniel Revell worked feverishly, pressing the edges of the panels that covered the walls of his dining room. He had had this small house built not ten years before; he had supervised the construction of this very room, these walls with their secret that until this night had remained hidden. He had sworn the architect and the builder to silence. A certain pressure of the fingers here, near the fireplace, along the molding, a secret spring lock—ah!

The paneling slid open to reveal a narrow passage. "Here!" he said to the Negro couple, "get in. You can walk most of the way, I have done it myself. At the end you will need to crawl—hurry!" For the pounding at the door had intensified, and any moment now those men must break their way in. They were federal commissioners empowered by the Fugitive Slave Act to arrest these two and send them south—and to arrest Daniel as well. If he were tried, the offense would be treason; if he were found guilty, he could be hanged.

Near perishing with fear, the two escapees scrambled to obey him. In a moment they were gone out of sight down the narrow dark passageway. It had been built to come out at a certain house not far away in the black district at the back of the Hill on Phillips Street—the house of another escaped slave, Lewis Hayden, who now daily risked his life to help his fellows coming north to freedom. But as Daniel slid shut the panel, he suffered a moment's doubt. He had not walked that passage since it was constructed. How did he know that it was still safe—that it had not collapsed, that the couple would not be trapped in airless darkness to suffocate, perhaps, before he could save them?

But there was no help for it. Pounding and pounding at the door—"All right! All right!" And even now as events crowded in on him, he wondered: who had revealed his secret? Who had informed on him, who had told the authorities that for the past two days he had harbored these two refugees from Hell?

Sometimes in the middle of the night, unable to sleep, tormented by his imagination, Daniel Revell paced the floor of his bedroom and allowed his thoughts to wander South (even as Henry Thoreau's meditations followed his jailer out of his jail cell)—to the burning sun of the cotton fields, to the slave auction, to the overseer's killing lash—ah, this cruelty was not to be borne! This foul outrage against God must end!

The fact that most churchmen hated Daniel and his fellow Abolitionists only gave him new strength. When in 1837 the Grimké sisters, Quakers from South Carolina, had addressed the Massachusetts Legislature on the evils of slavery, the Orthodox Congregationalist clergy the length and breadth of the state had erupted into a paroxysm of anger: women speaking in public? *Women?* On Abolition? Outrageous! They could not decide which was worse: shameless women or antislavery propaganda.

The clergy wanted to preserve the status quo—which included slavery in the South. Daniel and his fellow Abolitionists wanted to abolish slavery—an act that would mean that a good many men would lose a great deal of money, not just the value of the slaves themselves, but the value of their labor, which picked the cotton which fed the mills at Lowell and Lawrence and Fall River

and Chicopee—all those millions of bales of cotton that northern textile operatives—"factory slaves" in the parlance of the South—turned into millions of
yards of cotton cloth.

So the question of freeing the slave was not a moral one only, but an
economic one as well: and as Daniel Jackson Revell and William Lloyd Garrison
and their fellow Abolitionists learned, as Wendell Phillips and Theodore Parker
and the Nantucket Quakeress Lucretia Mott learned, and as Lydia Maria Child
and Theodore Weld and the noted humanitarian Dr. Samuel Gridley Howe
learned: when men's pocketbooks were affected, they lost their finer feelings in
a hurry.

In 1850 Congress threw a new ingredient into the bubbling cauldron of
national politics: the Fugitive Slave Act. Escaped slaves, the law said, must be
returned to their masters—forcibly if necessary. Federal officials in the North
must help slave catchers from the South to recover the missing "property."

Senator Daniel Webster of Massachusetts defended the act—part of a compromise to admit new states into the Union.

Some people thought that the shame of Webster's defense blackened the
state's name for all time—proud old state, leader in the Revolution, brought
down to this abomination, defending the Fugitive Slave Act!

It was, said the Abolitionists, an act written in the blood of four million
black slaves—a despicable, monstrous act, a covenant with Hell.

On the other hand, it was a useful propaganda tool.

Help the slave catchers? they cried.

Betray those desperate fugitives who turn to us for assistance?

Never!

The Underground Railroad doubled its business. The Abolitionists redoubled their efforts. All over the North people risked life and limb to help escaped
slaves stay free. In Boston a mob tried to help a slave named Sims, but the
federal marshals sent to get him called out the troops, and so poor Sims was
forcibly taken back to the South and beaten nearly to death as an example to
his fellows. The authorities were adamant: any man found helping slaves to
escape was subject to arrest and trial for treason, they said—and treason was a
capital crime.

Sleepless nights, long hours of darkness—and sometimes, tormented almost
beyond endurance by his thoughts, Daniel went downstairs to his little library
and lit his oil lamp and read for a while: antislavery tracts, or something more
lengthy, Prescott's *Conquest of Mexico* or, for a few memorable nights in 1851,
Uncle Tom's Cabin, a harrowing tale written by one of the Beechers, a woman
living up in Andover, a narrative written to show the human meaning of the
Fugitive Slave Act, a sensationally popular book (in the North, at least)—tens
of thousands of copies sold, so effectively fulfilling the author's purpose that a
decade later, in the midst of the Civil War, President Lincoln greeted her with,
"So you are the little lady who started this big war?"

On Thursday, May 22, Daniel Jackson Revell and one of his fellow Abolitionists, Albert Smith, walked through the lobby of the Revere House in Bowdoin Square. When Daniel wanted to stop to buy a newspaper, Smith urged him on—around a corner, away from the crowd.

"What is it?" said Daniel. "What's the matter?"

"The two men by the desk," said Smith. "They're the two who were askin' yesterday about—you know."

Daniel did know: Anthony Burns, an escaped slave who had taken refuge in Boston in the winter. "They are waiting for word from Washington," Smith went on. "The minute the Senate passes the bill and the news is telegraphed here, they'll pounce on him." He referred to a new version of the Fugitive Slave Act, a stricter version with harsher penalties for those who, like the Boston Vigilance Committee, would violate it.

"Then we must, ah, send the merchandise farther north," said Daniel. "I will notify the others and we will get him under way at once."

That night Daniel walked around to the back of Beacon Hill where the Negroes of Boston lived and knocked on Lewis Hayden's door—three knocks, pause, three again.

The door opened a crack. Hayden, who as an escaped slave himself was liable as any newcomer to be captured, generally harbored at least one fugitive under his roof.

Recognizing Daniel, Hayden opened the door to let him in. "Trouble?" said Hayden; the two men, long companions in their work, seldom wasted time on pleasantries.

"We have seen the slave catchers at the Revere House. We think they may be after Burns. Do you know where he is?"

"No."

"Can you find him? Warn him to get away? We will help him, of course, if he wishes it."

"I will try. I saw him on Monday. Not since."

"Do you know where he lives?"

"I know where he lived on Monday." Hayden's broad, black, homely face stared impassively at the white man standing before him. He knew Daniel Jackson Revell as well as he knew any white. He knew that Daniel, like Garrison, like Parker, like Phillips, would give up his life if that act would free the slaves. He knew that these men—and many women, too—gave every day all their energies, all their heartfelt strength to the great cause of Abolition.

And he knew that these whites, as well-meaning as they were, could never know the full truth of the horror that they so valiantly fought.

And further he knew that some of these same whites, good-hearted and compassionate as they were, had grown so frustrated at their failure to end the slave system that they grew more desperate every day—and that one day, not far off now, one of them would deliberately provoke an outrage the better to sway public opinion, to show the horrors of slave catching, and that outrage would involve a black man's life.

"Try to find him," said Daniel. "I have spoken to the committee. We have transportation ready."

"Tonight?"

"At any moment. We will get him to Canada—any place short of that is not safe now with this new act."

But Daniel's Vigilance Committee could not find the escaped slave, Anthony Burns. Instead, the slave catchers got him—the very next day, the day after the new and improved Fugitive Slave Act went into effect.

Afterward it struck some people as very strange indeed that Burns could have lived undetected for months and then all of a sudden be found by the very men he was trying to evade.

Perhaps his enemies betrayed him, people said.

Or perhaps his friends.

9

A warm May evening in Boston Town, a breeze blowing lightly off the harbor, new-leafed trees and springtime flowers scenting the air with their perfume.

But this night there is a different smell in men's nostrils: it is the smell of fear, it is the smell of degradation, and in Faneuil Hall the Abolitionists stride across the stage and shout to a full house as they whip up the crowd. Remember Webster's betrayal, they cry. Remember the fate of that poor wretch, Sims! Remember the Cotton Whigs—the mercantile and manufacturing men here in Massachusetts who get rich on slave labor!

The plan is this: at a prearranged signal the chief plotters of the rescue of Anthony Burns will make a dash from Faneuil Hall to the Court House, where a few companions await them. These men have laid in a supply of hatchets. Together they will hack down the doors. They will race upstairs to where Burns is being held, wrest him from the clutches of his captors, and secret him out of the city. The foremost devisers of this plan, the Reverend Thomas Wentworth Higginson and Daniel Jackson Revell, have been up all the previous night with the Vigilance Committee to coordinate the details of the action. They wait now in the twilight at the Court House door, straining their ears at each roar from Faneuil Hall as it drifts up the hill to where they stand.

Suddenly came the sound of running feet, the first of the crowd come to assist them.

Daniel clutched the handle of his ax and strained to peer through the gathering darkness. A few men coming at a good clip—but no, he did not recognize them, they were not the men he wanted to see.

"We are in trouble," muttered Higginson. "If we are to succeed, we must act quickly. These fellows are but the froth and scum of that meeting. Where are the others, where is Parker, where is Weld?"

"Trapped in the building, perhaps," said Daniel, "unable to get out. You know that the steps to the hall are steep and narrow. The crowd might have blocked them—"

Just then Daniel heard a familiar voice hail him: "Mr. Revell, we got a batterin' ram here!"

It was Lewis Hayden, calling from the west side of the huge granite building—the seemingly impregnable fortress whose locked doors kept them from rescuing the escapee.

"Better than axes!" cried Higginson. "Come on!"

And in a moment the two men had raced to the opposite side of the building, where Hayden stood at the head of a line of men holding a huge wooden beam. Daniel and Higginson found a place, and at Hayden's command—"Heave!"—the dozen or so men lifted the beam and at a half run, rammed it into the stout iron-barred wooden door. Once—twice—three times they rammed it, and at the third the door gave way.

"Come on!" cried Daniel as he and Higginson leaped through the door, now hanging off its hinges. But even as their companions surged in behind, the two men at the front were greeted by federal marshals wielding clubs, which they now set about using with indiscriminate fury. Left and right, *thwack!* and *thwack!* Daniel heard the sickening sound of hard wood cracking human bone, he saw men dropping all around him under the fierce assault of the authorities who had lain in wait. No hope for Burns—no hope even for these would-be rescuers.

All of a sudden a shot rang out, and then one of the marshals dropped dead, his face torn away by a bullet fired at close range.

The sound of the shot echoed through the hall. For a moment no one moved; each side seemed too stunned even to react.

Then, as if at an unspoken command, the Abolitionists fell back; they stumbled out the shattered door, they vanished into the darkness, not a man among them stout enough to go on with the attempt in the face of murder. For wasn't that what had happened? Murder?

No, Daniel would argue later; not murder but self-defense. One of us could as easily have been killed by those free-flying clubs.

But at the time it sobered them—brought them up short, sent them defeated into the night.

As he realized that they had failed, as he understood that Anthony Burns was still in chains, was still under sentence to return to his slavery, Daniel could not repress a cry of anguish that echoed into the rapidly dwindling crowd around the Court House.

"You cowards," he cried, "will you desert us now?"

No one answered him; no one bothered even to give him a wave of the hand.

Only old Bronson Alcott, the Transcendentalist philosopher, bucking the tide and coming up the steps while everyone else was running down: only he replied. Lifting his cane and waving it like a flagpole, he cried, "Why are we not within?"

No answer. Alcott stood bewildered, remembering perhaps a similar question between his friend Emerson and his friend Thoreau.

But then the troops came, briskly marching Marines from the Navy Yard at Charlestown, where some ladies had raised the money for a monument to the Battle of Bunker Hill that had helped to start the War for Independence and Liberty and Freedom for everyone who was white. (And for everyone who was male, Caroline Griffin Revell might have added; and some of the Abolitionists would have agreed with her.) And at the sight of the troops, the remnants of the crowd melted away.

Burns sat in his cell, awaiting his fate.

And through the Abolitionist circles of Boston was whispered the chilling verdict on the night's events: we have seen the first bloodshed of the war.

10

Five days later, a brilliant day in early summer, Daniel Jackson Revell and his thirteen-year-old son, Garrison, stood in the crowd lining State Street to watch the authorities march Anthony Burns down to the dock, where he would be put on a ship that would return him to his master in Virginia. Thousands of people were in that throng—as many as fifty thousand, some said later—and hundreds of armed troops as well, for once again, as in the time of the siege, the city of Boston was an armed camp, and her people lived under military rule. Many shopfronts were draped in black; many Stars and Stripes were flying, but flying upside down in the universal signal of distress—for this was indeed a day of distress, a day when the honor of the proud old town was badly soiled, and many of her citizens were ashamed of what was being done in their names.

"Here he comes! Make way!" came the cry echoing through the spectators. They craned their necks and jumped up and down to get a glimpse, for the street was lined by policemen with locked arms. Daniel saw the phalanx proceeding down the middle of the street: a hundred troops and marshals, at least, surrounded by mounted soldiers, and at their center the black man, his head held high, his face expressionless, walking steadily toward his brutal fate.

"Shame!" cried the crowd. "Shame! Set him free!" And then, as the procession neared Commercial Street, a few men managed to break through the police lines, and they made as if to charge at the cortege around Burns. They were driven back by the Marines, who assaulted them with drawn swords, badly wounding two or three.

Quickly the lines closed up again. Smug and vindictive in their little triumph, as the troops neared the wharf they began to sing: "Carry Me Back to Old Virginny," they sang, with broad grins on their ugly faces. But many strong men wept that day, Daniel Revell among them. He did not mind that his son saw him do so, for if a man could not weep at injustice, then he was not a man at all, but a mere husk of a thing, without conscience, without heart.

As Burns was put onto the ship, a tremendous shout went up, a cry of triumph, a cry of despair. The sound of it was like a knife through Daniel's own flesh. He stood for a moment numbed by the weight of his sorrow. He and the other Abolitionists had begun a kind of war. They had won a few early skirmishes, but now they had suffered a major defeat.

Slowly he turned away, and he and his son retraced their steps to West Cedar Street.

"Why is that man so important, Father?" the boy said—for it seemed to him that if the Queen of England herself had visited Boston, there would hardly have been more of a turnout.

"He is important because he had the bad luck to be here when they wanted to make a show of strength. They wanted to make an example of someone, to show that the law must be enforced."

"Even when it is a bad law?"

"Even then."

"Could someone here have bought the man and set him free?"

Daniel glanced at his son. A tall boy, with the Revell look to him—and now, it seemed, more than the usual quantity of brains.

"Of course that is the sensible thing to do," he said. "And I imagine that we will—we will get up a purse, and someone will go South and bargain with his master and buy him. If his master doesn't kill him first," he added grimly.

They came out onto the Common. The new fountain, put up by a wealthy benefactor to celebrate the piping-in of water to the city from the Cochituate Reservoir, gushed forth its pure, sparkling water in the bright June sunlight. A Sanitary Committee led by Dr. Lemuel Shattuck had recently investigated the city's fast-growing immigrant slums, Fort Hill and the North End. There had been famine in Ireland these past ten years, and half the population, it seemed, had fled to Boston. Fresh, pure water was almost impossible to obtain in those dark, festering warrens—but here it was for the taking, and, indeed, clusters of dirty little urchins were dabbling at the edges. They were Irish, of course, chattering in their strange Gaelic tongue—a dozen, two dozen, crowding around.

Daniel and his son walked on, up the Long Path to Joy Street where it came into Beacon. A few doors down, Hamilton Griffin Revell had recently built a fine new house. Daniel had heard that it had the most magnificent ballroom in Boston. Certainly he would never see it; he would never be invited there, for he and all his fellow Abolitionists were anathema to Cotton Whigs like the Griffin Revells, never mind their old family dispute. Recently the gentlemen of Boston had gotten up a club for themselves which they called the Somerset. All the best families were invited to join—and that meant all three branches of the Revells. Separated by their old feud, they were now split by this more urgent issue. But no matter. You could not invite one and not the other, for the Revells went back to the beginning of time, and if you were going to have a proper Boston club, you had to include them. Antiquity was what counted in Boston society—and money, too, of course. But plenty of more recent arrivals had money: money was not the most important thing. Antiquity—the tracing of the line right back to the beginning—why, the Revells had come over on the *Mayflower*! And if this country had an aristocracy at all, it was that of the *Mayflower*. No, no, you couldn't start the Somerset without all the Revells. Let 'em snub each other if they want, but get 'em on the membership rolls!

There seemed to be some disturbance at Hamilton Griffin Revell's door. A girl—a poor sort of girl, an immigrant girl—shouting at the butler? Could it be? They had no manners, these floods of newcomers, no sense of what was the proper way to behave. For a moment as he turned up Joy Street, Daniel was tempted to go back and see what the trouble was, but then he decided against.

Hamilton Griffin Revell's affairs were none of his.

11

Her name was Mary Margaret O'Donovan, and she had been told for a certainty that there was an open place at the home of Mr. Hamilton Griffin Revell at 43½ Beacon Street.

"Go right away," Bridget had said, "they'll have ten girls lookin' to get that one place, but if you get there first, they'll likely take you. Clean yer hands and face, mind, and—here—comb yer hair. They won't even talk to y' if y' don't look clean."

And so Mary Margaret O'Donovan had trudged through the streets on the day of Anthony Burns's martyrdom. She had paid no mind to the commotion all around her. She had a single purpose—a crucial, life-or-death errand to perform—and no one was going to keep her from performing it. Down from Fort Hill with its open sewers and foul courtyards, its filthy nooks and crannies, up to the Common and across it, hardly glancing at those same urchins who had momentarily distracted Daniel. Let them be. She was going to get a place at the grandest house in Boston—for sure she was!—and she would not have turned aside from her mission if the earth had opened at her feet and tried to swallow her. She would simply have skipped across the cracks and hurried on.

Despite her unladylike determination—the grit and gumption of the immigrant bent on survival—she was a pretty girl, seventeen or so, with curly brown hair and bright brown eyes and cheeks once rosy that held a trace of their former color. Some of her back teeth were decayed, but no matter; her smile was bright enough when she had something to smile about, and she had an air about her that said, "I am here, ready to make my place!"

So when she ran up the granite front steps of the grand Revell house fronting the Common—far grander than anything she had ever seen in her native village in County Cork—she was near to bursting with optimism, certain she would get the place. And she would make a success of it, see if she didn't!

She lifted the great brass ring on the knocker in the shape of a winged lion and brought it smartly down—once, twice, three times.

After a moment the door opened an inch or two. A man's face peered out. He didn't speak; just looked her up and down with fish-cold eyes and started to slam shut the door when Mary Margaret, realizing in that split second that she was about to lose her chance, said, "Please, sir, I've come about the place—"

And then, hearing her brogue as thick as a pot of porridge, he slammed the door anyway, narrowly missing her foot in its shabby boot.

Now Mary Margaret might have been the original inspiration for the phrase, "Get her Irish up." She wasn't going to let a fish-eye like that defeat her so easily. So she knocked again, harder this time.

And again the door opened, and before she could get out a word, the same man—who seemed to be wearing some kind of formal suit, although it was only midday—stared her up and down again with a look on his face as if he smelled something foul, and he said, "Get away."

"I've come about the place. Can I apply f'r it, please?"

"We don't want Irish here. Now get away with you."

And again he slammed shut the door.

Mary Margaret stood for a moment gathering her wits. She was not only determined, she was desperate. Over the past months she had survived a good deal to fetch up at last, like flotsam, on this particular front step on this particular street; and therefore, having come so far, and having so little to lose, she seized the brass ring again. Wouldn't see her? They must see her! Mother of God, they *had* to see her!

After a moment she gave up on the lion knocker and started to pound on the door. She heard the sound of her fists on the smooth white-painted wood, hammering, hammering—

"Hello!" she cried. "Are y'there? Hello!"

Hammering, hammering—her little fists ached with pounding, her voice cracked with the urgency of her message.

"Listen to me!" she cried. "Are y'listening? I am Mary Margaret O'Donovan from County Cork! D'y' hear me?"

Hammering, hammering—she was only a poor Irish girl, half starved, half wild, but already she had a sense of herself.

"Hello! Hello! D'you hear me?"

Hammering, hammering—

"Listen to me! I am Mary Margaret O'Donovan from County Cork, and I am here! I have come to work for you! Open up!"

O Revells! Listen to her! Do you not hear? Do you not know what she is? She is your destiny—your Fate! She has come to awaken you from your long dream of overlordship of this place! Listen to that fatal, echoing knock, insistent, peremptory, demanding to be heard, demanding to be recognized—listen! Can you hear her? She is calling to you! And as loud as that sound is now, it will be louder still for your children, and for their children coming after them—ah, listen!

She is your future coming to call on you, and you must let her in!

PART IV

"NO IRISH
NEED APPLY"

GRIFFIN REVELLS

Artemas
(1804–1873)

m.

Elizabeth Ropes
(1806–1876)

Nathaniel	Thomas	Harriet	Julia
(1833–1863)	(1834–1880)	(1836–1900)	(1837–1907)

Thomas
m.

Rose Standish
(1850–1874)

Lyman
(1840–1913)

Frederick
(1874–1936)

m.

Anna Gould
(1849–1918)

Winslow	Augusta	Fletcher
(1878–1968)	(1890–1977)	(1883–1950)

Caroline
(1805–1890)

Hamilton
(1809–1886)

m.

Alice Sargeant
(1815–1872)

Oliver	Theodore	Florence
(1840–1863)	(1845–1884)	(1846–1920)
	m.	m.
	Isabella Jackson Revell	Arthur Mifflin
	(1850–1936)	(1842–1863)

JACKSON REVELLS

Edward
(1822–1900)

m.

Elizabeth Cabot
(1828–1892)

Isabella
(1850–1936)

Four others

m.

Theodore Griffin Revell
(1845–1884)

Daniel
(1810–1884)

m.

Mary Parker
(1812–1872)

Garrison
(1839–1863)

Parker
(1840–1910)

Barrett
(1842–1864)

m.

Amelia
Weld
(1841–1890)

Edwin
(1863–1932)

ABBOTT REVELLS

William
(1825–1902)

m.

Katherine
Shaw
(1838–1863)

John
(1863–1930)

Francis Jr.
(1806–1881)

m.

Harriet Otis
(1815–1881)

Otis
(1849–1920)

Washington
(1811–1875)

m.

Celia Stoddard
(1819–1876)

Judson
(1850–1934)

m.

Louisa Richardson
(1855–1880)

Violet
(1880–1959)

SHAUGHNESSYS

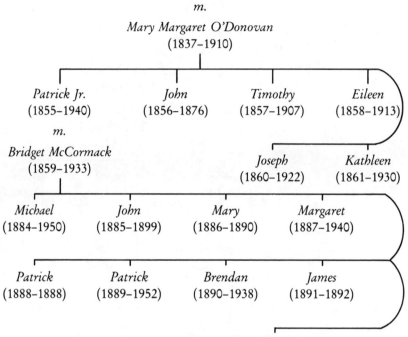

Patrick Shaughnessy
(1834–1863)

m.

Mary Margaret O'Donovan
(1837–1910)

Patrick Jr.
(1855–1940)

John
(1856–1876)

Timothy
(1857–1907)

Eileen
(1858–1913)

m.

Bridget McCormack
(1859–1933)

Joseph
(1860–1922)

Kathleen
(1861–1930)

Michael
(1884–1950)

John
(1885–1899)

Mary
(1886–1890)

Margaret
(1887–1940)

Patrick
(1888–1888)

Patrick
(1889–1952)

Brendan
(1890–1938)

James
(1891–1892)

Bridget
(1892–1961)

"The Yankee Brahmins are like the French Bourbons: they never learn and they never forget. They beat the British twice, but were conquered by a horde of invading Irish."

James Michael Curley

1. PILGRIMS

1

All the night in the foul, cramped quarters of the coffin ship, Mary Margaret had kept her vigil beside her new friend, and now, toward dawn, she saw that her friend was dying. Crouching because there was no headroom to stand, she went to the water barrel to get a cupful. Kathleen's lips were parched and cracked; at least, thought Mary, she could have that small comfort, brackish and foul though the water was.

"Here, Kathleen," she said, lifting the woman's head so that she might drink. But Kathleen had no strength even for that. Mary unknotted her own neckerchief, moistened a corner of it, and wiped the sweat from her friend's face and neck. After a moment the woman's eyes opened. "Thank you," she said. Her breath came hard and painful; in the dim light and shifting shadows of the oil lamp hanging in the passageway, Mary saw that her eyes had sunk back into her skull; she might have been a death's-head, a living skeleton, and suddenly Mary shivered with fear and crossed herself and breathed a prayer.

"Hush," she said. "Yer goin't'be all right. An' soon we'll be there, an' we'll get y'somethin't'help."

But Kathleen shook her head. Her lips were moving, but no sound came. Over the creak of the ship, and the constant wailing of the wind, and the snap and beat of the sails, and the moans and sobbing of her fellow passengers, Mary could not hear her. After a moment Kathleen closed her eyes. Mary held her hand. And after a while she knew that Kathleen had died.

Soon everyone else would know it, too: impossible to keep secrets in this nightmare of humans stacked like cordwood—a coffin ship it was, for sure, and this poor woman not the first and not the last to die on it. Fewer than one in three survived the voyage, she'd heard—not that that bit of news had stopped her from coming. She knew that Kathleen's husband had died the previous week. They'd had, she said, no children living.

And so in the little time Mary had before the ship's officer called the daily call for the dead, she felt along the hem of the dead woman's skirt, and along the seams at the side of the bodice, and at the waist for pockets. There. She felt them: four coins in a little pocket inside the waistband of the skirt. Kathleen had hinted as much. Quickly Mary worked them out and slipped them into the little money bag that she wore on a string around her neck. It held all the money she had in the world, only a few coins, adding up to not more than a couple of pounds. But now this woman, by dying, had given her this small bit extra, and Mary understood what it meant: it meant that she and her brother who lay in some other part of this foul, heaving ship had that much more chance to survive.

Not long after, the ship's officer came through. Without ceremony, without mourners, Kathleen would be cast over the side.

Mary went on deck to watch as Kathleen's corpse and five others were slipped into the water. She was glad that she had taken the coins. They would have done no good to anyone at the bottom of the sea—or in the officer's pocket.

The wind was bitter cold. She pulled her shawl more tightly around her. She did not want to go below, but she didn't know how long she could bear to stay on deck. The air hurt her lungs, and she was shivering so hard that her teeth chattered. She wished that she could visit her brother John, three years younger than she and not in very good health, coughing a great deal. But that was impossible: below decks the sexes were rigidly kept apart. She hadn't seen John for three days.

"Here."

She looked up, startled: a young man had thrown a jacket around her shoulders. She didn't remember seeing him before. She thought that perhaps she should refuse such a familiarity, but she didn't want to; the extra warmth felt good, and she was glad of a chance to stay on deck. And besides, he was good-looking—decent-looking, too. She liked his smile. "Thanks," she said.

He smiled down at her again. He'd seen her once or twice earlier in the voyage. She looked poorly now, more than before; but even so, she was, he thought, a fetching little thing.

"Yer welcome," he said. "My pleasure."

2

She was just seventeen, a pretty girl despite her pallor, the gaunt look of hunger that she shared with nearly all her countrymen. Until the spring of 1854 she had lived with her family and somehow survived the famine that had come in '46 and '47 and every year after. They had a comfortable farm near Fermoy,

County Cork. Their crop was not entirely potatoes, and so year after year, as they watched the population starve and sicken and die, or flee to safety in England or America, the family had managed to survive. But last year her mother and father and two older brothers had all died of some plague, they did not know what, and the landlord had raised the rent to make up for what he was losing on other properties, and at last Mary and John had been evicted. But the landlord was not a complete monster: he had given them tickets on this ship, and had wished them well. They had walked for two days, sleeping by the side of the road, and frightened to death to find that the man sleeping next to them had died in the night, so that they woke up next to a corpse. A bad omen, said Mary, and she had gone at a run down the road dragging John along behind her, not caring for the moment about the cough that near smothered him.

So at last, exhausted and wet and dirty, they had come in to the city and found the waterfront and the ship, and with a final visit to the church to pray for safe voyage, they boarded and found their places in the warren of pens below decks, and let themselves be carried away to the vast, unknown land across the water where, it was said, people had a better chance at life than here.

For the first few days the weather was fair, the sea calm, and Mary thought that the tales she had heard of nightmare voyages must have been exaggerations. But then a storm struck and the hatches were closed, and water seeped in underfoot, and rats by the dozen swarmed through the bunks, maddened by the smell of the food the passengers carried with them—although never enough, and what little they had soon rotted. People began to fall ill, and many of them died. Babies and children cried constantly, and the air grew ever more foul, and men fell to fighting over nothing, and the privy overflowed, and always the terrible cramped quarters, narrow sleeping pens, and even out in the center aisle, not enough headroom for a girl like Mary Margaret to stand, let alone a man.

The young man's name was Patrick Shaughnessy. He was cheerful in the way that most Irishmen were, which is to say she could sense the hardness, the hatred, very near the surface of his smile. But of course the hatred was not for her, and so she shrugged it off and smiled at him in return, and chatted for a while up there on the deck, both of them putting off as long as they could the return to the fetid Hell below.

He was from Cork City. All his family had died; he had an uncle in Boston, he said, who had promised to help him find work. And where was she headed, he wanted to know, and what were her plans?

She told him what little she could. She and John had the name of a family in Half Moon Place, wherever that was. Boston, she thought. She hoped that she and her brother both would find work. She'd heard the streets were paved with gold in America, but she didn't believe it. Yes, she said: she'd be glad to see him again, once their feet were on dry land.

3

The voyage over took six weeks, and by the time they staggered off the ship at the dock on Noddle's Island, they were no longer so cramped in their foul stinking berths, for many passengers had died and their bodies tossed overboard. Like all ships from Ireland, this one had a stench so great that the Boston Harbor master claimed that even if he were blind, he would always know when a coffin ship was coming in. Dear God, that stink!

It was a foggy day in mid-May, cool and damp just like home. Clutching her bundle of clothes and touching the coins in her pouch to make sure she hadn't lost them, Mary Margaret made her way down the gangplank onto the wharf. She and the others crowding close around her—but not John, she couldn't see him anywhere—were halted at a barrier, behind which stood several men in uniform examining the new arrivals one by one before allowing them in. To Mary's horror, she saw a woman turned back. Despite her loud wails of protest, the officials roughly shoved her away from the entrance. She was visibly ill, with open running sores on her face and neck, and a hacking cough. Mary shuddered.

"There's one for an early grave," muttered the woman behind her, nodding toward the ejected one. "When my sister came over in '49, she had to spend a month quarantined because the ship's fever was so bad, they wouldn't let anyone in."

At last it was Mary's turn. "Papers!" demanded the official.

She produced them.

He looked at them for a moment and handed them back. "Open!"

She opened her mouth and he looked down her throat. Then he looked into her eyes, peered into her ears. Finally he scribbled a word on a printed pass and thrust it at her. "Next!" he bawled.

She was in.

She looked around for John. He was not there. Frantically she began to search for him. At last she saw him at the end of the gangplank, recovering from a bout of coughing. After a moment he picked up his bundle and joined the slow, shuffling line of immigrants waiting to be examined.

If John seemed ill, they might not let him in. They would send him back to Ireland, and she would be left here alone. Mother of God! She bit her lips to keep from crying, but still her eyes filled with tears and she saw only a blurred, gray scene. But then she blinked and wiped her eyes, and there he was, coming through, almost at the head of the line now, and they were asking for his papers, and giving him a look, and passing him along as easy as you please, and he had done it, and they were both safe.

A throng of eager greeters stood awaiting the newcomers, and now Mary and John had to run the gauntlet of their cries: "Who's from Tipperary? Anyone from Galway? Galway here—come on, I've got a place for y', step right here!" A sharp-looking little fellow grabbed at John's arm. "Where'y'from, fella? I'll fix you up with your own people, I got a place f'r everybody." Mary understood that these men were sorting people out to match them with their neighbors from back home, but she and John had no use for them, for their destination lay across the harbor.

"Where'y'goin' Miss?"

"Half Moon Place. Can y'tell how to get there, please?"

A strange look crossed the man's face, as if he had seen some revolting thing crawl out from under a rock. "Y'sure? I can fix you up right away here, room in a clean house, honest landlord, he'll take y'right in."

But they must go where they had been instructed to go, and so he pointed the way to the ferry. It was not far from the shipyard of Donald McKay, whose clipper ship *Flying Cloud* had recently set a new record around the Horn and up the western coast of South America to California: eighty-nine days. But these newcomers knew nothing of such marvels. They wanted only the ferry; for two pennies each they were given a place on it, and so they came across the harbor and into the city of Boston.

The city of Boston, on that late spring day in 1854, did not want them. For years, now, ever since the first famine victims had begun to arrive in the forties, thousands upon thousands of starving, desperate peasants had been disgorged upon the streets of the prim Yankee city, so that by the time Mary and John arrived, the Nativist Know-Nothings had captured the state government and spread across the map their hatred of all things foreign, and particularly all things Irish and Catholic. "Enough!" they cried; we are drowning in Irish, we will be engulfed and overwhelmed by them, filthy, dirty bog-trotting serfs, the legions of the Pope, ignorant and superstitious, slaves to the Whore of Rome, filling every nook and cranny of our beautiful little city, fouling every spare inch. It is bad enough that they must land here, since Boston is the western terminus of the Cunard line, but must they stay? Can they not have the decency to move on, to go West?

But the Irish did not move on. Most of them had no money to move on, and in any case they would not have wanted a life on the vast prairies of the West, where a family lived and died in isolation. The Irish were congenial folk, great talkers, lovers of community. So they huddled together in Boston; if they must perish, they thought, let it be with our own. At the most, some of them, to keep from starving, went on railroad gangs as far away as Troy or Albany in New York State; others went on the corporations in the factory towns of Massachusetts: Lowell or Lawrence, Chicopee or Holyoke. The Yankee mill girls, once the pride of the manufacturers, had pretty much gone home by then, defeated by the constant speedups, the constant cutting of wages so that the owners' dividends might remain high. Their places were taken by the Irish, who were glad to get even that miserable chance to survive, and so inevitably conditions became even worse.

On a foggy evening in May, Mary and John arrived in Half Moon Place, off Broad Street. It was a foul, dark, airless courtyard reached by a narrow passage between the buildings that fronted the street. Over it towered Fort Hill. The warren of shanties and flimsy tenements were packed to overflowing with Irish: six, seven, ten to a room hardly big enough for one. A single privy served a hundred people. Most times it was clogged, so that the raw sewage ran down the middle of the courtyard; during heavy rains the courtyard became a stinking, poisonous pool of filth that overflowed into the basement rooms packed with immigrants.

At length the two newcomers found whom they sought: one Bridget Connor, a cousin of a neighbor back home. She seemed surprised to see them; apparently the message she had sent home sometime before, that all friends and family newly come ashore should stop to see her first, was badly out of date. She was a woman overburdened now, her two rooms jammed with paying guests. She didn't need more. On the other hand . . .

"All right," she said, cursing herself for her soft heart. "Y'can stay a week or two. But I'll have the rent in advance, if y'please, and I'll advise y' to look out f'r a new place as soon as y've found work."

4

The next morning one of their fellow boarders, a smart young lass with a squint and a bad complexion, gave them a cup of tea and a bit of advice: since John was so thin and small, and not very strong what with his cough, he wouldn't want to try for the usual type of job offered to an Irishman, which was hod carrying or ditch digging or similar heavy labor. But she'd heard that some of the city's hotels were hiring Irish—not as waiters, of course, for Irish waiters would drive away the gentlemen who dined there, but dishwashers, or busboys—try the Parker House, she said, up on Tremont Street.

Bridget overheard them. "That's right," she said. "And as for you, Mary . . ." She shrugged. "Y've got to get a place in someone's house. That or sewing shirts—that's all y'can do here. Now listen. Y'go out here, see, an'y'can walk together up State Street t'Cornhill. Then go left to School Street an'then go right. Up one block an'y'come to the Parker House. Then you, Mary, keep on goin' up the hill—it'll be Beacon Street then. An'y'just start knockin' on doors. A lot of 'em don't hire Irish, but I know three girls in the last month'v'found places. Th'American girls don't want to go into service, an' Canadians'r'gettin' scarce. So sooner or later they'll have fine Irish girls in every house on Beacon Hill, like it'r'not. Go on, now—an' good luck t'y'!"

John was in fact lucky that day: one of the busboys at the Parker House had just been fired, and so they hired him on the spot. Mary was not so fortunate: all day, until mid-afternoon when she was ready to drop from exhaustion and hunger, she walked the streets of Beacon Hill looking for work. She did not find it. By the time she returned to Half Moon Place she was ready to weep with frustration and humiliation—why, these people treated her as if she wasn't human! Time after time whoever answered the door took one look at her and slammed it shut in her face without even letting her finish what she had to say.

Bridget listened to her with a grim smile and a sour look. "I know, girl. It's hard. Once y'get a place, y'll do well, f'r I can see y'r a sharp lass and y'll do just fine. But it's gettin' that first job that's hard. I know it is. Well, keep tryin'."

Despite Mary's disappointment, she was cheered by John's success, and for a week or two her confidence stayed high. Every day she went out; every afternoon she came back defeated but not discouraged. They could stay for a week more, Bridget said; then she needed the room for her sister, due any day now with a flock of children.

One evening a girl working as a scullery maid at William Appleton's house on Beacon Street told Bridget that she had heard that at Mr. Hamilton Griffin Revell's house nearby they wanted a second upstairs girl.

"Go right away," Bridget said to Mary. "First thing in th'mornin'. They'll have ten girls lookin' to get that one place, but if you get there first, they'll likely take you. Clean yer hands and face, mind, and comb yer hair. They won't even talk to y' if y' don't look clean."

And so the next morning Mary Margaret set off once again for Beacon Hill. As she went she saw that some great excitement had gripped the city, for huge crowds lined the streets, and everywhere she looked she saw people openly crying, men as well as women, and after a while she saw a contingent of soldiers marching. She didn't care. She had her errand to perform, and nothing was going to prevent her from performing it.

She came to Beacon Street. She found the house: number 43½. She skipped up the steps and seized the large brass knocker in the shape of some fantastical mythical beast. Smartly she brought it down: *knock knock knock!*

The door opened an inch or two. A man's face peered out: narrow, hostile, with fish-cold eyes. At once he started to slam the door shut. All in an instant Mary Margaret realized that her chance was about to vanish, and she spoke up: "Please, sir, I've come about the place—"

And then, hearing her, he did slam the door shut, narrowly missing her foot.

Stupid old fish-eyes! Mary Margaret gritted her teeth and seized the knocker again and pounded harder.

The man was even more hostile this time, if that were possible, and he said, "Get away." And he wouldn't let her apply—not at all. "We don't want Irish here," he said. And slammed shut the door again.

It was a bright day in June. All down the Common the trees had sprouted, the vivid green of the leaves contrasting with the bright blue sky, the bright red-brick of the houses all around. Carriages came and went up and down the slope of Beacon Hill, children and governesses and matrons paraded the sidewalk, and all the world, so it seemed to Mary, was getting on with its business. Only she was stymied; only she was unable to get past this first great hurdle faced by all newcomers: finding a job. She felt her temper rise, and she gave up on the knocker and started to pound on the door.

"Listen to me!" she cried. "Are y'listenin'? I am Mary Margaret O'Donovan from County Cork! D'y' hear me?"

She pounded and pounded at the smooth white surface of the door, but no one came. After a while she gave up. Rubbing her sore hand, she went back down the steps and across to the edge of the sidewalk. She turned to look up at the house. Something caught her eye: the movement of a white curtain at an upstairs window. For a moment, a fraction of a second, she thought she saw a face. But almost before it could register, it was gone. They were looking at her, no doubt, to see what the butler had turned away. In a final gesture of defiance, Mary stuck out her tongue at the house. Nasty rich folks, too proud to take on a poor Irish girl. Well, it was their loss, she told herself, for she would have been a fine worker for them and they'd have been glad the day they hired her.

As she started to retrace her steps back up toward the State House and down lower Beacon Street, she saw a wagon from S.S. Pierce, the fancy grocers', turn into Walnut Street, and all in a flash she realized that perhaps she still had a chance. In an instant she darted into the narrow side street and along the alley that led to the back yard of number 43½. Her luck held: the grocer's boy was delivering to that very house, and he had left open the gate in the high board fence. Mary scooted in. The kitchen door was open. The boy was carrying in the sacks and parcels and bottles that made up the order, and he didn't notice her. She made herself scarce behind a small shed; after a moment she heard the boy's cheery "G'dday!" and he was gone, the door in the back fence shut behind him.

Mary took a deep breath. She was aware that she might be arrested for trespassing, but she was desperate enough to take that risk. She must get this job!

Softly she rapped on the back door of the house. Through the small panes she could see the room inside: the kitchen, it was, and a woman in a white coverall putting away the groceries. Another woman, wearing a black dress and a white bib apron, sat at the scrubbed deal table drinking something from a cup. Tea or coffee, Mary supposed; she wished she had some.

At the sound, the women looked up, startled; but when they saw only Mary, the coveralled one came.

"Yes? What is it, girl? You nearly scared me to death. What are you doing here, anyway? How did you get into the yard?"

So bombarded with questions, Mary felt free to pick and choose. "I came about the place, ma'am. I heard there was a vacancy."

Cook—for so she was—turned to the one at the table. "What about it, Mrs. Sanborn? She's here about the place. D'you want to talk to her?"

Mary felt the woman's hard, dark eyes. Then, after a long moment: "All right. I'll speak to her."

"She's Irish."

"I know."

"Come in, then, girl. I'll have flies all over my kitchen."

And with a little scuttling motion she waved Mary in and slammed the door shut. The room was filled with the fragrant smell of newly baked bread, and on the polished black range simmered a large pot of beef broth. Mary was famished, but she dared not show it, dared not show any weakness if she wanted this job.

"Come here, girl." Mrs. Sanborn's face was hard like her eyes. As Mary stepped in front of her she scanned her up and down while her face settled into an expression of dislike—disgust, even. "Now. How did you get into the yard?"

"Behind the delivery boy, ma'am."

"Don't you know that you were trespassing?"

"Yes, ma'am. I know it. But his nibs turned me away, and I wanted to ask for the place."

A slight softening of the housekeeper's expression. "You mean Mr. Dimwiddie? You knocked at the front door?"

"Yes, ma'am. He wouldn't even let me speak, and I thought, well, I'll just have a look around back."

A pause for further scrutiny. Then: "What is your name?"

"Mary Margaret O'Donovan, ma'am."

"And how long have you been in Boston, Mary?"

"Three weeks, ma'am."

"And in all that time you've not found a job?"

"No, ma'am. But my brother—he found a place at the Parker House right away."

"Did he? And who else came over besides your brother?"

"Oh, it was just us two, ma'am."

"Your family stayed behind, did they?"

"No, ma'am. Well—yes, in a manner of speakin'. They're all dead. The landlord gave John and me our passage money and wished us good luck and that was that. We'd nothin' to stay for, y'see. An' we heard it was pretty good over here. So we came."

"And where are you living?"

"Half Moon Place."

Mrs. Sanborn winced; she couldn't help it. She had never actually seen Half Moon Place, but she'd heard about it. And if Mr. Dimwiddie thought that the girl carried disease and death with her from the pesthole, very likely he was right. He couldn't be blamed for being too careful.

On the other hand, Mr. Dimwiddie did not have to deal with maintaining this house—cleaning it, seeing that things ran smoothly, the beds made, the fires kept up, meals prepared, cleaning and cleaning and cleaning—oh, yes, she badly needed an upstairs girl. The butler was right not to let the girl in at the front, but at least he should have sent her around to the back. But there: they did not get on, she and the butler. They jockeyed constantly for control of the household, and Mrs. Sanborn did not want to let him win this time. On the other hand, she needed to be careful.

She held up her right hand and waggled a few fingers at Mary. "How many, girl?"

"Three, ma'am."

The housekeeper stood and went to the pantry and returned in a moment with a small jar. "What's this, then? Can you read the label?"

Mary flushed. "No, ma'am."

In Yankee New England, with at least a primary school in every village, illiteracy was rare. But the natives knew enough about immigrants by this time not to be surprised that many of them could not read or write. Now Mrs. Sanborn thrust a pencil at Mary and a scrap of paper. "Can you write your name, then?"

"No, ma'am. But ma'am! I can work, ma'am! I don't need to read and write to work, do I? I've a strong back, and I can work with the best of them, that I can, ma'am. Just give me the chance, that's all I ask. Y'won't be sorry!"

The housekeeper pressed her lips together in what might have been an attempt to smother a smile. She opened the jar and dabbed a bit of its contents onto a cloth which she handed to Mary together with a small brass can. "Here's a bit of polish. Let's see how you do with it. That's right, just rub it on and then buff it up nice and shiny—that's it, very good."

She gazed at Mary in a contemplative way, trying to think how to proceed. They'd had a listing with the Intelligence Bureau for a week, and they'd advertised, and she'd spoken to everyone she knew, putting the word about that a place at the Revells' was open. Half a dozen Irish had applied; no Americans. This girl was the only one who seemed even halfway civilized. Mrs. Sanborn didn't know what the world was coming to when you couldn't even find help. The servant problem was becoming intolerable. She fancied herself a good judge of character. She'd been annoyed at first at this girl's cheek, coming into the yard so boldly without a by-your-leave. But now, having spoken to her, she thought she might do very well. They could try her for a week or two, at least. No harm in that. And then if she didn't work out, at least they would have had help for a while. And as for Mr. Dimwiddie . . .

She made up her mind. The butler would be angry, she knew, but he'd just have to make the best of it. She needed the help and that was that.

"Come on," she said. "I'll just take you upstairs to see the mistress, and we'll see what she says."

Ordinarily Mrs. Sanborn would not have troubled her employer or his wife with the thoroughly ordinary business of hiring an upstairs maid. But this was different; she wanted more authority than she had herself, to defy the uncooperative Dimwiddie. Not to mention taking on an Irish girl.

She led the way up the back stairs to the first floor, and then into the hall and up the main stairs. Mary was too apprehensive to look much about her, but what little she saw made her feel as though she were in a dream. Hamilton

Griffin Revell's house was a place of thick Turkey carpets and shining mahogany tables and gleaming brass and glittering crystal chandeliers, a place built with no regard to cost, the finest marble mantels, rare porcelains from the China Trade, plush furniture and silk draperies—a showplace, for sure, and to Mary Margaret, the nearest thing to a palace she ever hoped to see. She had heard that Queen Victoria lived in a palace, but Mary thought that not even the Queen's home could be as grand as this.

Up and up they went, their footsteps falling soundless on the thickly carpeted stairs. At last they rounded the graceful curve and came to the wide second-floor hall. A short way down they turned a corner and came to a narrow door. Mrs. Sanborn tapped.

"Come!"

Mrs. Sanborn turned the handle and they went in. They were in a small sitting room decorated in an extravagant floral-patterned wallpaper and matching upholstery, small tables crammed with little china whatnots and knick-knacks, the walls covered with paintings and etchings—a crowded room, a difficult room to clean.

"Excuse me, ma'am," said Mrs. Sanborn, dropping a little curtsey. "I've come about the second girl's place."

The creature who received them was unlike any female Mary had ever seen. Dressed in the height of fashion, she wore a day dress of sprigged blue sateen fitted close about the bodice and billowing out into an enormous hooped skirt that now, as she sat, surrounded her in a sea of fabric. Her pale brown hair was dressed in ringlets down the sides of her pale, delicate face and caught up in a knot in back; her small feet in black morocco shoes peeped from beneath her voluminous skirts and petticoats. The impression she gave was that she was simply a larger, animate version of the inanimate decorative objects strewn around the room.

She greeted the housekeeper with an expression of mild, ladylike surprise at what both of them understood to be a breach of etiquette, albeit a not very severe one.

"Yes, Mrs. Sanborn? What about it?"

"Beggin' your pardon, ma'am, but this here girl's come to ask for the job. An' Mr. Dimwiddie wouldn't see her. But we need someone, indeed we do. I thought perhaps you'd want to talk to her."

The lady smiled gently; her voice was gentle, too, as soft as a June breeze. It was instantly clear to Mary Margaret, as it was to all who met her, that Alice Sargeant Revell had never for one moment in her sheltered, luxurious life had to raise her voice for anything.

"It is Mr. Dimwiddie's job, and yours, to interview applicants," she said. Her voice carried no hint of censure, and she kept on smiling.

"Yes, ma'am. But he don't feel the brunt of it if he can't find someone. An' to tell you the truth, no one's applied except Irish, an' none of 'em any good. This one's Irish, too, but she seems better. But I didn't want to hire her without you knowin', an' at least seein' her."

Mrs. Hamilton Griffin Revell, who was the pampered daughter of one wealthy man and the pampered daughter-in-law of another, Nathaniel Griffin Revell, had no experience in hiring a second upstairs girl. She was not sure what the job required, beyond a strong back and an honest character. What she did know was that she had never in her thirty-nine years of life lived in a house that had Irish servants—and this girl was as Irish as Paddy's pig. Even if she did not say one word, that much was obvious. Mrs. Sanborn had not needed to say so.

"Yes," she said. "I understand. Well, girl, come here. What is your name? And how old are you?"

Mary told her that, and the rest of her little story. Mrs. Hamilton Griffin Revell nodded and smiled; her hesitant gaze traveled up and down Mary's shabby person. "Well, Mrs. Sanborn," she said at last, still gently, but with an air of having reached some important decision, "if you think she'll do."

"I think she's worth a try, missus. That's all I'm sayin'. A try."

Mrs. Hamilton Griffin Revell nodded. She smiled upon Mary. "You understand, Mary, that you must be a very good girl to work for Mrs. Sanborn. She is very strict. Do you understand that?"

"Yes, ma'am."

"You will live here, of course. So you must be considerate of the other girls, and you must keep yourself clean and neat."

"I'll send her to the bathhouse right off, ma'am," interjected the housekeeper.

"Yes," said Mrs. Revell. "Yes, you'd better do that."

And then they were excused from her presence, and Mary had a job.

5

Mary's first few weeks at 43½ Beacon Street were a blur of work and anxiety and constant worry that she wasn't performing well enough to be kept on. The butler, of course, was her devout enemy: one time she heard him through an open window, standing in the back yard and complaining to the coachman about how the housekeeper had overstepped herself in urging the mistress to hire the Irish girl.

Mrs. Sanborn taught Mary what she had to know, and so thoroughly did she work the girl that Mary threw herself into bed at night immediately after her supper of bread and milk. She would spend a few moments then thinking of John, wondering how he did, and then she was asleep and she slept like the dead until being awakened at five the next morning to begin the day's round of work again.

She was, Mrs. Sanborn said, responsible for cleaning the second-floor bedrooms; and for all of the third-floor rooms, including the nursery; and for the servants' quarters on the fourth floor, a low-ceilinged area under the roof that now, in early summer, was broiling hot, so hot that even the occasional sea breeze from the harbor could not cool it.

Soon, said Mrs. Sanborn, some of the servants—but not Mary—would accompany Mrs. Revell and the children on their annual summer's journey to the family cottage at Nahant; but Mr. Revell needed to be at his offices downtown, so he would stay at the Beacon Street house off and on during the entire summer. The house needed to be kept open, therefore, and the skeleton staff, of whom Mary would be one, always ready to receive him.

Mrs. Sanborn paused; she stared at the girl as if she could see through to her soul. Mary stared back. Mrs. Sanborn was a small, intense woman devoted to her job, which, as she saw it, was the highest calling possible—serving one of the First Families of Massachusetts. Like many servants, Mrs. Sanborn took her caste from her employers': she, too, was an exalted being because she worked for the Revells. One day when none of the Family were at home, she had taken Mary into the dining room. "There's something I want to show you," she said. "You see those portraits over the fireplace?"

"Yes, ma'am." Mary stared up at them: two portraits, a man and a woman, the man handsome and arrogant-looking, the woman a real beauty. They were dressed in costumes of long ago, but they had a freshness and vitality to them as if they had only just stepped out of this very room.

"Those are Mr. Hamilton Revell's grandparents. They lived in Boston during the Revolution. Look—see the hole just at her bosom? That's a bullet hole. It happened when British soldiers were quartered in the house. A bad time, that was. Mr. Revell's grandfather was a hero of the Revolution. He looks like a brave man, doesn't he? Yes, indeed."

Mary nodded. She could understand hatred for the British.

Now, in front of Mary's eyes, Mrs. Sanborn held up a key—a small, iron key such as was used for cabinets or closets. "This is the key to the silver closet," Mrs. Sanborn said. "I am taking it with me to Nahant. When I get back, in September, I will unlock the silver closet and I will count every piece in it—knives and forks and spoons, candlesticks, étagères, punch bowls, sugar and cream bowls, tea sets, coffee sets, salt cellars, some very old family pieces—everything! And I expect to find everything as I left it. Not a piece missing! Do you understand me? Don't go thinking that you can call in one of your friends to pick the lock while I'm gone, and get away with it! If so much as one piece is missing, I'll have you in prison for it, and you won't get out till you're dead! D'you hear me?"

"Yes, ma'am." Mary understood that this speech was intended to frighten her; it did not do that, but it did remind her that she was still on sufferance here, that she had not yet earned her place and probably would not do so for a long time.

6

One Thursday a month Mary was allowed several hours free. That first afternoon she went speeding down across the Common, her wages safely in her pouch, and made the equivalent of a triumphal visit to Half Moon Place and her erstwhile landlady. From her she learned that John was well, if somewhat overworked at the Parker House, and that while Bridget had had to let him go to make room for her new people coming in, he had found a bed at Peg Clancy's up on Fort Hill—a better place, as Mary saw, because it had a little breeze and more light. Otherwise it was as bad as Bridget's.

Peg Clancy eyed Mary suspiciously and told her that if she wanted to talk to her brother she could probably get to see him if she went to the back door of the hotel and asked for him. So Mary set off again, a small, resolute figure trudging through the city, retracing her footsteps up State Street, which had once been King Street, whose cobblestones had once resounded to the tramp of spit-and-polished British boots. Past the Massacre site, past the place where John Winthrop had once lived and Ann Hutchinson right across from him, up School Street where Samuel and James Revell had once gone sledding in the winter—and, stopped by the sentry, had gone to General Howe to demand their rights. Past Old South, where the Tea Party had been launched; past the offices of the Female Anti-slavery Society, where the fanatic, Garrison, had narrowly escaped lynching.

Surrounded by so much of the past, Mary knew nothing of it. Like all immigrants living on the edge of survival, she was concerned with the present: today, tonight, tomorrow—next week at the most. It was a warm summer day, brilliant sun, a few puffy clouds in the bright blue sky. On such days people who lived in Massachusetts forgot the rigors of winter, they forgot the cords of wood needing to be sawn, the winter vegetables laid by, animals slaughtered, bayberry candles and gallon jugs of whale oil put by. They thawed; they relaxed a bit.

The porter at the hotel was kind enough to fetch John without demanding a tip. Mary waited impatiently: a month since she'd seen him! And when he came out she gave him a great hug, and kissed his thin cheek, and laughed like she couldn't remember when.

He had only a moment, he said, since it was the dinner hour fast approaching—but of course he was delighted to see her, as well, and he'd think of some way they could have a proper visit.

She thought that he looked very tired. "I'm well enough," he said, his pale face alight with joy to see her. "It's hard work, but I don't mind it. They're decent enough. An' they say I'll be a waiter one day, if I look sharp."

7

By September, when the family returned to Beacon Street, Mary Margaret had learned her duties to a fare-thee-well, and although because she was Irish she got no praise from anyone, she understood that had her performance been remiss in any way, she would have been fired long since. So she began to relax a little, and even to take some pride in her work.

Her days were long, and she certainly earned every penny of the dollar a week they gave her. In the mornings, before she had her porridge, she set the master's breakfast tray and started his tea; whenever he rang, she was responsible for carrying the tray to his second-floor bedroom. In the fall, she was told, she would need to start fires in those bedrooms that were occupied. After breakfast she carried buckets of hot water to those same bedrooms; then she set about her day's housework: dusting and polishing the furniture and woodwork on the second and third floors; airing bedclothes and making beds; trimming lamp wicks; carrying trays where needed; sweeping—and that was just the mornings. After midday meal, and sometimes before it, despite her designation as "upstairs girl," she was expected to help wherever in the house she was needed: in the basement, ironing, if the laundress was behindhand; in the scullery plucking fowl if, say, Cook had to prepare dinner for company and the second cook was otherwise occupied. Cleaning up the kitchen after the meal; sewing—all of these tasks and more fell to Mary Margaret, for the second upstairs girl was a maid of all work, a servant to the servants.

As befitted their station, the Revells had many servants. They had the fish-eyed butler, Mr. Dimwiddie, and Evans the coachman, and the housekeeper, Mrs. Sanborn; they had Cook and her assistant and a scullery maid; they had a footman to help the butler, and a parlor maid and an upstairs maid and a second girl upstairs, who was Mary Margaret; they had a valet for Mr. Revell and the boys, and a ladies' maid for the mistress and for little Miss Florence when she was old enough; right now, at eight, Florence needed only Miss Wilcox, her governess.

So it was a big household for Mrs. Sanborn and the butler to manage, and the housekeeper had been understandably concerned that the other female servants would protest at taking on an Irish girl, for they would have to sleep with her, and eat with her, and as everyone knew the Irish were filthy, they brought disease and death with them from their benighted land across the sea, and any sensible American wanted to stay clear of them as much as he could.

On the other hand, if the Revell staff didn't want to do all the work themselves, they had no choice: they had to hire Mary Margaret or someone very like her.

Still, she had not been welcome. "I won't have her, Mrs. Sanborn," said Abba, the parlor maid. "Filthy thing! She can't even talk right! And she's a Papist, for sure. She'll have those juju beads in the house before you know it!"

Mrs. Sanborn had sent Mary to the bathhouse right away; about Mary's speech, and even more about her religion, she could do nothing. But Abba was not placated, and on the very first night that Mary slept at 43½ Beacon Street, Abba gave her a vicious pinch that left a black-and-blue mark on Mary's arm for days.

Mary Margaret was under no illusion at her good luck in getting the job at the Revells'—although she would have said that it was not luck but her own pluck that got it. Every day hundreds of new Irish immigrants poured into Boston. Many of them, unable to find work, thrown into the most hideous slums, quickly took sick and died. Epidemics of cholera and typhus thinned this surplus population with grim regularity: tuberculosis (or "consumption" as it was called—"the con," the Irish said) felled many others; and hunger and cold weakened the remainder so that they were hardly better off than their countrymen who stayed in Ireland.

In 1849, in the wake of a cholera epidemic, the city of Boston set up a committee, popularly known as the Cholera Committee, to investigate the conditions under which the flood of immigrants lived. The city of Boston was aware that it was rapidly losing its identity as a small, neat, homogeneous little city filled with spacious mansions and comely rows of more modest houses, ample gardens and lawns set about, a serviceable if eccentric and somewhat congested street pattern. Even the old North End, home to some of the first settlers and for a time in the eighteenth century a fashionable place to live, which had always been crowded in a not unpleasant way, now under the onslaught of immigrants became a warren of cut-up tenements, with hovels and shanties thrown up in every available space, courtyards and back alleys roofed over to shelter ten, twenty, fifty people, no air, no sanitation—a veritable pesthouse.

Under the direction of Dr. Lemuel Shattuck the Cholera Committee made its rounds. It discovered appalling conditions. The immigrants were living like beasts—worse than that, for no man would treat valuable livestock the way the Irish were treated in the slums and shanties and foul sewage-sodden courtyards and alleys of Boston. Naturally, said the committee, such conditions led to sickness, and it warned the city fathers that further outbreaks of cholera were inevitable. The disease would without doubt spread to the better-off districts. So even if only in self-interest, the city should try to clean up these slums, which were breeding grounds not only for disease and death, but for criminal behavior of the most vicious sort. We must civilize these people, Dr. Shattuck said, or they will destroy our decent American way of life.

8

One rainy day in September about a week after the Revells returned from Nahant, Mary Margaret was sweeping the third-floor hall when she heard the sound of sobbing from behind the closed nursery door.

Mary Margaret seldom saw the governess and her little charge, Miss Florence, because she had been instructed to clean the nursery only when they were out on their daily walk. But for the past two days the little girl had been ill, and so Mary had not gone into the room. "Leave it to Miss Wilcox," the housekeeper had said.

Mary Margaret stopped working and listened. Ten minutes ago she had seen Miss Wilcox go downstairs, probably to fetch the child's lunch tray. No doubt she was taking a cup of tea in the kitchen now with Mrs. Sanborn—a brief respite from her duties. Mary's first instinct was to go down herself to fetch Miss Wilcox, for the governess would not answer to a bell, but then she hesitated. Perhaps she should see what the matter was first.

Silently she stepped to the nursery door and turned the handle. She pushed open the door. The room was dim, the curtains drawn shut against the dreary day. In the high, canopied bed, almost lost in the mountain of puffy down-filled coverlets, Florence's little face could be seen against the pillows; it was crumpled, tear-streaked—a most miserable little face, the face of a child burdened by the world's sorrows.

Which of course was ridiculous.

Mary Margaret, who had seen more misery in her short life than any Revell could imagine, stifled her exclamation of annoyance and took a step or two into the room. Little Florence kept on crying, the tears squeezing out of her tight-shut eyes. Then, although Mary Margaret had made no sound, the child suddenly seemed to know that she was there, and with a little start she stopped crying, opened her eyes, and stared at Mary Margaret as if she were a ghost.

"What is it, now?" said Mary. "What's the matter?"

But little Florence had suddenly been struck dumb; she could not answer.

Mary Margaret looked around. The room was overwarm, she thought, a high fire blazing in the hearth, the windows shut and the curtains drawn. In the flickering light she saw the rocking horse in the corner, and it seemed as if he was rocking a little, all by himself; she saw the figures in the mural painted on the wall, little children dancing around a maypole, and it seemed as if they were really dancing, moving around and around; and the row of dolls on a low shelf, their bland faces painted on their bisque and china heads—were they not giggling and murmuring there, watching little Florence?

Stop it! Mary Margaret gave herself a shake and turned again to the child. "Well?" she said. "What is it?"

"I—I was afraid." Little Florence's reddened eyes peered at Mary from over the edge of her bedclothes.

"And whatever is there to be afraid of, I'd like to know?" Mary stood foursquare, hands on her hips, and turned her head from side to side as she peered in an exaggerated way around the room.

"The corner," said Florence.

"The corner! What about it?"

"I thought there was something there. Something that would come out and get me."

"Like what, child?"

"Like—oh, like the witch in *Hansel and Gretel.*"

"Pshaw," said Mary. "A witch is nothin'. Why, I could tell ye—" Just in time she stopped herself. She'd almost let spill the story of the banshee, the dreaded spirit that haunted the bogs and hills and hollows of her native land, and whose mournful keening foretold death. Now *that* was something to fear, she thought, repressing a shiver. But of course she couldn't tell such a tale to this weepy little thing. Mary didn't feel sorry for her—not exactly; what she felt was a kind of contempt. Here was a child who had had every luxury from the moment of her birth, and what good had it done her? Like most Irish, Mary admired toughness; a timid creature like little Florence Revell would never amount to anything, Mary thought, no matter how much money and social position she inherited.

"What?" said Florence. "What were you going to say?"

"Nothin'," said Mary. "I mean—I was goin' to say that I was frightened myself, one time, an' I got over it."

"Why?" said Florence. "Why were you afraid?"

"Oh, it was the lallygagger," said Mary. "That's what frightened me."

Florence giggled. "The *what*?" It was the funniest name she had ever heard, and she began to laugh uncontrollably.

"The lallygagger. Don't tell me you've never heard of the lallygagger."

Florence was laughing so much that she could hardly speak. "No," she gasped. "What is it?"

"Why, girl, the lallygagger's a creature that lives at the bottom of the sea, in a cave made of pearls, with mermaids all around—an' when I was on the boat comin' over, we had a storm, see, an' I thought for a bit that I'd be goin' down to the bottom to see the old lallygagger himself, sure I did, it was that bad."

"You came on a boat?" said Florence. "I was on a boat once, at Nahant. Was yours a sailboat?"

"Not exactly," said Mary.

"But you had a good time? I had a lovely time, when I went sailing. I didn't get sick a bit."

"Oh, yes, we had a lovely, lovely time. We had mostly fair weather, and a cabin all to ourselves—that's my brother an' me. An' we passed every day singin' an' playin' games, whilst the ship's cook made us the best meals you ever tasted."

"Just your brother? Why didn't your mother and father come?" Little Florence's eyes were dry by now, and alive with interest at the tale Mary was telling. She sat up straight in her bed, and smiled, and looked ready to chatter all afternoon with her newfound friend.

"Oh, they didn't want to. They had to stay to take care of our place. It's a big farm, they couldn't leave it." Suddenly Mary's words tasted like bile in her throat. Why was she wasting her time with this child of the rich who could never—oh, never in a thousand years understand what Mary's life had been, the bleak bitterness of it, the sorrow and pain of it, the illness and dying and fear and horror of it, stealing a few coins from a dead woman in order to survive—ah, what did these rich folks know about anything? An Irish child three years old knew more about the realities of life than any rich boy or girl on Beacon Street, that was the truth of it. Suddenly she remembered where she was. She'd get sacked for sure if Miss Wilcox found her here. She needed to get back to her work, she'd been foolish indeed to stop to talk to this one—

"What is this?" As Miss Wilcox's voice cut through her ruminations, Mary stiffened as if she had been struck. "I meant no harm, miss," she began; but before she could say more, the child intervened.

"She was telling me stories—wonderful stories," Florence said. "And you mustn't scold, really you mustn't. It was I who asked her to come in."

When Mary had been hired, Miss Wilcox had not taken sides; she didn't care one way or another if the family took in an Irish girl, she said, as long as she was honest and clean.

So now she did not scold Mary, but merely sent her on her way with a severe look that said, "Don't let me catch you in here again telling stories to Miss Florence." But the next day, as Mary was polishing the brass hardware in the third-floor hall, she heard a movement behind her and she turned, surprised, to see Miss Wilcox. "I want you to wash your hands," the governess said, "and come with me."

Miss Wilcox looked rather sour, Mary thought, but of course she had to obey. She followed the governess into the nursery, where once again she found little Florence with a tearstained face—but this time the child's face was splotched with color as well, as if she'd had a temper, Mary thought. And indeed this proved to be the case: Miss Florence, bored and fretful lying in bed, had asked to have the Irish girl come in again to amuse her, and when she had been told that it was not proper to request the company of a servant, let alone an Irish girl, she had become very angry. The mistress was out on some charitable errand, and so Miss Wilcox had taken it upon herself to accede, just this once, to the child's whim.

"Well, now," Mary said, approaching the bed. "What's this, then?"

And little Florence, given her way, promptly smiled and sat right up and demanded another story of the voyage over, or, if not that, then a story about the beautiful land from which Mary had come—a land of prosperous, happy people laughing and singing all day long.

And when Mary Margaret had complied, and had spent a half hour spinning tales out of her head—tales that had no more relation to reality than the first one she'd told—the child seemed positively recuperated. So Miss Wilcox said that, yes, Florence might be allowed to get up and get dressed for the afternoon; and tomorrow, if she continued to improve, she might very well be allowed to go out.

And so began Mary Margaret's daily visit to the youngest member of the household. She didn't exactly enjoy the time she spent with little Florence, but it gave her a curious kind of satisfaction; further, it fed her contempt for these rich folks, and in her own stunted, dreary, harsh world, contempt and its sisters, anger and resentment, could nourish one's will to survive better than anything else.

9

Autumn came. The leaves on the elm trees lining the walks of the Common turned brilliant yellow; scarlet runner on the brick walls of Beacon Hill gardens turned blood red in the October sun. Then the wind came from the northwest and the Common was a swirl of leaves; glancing from an upstairs window, Mary watched as gentlemen on the Long Path clutched their hats, and ladies struggled to control their voluminous skirts in the blustery gusts. The sight of the season's change made her realize that she had been in this new country for—what? Nearly five months. It seemed five years.

Now, as she turned away from the window, she rubbed her aching wrist. She'd been trying to black the hearths with her left hand, but it was slow going, terribly messy. Her right wrist hurt because Mrs. Sanborn had taken ill and died two weeks ago. Last week her replacement had come: a tall, black-haired harridan who'd taken an instant dislike to Mary Margaret. "Irish?" she'd said. "I don't know if I want to work in a house where they've got Irish. I don't know at all, I'm sure."

In the end she had taken the job, but she'd had an eye out for Mary ever since she set foot in the kitchen. Only this morning, when Mary was reaching for another piece of bread at breakfast, the housekeeper had slammed down a heavy iron ladle across her wrist. "One piece," she said, very angry.

Mary Margaret, in great pain, gasped that Mrs. Sanborn had always allowed her to eat as much as she pleased, whereupon the new one had made as if to swing at her again, and Mary had ducked only just in time.

"Mrs. Sanborn is dead!" the harridan had said with considerable venom; and Mary Margaret, to keep the woman from seeing her cry, had bolted out of the room.

She was sure the bone was broken; it throbbed and ached something awful, and certainly she couldn't work with that hand.

She heard footsteps just then, and she looked up to see Abba, who had become no friendlier despite the fact that they'd shared a bed for weeks.

"Mr. Dimwiddie wants you," Abba spat out, hardly pausing to speak before she went downstairs again.

The pain of Mary's wrist was like a red fog in her brain; she'd heard what Abba said, she knew she had to obey, but she felt distanced from herself, as if she were watching herself.

She went past little Florence's door; she hardly ever saw the child now, because Florence had begun to go to a school over on Chestnut Street. On down, through the first floor and past the magnificent ballroom she'd glimpsed only once, and like looking at a fairyland it had been, all glass and glitter and wide expanse of shining floor; on to the back stairs and down to the kitchen. He was waiting for her there; his face looked even more sour than usual, his eyes more fish-cold. He wore a big apron over his clothes, and a pair of white gloves stained with some dark stuff—tarnish, she realized, seeing the household silverware spread out on the table before him. The harridan stood on one side of him, the footman on the other, the downstairs parlor maid to one side. They all stared at her.

Her wrist throbbed, a hideous pain that seemed to travel up her arm and straight into her head. She stood straight and tried not to think about it.

"I'm just polishing this silver," said Mr. Dimwiddie, "counting it as I go, and I find we're a spoon short."

He paused, seeming to expect her to make some reply, but she had none.

"Well?" he said. "What d'you know about that?"

"Nothin', sir."

"Nothing? Mind you tell me the truth, girl."

Mary stood mute. The pain was making her sick to her stomach.

"Well?" He glared at her. She saw a little drop of saliva at the corner of his narrow mouth.

Well, what? she thought. She shook her head. "No sir, I don't know nothin' about that."

"Well, we will see what you know," he said. He spoke with a curious kind of triumph. "I am going to have a look upstairs. Robert, come with me. The rest of you stay here. Watch to see that she does not leave."

Mary was not sure how long he was gone; she sank onto a wooden bench by the wall and concentrated on not throwing up. After a while she heard Mr. Dimwiddie and the footman coming down the stairs.

"What did I tell you?" he said.

Mary opened her eyes. He was standing in front of her holding up a silver spoon. Mary blinked, she could think of nothing to say.

"Well? Do you know where I found this?"

"No, sir."

"No? Think a minute."

"No, sir. I—"

"Be careful, girl. The police can make you talk, y'know. They have ways."

The police! Mary clenched her teeth to keep from fainting. She was very frightened, even though she knew she had no reason to be, for she had stolen nothing. But she knew also that her word against Mr. Dimwiddie's was useless.

The butler stood before her, the spoon clenched in his hand. He was holding it so tightly that his knuckles were white. "Admit that you took this!" he snarled. "Tell us the truth!"

"No! I did not! As God is my witness, I did *not*!"

"Get out!" With his free hand he seized her arm—her right arm, the one that hurt—and pushed her toward the door. *"Aiee!"* She couldn't help herself, the pain was too great, and she shrieked with it as he hustled her along. Yanking open the door, he thrust her out into the back yard.

"Get out and stay out! Dirty Irish scum!"

Propelled by the force of his shove, she was halfway across the little yard before she caught herself from falling. She staggered on, reached the gate, opened it and went out.

Later, thinking back, she could not remember the long walk to John's room on Fort Hill; the journey was lost in a mist of pain and shock. They lied! They said she was a thief! And Mrs. Sanborn not there to defend her! Mr. Dimwiddie had never wanted her, had always resented her. Well, now he'd had his way.

When Peg Clancy saw her, she let out an exclamation of surprise that quickly turned to alarm. "My God, girl, what's the matter? You're as white as a sheet, an' y'look as if y'd been scared to death—what is it? Here, sit down. Yer arm? I can see it's swollen—it hurts that bad, does it?"

Peg had no medicines, so she gave Mary the next best thing: a good drink of whiskey. And just this once, because it was an emergency, she wouldn't charge for it.

By the time John returned from his job, around ten o'clock, Mary was half delirious. She lay on his pallet, moaning, and when John came in, the other four boarders in the little room told him that they didn't want to make more trouble for him than he had but she'd have to be quiet if she wanted to stay.

But there was noise enough in the Irish slum so that Mary's cries and moans that night were hardly noticed. Men cursing and shouting, women weeping and wailing, children screaming, dogs yapping and barking, the sound of a bottle crashing on the cobblestones, a weird, untuned fiddle playing a song of home— a land they loved, a land they hated, a land that had thrown them away, onto the cold charity of Anglo-Saxon America and particularly Anglo-Saxon Massachusetts, whose heart, never warm at the best of times, grew colder by the day as the starving Irish, desperate, kept coming in.

10

"But why?" said John. He tucked her hand into his arm as they walked, as if he were her older brother instead of younger. It was the Sunday morning after her ejection from the Hamilton Griffin Revell household; they had been to mass, and now, in the pale autumn sunshine, they enjoyed a sweet roll from the baker's as they walked back to Fort Hill.

"I don't know." It was her left arm that he held; she cradled the right— the injured one—against her as she went so as not to jostle it. Peg had rigged up a sling from an old shawl, but it didn't help much. "He never liked me, y'know. An' Mrs. Sanborn got me in under his nose, so to speak. She got the mistress to take me on, when he didn't want me. So when she passed away, why, he just wanted to have back at me."

She did not dwell on the injustice of it—not now. She did not have time for that now. Later, perhaps, when she had found a new job—and how she was to do that without a "character" from the Revells, she did not know. When she was secure, when she no longer lived on the edge of ruin—then she would settle with them. But not now.

The next morning she set off looking for a new place. But it was the same story as before: no proper Yankee household wanted to take in an Irish girl. Servants lived in close proximity with their masters, and the Irish were universally viewed as filthy, uncivilized peasants, creatures who would bring disease and corruption into the handsome parlors and well-stocked kitchens of the city's middle and upper classes. For nearly a week she hunted for a job, and then, temporarily defeated, she looked in on Tommy McNulty, who ran a barroom on Salem Street in the North End. He was a cousin of Peg's, always glad to help where he could.

"For certain, I can't use you here," he said. "But let me give it a think overnight. Betty Hanrahan's got a little shop, dry goods an' all. Perhaps she needs someone." He looked doubtfully at her. She had taken off the sling, of course, but she held her arm close to her body to protect it, and he could see right away that something was wrong with her. As she thanked him for his trouble and turned to leave, he stood on his step and watched her make her way through the teeming noisy street. He would have taken a wager, sure enough, that that girl now vanished into the crowd wasn't going to make it.

When Mary had been ejected from the Revell house, she had had one small bit of good fortune: she'd had her money with her, carried in a small string bag day and night around her neck. She never took it off, that little bit of cloth and string: it was her means to survival, everything she had in the world—seven dollars and twenty-five cents. Automatically now her hand went to it, to make sure it was still there; she touched it like a talisman. As long as she had her little savings, and the small stake from the woman on the ship coming over, she and John would be all right, see if they weren't.

So ran her thoughts as she made her way back to Fort Hill. Despite her situation, she was not yet desperate; barring further misfortune, she thought, they'd be all right.

She had a bit of meat pastie from a sidewalk vendor for her supper and a bit of Peg's whiskey for two pennies to ease the pain from her wrist. When John came home he stumbled a bit as he came into the room, and she saw right away that he wasn't well. His skin was hot and his nose was running. Mary felt a little shiver of fear cross her brain like a ripple on the surface of a pond in the first breeze of a storm. But she reassured herself: this was just a little cold he had, nothing more. She settled him right away—he'd had his supper at the hotel—and told him to go to sleep.

But in the night he went delirious, and by morning he was tossing and turning, raving, his eyes wild, a deep shuddering cough tearing his chest apart.

Peg took one look at him and delivered her verdict: "It's the cholera, for sure. Y'll have to go."

"Go! But—y'can't put us out now! Not when he's sick! An' it's not cholera, it's never that! Just a touch o'th'cold—" Mary forced herself to keep her voice calm; she could not show this woman her panic, or they'd be turned out for sure. "Just let's see how he does today," she said. "I'll get th'doctor for him, an'we'll see what he says."

But the only doctor known to the Irish was not to be found; his house-keeper didn't know when he'd be back, she said, looking at Mary with distaste.

By afternoon, when a single ray of sunlight had found its way into the room, they could see that John's skin had gone greenish—a sure sign, Peg said, of the cholera. There had been epidemics of it in Boston ever since the Irish began to arrive; she'd seen it before, she said, and she'd not have it in her place. They had to get out.

"All right," said Mary, "all right, we'll go in th' mornin', just let us stay the night." Anything, she thought. She was bargaining for their lives an hour at a time, and any small concession was a victory. Cholera! *Dear Mother of God, don't let him die, what will I do if he dies?*

All night she knelt by his side as he lay tossing; as she sponged his sweating face and body, she murmured a silent continuous prayer: *Please don't let him die, please dear God don't let him die . . .* She gave fifty cents to one of the lads to buy some beer and a measure of quinine, but John was unable to swallow. His features began to sharpen, as if his flesh were melting away before her eyes; in the light of the candle his eyes seemed black empty sockets, and his nostrils were distended as he tried to draw breath.

By morning Peg herself was ill, and that day three more of her boarders came down with the sickness. The miserable little rooms that were Peg's share of the tenement became a forbidden zone: no one would go near where the cholera was.

All that day and night Mary watched John as he died. He never knew she was there except for one brief moment when he seemed to come awake. He looked at her with clear, wide eyes; he smiled at her—and then he went uncon-scious again, and his breathing came hard and hoarse, and his body shuddered with fever, and the pain racked him.

Then he was gone.

11

"Mary! Mary! Are y'there, girl? Come quick—someone's lookin' f'r y'!"

Mary was so weak that she could hardly sit up, but after a minute she managed it. In the dim light she saw the woman who spoke to her: she couldn't remember her name. From across the way, she was; Mary didn't know her well.

"Who is it?" Mary said. Her throat ached; her mouth was so dry that she could hardly speak.

"I don't know," said the woman. "A fine young fella at the door downstairs, says he's lookin' house by house f'r Mary Margaret O'Donovan who came over last May on the *White Cloud*. Isn't that you?"

Mary's head hurt, and now as she tried to swing herself onto her knees and stand up, she felt dizzy and faint. The woman didn't move to help her; she stood just outside the door, reluctant to enter this room where, not a week ago, people had died of cholera.

"All right," Mary said. "Tell him I'll come down."

She managed to get as far as the stairs before her knees gave way. Clutching the balustrade, she sank down onto the top step and peered into the gloomy hall below.

"Mary?" Already he was coming up; in an instant he was beside her. She didn't know him.

"My God, girl, what happened to y'? No, don't try to get up—just stay where y'are. D'you remember me?"

Mary stared at him, and he saw that no, she did not remember.

"On the ship, girl! My name's Shaughnessy—Patrick Shaughnessy. D'y' remember, I said I'd look you up?"

And now, dimly, she did recall him. She had just enough time to tell him that before she fainted.

He'd been looking for her for days, ever since he came off the railroad gang where he'd been working, out in New York State. When at last he found her, he was appalled at her condition, and right away he borrowed a wagon and took her to his friend's place where he was staying, over beyond the back of Beacon Hill in the West End.

Over the next few weeks, as she recuperated, he told her his story: how he'd looked for her at the dock on Noddle's Island, where they had landed, and somehow had lost track of her in the chaos of their arrival; how he'd never found his uncle; how he'd signed up instead for the railroad gang. He'd come back as soon as he could because (with a wink) he'd had in his mind all that time the face of a certain young lady whom he was determined to find.

She gazed at him as he sat by her side and held her hand. She thought that perhaps she was dreaming, or hallucinating from her fever. She didn't remember all that had happened: why her wrist hurt, or how she'd injured it; she even forgot for a time that John had died. For the moment she was content to let this strong young man take charge. He would put things right; he was that kind of confident, capable person.

She went to sleep again, and the next time she awoke, she was able to eat a little stew and drink hot tea and whiskey, and begin to come back to her life again.

And then one day she wept for a long time, remembering at last poor dear John and how he had died—and why.

"If they hadn't sacked me," she sobbed, "I might have had the money to save him, Patrick." And she told him of Mr. Dimwiddie's unjust accusation, and how he'd fired her.

"Hush, now," Patrick said. "It was the will of God, hard as it is to bear. Everything happens just as God wills it, you know that. They were bad to y', sure enough, but y'can't say they gave yer brother the cholera."

But she did say it. Somehow, in her mind, the two things became cause and effect: she had been unjustly dismissed from service in the house of Hamilton Griffin Revell, and consequently her brother John had died.

And she cried and cried as if she could never stop, and Patrick held her in his arms and soothed her and promised her that she would never be alone in the world again to face her troubles. "I swear it to y', Mary Margaret O'Donovan, I'm here now for good. Y'have a man now to take care of y', that y'do."

And he kissed her tearstained face and made her promise him that as soon as ever she could, as soon as she had her land legs back again and could be up and about, she'd do him the honor—"the very great honor, indeed," as he put it—of becoming Mrs. Patrick Shaughnessy.

They were married just before Christmas. They had a room all to themselves on Garden Street, a few blocks from where Patrick found work as a porter at the Massachusetts General Hospital. Then a place on the docks opened up, and because it was twice the pay, he took it. Being a stevedore was good work, he said; he was proud of his strength, proud of his ability to provide for his Mary.

Their first child was born the following November. They named him Patrick Jr.

In the next six years Mary had a baby every year, and five of them survived. Sometimes at night when the children were sleeping, she would raise herself up from her bed and peer over to where they lay, the littlest one in his drawer which served as a cradle, the moonlight streaming in over the back alley and the refuse-strewn courtyard and its noisome privy, and she would say a silent prayer, not only to thank God, but to beg His continuing grace. Life was fragile—how much so, she remembered bitterly whenever she thought of her brother John.

In the winter of 1860 she got work sewing petticoats at home for a contractor in the North End. She paid a dollar a week rent for her sewing machine (a product of Elias Howe's ingenuity) and she made five cents for each garment she sewed. In a good week she could turn out five dozen.

In the fall of that year Patrick heard from their landlord that the man had a grocery store for rent, the tenant having died, and right there in the West End not two blocks away. Whoever rented the store could also have, for a reasonable sum, a three-room apartment upstairs. The landlord was a swamp

Yankee from Holyoke, with the Anglo-Saxon's distrust of the Celt, but he was not a fool, he knew a good tenant when he saw one. He'd teach Patrick the business, he said; nothing difficult about it if a man could add and subtract and keep a clean place.

And so Patrick became the proprietor of the West End Grocery. By the spring of 1861, after his first six months, he'd made more than he'd made in a year on the docks. In the evenings he would look around the supper table in the kitchen where they took their meals, and as he said grace he would silently thank God for allowing these, his dearly beloved, to survive so well.

"All right!" he would say then. "Tell us the news!"

And the children's bright little faces would smile back at him, each one, even the youngest, eager to respond; and Mary would choose which one would go first, a nod and a smile—ah, yes, she'd brought them up strict, they obeyed her as if she were a drill sergeant, and they loved her for it, they loved being cared for so deeply.

Six months at the store; and now it was spring again, and they'd got safely through another winter.

Mary smiled at him. And despite the poverty of their surroundings, he felt like a king.

12

By that time the southern firebrands had attacked Fort Sumter and war had begun—the real war so longed for, so dreaded, by both sides.

There had been, of course, a kind of de facto war going on for years. Northern men, Massachusetts men, had been sending out "Beecher's Bibles"—guns—to Kansas, "bloody Kansas," where northern settlers and southern settlers battled each other for the right to control the state, and the Abolitionist John Brown, like an avenging angel, swept down to massacre the settlers at Pottawatomie in reprisal for some outrage of theirs.

And the great Massachusetts senator, the Abolitionist Charles Sumner, had been beaten nearly to death on the floor of the Senate by one of those same South Carolinians who attacked the federal fort—beaten bloody and senseless by Preston Brooks wielding his gutta-percha cane. Brooks said that Sumner had insulted his honor and that of all southerners.

And finally there had been John Brown's raid on the federal arsenal at Harper's Ferry in Virginia—an outrageous act, and there were some Abolitionists in Massachusetts who fled to Canada when they heard of it, for fear of being hanged for treason as he was. They had helped old Brown, had collected money for him, entertained him in their homes: parlor radicals, excited at the thought of some action—any action—to end the crime of slavery after all these years of speechifying, letter writing, agitation to no avail.

And they sang for him, for the old fanatic; they mourned him after he was gone. "John Brown's body lies a-moldering in the grave," they sang; a haunting melody, mournful, insistent—you could not get it out of your head. "His soul goes marching on . . ."

The spring following Brown's execution, as if in anticipation of the conflict to come, the poet Longfellow paid a visit to the Old North Church on Patriot's Day and was inspired to write a poem. In 1860 the North End was not what it had been in Paul Revere's day; it had fallen on hard times, deserted by all but the poorest Yankees, taken over by the Irish. No matter. Longfellow's poem called to the patriotism of every reader, as if to say, the nation is soon to be tested even more severely than it was when Revere made his ride.

> Listen my children and you shall hear
> Of the midnight ride of Paul Revere . . .

People loved it. Practically overnight it became the most popular poem in the country. The editor of the *Atlantic Monthly* was delighted at its success—as was Longfellow, of course. As it happened, the poet lived in the very mansion over on Brattle Street, on "Tory Row," that had been General Washington's headquarters during the war that started with Revere's ride. He did not pay for this magnificent place out of his earnings as a poet, nor from his pay from the College, where he taught European literature; he had married the daughter of the textile king, Nathan Appleton, and it was textile money that supported him in such comfort.

So Longfellow immortalized Paul Revere; and Fort Sumter fell; and President Lincoln issued a call for 75,000 volunteers.

The Massachusetts Sixth Regiment had been drilling for months, eagerly awaiting the moment when they could march off to war. Within twenty-four hours their leader, Benjamin Butler, had rounded them up and paraded them through Boston on their way to Washington to answer the President's call. Butler was a cranky, brilliant self-promoter, a Lowell lawyer with political ambitions, who only the previous year had tried to make cause with southern Democrats. Smartly he and his men marched back and forth across the Common, making mud of the new grass. Caroline and her brother Hamilton watched them from the tall front windows of Hamilton's house on Beacon Street.

"Have you ever seen anything more ridiculous than Benjamin Franklin Butler on a horse!" exclaimed Hamilton.

"He wants Massachusetts to be first to respond," said Caroline. "He is a patriot."

Hamilton snorted. "He's an opportunist, pure and simple. He'll get all the publicity and personal glory that he can out of this expedition, and when he sees another chance to grab a little more glory, he'll jump at that, too. Why, less than a year ago he was with the slave owners in Charleston. Now he waves his sword and leads a regiment against them!"

The man in question—whom Hamilton would never have called a gentleman—was short, stout, bald, and wall-eyed. Despite his physical apparatus, he was as agile as a frog jumping to a favorite lily pad. He always acted as if he were as good as anybody—an infuriating trait. Privately, the men of the best families of Massachusetts loathed Butler; but they feared him also, for he had all the instincts of a demagogue, and his intelligence made him dangerous. So they held their tongues—and their noses—and wished him well as he rode off to war.

Now in the spring sunshine, Butler paraded his men back and forth; then they stood at attention as Governor Andrew praised them for bravery that they had not yet shown. As men often do, they looked forward to war. They longed to show the arrogant southerners what was what. They had no notion of war— no idea of what it was. After the ceremony they marched to the railroad station and boarded the cars. They were bumptious and jolly; they sang songs and told jokes and thought they were having a lark.

Hamilton had invited his sister to stay to dinner. She was, he thought, unwontedly quiet throughout the meal. Then, as if the food had given her new strength, she broke her news. "I am going to Washington, too," she said.

She might as well have said that she was going to the Sandwich Islands. They stared at her, shocked speechless: her niece, Florence, not quite fifteen; her nephew, Theo, not quite sixteen; her brother Hamilton; and her sister-in-law Alice, who had begun to cry—not as it turned out, for worry about Caroline, but in fear of the disgrace that she would bring upon a Family already tried to the breaking point by her adventures with Miss Dix.

"But—why?" said Hamilton at last. "What on earth—"

"To help," Caroline said simply.

"But—how?" said Hamilton. "What on earth can you do there that you cannot do here?"

"I don't know. Nothing, perhaps. But I must find out. Miss Dix has sent for me."

She smothered a smile. She understood their distress: she was incorrigible, a strong-willed New England maiden lady set in her ways, determined to do as her conscience dictated no matter how she offended her well-meaning but considerably more conventional relations.

Two days later the Massachusetts Sixth, marching from one train station to another in Baltimore on their way to guard the capital, was attacked by a mob of ten thousand men hostile to the northern cause. Four Massachusetts men were killed and dozens wounded. They were, as Benjamin Butler never tired of saying, the first bloodshed of the war. As Fate would have it, the deaths had occurred on the eighty-sixth anniversary of the Battle of Concord and Lexington—a sacred date in Massachusetts. People took it as an omen: of a long war, of many deaths to come, of eventual triumph.

13

The Civil War split the Commonwealth of Massachusetts, and in particular the city of Boston, as nothing had done since the Revolution. As the summer dragged by, and the First Bull Run failed to end the conflict, people realized that the nation was in for a protracted and bloody struggle.

Attitudes hardened on both sides. The Somerset Club had been founded not ten years before to provide, for the gentlemen of the First Families, a continuation of that happy club life that they had enjoyed at the College. Now the Somerset became well-nigh unbearable as Cotton Whigs frostily snubbed strong Union men, including a few Abolitionists like Daniel Jackson Revell. Feelings ran so high that in 1863, in the darkest hours of the war, a number of Somerset men split off and formed the Union Club. "Sambos," the Somerset men called them.

Eventually a scion of the first of the First Families recruited and supplied, at his own expense, a regiment of black men, and took them to fight in the South. This was an unheard of thing to do: conventional wisdom held that black men were, if not cowards, then at least undependable in battle. But Robert Gould Shaw, like William Lloyd Garrison and Wendell Phillips and Theodore Parker and Daniel Jackson Revell, put his convictions to the test. He turned out to have been right. His men fought well and bravely at the attack on Fort Webster in South Carolina and suffered a fifty-percent casualty rate. Shaw himself was killed. Some decades later a monument to him and his men was put up at the top of Boston Common on Beacon Street across from the Statehouse. And there the gallant Shaw rides in bronze bas-relief forever, the colonel at the head of his regiment of humble, plodding black soldiers whose blood, in the end, was as red as any white man's.

By that time, in that bloodiest of wars, President Lincoln could no longer rely on volunteers to fill the ranks of the Union Army, and so Congress had to resort to conscription. In the spring of 1863 a draft call went out. People looked at the battlefields soaked in blood and refused to answer. Congress renewed the call. Every ablebodied man between twenty and forty-five was eligible to be drafted, but any man could avoid service by paying a bounty of three hundred dollars minimum (some paid more), or by hiring a substitute. So rich men could avoid service with no opprobrium, while poor men had to risk their lives. This caused much unhappiness; people said that life was not fair, and that it was not right that a man die simply because he lacked the money to evade service.

Then, in early July, came the Battle of Gettysburg. In three days of fighting, fifty thousand men were killed or wounded. When news of this carnage got out, many men in New York City started a riot against the draft. They were for the most part Irishmen newly arrived. They may or may not have known that many of their countrymen formed some of the most gallant regiments in the Union Army. They did not care about gallantry. They wanted to stay alive and help their families to survive in this new land. They did not want to die for (as they saw it) millions of black slaves. The first thing they did when they rioted was to burn down a Negro orphanage. Then they went on a rampage, setting fires, smashing windows, looting—an orgy of violence and mayhem and murder that lasted for three days and left more than two hundred dead, many of them hapless blacks in the wrong place at the wrong time. The rioters blamed the war on the blacks more than on the white slaveholders; and in any case, the whites were far away, the blacks a handy target—and competitors for jobs. So enraged were the mobs that even Archbishop Hughes was unable to quiet them; at length the National Guard was called out and peace was restored.

14

In Boston, that hot July, Patrick Shaughnessy tended his store and watched over his family and thought that if the Massachusetts quota was not reached, and he was called to go, he could probably find a substitute. He had no intention of leaving Mary alone: she had been sickly with another pregnancy, and for the past few days she'd spotted a little blood. She was supposed to stay off her feet, but with the little ones running in and out, that was impossible. So she rested in snatches, and Nora Fogarty from upstairs helped as much as she could, what with her own brood; somehow, Patrick thought, they'd be all right. He felt very strongly that the worst of it was behind them: the voyage over, the brutal first months, finding shelter, finding work, the hard years of chipping away, chipping away, to make a little niche for themselves—a home, a job, the start of a fine family. He was not going to endanger it all now by marching off to fight a war that was no concern of his. He didn't give a damn about the blacks. Why, he'd heard of a black family up on the back of Beacon Hill that had complained when an Irishman moved next door! Imagine it! No, there would be no blood sacrifice by Patrick Shaughnessy this time around; if it were a fight to free his homeland from the British, he might think differently, but even there, he wasn't sure he'd join up. He had too much at stake.

The day after the newspapers carried word of the riots in New York, Patrick was behind the counter waiting on a customer when he heard the sound of shouts, men's voices raised in angry tones—and then the sound of shattering glass as someone heaved a rock through a window. He gave the customer her parcel and her change and, calling to his clerk to take charge, he ran out to the street so quick that he did not stop to remove his big white apron.

It was a blinding hot day, the sun beating mercilessly on the red-brick tenements and cobblestoned streets of the West End. The noise came from Fruit Street, near the hospital. That morning Mary had at last consented to go to see a doctor there about her condition, the bleeding and cramping that she'd been suffering. She'd never had a doctor in pregnancy; a midwife was far preferable, she said, and much more modest, too. She couldn't bear the thought of a man examining her. But Patrick had insisted, and so off she'd gone with Nora to help her, hours ago now and not yet returned. If she came out and found herself in the midst of a mob . . .

The noise increased. He began to run. He turned a corner, and then another, dodging a horse and wagon as he ran down the middle of the street. He heard the sound of many voices, angry men roaring and rampaging, more glass breaking, a pistol fired, a panicked horse neighing—

He turned another corner, and before he knew it, they were upon him. They bore him no hostility; he was not the enemy, the government was the enemy, and rich men as well, but he was in the way, and so with no ill will toward him at all, they stampeded over him. They hit him like a tidal wave; they ran him down without even seeing him. No man, no matter how powerful, could have withstood them; there were five hundred men, at least, in that mob, and those who did not have guns had brickbats and cobblestones and bricks, ready to charge, ready to do damage wherever they could, and for the same reason as their brethren in New York: they would not be drafted! Never! The draft system was unfair, it let rich men evade battle while poor men died in their places.

When Patrick fell, his head struck the cobblestones. After the mob hurtled on, he lay unconscious in the broiling sun, blood trickling from his mouth, a dark bruise forming at the side of his forehead, his leg bent at a queer angle.

Mary found him a short time later, when it was safe to go into the streets again and she was on her way home from the hospital. Of course she recognized him at once. With a little cry of terror she sank to her knees and touched his face, tried to lift his head—

"Patrick? *Patrick!*"

His eyes would not open; he hardly seemed to breathe.

"Nora—go get help—" But Nora did not need to be told. Already she was off at a run, and Mary sat in the middle of the street in the broiling sun and tried to give her husband a little shade, tried to wipe the blood from his face—"Oh, my God, Patrick, what happened, y're all bloody, what did they do t'y', oh my God, *Patrick*—"

By the time Nora came back—without a doctor; a doctor wouldn't come—Patrick was dead, and so all they could do was to get a wagon to carry him home. They laid him out in the front room, and the neighbors and the priest came in to mourn him.

The day after the funeral Mary miscarried; as sorry as she was to lose this last child of Patrick's, in some secret place in her heart she acknowledged to herself, if to no one else, that perhaps, if she had to lose her husband, it was best that she not be burdened with one more mouth to feed, never mind the difficulties of pregnancy and birth. A hard thing to admit: but then, life was hard. It was only fools who thought otherwise—fools or rich people.

And since she was neither, she gritted her teeth and gathered her children around her and promised herself that somehow—somehow, she didn't know how—she would keep them together, and alive.

15

"I can't rent to a woman," said Robertson. "And besides, it's not possible for you to run the business by yourself."

"Just let me try," said Mary. Her head ached from weeping—and, if the truth be told, from the considerable quantity of whiskey she'd drunk the night before. Three days since she'd buried her husband, two since she'd miscarried. Now she needed to take up the burden of her life, hers and the children's, without him. The first task was to persuade the landlord, through his agent standing here before her, to continue to rent the store to her. Of course, it was Patrick who had made it go; without him, she thought, she'd have the devil's own time, but she must try. What else could she do, with six little mouths to feed? The eldest, Patrick Jr., would turn eight in November. Mother of God! Six babies to feed, and her man six feet under!

She bit her lips to keep from crying, for Robertson must not see her weep, he must not see that she was frightened. She must make him think that she was capable and strong.

"How can you run a store?" he said. "Can you read and write? Can you keep accounts?"

"Some," she said; and it was true, Patrick had begun to teach her. She'd learned quickly.

"Some! How much?"

"Enough. Enough. I can manage. I know I can. Let me try it for six months," she said. "You know we've been good tenants, we've paid the rent on the first of the month and never a day late. It's not much I'm askin', just give me a chance."

She would find someone just off the boat, she thought, and give her a place to sleep, and three meals a day and perhaps a few pennies over, to mind the children while she herself tended to the store. And she'd have to pay someone with a strong back to go to the wholesale market for her, to keep up her supplies.

She straightened her shoulders and gave Robertson a firm handshake. Her eyes were dry. Weeping took strength, and she had no strength to spare now. "I'll make a go of it," she said. "See if I don't."

Reluctantly he agreed. "But six months only," he said. "If you're not makin' it by then, I can't afford to keep y'."

16

Willard's Hotel
Washington City
November 24, 1863

My Dear Cousin Daniel,

I have wanted to write to you for many weeks, but the right words would not come, and I did not want to put pen to paper until they did.

Dr. William came to take tea with me today, and he told me that your boy was buried at Mt. Auburn in the summer. He heard this only last week from Cousin Edward Jackson Revell. As you may know, Dr. William has been working day and night for months, ever since the battle, and has been, as he put it, "out of touch." But now he is going home to that saddest of tasks, to bury his dear wife, and he has promised to carry this letter with him, next to his heart, and to deliver it to you in person. He is exhausted, poor man, and I cannot imagine how he bears this new burden of grief after all he has seen. At least he has a son now, although in his present condition he cannot appreciate his good fortune.

But I was going to tell you about Garrison. You know, perhaps, that I was with him when he died. His last words were of you and his mother—and of course his dear wife Amelia. "Tell them that I love and honor them," he said, "and that I am sorry only that I did not live to fight again."

He suffered little at the end, and the pain he endured, he endured bravely and well. You must be proud of him, dear Daniel, for he was the noblest type of man.

As you see, I have put aside the Family quarrel. It seems ridiculous to me to continue it in the face of this larger, all-devouring family quarrel that the nation suffers now. You and your boy are my flesh and blood, and nothing can change that. So please let me speak to you now, and let us two, at least, bury the old dispute.

As you know, I have worked with the Army of the Potomac Hospital Corps since the summer of '61. I was able to receive an appointment as a Nurse very promptly because of my long association with Miss Dix, who in June of '61 was appointed Superintendent of Nurses. At first I did not go into the field, but worked with her here in Washington. She was besieged by women wanting appointments as nurses. Many of them were honest, patriotic souls who wanted only to serve their country, but some were of poor character, wholly unsuitable for the exacting duties that would confront them.

So Miss Dix had to be extremely careful whom she allowed to serve. Inevitably she made many enemies, but she laid down her laws and stuck to them: a woman must be between thirty-five and fifty, and "not beautiful." I was a bit too old on the first count (she made an exception for me), but I certainly fitted the second! Then she must be industrious, neat, sober, and strong. She must provide two letters of recommendation as to her good moral character. Despite these stringent rules, we recruited many nurses during the first few months.

At length I got into service. By the time the Gettysburg battle took place, I had been working in the field hospitals for over a year. So I knew what needed to be done, and I was pretty competent at doing it.

The day after the battle (which as you know actually lasted three days) was July 4—what an irony! After three fine, hot, sunny days while men killed each other, it seemed that on that day the Heavens wept, for it began to rain before dawn and continued through the day. Never have I seen such downpours! We tried to venture out onto the field, but the rain came so hard that we were soon mired in mud, the wagons stuck, the horses unable to move. So we had to give up until the next day, which was Sunday, and I know that the Lord forgave us as we worked on His day, for never did such work more need to be done. For hours upon hours we walked among the wounded, bringing food and drink. The ground was soaked with blood and strewn with abandoned knapsacks, rifles, cannon, caissons, dead horses whose bloody open wounds were alive with flies, the carcasses bloating and exploding in the heat. From all sides came the cries and moans of the survivors, but some men, while still alive, were unconscious and could not call to us. So we had to look at every body to see whether it should belong to the burial detail or to us. Many of the dead, and some of the living as well if you can believe it, had been robbed of their shoes and boots by scavenging rebels. We heard that they came to Gettysburg originally not to fight but to find shoes at the factories there—poor barefoot boys! The sun was hot—far hotter than any sun in Massachusetts—but despite the clear blue sky, I felt the presence of a shadow over the battlefield, and I believe that it was the spirit of Mars, the old god of war, lusting for his blood tribute. Well, he certainly had it at Gettysburg.

The litter bearers took the wounded to the wagons, which carried them to the field hospital. This was three large tents hastily put up that day, no floor but the bloody mud, but at least we were near the town and could get our supplies when the Sanitary Commission sent them in, which it did promptly.

As the men were brought in to the hospital, our first task was to wash them, for they were caked with mud, and the doctors could not see their wounds to treat them. The surgeons were mostly good men, although one of them drank to excess, so that his hands trembled and he could hardly hold his knife. The doctor who worked on Garrison was Dr. William Abbott Revell. Garrison was brought in on the Monday. His leg was shattered above the knee by a minié ball. Dr. William had no choice but to amputate, and that he did with dispatch. We had no ether or chloroform, but Garrison was given a good swig of whiskey, and he gritted his teeth and gallantly bore his pain. Dr. William is the kindest of men, and a wonderfully skilled surgeon as well. You must believe that he did everything in his power to save your boy. No one could have done more.

Garrison lived for a week after the operation. He was always terribly thirsty;

I gave him a drink many times a day, and at night as well, for I was on duty around the clock those first awful days, and slept only a few hours at a time. At the end, as I said, he asked me to send his dearest love to you and his mother, and to his wife. He said he regretted not seeing his child. Has it been born? He or she will be some comfort to you, at least.

I enclose several locks of Garrison's hair, and the photographs that he carried of all of you. William will bring his sword.

And I grieve with you, and for you, for the terrible loss you have suffered.

O Daniel! What a tragedy is this war! And yet we had to fight it, didn't we? I know that people say that Mr. Garrison and Mr. Phillips and all of you who argued the Abolitionist cause brought this war to pass. But you could have done nothing else. You were right; and you have the comfort at least of knowing that your boy did not die in vain. He died for a noble cause, as Mr. Lincoln said last week.

And yet, it is very hard, this business of war. I have seen men driven mad by their experiences on the battlefield, and they lie raving on their hospital cots.

I have seen women coming through the wards, searching, searching—for their sons, for their brothers, their husbands. And going away still searching, for some who will perhaps never be found.

Miss Clara Barton, who has done so splendidly with the Sanitary Commission, raising millions of dollars and providing tons of supplies to our hospitals, has told me that she intends to set up a registry of missing men to help families find their loved ones. She comes from Massachusetts, from Oxford, near Worcester. They would do well to put up a memorial to her, for she is surely one of the heroines of this war.

In August we moved to a general hospital—a proper building instead of a tent—and after the dedication of the National Cemetery, which took place last week, the hospital closed and we will be here in Washington for the winter.

The President spoke at the ceremony—President Lincoln, I mean, although President Everett of the College spoke also, on and on, for two hours and more! I know that he is supposed to be the greatest orator of our time, but he went on far too long. That is heresy, I suppose. Mr. Lincoln, brief as he was—really only a few minutes—had a much better speech.

And now I will tell you how I met Mr. Lincoln. Since I have been in Washington I have been restless and out of sorts—I feel strange because I have only a normal workday, and life here is not one crisis after another as it is in the hospitals. So I have slept badly, and because the weather has been very mild, I have risen early and walked out before breakfast. Few people are about then, and I can walk and think and even talk out loud if I wish—a slightly batty old woman, but harmless!

Yesterday morning when I went out, I turned my steps toward the White House almost without realizing where I went. Soon I was in the garden, which, since it was yet so early, I had to myself—or so I thought. But then I heard a step behind me on the graveled walk, and I turned to see Mr. Lincoln himself.

He seemed almost as startled as I; he had been walking deep in thought, his head down, hands clasped behind him—but without his familiar stovepipe hat atop his head. Since he is so tall, I had to tilt my head at quite an angle to meet his eyes. We shook hands, and I apologized for disturbing him. He said that I had not done so (really he is a very kind man, with a great heart that is, I think, slowly breaking over this war). We talked for some minutes. He learned who I am, what I had been doing; he thanked me for my hospital service, although of course he hardly needed to do so. When I told him about Garrison, he asked me to send his sympathy to you. And as we parted he told me to come back any time, that I was always welcome to walk in the garden there. Wasn't that kind? If you can get to Washington, and if I am here, we should go to one of his Thursday afternoons. He holds open house, and people line up around the block to see him and talk to him and shake his hand. He looks exhausted, as well he might, but he will not spare himself this weekly ordeal.

And lastly I will tell you about Mrs. Howe. You know Dr. Samuel Gridley Howe, of course, and his work with the blind—and of course he is an Aboli-tionist, too, isn't he? I don't know if you ever met his wife, Julia Ward. She is from New York originally but has lived in Boston these many years. Well, she has written a most splendid hymn—to the tune of "John Brown's Body," no less—and I urge you to get a copy of it as soon as you can because it is really a magnificent piece. She said that it came to her in a dream. She and Dr. Samuel had come to Washington on the cars, I don't remember why, and it was night as they came in, and they passed the campfires of the soldiers bivouacked out-side the city. The image of these stayed in her mind, and early the next morning before dawn she awakened with all the verses all written out in her mind, as it were, and she got up and lighted a candle right there in their hotel room—in this hotel, in fact—and put the lines down on a sheet of paper just as if she were taking dictation. I believe she tells this story so as to convince people that the hymn was divinely inspired—as indeed it may well have been.

> Mine Eyes have seen the Glory
> of the coming of the Lord;
> He is trampling out the vintage
> Where the grapes of wrath are stored;
> He hath loosed the fateful lightning
> Of His terrible swift sword . . .

It would be a wonderful thing for the choir at Emmanuel (is that where you go to church?) or anywhere else, for that matter:

> I have seen Him in the watch-fires of a hundred
> circling camps;
> I can read His righteous sentence by the dim and
> flaring lamps . . .

And then the magnificent chorus:

> Glory, Glory Hallelujah!
> His truth is marching on . . .

Really, it is a most extraordinary hymn, and it will help us to win this war. She calls it "The Battle Hymn of the Republic," and indeed that is what it is.

And now, dear Daniel, I must end this letter and seal it up and give it to Dr. William to deliver to you.

My heart goes out to you and all your family. When I return to Boston I will take the liberty of calling on you. As far as I am concerned, the quarrel need not exist between us, no matter how the others feel.

With love,
Your Cousin Caroline

17

Mary Margaret had been unable to find a dependable girl to mind the children, and it was hard to manage the store and the children both. And then in December she'd taken ill, not the consumption as she had feared, but a bad case of pneumonia, and she'd been unable to open the store at all. By the New Year she was through. She lay in her bed, the two littlest ones alongside her to keep them from freezing, and drifted in and out of an exhausted sleep.

At last, one bitter January noon, she felt well enough to get up and put on once more the black clothes of mourning that she knew she would wear to the end of her life. She went out into the blinding day. A foot of snow had fallen in the night; now the sky was clear deep blue, the sun brilliant but without warmth, the temperature at five degrees and the wind cutting through her like a knife.

It was a brief interview she had, both sides knowing how it would end. The landlord was going to evict them. The apartment went with the store; he'd want to let it to the next one who took over. But the agent was not entirely without compassion; he'd let her stay to the end of the month, he said, and give her a chance to find another place. She didn't have the money to rent another place, but she didn't tell him that.

"Don't you have family—anyone who could help you?" he said.

"No." Something ticked at the back of her brain; she couldn't quite grasp it.

Outside once again, she stood for a moment shivering in the brutal wind. Across Cambridge Street rose the back side of Beacon Hill, no longer the slum it was only a few years ago, but beginning to be built up with neat rows of modest brick houses, nothing so grand as the southern slope facing the Common, but vastly better than the shantytown they replaced. Like most people of her sort, Mary seldom ventured far afield; it had been a long time since she had been more than a few blocks from home. Now, disoriented from her illness, from her impending eviction, she looked around as if she were searching for some solution to her difficulties, some path to follow that would lead her away from the bitter struggle that her life had become since Patrick died.

Don't you have family—anyone who could help you?

When she'd come to America—ten years ago, now, it was—she'd had a brother. If he were alive now, he could help her. He was not alive; he had died because the Revells had fired her. Many times Patrick had tried to argue her out of that conviction, but he had never succeeded: it had, by this time, become an article of faith for her, and she would believe it until she died.

For her, it was the same as saying, the Revells killed him.

And if that were so, then in all fairness they must pay some reparation; somehow they must make it up to her, or at least try to do so.

Suddenly filled with new determination, she made her way across Cambridge Street—a broad, busy thoroughfare filled with carts and carriages and teamsters and omnibuses. She walked up the steep incline of South Russell Street, then left on Myrtle and right onto Joy. As she slipped and slid, first up and then down Joy toward Beacon, she saw the blinding white expanse of the Common at the end of the street. At the corner of Beacon she turned right, headed for number 43½.

A mourning wreath adorned the gleaming white door, and far back in her mind flickered the question: who died here? But she did not care; as long as the person she wanted to see was still living, she did not care who else of the family had gone. She was in fact glad that they were bereaved; she hoped that they suffered as much at their loss as she had at hers.

She climbed the neatly shoveled steps, lifted the knocker in the shape of a griffin and brought it down smartly: *rap-rap-rap!* Even as she did so, she wondered if her old nemesis, Mr. Dimwiddie, would answer. But no: the door was opened by a maid, no one Mary recognized.

"Is Mrs. Revell in?"

"Y'll have to ask at the back."

"I don't want to ask at the back. I'm askin' here." Mary felt strange standing here, in the very place where once she had been a frightened immigrant girl. Well, she wasn't a girl any longer; and she wasn't frightened, either.

"Y'll have to wait, then," the girl said, and shut the door.

Mary stood on the step, shivering: five minutes, ten, shifting her weight from one foot to the other to try to keep from freezing. She tried to rehearse in her mind what she would say: I don't know if you'd remember me, ma'am, but I used to work here, Mr. Dimwiddie said I stole a silver spoon, but I didn't and that's the God's truth.

Or perhaps Mrs. Revell was not at home, after all, and it would be Miss Florence who saw her—little frightened Florence who would now be a young woman grown. Mary wondered if Florence would remember how cheered she'd been by Mary's stories, how distracted from her fears.

Fifteen minutes, and Mary realized that the girl wasn't coming back; they weren't even going to give her the courtesy of a reply.

Damn them!

She felt weak again; she was not completely recovered from her illness, she couldn't stand and pound the door as she had done once long ago, when she was a greenhorn girl just off the boat.

She went down the steps and along the little path shoveled across the pavement. She stood at the curb and looked up at the handsome brick facade of the Hamilton Griffin Revell house. The bitter wind stung her eyes, and so when her tears fell, no one noticed, and no one paid particular attention, either, as she muttered to herself. The Irish were known to be strange, with their charms and their curses.

Eventually she moved on. She had neither time nor energy to waste, now, ruminating on her hatred of these people. She had urgent business to attend to—the business of survival. Her hatred must wait. She pushed it to the back of her mind and slammed shut the door on it. She would keep it there; it would stay alive, it would even grow and flourish there. And when the time was right, she would take it out and welcome it like an old friend.

18

By the end of the month Mary and her children were homeless.

"Come along, then," said the priest at St. Joseph's. "F'r a couple of nights, anyway. Y'can't sleep out of doors in this weather." This was not the first family he'd helped, nor would it be the last. "An'y' can put your things in the yard in back. Chances are no one'll steal them for a bit, anyway." A couple of trunks, bedding, a few pots and pans—not much. Mary left the younger ones with Patrick Jr., aged eight, while she went out searching for a place to live. If they had been evicted in the summer, they could have camped out on a vacant lot somewhere, she'd seen people doing it, but not now, not in the bitter Massachusetts winter when the temperature hovered below ten degrees during the days and below zero at night.

In the end it was the priest who heard of a place, a woman in Malvern Court, he said, who'd let them have a room all to themselves. She was healthy as far as he knew. Without even going to inspect it, Mary said yes. No matter how bad it was, she thought, they'd manage somehow. But when they arrived, her heart dropped and she thought that they shouldn't take it after all, it was too grim—too much like Half Moon Street—and what it would smell like in the summer she could imagine only too well.

Her new landlady, whose name was Betty Maguire, took the rent in advance and demanded fifty cents extra for a pail of coal.

"All right." Mary was exhausted—too worn out to carry on a conversation, much less argue about the extra expense. She settled herself on the floor and took the baby, Kathleen, onto her lap and began to sing her to sleep. In the morning, she thought, she would start looking for work.

When Mary and her little brood moved into Malvern Court—a narrow, refuse-strewn cul-de-sac not far from the hospital—she had five dollars and seventy-two cents. She figured that they could live for a month on that. So she needed to find work right away, and she'd have to depend on Patrick, so she told him, to take care of his younger brothers and sisters: Tim and Joe and John, and Eileen, and the baby, Kathleen. Within a week she'd found a job: scrubbing floors at the hospital. It didn't pay much, but they could live on it: two dollars a week. And it was mostly night work, so she could at least be on hand during the days, ready to awaken if any emergency came up.

They survived the spring. Mary was tired all the time; she'd lost her former stamina with her illness in the winter, and hadn't gotten it back, but she could manage, she thought. Being tired all the time wasn't the worst thing in the world. Patrick was a good boy, very responsible, already a little man; she didn't know what she'd have done without him, and that was the God's honest truth. Of course, his duties meant that he couldn't go to school, but that couldn't be helped. Perhaps next year.

19

Florence Griffin Revell, who once upon a time had been entertained by the cheerful conversation of her family's Irish maid, had recently endured a sorrow that no cheerful companion could assuage. Like many young women in those war years, she had married her fiancé before he went to the battlefield, and in a matter of months she was a widow. A few weeks after her husband's death had come word that her oldest brother, Oliver, had also been killed in action. So the mourning wreath that Mary Shaughnessy had seen at the Hamilton Griffin Revell house had had double meaning, and the inhabitants of that house were devastated by a double loss.

Eventually, however, Florence began to recover, even if her parents did not. Together with her surviving brother, Theo, Florence began to go out into the world again, to church, to her sewing circle, to pay calls to family members.

One day one of her cousins on her mother's side mentioned that on Easter Sunday charitable baskets—food and clothing—were going to be distributed to the city's poor, and if Florence would like to make up a basket, the committee would be most appreciative. She wouldn't have to distribute it herself, of course, and she could even remain anonymous if she wished.

Florence was glad of this chance to escape her grief, if only for a little while, and when she delivered her basket to the office of the Committee to

Distribute Charity to the Poor, she tucked in a little slip of pasteboard with her name on it: Florence Revell Mifflin.

Since she and her late husband had never had a chance to establish a home of their own, Florence still lived at 43½ Beacon Street. A few days after Easter the gentleman from the charity committee paid her a call.

"I am very sorry to disturb you, madam," he said, "but I have been requested most urgently to contact you by one of the recipients of our recent campaign." Nervously he cleared his throat. "Does the name Mary Shaughnessy mean anything to you?"

Florence frowned, trying to think. "No," she said at last. "No, I can't say that it does."

"I see. Well, no matter. I promised that I would inquire, nothing more." He rose to leave. "Thank you for—"

"Wait." Florence motioned him to stay. "Why do you—what is the trouble, why am I asked such a thing? Who is this person—this Mary Shaughnessy?"

"She was the recipient of your charitable basket, madam. She reads only a little, I think, because when she saw your card, she sounded out your name and then she asked me if she was correct. I said she was."

"And what was her reaction to that?" said Florence.

"She seemed very surprised—and pleased, I think. She asked me to come to see you, to ask you if you remembered her. She said she used to work for your family. When you were quite young, she used to tell you stories to amuse you, she said."

"Ah ..." Florence put her hand to her mouth in astonishment. "Yes—I do remember that girl, although I couldn't have told you her name. She was a delightful girl, a lovely girl. I always wondered what had happened to her. Mercy! Is she in such a bad way that she needs charitable donations?"

"She looks to be pretty badly off, madam."

"I shall go to see her at once," Florence said. "Where is she?"

"I don't know if you want to do that, madam. Those places over in the West End are pretty grim. No place for a lady like yourself."

"Nonsense," said Florence. "I shall go to her at once, and you, if you will be so kind, will take me!"

"Mary? Is that you?"

The voice came at her from out of the fog of sleep, and for a moment she thought she was dreaming. She saw a pale face framed in a black bonnet brim, she caught a whiff of fresh scent, she felt the touch of a gentle hand upon her arm. Yes; she was certainly dreaming. No such creature belonged here.

"Mary, can you hear me? It's Florence Revell—Florence Mifflin now. Do you remember me?"

Mary struggled up. Even in the daytime the light in the crowded little room was dim. And in any case the Florence Revell she had known had been a child no older than Patrick was now. So she could hardly be expected to recognize the adult—that faceless stranger she had asked for from the committee man.

"Oh, Mary, Mr. White told me that you asked for me. I'm so glad you did! I'm sorry you're ill—"

"No—no, I'm not ill. I work nights, I got to sleep in the day." Mary was fully awake now, and she scrambled up, wincing as she leaned on her right arm for balance and felt the old pain in her wrist, a broken wrist she'd gotten at this woman's house. She smoothed her hair and straightened her dress and said, "We'd best go outside, we can talk better there." By which she meant she wanted to be away from the humiliation of the wretched room, the squalid house where she had to live because she could afford nothing better. As they made their way slowly down the street, Mary cast repeated glances at her companion. She never would have recognized her, she thought, all grown up.

"Oh, Mary, I'm so glad to see you! You know, I've never forgotten how kind you were to me. And I never knew why you left us, except that there was some trouble—"

"They said I stole a spoon," Mary said slowly, glancing at Florence to see her reaction. She hadn't expected Florence to come so quickly; she should have been up and ready for her, she thought, instead of lying in bed half asleep. But too late now, she'd have to do her best with this God-given bit of luck: to find Florence, after the family turned her away.

"Did you?" said Florence. "Did you take it, Mary?"

"No. I never did." And Mary spoke with such conviction, such eye-to-eye honesty, that Florence believed her.

"It's odd, isn't it, the way things happen sometimes," said Florence. "Perhaps I shouldn't tell you this, but some years ago Mr. Dimwiddie was fired, himself—for stealing. But never mind, that's all done with now. Don't you see? I've come to help you! Oh, Mary—this terrible war, and so much cruelty! If there is a lesson in it anywhere, it is that we must love our brothers and sisters all the more, don't you agree?"

Mary might have replied that a slum dweller like herself hardly had time for brotherly and sisterly love of humankind, but she did not. She let Florence prattle on; from time to time she made appropriate responses. She had sent to Florence for help; she thought that after a while Florence would get to the point.

"But of course we are going to help you, Mary. The only question is, how? We must get you and the children out of that hideous room, certainly. But what can you do? Let's think for a minute. I don't suppose there is anything you could teach, and in any case—"

In any case, no one would want an Irish teacher. Quickly Florence recovered from her gaffe and went on. "So we must think about it. I don't suppose—well, no, governessing wouldn't do, would it? What can you do, Mary? Let's really think hard now."

"I can sew a bit," Mary offered. "I did petticoats for a bit. But I don't want to do that again, it's worse than scrubbing floors."

"Ah! But the point is, you can sew! You used a machine?"

"Yes, I—"

"Well, then! Why don't we set you up in dressmaking?"

"Dressmaking?" A dress was a complicated thing, yards and yards of fabric, intricate detail—

"Absolutely! That is what we are going to do! I know a woman who can teach you everything you need to know. She's done our dresses for years."

Then she won't want to help the competition, thought Mary, but she said nothing.

"I will tell her to get out a few Godey patterns, and I'll supply the fabric, you can make two dresses for me as practice, and then I will be a walking advertisement for you. I know plenty of women whose husbands have made enormous sums in this war. They are longing for new dresses. They can't get M. Worth from Paris, of course, but they'll give their business to you, see if they don't— Oh, Mary! Think of it! Mary Shaughnessy, Dressmaker! Why, you'll be a marvelous success in no time!"

2. THE LOVERS

1

"Marry him?" said Mrs. Edward Jackson Revell. "What are you talking about? Marry him? You don't even know him! None of us know the Griffin Revells! We're not supposed to! We don't acknowledge their existence! You know that! I told you myself, I distinctly remember— *Marry him?* Have you gone mad? Speak to me, Isabella! Don't just stand there gawking like a silly sheep! Answer me when I— Where did you meet him? And how did you— Oh, I am going to faint! I feel it coming on, I can always tell. Ellen! Ellen!" She tried to rise from her chair and get to the bell pull to summon her maid, but she could not; her corset held her in its iron grip, asphyxiating her, and in any case her lower limbs had turned to water at her daughter's announcement.

Isabella—marrying a Griffin Revell? Edward would die, she thought. And before he died, he would horsewhip young Theodore Griffin Revell, and he would shout and rave and make a scene, blaming her, no doubt, for lax supervision of their daughter, the beautiful, the irrepressible, the very stubborn young lady who stood before her now, her lovely face set in lines of grim determination.

"Isabella—fetch Ellen," Mrs. Revell gasped. "I am going to faint. I cannot see, I cannot breathe—"

Isabella stared at the panting, swooning woman before her. She loved her mother, of course, but she loved both herself and Theodore more.

"I will fetch Ellen in a moment, Mother," she said. "But before I do, I want you to promise me that you will have him to dinner next Tuesday. I told him you would."

"Have him to dinner!" moaned Mrs. Revell. "Your father will die. Yes, he will. Why, that young man's father cut your father dead only six months ago in State Street. It was because of the clubs. None of the men in the Somerset speak to the men who broke away to found the Union."

"Well, there you are," said Isabella. "They are squabbling over the war, and the war was over four years ago. Nothing to do with the Family quarrel. It's a stupid thing, anyway. Both Grandfather and Great-Uncle Nathaniel are dead—"

"Isabella," moaned her mother, "don't use such language. Say 'passed away,' or 'went to their reward.' "

"The point is, they are both gone. Why should we have to carry on their disagreement, whatever it was?"

Her daughter's remorseless logic failed to persuade Mrs. Revell, however, and she kept on saying no until she did indeed faint from sheer exhaustion, and the elusive Ellen came running in at last to rescue her from the cruelties of Miss Isabella who was, as they all agreed below stairs, a most unsuitably headstrong and overindulged young lady.

At around the same time, Hamilton Griffin Revell sat in the library of his house at number 43½ Beacon Street and granted his younger and only surviving son, Theodore, the interview the young man had requested. Since the death of Theo's older brother Oliver in the winter of '63, Theo had become all the more precious to his father, for there had been only two boys, three children in all: Florence the youngest, this lad the middle child; he could remember the night he was born, a terrible blizzard, the doctor stranded coming back from Brookline . . .

Hamilton shook his head. More and more he found himself musing about the past, instead of paying attention to the present. Getting old! He would turn sixty in October. His best years were behind him. He wanted to see a grandchild before he died. And since Oliver had been killed in the war, and Florrie was a childless widow because of that same war, at the moment it looked as though this young man in front of him was his only hope for producing a new generation. Hamilton's elder brother Artemas had half a dozen grandchildren at least. Hamilton felt a nasty twinge of envy whenever he thought about that. It wasn't fair that Artemas had so many and he, Hamilton, did not have even one.

"Well?" he said to his son. "What was it you wanted to see me about?"

"I wanted to ask something of you, Father." Theo was a tall, well-put-together young man who was a Revell through and through, not a weak bone in his body, never a day of sickness, and thank God he'd been of a mind to buy a substitute, an Irish lad, they'd never heard what happened to him. One son was enough—although Hamilton knew of many families who had lost two and three and even, in the case of Mrs. Bixby, four. Four sons killed! President Lincoln had written a beautiful letter to her. Small comfort!

Now, looking at his boy, twenty-four he was and not a boy any longer, Hamilton's face softened and he smiled a little. He felt in an indulgent mood. Ah, yes, he was fortunate to have this boy left to him! And if he spoiled him a bit, what was the matter with that? Anything the boy wanted he could have, within reason of course: a new sailboat, a new horse, a membership in a new club. "What is it?" he said. He thought that the sun, streaming through the window onto Theo's hair, shone like the gold he had once seen on an illuminated manuscript in France. Beautiful!

"I want you to speak to Mr. Edward Jackson Revell," said Theo.

Hamilton blinked. The sun was very bright. Perhaps he was so dazzled by its glare that he misunderstood what his son was saying.

"What do you mean, 'speak to him'? I never speak to him. Never spoke to him in my life. You know that."

"Yes. I do. But now . . . Father, I want to ask him for the hand of his daughter. Her name is Isabella. And I thought—well, I thought that it would be, ah, more diplomatic perhaps if you went to him on your own, since you carry more weight, more moral weight, I mean, more weight of character, you have more stature, I mean, and if you could convince him that I am absolutely sincere, and that also I am a man of good character, I mean I think I can convince him of that myself, but if you just put in a word for me . . ."

He couldn't seem to stop talking. His father said not a word more, just sat and stared at him as if he had suddenly turned green, or sprouted antlers—as if he were some kind of freak.

After a while Hamilton got up and, touching his son on the arm, bade him come along. They would walk down to the Union Oyster House and have a plate of cherrystones and a glass of good dark beer and they would talk business. Real business, not this nonsense about Isabella Jackson Revell. Why, only the other day he'd heard about Professor Agassiz' boy, young Alexander, and the way he was going to sell shares in his copper mine out in Michigan, what was it called? Calumet-Hecla, that was it. And railroads—yes! Perhaps Theo was too cooped up in the Family office here. He should go West, see for himself how Boston men were going to get rich now that the railroad had been laid coast to coast, only this past May the golden spike uniting the lines driven in at Promontory Point in the Rockies. The Credit-Mobilier scandal, which had unfolded in the course of that achievement and had forced a Massachusetts congressman to retire, was nothing—just a little hiccup in the grand march of progress.

He heard his voice ringing in his head as they climbed the hill to the State House and followed Beacon Street down again to Tremont and on down to Blackstone Street, where the Oyster House was. His son didn't say much; but when they had settled themselves at the big curved, oaken bar and had their plates in front of them, slipping the little delicacies down their throats, Theo spoke again, and it was as if his father had never said a word.

"Father, I want to marry Miss Revell."

"Impossible." Hamilton swallowed the last little clam and raised his eyebrow at the barkeep, signaling for another plateful.

"Why? Because of the blood relationship? We are second cousins at worst, and we are far less than that in fact, because Grandfather Nathaniel and Samuel Jackson Revell were only half brothers."

"You know perfectly well that it is not because of the relationship. You know that there is a breach, that we do not acknowledge them—"

"But why? For something that happened years ago? Isn't that foolish? Whatever it was that started this—this split, this silly breach—happened long before any of us were even born! How can we be expected to keep it up?"

Hamilton turned his cold blue gaze upon his son and said, more sternly perhaps than he had intended, "We keep it up because my father chose to do so. And I must follow his wishes, and so must you. Samuel Jackson Revell did my father a great wrong, a very great wrong indeed, and we cannot forget it."

"That is ridiculous!" Theo spoke so vehemently that several gentlemen turned to stare at them.

He apologized at once for his rudeness, of course, and for a while they sat silent, working their way through another plateful. Then Hamilton turned to his son and said, ruefully, "I am sorry, my boy. It simply won't do."

2

The announcement that brought such grief to Mrs. Edward Jackson Revell and Mr. Hamilton Griffin Revell—that their children wished to repair the breach that had divided the Family for some seven decades—came about because earlier that year, an Irish bandmaster named Patrick Sarsfield Gilmore had proposed a Great Peace Jubilee to be held on the newly filled land of the Back Bay in St. James' Square.

The businessmen of Boston, the hoteliers, the restaurateurs, railroad officials, merchants, agreed that a Peace Jubilee was a splendid idea. Some of them wanted to hold the jubilee on the Common, but others objected, and so—because this was a festival of Peace, after all—they selected a site in the wasteland of the Back Bay that would eventually become Copley Square. Then Gilmore set to work. He turned out to be not only an excellent musician—during the war he had written "When Johnny Comes Marching Home Again," a song that was unfortunately destined to become a perennial favorite—but a superb organizer as well. He enlisted an orchestra of one thousand and a chorus of ten thousand, all Americans. He solicited help from around the world, and they came: the "king of violinists," the Norwegian, Ole Bull; the opera soprano Madame Parepa Rosa; the Grenadier Guards band from London; the band of LaGarde Republicaine of Paris; the Emperor's Quartet from Berlin; and, from Vienna, the waltz king himself, Johann Strauss and his orchestra. The director of the Handel and Haydn Society of Boston helped Gilmore to rehearse the chorus so that the Americans would not disgrace themselves in the face of all that foreign talent.

When in June of 1869 the citizens of Boston, and the citizens of much of New England and even farther afield, sat themselves down in the huge, newly erected Coliseum that seated fifty thousand, they saw at once from the splendor of the decor, the draped flags and bunting, the arms of the states displayed around the galleries, that this was indeed what Gilmore had promised, the greatest musical and patriotic display in history.

The proceedings were opened by an eloquent prayer from the noted minister and author of the popular patriotic story, "The Man Without a Country," Edward Everett Hale. Then came the music, including a Hymn of Peace written especially for the occasion by Dr. Oliver Wendell Holmes; Gounod's "Ave Maria"; *Tannhaüser*; the "Gloria" from a Mozart mass; and not one, but two pièces de résistance: the "Anvil Chorus," played to the accompaniment of one hundred Boston firemen dressed in black pants, red shirts, and white caps, beating time on one hundred anvils; and "The Star Spangled Banner," also with full chorus and orchestra, the great organ, military bands, and—set off by electricity in perfect synchronization—infantry firing and cannonades, together with all the church bells in the city.

The two young Revells met on the second day of the four-day festival, the day on which a thunderous welcome was given to President Ulysses S. Grant and all his cabinet as they entered the hall to the strains of "Hail the Conquering Hero." The audience that day was even more uplifted, more inspired, than it had been on the first day, and so people were a bit more careless, perhaps, about how they made their exits. Their heads were still in the clouds, so to speak, and so their feet trod carelessly. And so when Isabella tripped and fell to the floor in the middle of the crowded aisle, she might well have been trampled.

Theo saw her go down. He had no idea who she was, of course—just a girl about to be seriously hurt. He had been well trained in chivalric conduct by his mother and father both, and he was a strong man, a good athlete. In an instant he had pushed through to where she had fallen. He threw himself in the way of the oncoming crowd, thus making a little space for her, and reached for her hand to lift her to her feet.

"Look here!" he shouted against the roar of excited voices all around them. "Hold fast—I'll get you out safe!"—for the crowd was fifty thousand strong and it had been sitting for some hours. Now it was determined to make its getaway; even the presence of three hundred Boston policemen could not stop it.

He felt her hand grip his as they made their way out. The crowd pressed so thick around them that even when he managed to turn his head, he could hardly see her, and not until they got outside was he able to get a good look at her. And then he stared as if he could not take his eyes from her. She was a beauty, he thought as he gazed at the late afternoon sun glinting off her golden hair a shade lighter than his own, the perfect oval of her face accented by high cheekbones and well-marked brows, and was there not something familiar about the set of her chin, the deep blue of her eyes . . . ?

She shook herself together, smoothing her hair, repositioning her flat little hat, adjusting the ruffles of her white dress. She was tall for a girl, and slender, with a certain carriage that spoke of gentle birth—like a prize filly, he thought: she had good lines, and a bit of temperament. Theo was known to his Porcellian chums, if not to his family, as a hot-blooded young man who more than once had led a delegation to visit a house where lived certain ladies of the night. Of course, he had never so much as kissed a decent girl, a girl of good Boston or Cambridge family, for such things were not permitted in the tight little world that he inhabited. Once, on a trip abroad, he had struck up an acquaintance with a little French girl, but since everyone knew that the French were hopelessly decadent, she had had, as it were, no honor to compromise.

But a proper Boston young lady was a different kettle of fish altogether, and so now Theo, all his antennae alert to a prize catch, stood before this delectable creature whom he had rescued and took her hand and bowed over it a little in a deliberate display of punctilious good manners, and said,

"Allow me to introduce myself. I am Theodore Griffin Revell. May I ask your name?"

As he straightened he saw her hesitate. She had been quite pale, understandably, but now a little rosy color came to her cheeks, and she looked suddenly shocked.

He kept hold of her hand. "Well?" he said. "May I?"

She seemed to come to some decision. To his surprise, she took back her hand; she stared at him with a look that, in most women, would not have been quite ladylike: it was too direct, too forthright. All around them came the crowd streaming out of the Coliseum, their faces alight with the splendor of the performance, their hearts aflame for Peace. It was an impossible place for a tête-à-tête.

"Come," he said, his voice raised against the noise of the crowd. "Let me see you—where? Home?"

She threw him that strange look, as if she knew something that he did not. In a girl less attractive, such behavior might have cooled his interest; but this girl was far too beautiful to let go, no matter how strangely she behaved.

"I—I came with friends," she said. She looked helplessly around at the thousands of people surrounding them.

"Well, you've obviously lost them. Can't be helped. Come on."

At last she allowed him to lead her away, and they made their way down Boylston Street to the Public Garden, just now, in mid-June, at the height of its bloom. And it was not until they were safely apart from the main body of the crowd, making their way along one of the winding paths that led around the lagoon, that he ventured his question again: "May I ask your name?"

She came to a full stop so suddenly that the frothy hem of her skirts and petticoats swirled around her ankles. She turned to face him. Under the direct blue gaze of those lovely eyes, he felt a little *frisson*.

"My name, Mr. Revell, is the same as yours." She could not repress a little smile as she spoke, and even as her words registered he found himself wondering how it would be to kiss that luscious mouth. Heaven, he thought: pure bliss. "My last name, that is," she added. Suddenly her face went solemn—somber, even, and she frowned and turned away from him. "And you know as well as

I do that we should not be walking together," she went on. "Think how angry my father would be if he knew—and yours, too, I suppose."

He was so dazzled by her, all golden and glowing as she was, that he was at a loss for words. But then he somehow found a few, at least, and he said, "What do you mean?"

"My name is Isabella Jackson Revell," she said. She had faced him again, and now, seeing his dumbfounded look, she could not help but laugh. "Don't you know about the Jackson Revells?" she said. "We don't speak to the Griffins, and they don't speak to us. It goes back to my grandfather Samuel and your grandfather Nathaniel. The way I heard it, Great-Uncle Nathaniel insulted Grandfather Samuel."

"I heard it was the other way around," he said, and at that they both began to laugh. Isabella stopped first. "It is very wrong of me to walk with you," she said. "I am grateful to you for rescuing me, truly I am, but I cannot stay with you. Good day."

Abruptly she turned and began to walk away. Theo hurried after her. "No—wait! Let me see you home! Where do you live?"

She waved her hand toward Commonwealth Avenue. "Up there—just beyond Berkeley."

"Well, then. Let me walk with you."

"Oh, no! You mustn't!"

"But I must. Indeed I must. You cannot walk the streets alone. Your family will be alarmed, they will be looking for you. I will see you home, and perhaps I may speak to your father."

"No!" She was appalled—horrified at his suggestion. Speak to her father—never!

"But of course I must speak to him. How else may I come to call on you?"

"You cannot come to call on me. It is out of the question! We do not speak to the Griffin Revells, you know that!"

"I know that I am speaking to you, and no harm has come of it."

"Oh, but it will. It will! You must go away, we cannot be seen together—"

And she turned and began to hurry away, toward the Arlington Street gate and the safety of Commonwealth Avenue, the long dusty street divided by the embryonic mall planted with a few spindly saplings.

Theo went right along beside her; nothing could have pried him away. He did not care she did not want him there. She was mistaken: no possible harm could come from their association, and besides, even if it did, he would not be deterred. He knew that on this day he had found the love of his life; he did not intend to give her up, and certainly not for a stupid ancient family disagreement entered into long before either he or the beauteous Isabella was born.

But at last, at the corner of Berkeley Street, he saw that she was crying—with fear, with frustration at his stubbornness, he did not know what. And so he agreed to leave her, but only temporarily. "I must see you," he said. "And if you cannot think of a way to arrange it, I will march up to your door and present myself. You have had your coming out—yes?—and so you are entitled to receive callers. I will be one of them."

She made no reply, just threw him an imploring look. What she implored—what she wanted—he hadn't a clue. He watched her go: a tall, elegant, bewitching figure of a girl walking down the half-finished row of attached brick and brownstone town houses that would, one day, be the most handsome street in America. Just now it was like a gap-toothed smile: a house, a vacant lot, two or three houses, another vacant lot. But Theo was not thinking about the landscape just now; he was trying to think of ways to see Isabella without arousing the wrath of either of their families.

3

"Say, friend, how do I get to Walden Pond?"

"Walden Pond? Well, now, it's not too hard. Get yourself to Harvard Square—just over the bridge and up Mass. Ave. Then go on out from there toward Arlington and keep on going to Lexington. Then—well, you'd better ask at Lexington Green. I think you go toward Lincoln, but I'm not sure."

4

A warm summer's day, a perfect day for a stroll around the pond made famous by the late eccentric, Henry David Thoreau. He had died some years before, but people still remembered him, still thought of him in connection with this place. All traces of his hut save for the hearthstones had long disappeared, but only the previous fall Bronson Alcott, the Transcendentalist philosopher and father of the author of the extraordinary success, *Little Women*, had begun the custom of depositing a stone on the site. There was quite a little cairn now, a memorial of sorts to the pond's Yankee patron saint.

But neither Theo nor Isabella had any thought for Henry Thoreau this day. They walked slowly around the pond, the water sparkling in the sunlight, a little breeze riffling the surface and stirring the leaves of the surrounding forest. After a while, when they reached a spot well away from any prying eyes, they stopped. He lifted her hand to his lips. As he kissed it, he felt the shudder that passed through her slender body, and he took it as a sign that she wanted him to go on kissing her, that she wanted him to kiss some other portion of her anatomy than her hand, that she was in fact as much in love with him as he was with her.

He took her in his arms and pressed his mouth on hers—that lovely, ruby mouth that had so enticed him the first day they met, a month and more ago.

This meeting today was only their third. He had had the devil's own time to arrange it, for Isabella had refused for days to see him, to have any contact with him. Three times he had sent her notes, and three times she had sent them back unopened. He could not believe that she had so hard a heart. At last he had employed the services of a spy—his cousin Mildred, his mother's niece, a spinster lady on good terms with the Edward Jackson Revells. She had discovered for him that the fair Isabella was to visit a friend she had met at Miss Slater's School for Young Ladies; the friend lived in Concord, and Isabella was to be there about a week.

Miss Mildred was very surprised indeed when Theo impulsively seized her and kissed her withered cheek. "Splendid, cousin! I am in your debt! If ever there is any service—any service at all I can do for you—Concord! Wonderful!"

There would be difficulties enough, but she was out from under her family's supervision, that was the main thing. The rest of them had gone to Nahant, where she would join them at the end of July. So he had very little time to make his case. This picnic today at Walden was his first chance. He had driven out early in the morning in a rented buggy; he had written to her to alert her, saying that he would present himself and he hoped that she would relent and give him a little of her time.

She had done so: thus her position now, held fast in his arms. She had no idea what had come over her. She thought that if anyone saw them, she would be ruined. She did not care. She wanted him to go on kissing her forever. Like all young girls, she had chattered and giggled with her schoolgirl friends about whom they would allow to court them, whom they would allow to marry them. She understood now that all of that chatter had been a waste of time. How could mere schoolgirls possibly know what she knew now—what she felt, what she desired at the hands of this insistent young man so like herself, tall and fair and handsome, and yet so different because he was that mysterious thing, a man.

"Marry me," he said, taking his mouth from hers for an excruciating instant.

But of course she had no choice, she had to marry him, for in kissing him she had compromised herself beyond all redemption.

"Yes," she said. From somewhere back in a corner of her mind she heard her voice say: "But you do not know him. And in any case, he is a Griffin Revell." She told the voice to be quiet; she went on kissing him.

5

Inevitably someone snitched on them. When Mrs. Edward Jackson Revell, in summer residence at Nahant, heard that her daughter Isabella had been seen in the company of one of the Griffin Revell boys, she fainted. Then she got up and sent a manservant with the carriage to fetch Isabella home. When Isabella arrived, Mrs. Revell sent her to her room. Ordinarily a voluble, cheerful woman, Mrs. Revell was now a figure of somber taciturnity. She did not speak to her daughter. She spent the next day writing a series of notes. She sent a sum of money to the Cunard Line to reserve a double stateroom. She ordered her maid to go to Boston and pack several trunks. She wrote lies to hostesses who had invited her and Isabella to attend social affairs in the coming weeks. Then, when all was ready, she sent for her daughter and informed her that the two of them, plus a maid, were taking an extended trip to Europe. Isabella's father and her younger brothers and sisters would join them when it was convenient. She never so much as mentioned the name of the offending young man, or even the reason for their going, thereby making her dictates seem all the more mysterious, all the more frightening.

There was of course no chance for Isabella to say good-bye to her beloved before she left. Weeping, stunned into obedience by the swiftness and ruthlessness of her mother's battle plan, she walked up the gangplank on a muggy August day and steeled herself for an indefinite period of exile and misery.

It was not until they were on the high seas, well away from Boston Harbor, that Mrs. Revell spoke of the matter that hung between them like a sword.

"You must promise me," she said, "that you will not attempt to communicate with that young man."

"Yes, Mother." Isabella had read a story once about a girl who had died of a broken heart. She wondered if she herself would survive. At the moment she hardly cared.

She turned away so that her mother would not see her tears—bitter, burning tears that she could not stop. They were at the rail of the ship; as strong as the wind was, it could not dry her face. After a moment she felt her mother's arm about her trembling shoulders. "My dear, please try not to grieve too much. You think that I do not know what you suffer, but I do. When I was a girl hardly older than you, I—well, I was attracted to a young man who—" Her voice broke, and she paused to collect herself. "He was ill. He . . . died. I felt as though I had died, too. But life is not so cruel as all that. And when I met your father, I was glad that I had lived. Isabella, you are young, you are beautiful, you have your life ahead of you. Weep for this little time if you must, but believe me, life will call you back, and you must answer."

Isabella's mother spoke more truly than she knew. They wintered in Italy that year, settling in with the American colony in Rome, and before many weeks had passed, Isabella had indeed begun to recover. What was more, in the company of the Misses Caldwell, the daughters of the noted sculptor Elihu Caldwell, she began her education in a new love that was to stay with her all her life: the paint and canvas and blocks of marble and tons of bronze that artists like Elihu and his brethren, particularly his brethren of the Renaissance centuries before, had transformed into works of art. She became infatuated: she haunted the galleries and studios of the city as if she were going to a rendezvous, as in a way she was; and when for the moment Rome had given her what it had to offer in the way of visual delight, she ventured to Florence, to Siena, to

Venice—all of Italy became the country of her heart, and she roamed it with a lover's passion.

Soon she began to want to own something—some small item representative of the whole: a little Leonardo, a small Raphael. By that time, not long after Christmas, she and her mother had been joined by the rest of the family. So any decision about money could be made at once, her father of course having the final word. Edward Jackson Revell did not care a pin about art. One day Isabella took him to see a painting at a dealer's off the Via Garibaldi. It was a Madonna and child, not large, about fifteen by seventeen inches. The dealer assured him that its provenance was unimpeachable, but of course those fellows would say anything to get a sale. For all he, Edward Jackson Revell, knew, the thing was a fake, newly painted only the previous week in some freezing studio by an impecunious second-rater needing money to buy food and fuel.

The dealer stood by, suave and ingratiating, with just the necessary touch of hauteur. These rich American barbarians were easy to fool, but such trickery was beneath him. This painting by Raphael was genuine. The many thousands of lira that he was asking for it was not an outrageous sum.

Edward thought of his daughter. She seemed to have recovered from her near disaster with young what's-his-name—the Griffin Revell. Her mother had been right to bring her to Rome; and if this little bit of paint and gilt on wood might serve to complete Isabella's cure, it was cheap at the price.

"Very well," he said. "I'll take it."

Foolish man! He had no idea what he had done. For of course Isabella would not be satisfied with that one small painting. She had been aroused—as strongly as any woman suffering through a passionate love affair. She and her family would return to America not many months ahead, but she would leave a bit of her heart—her very soul—here in Italy. At home, in Massachusetts, she would feed her addiction by beginning to study works of art, and particularly works of the Renaissance, that glorious burst of human achievement that approached the divine—ah, Rome! Italy! How she loved it! How grateful she was to her mother for taking her there! She planned to visit Italy again—many times.

By May they were back in Boston. Commonwealth Avenue seemed much less grand than before, but Edward was glad to be home. Damned foreigners! With their gabbling, incomprehensible language and their hands always out for a tip!

Nevertheless, the trip had been worthwhile: his daughter had been cured of her affliction.

The day after he set foot in his office in State Street, he had a nasty shock when, walking home for dinner, he passed the Old Corner Bookstore at the corner of School and Washington Streets—the site of Ann Hutchinson's house, but he did not know that—and he saw in the window a new book, just published: *The Lovers: or, Romeo and Juliet*, by Washington Abbott Revell. Edward went in; he picked up a copy to look at it. He had always enjoyed his cousin's writings: having a literary man in the family was not a bad thing, it lent a nice air—and Washington was not so literary that a man couldn't understand him.

After a moment, standing at the display and reading a line here and there, he began to sense that something was wrong. He began to read more slowly, and to read every line. The clerk, glancing at the tall gentleman perusing the new romance by Washington Abbott Revell, saw that the gentleman's face was bright red, and his mouth was working as if he were silently cursing his bitterest enemy.

Edward could not believe it. That damned scribbler had taken the story of his daughter's attachment to a totally unsuitable young man—never mind that he was a Revell—and turned it into a story. Romeo and Juliet, indeed! Slander and libel was more like it! What was the fellow thinking about? To use people's private affairs, spread them all across the page for anyone to see—outrageous!

Hurriedly he fished a couple of bills from his pocket, threw them at the startled clerk, and, carrying a copy of the offending book, stalked out. He would give that fellow a piece of his mind, see if he didn't! At home, before he took a bite of food, he went to his library to dash off a blistering note to Washington out in Concord.

Unfortunately (from the point of view of the Edward Jackson Revells) *The Lovers* had a big sale. People thought it was an enchanting tale; many of them were aware of the rumor that it was based on a true story. Inevitably, Isabella got hold of it; she saw it at a friend's and asked if she might borrow it. She read it quickly, read it again more slowly, and did not know whether to laugh or cry. Clever, clever Washington to know the secrets of a young woman's heart, and to put them on paper for everyone to see!

In Washington's story, the young lovers eventually married.

Isabella thought about that. Was she still in love with Theo? Did she even want to see him? Had her new love—the splendors of Italy—taken her heart entirely, or did that heart still have room for him?

On a warm afternoon in late May, only Isabella and her mother were at home when, shortly after one o'clock, an urgent message came for Mrs. Revell from the Ladies Visiting Committee at her church, Emmanuel, an Episcopal church on lower Newbury Street. This committee kept a list of the deserving poor; now, it seemed, one of them needed help, and it was Mrs. Edward Jackson Revell's turn to go. She took her church duties very seriously, for she was a good Christian woman; so she summoned her maid to accompany her, and the two of them set off to the South End, where the trouble was.

Isabella was sitting under the shade of a hawthorn tree in the small walled garden at the rear of the house, trying to concentrate on *Little Women*, a tremendously popular novel by one of the Alcott girls. But her attention drifted; she couldn't keep track of the story. From within the house she heard the door bell ring; after a moment Barker went to answer. She heard nothing more: some caller for her mother, she supposed, who would leave her card and call again another day. A bumblebee noisily dove at a blossom above her head;

from the kitchen she heard a crash of crockery onto the stone floor, followed by Cook's voice scolding the scullery maid.

And yet . . . Amid the humdrum normality of the day, something was not right.

Isabella was sitting with her back to the house. Now, for no reason at all that she could identify, and despite the warmth of the day, she felt a chill run up her neck, and with a little shiver she turned to see—what, she did not know, but something was there, someone—

The sun glinted on his hair, making it a cap of gold, and his eyes held a longing, a hunger for her that even his polite smile could not disguise.

For a moment she was so startled that she could not move. Then, as if she were propelled by some force outside herself, she sprang to her feet, she sobbed aloud in joy, and she ran to his arms as if they offered the only refuge in the world for her lonely heart. A year ago they had met, had fallen in love; for long months they had been separated. How could she have thought that anything could replace him in her heart? No painting, no work of art, no exquisitely sung opera mattered a bit to her now that he held her close, now that he kissed her and kissed her— Ah, how she loved him!

"Yes," she said, "yes, yes, yes!"

Later, remembering, they laughed as they agreed that she had almost certainly given the answer well before he had had a chance, this second time, to ask the question.

6

Early the next morning the clerk put his head around the door of Edward Jackson Revell's inner office. "Young gentleman to see you, sir."

"Yes? Who is it, Junius?"

"His card, sir."

Edward stared at it: Theodore Griffin Revell. He pressed his lips in annoyance. Bothersome young scamp! It would be an unpleasant interview; he might as well get it over with.

"All right."

The young man was not what he expected. He had expected someone more—flippant. More lightweight. This young man seemed quite serious. As well any young man might be, who aspired to marry Isabella. But in particular Edward had thought that the Griffin Revell who knowingly broke the Family taboo would be a taboo-breaking type: insolent, perhaps. Shifty. A criminal look to him, perhaps.

But this young man looked perfectly presentable, perfectly upright and honest.

He advanced with his hand outstretched. Edward did not take it; nor did he invite the young man to sit in the chair opposite his massive desk. Instead, he stood up. "What do you want?" he said—an unnecessary question, since both of them knew perfectly well what Theodore wanted.

"I want permission to marry Isabella, sir." The young man had a steady gaze, his blue eyes reflecting intelligence, a firm character. His chin was firm, too, and his features nicely clean-cut. No big surprise in that: he was a Revell, after all.

But he was not going to have Isabella. Never.

"Out of the question," said Edward.

"With respect, sir, I understand how you feel—"

"Nonsense. You haven't a clue about how I feel."

"Sir, please hear me out." Theo was getting a little pink in the face, and he was starting to perspire rather heavily. "I don't—I find it difficult to express to you the extent of my devotion to your daughter. All I can say to you is that no one in the world will care for her better than I will. I understand your concern—"

Edward moved his hand impatiently, as if to flick invisible specks of dust from the air. "Don't tell me again, young man, that you understand. You do *not* understand. I am the one who understands. And what I understand is that this—this request of yours is impossible."

"Because . . . ?"

"Don't be impudent with me, young man. You know perfectly well—"

"The old quarrel? But that was—what? Nearly seventy years ago? How can we keep on with something that old, that long forgotten? Mr. Revell, listen to me. You have undoubtedly heard of the theories of the naturalist, Charles Darwin."

"Atheistic rubbish."

"Yes—well—but if you grant him his premise—"

"Which I do not."

"Yes, but if you will, for a moment. Many eminent scientists agree with him. I am sure you are acquainted with Dr. William Abbott Revell, and he is one of the most eminent doctors in the country, and he thinks—"

"I am not interested in what Dr. William thinks. He is at liberty to think whatever he likes. That has nothing to do with what you ask of me."

"Well, no, in fact it doesn't, but the point that I am trying to make is that if—I repeat *if*—we are indeed an evolved species, then we have evolved a brain large enough to, ah, rise above these petty quarrels, and we can learn to forgive—"

"It is not a question of forgiveness, young man, any more than it is a question of species or whatever rubbish it is that you are trying to drag into this discussion. You may not marry Isabella, and that is final. Do you understand me?"

"Yes, sir, I understand you. But I do not accept your verdict. I have to tell you that she has sworn to me that if you do not allow her to marry me, she will never marry anyone. Would you condemn her to a life of solitude, without a husband, without children?"

Edward felt the flush rising over his face. "Are you threatening me?"

"No, sir. I would never do that. I am simply telling you what she told me."

"You extract a promise like that from her, and you expect me to believe it was a voluntary—"

"I did not extract it, sir. She did indeed offer it freely. What I am trying to do is to make you see the absolute determination that we have, both of us. I know that it is difficult for you to cast aside three generations and more of antagonism. But at the same time, I will say that I think it very unfair for our ancestors—our mutual ancestors, if you will—to burden us with their old quarrels. Don't you agree?"

Edward did not agree, not yet. But that afternoon when he arrived home, Isabella went directly to him. He saw shadows under her lovely eyes, and a worried frown creasing her lovely forehead, and he felt a faint sense of unease.

"Father? Did he—did Theo speak to you?"

"He did."

"And did you give him your answer?"

"Yes."

"And may I know what it was?"

"I think you do already."

She stared at him. She could not believe that he would willfully ruin her life in this way. Since the Jackson Revells had had no contact with the Griffin Revells for decades, she did not know the story of her aunt Caroline's ill-fated adventure of the heart more than thirty years before. Had she known it, she would have held it up to her father as an example of a ruined life which she would not emulate. Had he known of it, he would have done the same: Nathaniel had been right to refuse, just as he, Edward, was right this time.

"Father, I—"

"Isabella, before you say anything, let me remind you that I have your best interests at heart. Even though you may not think so at this moment."

She stared at him. Her eyes grew large, her face paled, her hands clenched at the stuff of her skirt as if she would rip it to shreds. Finally: "I intend to marry him, Father."

"No. You will not."

A deadly silence lay between them. Then she turned and hastened from the room, nearly colliding with her mother, who had been listening at the door. "Tell him," Isabella spat out, "that if he does not consent, I will elope. That will bring more disgrace on the Family than anything—certainly more than healing an old quarrel will bring. Tell him! You have to do it, because I will no longer speak to him!"

Mrs. Revell paused for a moment, trying to think where she had failed in her maternal duties, to have confronting her now this implacable young woman who seemed never to have been taught the rudiments of proper respect for her parents. Then she went to have a word with her husband.

A short while later he was pounding on the front door of the minister's residence. Edward had remained faithful to King's Chapel even though he had moved way out to the Back Bay. The minister was home, working on his sermon. He welcomed Edward (a faithful parishioner, a generous donor) and, when he saw how distraught he was, gave him a drink of brandy. He heard Edward's tale; he thought about it for a few moments; then he gave his opinion. Forgiveness was entirely within the Christian tradition, he said; so was peace-making.

So the next day, which was Sunday, Edward sent his footman up to 43½ Beacon Street with a note inviting Mr. Hamilton Griffin Revell to call at 57 Commonwealth Avenue the following afternoon at four o'clock. He was not entirely sure of the protocol for such a situation, so he made it up as he went along. To his great relief, Hamilton accepted. Promptly at four the next day he appeared. Edward was startled to see that he was nearly an old man. He walked with a little limp, and his eyes were faded and rheumy. As they went into the drawing room, Edward caught a glimpse of movement at the top of the landing. Isabella, no doubt, spying on him, wanting a peek at her future father-in-law.

7

On the afternoon of July 23, 1870, Edward Jackson Revell stood in the doorway of his double drawing room in his house at 57 Commonwealth Avenue in the Back Bay and surveyed the first gathering of all three branches of the Revell Family in nearly three-quarters of a century.

It was, he admitted to himself, an impressive sight. The Griffins, the Jacksons, the Abbotts—how strong the Family resemblance was, not only the facial resemblance, but also the tall, thin physical frame. Some, like Hamilton's daughter Florence, were not so blond as the rest; others, like Artemas Griffin's daughters, were plumper than the norm; and (so Edward noted with interest) Artemas's son Lyman was already developing a little bald spot at the back of his head. Lyman walked with a limp, which he'd gotten at the Battle of the Wilderness in '64. And there was Artemas's and Hamilton's sister, the redoubtable Caroline, her hair pure white now under her little lace cap, but her eyes as fierce as ever, missing nothing, speaking forcefully to her niece Florence even as she kept a watchful glare on the assembly. The Abbott Revells were there, Dr. William and his little son John; and Judson, the novelist's son, a tall, thin, sickly-looking lad, looked like he needed a year out West to toughen him up. Washington had sent his regrets—no wonder, given the trouble he'd caused with his book! And there was Cousin Daniel Jackson Revell, the Abolitionist, and his little grandson, Edwin, posthumous to Daniel's son Garrison. Another of

Daniel's sons, Barrett, had also been killed in the war; his third, Parker, had bought a substitute. People said that Daniel no longer spoke to Parker for that.

Caroline came up to Edward now and gave him a grim, approving smile. "Have you heard from Wash?" she said.

"Ah—no."

"He said he'd send you a note. I'm sure he will. I think he's a bit embarrassed. He and I are great friends, you know."

"So I've heard."

"So I can speak frankly to him."

Edward wondered if there were any person on earth to whom Caroline Griffin Revell could not speak frankly.

"He always said he couldn't write about the real world—the modern life all around us. He was more comfortable in the past, he said. And now when he had this one try at a real-life story, what a mess he made! I told him so. I spoke very honestly to him. I told him that he was meddling in people's private affairs. He said he couldn't help it. He had to write what came to his head, and Isabella's and Theo's story enchanted him, he said. I told him he had no right to put people's love affairs—and difficult ones, at that—into a book for the whole world to read. I wanted you to know that he is sorry if he made any trouble. On the other hand . . ." Her forbidding, hawkish face brightened. "Perhaps he has helped to make a real love match. With a happier ending than the original Romeo and Juliet, I mean. It really is very fortuitous, don't you think?" And she waved her hand at the assembled crowd. "Look at them all," she said. "They are a fine-looking bunch, are they not? And why should we always keep separate, like—like warring clans in the primitive Highlands of Scotland, or some obscure African tribe? Think of it, Cousin Edward. We are the Revells of Boston. We have been here forever—two hundred and fifty years we have been here! Why should we allow ourselves to be separated from each other by a foolish quarrel—well, perhaps it wasn't foolish when it began, but to carry it on, decade after decade—*that* is foolish. Mark my words: your daughter will go down in the Family history book as a peacemaker—'blessed be the peacemakers,' isn't that right? I think that you are a very brave man, a great man, to make such a magnificent gesture."

Edward had not thought of himself in precisely those terms. "A great man?" Well: she was right, he supposed. The Family was together again, was it not? He cleared his throat; he signaled to the butler, who rang the little silver dinner bell. He had written a short speech, and memorized it pretty well. He nodded in a friendly way at the two-score faces in front of him: all so much alike (save for a few of the in-laws)—and all Family, that was the thing! They were all one flesh and blood, and it was time now—even as the nation had bound up its wounds—time to reconcile, to become one again. He well remembered his father's hatred of Nathaniel; he'd had to assume it was reciprocated. All nonsense. Foolishness! Time to be done with it, put the old hatreds aside. Beckoning to Hamilton, he said, "Yes—cousin—come stand beside me."

Heads turned, and a little whisper of excitement filled the room as Hamilton Griffin Revell made his way through the crowd and then joined Edward on the lower steps of the staircase so that everyone could see them together. Side by side they stood, while Edward spoke: of the importance of Family, of reconciliation, of the plain good sense not to carry on a quarrel beyond its time—and surely nearly three-quarters of a century was time enough for any quarrel.

Then Hamilton spoke, only a few words, but the sentiment was there; people felt it, they heard his voice tremble, they saw a telltale moisture in his eyes. Then Theo and Isabella were introduced, and a rousing three cheers given them, and people said what a splendid couple they were, and wasn't it grand that Cousin Edward had made such a magnificent gesture and put the old quarrel to rest?

It was, after all, only five years since the end of the bloody, fratricidal war; and only three since the varmint, the new congressman Benjamin Franklin Butler of Lowell, the erstwhile "Beast of New Orleans," had threatened the foundations of the hard-won peace by helping to impeach President Johnson. He'd failed to get the necessary votes, but only just barely. People in his home state viewed him as an ever-present danger, like a keg of dynamite waiting to explode. Certainly he had a short fuse. His very existence was a threat to that domestic tranquility that the Founders had espoused. How could anyone be tranquil when Ben Butler, Esq., was on the prowl?

So now the Family felt that their own civil war had been settled, even if the national quarrel still festered. They were, they thought, setting a splendid example for everyone else, North and South, to follow.

8

By that time, the summer of 1870, Mary Shaughnessy had been in business for six years. She was prospering: only the previous spring she had moved into a showroom in Washington Street not far from Eban Jordan's department store.

Her clients were the wives and daughters of rich men. Some of them were men who had made money honestly from government war contracts—for uniforms from a woolen factory in Fall River, for example. Others had made their money profiteering—men who manufactured shoes with paper soles, or rifles that could not shoot, or—in one notorious instance—a man who manufactured dark blue overcoats for the troops, whose dye ran the first time it rained, staining the soldiers as dark as any Negro.

Florence Revell found these customers for Mary, of course. It was perhaps not entirely proper for Florence to associate with such people, but she had connections everywhere, and in her newfound zeal to help Mary Shaughnessy, she did not mind soiling her own hands a bit. If a woman had money, and looked to be the type of woman who wanted new clothing—and what woman did not—Florence wangled an introduction to her and convinced her that Mrs. Shaughnessy was the finest dressmaker this side of M. Worth, in Paris.

As Mary had foreseen, the Revells' dressmaker was an unwilling instructor, but Mary learned quickly, and in six months she no longer had need of a tutor. What was more, she proved to have a heretofore untapped sense of style and color, which rapidly gave her an excellent reputation. That Mrs. Shaughnessy is a clever one, women said; she suggested Nile green for Delia Goodrich's new ball gown, and it turned out to be the perfect color. Delia said she'd never have thought of it herself. And Mrs. Shaughnessy is so deft and quick, she almost never needs to take a second fitting. Would I recommend her? Definitely!

Even before she was properly started, Mary sold a dress to one of Florence's friends and came away with twenty dollars profit. At once she found a new place to live, an apartment on North Anderson Street with a small extra room for her business. The rent was high, but no matter; she understood that if she and the children were to survive, they must move on.

9

Theo and Isabella were married in October. The wedding went off splendidly. The newlyweds went to Italy on their honeymoon—of course—and when they returned to Boston the following spring, they set up housekeeping in a stylish new town house that their fathers jointly financed on the water side of Beacon Street.

On their first evening in their new home, Isabella stood at the tall windows at the rear of the second floor, in the small room that would be her private sitting room, and gazed out at the sunset over the river, and leaned back into her husband's arms as he stepped up behind to embrace her. Tall as she was, he was taller. He buried his face in her thick, coiled hair and inhaled her special scent which was not perfume.

"It's not quite the Grand Canal, is it?" he said.

"No, but it's lovely, all the same."

"You like the house? Everything is suitable?"

"Yes. Everything is perfect." *As long as I have you*, she thought.

"Because if you want to change anything, you have only to say so."

"I know. But I don't want to."

He had begun to kiss the side of her neck, just below her ear. She felt herself go giddy, the way she always did when he kissed her. She turned to embrace him. The glowing red sun descended into a bank of purple clouds. The room darkened. Boston on a spring evening was not Venice, he thought: it was better than Venice, better than any place in the world. It was home.

The following year, no offspring having appeared, Isabella and Theo went abroad again, to Italy again, and the year after as well. Isabella began to be somewhat comfortable with the language (although Theo never was; he had no ear for it, he said. Plain English—by which he meant Boston English—was good enough for him). And so they missed the Great Fire that ravaged Boston in November of 1872: the entire business district burned from the water to the Common, and Henry Lee Higginson himself, the future founder of the Boston Symphony, stood guard with a shotgun at the rubble-filled doorway of his family's investment firm, not against looters from the slums, but against the men of his own class who wanted to break in and retrieve their precious pieces of paper, their millions in securities.

The Revells were hurt by the Fire, some more than others, but it made far less of an impression on Isabella's life than did a visitor in the winter of 1874, not long after she and Theo returned from what had become their annual journey to the land of Michelangelo and Leonardo. She didn't have a Leonardo—not yet—but she did have crates and crates of other things that she had bought: paintings, statues, bits and fragments of architecture, a door, a mantel—even, this time, an entire room from a palace in Venice that had been rotting away, nearly falling into a canal.

Her caller, this dull December day, was Lyman Griffin Revell—Theo's cousin, his elder by five years or so, but so cut and dried and tightly wrapped in his somber clothes, unrelieved by so much as a gold stickpin, that he seemed like a man of sixty. Lyman was known as a rising man whose prospects, even granted that he had been born to great wealth, were without limit because of his talent—his very great talent, widely acknowledged—for making money. His father, old Artemas, had died the previous year. The elder Revell had been known as a hard man. A fair judgment: business was hard, and only hard men survived in it. Lyman had learned business at his father's knee; moreover, he had had, all along, ideas of his own about how the Family's affairs should be run: the textile mills, the railroad speculations, the insurance company, the proper degree of investment in a copper mine that young Alex Agassiz was operating out in Michigan. All of these and more, including some interesting real estate ventures, had come to Lyman's hand upon his father's death, for his eldest brother had died in the war, and his next eldest, the subject of his visit to Isabella today, had abandoned the Family in a way different from death, but no less painful. So now all the burden of Artemas Griffin Revell's family fell upon the shoulders of his youngest son, Lyman; and it was to fulfill part of that duty that he had come today to see this woman who had been the subject of so much speculation, so much talk. Already she had the reputation of being something of a spendthrift—a character trait that Lyman, who worked so hard to accumulate money, found distasteful indeed.

This was not one of her days "at home," but to him, of course, she was. She received him in her little upstairs sitting room—a private place where she could conduct her têtes-à-têtes in cozy comfort instead of the formal, rather chilly drawing room. Now, as she gave him her hand, she repressed a smile as she saw that he hardly knew what to do with it. Shortly he gave it back to her and lowered his tall, spare frame into a little tufted rose velvet chair by the fire, opposite hers.

At just past four o'clock it was already growing dark, and so she summoned her little maid to draw the curtains of the windows that gave out over the Charles, lights twinkling now on the Cambridge shore, the river already frozen and covered with a light dusting of snow. A fire burned cheerily in the hearth; the tea table held a tray laden with an imposing array of delicacies, scones and tiny sandwiches and pound cake sliced thin, and Cook's wonderful lace cookies.

Lyman seemed tongue-tied, very ill at ease, Isabella thought. She was fond of men; she preferred their company to that of women, whose conversation was often stultifying. Men spoke of interesting things—politics and money and art and music—all the things that made it worth one's while to get up in the morning. And, being fond of men, Isabella understood them. She understood, for instance, that there were some men who disapproved of her: who thought perhaps that she wore her gowns cut too low, who thought perhaps that she attended too many social functions; certainly there were some who thought that she spent too much money, and that she persuaded her husband to spend too much also—who thought, in short, that Isabella lived a life far too self-indulgent, far too free. But what did they expect of her? What was she supposed to do with herself? As yet, she and Theo had not been blessed with a child, and she had to fill her days and nights somehow. So she would go on as she wished, and pay no attention to those who criticized.

Her visitor had very little aesthetic sense, but he thought as he watched her now that he understood a little better why Theo had insisted on having her. The ruddy firelight played over her thick, smooth hair, the color of old gold, which she wore pulled high to the crown of her head, not bothering with the frizzy little bangs that were the fashion just now. She had the look of a statue he had once seen in some European museum, he could not remember where, and yet she was so very lifelike, so warm and vital, her skin like satin, her mouth deliciously full, her tight-fitting bodice showing her womanly shape, never mind that she was in mourning as they all were—and that reminded him of the purpose of his visit.

She was saying something, and he'd missed it. She looked amused. "I was just saying, Cousin Lyman, that we don't see enough of you. And, ah, but you have no wife, isn't that correct? So I cannot ask for her health. Just your own." And, having given him his tea, she raised her cup and made him a little mocking toast with it.

Lyman felt himself flush. He was never comfortable with women; he was here today only at the behest of his aunt Caroline, that indomitable personage whose direct order he could not refuse.

"I insist that you speak to Isabella and Theo," she had said. "It is the only sensible thing to do."

He cleared his throat. He took a sip of tea. It was too hot; it scalded his tongue. He put down his cup and, resting his elbows on his rather bony knees, clasped his hands and peered earnestly at Isabella for a moment before he spoke. And in that moment she noted how oddly he looked like her dear husband: the same Family coloring—her own, to be sure—and general physiognomy, and yet such a different look to him! For where Theo was warm and loving, enjoying the good things of the world as much as she did, food and wine and music and art, this man before her was as cold as cold, he seemed aged beyond his years—about thirty-five, she thought.

"Isabella—" He felt awkward, calling her that, but what else was he supposed to call her? "Isabella, you know that we suffered a grievous loss while you were away."

No hint of reproach in his words, she thought, and yet she saw something in his eyes.

"Yes. I am so sorry." But of course she knew: why else would she be in mourning? Lyman's sister-in-law, his elder brother Thomas's wife, had died giving birth to a son. To escape his grief, Thomas had fled to the West, to oversee some of the Family's railroad interests.

"I had a letter from Thomas yesterday. He says he will settle out there. He has no room in his life for a child, he says. He wants the boy kept in the Family—among us, if possible. The Griffins."

"I don't think—"

"Isabella." The second time was no easier. "I wanted to talk to you alone, before Theo comes home. Because it would be your role, far more than his, to care for this child."

He saw, with some small satisfaction, that he had succeeded in unsettling her equanimity. "Yes," he went on. "That is why I have come. To ask you to take on this Family obligation. Who else could I ask? My eldest brother is dead in the war. Only one of my two sisters is married, thanks in no small part to that same war, and she has four children already. Uncle Hamilton's eldest son—Theo's brother—is dead also. Theo's sister Florence is a widow. Who else is there? Only Theo and you. And you, ah . . ." Gently reared as he had been, he did not know how to put to her the issue of her own childlessness.

She put her hands around her cup as if to warm them; although, he thought, it had been some few minutes since she had poured, and her tea must be cooled by now.

"Since you put it to me in that way, Cousin Lyman, I can hardly refuse." She stared straight at him, her dark blue eyes direct and intelligent under her thick, straight brows.

Yes, a beauty, but perhaps too forthright, he thought. Women should be more hesitant—more oblique. Bluntness in a woman was decidedly unfeminine. Still, she was a Revell twice over, a Griffin Revell by marriage: he and Thomas couldn't ask for a better home for little Frederick. And perhaps taking on the responsibility of a child would cramp her style a bit, and that wouldn't be a bad thing. As handsome and dashing as she was (and what a fine figure she'd cut on horseback!) she was a bit too—well, too showy. Revell women were usually cut from plainer cloth; despite their wealth, despite their unassailable position at the very pinnacle of Boston Society, they were a modest lot, demure and self-contained. Once upon a time, of course, there had been the beauteous Emilie: but that had been a different world. Nowadays, Revell women didn't believe in making a splash: that was for the new rich, war profiteers and the like. He didn't know where Isabella had got her streak of exhibitionism—buying all those Italian things, befriending a female opera singer last spring right here in Boston. The woman had had three lovers at once, and Isabella had invited her to dinner all the same, and one of the lovers to boot.

His ruminations were interrupted just then as Theo came in, having lingered late over his lunch at the Somerset Club and eager now, as he always was, to spend a little time alone with Isabella before they needed to dress for their evening's engagement. Although Boston was a small place, with an even smaller social circle, the two cousins seldom came across each other; they moved in different pathways, Lyman choosing to attend to his business affairs, Theo just as wealthy, but of an entirely different temperament, free to live a more leisurely life.

And so Lyman stated the matter again, and this time he saw that Isabella was more receptive, and Theo was in fact quite enthusiastic about the idea. "The very thing! We'll raise him up as if he were our own!"

Caroline was very pleased. "You see," she said, "blood will always tell!"

10

If Lyman or any other Revell thought that the addition of an infant to the Theodore Griffin Revell household would alter the lifestyle of that happy couple, they were mistaken. Isabella hired a delightful English nanny; she played with the baby for a few minutes every day, but did not disrupt her social schedule in order to do so; and she and Theo continued to make their annual trip just as they always did, but now they brought their young charge with them, nanny and all. Little Frederick seemed to thrive in this atmosphere. He grew tall and strong, a sociable lad with many friends; he was, people said, the perfect all-around boy, good at his studies, good at athletics, at ease in any social situation—and yet not so talented, not so brilliant as to be an oddity.

Lyman eventually married. His wife was pretty in a conventional way, quiet, brown-haired, somewhat retiring—a perfect lady, people said, a sweet little thing who looked to her husband for direction at all times, who would never dream of asserting herself. Modest, gentle, a devoted wife and, in time, mother.

And yet, despite the fact that he had courted her and married her and decided all on his own to make her his life's companion—despite all this, Lyman admitted to himself that she did not please him. She did not, ah, interest him. She was too demure: too dull, if the truth be told. He had not been married six months when he discovered this fact: she was unutterably, undeniably dull. She wanted nothing except to do as he wished—a marital condition that most men would have found bliss. So he would tell her what to do, what to wear, what to serve at dinner; and she would obey him; and he would find fault.

For a long time he did not know why: he could not understand why this good, obedient, loving woman did not satisfy him. But then one evening he saw Isabella at a dance. She was "chandeliering" with a string of young men, one after the other, most of them younger than she—waltzing around and around under the glittering chandelier, all eyes upon them, her figure encased in some golden stuff that made her seem a vision of gold from head to toe; and she was so beautiful, so extravagantly beautiful, laughing and flirting with the lucky devil who had her in his arms—and Theo smiling on from the sidelines, secure in her love, knowing that she was only amusing herself, none of it meant anything because she adored him and him only, Romeo to her Juliet. And it was on that evening that Lyman realized what was wrong with his marriage: not that he wanted Isabella, for he did not—but he wanted someone like her, someone joyously alive, and greedy as she was for life and all its good things. At that moment he forgot that he disapproved of her extravagance, her self-indulgence. He remembered only that he seemed to have missed something from life, but he did not know what it was—never mind how to go about finding it.

11

By 1876 Patrick Shaughnessy Jr. had been employed at the Parker House for seven years, first as a busboy (even as his Uncle John had been), and then as a waiter.

He was a bright lad, a look-sharp lad: the headwaiter told the manager that if he had ten men like young Shaughnessy, they'd have an easier time of it running the dining room, which was always busy, a popular gathering place for the Literati, for politicians, theater folk, travelers, and just about everyone else in the world, so it seemed. On a good night Patrick earned double his salary in tips.

In his spare time, mornings, odd afternoons, Sundays, he worked for Mickey Flanagan at the Hibernian Club on Cambridge Street in the West End. Mickey controlled the West End ward. He was a cadaverous man of indeterminate age, forty, fifty, with thin black hair and a thin pale face and eyes that never smiled. From their first meeting, when Patrick was still a small boy, Flanagan had spotted him: bright, energetic, willing to learn. At ten and eleven years old, Patrick had become a runner for Mickey. Every day after school he would check in at the small storefront room that served as the clubhouse, ready to perform whatever errand awaited him: to run with a message to the North End, to run with a note for the man at the Water Department at the new city hall on School Street hard by King's Chapel; to run with a bucket of beer for old Jack McCarthy, whose wife passed away last month and the old man still grieving.

But even a grieving old man had a vote worth cultivating and keeping: so beer for McCarthy, and a job for Brendan Finnerty's boy, and a word to the authorities on behalf of the new family on Lynde Street, and a basket for the Widow Kerrigan at Thanksgiving to feed her eleven children, three of whom were fine stout lads almost old enough to vote.

Because that was what it was all about, all Flanagan's activity: the vote. The vote was power. And while the Irish were a long way from having the Yankee's wealth or social position, already they had the power of the ballot box. If they stuck together, that power was theirs for the taking. Aldermen, state legislators—even the mayor's seat, even the governorship, one day would be theirs.

So vote early and often became the rule of the ward heelers, the bosses with their separate little fiefdoms: P. J. Kennedy over in East Boston and "Honey Fitz" in the North End and Smiling Jim Donovan in the South End. Come election day and they got out their "mattress vote"—a man with his bedroll who showed up at Mrs. O'Hanrahan's boarding house, say, and for the fifty cents they paid him, swore to the annual census takers that this was his permanent residence, and that yes, he would vote in this precinct. Sometimes, in a hot contest, even stranger things happened. The dead voted from their graves. Poll workers for the wrong candidate might be arrested as they gathered at the polling place, and at the end of the day, when the election was over, just as miraculously be released. Or a candidate running on stickers would find that somehow the thousands of small gummed pieces of paper that he had ordered had been printed up with his name perfectly legible in big type, but without glue on the back—and too late now to order replacements.

One of the first tasks that Patrick performed for his mentor was to run an errand down to Scollay Square to a wholesaler of imported goods. He carried a note to the proprietor; and when he had returned with the answer, Flanagan gave him an approving nod and said, "Tell me when the delivery's made, boy, an' I'll show you a trick or two."

And sure enough, the next day a large carton arrived, and Flanagan pulled back the lid to reveal—tortoiseshell combs. Patrick was mystified. Why would Mickey Flanagan want hundreds and hundreds of combs? Was he going to instruct every man in the ward how to keep his hair neat?

"Now watch, boy," said Mickey with a wink. "This is what I want y'to do." And he took a comb, and at irregular intervals he snapped off its teeth. "Now you do that to all the rest of 'em," said Mickey. And seeing the expression on Patrick's face, he added, "Here! This is why!" And he held up the gap-toothed comb to a ballot printed with the names of the candidates, and lo and behold, certain names were blacked out and certain ones showed through—the very ones Mickey wanted to win.

A rare smile flitted across Flanagan's somber face as he saw the boy's delight in the trick. "All right, then," he said. "Go to it. An'y'll be helpin' to win this important election, boy, even if nobody's hair gets combed right."

And on election morning Patrick was allowed to stand with the other poll workers at the polling place and hand out the combs, and each man receiving one was shown how to place it on the ballot so that the right names showed, so even an illiterate man would know how to vote.

By the time Patrick reached fourteen, school-leaving age, he was as likely a lad as Flanagan had ever seen. He was middling tall, brown-haired, with his mother Mary's bright brown eyes and rather pugnacious—if charming—expression. He knew everyone in the West End down to the most recent arrivals. He could listen to a man for five minutes explaining himself to Mickey, and tell you whether that man was honest or a thief, hardworking or shiftless. He could visit a family in their miserable, airless room and tell you whether that family, given decent luck, would survive or perish. He knew who Mickey Flanagan trusted (almost no one) and whom he admired (six or seven Irishmen and two Yankees).

From time to time Flanagan allowed Patrick to accompany him to the immigration office in East Boston to welcome newcomers off the boat. This was always a riotous scene, one which Flanagan, a County Galway man, remembered very well from his own arrival. "Y'see, it's all a matter of stickin' together," he would say as he loped along, Patrick trotting at his side to keep up. "I remember when I came over. I didn't know where to go, I didn't have anyone to go to, an' then I was taken up by one of Patsy Neville's runners. You never knew Patsy, but he was a lovely man. A lovely man." In Flanagan's lexicon, there was no higher praise. "An' he took me in, green as I was, an' he taught me everythin' I know today. He could'v'been th'Sewer Commissioner, Patsy could've, if the good Lord had spared him. He died of lockjaw. Durin' the war, it was. He suffered somethin' terrible. Ah, well. Hop to, boy. There's no rest for the wicked." On the ferry across to the immigration depot, Flanagan would retreat into silence as he smoked his pipe, and Patrick would watch, fascinated, as the ferryman piloted the small boat among the heavy water traffic in the harbor. From this perspective the crowded little city of Boston looked impenetrable. Church spires rose like stalagmites; the State House dome, which had recently been gilded, shone in the sunlight like a beacon. Patrick, never having known any other place in the world, thought of the city and its inhabitants as easy to deal with. Nothing frightening about it. But he had seen enough of the immigrants' bewilderment and terror to understand that to a peasant just off the land, the city was a fearsome place.

Whatever else they learned in their first weeks in the New World, the immigrants knew one thing for sure: Mickey Flanagan was their friend and salvation, and whatever he commanded them to do, they did. Usually he asked for nothing but the men's vote, once they become citizens, and this they gladly gave him.

Thus as the years passed he built an enviable organization in his ward. Hundreds of people owed their very existence to him—a job, a place to live, a word to the police when a boy got into trouble, a husband pulled out of a barroom and delivered to his family, a basket of food, a pair of shoes, a bundle of firewood or a bushel of coal. He remembered every good turn he had ever done for anyone, and on election days he called in his favors. He was the subject of considerable awe because he could estimate within a half dozen how many votes he could deliver in any given election—a more accurate figure than any other ward boss in the city could provide.

When Patrick turned twenty-one, Mickey asked him to work full-time for the Hibernian Club—which meant, for Mickey. "It'd be longer hours than the hotel," said Mickey, "but not so much heavy liftin'."

When Patrick told his mother of Flanagan's offer, she frowned and shook her head. She had higher aspirations for her eldest son than that; and while she respected Mickey Flanagan, and readily acknowledged all the good that he did, still she wanted something more for Patrick. By which she meant, more lucrative.

"I'd ask you to wait awhile," she said. "Don't be too quick to give up your job at the Parker House. Y'never know what's goin' to turn up."

Patrick smiled at her. She was a small, plump woman, the first strands of gray showing in her hair, always neatly garbed as befitted her station as the proprietress of a prosperous dressmaking establishment, always in black, for she had never ceased to mourn her husband. She worked harder than anyone Patrick knew, and she managed her business and her family both with an iron hand. Thus she had survived, and her children with her. If every Irish immigrant had had his mother's strength and determination, he thought, they would have seized control from the Yankees years ago. As it was, she served as an inspiration—or a terror—to those who knew her, and her son would no more have thought of quitting his job to take another without first consulting her, than he would have thought of abandoning the family to seek his fortune in, say, California.

"What d'y'mean?" he said. It was late on a warm summer night, the two of them sitting at the kitchen table with a glass of beer each and a cigar for Patrick.

"I mean, it's too early yet to make that kind of decision. You're young yet. I know Mickey's a good man, and he'll teach y'every trick in the book if he hasn't already. But . . ."

"What?" He watched her. Not for the first time, he thought how odd it was that an Irishman—or woman—could blather on for hours about nothing at all, but when it came time to speak a few important words, he—or she—was as tongue-tied as any Yankee.

"There's no money in it," she said at last. "Not if a man is honest. And I think Mickey is, and I know you are. So at the end of the day, what does he have to show f'r it? A thousand votes, to get someone else elected? What's he live on, anyway?"

"The members pay dues."

Mary snorted. "Dues! An' he takes his pay out of that?"

"He's honest, Ma. A dishonest man could have a fortune in graft, I'll grant you."

"You know as well as I do that honesty's no substitute f'r experience."

He laughed; he couldn't help it. Many women got through life by denying reality; his mother always seemed to embrace it.

Sharply she shook her head; she reached out and patted his hand. "Stay on at the hotel for a bit. Something will turn up. And I don't say break off with Mickey. No sense in doin' that. But just say yer old ma put her foot down, so he won't blame you. I don't want to make an enemy of him, because we might need him someday. But you'll do better than Mickey Flanagan and the Hibernian Club, see if you don't."

Some months later she heard of a small saloon for sale down by the Haymarket. The man who owned it was in financial difficulties and was willing to let it go cheap. By that time Mary had amassed a considerable savings, and she was able to convince the Columbia Bank in South Boston that Patrick was good for the balance once she'd put down half the purchase price.

So Patrick left the Parker House, and became the youngest saloon proprietor in Boston. The first week that he was open, he had a bit of trouble with the spalpeens, the boyos who wanted to drink and not pay. They were testing him, he knew, to see what they could get away with. So he summoned Mickey and his goon squad, and after one night they had things sorted out. The boyos understood: if you wanted to have a drink at Patrick Shaughnessy's saloon, you paid as you drank, and no fighting allowed.

After that he had no trouble. And from the beginning he showed a profit: men came to gawk at him, and while they gawked they drank, and by the time he ceased to be a novelty, the boy saloon keeper, his customers had formed the habit of coming to him. And besides, he had the reputation of running a reliable place, the best beer, the best whiskey, and half a dozen strongarm boys standing by to keep out the troublemakers—and, therefore, the police. A man could drink in peace at Patrick Shaughnessy's.

In the fall of 1882, shortly before his twenty-seventh birthday, Patrick attended a Sunday-evening social at the parish hall, and there he met a handsome black-haired young woman from Dorchester. Her name was Bridget McCormack. Behind her back—never to her face—people called her "the striver." It was not a criticism: in Brahmin Boston, the world of "No Irish Need Apply," only the strivers succeeded. For Bridget, as for every other woman in the world, success depended a very great deal on who she married. She was twenty-two years old, and she had not yet encountered a man who met her qualifications. But within half an hour of meeting Patrick, she knew that she had done so at last, and so while the fiddler played, she sang and danced her very best, and knew that he was watching her, and at last he joined her, and before the evening was done the course of her life was settled forever.

Shortly after Christmas they became engaged, and they married in the spring.

12

On an afternoon in June 1884, Theodore Griffin Revell, Isabella's beloved Theo, aged thirty-nine, was thrown from his horse during an afternoon's ride with his wife and several friends at his new summer place in Brookline.

He died instantly of a broken neck.

After the funeral, Isabella sent Frederick to stay with the Lyman Griffin Revells at Nahant, and she herself spent the summer not in Brookline, but in the house on Beacon Street.

She was numb: dazed, mortally wounded, she felt as though she, too, had died. She lay awake all the nights and swooned into unconsciousness during the day. It did not seem possible that Theo was gone—her beloved husband, so filled with the joy of life, with the joy of *her*—dead!

And she herself was condemned to live.

All summer she stayed in her darkened sitting room, the draperies drawn, the house shuttered and quiet. She did not want the view, she did not want company. She turned away all callers, even her own parents. At last, one day, her mother pushed her way past the startled butler and went upstairs.

"Isabella! My dear! You must stop this!" Privately, Mrs. Revell thought that her daughter had taken leave of her senses. Nothing she could say would console Isabella. And so at last she went away and ordered her doctor to call, but Isabella would not let him in.

At last one day in late August Isabella caught sight of herself in the pier glass in her bedroom and for a moment she was startled: who was this stranger— this ugly, bedraggled wraith? Why, that was Isabella Jackson Griffin Revell: once a great beauty, now a pathetic, broken creature, left behind by her husband to live out her life alone. . . .

For a moment she stared at herself in the harsh light of the gas lamps, hardly able to believe what she saw. Then in the fog of grief and pain that enshrouded her, she pushed back the heavy strands of golden hair that fell across her swollen, tearstained face. She stared into her once lovely eyes, red-rimmed and bloodshot, sunk far back into her head; and as she did so, a silent message passed between herself and her reflection: you are young, you have your life ahead of you. It is time to leave your grieving now. Come back into the world: there is much here for you, much for you to do!

A silent message; and yet the words reverberated in her head as if they had been spoken aloud.

Leave your grieving now . . .

She felt—literally felt—the weight of her sadness lifting from her shoulders.

Come back into the world . . .

She felt as though she stood at a turning in the road that was her life's journey, and now she must make the choice: right or left, life or death?

She pulled aside the heavy draperies at the windows. It was a golden day in late summer. Up and down Beacon Street carriages and wagons skirted the

trolley, and on the sidewalks children skipped and nursemaids pushed peram-
bulators and gossiped as they walked together in the sunshine.

She breathed the fresh, cool air. Her eye fell on a young man below who
seemed to be waving at her. For a moment she did not recognize him, but then
she did: Edwin Jackson Revell, grandson of Daniel the Abolitionist, her second
cousin once removed—or perhaps he was her third cousin, if such a condition
of cousinhood existed; she didn't know.

But in any case she waved back.

"Hallo, Isabella! Glorious day!"

His enthusiasm and jollity were so infectious that she could not help smiling, too. He made a little mock bow and tipped his straw boater to her, and
for no reason at all she laughed. She could not remember the last time she had
done that. She waved at him again. She was glad to have seen him. She could
not remember when she had been glad about anything. Then, turning from the
window and filled with sudden resolution, she rang for her maid and ordered
a bath. Then she put on one of the new mourning dresses that she had not yet
worn—a well-made dress, she noted, done by some Irish seamstress whom Florence knew. Then she summoned that same sister-in-law from 43½ Beacon Street.

Florence was delighted at the message. Like all the rest of the Family, and
despite her own sorrow at the death of Theo, her only surviving brother, she
had been extremely worried about Isabella, whose grief, like everything else
about her, had been lavish and extravagant.

"Dear heart! How glad I am to see you up and around!" Florence embraced
Isabella and then sat beside her on the little velvet sofa. The draperies were
drawn back, and from the river a cool breeze came in, harbinger of the autumn
to come. The water sparkled blue in the sunlight; sailboats skimmed the surface,
and back and forth across the bridge they could see a steady stream of traffic,
carriages and wagons and omnibuses—all the world going about its business.

And now Isabella wanted to be back in that world again, no matter how
painful her memories, how wounded her heart. She was young, she was alive—
and life called to her, raised her up from her sorrow.

"Florrie, I have just looked at myself in the mirror," she said. "I know
that I am in mourning. I don't have to tell you that in a sense I will be in
mourning for the rest of my life. But I am a wreck, Florrie, and Theo wouldn't
want it. You know that he wouldn't."

At the mention of her brother's name, Florence felt herself weaken, and
although she had promised herself that she would not, she began to cry.

"Stop it, Florrie. Stop it! He wouldn't want you to. And he wouldn't want
me to pine away here, either. I know it. He'd say to me, 'Go ahead, get on
with your life. Don't waste your time crying for me. Go—do whatever you
want! Buy me a picture! Sing me a song! I'll be watching you, I'll be loving you
for all time. So go ahead and live. Do it for me!' You see, Florrie? That's what
he'd want. I know it! I knew him better than I do myself. And he'd be furious
with me for turning my back on life. And I'm not going to do it anymore. I
made up my mind. I'm going abroad as soon as Frederick is settled in school—

about the middle of September. Will you come with me? We can go for the cure at Baden-Baden. They say it's wonderful. And then we'll travel down through the Alps to Venice. You've never seen the Alps? Oh, but you must! And I've had a letter from an agent in Venice; he offers a palace for rent at a bargain price, just off the Grand Canal. Oh, Florrie, say you'll come!"

Florence was taken aback by this onslaught, to say the least, but after a day or two, and after she discussed it with her mother and Isabella's as well, she acquiesced. And lest she disturb her New England conscience by enjoying herself too much, she resolved to make good use of her time abroad by hiring tutors along the way to teach her the languages. Florence had taken an interest in social work, and what with the increasing floods of immigrants pouring into the city, she was often at a loss to communicate with her charges. Italian, she thought, would be particularly helpful.

Isabella sniffed when she heard Florence's plan. "To work in the immigrant slums of Boston," she said, "the only foreign language you need to know is Gaelic! But if studying will make you happy—by all means, study away!"

3. COUSIN ISABELLA

1

On a cold and cloudy Friday afternoon a few weeks before Thanksgiving in 1889, Isabella Jackson Griffin Revell made her entrance at the Music Hall to take her seat at Symphony. She wore a plum-colored jacket and skirt of fine broadcloth, a gray silk blouse with a high collar trimmed in matching lace, and a plum-colored hat with gray ostrich feathers sweeping down the side of her cheek. Her high-button shoes and her gloves were of fine black kidskin; her muff was gray fox.

She was thirty-nine years old. People said she was the most beautiful woman in Boston. Certainly the young man who accompanied her seemed to think so: as they seated themselves, he kept his eyes fixed upon her as if he were mesmerized.

Heads turned as people watched her. She paid no attention: she was used to being observed. All the autumn just past, while she had sat for her portrait, the artist had looked and looked at her as if he would penetrate to her very soul. She hadn't minded. She'd liked it, in fact: his looking at her that way. For those hours, she'd felt as though she existed—as though she was truly alive. She had thought the end result splendid: full length, full face, her figure sharply outlined in its black velvet decolleté gown. Most women's clothing looked like upholstery, but such was the genius of John Singer Sargent that he had painted the dress to look as though it clung to her body with very little underneath.

The audience quieted; to a wave of applause, the conductor strode onstage. He was a German named Wilhelm Gericke. Henry Lee Higginson, who was single-handedly responsible for the Boston Symphony, had hired him several years ago.

Gericke lifted his baton. Then he sharply brought it down, and the first notes of the *Eroica* came spilling out. Isabella felt the little thrill that always came when the music began. Not Venice, not the reading of Dante, not even her growing collection of pictures gave her the deep, visceral satisfaction that Symphony did. She was aware that beside her the young man sat with tightly clenched hands. No doubt he was preparing a declaration of devotion similar to many others that she had heard. She had told him that he could stay to dinner—she had invited a dozen guests, as she generally did on Friday evenings—but if he was going to be a bore, she would tell him to go away.

She realized that her concentration had broken. Annoyed, she looked around the dimly lit auditorium. She recognized most of the faces in the audience, for Friday afternoons were the special time for people like herself—people whom Dr. Holmes had christened "Boston Brahmins." Three rows down and a few seats in from the aisle, she saw someone she knew, but who had never to her knowledge come to Symphony: Judson Abbott Revell's nine-year-old daughter Violet. Judson was with her, of course; as the son of the late, great Washington Abbott Revell, he prided himself on his connoisseurship of all things artistic. At a Family gathering not long ago, in fact, Isabella had had a spirited discussion with him on the relative merits of her beloved Italian Renaissance versus the modern French painters whom Judson preferred—painters who went out of doors to set up their easels and paint Nature from Nature. Also, Judson was a prissy sort, a widower whose life centered entirely on his daughter. As a result, Isabella thought, the child was abnormally unchildlike, with a long, pale Revell face and sad, wary eyes.

Gericke brought the music to a close for the moment of silence between the first and second movements. Thank God, thought Isabella, that no one clapped. In the first few years of Symphony, some people in the audience, musically innocent, would applaud at the wrong time. Henry Higginson himself would rise from his seat in the front and angrily wave his arms for silence.

The music began again, passionate, intoxicating. Her young man seemed to be leaning on her, and with an annoyed shrug she put him away. Her glance, distracted from the orchestra, met that of Judson, who had turned to look at her. He smiled and ducked his head in greeting, and she nodded in return. She didn't dislike him; she merely found him tedious. As were all men, she thought. Since Theo died, she had not met a man who interested her.

Some time ago Judson had taken her to the North Shore on the pretext of showing her Revell Hall, the rapidly disintegrating house built by his grandfather, Elias. Built to imprison a beautiful woman, Judson said, but that was not true, that was only a story that Washington had written. Judson had said that Isabella, whose wealth was so much greater than his own, might want to buy Revell Hall and restore it to its original beauty. Even more, she thought, he had wanted to make some sort of proposal to her. But he had not done so: he lacked the courage, she thought—or perhaps, after all, he was content to spend his life with his daughter. During the winters they lived in a small, charming house in Clarendon Street; summers, they decamped to a rather elaborate cottage in Lenox. The child benefitted from the fresh air, while Judson held court for the small coterie of artists and writers who went annually to the Berkshires.

Isabella had not liked Revell Hall—a wreck of a place, squirrels running about, cobwebs everywhere, rotting plaster. Certainly she hadn't wanted to take it on as a project. So the day had been only a day in the country, nothing more. She hadn't minded.

The music surged to its climax. What a passionate man Beethoven must have been! She had said that once to a very proper Boston lady, and instantly had realized her mistake when the woman, a notorious chatterer, turned bright pink and went speechless. Isabella hadn't minded that, either.

Nor did she mind that people talked about her. Let them talk if they had nothing better to do. She had decided, after Theo's death, and after her own resolve to try to live, that she would do as she pleased. Despite her determination, she felt dead herself, much of the time. She was looking for something—someone—to revive her. She had all the money in the world—more money than she would ever be able to spend, two-thirds of the Hamilton Griffin Revell fortune. Sooner or later, in addition to all her works of art, all her clothes and jewels and travel, her money would bring her a new life as well. She had to believe that.

After the concert Isabella suffered her youthful escort to accompany her home. He could amuse himself in the library, she thought, while she retreated to her room and smoked a cigarette.

Merton, the butler, greeted her with an announcement: "Master Frederick has arrived, ma'am."

"Ah . . ." She had forgotten: Frederick had his midterm break from Groton, and had arranged to bring a friend home with him.

"Very well, Merton. Show Mr. Longworth here into the library, see that he has his tea, and tell Master Frederick to come to my room." With a wave of her hand, she dismissed the hapless Longworth, who, with a despairing glance at her, reluctantly followed the butler away to the rear of the house. He was becoming a bore, she thought; she couldn't remember why she'd thought he was worth bothering with.

As she ascended the stairs, she felt the little stab of pleasure that she always did when she gazed at the paintings that covered her walls. She had many paintings by now—dozens, she supposed—for her buying had passed the point of being mere collecting: it had become an obsession. One entire room at the top of the house, in fact, had become a storage room for canvases and objets d'art that she had no room to display, and so for the past few years she had rotated the paintings on view, just as the Museum did. Recently, in fact, she had begun to consider building a museum herself—a proper place for all this relentlessly accumulating treasure.

She opened the door of her bedroom where her maid awaited her. She allowed herself to be unlaced. Then, comfortable in her peignoir and having lighted her cigarette and tasted her first sip of tea, she remembered that Frederick was supposed to come to her. It was unusual for him not to obey promptly.

"Marie, would you go fetch Master Frederick for me, please?" She remembered the friend. "Tell him to come alone, and I'll meet his friend later."

While she waited she rested on her green velvet chaise longue and tried to remember what she had ordered for dinner. Oysters, she thought, and roasted quail, and saddle of lamb. Several of the young men—her protégés all—would undoubtedly want to make toasts, so Merton would have to make sure that there was plenty of wine. But Merton would do that without being told; he was very dependable. One of the young men, she remembered, had just completed a cycle of verses, which—if he could find a publisher—he planned to dedicate to her. Another was working on an opera; perhaps, at the piano, he would play an aria or two. She hadn't the heart to tell him that Americans were no good at opera: you needed to be Italian, or German. Italian was far better. She'd heard German opera at Munich and hadn't liked it: too gloomy.

All of the young men, including poor Longworth languishing in the library, were in love with her, of course. It was good for them, she thought, to be in love with a woman so beautiful, so elegant, so worldly—and no danger of any of them, including herself, being trapped into marriage.

A tap on the door, and Frederick entered. He was a tall boy, fifteen this past summer, now in his second year at Groton—the fourth form, as they called it. The Reverend Mr. Peabody had modeled the school on the great English "public" schools, Eton and Harrow, but with a dash of stern Yankee Puritanism that would chasten the sons of the rich who were his students. Life at Groton was New England "plain living and high thinking" carried to an extreme degree, but so far Frederick seemed to like it.

Now, however, she saw that his face was somber. Dutifully he came to her and kissed her cheek as he always did; then he perched on a chair next to her.

"Well, my dear! I am delighted to see you. How is the academic world?"

"All right."

"Just all right? Is Dr. Peabody keeping you busy? And how about your friend? Did you bring him?"

"No."

"Why not? Is he sick?"

"No."

"Not sick. Then why—"

"He just—couldn't come." Frederick had gone very red in the face, and now, looking closely, she saw that his eyes were filled with tears. She was appalled. He was a strong boy—a strong human being. He hadn't cried since he was a toddler. For him to do so now meant some kind of real trouble.

"Frederick—what is wrong? I can see that you are upset. Is it something at school?"

"No." He stared at the patterned carpet, reluctant to meet her eyes. "It's nothing, really. I'm fine. School is fine. Dr. Peabody sends his regards. He said he'll stop in to see your new pictures the next time he is in Boston." He stood up. "May I be excused, please?"

She was so dismayed that she gave her consent without thinking. What had happened? For certainly something had gone wrong for him. At school, undoubtedly. Where else was there, for him? She'd get to the bottom of it.

Later, at dinner, she was pleased to see that Frederick spent some time talking to Edwin Jackson Revell, grandson of the Abolitionist, Daniel; Edwin was in his mid-twenties and just finishing up at Harvard. He had taken a few years off to travel—"to find himself," as the saying went. Isabella frequently had Harvard boys—or men, as they liked to be called—to dinner. Edwin was often among them. She'd never forgotten his happy salute to her the day she came back to life. Men almost always outnumbered women at Isabella's table, so now Edwin and Frederick sat side by side.

It was not until after the music that Isabella herself had a chance to speak to Edwin. He smiled at her and lifted his brandy glass in greeting. "Cousin Isabella. A splendid dinner."

"Thank you. I saw you talking to Frederick. How did you find him?"

"Rather sober."

"Yes. I thought so, too. Have you any idea what is wrong?"

"No. D'you want me to take him out tomorrow and have a chat in private?"

"Would you? That would help enormously." She smiled at him. He was as vulnerable to that smile as every other man in the world. "Sometimes—I don't know how to put it—sometimes I miss Theo more than other times," she said. "I mean, I always miss him, but when problems arise with Frederick—which I must say is not often, but when they do . . ."

Accordingly, the next day, Edwin invited his young relation to dine: not at his club at Harvard, which was a rowdy place, but at home—the house on West Cedar Street that he and his mother had inherited from his grandfather. At Edwin's request, his mother left the two young men to eat alone. It was not long before Edwin discovered what the matter was.

"Damn and blast 'em!" he said. "You mean they're razzin' you about it?"

Frederick nodded. He was once again on the verge of tears, and in his fifteen-year-old heart he wondered if he was what Dr. Peabody always referred to contemptuously as a "weakling."

"That's not right," Edwin said. He had a strong sense of injustice; he could never understand indifference to the world's sorrows. "It's not right at all. So your, ah, friend was bein' unpleasant, as well, and you just disinvited him, eh?"

"Yes." Frederick cleared his throat and went on. "And I gave him a good dust-up, too. Teach him to keep a civil tongue in his head."

"Lucky for you the good reverend didn't catch you. I hear he's death on fighting. All the same—good for you, boy! Nothing more admirable than a gentleman defending a woman's honor—particularly when that woman's his mother! Well! Let me think. I'll talk to Judson. I imagine he can help."

Privately, however, Edwin was not so sanguine. A nasty mess, this: and Isabella likely to find herself drummed out of decent Boston Society if she didn't watch out.

The next afternoon, a Sunday, he went around to Judson's house in Clarendon Street. This was a new place built in the popular medieval style, with a Gothic arched door and a miniature turret. Judson was in the library playing draughts with Violet. She seemed relieved when her father sent her away; Edwin caught a glimpse in the hall of a pleasant-looking young woman who was, he assumed, the child's governess.

"Well, m'boy! What can I do for you?"

"Ah, it's about your club, actually." Edwin ran his eyes over the shelves of books that lined the walls. Some of those titles were undoubtedly the tales and novels written by Judson's father, Washington. Edwin had never liked them: they were too fanciful, too remote from the real world.

"Which one? Somerset? You want me to put up your name?"

"No. No—thanks. It's about the St. Botolph, actually."

"Ah. Jolly fellows, those. Not so lively as the Tavern Club, though. Ever seen one of our revues at the Tavern? I'll send you a chit next spring when it goes on. We do even better stuff than we used to do at the Hasty Pudding when I was at the College. We dance—oh, yes. Better than the gals at the Folies Bergère, would you believe it? Hah! You should see Johnny Russell in his costume, tights and all! Jolly fun! Well! What is it?"

"It's about the exhibition."

"At the St. Botolph? Oh! You mean the Sargent canvases. I don't like him, myself. Too, ah, *rude*, if you know what I mean."

"But you've seen it."

"Oh, yes. It's been up for the better part of a month, I should think."

"And you've seen the portrait of Cousin Isabella."

A faint expression of distaste flitted across Judson's face. "How could I help seeing it? They gave it the place of honor. Y'want to take a look? Come along, it's just over on Newbury Street."

The day was gray and raw, with an east wind coming off the harbor to cut like a knife through the stoutest woolen overcoat. The two men hurried around the corner to the narrow red-brick building that housed the St. Botolph Club, named for the English saint who had given his contracted name to both the English and the Massachusetts towns.

The Back Bay had been building for thirty years and more now, and at last it had begun to look as it was intended to look: like the long, elegant boulevards of Baron Haussman's Paris. Many of the houses had the new French mansard roof; many others were built in styles varying from Gothic to Renaissance to a bastard melding of the two, limestone, panel brick, or perhaps the new and very fashionable brownstone. They were all attached, all in a row from block to block down the long straight vistas of Newbury and Commonwealth and Marlborough and Beacon; and yet, varying in design as they did, they all somehow blended into a harmonious and unified whole. In that age of restless, ruthless individualism, every architect here bent his ego to the demands of the entire streetscape; it would have been thought bad manners indeed to attempt a design that did not fit. Even the Trinity Church rectory a block or so from

Judson's place, even the vast white Vendome Hotel a block up on Common-wealth, were designed to match their settings rather than quarrel with them.

At the St. Botolph the members lounged in lazy comfort. The air was thick with smoke from expensive cigars; the sound of well-bred conversation hummed from a dozen or so leather chairs in the downstairs lounge, while from some-where overhead came the faint *click-click* of a game of billiards.

"This way," said Judson. He led Edwin to the back, to a large, skylit exhibition room whose walls were lined with pictures, mostly portraits, all done in the extravagant, unmistakable style of John Singer Sargent.

And in the center of the back wall, set a little apart from the others and obviously intended to have the place of honor, was the portrait of Cousin Isabella.

Edwin was hardly a connoisseur; he was interested in the real world, not in its distillation through someone's eyes. But even he could see that the artist with typical boldness had portrayed Isabella in a most shocking way. She might as well have been naked, so suggestive was Sargent's portrayal. Edwin wondered if, posing, she had really had that intriguing, inviting smile, if her lovely blue eyes had been shining with just that irresistible promise. And the dress—!

"Well, there it is," muttered Judson. "Bit too much, what?"

For the moment they were alone in the little gallery. Edwin was glad that no stranger was at his elbow to see his reaction; he could not take his eyes away, and yet his face was hot, he was sure that he was blushing.

"I think Billy Sears's boy is at Groton," said Judson. "That's probably how they got wind of it. They're razzin' Frederick, y'say? Understandable. It's too bad, but understandable."

By now, after the first shock of it, Edwin had had time to examine the portrait more carefully. He saw, for instance, that the artist had included, on a gleaming wooden chest of drawers in the background, a pair of silver candle-sticks. "I say—are those the ones in the Copley portraits at Cousin Lyman's?"

"That's right." Judson tasted the sour tang of envy as he spoke; he thought that of all the pieces that old Jedediah Revell had made, two centuries ago, those candlesticks were the finest. He had always coveted them. "She wanted 'em in the picture, so Lyman lent 'em to her." It was not fair that they always stayed with the Griffin Revells; they should rotate, he thought. Before you knew it, they would be whisked away from the Family altogether and deposited in the Museum, and he would have to share them with everyone in the world.

"Lyman has the Copleys and he has the candlesticks as well," he said. "Hardly seems fair, what?"

But Edwin did not care to pursue the issue he had raised. The purpose of this visit today was to inspect Isabella's portrait and see what could be done to extricate young Frederick from a predicament not of his making.

"I think we should speak to Mr. Sargent," he said. "I believe he's in town?"

"Yes—yes, he is," Judson replied. "Ah, what will we say? That we think the thing's indecent? And what about Cousin Isabella? She'll surely have a word or two to contribute."

She did, of course. The word was "Nonsense!" But as she came to see that Frederick really was suffering under the gibes of his schoolmates—"filthy little buggers, but there you are, boys will be boys," said Edwin—she agreed at last to ask the artist to remove her portrait from the exhibition at the St. Botolph Club.

The artist was no happier than she about the necessity to take it down, but he could hardly refuse: he wanted commissions from these rich folks of Boston, and if he proved too stubborn, they would take their business elsewhere.

So the canvas was removed, and Isabella stored it away in her attic. Those who knew about the affair praised her for her good sense; they would have been less approving had they known that far from intimidating her, the contretemps only stiffened her resolution to make a proper home for her acquisitions, including the Sargent portrait of herself.

At Groton the boys found something else to snicker about, and Frederick was left in peace. Dr. Peabody heard about the affair, of course, and the next time he was in Boston he called on Isabella, insisted on seeing the picture, and told her she had done the right thing. "Too, ah, European, my dear," he said. "It looks rather French, y'know. Not the type of thing for Boston at all."

Isabella gritted her teeth as she smiled at him. She did not mention her plan; she lowered her eyes and assumed a modest air and wondered how long it would be before he went away and left her in peace. From now on, she thought, she would abandon the custom of being "at home" one or two afternoons a week; you were at the mercy of anyone who chose to inflict himself on you, and no matter how annoyed you were, you had to be polite. She was tired of being polite; the older she grew, the more she wanted to be herself.

Whoever that was.

2

Those were good times, the decades after the Civil War. While the rest of the nation was caught up in the hustle and bustle of building—expanding across the continent, railroads crisscrossing the plains, coal being mined, steel being born from the great roaring furnaces of what was already the industrial heartland, Wall Street jugglers playing fast and loose with their stocks and their bonds— while all this was going on, Massachusetts basked in the contented glow of past accomplishments. Massachusetts had no need to hustle. People there had already done their hustling. Now they could rest easy, and collect their dividends: for it was Massachusetts money that was financing the nation in its industrial expansion.

They grew a trifle smug. William Tudor, whose brother Frederick had made a fortune selling ice to the tropics as far away as India, said that Boston was the Athens of America. Dr. Oliver Wendell Holmes said that the State-house was the hub of the solar system.

Everyone was extremely genteel: and the more the feisty, brawling Irish crowded in, pushing and shoving their way up the ladder, the more genteel the Anglo-Saxons became. They withdrew, they retreated into their own world of clubs and corporations and cultural and charitable boards of trustees, into exclusive suburbs where the Irish were not allowed except as servants—Chestnut Hill and Milton and Pride's Crossing and Beverly Farms.

And year by year, house by house, block by block, the Back Bay went up: long avenues of brick and brownstone, elegant town houses punctuated by occasional churches that had forsaken the theological passions that rocked them once upon a time. Now, they were as genteel as their parishioners.

But the theological giants had gone, and the others as well: the men who made the American Revolution, who founded the China Trade and birthed the Industrial Revolution.

And the literary giants were all dead, too, or nearly so: Hawthorne and Longfellow and Whittier, and poor Melville; and their friends the Transcendentalists of the School of Concord, Emerson and old Bronson Alcott. Now remained old Bronson's daughter, Louisa May, with her moral tales and her heavy mantle of respectability and duty and the suppression of female anger. Miss Alcott tried to keep *Huckleberry Finn* out of the Concord Public Library. *Huckleberry*, she said, was not the sort of story to give to our pure-minded boys and girls. Many people, including *Huck*'s author, were sorry when she failed. The publicity resulting from her attempt, he said, was wonderful—better than anything.

Boston, too, seemed a twilight place now; and it was at this time that the American impressionist Childe Hassam looked out the window of his studio at 143 Tremont Street and painted the quintessential Boston picture, *Boston Common at Twilight*: an exquisite, romantic scene of snow and rosy western sky, leafless black trees silhouetted against the horizon, a little girl feeding winter birds along the Tremont Street mall.

In those days the most widely read authors were two men somewhat less literary than the Concord lights, or even than the realist William Dean Howells, who edited the *Atlantic Monthly*. Emily Dickinson, of course, was better than any of them, but no one knew about her then. She died in 1886; like Melville, she had to wait another fifty years for recognition.

Together the two new authors embodied the two strains of character that had existed uneasily side by side ever since the first Pilgrim set foot on Cape Cod two and a half centuries before: Yankee/energetic/worldly hustler-for-a-dollar; and Utopian/dreamer/seeker of a better world.

They were both sons of clergymen. Other than that, they had nothing in common.

The first, Horatio Alger, was born in Revere, just up the coast from Boston. After attending Harvard Divinity School, he went to Paris. He did something there—no one knew exactly what—that led him to renounce the ministry. He came home and began to write moralistic little tracts. His name became synonymous with the American Dream: simpleminded tales of wish fulfillment in which a plucky, energetic poor boy with an eye for the main chance makes good. *Tattered Tom, Ragged Dick, From Canal Boy to President, From Farm Boy to Senator*—like many writers, he had but one story to tell, and he told it over and over again. And, like his heroes, he got rich. Unlike them, he spent all his money and died poor.

The second, Edward Bellamy, was born in the factory town of Chicopee, just north of Springfield on the Connecticut River. In 1888 he published *Looking Backward*—a Utopian novel set in the Boston of the year 2000. Its thesis was that the predatory capitalism of the Gilded Age was not only self-defeating, but ultimately unworkable. It was a book that the public was waiting for, it seemed, because within a few years it had sold a million copies—making Bellamy even richer than Alger—and had been published around the world, translated into German and French and Arabic, Italian and Russian, and even Bulgarian—languages that sounded very strange indeed to the Yankee ear.

One of the most enduring literary efforts from those years came from the streets: a bit of doggerel out of Fall River. It concerned the murder of Asa Borden and his wife one hot day in August 1892. They were butchered—hacked to death. People were horrified—and they were even more horrified when Asa's daughter was arrested and charged with the crime. True, she hadn't liked her stepmother. But not liking was one thing, murder another. Eventually she was tried and acquitted, but people never stopped arguing about the case. She lived the rest of her life as a recluse, right there in Fall River. Sometimes the neighborhood children, who like all children could be very cruel, would stand outside the gate of her house on warm summer evenings and chant:

> Lizzie Borden took an ax
> And gave her father forty whacks,
> And when she saw what she had done
> She gave her mother forty-one.

3

"The Boston Brahmin is a curious beast," said Edwin Jackson Revell. He was slightly drunk; as he stood at the members' bar of the Union Club in Park Street, he put his hand on the polished mahogany surface to steady himself. "Consider: the Boston Brahmin has the brain of an elephant for his memory. He has the body of a mule for his strength. He has the shell of a turtle, for not only is he that slow, he has that imperviousness to the world's slings and arrows. He has the feet of a camel, for he can walk great distances. And lastly, my friends, he has an instrument of Nature as mighty as the whale's, for the Brahmin, like the Irish he despises, is a prolific procreator!"

Dead silence. A dozen pale faces watched him; they seemed to sway up and down. Or perhaps it was the floor under his feet that swayed, he didn't know.

After a time, he couldn't tell how long, a low hum of conversation filled the room; drunk as he was, he was aware that none of it was directed toward him.

His grandfather, Daniel the Abolitionist, had been a founding member of the Union Club during the war, when the Cotton Whigs of the Somerset had proved too sympathetic to the southern side. That generation—the Civil War generation—had been made of sterner stuff than Edwin's own. He was aware that many of his contemporaries lived the life of the idle rich, comfortable on the proceeds of their trust funds, no matter that some of those trusts were of the "spendthrift" variety, set up by vigilant fathers and grandfathers with stingy terms to ensure that their descendents did not run through the family fortune. He himself was the beneficiary of two such trusts, whose small income allowed him to be here this evening, drinking too much, talking too much, putting off the day of reckoning when he would need to decide what to do with the rest of his life.

He felt suddenly sick of the Union Club; or perhaps he was sick of himself, he didn't know. He turned and walked carefully into the hall and down the stairs to collect his hat and his cane from the porter.

"Good night, Sam."

"Evenin', Mr. Revell."

He stood on the front steps. To his right, a few hundred yards up the sharply sloping street, loomed the State House. They'd gilded the dome in '74, and now in the moonlight it gleamed softly above the colonnaded front. Ahead of him was the darkness of the Common, picked out with occasional street-lamps. The Common was formerly safe at night, but in recent years, with the arrival of so many poverty-stricken immigrants, you walked there after dark at your peril.

He went up Park to Beacon and turned left. It was an October night, not cold, but the wind brisk enough to remind him that the long New England winter lay ahead. He didn't mind winter; rather liked it, in fact.

His head cleared as he negotiated the uneven brick sidewalk down Beacon Street. In the tall, elegant town houses that lined the way, he could see through open shutters into the tastefully decorated parlors; several times he saw the inhabitants, well-dressed men and women, many of whom he knew. By the time he reached Charles Street he was pretty well sobered up. If he were headed home, he'd turn right at this corner. He did not want to go home; he lived alone since his mother died, not long after he graduated from the College, so no one waited up for him. He walked on. Now to his left stretched the Public Garden, as dark as the Common. A pleasant place in the daytime, with the swan boats plying the little lagoon, back and forth under the miniature suspension bridge. But not at night, no more than the Common.

Past Arlington Street, past Berkeley. He'd had a destination all along, but he'd not wanted to admit it even to himself: Isabella's house. He came to it; he stopped. All dark except a light in a small window on the top floor, which was probably the housekeeper's room. Isabella was abroad. He had known that. He had walked to her house on the wild hope that perhaps unexpectedly she'd come back. He was sober now, and yet just at that moment he felt a little giddy, thinking of Isabella, thinking of her slender, graceful hands pouring out his tea, her beautiful eyes smiling at him—

Stop it! He shook his head and turned and began rapidly to walk home to West Cedar Street.

And the next morning he went to the offices of the Boston *Transcript* where, the previous week, he'd had a chat with the editor. Now, he said, he was ready to take the job that had been offered him: staff reporter. For a long time he'd been restless—bored, dissatisfied with his comfortable existence, want-ing—what? Something else, he thought. He had no idea what. This job—far too humble for a Boston Revell—might be the means to find out.

4

"On the other hand," said Isabella, "I want it. And if I want it, I see no reason why I shouldn't have it."

"No reason at all," said her companion. He took her hand and held it to his lips; after a moment, when he did not let go, she took it back. "La grande Isabella should have anything in the world she desires. Bella, bella, Isabella." He took her hand again, and this time he turned it over and kissed her palm and then her wrist.

She let him. She didn't mind. He was a good-looking youth, twenty-five years old, a southerner. His family had sent him to Europe to take the Grand Tour. So far he had seen London, where he had met Isabella in the winter, and Venice, where he had traveled with her and where he had spent most of his waking hours at her rented palace just off the Grand Canal.

That afternoon, Isabella had had a visit from a picture dealer. He had of-fered a Botticelli Madonna with an impeccable provenance: it was owned by a prince, a genuine prince whose family, centuries ago, had commissioned it from the artist.

Now the prince, on hard times, was prepared to offer to the very rich American lady this finest fruit of the Italian Renaissance. There were not very many genuine Botticellis available: a devoted and addicted collector like herself could hardly refuse such an opportunity.

Ah, he was clever, that prince—and the dealer, too: they knew Isabella, they knew that she could well afford to indulge herself.

The dealer had had a photograph prepared. He slid it from its envelope with great care, as if he handled the painting itself. "There," he said. "Even in a photograph you can see how splendid it is."

Isabella took it and studied it for a moment. He was right, of course: if it was the real thing, which it probably was, she had to have it.

She agreed to go to look at it the following day. By now she had a repu-tation the length and breadth of Italy: she was insatiably acquisitive, and she was very very rich. Neither she nor the dealer was so crass as to mention money, but she knew that the price, when it was announced, would be a fine high one.

A breeze from the canal set the candle flames to dancing. A gondolier's song drifted up to them. The young man's lips caressed her skin. Truth to tell—and Isabella was surprisingly honest with herself, if not with others—she wanted that scrap of paint and canvas far more than she wanted him. That was where her lust directed her: to works of art, works of genius, inanimate things. She watched his handsome head bent over her hand. He was good-looking, but really something of a bore. For one terrible moment, as she watched him, she realized that she could not remember his name. That had never happened to her; she had had many admirers over the years, young and not young, and she had always been able to keep them sorted out, their names, their native cities, the reasons why she allowed them to approach her, and sometimes to make love to her as this young man was attempting to do now.

But he wasn't very interesting at all. She was tired of him. With a gesture of irritation, she shook him off. He lifted mournful eyes, begging her to be kind. They all did that: the more she shooed them away, the more they cast themselves at her feet.

"Please," he murmured. "Please." In one swift movement he slid from his chair opposite her and knelt before her, burying his pretty face in her silken lap.

Sometimes when a young man did that, she felt a faint, answering tremor of arousal within herself, and so she would let him continue. But most of the time she felt the way she did now: dead, or at least deep asleep—incapable of being awakened.

"Stop it," she said.

But she always allowed the next one to try, or at least to begin—to see if he could call from within her that glorious, joyful arousal that she had experienced with her husband, and that she had not felt since he died.

She couldn't feel anything: that was the frightening part. Couldn't feel joy, or sorrow, or fear—nothing. That was why she kept a string of young men around her (much to the outrage of proper Boston Society back home), and that was why she traveled so restlessly and why she spent so recklessly—trying to bring herself back to life, trying to feel something—anything!—once again. As she had done when Theo was alive. As she had done when Theo made love to her. Aside from music, the only activity that gave her anything like it was the buying of pictures and statues and tapestries and—one time—a magnificent illuminated manuscript. At those times she came a little bit alive again.

She had tried to explain, once, to Florence. But Florence hadn't understood; she'd loved Theo as a sister, of course, and apparently her relationship with her own husband, short-lived as it had been, had not been what Isabella's had been with Theo.

And so Isabella sat in a rented, decaying Venetian palace with a young man who hadn't the faintest idea how to handle her—he was as incompetent as any smooth-faced schoolboy—and mourned once again what she had lost.

Ah, Theo, why did you leave me?

She heard her voice in her ears so loud that she thought for a moment that she must have cried out. But apparently she had not. The servant had come in to clear the remains of their supper, and his dark, impenetrable face was as expressionless as ever. The young man had not bothered to rise, but now Isabella, annoyed, kicked at him and pushed him away with a little exclamation. The servant didn't seem to notice that, either. He lifted the tray laden with dirty dishes and silently went away. Isabella looked at the pendant watch pinned to her bosom: eleven-thirty. The whole long night to get through. She hated the nights.

The young man bent over her, his hands clasping her bare shoulders. Longingly he peered into her face. "Please," he whispered.

"Please what?" she snapped. Really, he was very irritating. But at least now she had remembered his name. "Sidney," she added.

He bent and kissed her neck. "Let me come to you tonight," he whispered.

Eleven thirty-five: hours and hours to endure before tomorrow. When perhaps at last she would find—what?

She remembered the Botticelli. Yes: she had that to look forward to, at least.

And in the meantime . . .

"All right," she said. "Just this once."

And turned her face away so that he would not see her expression of contempt, or the tears that suddenly threatened to spill from her beautiful eyes.

5

For the most part, the Revells didn't mind that Edwin took an ordinary job like that of journalist. They viewed it as evidence of his eccentricity; and eccentricity was perfectly acceptable, every New England family had its share of eccentrics.

The activities of Dr. William's son, John, were another matter. John had graduated from the College in '83. He was a clever boy, people said; too clever, perhaps. Like his father, he had a pronounced scientific bent. At the College he'd gotten a lesser education than Boston Tech would have given him, but no matter. He was an indifferent student impatient with the drudgery of classwork. His chums at the Porcellian had always found John rather arrogant, and if he was arrogant to Porcellians, he was well-nigh unbearable to ordinary mortals. He had the sense that as the century drew to a close, great things were going to happen—scientific things. A New Age was dawning. He wanted to be part of it.

He'd never forgotten the night some years ago when his father took him to a preview, as it were, of that bright dawn: a meeting of the American Academy of Arts and Sciences, a demonstration of an amazing new machine. Dr. William Abbott Revell had spent years working with deaf and blind children at the Perkins Institute; meanwhile, Professor Alexander Graham Bell, who taught at Boston University, had been trying to invent a device that would help the deaf to hear. Instead, he had developed a device that promised to revolutionize the world.

He called it the electric speaking telephone. In the months since he had received his patent for it, he had given a series of public demonstrations, including one at the Centennial Exhibition at Philadelphia for which he received the gold medal. Now, on this mild spring night, his expectant audience gathered to see the new wonder for themselves.

In his pronounced Scots accent, Professor Bell explained that two miles away in East Cambridge his assistant, Thomas Watson, awaited the signal to speak. Then he held up an odd-looking bit of machinery and spoke into it:

"Do you hear what I say, Watson?"

And from far across the river—no, from the piece of machinery!—came a voice that those who knew Watson recognized as his: "I do."

"Would you speak to us, please?"

There was the sound of a throat being cleared—Watson had recently recovered from typhoid fever—and then came his voice again, eerie, disembodied, and yet indisputably his:

> "To be or not to be: that is the question:
> Whether 'tis nobler in the mind to suffer
> The slings and arrows of outrageous fortune,
> Or to take arms against a sea of troubles,
> And by opposing, end them? . . ."

The gentlemen of the Academy looked at each other in amazement. This was much better even than a séance! This was—absolutely astounding! And—if the machine could be made to work reliably—a sure-fire moneymaker!

In the fall of '83 John took ship around the Horn, just as his ancestors had done, but for different reasons. John hadn't been interested in trade: he'd simply wanted to live as far away from Massachusetts as possible.

That wasn't eccentricity, said the Family. That was insanity.

He'd been gone for seven years. He'd lived in Japan—lived like a Japanese, learned the language—even written a book about the place. He seemed to believe that the West should pay special attention to that small, inward-looking country so alien to the Yankee world. He'd sent back crates and crates of pottery and statues and paintings and all kinds of artifacts which he'd given to the Museum in Copley Square. But the Museum had no room to display them, and so only a few pieces were on view; the rest were stored in the basement.

When John came home at last, he announced that he'd developed a new interest: astronomy. He set up a telescope in the cupola of his father's house in Cambridge. For two years he made observations of the planet Mars, but he was unhappy with his progress. The Massachusetts sky was cloudy more often than not, the atmosphere less than pure. His work was proceeding too slowly. Moreover, he needed a larger refractor. Already he'd made an exploratory trip to Arizona to search for a place to build an observatory. In the summer of 1894 Mars would be in conjunction with Earth. He planned to be ready for it.

6

"Here we are, sir. The completed statements for the year."

Lyman Griffin Revell nodded as the accountant placed the heavy volume on the polished table: the year's profit and loss statement for the enterprise that his grandfather, Nathaniel, had founded, the Commonwealth Mill in Lowell.

"And what is the final tally?" Like a good trial lawyer, Lyman knew the answer before he asked the question.

"Ah, we're up a bit. Not what we were before the crash, of course. Dividends at two percent."

The stock market crash of the previous year, 1893, had been disastrous; the resulting depression showed no signs of abating. Lyman knew that he was fortunate to have even two percent. Nevertheless, it was hardly enough. He felt compelled to make a better showing than that to his stockholders.

"All right. I'll take a look."

For several hours that morning he studied the long columns of figures, page after page of expenses, the price of raw cotton, the cost of dyes, the cost of machinery, the price of waterpower. All of his expenses were fixed. The only place where he could cut costs, and therefore raise the stockholders' dividends, was the cost of wages.

Accordingly, he made his decision. That afternoon he sent word to the resident agent in Lowell: the following week, institute a pay cut of ten percent.

Somehow word got out; within twenty-four hours every operative on the corporation knew that his or her wages were going down. Some of the hands thought that this would be an appropriate time for a show of strength.

Someone tipped off the journalist Edwin Jackson Revell, too, and so he went to Lowell and took a room at the Merrimack House so as to be on the scene early Monday morning when the workers turned out. He was bored with writing up the activities of the Boston Common Council; this, he thought, was a much more interesting story. Now, in the gray half-light, he walked the short distance to the mill. A fine, stinging snow had begun to whiten the streets; the muffled figures of the mill hands hurried past him to get to their places before the gates were locked. From the white belfry atop the huge, red-brick mill complex, the bell tolled them in. These folks, Edwin thought, must be the unskilled hands, who were not organized.

He hurried along, propelled by the wind. At the end of the street loomed the mill buildings. A crowd had begun to form at the gates, and now Edwin saw that the workers were not going in after all, for the gates were shut. The hands thronged in a growing crowd, voices rising in anger and confusion. "What's goin' on? Let us in! This is none of our affair—let us work!" And many of the voices cried out in foreign tongues, strange-sounding languages that Edwin had never heard, and the faces of the crowd were foreign-looking faces, swarthy and dark-eyed.

Now at the mill gate a man leaped onto the back of a wagon and held up his hands for silence. Around him, others held up signs: "MULE-SPINNERS OF THE U.S. ON STRIKE."

"Fellow workers! Fellow factory slaves! Listen to me! We will take no wage cut from the Commonwealth Corporation! Even as I speak to you here, the mule-spinners in every mill in Lowell are turning out! We will stay out until our wages are restored! They bleed us to death and grow fat on us, and I tell you that we will have no more of it! Workers of the world, unite! You have nothing to lose but yer chains!"

With a dramatic flourish he turned to the closed gates, shook his fist and shouted, "You greedy bloodsuckers! I know yer there! An' you can hear me! An' you can tell yer high muckety-muck, yer high an' mighty treasurer, Mr. Lyman Griffin Revell, that we can wait him out, because he's losin' a lot more money than we are!"

A few ragged cheers greeted his words, but most of the crowd, which by now numbered several hundred at least, stood silent and sullen in the rapidly thickening snow. Then someone cried, "Let us in! We want to work!" Some of his fellows tried to shush him, but others joined in: "That's right! We are weavers!"—or dyers, or sweepers, or cutters—"and we are not on strike! Let us in to work!"

There was no response. The gates stayed shut and locked. Another striker got up to harangue the crowd, to plead for its support, and then another— coughing as the cold air seared their damaged lungs, shivering in their thin coats. Some of the onlookers cried their support for the turnout, but most did not. They were poor folk, living from week to week on their meager pay, never able to make ends meet, always in debt to the landlord or the grocer or the doctor. They wanted no part of a strike, most of them—and they knew all too well that they would suffer along with the instigators, the militants of the mule-spinners' union, which never since its inception two decades before had had a successful strike, not in Lowell or any other mill town. To strike was to court death: everyone understood that. Not only was the striker dismissed; he or she was blacklisted, never to work in this city again. To find work, he needed to move himself and his family to some other place—an almost unthinkable task for an immigrant who found security in this new land only by congregating with his fellow countrymen. And sometimes the strikers' names were sent around on a blacklist, so that not even in a new town could they find a job.

So despite the speedups and the wage cuts and no guarantee of steady work, there were few successful strikes—not in the Massachusetts mills, not in the mines farther south, not in the machine shops all across the land making the engines of this mighty new industrial nation whose way to greatness, whose own native Industrial Revolution, had begun here on the banks of the Merrimack, just as her political revolution had begun in the narrow streets of Boston Town a century and more before.

Indeed, when Lyman Griffin Revell learned that the mule-spinners on the Commonwealth Corporation had called a strike, he sent word at once to the resident agent in Lowell: lock everyone out. In his years at the head of one or another of a dozen cotton manufacturing corporations, he had learned one lesson and learned it well: he and he alone would dictate the terms on which the mills would run, and he would tolerate no trouble from his employees. When, in order to preserve their dividends, he and his board of directors decided that wages must be cut, then wages must be cut. The mill hands must accept the new rate of pay or look for work elsewhere.

This was not the first strike he'd had to deal with: far from it. Over the years, he'd had literally hundreds of slowdowns, work stoppages, out-and-out strikes—and he'd never been beaten. Never once. By now he had a reputation: he's a hard, hard man, people said. Never gives an inch. Bad working conditions? Low pay? Go elsewhere to work, he'd say. Perhaps some other corporation will let you start a union, but you won't start one here. In recent years, he knew, some of the skilled hands had tried to form a nationwide union. The National Mule-Spinners? he said. I don't allow unions. They won't organize here. Any man who says he's a member will never work on any corporation of mine again.

On the morning of the strike, Lyman breakfasted as usual at seven o'clock in his house on Louisburg Square, Boston. Afterward, instead of walking down to his offices in State Street, he walked in the opposite direction to the depot and caught the eight-fifteen train to Lowell; by nine o'clock he was on the scene, looking down past a sea of heads toward the closed and locked factory gates. Two Pinkerton security guards fell into step at his side as he began to make his way down Dutton Street through the crowd.

Not one in a hundred people knew who he was, of course. Not one in two hundred. But in his black top hat and his dark gray Inverness cape, he made an imposing figure. They could see that he was someone of importance, and therefore possibly someone who could help them. For that was what they wanted: help. They didn't want to strike, not the majority of them. They simply wanted to get back to work so that at the end of the week they could take home their pay, miserable though it was, and help their families to survive in this harsh new world so different from the old, and yet, in its harshness, not so different after all.

"Hey, mister," some of them called, not in a rude way, nothing uppity—rather, they were pleading, begging him to listen to them, to help them. "Hey, mister! Tell 'em to open the gates! Tell 'em we want to work."

He paid no attention. He knew how to break a strike, and talking to operatives in the street was not it. He lifted his blackthorn walking stick and rapped sharply at the gate—to have rung the bell would have made him seem like any ordinary person. From their perch on the wagon the strike leaders were still trying to whip up support from the crowd, but they could not: the sullen throng simply stood quietly, uneasily, knowing that with every passing minute their chances to keep their jobs, and therefore their lives, were ebbing like a fast tide. Some of these people, Lyman reflected, might have heard of the recent unpleasantness in Illinois, where the Pullman Palace Car Company had broken a bloody strike using Pinkerton guards just like the ones who stood by him now, and military troops as well.

Once inside, he received the agent's report. The resident manager of the mill—the man who lived in Lowell to oversee the day-to-day operation of the factory—was a little martinet with a nervous twitch in his left eye. Yes, he said: he knew the names of the troublemakers. He thought that he could find at least a skeleton crew of spinners to replace them. Give him a day or two and he thought he might be able to start up the works again. These troublemakers would be fired—yes, yes, of course, fired and blacklisted as well. They'd never work in any mill in Lowell again—or Lawrence or Fall River or Chicopee, either.

Lyman nodded. That's right—teach 'em a lesson one more time. It was odd, he thought, how the lesson never seemed to stick. *He would not tolerate a strike.* Further, he would not tolerate a union of any kind. He made the rules; others obeyed them.

Through the windows of the agent's little office he saw half a dozen men: the overseers, come to get their orders. He went out to speak to them. Then, accompanied by his guards, he left the mill yard and walked back down Dutton Street. The throng was silent this time, watching him go. He kept his head high, not meeting anyone's eye; but just as he reached the corner of Merrimack Street, for some reason he glanced at a row of men, and one of the faces leaped out at him. A familiar-looking face: a Revell face, in fact.

Edwin Jackson Revell. He met Lyman's eyes for no more than an instant and then abruptly turned away.

Damned impudence! Lyman was old enough to remember a time when Griffin Revells did not speak to Jackson Revells. Apparently Edwin wanted to revive it.

But then he remembered also that Edwin had a job—an ordinary job, not a position in one of the Family firms. Journalism, it was: no fit work for a gentleman. Why was he here? What was of any interest to him in Lowell? For surely he wasn't going to be foolish enough to write about the events of this day. No one would read that stuff!

Lyman realized that the sight of his young relative had unnerved him—as much as a hard-headed old Yankee like himself could be unnerved. With a curt word he dismissed his guards at the depot and boarded the train for Boston.

Some time later Edwin went back to the *Transcript* office and handed in his account of the events in Lowell.

"Are you out of your mind?" said his editor. "Who told you to write this?"

He slapped the sheets of paper with the back of his hand and thrust them under Edwin's nose. "Well? What about it?"

"I thought it was a good story," said Edwin.

"Good story? For the *Globe*, perhaps. Not for us. Our readers don't want to read about things like this. Our readers are ladies and gentlemen, in case you had forgotten."

"Many of whom have stock in the mills."

"And who depend on the managers to look out for their interests! They don't need the likes of you, stirring up trouble! Why, it's your very own folks, some of 'em, that own those mills, don't they? So what're you doin' writin' about the damned troublemakers?"

"I thought it was a good story," Edwin said again.

"It's not your business to think! Don't talk back to me, Revell, or I'll have your job so fast it'll make your head spin!"

After which, it was really impossible for Edwin to stay on at the *Transcript*. And so he left, and he took his story with him. Several weeks later, when it was no longer news, he finally got it published in an obscure radical sheet in New York.

By that time the management of the Commonwealth Mill had broken the strike and fired its ringleaders. Those workers who were allowed to return to their jobs returned at the new rate of pay: ten percent less.

7

"I'm tellin' y', so help me God," said Hennessey. "I saw him with my own eyes, walkin' down Bowdoin Street."

Patrick wanted to laugh, but on the other hand the matter was too serious for that, and so he struggled to keep a straight face.

"And you say, he wants to be on the ballot?" he said.

"That's right. Thomas N. Kavanagh for mayor—on the Republican ticket! Did y'ever hear the like? He'll be struck down dead, see if he isn't. A Republican Irishman!"

Hennessey's broad, freckled face was slack with astonishment. He'd seen a two-headed calf once, but that was nothing compared to the amazing Kavanagh.

"Why, that's wonderful news yer bringin' me, lad." Patrick grinned as he pulled the tap handle, filled a thick glass mug with his best beer, and set it in front of his informant. "Here—on the house. Good news! With the Republicans at each other's throats we have a chance t'win! So here's t'yer health, an' we'll all do our best!"

It was a bitter battle, that time around, and Patrick and his fellow ward bosses fought with every weapon at their disposal. Patrick's lieutenants scoured the district for every last man to put his name on the voting lists, and every boss in the city had troops of reinforcements from outlying towns ready to pack the boardinghouses in a "mattress vote"—that miraculous population explosion that took place in so many Irish enclaves as election day approached. Names were lifted from tombstones and signed upon the lists as long-lost friends and relations were resurrected. And on election day little groups of repeaters started on their rounds as soon as the polls opened. "Vote early and often" was the watchword, and at fifty cents a vote it was well worth a man's time to cast as many ballots as he could.

Despite all this, they lost—barely.

"A close vote! Less than a thousand, by God!" cried Patrick. He had predicted the vote in his ward to within half a dozen—a mathematical wizardry learned from his late mentor, Flanagan, that never failed to astonish. "Will we demand a recount?"

"We have the Common Council," said Smiling Jim Donovan, the dour, grim-faced boss of the South End. "We can run the city on our own. We don't need a mayor to do it." The ghost of a smile crossed his forbidding visage. "An' if anything goes wrong, we'll blame it on th'high muckety-muck Repooblik-kins!"

Smiling Jim was right, of course: the Irish ward bosses, after some three decades of clawing their way to power, by now had firm control of most of the crucial levers that made the city run. The City Health Commissioner was an Irishman (innocent of medical training), and the Superintendent of Streets— a key position from which to pad the payroll with deserving laborers. The Board of Assessors was controlled by the Irish, and of course most of the city's administrative bureaus were largely Irish by now. There were even a good many Irish policemen.

So they could afford to let the mayor's office go to the Republican candidate (not the hapless Kavanagh). They'd elected an Irishman, Hugh O'Brien, in 1884; inevitably, the next time, or the time after that, they would elect another.

That winter, as the nationwide depression continued, upward of five thousand more Irishmen were added to the city's payrolls. When the municipal treasury ran dry, the Board of Assessors imposed new taxes on the largest and most profitable businesses—which were, of course, those run by Anglo-Saxons.

Howls of outrage could be heard as far as Worcester. It is bad enough, people said, that these intruders have very nearly pushed us out of our fair little city, ruining the neighborhoods, flooding the schools. Now we are expected to perform as a charitable organization as well? Outrageous! Here is an Inspector of Sidewalks! What does he do? And a night porter! And seventy-three pound keepers! *Seventy-three!*

And so, very soon, a group of civic-minded men decided to act to save their city.

On an afternoon in March a group of them gathered in the offices of Otis Abbott Revell, who was, among other things, Judson Abbott Revell's second cousin, and more important, president of the largest insurance company in the state. A steady sleet hissed and spat against the windows as he and his associates pondered their dilemma: after 250 years, their beloved little city, and indeed their grand old Commonwealth, were in danger of being snatched from under their noses by a gang of greedy peasants who cared nothing for civic virtue, who had no civic pride, no sense of obligation except to enrich themselves and to buy thousands of votes to keep themselves in power.

The conferees began to make suggestions. Short of wholesale deportation of the Irish, there seemed to be no solution to their problem. At last, long after the windowpanes had gone dark and the cleaning women had come into the building, and were even now on their knees scrubbing, someone suggested that the group start up a City Improvement Association—CIA for short. Exhibitions could be held, pamphlets written, citizens of proper Yankee extraction exhorted to exert themselves in the name of good government. Don't forget the birthrate, said someone, but none of the men in the room had the faintest idea how bluntly to tell Yankee women to produce more babies to match the fecund Irish, and so the matter was left to the Legislature to forbid the use, demonstration, sale, or other manifestation of contraceptive devices.

When Patrick Shaughnessy heard about the CIA he hooted with laughter. "City Improvement Association? Yer pullin' my leg. Improvement, is it? They want improvements? We'll give 'em improvements till they don't know what hit 'em, but they'll have to pay f'r'em! Yessir! Th'tax rate'll go sky high, but those gents can afford it. Why, we haven't had a chance like this in I don't know when!"

His mother Mary laughed, too, when he told her about the CIA. She sat at her kitchen table rubbing her wrist that often ached in the cold damp Boston winters, and she sipped her tea and smiled at him as she never smiled at anyone else. She was a success now, had been a success for many years, with a showroom right downtown on Washington Street near Jordan Marsh. She had a faithful clientele, and a reputation as an honest woman with a good sense of style, and by now she had enough business to employ three seamstresses and bring in extras at busy times.

"They're supposed to be so smart," she said, "but here they are starin' at the facts of life, an' they can't see 'em. They'll never get rid of us now, it's too late f'r that."

"The truth is, I enjoy fight'n'em," said Patrick. "Makes it a pleasure to get up in the mornin', knowin' I'm goin' to beat out a Yankee that day."

And then he saw Mary's expression darken, as it often did, suddenly, when they spoke of the ruling class, and he changed the subject. He told her a funny story about one of his regulars at the saloon, and by the time he left her to go home, she was cheerful again.

But the issue of Yankee versus Irish could not be done away with so easily, and in the next couple of years each side dug in its heels and hardened its attitudes. Matters came to a head in the summer of 1896, when an epidemic of cholera swept through the Boston slums, and immigrant children of all kinds, and of course many Irish as well, began to die in even greater numbers than usual. The Irish street keepers laid down carpets of lime on the city's thoroughfares to damp down the spread of the infection, but their efforts did little good. Those people who could, left the city, escaping to the pure air of the mountains or the seacoast, but the poor, as always, were trapped.

Boston City Hospital rapidly filled to overflowing, and soon it had to turn people away. This gave rise to some agitation, and by the end of the summer it was decided to raise property taxes in order to pay for a new hospital building.

The City Improvement Association, whose members were still feeling the effects of the depression, protested the tax. They would not pay it, they said. The city's Republican mayor sided with his brethren, of course, but the members of the Common Council had the votes to do what they would.

They voted the tax. Then they voted a bond issue as well, to make sure that there would be money enough for many Irish workmen to be hired on the hospital project, and the thing was as good as done.

One day not long after, word went out among the bosses that the CIA wanted to have a chat with them.

"Well, now," said Patrick. "What about, I wonder?"

But of course he knew. He arrived in Otis Abbott Revell's less than lavish office to find a row of stern-faced Yankees confronting him and his companions, and before any one of them could say a word, Patrick knew what was coming.

Without a word of pleasant greeting, Revell came to the point. "We cannot bear this new tax," he said, "and we will not. You say that the City Hospital is filled. Keep in mind that there is also Massachusetts General Hospital. And of course Boston Floating Hospital, which was set up only a few years ago to deal with this very thing—an outbreak of cholera."

They had taken an unused barge in the Fort Point Channel to use as a hospital for slum children. That had been several summers ago, during a particularly vicious heat wave. Shortly thereafter a small building had been put up, but it was nowhere near large enough for the present necessity.

And besides—"That's only for children," said Patrick. "It's good enough as far as it goes, but no adult can get treatment there. And Massachusetts General is a fine place, but many folks can't pay f'r it. So we need more room at Boston City, an' we intend to get it. We can start construction by the end of the month, and next year this time we'll have a grand new building."

Otis Abbott Revell was not a cruel man, and certainly not a stupid one. What he lacked was imagination. He was incapable of imagining that any Irish parent, or anyone not of his own caste and class, had feelings like his—a horror of losing a child, a deep love for a husband or wife, father or mother.

Now, with a little pulse of anger throbbing at his temple, he replied to the inferior creature standing before him. "I tell you, we cannot bear it. We have not yet recovered from the crash. Keep in mind that if you bankrupt us, we will be of no use to you at all."

"I think yer a long way from bankruptcy, Mister, ah—what'd'y'say yer name was?"

Revell did not rise to that bait. "Let me say again, to all of you"—and his stern gaze swept around the little half-circle of Irishmen—"we will not finance this boondoggle. That is what it is—a make-work project. And when I say to you—"

"Wait a minute." Patrick's voice was low, but compelling in its very softness. "You seem to have bad information. This is not a make-work project we're talkin' about here. This is an expansion of the City Hospital. We have a lot of people sick, a lot of people who don't have th'money to pay the doctor. An' we want t'give 'em a chance, see? So we need more space. An' we're goin't'have it. If you don't like this new tax, we can give y'another one that'll be twice as big, an'we'll see how y'like that."

Otis Abbott Revell felt his face flush. He was glad that his father and his uncles were dead in their graves, rather than survive into a world where a common Irishman spoke in such a way to his betters.

"Now wait a minute—" he began.

"No! I will not! It is your turn to wait a minute, mister! If you are so concerned about payin' a little more tax, why don't you just lower yer dividends? Y'can do with a point less. Y'won't starve. But if we don't get this new hospital wing, there's a lot of folks'll die, and they'll die in the next epidemic and the next . . . Oh, yes, mister. We got t'have this place built. An' we're not goin't'stop it f'r th'likes of you! City Improvement Association. Don't make me laugh! What th'hell d'y'think a hospital does? Doesn't a hospital improve the city? Y'blind stupid—Yankee! Take the tax out of yer dividends, and don't ever let us hear you again complainin', or we'll show you what a tax really is!"

8

The morning dawned cool and damp, with a fog so thick that for a while the day's planned event was in danger of being canceled. But at last the weather cleared a bit, the officials gave the go-ahead, and the fifteen participants lined up at the starting point and waited for the starter's pistol. They wore stout boots and odd-looking pants that ended at the calf.

Frederick was third in from the right. He crouched at the ready, every muscle tensed to spring to action.

Bang!

They were off: running easily for this first stretch, knowing that they needed to conserve their stamina for the end, for the brutal punishing last few miles.

Frederick was a second-year student at the Law School. He found the work interesting enough but not terribly exciting. When he'd heard that the Boston Athletic Association was organizing a marathon to be run in celebration of the resumption of the Olympic Games in Greece, he'd signed up at once. He couldn't have said why the idea appealed to him: a run of twenty-six miles through the countryside from Metcalfe's Mill in Ashland to Boston, on narrow country dirt roads hardly designed for running, uphill and down, into the more thickly populated towns near Boston, Framingham and Natick and Wellesley, on through to Commonwealth Avenue and the Newton Hills near Boston College, the last of which came to be known as Heartbreak Hill—a punishing run, but no more so, he supposed, than the original. He'd done it twice in practice, all near three hours. Now he loped along feeling the moist air on his skin, aware of the world around him, a blurred soft gray and spring green. After a while he realized that he was alone: one runner ran far ahead of him, out of sight and hearing, and he could not distinguish the sound of pounding feet behind: only his own, thud-thudding against the road. On and on he went, past fields and farms, an occasional house, once a woman peering at him from her front porch as if he were crazy, as if she were frightened of him—a half-clad stranger running by.

All alone: he might have been the last man alive, pounding, pounding—but now he was aware that someone was gaining on him. He heard labored breathing from behind. His peripheral vision picked up a competitor, and after a few moments the fellow overtook him.

Frederick ran on. Not the winning but the running was the point of this race.

And in fact he did not win. That honor went to one John McDermott of New York City, age twenty-five, occupation unknown. His time was two hours, fifty-five minutes and ten seconds. Heartbreak Hill nearly did him in: he needed to stop to rest five times between Boston College and the finish line at the Irvington Street Oval in Boston. During the run he lost ten pounds.

Frederick came in a very respectable fourth, in three hours and fourteen minutes.

He was very pleased, as was Isabella. Fourth place was just fine. What she couldn't understand was why he wanted to do such an odd thing at all.

9

Isabella, those days, had more important things to occupy her mind than the fledgling Boston Marathon—more important even than the fortunes of the Boston Redstockings, whose ardent fan she had become. Every spring and summer day that she was in town, up until this year, she had gone to the games with a party of young men and some young women, too, and cheered loudly and in a very unladylike way as the "Heavenly Twins," Tommy McCarthy and Hughie Duffy, practiced their rowdy art.

This year, however, she had taken a step that she had long wanted to take, and she couldn't tell how many baseball games she would attend—even though, by July, the Redstockings (or the "Beaneaters," as they were known) were locked in a pennant race with John McGraw and his rambunctious Baltimore Orioles.

Out in the Fens, a muddy, undeveloped tract west of the Back Bay, a link in the Emerald Necklace that Frederick Law Olmstead had designed for Boston, she had purchased a piece of land and made her announcement: "I am going to build a palace!"

What she meant was that at long last, and after years of insatiable buying of the treasures of Europe, and most particularly of Italy, she was going to give them a proper home. What she had in mind was a more or less faithful copy of a Venetian palazzo: a square building of pale brick with a red-tile roof and a glass-roofed central court. Each of the display rooms would have its own theme: the Gothic Room, the Titian Room, and so on. At the top, on the fourth floor, would be a cozy apartment for her to live in. And she would open the palace to the public. It would be her gift to them.

By the fall the workmen had dug the foundation and begun to lay the stones and pour the concrete for the cellar. Every day she drove out to see them, carrying a picnic lunch and a bottle of wine. At first the men laughed at her: the rich lady so out of place at a construction site, even if that site was her own. But soon enough they learned to take her seriously, for if she saw a man slacking on the job, she ordered that he be fired; and when she realized that three or four of them, on their lunch break, were mocking her, she dismissed them on the spot. After that the men greeted her respectfully, lifting their caps as she passed, and in time they came to have a feeling of admiration for her: there was a woman who knew what she wanted, by God, and she was as insistent as any man upon having it!

One mild October day Lyman drove out with her. She'd instructed Cook to pack enough food for two, and now in the warming sunshine they sat in Isabella's open landau and lunched on cold chicken and salad and French bread and butter, and a bottle of Graves, not quite chilled enough, but perfectly acceptable.

"The quarterly statements are in," said Lyman. He gazed out across the dusty wasteland where Isabella's palace would rise.

"And are they acceptable?"

"Oh, yes. Perfectly acceptable."

Like all his kind, Lyman was never forthcoming with information. Therefore, after a moment, she said, "And what will I have for the year, do you think?"

She could see from his slightly startled expression that her query was not entirely proper. Gentlewomen were not supposed to ask such specific questions. Too bad, she thought. It is my money; I have a right to know about it.

"Hard to say," he responded.

"Try."

"Really very difficult to predict these things."

"Just a rough estimate. How, for instance, is the Calumet-Hecla doing?"

"Oh, you've no worries there."

Shortly after the war, young Alexander Agassiz, the son of Harvard's famous biologist, had gotten control of a patch of ground in Michigan that looked promising to him. He'd offered shares to his family and friends. Because Boston was a close-knit place, families intertwined, friendships lifelong, people had taken shares to help him out—such a nice young man, and his father so distinguished, a stalwart in the fight against the Darwinians.

Now, three decades later, the Calumet-Hecla mine was better than a gold mine. Year after year it gave up its copper ore and returned rich dividends.

"And the Commonwealth Mill?"

"That, too."

"And Bell Telephone?"

"Oh, yes, you're all right there."

"And the Massachusetts Hospital Life Insurance Company? And the United Fruit Company? And the—what was it, I can never remember the name of the railroad."

"Isabella, believe me. If I thought you had any worries financially, I would insist that you stop this"—he waved his hand—"this folly that you insist upon having."

"Which I can well afford."

"At the moment."

She smiled at him—a gesture of forgiveness for his grudging assistance—and patted his hand. She knew that he disapproved of women having control of their money. Fortunately for her, both Theo and her father had thought differently. And so now she was able to indulge her fancy, even to the tune of the million or more that this place would consume. It was like a devouring beast, she thought: already they were over budget, and they'd been at work only a few months. She would ask Mr. Codman to bring her the account books tomorrow, and if she couldn't understand them, she'd find someone—but not Lyman—to explain them to her. And she would simply have to insist on economy.

Probably Codman underestimated her, she thought. It was not surprising. The landscape of Massachusetts and half of Europe, too, was littered with the bodies of men who had underestimated her—who had thought that because she was an attractive woman, she was also a typical one, reluctant to insist upon what she wanted, hesitant to exert her will.

But she was not reluctant, she was not hesitant, she knew what she wanted, and she meant to have it.

Lyman glanced at her. Under the brim of her hat, just one shade darker blue than her eyes, her face was serene, her exquisite mouth curved into a contented smile.

10

"Life on Mars? But of course there is life on Mars, gentlemen. I have seen it— or proof of it, at any rate."

A blustery October night when the leaves of the elm trees on the Common blew thick across the Long Path, and people huddled by their fires at this first reminder of the long winter to come, and the stars in the black heavens glittered with new intensity—thousands and thousands of stars, and who was to say that not one of them was inhabited?

In the cozy confines of the Somerset Club, a few of the members were having a go at John Abbott Revell, whose new book, *Mars*, was causing a sensation. He had seen, he said, canals on Mars. Canals—that is, not natural channels, but man-made waterways. On either side of many of these canals, he had observed what looked like vegetation; as the seasons passed, it changed color, disappeared, and then seemed to spring to life again—just as crops could if they were planted alongside irrigation canals.

Ever since the book's publication the previous May, John Abbott Revell had been besieged with invitations to speak, to present his views to audiences of varying degrees of scientific sophistication. Naturally he met with considerable scoffing, particularly from astronomers, but he was a hard-headed man, a stubborn man, and was not going to allow himself to be deterred. He had made one of the most important discoveries in the history of mankind; it was his duty to defend it, promote it, and expand it.

He stood at his ease now, one elbow resting on the mantel of the blazing hearth, puffing at his pipe with a sardonic smile on his handsome face as he watched the members lounging around the room try to come to grips with the implications of what he said.

"My dear fellow," said Harry Chadwick. "If what you say is true, then those of us who are believing Christians might as well give it up. Religion, I mean."

"I don't see why."

"But of course you do. Why, this is worse than Darwin, damn it! How can we be God's special creation, if He's got another population on another planet?"

"That just makes Him a mightier God, I should think." John understood this objection, since it was the primary one given to him everywhere, but he did not sympathize with it. He was a man of very little religious faith, and he was not going to allow his work to be deterred by people whose minds were— as he saw it—shackled in medieval superstition.

"How many books have y'sold now, Revell?" Simpson Russell, a wizened little man, always wanting to put matters into dollars and cents.

"I haven't checked, actually." Not true: he had been around to the offices of Houghton and Mifflin only that afternoon. It never ceased to amaze him that perfectly well-mannered people, who would never think of asking their doctor's income, or their lawyer's, thought nothing of asking an author how many books he had sold. As of the previous week, the publisher had said, *Mars* had sold over a hundred thousand copies—an astonishing figure, particularly for a work of science.

Pseudoscience, some of the professors at Boston Tech would have said, but no matter. The professors at Boston Tech had no imagination; they were academic drones, chained to their classrooms, unable by the very nature of their work to allow their spirits to roam free through the heavens, sighting out new worlds, expanding man's horizons. It was in the nature of Man, John said, to move on. Columbus; the settlers of the New World; the push to span the continent, to voyage to the Orient; the great expeditions to map and chart the vast white spaces on the maps of the continents of Africa and South America— all of these were Man's nature. And the inevitable next step in the scientific tradition going back through the heretic Galileo all the way to the Greeks, was to learn what existed beyond their own planet.

So he dealt easily with his audience this night, secure in his own beliefs, and when October came to an end, he boarded the train once again for his observatory at Flagstaff, there to spend the winter refining his observations. He was right—he knew he was right! Nothing would ever shake that conviction.

From that time, the fascination of the idea of life on Mars—an intense Mars Mania—seized the popular imagination and never let go. The year after John's book appeared, George DuMaurier, the creator of the character of Svengali, wrote a sensational novel called *The Martian*. The year after that, the noted science fiction writer H. G. Wells wrote an even more sensational Martian novel, *The War of the Worlds*. A dozen lesser talents, as they always do, hastened to grind out imitations. Then, in the next decade, the first of the new century, the last century of the millennium, the science fiction pulp writer Edgar Rice Burroughs introduced Mars to his Tarzan fans in *A Princess of Mars*. In the thirties, in the heyday of comic books, Buck Rogers and Flash Gordon encountered Martians in episode after episode. Meanwhile the boy genius, Orson Welles (no relation to H.G.), scared the bejeezus out of millions of people on Hallowe'en, 1938, by broadcasting a radio play adapted from Wells's novel. Many people thought it was not a radio play but a news broadcast, and for a few hours that night the public, or at least a large portion of it, went crazy with fear. The Martians are coming! The Martians are coming! Not many years later, Ray Bradbury produced one of the most haunting works about the red planet, *The Martian Chronicles*. The UFO craze that swept the nation beginning in 1947 was predicated on the notion of "little green men"—Martians.

Life on Mars. The idea haunted earthlings; it would not go away.

Was life there now? Or had life been there once, long ago? And if life had been there once, how and why had it died?

And if life had died on Mars, would it die on Earth as well?

Was the secret of Martian life the secret of our own fate?

11

When in 1890 Lyman Griffin Revell had passed the half-century mark, he felt no breath of mortality hot against the back of his neck. He went on working, managing his factories, piling up his fortune just as he had always done. In what little time he had to spare, he cultivated his gardens—a large one at his summer place in Brookline, a very small one behind his house in Louisburg Square, Beacon Hill. He liked to work the soil; he liked to see green shoots poking their heads up after the long winter, and the beautiful bright colors of the blooms. In the greenhouses at Brookline, he carefully nurtured early seedlings until he could put them outdoors, thus always assuring himself of the first tomatoes, the first primroses and carnations. He was particularly fond of his roses, and he was proud when he began to win prizes for them. He loved to show off his rose garden. He would take little Revell children, visiting nieces and nephews, by the hand and lead them along the paths, warning them about the thorns, pointing out the choicest blooms. He liked to see the new generation coming along. Soon his own children would give him some grandchildren.

When he walked to the depot in the North End, he was sometimes overcome with disgust at the sight of the hordes of immigrant children swarming over the streets—dirty, raucous, jabbering in strange tongues. Once, Gaelic had been the only foreign language heard in Boston. Now, one heard Italian and Yiddish, Russian and Polish, and who knew what all. This was his country—his and his Family's—but sometimes now he felt as though he was being pushed out by all these strange-sounding newcomers. If he and his kind didn't watch out, he thought, the day would come when they'd be outnumbered—denied their birthright by all these latecomers, who, unfortunately, had the vote. Every man who had his naturalization papers could go to the ballot box just as Lyman did himself.

Not long ago some of the fellows over at the College had started up an Immigration Restriction League. Henry Holt and Abbott Lawrence Lowell were prime movers. Lyman made up his mind to ask Lowell about it the next time they met at the Somerset. The anti-immigrationists had put out a book whose argument was that the Anglo-Saxon, Northern European stock was racially superior to that of Eastern and Southern Europe. They claimed that that old American stock—that Anglo-Saxon New England stock—was in danger of being obliterated by the hordes of swarthy, strange-sounding newcomers flooding into the slums of Boston and many other cities along the northeastern seaboard.

Decades of Irish had been bad enough; these most recent arrivals were the last straw. The Immigration Restriction League wanted—at last—to limit immigration. Only the previous month Senator Henry Cabot Lodge had made a magnificent speech to the Senate in which he argued for restrictions on immigration. Lyman thought it an idea whose time had come.

Always, he was conscious of the newcomers' dark, unfathomable eyes upon him as he strode through his city—*his* city, the city that his ancestors had helped to build, and the commonwealth as well. He knew what these interlopers thought as they watched him: they wanted what was his. They were full of radical ideas, alien beliefs, socialism, atheism, Papism, Judaism, anarchism, crackpot schemes to overthrow the moneyed classes.

And if they continued to breed the hordes of children that he saw, they would soon take power.

As the last decade of the century wound down, because he felt so threatened, he did what people often do when they feel unhappy with their present circumstances and powerless to change them: he turned to the past, and specifically to his own and his Family's past, and he became an amateur genealogist. Soon he was regaling family and friends alike with his discoveries. Much was already known, of course: the writings of Washington Abbott Revell gave considerable information, and Catherine Mayhew Revell's account of her captivity and the three Family bibles were treasures. He consulted several times with the staff of the New England Historical Genealogical Society. He began to experiment with charts and trees. He made wonderful, astonishing discoveries; he enjoyed himself immensely.

So Remonstrance Griffin had been born on the wrong side of the blanket! About his father, nothing was known except his name. About his mother— well, everyone knew that the witchcraft had been mass delusion, ancient superstition. There was in fact even something of a cachet in having a witch in your family tree, particularly a Salem witch, than whom none were more famous.

But faceless, elusive Phineas—he was a problem.

And then one day Lyman found something even more interesting than Rebecca Sparhawk and shadowy Phineas and their son Remonstrance.

Word had gotten about, of course, that Lyman Griffin Revell was on the lookout for genealogical tidbits. One day he had a note from a dealer in rare books and manuscripts; the man said that he'd turned up something that Lyman might like to see.

Such an offer was like catnip to a cat: Lyman was in the man's shop the next morning.

"Yes, sir. This just came in the other day. I have an agent in England, y'know, who buys up odd lots and whatnot, goes to auctions, reads the death notices and buys what the inheritors want to get rid of. He sent me a box of miscellaneous items not long ago, and I was just cataloguing them, and I found this. Really fortuitous, wouldn't you say? Have a look."

Lyman looked. It was a letter, part of its sealing wax still adhering, its brown ink remarkably legible.

He read:

Harefield House
Surrey
10 Aug 1796

Mrs. Ebenezer Revell

Dear Sister Abigail,

I cannot Believe that it is more than twenty years since I sailed from those shores. But time always goes Quick, don't it, when you are young.

I will not tire you with a recital of all that has happened to me since I evacuated Boston, except to say that in 1777, before I came out to England, I bore a son to General Howe. That son is now a fine strapping lad, and his father has bought him a Commission in the Army.

For myself, I am much alone here, and I think often of my youth, my Childhood and my Days in Boston. I am sorry, dear Sister, that we never knew each other. I think our Mother was greatly at Fault to keep us apart, Tho I fear, had we been close, and I not in a position to do what I did, perhaps your step-son Thomas would not have been able to perform his brave Deed. Yes, I know about that.

And now I must tell you that I have fallen into pitiful pecuniary Circumstances, dear Abigail, and I must ask your help. You have Agents, I believe, if not here then on the Continent. Could you ask your Husband to instruct them to make an advance to me—3 or 4 hundred £ would see me through the Winter & if All goes as I expect, I will be able to pay it back next Spring or Summer at the Latest.

You may be Certain, dear Abigail, that not a Person here in England, or in America, has ever Learned from me, & None ever shall, of our Relationship.

That every Blessing which Heaven can bestow light on you, and yours, is the sincere Wish of your Affecte Sister

Betsey Loring

Joshua is dead.

Lyman looked up at the dealer, who was watching him with great interest. He met the man's eyes, and then he looked away.

What on earth!

He realized that his hands were trembling. "Where did you say you got this? From England?"

"That's right."

"Where in England?"

"From the estate of a Mr. Henry Albright, Kensington Gardens."

"And who was he?"

"He was a barrister, lived and died a bachelor. His library and furniture were sold after his death. This letter was in the drawer of a desk."

Lyman's heart was all a-flutter. What did it mean? What could it possibly mean? Betsey Loring had been no better than a—than a woman of the streets! Why, she had been notorious! Living openly with General Howe as his mistress, betraying the American cause—everyone knew about Betsey Loring! The Boston Lorings had gone to great pains, some years ago, to distinguish their branch of the family from hers.

What was more, apparently, she had been a blackmailer as well as a—a loose woman. Yes, that was certainly a strong hint, "not a Person has ever Learned . . ."

And if this letter was genuine, was he to infer that Betsey Loring had been related to his great-grandfather Ebenezer's wife, Abigail Abbott Revell? The highest type of patriotic woman, a woman who brought up his grandfather Nathaniel—a man whom Lyman remembered meeting—as if he'd been her own boy!

Canny, cautious Yankee that he was, Lyman did not buy the letter that day. Instead he told the dealer to hold it for him. He went from the dealer's directly to the offices of the New England Historic Genealogical Society. Late that afternoon he went home. As he climbed Mt. Vernon Street he pondered the day's events. Incredible! Betsey Loring—a relation!

It could not be. It *must* not be. Not after all his work to put together the story of the Revells: merchants, patriots, men of honor.

For two days he thought about the letter purported to be Betsey Loring's. Then he returned to the dealer. He would buy it, he said, and for once he did not haggle about the price.

"Have you told anyone else about this letter?" he said as the dealer wrote out his receipt.

"No, Mr. Revell, I haven't." The dealer was an obsequious little man, certain to want to do further business with Lyman Griffin Revell.

"Then see that you don't," said Lyman, and abruptly, taking his purchase, he turned and hurried out of the shop.

He went directly home. In his second-floor study he had a small safe. He opened it, put the letter inside, and closed and locked it.

As far as he was concerned, that letter had never existed.

That summer, Lyman surprised his wife by proposing a trip to England. While he was there, he visited Somerset House to investigate its birth and death records, and then, leaving his wife and daughter to enjoy the delights of the London season, he went north to York. When he returned, well satisfied with his journey, he carried with him indisputable proof, bought and paid for from a cooperative genealogist, of the ancestry of Phineas Griffin of London, who was, it turned out, a descendant, albeit illegitimate, of a distantly royal personage.

And of course now nothing would do but that he must order a coat of arms. So the Griffins were royalty! Ha! That would put the noses of the Jacksons and the Abbotts out of joint!

The escutcheon arrived in Boston some weeks after Lyman and his family returned. It was a handsome thing, red, black, gold, and white. It showed a griffin with its front, or eagle's, claws clutching fascines or sheaves of wheat—to symbolize wealth; its hindquarters, which were those of a lion, rested on a globe, to show the far-flung commercial dealings of the Family. He had two large copies made in wood for the doors of his carriage, and slightly smaller ones for the landau; his wife worked one in embroidery silks on the breast pocket of his dressing gown; he had stationery printed up showing it in miniature, and so on. He even had a quite large one, three feet by three feet, made to hang over the mantel in his study in the Louisburg Square house.

Of course, everyone admired what he had done—all the research, the undeniably handsome results. And so by the end of the decade he was somewhat more at ease. He felt that somehow he had solidified the Family's place in the world. Let the foreigners come in; they'd never usurp the Revells' place at the top of the natural order!

That Christmas of 1898, properly to show off his brand new coats of arms, Lyman instructed his wife to invite all three branches of the Family to a Christmas Eve party. What with all the in-laws, nearly two hundred people came. Lyman was delighted. He stood in his front parlor with its Christmas tree reaching to the tall ceiling, and he and his wife and his eldest son, Winslow, greeted their guests. His second son, Fletcher, age fifteen, was in charge of overseeing the adolescent cousins. Augusta, age eight, was perched on the landing, elegant in her new Christmas dress with small puffed sleeves and velvet trim, content for the moment to watch the proceedings. She was his only daughter, his last, late blossom; as much as he was able, he loved her.

Isabella came with Frederick and the delightful young woman who was his fiancée, Elinor Forbes; and Dr. William came with his son John. William had been the heart and soul of the Perkins Institute for decades; his work with the blind was internationally known. And William's son, the even more famous John, the astronomer—a handsome fellow, damned if he wasn't. All that business about Mars! And a whole pride of Jackson Revells—or perhaps they were a gaggle, thought Lyman: old Edward, Isabella's father, and his sister Lavinia, and Edwin, and Edwin's uncle Parker and his three children and their families....

Some of the late arrivals, he noticed, had to brush snow from their cloaks and hats, and so when the last of them had come in and were safely settled amongst their relatives—the place where a Revell felt most comfortable—Lyman stepped outside and stood for a moment on the front stoop looking out across the little square (which was not a square but a rectangle, with an oval patch of grass and trees in the center, protected by a fence made of tall iron spikes). Yes: it was snowing. A soft, steady fall, perfectly straight in the windless night. The streetlamps glowed softly, each one with its aureole of light in the falling whiteness. In the tall brick houses ringed around the square he saw lighted windows and a Christmas tree or two; and in the still night air, softened by the snow, he heard snatches of laughter and music as his neighbors celebrated the holiday.

"Isn't it beautiful?" said a girl's voice at his side; and he turned to see Violet, Judson Abbott's daughter, who had just made her debut and so was now officially on the marriage market. Poor thing: she was very plain, plainer even than Aunt Caroline had been. Her high forehead sloped back to her uneven hairline; her long, pointed nose had a pronounced bump in its middle; her teeth were prominent and her chin receding; her eyes were a nice enough blue, but the lashes were so pale as to be invisible; and she was tall and awkward and rangy, like a badly bred horse. No, she'd have a time of it, he thought, and perhaps not so much money as people thought, since Judson's income was not what it should be, if he guessed right. Judson was an ineffectual fellow who fancied himself an artistic type like his father, the renowned Washington. But while Washington had indeed had some ability, Judson did not. He had spent his twenties in Paris learning that he could not paint; he had spent his thirties, off and on, at his cottage in the Berkshires learning that he could not write. Now, in his forties, he seemed to have no idea how to get through the rest of his days. Apparently he hadn't done too well by this girl, either: she was as awkward as a twelve-year-old, and she had a silly neighing laugh that set Lyman's teeth on edge. No grace, no charm—even if a woman were unlucky enough to be homely, she could at least cultivate her inborn feminine qualities. Violet's mother had died when Violet was born; she'd been brought up by governesses, and this was the sad result.

Lyman was not accustomed to feeling sorry for anyone, let alone anyone lucky enough to be born a Revell; but now he glanced down at this hapless creature, who did not even seem to know just how hapless, how utterly unsuitable she was, and he felt suddenly kindly toward her, as if he wanted to do her some small favor, he didn't know what.

"Go and fetch a cloak," he said. "Anyone's—doesn't matter. We'll take a turn around the square before the snow gets chopped up by the horses."

She obeyed him; and within minutes they were strolling past the brightly lighted houses, hearing the laughter and singing, feeling delightfully naughty as they escaped their own party to have this little adventure together.

From number 16 they heard, "Silent night, holy night . . ." Lyman hummed along; and suddenly he was surprised to hear Violet sing as well—not a discreet hum, but a lovely, sweet soprano; " 'Round yon Virgin, Mother and Child . . ."

Violet sang softly, not loud enough to call attention to herself, but confidently, as if at last she felt comfortable in the world.

"Sleep in Heavenly peace . . ." In the light streaming from the windows, he could see her face alive with joy, her eyes shining—altogether a different person from what she had been a moment ago in his front parlor.

"Sleep in Heavenly peace . . ." He heard voices behind them, joining in. He turned to see three people he thought he recognized, from somewhere on the Hill: a man and two women. As the song ended, Violet began another: "O come, all ye faithful . . ." At once the others took it up, and now the door of the house where they stood was flung open, and three young folks, two girls and a boy, the Richardson children, joined in the singing: "O come ye, O come ye . . ." And now another group from the next house came out, the women wrapped in shawls against the snowy night. Violet moved on, and the little crowd followed her down the narrow sidewalk to the house beyond, where again the door was flung open, and again two or three people came out to join them. "O come let us adore Him . . ." Soon there was a crowd of at least twenty, and when Violet began to make her way down Mt. Vernon and along West Cedar to Chestnut, they followed her and welcomed more to their ranks.

For the better part of an hour they went up and down the narrow, cobbled streets and brick sidewalks of Beacon Hill singing Christmas carols. Some of those who came brought lanterns, or shaded candles, so that they seemed not a threatening crowd, but what they were—bearers of good tidings.

And so began the custom of Christmas Eve caroling on Beacon Hill. The following year Lyman did not have a large party, but he did invite a few people in for eggnog, Violet among them, and shortly after seven they set off on their singing rounds. As before, people came out to join them—more than a hundred, Violet thought. And the next year after that they went out again, and as she said, three years in a row made the custom: on Christmas Eve you went caroling around Beacon Hill. It was in that year that Lyman suggested to some of his neighbors that they put lighted candles in their windows, and they did; and so the carolers were welcomed by points of light gleaming from the windows of the mellow old red-brick houses. The whole southern half of the Hill was aglow with the spirit of the season, evergreen wreaths on every door, Christmas trees glittering inside—a lovely season, and Violet had helped to make it better. Blushing, she declined any credit. It was all Uncle Lyman's doing, she said; she'd heard him humming along, and she had simply taken her cue.

No matter. By the time the feature writer for the *Transcript* put out a little story, it was well into the middle of the next decade—the new century—and the facts of the case had settled into myth. It was Miss Violet Abbott Revell of Clarendon Street, Boston, and The Manse, Lenox, who had begun the delightful custom of Christmas Eve caroling on Beacon Hill. As shy and self-effacing as she was, she could not deny it.

12

At around the time that Lyman and Violet were setting out that first Christmas Eve, Patrick Shaughnessy pushed his chair back from the table in his dining room, beckoned to his eldest son, Michael, and announced to his wife and the younger children that the two of them were going to get a bit of air. They'd be back soon, he said. He stopped at the kitchen to pick up a basket he'd packed himself earlier in the day and gave it to Michael to carry.

A soft light snow was falling steadily as they went down the granite steps of the Shaughnessys' well-kept tenement that Patrick had bought not long after his marriage. After Brendan's birth in 1890, the family had taken two floors instead of one, so they had always been comfortable. Now without hesitation Patrick turned and headed down the street, and it was obvious to his son that this was not a casual stroll but a definite errand.

They walked in silence. They were perfectly amicable; they did not need to make small talk. Michael was in his next to last year at the Latin School— one of only two Irish boys in his class, and often enough he'd had to fight his way into the building. Much to the disgust of the priest at St. Joseph's, Patrick was determined to send the boy to Harvard, if they'd have him. Bridget felt the same. The priest had argued for Boston College and the Jesuits, but Patrick had had enough of second-class citizenship. A degree from the Jebbies stigmatized a man for life: Irish Catholic. A degree from Harvard was, if not a ticket to the power structure that Harvard produced, at least a kind of statement: I grant you nothing, you rich Anglo-Saxons who happen at this moment to rule our little world up here in this small corner of the nation. But you will not rule it always: more and more of us are coming in, we who are not rich, who are not Anglo-Saxon. Sooner or later we will have what you have.

He smiled to himself as he always did when his thoughts became too large. Nothing worse in the world to the Yankees than an uppity Irishman, a mighty Mick dreaming his foolish dreams. "No Irish Need Apply" was still a byword in Yankee Boston—and doubtless at Harvard as well.

Nevertheless. The boy was as sharp as could be; he learned his lessons in no time, and all his teachers said he had a good chance to be admitted. True, Harvard filled its classes first with the sons of alumni; then nephews; then especially recommended friends, and so on. If there happened to be a few places vacant, they might take an occasional Jew or Irishman. Worth a try.

They went on. The night was silent, mysterious as darkness always is, and particularly when it is filled with snow. Little traffic: everyone home for the holiday. They turned at a corner; turned again at the next. A short way down, Patrick stopped. They were at the entrance to a courtyard: Malvern Court, the sign read—a rotting wooden sign nailed to the corner of a rotting wooden building, barely visible in the dim light from the streetlamp.

"Here we are," said Patrick. He reached out and took the basket from Michael's hand. "I'll tell you now why I've brought you here. Two birds with one stone, y'might say. Y'see this place"—he gestured toward the narrow, dark alleyway—"this was where I lived, once upon a time. With Grammy. Oh, yes. My father died, as you know, when I was just eight. An' we had some hard years after that." He started into the courtyard, and his son followed. The way was lined with tenements; in the little light from the streetlamp and the reflected light of the snow, Michael saw that these were poor buildings, badly kept, with gaping wooden stairs, doors half off their hinges, and here and there a boarded-up window. He could hear the sound of a fierce argument, a man and a woman shouting, and from another building a drunk singing a loud, slurred song in what might have been Gaelic.

At the far end of the court they came to a building whose windows were entirely dark save for a glimmer at the first floor. Patrick went up the steps, feeling his way lest the snow hide a hole, and pushed open the door into the hallway. Pitch-black. Cautiously he stepped inside; when he found a door, he rapped.

No answer. He rapped again, a little louder, and called, "Hello?"

This time a voice replied, but in a tongue that neither of them could understand—not Gaelic, something stranger even than that.

"I am a friend," Patrick called. And, in an aside to his son: "They fear the bill collector, even on Christmas Eve!"

The door opened a crack. In the dim light from within they saw a young woman with a shawl around her shoulders, a whimpering baby in her arms. Two toddlers clutched at her skirts. Her hair was straggling down around her thin face, and as she moved back to let them in, Michael noticed that her feet were bare. The room was as cold as outdoors, no fire, no stove, a few pallets on the floor and a crude table and two chairs. No sign of a husband.

Patrick made a little bow. The woman watched him, expressionless; Michael thought that like many of the poor, she was more or less numb from the repeated blows dealt to her by a hostile fate.

"I apologize for intruding," said Patrick in what Michael recognized as his best campaign voice: friendly, warm, a voice that sounded confidential even at a rally of a thousand people and more. "Allow me to introduce myself. I am Patrick Shaughnessy, and this is my son Michael." The woman made no reaction. "Ah, in this Christmas season," Patrick went on, "I was overcome by the memory of my childhood. Once upon a time, I lived in this very room. We had the whole first floor then, before they cut it up." He smiled at her now, acknowledging her first show of interest in his words. "Yes, when I was a lad only a bit bigger than your own, my mother and I and five younger ones lived right here in Malvern Court. And so, in accordance with the season, I thought I'd bring to the person living here now—that is, to you—a Christmas basket." With a small flourish, he set it on the rickety table, which threatened to collapse under its weight. It was a heavy basket, for it contained a large turkey and a dozen potatoes and three squashes and a jar of cranberry relish and a plum pudding and a bottle of hard sauce and a dozen day-old Parker House rolls that Patrick had requisitioned from one of his old friends at the hotel.

The woman did not move to examine it, so Patrick folded back the cotton cloth. "Y'see, here it all is—your Christmas dinner. D'you have an oven?" For he admitted to himself now that perhaps he should have had Bridget cook the dinner instead of bringing it raw. It had not occurred to him that the occupant of his former home might not have a stove. As poor as the Shaughnessys had been, they had never, in his lifetime at least, been without a stove. His mother, he knew, had seen harder times; he remembered her tales of the old country in the famine, and the terrible days in Half Moon Place and Fort Hill.

"Well!" he said. "Can you cook here? Or should I take it back and have my wife cook it up for you?"

The woman looked at him, then at the basket of food, then at him once more. If he had been Father Christmas himself, he would not have been a more amazing sight. But then, thought Michael, Christmas was a time for miracles, and to this poor creature he and his father must have seemed one.

And now at last she found her tongue. Suddenly her pale face lighted up and her mouth opened in a gap-toothed smile. She jabbered in her incomprehensible tongue and nodded her head toward the rear of the house. As if she were afraid that he would snatch the basket away, she grasped the handle.

"All right, then," said Patrick. "We'll be on our way, and a happy Christmas to you." At the risk of catching whatever disease she might have carried, he put out his hand, but she did not take it. She simply stared at him, witless once more. Michael was glad when they left.

They made their way out of the courtyard; they passed the corner that would have taken them home, and stood at the crossing at Cambridge Street. "Let's walk a bit," said Patrick. As always, the family would go to midnight mass, but it was early yet, just past eight. They crossed the nearly empty street, one lone hack and its swaybacked nag waiting for a fare, and walked down the other side.

And now at last, as if walking somehow loosened his tongue and stirred up his memory, Patrick said, "That was a good thing to do. To visit that poor woman, I mean. No tellin' when that place'll fall down all by itself—or be torn down by the Board of Health. An' I wanted y't'see it. I expect y'll be goin' over t'Harvard year after next—oh, yes, I think they'll take you, I'd be surprised if they didn't—an' you'll meet up with some pretty fancy folks over there, leastways they think they are. An' I wanted you to remember where we come from. Where we pulled ourselves up from, more like it. When my father died, the landlord wouldn't give Grammy so much as a month's grace on the rent. We had a little store, y'know, and Grammy tried to run it while I minded the little ones. But the store failed, an' we got put out. An' we came to Malvern Court. Grammy got a job scrubbin' floors at th' hospital. We never had enough to eat, that winter and spring. I can remember very well how it feels to go to bed so hungry you can't sleep." His voice had oddly changed, Michael thought: it seemed a stranger's voice, dry and thin. "An' then Grammy got some help, an' she was able to start her dressmakin' business. Lucky for all of us she had that much spunk."

They came to West Cedar Street, which would take them to Pinckney. They turned up it. And after a while, in his normal voice, Patrick said, "It looks as if we're goin't'take th' Common Council again in th'next election. It'll mean a lot more jobs f'r th'boyos. D'y'understand? D'y'see the connection with what I've just been tellin'y'? We came from that"—and he waved his hand back toward Malvern Court—"an' now we control the city, or pretty near. We fought our way up, an' we're still fightin', an' will be when your boys have boys of their own. No one ever made anything easy f'r the Boston Irish, not that we wanted easy, but we wouldn't have minded a fair fight. An' we didn't get it."

They passed under a streetlamp. Michael glanced at his father's face. Underneath the snow-covered brim of his black bowler, Patrick's thin, sharp features were drawn down into an expression that his son had never seen: hatred, pure and simple—for the Yankees? Michael liked them no more than his father did, but such an expenditure of feeling seemed a waste of energy.

"Sooner or later," said Patrick, "one of those fancy folks over across the river'll throw it up t'y' that y'r father's a ward boss. When he says it, he'll have an expression on his face as if he's smellin' somethin' bad. An' you just stand up f'r me, y'understand? I don't ever want to hear that y're ashamed—not of me, not of y'rself or anyone in y'r family—or none of the lads, either, Johnny Fitzpatrick and P. J. Kennedy and Martin Lomasny, an' even that young fella, Curley, the one that went to jail for takin' a civil service examination f'r his friend. Did y'hear about that? That young man's got more brass than the State Street Bank, but more power to him, I say. He's just doin' what we all have to do. Helpin' each other to survive, that's what."

When they were halfway up Pinckney Street's steep incline, they heard the sound of voices singing "O Little Town of Bethlehem," and when they reached Louisburg Square they saw carolers stopped in front of one of the big houses, the happy, well-fed faces glowing in the light of lanterns and candles, everyone filled with the spirit of Christmas.

Patrick and Michael stopped on the far side of Pinckney Street to watch. None of the carolers noticed the two dark-clad figures standing in the thickening snow, silent spectators to this impromptu concert.

And after a while Patrick turned and led the way, really treacherous now, on up to the top of the Hill and down Anderson Street through the humble Jewish quarter at the back, and so down to Cambridge Street again and their own West End.

And all the while, as they walked through the white, silent night, Patrick thought of his son going off to Harvard, and he thought of his tens of thousands of countrymen who would never have that chance. So they'd have to depend on Michael, and a few others like him, to make things right for them all: to get the knowledge to fight the Yankees on their own turf, to get to the centers of power, the banks and the law firms—and, failing those, to solidify their political power.

His wife never got angry the way he did. It's a waste of time to get angry, she'd say. He'd lose his temper at some infuriating item in the *Globe*, or he'd hear about some poor family being evicted by their Yankee landlord, and he'd blow up. Not worth it, she'd say. Don't get mad, Patrick. Get even.

And that was what he meant to do.

13

"Isabella. Congratulations. It is—simply overwhelming. How can I . . . ?" He gave up, waved his hand at their surroundings and shook his head.

She knew that Lyman Griffin Revell had never been a man to show his feelings; she hardly expected him to do so now. It was enough that she had made him speechless, she thought.

So she laughed at him, giving a little flutter to his heart, and pressed his hands between her own, and passed him along so that she could tend to the rest of her guests, a long line of them stretching down the corridor to the door. It was a bitter, windy night: New Year's Eve 1899. She lifted her hand, and a footman came running. "Make sure that no one is waiting outside," she said. She meant her guests, of course; for the coachmen and their horses she had no thought.

"Yes, madam."

She returned to her duties: receiving her guests. She stood at the midpoint of her grand staircase, at the place where it split into two. To one side of her stood her nephew and adopted son, Frederick, and his fiancée; to the other her cousin and dearest friend of thirty years, her sister-in-law Florence. Through the huge double doors of her palace—oak, Venetian, XVIth century—streamed the whole of Boston, or so it seemed. Actually, of course, it was only a very small percentage of Boston, and a representative smattering from places like Cambridge and Concord and Salem and Beverly Farms. All the Family, of course—every last in-law of every last great-great-something-or-other; and the assorted pillars of Boston Society, such as it was—nothing to compare with the ostentation and vulgarity of New York, thank heaven; and a good smattering of the city's cultural elite, patrons of the Museum, the Boston Symphony, proprietors of the Athenaeum. And from across the river a few gentlemen from the College: her dear Professor Norton with whom she read Dante; and Mr. Eliot, whom she didn't know terribly well, but he was the president and you couldn't not invite him. And there, just now coming up, was the so very interesting Professor William James, who was rumored to have an interest in psychic phenomena.

"Professor, how delightful to see you . . ." and behind him, the imposing figure of the Episcopal bishop of Massachusetts, William Lawrence, and behind him, Dr. William Abbott Revell. Isabella had always liked Dr. William; he was astonishingly modest for a man of his fame, and kind and gentle—a real saint, people said. If the Unitarians had saints, which they did not. She wondered why he had never remarried; for the same reason, perhaps, that she herself had not. Having had a happy marriage, one hesitated to tempt Fate again.

It was after ten. Soon everyone would be here, and she would go upstairs and lead the way into the Music Room, where she had arranged for some Symphony players to perform a few selections. Then Lyman would say a few words, and Frederick as well, and they would all take a glass of champagne from the waiters bearing trays and toast the New Year—the new century. Frederick had tried to explain to her that in fact the year 1900 was the last of the old century, not the first of the new, but she had not understood him. "We are no longer going to write eighteen hundred and ninety-something on our letters, are we?" she had said. "We are going to write January seventeenth, nineteen hundred. As far as I am concerned, that is the new century. And I am going to welcome it with a grand open house. So there!"

She had not received one refusal of the several hundred invitations she had sent out. Everyone was eager to see the place she had built. For nearly three years now people had gossiped and speculated and wondered. A palace? In the Fens? But it would cost a fortune! Granted, Isabella Jackson Revell was in possession of a fortune, a very comfortable fortune indeed, inherited not only from her father and separately from her mother, who was a Cabot, but also from her husband and, via him, from her husband's father, who had been one of the richest men not only in Boston, not only in Massachusetts, but in all of America. But still. It seemed not only an eccentric thing to do, but an ostentatious one, and ostentation, to the New England conscience, was bad form.

To some people, of course, it had been obvious years ago that sooner or later she was going to need a place to display her treasures. Now, in the vast, echoing rooms of her version of a Venetian palace, hung paintings by Raphael and Giotto, Rubens and Crivelli, Vermeer and Cellini, Botticelli and Velasquez and Fra Angelico. The most magnificent Titian this side of the Atlantic, the *Rape of Europa*, hung in its own special room surrounded by tapestries and stained glass; in other rooms were rare books and manuscripts, antique furniture and silver and enamels, bas-reliefs and paneling and mosaics—a treasure house, this was, and the people of this prim, cold little city had never seen anything like it in all America. In Europe, yes—but that was the point, wasn't it? Rather than spend the rest of her days in Italy, she had, at great expense and effort, brought Italy here, and a bit of other countries as well. And now at last it was ready, her very own palace, and to celebrate its completion, as well as the coming of the new century, she had put on this magnificent party.

The journalist Edwin Jackson Revell walked out to it from his apartment in the new Hotel Agassiz on Commonwealth Avenue. For some weeks now he had been struggling with a piece of writing that would not come right, and he thought that the walk, two miles and more, would help him to think. He didn't mind the cold, it cleared his brain. As he approached through the dark, frozen Fens he saw the palace shimmering like a jewel in the night, illumination streaming from every window. A long line of carriages stretched down the road, carriage lamps flaring, the coachmen warming themselves in little groups, no doubt with liquor flasks well at hand. The bitter wind tore at Edwin's tall hat and his evening cape as he loped along. Overhead the night sky glittered with a thousand stars; a gibbous moon hung low. The wind whipped across the open space of the Fens and battered him so that he nearly stumbled. No matter: he liked a good fight, with the wind as well as anything—or anyone—else. He came near, saw the crowd going in, the building like a vision from a fairy tale, and then inside, warmth and light and people's excited voices, laughter and chatter. He handed in his things and in the press of the crowd allowed himself to be moved along. What he saw astonished him: an enormous courtyard four stories high topped by a glass roof. Despite the season, despite the temperature, the space was filled with trees and flowers: lilies and poinsettias, roses and gladioli and some whose name Edwin did not know. Statuary stood along the graveled walks; at the far end, water trickled from the mouth of a stone dolphin. And in the center of the floor, a magnificent mosaic, Bacchus and his nymphs. Edwin took a deep breath, inhaling the delicious fragrance from the blossoms. Truly, this was a magical place in the middle of a Boston winter.

And waiting to greet him, resplendent in a shimmering blue gown, diamonds at her ears and throat, her beautiful eyes glowing with the triumph of this night, stood Isabella. His heart skipped a beat as he went to her. She was the most intriguing woman he had ever met, and what a shame that she had never remarried. On the other hand, he despised the life of excessive spending that she led.

In fact, if it hadn't been Isabella whose place this was, he would have hated it. He had recently been to Newport, where the Vanderbilts and the Astors and others trying to ape them had begun to build vulgar and ostentatious summer "cottages" that were miniature French chateaux, or Scottish castles, or similar inappropriate ornaments for the Rhode Island shore. From Newport he had returned to Boston. It had been midsummer, very hot. He had walked down Commonwealth Avenue gazing at the magnificent town houses that lined the center mall. Most of them were empty, their owners fled to the seashore and the mountains. In the slums of the North End children ran half naked in the streets and died of typhus and dysentery and infection and malnutrition. What Mrs. Vanderbilt—or Isabella Revell, for that matter—spent on a new dress would feed a poor family for a year. He admitted to himself that the rich people of Boston, of Massachusetts, were hardly the equal in vulgarity and ostentation of the New York rich, but all the same, it disturbed him to know that members of his own family spent as much as they pleased while the children of the poor struggled to survive.

And it was not only a matter of spending. His eye fell on Lyman Griffin Revell. The older man met his gaze and stonily returned it. He had not forgotten, Edwin knew, the episode of the strike at his mill.

"Dear Edwin! How good of you to come!" Isabella smiled her lovely smile at him. "Come to tea tomorrow and tell me what you think. Will you?"

He laughed with pleasure at the thought. He was aware that the man next to him, whom he did not know, was looking at him enviously. He pressed

Isabella's hands between his own. "I'll tell you right now what I think. It's magnificent! But you know that, you don't need me to say it."

"Ah, but I love to hear it! And from such a critic as you—wonderful!"

She laughed at him and passed him along to Florence. Dear Florence, a half-lived life, and yet Florence was, for Edwin, the conscience of the Family, the one who, like her aunt Caroline, had seemed to feel the need to make repayment for the fact that she had been born a Revell, born to great wealth. She looked thin, he thought. He'd heard that she'd funded a settlement house and worked there long hours. He resolved to visit it; when he told her so, her face lighted up and, despite her years, she looked almost pretty.

Then on into the Music Room to await the concert. Everywhere his eye came to rest, he saw something more to wonder at. The magnificence of Isabella's achievement was staggering, he thought. He hoped she had the sense to hire guards—not just for tonight, but permanently. Unprotected, this place was an invitation to theft. As he took a seat he looked at his fellow guests. He saw Judson and his daughter Violet. One of Isabella's brothers and his wife. One of Lyman's sons. Old Edward Jackson Revell, Isabella's father. And then, right at his elbow, Professor James. Edwin was a great admirer of the Professor's brother, Henry. He thought it would not be too forward if he asked if he might meet Henry the next time he came to Boston. Edwin had heard that Professor James was one of the founders of the American Society for Psychical Research. Perhaps that was why he looked so intently at Edwin as they spoke: he was trying, perhaps, to see if Edwin had any visible talent for parapsychology. Perhaps, Edwin thought, he should have asked to attend a séance instead.

There was a little stir at the door, and a ripple of excitement passed through the audience like wind across a field of wheat. But it was not Isabella who came in, nor even the musicians hired for the evening; rather, the Family's most famous member, the astronomer John Abbott Revell, was about to make his entrance. He was indisputably the most handsome male in the Family: well over six feet tall, with an athlete's build and a matinee idol's looks, and an air of arrogance that seemed to draw people toward him rather than repel them. For a moment he surveyed the crowd; then he made his way, nodding and smiling in greeting, to an empty seat beside Edwin.

"I say, cousin." John eased himself onto the small gilt chair and absent-mindedly ran his hand over his crown of golden hair. "This is something, is it not?"

Edwin laughed. "Something! More than that, I'd say!"

"You writing it up for one of your papers?"

"Oh, no. It's not my kind of story. There are plenty of Society writers who'll be glad to have a fling at it."

"If she lets 'em in," snorted John. "She'd not terribly fond of the press, y'know. Present company excepted, of course."

No more than you, thought Edwin, but he held his tongue. John had recently returned from London, where he had ascended in a balloon over Hyde Park so as to photograph the paths from a height and compare them to what he saw on Mars. The press had gone wild over this exploit, and John had made headlines in Boston and New York as well as in London. Of course he was now linked irrevocably to the wildest inventions of the scribblers of science fantasy, Martian invaders and all the rest. The only way he could combat their pernicious influence, their trivializing of his work, was to keep on working in his serious way. It was not his fault if the gullible public wanted to read embroideries on his findings; the findings themselves were fantastic enough without some fantasist's meddling.

And now at last the musicians filed in to take their places on the little stage; and Isabella, aglow with triumph, signaled Herr Gericke to begin. In the sudden, expectant hush, the first notes floated out, the nearly unendurable beauty of an air composed by Johann Sebastian Bach more than a hundred and fifty years ago. A long time!—and yet the notes unfolded as fresh and compelling as if they had been written only the day before. Isabella sat a little to one side, nodding her head ever so slightly, looking out over her audience. Her open house was far from over—in fact it had barely begun—but she knew that it was a great success. Just as people launched their daughters into society, she had launched her palace. It was famous now: secure in the annals of the city. And all the people who disapproved of her—and there were many—now would have to acknowledge that.

She wished—oh, how desperately she wished!—that Theo was here to see it, too.

PART V

AUTUMN HARVEST

GRIFFIN REVELLS

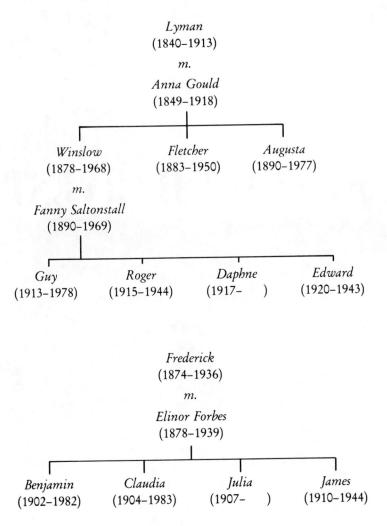

Lyman
(1840–1913)

m.

Anna Gould
(1849–1918)

Winslow   Fletcher   Augusta
(1878–1968)   (1883–1950)   (1890–1977)

m.

Fanny Saltonstall
(1890–1969)

Guy   Roger   Daphne   Edward
(1913–1978)   (1915–1944)   (1917–   )   (1920–1943)

Frederick
(1874–1936)

m.

Elinor Forbes
(1878–1939)

Benjamin   Claudia   Julia   James
(1902–1982)   (1904–1983)   (1907–   )   (1910–1944)

JACKSON REVELLS

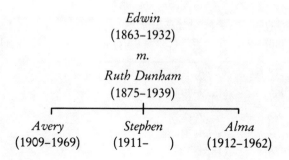

Isabella Jackson Griffin Revell
(1850–1936)

Edwin
(1863–1932)

m.

Ruth Dunham
(1875–1939)

Avery	*Stephen*	*Alma*
(1909–1969)	(1911–)	(1912–1962)

ABBOTT REVELLS

Judson
(1850–1934)

m.

Louisa Richardson
(1855–1880)

Violet
(1880–1959)

m.

Alex Korsakoff
(1891–1976)

Otis
(1849–1899)

m.

Margaret Henry
(1855–1907)

Henry   *Six others*
(1879–1943)

m.

Marian Motley
(1881–1942)

Lawrence
(1909–   )

John
(1863–1930)

m.

Evelyn Sohier
(1875–1933)

Dwight
(1910–   )

SHAUGHNESSYS

Michael
(1884–1950)

m.

Kathleen Costello
(1885–1951)

Michael Jr.   *Jane*   *Four others*
(1912–1974)   (1914–1980)

And this is good old Boston,
The home of the bean and the cod,
Where the Lowells talk to the Cabots
And the Cabots talk only to God.

John Collins Bossidy
Toast, Holy Cross College
Alumni Dinner, 1910

1. BREAD AND ROSES

1

"I say, Shaughnessy! Hold up a minute!" The voice came out of the late afternoon dusk, someone calling to him from across the Yard. Michael Shaughnessy halted on the narrow path trodden through the snow. The bare black branches of the tall elms were silhouetted against the pink-tinged sunset sky; lights had come on in the buildings. At such times (and at few others) he felt a curious affection for Harvard: not the familial affection felt by most of his classmates, but a feeling of amiable contempt for a place whose standards and values, while charming and rather endearing, were largely irrelevant to life in the real world— life as he knew it, thanks to his father.

He nodded now as Fletcher Revell came puffing up. Fletcher was a thin, languorous youth who sat one seat in front of Michael in their Renaissance History class. A pleasant enough fellow, Michael thought, but hardly a serious person.

"Hallo. Where's the fire?" he said.

"No fire." Fletcher still panted. "But a bit of a clutch. I say, are you free tonight?"

Michael frowned. He had planned to have an early supper and finish writing a paper.

"Might be. Why?"

"My cousin's having a bud party."

"A what?"

"Debutantes. They call 'em buds, don't ask why. I told her I'd bring a few fellows. But *la grippe* has laid 'em low, and I am desperate, old boy. Could you do a chap a favor an' come on over? Just across the river, won't last long. Good food, pretty girls—an hour or two of your time, that's all. Can't bear to let the girls down, y'know."

537

Michael would not have been more amazed—and amused—if Fletcher Revell had invited him to join the Porcellian. He must be desperate indeed, he thought, if he invites an Irishman to a Boston debutante party!

He was struck by a sudden curiosity, as if someone from the Peabody Museum of Ethnology had invited him to observe a tribe of natives deep in the Amazon jungle. This might be the only chance he would ever have to see genuine Boston Brahmins in action on their home turf.

"I'd be glad to," he said. "Thanks. What time?"

"Oh, about eight. Say, that's really good of you. I'm in your debt." Fletcher was all smiles. "I'll come by and pick you up. We'll get a cab over. D'you have a dinner jacket?"

"Yes."

"Good. And, ah . . ."

In the rapidly gathering dusk Michael saw the other's face twist into a grimace of embarrassment. Or perhaps it wasn't that; perhaps it was simply cowardice.

In any case: "One more thing, old chap. If anyone asks you, could you, ah, say you're from, ah, New York? Or anywhere, doesn't matter, but not, ah . . ." He laughed a little nervous laugh.

The significance of his request, the sheer outrageous nerve of it, hit Michael like a slap across his face. He caught his breath; he smiled to conceal his anger. "But not from Boston, right? You don't want me to be a Boston Irishman."

Fletcher nodded so enthusiastically that a lock of straight blond hair fell across his forehead. He was grateful that Michael understood. "No hard feelings, old boy, but it's just that—"

"Don't try to explain." Michael could feel the stiffness of his mouth, stiff from smiling, smiling—the bloody nerve of this twerp, who in hell did he think he was, coming right out with it, don't *be* what you *are*, you might offend someone . . . ?

Still smiling, Michael said, "I'll see you, then."

Michael watched him go; then, feeling sick to his stomach with anger, he returned to his house and went to his suite, and without speaking to his roommate, a gloomy German boy, went into his bedroom and lay down. His heart was hammering at his ribs, and he could feel his anger rising so that it threatened to split his skull. He'd said yes only because he had been so shocked. But now, reflecting, he didn't think that he could go through with it. Pretend to be what he was not? But he was perfectly happy with what he was. Why should he have to pretend to be something else?

For the better part of an hour he lay in the dark, thinking about the evening ahead. He hated Fletcher Revell. More, he hated himself. He should have returned Revell's insult with one of his own. Now he needed to find some better method of revenge. *Don't get mad,* his mother had always said, *get even.* At last he got up, went down to supper, returned, and changed his clothes. While he combed his hair he looked at himself as a stranger might. Could you tell what Michael Shaughnessy was, just by looking at him? Well: perhaps.

There was a certain type of Irish, black Irish they called it—black-haired, blue-eyed—and that was what he was. Like his mother.

Not good enough for Fletcher Revell, was he?

Well, he would see about that.

At the party, which was held at a large, handsome house on lower Marlborough Street, Michael was introduced to a series of pleasant-looking young women who were accustomed to having Harvard boys fill out the guest lists of debutante parties. Each time he heard his last name announced, Michael watched to see the reaction. Sometimes there was a flicker of interest, Shaughnessy not being a name that was heard at Boston debutante parties; but no more than that. He was said to be from New York; for all anyone here knew, his father was the Irish consul. And so because Fletcher Revell had vouched for him, they accepted him well enough, and he even had a little show of interest from one or two of the young ladies who were, as they had been brought up to be, always on the lookout for a prospective husband.

He played his part; he bided his time. Fletcher Revell's insult still rankled, worse and worse as the evening passed; but the moment must be just exactly right . . .

He watched the crowd, even as he danced and talked and sipped the rather warm fruit punch. He had never had the opportunity to see so many Yankee females all together. They were, he thought, not half so interesting as the Irish girls he knew—granted that he was prejudiced in favor of his own kind. But at the same time, neither the young men nor the young women here tonight seemed worthy of the kind of hatred that his grandmother had lavished on them over the years; they didn't seem substantial enough. They seemed like people of no consequence—silly, shallow people with no sense of the seriousness of life.

But even as he made that judgment, he knew that it was wrong. These young folks came from families that ruled not only the city of Boston, but the Commonwealth of Massachusetts and, indeed, a good part of the nation—ruled financially, ruled socially, and still, as his father would attest, ruled politically, despite the inroads of Patrick Shaughnessy and his fellow ward bosses.

"Michael?" Fletcher Revell stood before him. At his side was an absolutely stunning girl who, despite her beauty, bore a faint resemblance to Fletcher. "I'd like you to meet my cousin, Blanche Winslow Brown."

Michael took her hand and felt its strength, its warmth; he looked into her beautiful blue eyes and saw dancing merriment, a challenge to excite any man.

And now, he knew, his moment had come.

He put on his most ingratiating smile. He gazed into her eyes as if he and she were alone, just the two of them. He saw the spark of her response.

"Sure, now," he said, "it's a lovely colleen I see here. An' did'y'come over recently, m'dear? Yer as pretty as the Rose of Tralee, sure y'are."

He saw the smile freeze on her face. Fletcher's mouth had dropped open, even as an angry flush rose to his cheeks. People standing nearby, who had overheard, paused in their conversations to stare, to wonder if indeed they had heard correctly. It was as if—well, as if a pigtailed Chinaman had suddenly dropped down into their midst and started jabbering at them.

"I'm from Bhaaston," Michael went on in his lilting brogue. "How about yerself, dearie?"

It was a question so crudely put, so loudly and embarrassingly put, that really the only thing that Fletcher could think of to do was to put his hand under Michael's elbow and steer him none too gently across the room under the shocked, outraged, disbelieving eyes of some of the very best people in Boston, many of them related to Fletcher—and wouldn't he have the devil's own time explaining to his aunt and his mother how on earth he came to be stupid enough to bring along this young man who was—"*Really*, Fletcher!"— an Irish boy from God knew what slum. Irish! He might better have been Negro. He might better have been that pigtailed Chinaman. Then at least he might have aroused some charitable feelings in the white folks assembled to gawk at him as if—even in his dinner jacket—he were some vagrant savage, some poor lost aborigine.

Outside, in the bitter January night, Fletcher kept on going down the narrow shoveled path until he reached the street with its long line of waiting carriages. Then he stopped and faced the acquaintance who had so horribly embarrassed him.

"I say, Shaughnessy, that was a low blow." Fletcher was trembling, more from fury than from the cold. "You promised to behave decently, you know. If I'd known you were such a cad, I'd never have brought you."

Michael knew that the sour taste in his mouth was contempt. "I did behave decently. If you can't take a little joke, that's your problem."

"Little joke! Why, you insulted everyone in that room! Behaving like a— like a—"

"Like what I am!" He heard his grandmother's voice: *Just remember, they don't give any more credit to an Irishman than they do to a horse. More to the horse, if you ask me. You're not human to them, never forget it.*

Fletcher made an involuntary movement, as if to cuff Michael on the chin; and then he stopped, remembering that Michael was a star member of the college boxing team.

Automatically, Michael flexed his fists, but he had no need to do so; this young man was not about to risk having his teeth shoved down his throat, not even to salvage the Family honor.

Abruptly Michael turned and walked at a rapid clip down the middle of the snowy street.

Eventually, Fletcher Revell's relatives forgave him for the embarrassment he had caused them; they understood that he had only been trying to be helpful. Silly boy, they said. Next time, come by yourself.

Patrick was less forgiving than the Revells.

" 'Twas a stupid thing to do," he said. "We've enough trouble with 'em in the ordinary course of events. We don't need to go out of our way to make enemies of 'em."

It was a Saturday afternoon, closing time at the Hendricks Club, the Ward Eight meeting place. As he did almost every week, Michael had spent the day at his father's side as the folks from the ward came by to ask Patrick's help. Patrick thought of the process as a form of buying on credit: people were borrowing from him, borrowing his time, his energy, his expertise in the ways the world worked. And inevitably, on election day, he would call in the debts. And they would pay with their votes, and then the process would begin again.

2

The unease that Edwin had experienced at Isabella's housewarming on New Year's Eve, 1899, stayed with him well into the next decade. He worked as a freelance journalist, an inhabitant of Grub Street; often he wrote about poor people—people oppressed by the wealthy classes. The meager fees he earned would not have kept him in tobacco, let alone paid for food and shelter. Fortunately he had income from his Family trusts.

The fact of his own wealth sometimes gave him more than a twinge of guilt. He acknowledged that he could not possibly have endured the lives of his subjects—oppressed people, impoverished people, factory workers and immigrants and sweated labor in the tenement districts of every sizable city in the state. Sometimes he went far afield to find his stories, to New York, with its sweatshops; or into the South, where the cotton factories had begun to relocate; or into the heartland, to Pittsburgh and the industrial cities of the Midwest, to mining camps and migrant worker camps in the Far West—to all the nation's oppressed, Edwin Jackson Revell paid his visits, and he wrote his stories and sold them to muckraking magazines.

And year after year his anger grew—anger at the titans of industry who squeezed the life out of their workers and fought the growth of the unions tooth and nail; anger at the complacent public, who tolerated such conditions; anger at the legislators who took lobbyists' money and refused to control the ways in which corporations exploited their labor.

He became, in short, that most toothless of tigers, a parlor radical. He played the part well. He let his hair grow until it touched the collar of his velvet jacket; he used an ivory holder to smoke his cigarettes; he wore a flowing tie and, in winter, a cape and a low-crowned, broad-brimmed hat so that he looked more like a bohemian painter than a scribbler. Most of all, he had about him an élan, a quality of style and verve that seemed to grow, year by year, the angrier he became, the more convinced he became that the system and all its attendant ills needed to be radically changed.

In the summer of 1905, while on a visit to Newport, he underwent a revelation in both his personal and professional lives. His hostess was the chatelaine of one of the palatial summer "cottages" that had sprung up along Bellevue Avenue and Ocean Drive. She liked to surround herself with people whom she judged to be "interesting"—artistic types, often enough, who could be counted upon to keep a lively conversation going at the dinner table. And so, on his first evening, Edwin found himself seated beside a bright-looking young woman who announced that she was a dancer in the style of Isadora Duncan, and that she had no qualms about taking a lover whenever she pleased.

True to his principles, Edwin admired such a liberated female; and later than night, lying on his palatial bed in his palatial room and trying, after his full meal, to read the latest installment of *The Jungle*—a nauseating exposé of the conditions in the Chicago stockyards—Edwin discovered that he could not get the engaging young lady out of his mind. He put down the obscure socialist periodical in which Upton Sinclair's story was printed, and in his stockinged feet tiptoed out of his room and down the corridor to where he thought the demoiselle was quartered.

He was right. What was more, she was as sleepless as he, and very glad to see him. And after they had gotten to know each other considerably better, they talked for a while. She was, it turned out, as put off as he was by the ostentation surrounding them in this pile of masonry and gilded woodwork and marble that perched on the edge of Narragansett Bay like a gaudy bauble. What a waste of money, to build a place like this! Newport was full of them. What they cost could feed thousands of tenement families for a lifetime.

Earnestly, the young woman gazed into Edwin's eyes. She thought he was wonderful. What eloquence! What a splendid lover!

Three months later they were married, and Edwin, stung by Upton Sinclair's success, embarked on his own exposé. *The Shame of the Rich*, he called it—an account of the way the nation's wealthy men had acquired their fortunes, ill-gotten and then often squandered, while all around lay the seeds of revolution in the persons of millions of poor. The growing gap between the haves and the have-nots, he wrote, could result in only the gravest consequences for the nation; somehow, Congress must take action to lessen the extremes of wealth and poverty before a second revolution, much more bloody than the first, was undertaken.

He was not content to deal with the present only; he went far back into the past, which meant into the past of his own family as well as others, and dredged up the business of slave trading, and the business of opium trading; more recently came the tales of worker exploitation, and the business of union breaking, and the business of slumlording—all those unpleasant truths, and more, he put into his book.

He had thought that such an exercise would free him of the guilt he felt at living off his Family trusts, but he was wrong. He still felt it, all the more because he couldn't bring himself to give up his comfortable life.

What was worse, the book was not a great success. The upshot of the affair was that on the one hand he succeeded in alienating—permanently—the majority of his Family, who were outraged at what they considered his betrayal, while on the other he failed to set in motion the reforms that he had outlined in his book as necessary to save the Republic from Red Revolution.

3

It was the feast day of St. Brendan the Navigator, who as everyone knew was the real discoverer of America, and in the soft May night the boyos flocked to Patrick's saloon to drink the health of the ancient explorer.

But Patrick was not with them, for his mother was dying. He sat by her bed, holding her hand, and his thoughts were far from the riotous celebrations at drinking places all over the Northeast.

So now he sat with her in her small bedroom on the first floor of the tenement she owned on Chambers Street, and kept what he knew was the death watch, and waited for the moment when her eyes came open again so that he could say to her what needed to be said. Like most Irish men, he disguised his feelings behind a mask of hearty conviviality which kept people at a distance even as it enabled him to get through his life with a minimum of difficulty. In the front room were his own children, and his sisters and his brothers and their children, and several neighbors—a regular crowd, it was, and from the looks of her, it wouldn't be possible to have them all in before she went.

Her face was pale, remarkably unlined for a woman of seventy who had, as she had, survived a difficult life. She looked unreal to him, lying there so still. A large portion of her charm—and she had had charm, indisputably—had always been her vivacity, her sharp intelligence reflected in her face.

Absentmindedly he patted her hand. As if in response, her eyes opened. She looked at him blankly for a moment; then she knew who he was. She managed a little smile.

"Well, now," she said. "An' how are we today?"

He felt hot tears sting his eyes. "All right," he said, blinking rapidly. "We're doin' grand, Ma. How about yourself?"

Her tumor was inoperable, the doctor had said; he had given her morphia to dull the pain, and so she was somewhat numb, with slurry speech, her good sharp brain fatally slowed.

"I'm goin'," she said. "It doesn't matter. I'm glad to go, to be with your father again."

He had only a few memories of his father, and all of them worn soft and round by memory, as the sea wears smooth a pebble: his father holding his hand as they went for a walk to the Common, his father lifting him high to see a Fourth of July parade, and presiding at Christmas dinner, or perhaps it was Thanksgiving. . . .

She pressed his hand a little.

"What is it, Ma? D'you want to see someone? Michael?"

Almost imperceptibly she nodded. Michael was her first and always her favorite grandchild; they all knew that, and accepted it. It was as if his birth had meant, to her, that the roots she and her husband had planted had taken hold, and that the family would stay: two generations born here, and they were here for good.

At her funeral a good many people who came wondered, to themselves if not out loud, whether that good-looking Harvard-educated boy was going to follow in his father's footsteps and take up politics. Michael was aware of this speculation, if hardly influenced by it. He had no intention of going into politics. He had no liking for it—endless horse trading, counting votes, remembering favors, holding grudges. "Every time I get someone a good political appointment," Patrick had told him once, "I make ten enemies and one ingrate."

And so while Michael knew perfectly well that politics had nurtured his father's generation into life in America, and was performing the same function for his own, he had a different way to gain acceptance. He was going to make money, and buy his way in.

4

"Say, friend! How do I get to Walden Pond?"

"Well, now—we're here in Jamaica Plain, you got to get to the railroad station. So you just go along Centre Street a bit and take a right on Boylston. That'll bring you to Boylston Station, about half a mile. Take the train in town to the Park Square Station. Then you got to get to Causeway Street, you can either hoof it or take a hack. You want the station for the Fitchburg railroad. First stop after Lincoln Station is Walden. I've done it myself with the family. It's not a bad trip—maybe two or three hours, depending on connections."

5

"If y'want my support," said Patrick, "y'll have to promise the jobs, otherwise I can't do it. I have my people I have to take care of. They know I'll save 'em from the inquisitorial terrors of organized charity. There's a fate worse than death, for sure. Organized charity my foot! There'll be no social workers trampin' around my bailiwick, no, sir! Meanwhile I got this Christmas party to run, see, an' I want Mr. Edward Filene himself to show up. An' I want him to be bringin' with him five hundred pairs of mittens an' five hundred little knitted caps, like this, see? An' if he doesn't want to do that, I think we're goin' to have to reassess his property. Hasn't he just opened his Automatic Bargain Basement? Very profitable, isn't it? I think maybe his taxes will have to go up."

There was now something called the "Good Government Association." It had been organized after the rapid demise of the old, impotent CIA. Like that group, this was a Yankee creation designed to torment the Irish. It failed to do so. By this first decade in the new century, the Irish were everywhere, unstoppable, unbeatable—a punishment from God, it seemed, on the descendants of the Catholic-hating Puritans who had founded the colony.

When Patrick Shaughnessy heard about the Good Government Association he laughed out loud—something he rarely did. "Good Government Association, is it? I'll show y'what good government is, that I will! Goo-goos, that's what they are! Well, let'm'have their association, if they want. We'll have one, too. An' we'll call it the 'Better Government Association'!"

6

On January 11, 1912, the female weavers at the Everett Cotton Mill in Lawrence, Massachusetts, opened their pay envelopes to find thirty-two cents less than the previous week's pay.

At once they stopped their looms. Then they walked out, shouting—in their native tongue, which was Polish—"Short pay! Short pay!" The company brought in its interpreters to try to explain to the weavers why their pay had been cut, but the women would not listen. Thirty-two cents out of a weekly pay that averaged six dollars was a sizable amount. Thirty-two cents would buy five loaves of bread. Few workers in Lawrence could afford meat, but almost everyone had bread. Now the corporations wanted to take that away, too.

The weavers' pay was short because the Massachusetts Legislature, responding to public pressure, had reduced the work week for women and children from fifty-six hours to fifty-four. The Legislature had acted similarly in 1910, when women's and children's hours were cut from fifty-eight to fifty-six per week. Pay had not been cut then; with the passage of this new law, the workers had been concerned that this time they would lose money. They could not afford to. A few of them sent a special delivery letter to the corporation managers to ask about the company's plans. They had no reply. The men who had written the letter were members of a fledgling labor union that called itself the International Workers of the World—the IWW, Wobblies for short. They aimed to organize all the unskilled workers left out of the American Federation of Labor, which was made up of craft unions. The Wobblies were known as radicals—very dangerous. People were afraid to sign up with them. In Lawrence they had only a couple of hundred members.

Word spread quickly that night in Lawrence that the Polish women had walked out, and the next morning, at another mill, some Italian men walked out, too, and started a rampage that left considerable property damage. For the first time in the city's history, the bells rang a riot alarm.

That afternoon a mass meeting was held in the Franco-Belgian Hall. Starting a strike was one thing; keeping it going was another. The workers knew that they needed help. They sent a telegram to New York, to ask for Joe Ettor. He was a young man, but already a veteran labor organizer. Although he was a native-born American, he spoke not only English, but Italian and Polish, and could get along in Yiddish and Hungarian—just the man for a polyglot place like Lawrence.

By Saturday afternoon he was in the city at the hall addressing the strikers. They were many hundreds now, eager to follow his orders. He set up a strike committee and explained how a picket line and a soup kitchen should be run.

On Monday morning pickets ringed several of the mills. Some people crossed them to go to their jobs, but as the week wore on, fewer and fewer did so. For one thing, they were threatened with violence—beating or worse. For another, they thought that if the strike kept up, it might succeed. By the end of the second week membership in the IWW local had mushroomed to ten thousand.

But it is hard to keep a strike going, particularly in the middle of winter when an empty belly seems all the more empty. And of course the authorities did not sit idly by and watch the strikers parade every day. They mobilized the state militia to assist the local police. Many Harvard boys were in the National Guard; they viewed going up to Lawrence as a lark—a chance to cut classes for a worthy cause, a chance to keep the lower orders in their place.

The main thing, said the mill managers, is to stop the picketing. So the militia and the police attacked the picketers with streams of water from fire hoses. The pickets would disperse, but then they would line up again and start marching again, waving their signs—and singing! That was the worst of it, the singing. The authorities realized all too well that songs were a powerful builder of morale.

The strike leaders warned the strikers over and over again that they must be nonviolent. Any blood that is spilled will be your blood, they said. It turned out that they were right, for as the police harassed the picketers day after day, blocking their path, herding them away from the mills, it was inevitable that the strikers' discipline, which had been pretty good, would break. One night, when the police charged a picket line, flailing left and right with their billy clubs, some of the strikers and their supporters on the sidelines began to throw snowballs and rocks at the police. Shots rang out. One of the strikers, a woman, fell dead.

The mill owners were not displeased. Now the world will see, they said, how these red radical anarchists have brought nothing but death and destruction to our fair city.

Joe Ettor was arrested for the crime. He had an alibi: he had been at a meeting of German workers several miles from the incident. No matter, said the authorities: he incited and provoked and counseled the person who did commit the murder—and that was not the police.

They put Lawrence under martial law; they forbade all public meetings; they called out twenty-two more militia companies; and they sent Ettor to the Salem jail, where he was held for months without a hearing, without bail. He continued to protest his innocence. I was arrested not for any crime I committed, he said, but for the political beliefs that I hold. They don't like anarchists; they think we are their enemy. They are right in that, at least: we are.

7

When the Lawrence strike began, Edwin Jackson Revell was in North Carolina writing a series on child labor in the cotton mills—many of which had come from the north to take advantage of labor cheaper even than in Lowell or Chicopee or Lawrence, Massachusetts.

His editor in New York sent him a copy of the *Times* with the account of the strike and the picketing. Edwin did not know Joe Ettor, but he had heard about the IWW. He knew that, given the right dispute, the union had great potential for radical reform. This, his editor said, might be it.

Edwin agreed. He got into his buggy and drove to the nearest railroad station and took the first train north.

He stopped off in Boston to see his wife and children. His wife had not danced professionally since the birth of their first child, a boy. After that came another boy, and then a girl. Edwin loved his wife, but as he admitted to himself, she was not the passionate, exciting, emancipated young woman whom he had married. After their daughter's birth, she had announced to him that she wanted no more children, and so their marital relations had stopped. Edwin had had an intimate relationship with only one woman since then, a redhead whom he'd met at a party in Greenwich Village. She had had bad body odor and he hadn't enjoyed himself.

The next morning he went up to Lawrence on the train. It was a bright, bitter January day. Snow lay deep and spotless white in the countryside, but in the city it was pounded down into what seemed like gray rock. The place was tense, police everywhere, people's faces drawn and angry. He walked along until he came to the picketing. Around and around the huge red-brick mills—a thousand people, at least. He was surprised that there were so many. They carried signs, and as they marched they sang:

> As we come marching, marching in the
> beauty of the day,
> A million darkened kitchens,
> a thousand mill lofts gray,

> Are touched with all the radiance
>   that a sudden sun discloses,
> For the people hear us singing: "Bread
>   and roses! Bread and roses!"
>
> As we come marching, marching,
>   unnumbered women dead
> Go crying through our singing
>   their ancient cry for bread.
> Small art and love and beauty
>   their drudging spirits knew
> Yes, it is bread we fight for—
>   but we fight for roses, too!

At the end of the street stood a phalanx of police and militia, bayonets drawn and at the ready. At a shouted order, they began to move forward in lockstep. The picketers had no place to retreat to. When they were safely penned up, another order was shouted, and all at once the clean air, the sparkling, windless day was clouded by a fog of tear gas. People shrieked in panic; they tried to run away but they could not because of the bayonets. A number of picketers were wounded; Edwin saw at least three militiamen deliberately stab civilians.

Silence fell over the scene—an appalled hush, as people realized what had happened, as they tried to breathe in the poisoned air. Slowly they regrouped. Each one found a partner; they clasped hands, they formed their picket line again; and as they slowly began to walk, they began to sing as well:

> As we come marching, marching,
>   we bring the greater days.
> The rising of the women means
>   rising of the race.
> No more the drudge and idler—ten that
>   toil where one reposes,
> But a sharing of life's glories: Bread
>   and roses! Bread and roses!

Edwin was gasping, his eyes watering so that he could hardly see. He couldn't understand how they could sing; he could not have choked out a word if his life had depended on it. And so after a few moments he hurried away and found a barroom where he could soothe his throat with a glass of cold beer.

That afternoon he went to the Franco-Belgian Hall. A meeting of the strike committee was in progress: no outsiders allowed. All the same, a few journalists hung about. They knew that the strikers depended on them for publicity and would therefore give them at least some tidbits before the day was through.

But there was no time, it seemed. The door to the small meeting room was flung open and the men came hurrying out. "Come on! Big Bill's comin' in, we're goin' to meet him!"

So the newspapermen joined in, and everyone headed for the railroad station. Shortly the train came puffing in. There were thousands of workers gathered, spilling from the platform and waiting room out into the street. They looked happy, they looked as though they were at a celebration. Despite the agonies of the past weeks, they were jubilant.

The train stopped. A man appeared at the door. He was huge—over six feet tall, as broad as a barn door. A shout went up. "There he is! It's Big Bill! Hey, Bill! Welcome to Lawrence!"

The man grinned and waved his Stetson hat at the crowd. "Thanks! Thanks very much! We've come to do a little job of work here, an' it ain't in the mills!" The crowd roared. He put his hat back on his leonine head, clasped his hands above it like a champion prizefighter, and wedged his burly body down the narrow iron steps onto the platform. Behind him came a woman and two men.

The reporter standing next to Edwin during this little show was a sharp-looking fellow from the *New York World*—Pulitzer's sheet. He turned to Edwin. "That's Big Bill Haywood, all right," he said, "but who's that with him?"

"Elizabeth Gurley Flynn. And the foreign-looking man is the anarchist Tresca. I don't know who the third one is."

The reporter let out a low whistle which came soundless in the uproar around them. Haywood and his companions were making their way as if they were royalty in a progress. People reached out to clasp their hands, to shout a greeting, bestow a hug. Every last soul was convinced that now the strike would be won, now that these near legendary figures had shown up. Their presence meant that this was no longer a local affair. National attention would be paid, now that Big Bill Haywood had come with his best organizers.

That night, Haywood outlined his strategy to the strike committee, and over the next few days they began to put it into action. Mainly, he said, you need to keep the public's attention. The murder and the bayonet attacks on the pickets are all well and good as far as they go, but we can do more. You have the public's attention now—look at all these reporters, do you think they are here for their health? So here's what we're going to do.

A week later Edwin found himself at the railroad station again, this time to watch a departure. A crowd of workers, women mostly, had gathered on the platform. Each one held the hand of a child. Each child had pinned to its coat a white cardboard label that gave its name and its destination. All of them were going to New York City.

Many of the women wept. When would they see their beloved babies again? As Haywood had explained to Edwin and a few of the other reporters, these children, as anyone could see, were badly undernourished. Most of them—*most of them, mind!*—had rickets. Their little bones were twisted and malformed—crippled from birth, crippled from before birth because neither they nor their mothers had ever had enough to eat. Look at them! These innocent little victims of capitalist greed! Wages are so low in Lawrence that no one on the corporations can survive! These children have starved all their lives, they starved in their mothers' wombs, and their mothers starved before the children were conceived! Look at them! There's your capitalism for you—starving children!

The reporters scribbled assiduously. When they wrote their articles, they added many facts: of every thousand children in Lawrence, 176 died before their first birthdays. One out of three mill workers died before reaching the age of 25. Average life for a mill operative was 39.6 years, for spinners 36 years—this compared to an average life for a lawyer or a clergyman of 65.4 years. Average price of a room in Lawrence, one to six dollars a week. Average week's pay, $8.76 for men; one-third less for women. No one worked a full year. One in four mill workers suffered from tuberculosis.

And so on. By the time the children reached New York, the stories were written, and they appeared the next day alongside pictures of the little waifs being greeted tumultuously by crowds singing the "Internationale."

One hundred and twenty children were evacuated that day—ostensibly to get them into stable homes where they could be warm and well fed for a little while at least, while the strike ground on. It was noted that many of these children, malnourished, sickly, were dressed in little more than rags. Only a few had any underwear. In their misery, in their victimization, they caught the public's fancy as nothing else had done.

Capitalist swine! Squeezing the life out of these innocents!

Two weeks later, ninety-two more children were evacuated, again to New York. Hundreds of families had signed up, asking to take a child; there were more applicants than there were children. One of the women who helped to organize the operation was a nurse named Margaret Sanger. She shepherded the children that cold February afternoon in a parade down Fifth Avenue. People waved and cheered them from the sidelines. Many of the children were confused; they had no idea where they were, or why.

No matter. They had served their purpose. They were a tremendous success. Brave little troupers!

The name of Lawrence, Massachusetts, began to have a bad smell to it. The newspapers had stirred up the public, which in turn had stirred up Congress. Hearings were scheduled. If conditions in the mills were as bad as advertised, perhaps some kind of regulatory legislation ought to be passed.

The mill owners shuddered, as did the city fathers of Lawrence. They realized that the red radical anarchist syndicalist Wobbly troublemakers, the outside agitators coming in to stir up trouble amongst the peaceful working folks of Lawrence, had succeeded.

One night not long after, Big Bill sat with one of his lieutenants, William Trautmann, and one of his allies, the anarchist Carlo Tresca, and gave a frank and largely off the record interview to several of the journalists who had been covering the strike. Big Bill was in an optimistic mood; the strike was going well. The soup kitchen was keeping up with the demand. Donations were coming in at a good clip. The children had provided tremendous publicity for the strikers, and next week another group would go out.

Suddenly the door burst open. Three people came running in: two young men and a girl who was perhaps twelve years old. In a flood of rapid Italian they cried out their warning; after a moment, Tresca held up his hand and, speaking in their native tongue—and his—asked them to tell him what the trouble was and he would interpret to the *Americani*.

There was a tense exchange, and then another. Then the girl let out a stream of words, very fast. She was obviously frightened, but more than that, she was extremely angry. Tresca might have been expected to reprimand her, since anger was unseemly in a female. Instead he put his hand on her dark, tangled curls; he spoke gently, softly, trying to calm her, to ease her fears, perhaps. And he succeeded: she quieted; she even found the heart to smile at him a little, nodding her head. Edwin noticed how her face lighted up when she smiled; her dark eyes glowed, she seemed a different person.

"Good," said Tresca. He turned to the others in the room. "She says that the women are marching tonight. They know that the police will club the marchers, but they march all the same. Many of the women are pregnant." To indicate his delicacy, he used the Italian word—*incinta*. "They say that the police will not club them, because they will tell the police about their condition. But Lucia here does not trust the police. Her mother is on the picket line. She asks that we come to help."

Haywood grunted. "We've got to stay nonviolent. So all we can do is observe. We can't get into a battle—and we can't let the picketers, either."

Nevertheless, within ten minutes they were at the site. A long line of women stretched down the street beside the canal; on the other side loomed the great, grim mill buildings. It was dark. Men walked along beside the marchers holding flaring torches. Most of the picketers were women, and many of them, as predicted, were visibly pregnant. They carried their signs, they sang their songs, and in the darkness of the cold winter night they seemed a greater rebuke than any daytime picketers. Proudly they thrust out their swollen bellies as if to say, "You see! We carry the next generation! And we will not have them suffer as we do!"

A line of police watched them; behind the police stood a company of National Guard. If Edwin had looked closely, he might have seen someone he knew, for the boys at Harvard were enthusiastic supporters of the mill owners of Lawrence, and they eagerly went to perform their strike-breaking duties.

Suddenly, as if on command, the police charged. Billy clubs flailing, they fell on the women and beat them, right and left, with all their strength. Shrieks of pain filled the cold night air, cries of outrage from the women's male supporters, the hoarse voices of the troops as they, too, set upon the pickets.

In five minutes it was all over. Scores of women lay on the ground, moaning, bleeding. One woman miscarried right there on the street; others, taken to their homes, lost their babies later that night, or the next day, or the next. Two of the women died, one of them the mother of the girl who had come running for help.

Big Bill's fleshy face was grim as he spoke to the journalists. "Write it down, boys," he said, "write it up. In Lawrence, Massachusetts, in the year of their Lord nineteen hundred and twelve, they set the cops onto pregnant women. They beat up those women, here in Lawrence. And why? Because the women want enough pay to feed their families, that's why. They ain't asking for a handout. They'll work—they'll work as hard as anyone. But they want enough to live on. That's all. They don't want to be cut down and cut down, while some damn millionaire buys another yacht. You know William Wood? He's the head of the American Woolen Mills, right here in Lawrence. Yessir. And you know how many automobiles he has? He said to the newspapers the other day, he don't know how many he has, he's too busy to count 'em. Busy doin' what, I'd like to know. Beatin' up pregnant women?"

All of which made good reading for the public. But the story got better— or worse—when, the next week, the third contingent of children prepared to ship out, this time to foster homes in Philadelphia. As before, they gathered at the railroad station, pathetic little things, thin, ragged, some crying, some glad to have this adventure in their starved little lives.

Across the street a contingent of police drew up. In the other direction appeared two militia companies. The authorities had decided that the hemorrhage of bad publicity must stop: no more children could be evacuated.

Some of the children seemed to sense trouble. They clung to their mothers' hands, they cringed at the sight of all the strange adults confronting them—and then in the instant the attack began, they started to wail and cower, with nowhere to hide as the police and soldiers set on them with clubs and bayonets. The children were torn from their mothers' grasp and thrown into the paddy wagons pell-mell, a heap of screaming humanity, mothers frantic as they lost their little ones, reporters scribbling madly, photographers setting off their flashes—oh, it was magnificent! Magnificent! A real coup for the strikers, intensive nationwide publicity—see how we are attacked, innocent children beaten down, see what cowards our enemies are, that they make war on women and children!

The next day, when Edwin tried to walk into a meeting of the strike committee, a meeting to which journalists had been invited, he found his way barred at the door by a thickset, combative-looking man.

"Excuse me," said Edwin, but the man would not budge.

"I'm expected inside," said Edwin. He tried to shove past, but the man barred the way.

Just then one of the IWW organizers came up, and Edwin asked to see the man in charge, an Italian-born weaver who spoke good English.

After a moment the man came out. His name was Giovanni. Although he had been cordial enough in the last few weeks, now he looked distinctly unfriendly.

"What's wrong?" said Edwin. "Why won't they let me in?"

Giovanni glowered at him. His black eyes were stone cold. "We found out about you," he said.

"What do you mean, you found out about me?"

"We know who you are now. You aren't any newspaper writer. You're a spy, that's what you are. Mr. Edwin Jackson Revell. A corporation spy!"

"I don't know what you're talking about." But he did, and Giovanni knew it.

"Your family own stock in the Atlantic Cotton Mills," said Giovanni. "A lot of stock. You got twenty people in your family who own it. What do you say to that, eh? All your family is owners of this corporation, Mr. Revell! An' you want me to let you into the meeting where we're organizing our strike? You got to be crazy, mister. You got to be out of your mind. You ain't coming into any more of our meetings, you unnerstan'? No more. We may be dumb guineas, but we ain't that dumb."

He spat into the street, narrowly missing Edwin's shoe. Then he turned and went back inside, slamming the door behind him.

Edwin was not willing to admit defeat so easily, of course. He went to see Big Bill Haywood. Big Bill had read *The Shame of the Rich*. He knew that Edwin's heart was in the right place, even if he felt some contempt for a man who could not divest himself of shameful holdings like stock in the Atlantic Cotton Mills.

Big Bill said that he would do what he could, but it turned out to be nothing much. The Lawrence strikers thought that Edwin was a spy, and nothing that Big Bill said would change their minds.

Public sentiment was now thoroughly aroused. A congressional investigation was scheduled at once. Henry Cabot Lodge blocked any Senate inquiry, but the House Committee on Rules heard testimony from many workers, including children. So high was public interest that President Taft's wife attended the hearings. For a while it looked as though the corporations would lose their protective tariff. Not wanting that catastrophe, they gave in and restored the workers' pay to what it had been before the fifty-four-hour week took effect.

But the corporations won in the end, because by 1914 they forced workers to tend twelve looms instead of seven, with no increase in pay.

Meanwhile, the *Titanic* went down, an unthinkable disaster, headlines six inches high, fifteen hundred people lost. And in the South End a gruesome murder took place, a woman and her child killed, transfixing the public for days. College commencements were held—always a busy time in Massachusetts. The maverick, James Michael Curley, made noises that indicated he might run for mayor. Life went on. People's interest in the Lawrence strike faded.

For months that spring and summer Joe Ettor and two other IWW organizers arrested with him, all of them Italians or of Italian descent, sat in the Salem jail—no bail, no hearing, no trial. In September 15,000 textile workers in Lawrence held a one-day walkout to protest the treatment of the three prisoners. A gigantic rally was held on Boston Common. Big Bill Haywood spoke to the crowd, rousing them to great excitement; then he walked cheerfully into the arms of the police waiting to arrest him.

At last a trial was held. One of Ettor's lawyers was Fred Moore, a veteran IWW defender from the Midwest. The trial took two months. At the end, Ettor asked for permission to make a statement. In it he said that he was being tried for his political beliefs. But public opinion, he said, was on his side. After that the jury went out and came back shortly with an acquittal.

People said that the Ettor case proved that even the humblest workingman, even someone who was "foreign," who held radical ideas, could get a fair trial in Massachusetts.

8

Now pay attention, sports fans—you Royal Red Sox Rooters:

That year, 1912, we won the World Series. Beat the New York Giants.

You don't believe it? Here's how it happened:

We're in extra innings, top of the tenth. This is the last game of the series, and it is the eighth game because Game Two was tied and stopped for darkness after eleven innings. But the stands are only half full: in this grand new baseball stadium, Fenway Park, built to hold 35,000, located in a town of rabid sports fans, we have an attendance of 17,000 tops.

Why?

Because the previous day the Boston Royal Rooters, led by "Nuff Ced" McGreevey, a South End saloon keeper, caused a near riot when they found that their three-hundred-ticket allotment had been sold out from under them. So this day, this crucial final day, this excruciating time of suspense—this day, there is a picket line of 10,000 angry fans outside, and a half-empty stadium.

Never mind. Here we are:

Smokey Joe Wood, who has won 34 games for the Red Sox this season, is on the mound. The score is 1–1. After one out, Red Murray doubles to left, and Fred Merkle brings him home with a single. The Giants lead 2–1. Smokey Joe makes a brilliant bare-handed stop of a sharply hit ball back to the box to make the final out of the inning. He was scheduled to lead off in the bottom of the tenth, but his hand is so badly damaged that he can't swing the bat.

Clyde Engle comes in as pinch hitter for the Sox to face Christy Matthewson. Christy is the greatest pitcher in the history of baseball. He makes $5000 a year. He has been on the mound for the entire game. Now, in this crucial hour, he never allows his shoots to rise above knee level. Engle hits a long, lazy fly to left center. Fred Snodgrass drifts under it, raises his glove, and *the ball bounces away*. It is the fifth Giants error of the game.

With Engle on second base and Harry Hooper up, Hooper reaches out and drives a pitch deep into center field. This time Snodgrass makes the catch: makes it running back toward the Wall, makes it *over his shoulder*, makes it, makes it—a miracle! He has robbed Hooper of a sure triple that would have tied the game.

Next, still keeping his pitches low and working carefully, Matthewson walks Yerkes.

The next batter up is Tris Speaker. He has the highest salary in baseball—$9000 a year. He gets a life when he hits a pop foul a few yards from first base. Fred Merkle and Chief Meyers allow it to drop between them. Matthewson shouts for Meyers to take the catch, but he is drowned out by the roar of the crowd.

Speaker gets a second chance. He singles and brings Engle home from second base. The game is tied.

The crowd is suddenly quiet, very tense. Matthewson is pitching to Duffy Lewis. He pitches very carefully—too carefully. Lewis walks. The bases are loaded. Yessir, Matty sure used his old headpiece that time!

Now Larry Gardner steps up to the plate.

Larry Gardner is a man who at this moment feels the weight of the world on his shoulders. He feels the tension crackling all around the park like lightning—although the weather has turned cold, there will be no lightning this day. He understands all too well what is riding on the next few seconds.

He says a wordless prayer, assumes his stance, summons up all the strength and cunning and skill that he has acquired over these past rough years in this rough game, squints, spits, crouches—and the pitch comes in over the inside corner and he hits it, he hits it, oh my God he hit it, look how he hit it, the ball goes flying into right field, he did it, he did it, oh my God Steve Yerkes is coming in, *he's coming in*, they did it, they did it, they won, ohmyGod-Idon'tbelieveit!!!

Well, the old town of Boston went crazy that day and night, and the next day, too. Down in Newspaper Row, in lower Washington Street, ten thousand fans crowded around as the megaphone man, listening for the "tick" of the bulletin-board ticker, shouted out the progress of the game. When the home-town boys won, pandemonium broke out. The crowd gave a fierce yell that no one who heard it would ever forget. All over Boston—indeed, all over much of eastern Massachusetts—all business ceased. Not even the dispatch of American troops into Cuba, not even the news of the attempted assassination of the Bull Moose himself, Teddy Roosevelt, could distract people from their craziness over the Red Sox.

The next day, the ball players came in a twelve-car caravan from Fenway Park to Park Square, thence to Boylston Street to Tremont to Cornhill to Dock Square. Faneuil Hall was jammed. The crush was terrible. Men fought to get inside, and women were tossed about like chaff. Mayor John J. "Honey Fitz" Fitzgerald drove in the lead car—his own—dressed in a big ulster over a frock coat, a glossy top hat perched on his head. When the team picture was taken—with the players in street clothes—the mayor sat in the middle. He promised them a fine silver cup. The band played "Tessie" twice: the significance of that

particular tune was known not only to the mayor, but to everyone in attendance. No matter. This was a day not for tattling, but for celebration.

Huzzah! The Boston Red Sox were the World Champions!

The winning players got a bonus of $1300 each. Both the Boston and the
New York clubs got $147,000.

Everyone was very happy.

9

The year after the Lawrence strike, in the fall of 1913, Congress put into effect
the number-two demand made by Karl Marx in the *Communist Manifesto*: the
progressive income tax. Bachelors with an income above $3000 per year, and
married couples above $4000, would pay a tax of one percent on the excess.
The top rate, six percent, applied to incomes over $500,000.

Congress had tried something of the kind once before, but the Supreme
Court had struck it down in 1895, saying that an income tax violated the right
of property. It was that legislation, perhaps, that led Samuel L. Clemens to
remark that no man's life or property was safe while Congress was in session.

When Lyman Griffin Revell first learned of the proposed law, which was
in fact the sixteenth amendment to the Constitution, he became extremely
agitated. It was in late July of 1909. He was at his summer place in Brookline.
On fine days he took his morning coffee on the terrace within sight of his
beloved rose garden. He sat there and read his morning *Herald*; this morning,
when he came to the article about the progressive income tax amendment passed
by Congress and sent out to be ratified by the states, he choked on his coffee
and splattered his clean white shirt. His son Nathaniel, visiting for a few days,
found him in a highly agitated state—very unhealthy for a man Lyman's age.
He had just turned sixty-nine. He was still active, going in to his office from
Brookline two or three times a week, and every day when he was in residence
at Louisburg Square. He was tall and alert, with the familiar Revell glint in his
eye. He could calculate a profit in his head quicker than one of his junior clerks
could do it on paper. In his lifetime of tending to his family's business, he had
increased his own wealth ten times over, and that of most of his relations nearly
as much. Now this pernicious law was going to take it all away—everything he
had worked for. The power to tax was the power to destroy. Who would
bother to accumulate property, if the government could take it away? Wasn't
that why Revells had fought in the Revolution—to protect their property? To
protest unjust taxes? Crippling taxes, that robbed a man of his livelihood, of
his initiative? That was what this country was all about, wasn't it? Initiative?
Wasn't that why everyone had come here in the first place? To be free of work,
to accumulate what he could? Now every penny was in danger!

As these dark thoughts passed through his mind, he wondered how difficult
it would be to stage another Boston Tea Party. It was one thing to defy King

George III, who was far across the sea and lived in the age of sail, weeks away; it was another to defy Congress, a day's train ride down to Washington. Probably, he thought, a second Revolution against unjust taxes would not succeed. There were too many radicals now, too many anarchists and socialists, levelers who wanted the rich to give away all their money so that everyone could share the same low level of existence. That Jackson Revell fellow, Edwin, was one of them. Ah, they had always been trouble, those Jackson Revells! Even Isabella— No. Lyman was a gentleman. Even in his own private thoughts, he would not criticize dear Isabella.

Early in the new year, he went into a decline. In March he had a stroke and went into a coma. Thus he was spared the indignity of actually paying his tax for five-sixths of 1913, which was what the law required that first year.

He died in early April. People said that an era had come to an end, now that Lyman Griffin Revell was gone. Half the city, it seemed, came to his funeral, and many people from outlying areas as well. Both the *Herald* and the *Transcript* published an editorial about him; the Family held a memorial service in Trinity Church that was so crowded that you could not find a seat. When his will was made known, it was discovered that he left considerable sums of money to all manner of good causes: to his cousin Florence's settlement house in the South End, to the new Museum of Fine Arts out on Huntington Avenue, to a summer camp for slum children, to the Boston Symphony. In addition, he left a fund to establish a series of public lectures—something like the Lowell Institute—that were to be open to the public with free admission.

None of this was terribly surprising. He was a public-spirited man, he loved his city, his state—why, he had often said that Massachusetts was the best place in the world to live, he couldn't imagine living anyplace else.

No one bothered to find out the reaction of his employees—his thousands and thousands of mill hands, who would have been surprised to know that Lyman Griffin Revell had a charitable bone in his body.

10

The next year, the year of the assassination at Sarajevo, Isabella had a piece of misfortune that turned out to be very good luck indeed. She had planned to take the cure at Baden-Baden, as she so frequently did, before journeying on to Venice. But in May she stumbled on a marble step at her palace and broke a bone in her foot. It was extremely painful; what was more, her doctor said that she would be unable to walk for months. She saw no point in traveling if she could not walk, and so she canceled her reservation at Brenner's Hotel and sent word to Venice that the palace she usually rented there should be let, and she resigned herself to staying home. Thus she avoided being trapped in the midst of a war. By July she was well enough to accept Judson's invitation to stay with him and Violet for a while in Lenox. "We rough it," he said, "but the air is marvelous, and we can take you out every day in the open car so you won't feel cooped up."

So she went. Judson and Violet had a place on the outskirts of the village. It had a wide piazza and a panoramic view of the mountains. It was not far from where Judson's father, the famous Washington Abbott Revell, had lived and worked one winter more than sixty years before.

Judson was a shy, kindly man, tall and thin in the Revell way, but lacking completely the qualities of character that made the Revell men interesting. He was not bold, or adventurous, or brilliant; he lacked even Lyman's single-minded determination to get richer. He was simply a famous writer's son, doomed to live out his life in his father's shadow, afflicted with the ability to recognize not only the talents of others, but also his own lack of them.

Isabella had always been impatient with Judson's attitude of injured self-importance. Now, in her usual fashion, she confronted him directly.

"You are a fool, Judson Abbott Revell," she said. They were sitting on the piazza. Remnants of their tea lay on a small, low table; the golden light of the late, warm afternoon spilled across the lawns and gardens that surrounded the house, and shimmered on the mountains in the distance.

Judson grimaced to hide his discomfort. He had invited her on a whim, not expecting her to accept; he had forgotten how blunt she could be. Now, too late, he remembered.

"How is that, dear cousin?" he said.

"You should have educated that daughter of yours, for one thing. And for another, you should have been buying up the new painters you like, all these years you've been going to Paris. I know they're not the equal of my Italians, my Raphaels and Fra Angelicos, but they will grow, in time. Already their price is going up."

He chose what seemed the more dubious of her statements. "What do you mean, I should have educated Violet? She had a perfectly good education at Dana Hall."

"Ah, but it ended there, didn't it? Why didn't you send her to Wellesley? Or to Mt. Holyoke? I believe Theo's Aunt Caroline was a friend of the woman who founded Mt. Holyoke. We're going to have the vote any day now, you know. The younger generation of women must be educated."

Judson felt as though he were under siege. To fend off further attack, he suggested that he and Isabella and Violet take a drive to see Mrs. Wharton's place, a magnificent reproduction of an English Georgian manor house. Mrs. Wharton was no longer there, having divorced her husband and returned permanently to Europe to live. The house was empty except for the caretaker, who would allow them to drive into the grounds, at least.

"I didn't like that book of hers that you gave me to read," said Isabella. Judson was not sure whether this was acceptance or refusal of his suggestion. "It was so grim. So terribly depressing." Isabella was an uncompromising realist in life; when she read fiction, she preferred it to be happy and delightful—which is to say, unrealistic. *Ethan Frome*, a novel that Mrs. Wharton had set in the hill villages of the Berkshires, and which portrayed the barren, stunted lives of the people who lived there, was for the novelist an exercise in technique—a Conradian layering of narrative that drew the reader inexorably into the haunting tale that she had to tell. Many people would come to regard it as her finest work. But for the seekers of pleasant escape, it was a nasty shock. Isabella knew that people like Ethan Frome existed, living out their bleak lives tucked away in godforsaken corners of the mountains. But she did not want to be reminded of them, any more than she wanted to be reminded of the lives of the mill workers whose labors paid her such handsome dividends.

"All right," she said after a moment. "Yes—let's go. Where is Violet?"

Violet was painting in the far end of the garden, where she had a good view of the same Mt. Greylock that her grandfather had seen when he went to call on Herman Melville. Violet had never heard of Herman Melville, and not only because of her abbreviated education. He had sunk into obscurity half a century before, and it would be nearly another decade before an enterprising academic rescued him and presented his tale of the white whale to a world ready at last to read it. Melville had died in 1891, and so he was unable to enjoy his posthumous popularity—not to mention his posthumous royalties.

Summoned by her father, Violet obediently trundled up to the house carrying her canvas in one hand and her paint box in the other. She was tall and blond; like Caroline Griffin Revell, she was very plain, and in fact she bore a striking physical resemblance to that indomitable female. But it was a physical resemblance only, for Violet lacked Caroline's strong character. The fact that she had begun—with Lyman's help—the custom of Christmas Eve caroling on Beacon Hill was unimpressive, she thought, compared to Caroline's labors during the war. She had read Caroline's reminiscences. Even on the printed page Violet had found Caroline intimidating; in person, she remembered an ancient woman in a dark dress and white lace cap in the old-fashioned style. Violet had been too shy to say anything much, and Caroline, with the impatience permitted to old age, had soon—to Violet's relief—turned her attention elsewhere. The one impression that Violet had carried away with her was that Caroline didn't think she was very interesting or important—a sentiment that Violet herself shared.

"Progress?" said Isabella, still smiling. "How industrious you are, my dear. I could never bear to sit out in this heat for so long."

Violet gave her a tentative smile in return. She was not comfortable in Isabella's showy presence. Even now, when Isabella was well past middle age (Violet thought she was at least sixty, which she was—sixty-four, in fact), she made an impression of glamour, of feminine beauty and charm which Violet herself had never possessed. She never felt the way she thought Isabella must feel: attractive, enchanting, the center of attention. Violet had never wanted to be the center of attention, but she wished that she might at least have had a beau or two. She never had. Plain and shy, she had endured the debutante parties of her youth and watched as the other girls, one by one, married off. For some years past, now, she had felt a curious sense of relief. For a while she had hoped that she would marry also; but since her mid-twenties, she knew that she should hope no longer. She had relaxed into the routine of her life, resigned to the knowledge that no man would choose her, and had set about finding ways to fill her time. For the most part she succeeded. A little painting, a little music, a little charitable work, a little travel—it was an uneventful life, to be sure, but not unpleasant. She was thirty-four years old. She expected that she would live this life until she died.

In the green-and-gold late afternoon, they drove out in Judson's Stanley Steamer. Over the roar of the engine, with its occasional little *pops*, Judson confided to Isabella that he had at last, after all these years, found a buyer for Revell Hall.

"What do you mean, a buyer?" said Isabella. "You don't mean you're going to sell it?"

Judson remembered his unsuccessful attempt, many years before, to convince Isabella to take the place off his hands. He pressed his lips together in irritation and pondered the fickle organ that was a woman's heart. She wouldn't buy it herself, but she didn't want him to sell it to someone else.

"I have to," he said. "I made some repairs, but it needs constant work—constant attention. Someone should restore it properly, from top to bottom. I haven't the means to do that, never mind the interest."

It was true that Judson was not so wealthy as some of the Family. But money was not the point, thought Isabella. The money could be found, if she could persuade him to do what he ought, keep the property in the Family and bring it back to what it once had been. Since Isabella had built her own place, her magnificent palace on the Fenway, she had come to have a healthier respect for the things in life that lasted. Bricks and mortar lasted: look at Venice! And her palace would last, too. She had made provision for its upkeep in her lengthy and detailed will.

From under the brim of her white straw hat, she fixed Judson with her brilliant eyes—those eyes that had turned so many men's knees to water. "I think," she said, "that you should not sell it. I think that you and Violet should restore it." As soon as she said the words, she knew that they were absolutely correct. It was a wonderful idea—a real project for Violet, instead of the make-work with which she filled her life.

"Didn't you tell me that Samuel McIntyre built that house?" she went on. She was aware that Violet was watching apprehensively. She didn't care what Violet thought, not at the moment.

"Yes."

"If I remember correctly, you showed me a set of plans—his drawings. Isn't that so?"

"Yes, I—"

"Judson, I find it perfectly ridiculous that you would allow such a treasure to slip through your fingers. McIntyre was a genius second only to Bulfinch. Why, he practically brought Salem into being! Haven't you any Family sense at all?"

Feebly, he tried to defend himself. "Isabella, I seem to remember a time when I offered Revell Hall to you, and you wanted nothing to do with it."

"Of course I wanted nothing to do with it! I wasn't ready then. I was too young. I didn't know enough."

"And now ...?"

"And now I am too old. Far too old." It was the first time she had described herself in that way, and saying the words gave her pause. Then, flushing slightly, she went on: "And besides, I have to tend to my own property. You have no idea how much attention that place needs! But as a project for you, and even more for Violet—oh, Judson, it would be perfect! There isn't much interest in historic preservation nowadays, but mark my words, there will be!"

Violet, in her uncomfortable position on the jump seat, realized that her life—or a considerable portion of it, at least—was being accounted for. What if she didn't want to restore Revell Hall? For as long as she could remember, it had been tenanted by various cousins, or sometimes by strangers if no cousins were available. Her father had always regarded it as nothing so much as a burden. She had no special affection for it. Why, now, should she suddenly devote herself to it?

Isabella said no more that day, but all the rest of the afternoon and into the evening her thoughts were filled with the idea of Revell Hall, and how Violet could rescue it. And of course she, Isabella, could provide a long list of people to help—craftsmen to duplicate original carving and plasterwork, artists to design or reproduce hand-painted wallpaper, landscape gardeners to bring back the grounds and plant them with their original trees and shrubs and flowers— Ah, it was a wonderful project! And she would see to it that Violet had plenty of Family money to work with. They would all contribute; why shouldn't they? It was a Family treasure, wasn't it? And when it was finished, she'd get Winslow to buy it: he'd inherited enough from Lyman to do that a dozen times over.

When she returned to Boston and saw Frederick not long after, he remarked dryly that one woman's treasure was another's white elephant. "And besides, Mother, do you really think that Violet is capable of such a task? She never struck me as being particularly enterprising."

"She's not. But that doesn't matter. She'll have me to help her, and Lord knows I am enterprising enough for two! I'll find her all the experts she needs." Comfortably they laughed together; Frederick reached out and patted her hand. He loved her very much; he could not have loved her more had she been his natural mother instead of his adoptive one. At the end of the month he would turn forty. Despite his law degree, he had chosen business. He was president of the largest bank in Massachusetts—in New England, for that matter. He sat on a dozen boards; he chaired several charitable institutions; he had a loving wife, fine children, plenty of money. He knew perfectly well that his life might have worked out very differently. He had been no better than an orphan. The eugenicists, he knew, put great emphasis on heredity; but Frederick thought that upbringing was equally important. This woman before him, still laughing and vigorous at sixty-odd, had given him a splendid upbringing, and had continued to do so after her own great bereavement. Frederick knew all too well that in those dark days after her husband's death, she might have packed him off to some other Revell family, some cousin or in-law. But she had chosen to keep him—had remained faithful to him, as he saw it. He could never do less for her.

It was a warm evening in August. They sat in the glass-roofed central court of Isabella's palace. Frederick's wife and children were at Northeast Harbor, where he would join them at the end of the week. That day the papers had carried the news of the Kaiser's invasion of Belgium. As Frederick read the long, densely printed columns, he had had the sense that he was reading an obituary—the death notice of an era. In the background, if he listened carefully, he might have heard the muffled drums of the funeral procession.

War! Bad for business!

"To Violet," said Isabella, laughing. "And to Revell Hall!"

2. JUSTICE CRUCIFIED

1

On the afternoon of April 15, 1920, the paymaster for the Slater & Morrill Shoe Manufacturing Company in South Braintree, Massachusetts, together with his guard, was shot and killed and the payroll stolen—$15,776.51.

Witnesses said that two dark, foreign-looking men committed the crime. They jumped out of a dark Buick sedan and ran to Parmenter and his guard, Berardelli; after the killing, they jumped back in, carrying the boxes of money, to make their escape. At least three other men were in the car. Two of them were also dark and foreign-looking; one, the driver, was pale and blond. One witness to the crime said that he knew the killers were foreigners because of the way they ran. Another said that they were not foreigners because one of the two robbers, who took a shot at him, shouted in perfect English. Everyone agreed, however, that none of the gang wore gloves.

On May 5 two foreigners—Italians—were arrested and eventually charged with the crime. Because they understood little English, it was unclear whether they grasped the details or the significance of the questions they were asked. What they did understand was that they were in a great deal of trouble.

The police chief of the town where they were arrested—Brockton—said that he was sure that these were the right fellows because when they were arrested they were carrying not only pistols and ammunition, but a considerable amount of anarchist literature, pamphlets and such, which no doubt they had intended to distribute.

Despite its sudden savagery, the South Braintree robbery-murder was an obscure crime, of some interest locally but hardly noteworthy in a nation that was in the midst of a crime wave, gangsters running loose everywhere, and strikers, too, causing endless disruption, and red radical anarchists spouting their nonsense from every street corner. A bad time, a difficult time everywhere, and nowhere more than in Massachusetts. Only the previous year the Boston police had gone on strike. People had cowered in their houses, fearing the worst—robbery, looting, rape, murder. Governor Calvin Coolidge had saved the day. He called out the militia, he kept the streets safe. If the criminal element thought that it could take advantage of the good people of Boston in this emergency, it had another think coming.

Later, when Coolidge got to be Vice-President and then President, people understood that it was the Boston police strike, and his prompt, decisive handling of it—his show of manly strength—that won him those elections. Intransigence in the face of threatened anarchy: that was what had done it for "Silent Cal." The lesson was not lost on another aspiring politician in the Bay State, a car dealer named Alvan Fuller.

The police strike occurred in the summer and fall of 1919. It frightened people—really unnerved them. Ever since the war had ended the previous year, the world, which had been made safe for democracy, had suffered one peril after another. The United States had invaded Russia to try to subvert its revolution. The Spanish influenza had devastated large portions of the world's population, more deadly than the great plagues of the Middle Ages. All across the nation, workers struck and struck again—not only the textile workers of New England, who were increasingly restless, but miners and steelworkers and lumberjacks—and it was the reds who stirred them up to it! Not content with their victory over the czar, they wanted to export their revolution worldwide. Damned troublemakers! Un-American, that's what they were. Foreigners, anarchists, Communists, red radicals—go back where you came from, people said, and leave us alone.

So it had come as a particular relief when, in the late fall of 1919 and the early days of January 1920, the Attorney General of the United States, Mitchell Palmer, staged a series of raids on reds and radicals all over the country. Hundreds, thousands, were rounded up, and many of them were deported under the emergency laws enacted a few years previous, during the war. Patriotism had become a big issue then, even before the nation was actually sending over troops to fight the Hun. Anyone who criticized the war effort was likely to be arrested and sent to jail. Everyone was hysterical with fear of things German. Anyone of German descent was likely to be labeled a spy. The music of Beethoven was banned as subversive. German was no longer taught in the public schools. Sauerkraut became "liberty cabbage." Karl Muck, the distinguished German conductor of the Boston Symphony Orchestra, was asked to play "The Star-Spangled Banner" at the beginning of each concert. He refused. It was musically inappropriate, he said. He was arrested and put into prison on a trumped-up charge of espionage. Many of the orchestra's musicians were enemy aliens. Those who declined to take out their first naturalization papers were dismissed. They were replaced, by and large, by Frenchmen, who were musically inferior but politically correct. Free speech? Never heard of it. Shut up and buy another war bond.

Thus did the Kaiser win, even as he lost.

In Massachusetts, Palmer's raiders arrested people in Brockton and Chicopee Falls, in Fitchburg, Lowell, Lawrence, Holyoke, Haverhill, Worcester, Springfield, Norwood, and Chelsea. And in Boston, of course. In Boston, that bitter January night, they herded the reds across the city, and they draped them in chains for the benefit of the newspaper photographers who scurried alongside. The hapless detainees were interned on Deer Island—just like the Indians sequestered there two and a half centuries before during King Philip's War. Like those unfortunates, many of these people did not have a happy outcome to their story. Many of them never saw home again. On the other hand, many of them had their cases thrown out of court, particularly the ones who had been arrested without a warrant.

In any case, it was an unsettled time—a time when people wanted to be sure that red radical anarchists did not subvert the country. Native Americans (which, at that time, did not mean American Indians) looked again to the Congress to erect tough immigration barriers—particularly for those folks from Eastern and Southern Europe, almost all of them Catholics or Jews or Orthodox, whatever that was—it once had meant good stout Puritanism, but no longer—and none of them white Anglo-Saxon Protestants, which as everyone knew was the race that had built the nation and would be the race that saved her from degeneracy and race suicide. When it became known that President Abbott Lawrence Lowell, over at Harvard, had joined the presidents of other distinguished colleges and initiated a strict quota for Jews, people nodded approval. If you didn't watch out, those foreigners would take over everything.

2

In August of that year—the year of the South Braintree holdup—Isabella turned seventy. Since she was in her way as strong-minded as any Revell woman who had ever lived, she had never made any attempt to hide her age. Hiding your age was ridiculous, she thought. She adopted instead, she said, the Oriental view: age was to be respected and even revered; each additional year was a triumph. Nevertheless, she had begun to use a little makeup.

"You should visit Japan, cousin," said John, smiling at her as he lifted his glass of bootleg champagne to toast her health. "When I lived there, I learned a great deal about their beliefs. Not only do they respect their elders, they also worship their ancestors."

Isabella laughed. "Just like all the First Families of Massachusetts!" she said.

It was late on a warm afternoon, cloudy, humid, a thunderstorm threatening. The courtyard of her palace was thronged with people, most of them more or less related to her—two hundred at least, her secretary had said. Some of them had brought, with permission, people not yet married into the Family. She didn't mind. She didn't mind anything much, anymore. That morning she had gone, as she always did on both their birthdays, to visit Theo's grave.

Thirty-six years ago it had been—that dreadful day when he died. She still missed him, of course—she would miss him every day of her life—but the terrible pain was gone, the pain that had driven her to seek solace elsewhere. She had never found it. Not with any of her young men, at least. This place—this magnificent palace—had done more to give her a new life than any of them.

Now she surveyed them from her tall-backed gilt-and-red-painted chair: handsome Cousin John, the famous astronomer, and his boy Dwight; and Edwin the journalist with his three, Avery and Stephen, and the girl, what was her name? And dear Augusta, Lyman's daughter. Thank God she had married at last. In the winter of 1917 she had severely upset her mother and everyone else in the Family when she had gone to Washington with Alice Paul and the radical suffragettes and chained herself to the White House gates. Along with many others, she had been arrested. She was too adventuresome, Augusta was. Last year Harry Trowbridge had married her, and a good thing, too. Settle her down a bit. Thank Heaven Lyman had not lived to see her in jail.

Now she came up to say hello. "Happy birthday, Cousin Isabella. How well you look."

"Congratulations yourself. Any day now, right?"

She might have been speaking of, say, the imminent arrival of a baby, but she was not. She referred—as Augusta understood—to the imminent passage of the Nineteenth Amendment, for which Augusta had worked so hard.

"Right." Augusta smiled broadly.

A young man came up to Isabella then with a glass of champagne. She could not remember his name, but she smiled at him nevertheless. He congratulated her; Augusta drifted away; Isabella chatted with the young man.

She was having a very good time.

The next day, when the air had been cleared by a night of thunderstorms, Isabella allowed Violet to drive her up to Salem to see how Revell Hall was coming along. It was a glorious day, bright and sunny. Isabella watched admiringly as Violet handled her new little runabout. "How do you do it?" said Isabella. "I'd be all over the road, I could never steer so neatly."

"Nonsense, cousin," laughed Violet. "I'm sure you could do it if you tried. Would you like me to teach you?"

Violet was the first person ever to suggest such a thing to Isabella, and after a moment's consideration, she found that she liked the idea. Well before they reached Revell Hall, they had agreed on a schedule: every Sunday afternoon, Violet would come to fetch Isabella, and they would set out. "Of course you can do it," said Violet. "If I can, anyone can."

Which was perfectly true, thought Isabella. Violet had been the most timid little thing on earth, but lately she had acquired much more spunk.

"I can tell that you are looking at me," said Violet, not taking her eyes from the road. "What's wrong? Do I have a smudge of dirt on my face?"

"No, of course not!" laughed Isabella. "I was just thinking how, ah, how very good you look. You are much more lively than you used to be." And it was true: Violet's Revell-blue eyes had a little sparkle, and her chin tilted up at a jaunty angle; and—yes—she laughed more. Something as simple as that: yesterday, at the party, Isabella had seen and heard Violet laughing quite loud.

As if on cue, Violet laughed now. "I've been working myself silly for months now. It must agree with me."

"You enjoy it?"

"Of course. I realize now that I hated being idle all those years—having no real work to do."

They rounded a curve and came out onto the coast road. Far away to the horizon stretched the sea, shifting, shimmering blue in the sun. How many times had Isabella cast herself upon the bosom of those waters! She had not been to Europe, to her beloved Italy, since before the war. Now she was suddenly seized with a longing to board one of the sleek, luxurious vessels with its charming captain and its interesting passenger list and its attentive stewards. Yes, she thought: I will go again, I will book passage the moment I return to Boston. The driving lessons can wait.

She realized that Violet was talking, and she had missed she didn't know how much: ". . . as you remember, it took a long time to get started, have the plans drawn up, find the right materials—and in fact many of those materials had to come from Europe, and so they were impossible to get, what with the war. And then we got into the war, too, and so I simply had to call a halt, I couldn't get two workmen let alone the fifteen or twenty that I needed. *Then* I thought I'd be able to get a crew right away—the week after Armistice Day. But of course I couldn't. And then the flu came, so it's really been just this spring that we got started. There's not much to see yet, I'm afraid—but at least it will be interesting for you to see before and after."

"That's all right," said Isabella. "You've begun, that's the main thing."

Soon they came to the road to Revell Hall, and then to the tall iron gates now rusted permanently open.

"This allée will be cleared up, of course," said Violet as they jounced down the long-neglected drive. "For the moment all we need is a road for the trucks."

The house stood as Isabella remembered it, a sadly neglected pile in an overgrown thicket of shrubbery.

"The first thing we did was to repair the roof," said Violet. "We'll paint the outside and tear down all this growth after we finish the interior."

She pulled up under the portico and led the way in. The entrance hall was filled with the sound of hammering and sawing, and a harsh scraping sound as century-old paint was removed. A cloud of dust hung in the air.

"You see," said Violet, raising her voice above the din and leading Isabella into the front parlor, "we have enough of the original wallpaper to have it duplicated." Isabella stared at the stained and faded wallcovering, some of it peeling off in strips from the damp. She could see that the original color showed at the edges that had been covered by molding. "Now come upstairs," said Violet. "I want your advice on the colors in the master bedroom."

Treading carefully amongst the debris and around the ladders and scaffolding, they made their way up the curving staircase, which even in its decrepitude retained a good deal of its former grace and beauty.

"The paper that is on the walls here, ruined as it is, is not something I think we should duplicate," said Violet. "It isn't the right period. Someone papered over the original. I've been able to find a little scrap of that over by the windows, but you can't really tell the color. But it's a lovely design, urns and garlands, why do you suppose they covered it with these hideous cabbage roses? Stained, I suppose. Now what do you think, Isabella? I like the pale blue and gold, don't you?" She held up two samples for Isabella to inspect, artist's renderings of wallpaper.

As Violet conferred with the workmen, Isabella went exploring, and soon she came to a narrow door at the back of the upstairs hall. It was stuck; with an effort that belied her age, she got it open. Gathering her skirts in her left hand (for she had no intention of adopting the new, shorter styles that had come in since the war), she peered up the narrow, steep stairway that led, presumably, to the attic. Then, carefully feeling her way, she started up.

"Isabella?" Violet's voice echoed up the stairway.

"I'm looking around. All right?"

"There's nothing up there but some old furniture. I looked when they were fixing the roof and we had to find all the leaks. Mind you don't trip." Violet hated the attic, dirty and harboring God knew what wildlife, but she felt a responsibility toward Isabella to see that she came to no harm on this expedition. The fact that Isabella was an intrepid traveler who had often set off halfway around the world by herself was beside the point.

It was warm in the attic, with only a dim light from the small high windows. As her eyes adjusted to the gloom, Isabella saw discarded pieces of furniture: an old Winthrop desk, a settee with its upholstery rotting off, a tall armoire with one door hanging open.

"Careful," said Violet, panting up behind her. "There's nothing of any interest whatsoever up here, Isabella. I don't think you should—"

"Your great-grandfather Elias spent a great deal of money on this house," said Isabella. "Who knows what we might find? It's worth a look, I'd say."

She stood for a moment in the middle of the low-ceilinged room, like a general surveying a potential battlefield. Then, with an instinct honed by decades of treasure-hunting through the art capitals of Europe, she headed for the settee. In itself it was of value only if it could be restored; what interested Isabella was that it stood away from the wall a little. It had an awkward look to it, as if it didn't quite fit. She pulled one end a little farther out and peered into the gloom behind. Then, with a little cry of triumph, she pulled a little more and pounced on what seemed to be a small trunk.

"Here!" she exclaimed. "Just as I thought! Come and help me, Violet, I think we've found something!"

"All right—all right. Watch out, you'll hurt your back, let me do it—" Sneezing from the tremendous amount of dust being raised, Violet reached behind the settee and pulled out the trunk. It was nail-studded leather, about two feet long, a foot high.

"There!" said Isabella. "I knew we'd find something! Let's see if we can get it open." She was heedless of the dirt and dust now, greedy as a collector always is, hoping for that one spectacular find.

They could not get the lock open, however, and so they went back down the narrow, high-risered stairs and sent one of the carpenters to fetch it down to the sun-filled upstairs hall. Then Violet borrowed his hammer and struck at the lock. On the third try it burst open. She lifted the slightly domed lid. Inside was a folded dress, once white, now pale yellow. As Violet went to lift it out—"Careful!" warned Isabella—the fabric cracked a little. They caught a faint scent, of old roses, perhaps.

"Why, it's a wedding gown!" said Violet. "Look, Isabella! This lace at the neckline, have you ever seen anything like it? And so tiny—whose was it, d'you suppose?"

"And look here!" said Isabella. Old gowns were all very well, but they hardly counted compared to some objet d'art. "Now here is something—oh, look, Violet!"

With a swift thrust of her hand she reached down and pulled out a small parcel of brittle brown paper tied with rotting string. She unwrapped it and brought forth a metallic object, black with tarnish—probably silver. It was a small box with a hinged lid. Opening it, she found a folded note. "Listen!" she said. She moved closer to the window to see the faded brown ink. "From Elias Abbott Revell to Dolly Kendall, on their wedding day. October 16, 1807.

"Oh, Violet—how exciting! Elias was your great-grandfather—Washington's father! Do you know, I heard my father-in-law talking once about the candlesticks—you know, the ones that are in the Copley portraits and in my Sargent as well, made by Jedediah Revell. And Father-in-law said that there was also a sugar box made by Jedediah at the same time, 'way back, and that it had disappeared. Everyone thought that it had been lost in the Revolution. Why, this is worth *thousands*!—but of course we aren't going to sell it, we couldn't possibly do that. This is an irreplaceable heirloom. Fantastic, really. Just imagine, a piece of old Jedediah's silver! There are only four or five pieces known to exist, aside from the candlesticks. What the Museum wouldn't give to have it!"

She put the box, wrapping and all, into her pouch bag, and for the rest of the day she carried it around with her. And when she and Violet drove back to Boston, she marched up the front steps of Judson's Clarendon Street house and plunked it down in front of his mild, startled eyes and said, "There, Judson Abbott Revell! You see what you nearly lost? This is your reward for taking my advice, and I hope you have the sense to care for it properly. Believe me, if you don't want it, I'll be happy to give it a home."

But Judson was of course delighted to have it, and when he had polished it well, he ordered a special cabinet made to hold it and a new set of locks for his house.

3

On May 31, 1921, the day after Decoration Day (which is what Memorial Day used to be called, because that was the day when people went to cemeteries to decorate with flowers and small flags the graves of the war dead), the two men charged with the murder-holdup at South Braintree went on trial for the crime at the Norfolk County Court in Dedham, Massachusetts. In the course of the testimony, it came out that not only were the two defendants anarchists, they were also draft evaders.

After six weeks the case went to the jury. In his charge, the judge made a big issue of patriotism—of being willing to fight for one's country. The twelve men took just five hours to reach their verdict: guilty.

Although the two prisoners were the lowest of the low, Italian immigrants barely able to speak English, one of them, a fish peddler, very poor; the other, a shoemaker, somewhat less poor, both of them devout anarchists (a belief that put them, to say the least, at odds with mainstream Republican and Democratic America)—despite those facts, the two men were not without resources, not without friends. They had, in fact, something that few prisoners had: a Defense Committee. Already this committee had raised money and hired a lawyer who—as it turned out—did such a poor job.

Now the Defense Committee redoubled its efforts. It was inconceivable that the two men had been found guilty, but of course the fight would go on, more fiercely than before—a new set of lawyers, new evidence, a new trial. From the headquarters on Hanover Street in Boston's North End came an endless stream of pamphlets, correspondence, petitions, appeals—all of the paraphernalia that such committees generated. Influential people were approached for help; a subcommittee of socially prominent Boston women was formed, high-minded, altruistic women of the type who had worked for abolition and suffrage. All of them, Italians and Americans alike, firmly believed that in the end they would win.

4

"My dear Augusta—do you really think that you want to become involved in something like this? I thought you were going to settle down with Harry into happy domesticity, now that you have the vote."

She gritted her teeth; then she relaxed her jaw and forced herself to smile at him: her second cousin, Edwin Jackson Revell, or perhaps he was her third, she didn't know. They were walking around the lagoon in the Public Garden. It was a warm day, bright flowers blooming in the carefully laid-out beds, the swan boats making their stately way around the little lake, each propelled by its boy working the pedals.

"I didn't choose to become involved," she said. "Mrs. Evans asked me. And since her husband is in a position to be helpful to Harry, I don't want to offend her." This last was not altogether true, but she thought that it helped her to make her case.

"And why, may I ask, is a proper Boston lady like Mrs. Glendower Evans intruding herself into the Sacco-Vanzetti case? Never mind that she asks other proper Boston ladies like you—you *are* behaving properly these days, aren't you, my dear?—to intrude themselves also."

They came to a bench and sat down. "Please don't condescend to me, Edwin. Sacco and Vanzetti must have a new trial."

"And a new lawyer, too, I should think. The one they have did a terrible job of defending them. What's his name? Fred Moore?"

She nodded emphatically. "Yes. He's simply dreadful. He wants more and more money, and then he loses the case! He won't even get a haircut. Walks around in the courtroom in his socks. Says he's making a statement to the Establishment."

Edwin smiled to himself. He, too, had tried to make a statement to the Establishment many years ago: he had written a book called *The Shame of the Rich*, he had turned out article after muckraking article. The establishment had paid him no heed—no more than it paid to Sacco and Vanzetti's unorthodox lawyer.

"Edwin, listen to me." She turned to face him. She was not pretty, but she was handsome in the angular, intelligent-looking way of so many Revell women. He had always admired her for her part in the suffrage fight.

"I am listening, my dear. I simply don't know what you want me to do."

"I want you to help us."

"How?"

"I don't know. Anything. You can write, you get around, you know a lot of people. Who knows what you can do? Are you working on something now? Perhaps you could put it aside—"

"No. I'm not working on anything." After the Lawrence strike, his energy had flagged; for years, now, he'd done nothing more than a few human-interest pieces for the *Herald-Traveler*.

"All right, then. Just look into it, that's all I'm asking. Go to the committee office in Hanover Street. Talk to Aldino Felicani, he's the man who organized it. Ask him who else you should speak to. I have a scrapbook of clippings that you can look at, if you want. Fill you in on the details."

He sat silent for a moment, thinking. It was true that the two men had not had a fair trial. No anarchist could, in the current climate. The foreman of the jury had been heard to proclaim their guilt before their trial had hardly begun; worse, the judge, Webster Thayer, held forth upon the case of what he called "those two anarchist bastards" at every opportunity—on the golf links, at the University Club—wherever he could find a sympathetic ear.

"Very well," Edwin said. "I will see what I can do."

The next day he went around to the Defense Committee's office in Hanover Street. This was a small, stuffy room, fifteen people crowded in at least, all talking very fast in Italian while two or three typewriters clattered in the background and the phone rang and rang, and was answered, and then rang again.

"Mr. Felicani?"

"Who wants to see him?" A small, intense-looking man whose black hair showed streaks of gray.

"My name is Edwin Jackson Revell. I was asked to come here by Mrs. Augusta Trowbridge. She is a friend of Mrs. Evans."

"What'd'you want with Felicani?"

"I'd like to talk to him."

"That's what you're doin'."

"Ah! Yes—of course. Well, you see, I'd like to ask you a few questions about the case."

"Such as?"

"Well, for instance—about the stolen money. I don't believe it was ever found?"

"That's right."

"And if I were to, ah, write something about the case—"

"You're a writer?"

"Yes."

"We need somebody always to write for us, you know. Pamphlets and such." He picked up an example from a table and gave it to Edwin. It was an unimpressive-looking piece of work, badly printed, shoddy paper. If these people were going to appeal to a wider circle than that of immigrant anarchists, they would have to learn to present themselves better, Edwin thought.

"Yes. I see. Well—if I were to write something, I would need to talk to someone like you familiar with the case, and with the lawyers—and I'd like to see the transcript when it is available."

Felicani nodded. "That's all okay. You can do that."

"And, ah, I'd like to talk with, ah, Mr. Sacco and Mr. Vanzetti. D'you think that would be possible?"

Felicani shrugged. "You can try. I don't know."

"Aldino! Telephone!"

"Excuse me." Felicani held out his hand. "You can come back tomorrow. I can't talk no more today. But you can go see Moore if you want to. He lives on Rollins Place. You know where that is?"

"Yes." Rollins Place was not far from where he lived, higher up the hill, but on the poorer side.

Accordingly, Edwin walked back from the North End and made his way to Revere Street, which paralleled Pinckney and Mt. Vernon but was not nearly so elegant. Several narrow courtyards led off the street, and they in turn were lined with tiny four-story town houses barely fifteen feet wide. A century ago they had been built as single-family homes, but some of them had been cut up into even tinier apartments. Rollins Place was different from the others because across the far end of the courtyard stretched what appeared to be a house—a southern mansion, in fact, with little columns arrayed across its narrow front porch. But it was only a facade—a false front coverup for the precipitous drop behind it, for between Revere Street and the next street over, Phillips, was a high, steep cliff.

Edwin scanned the nameplates on the mailboxes of the little brick houses lining the cul-de-sac. The last house on the left had none; but from its windows, this warm summer afternoon, came the sound of music from a gramophone and high-pitched female laughter. He mounted the narrow, steep steps and pressed the buzzer. When after a moment no one answered, he tried the door. It was in need of paint, but still handsome, a double door, in fact, with ovals of etched and frosted glass. It opened. The music and laughter came from the second floor. He went up the narrow, curving stairway—like everything else, a perfect miniature. A door on the tiny second-floor landing stood ajar. He tapped on it; then he pushed it open.

A man lay on a sofa. His long hair was uncombed—greasy and matted. His dingy shirt had no collar. His trousers had no suspenders. His feet had no shoes or stockings. He held a glass of what looked like whiskey in one hand; the other was clutching the breast of a girl who sat on the floor beside him.

For a moment no one spoke. The gramophone, having run out of its tune, rasped and rasped. A shaft of sunlight filled with dust motes illuminated a filthy, littered little apartment, one tiny room front, one back, very warm on this warm day.

"Mr. Moore?"

"Who wants to see him?"

Felicani's line; had he learned it from this man?

"My name is Edwin Revell. Aldino Felicani sent me to see you."

"Why?"

"I am a journalist. I may be writing something about the case." Both men understood that he did not need to say what case. Moore grunted, took his hand away from the girl, put down the glass and swung his feet onto the floor. After a moment he heaved himself up. He did not look healthy. His hands trembled; his eyes watered; his face was pasty-looking. His speech was slightly slurred. He held out his hand; reluctantly, Edwin took it.

"I know the name," said Moore. "Didn't you write about the Lawrence strike?"

"Yes."

"I was counsel for Joe Ettor. Got him off, too."

"Right."

"We had a better jury that time. Better judge, too. Bastard." He waved his hand. "Sit down. What can I get you?"

"Nothing, thanks. I just wanted to ask you a few questions."

"Shoot." Moore reached out and pulled a straight-backed chair close to the sofa. "And sit down. Too hot to stand."

"When do you think the trial transcript will be ready so that I can read it?"

Moore shrugged. "Dunno. It's going to cost a lot of money to get it done. Lots of defendants never get their transcript. Can't afford it. I told the committee, they got to get cracking. We need double what they're taking in. Case like this'll run you dry in no time."

"Would you care to give me an estimate of how much has been spent up to this point?"

"No. I would not. That's confidential. But I will tell you this. Costs a lot of money to run a good defense. I got expenses like you wouldn't believe. Expert witnesses, secretarial help—"

He was interrupted by the young woman, who handed him a fresh glass. He grinned. "You take Maisie, here. She's worth her weight in gold, Maisie is. An' I have to pay her, don't I?"

He took several swallows and wiped his mouth with the back of his hand.

"When will you file the appeal?" said Edwin.

"Oh—couple'a months. We got some new leads we got to develop."

"You mean new evidence? That you didn't use in Dedham?"

Moore shook his head. "If you want to write about this case, Mister, ah . . ."

"Revell."

"Mr. Revell, you have to understand one thing. This is not a case that can be won on the evidence."

"How do you mean?"

"I mean, look at the verdict. The other side won, right? For the moment, at least. But they didn't win on the evidence, because the evidence was nothing."

A fact that you failed to demonstrate to the jury, thought Edwin.

"No," Moore went on, "this is a case that will be won in the streets. In the court of public opinion, that's where it'll be won. You know that a number of very prominent people have offered to help. The best families, very wealthy. Yes, indeed. An' I told 'em, we need your support. Financial and otherwise, I said. Talk to your state representatives, talk to your governor. Talk to the newspapers. Public opinion, that's what's going to do it. We've got to turn public opinion in Sacco and Vanzetti's favor. They were convicted, not because the evidence showed they were guilty, but because of what they believed. Sacco and Vanzetti are anarchists, you know. Most people think an anarchist is some wild-eyed fellow ready to throw a bomb, but you and I know different. They're really very peaceful fellows, Sacco and Vanzetti. Wouldn't hurt a fly, particularly Vanzetti. But they have their own political beliefs, an' they aren't the beliefs of most of the population. But isn't that what this country is all about? That a man can believe what he wants? That's why they came here, isn't it? To be free? They weren't on trial for murder these past six weeks, my friend, no matter what the indictment said. They were on trial for their political beliefs, which aren't exactly popular. The day after they were indicted, last September, some damn fool threw a bomb into the Stock Exchange down in Wall Street. I always thought that was the worst damn timing. People remembered it, an' they held it against these two. They had nothing to do with it, of course. But the perception in people's minds was, anarchists did that bombing—or so the police said—and Sacco and Vanzetti are anarchists, therefore they must be capable of murder.

"You know, I've been with the IWW for a long time. That's why Tresca and Felicani brought me in. They knew right away that this would be a political trial. And they wanted someone like me, who was familiar with the anarchist and socialist point of view. Now I done most of my work out West—with the exception of the Lawrence business—but I know how to handle public opinion because that's the same wherever you go. So now we got to raise more money, and really stir up the public an' get 'em to see the injustice that's being done here. So if you want to write us up, go right ahead."

"I'd like to interview them."

"You're welcome to try. Don't think the warden'll let you, though."

"They're at Charlestown?"

"Only Vanzetti's there. Sacco's at Dedham."

As Edwin got up to leave, Moore stood up as well, and put a hand on Edwin's arm. "Just remember one thing. Remember that I am in charge of this case. Not Felicani, not any other lawyer, not the Defense Committee."

"How about Sacco and Vanzetti?"

"No, sir. Not even them. This case runs the way I say it will run. You can print that, if you like. It's a political case from first to last, and that's what it'll always be."

5

When Edwin Jackson Revell began his investigation into the case of the Commonwealth of Massachusetts vs. Nicola Sacco and Bartolomeo Vanzetti, he had no idea whether he himself considered the two men innocent or guilty. He was aware, of course, that there had been considerable agitation on behalf of the two men, the main thrust of which was, as Fred Moore had stated, that they were being tried for their political beliefs. On the other hand, skeptical journalist though he was, he was nevertheless conventional enough, or unimaginative enough, to believe that most people who were arrested and indicted for a crime were guilty. True, some trials ended in acquittals. But in general, he thought, the police were not so sloppy in their methods as to arrest people for no reason. The warrant, the arrest, the fact of going on trial, in themselves cast a presumption of guilt, no matter the principle of innocent until proven guilty.

After six months, talking to everyone whom he could think of and many who were suggested to him, he was convinced that Sacco and Vanzetti were, if not innocent, then at least victims of prejudice who had not had a fair trial.

One of his first and most persuasive informants was Augusta's friend, Mrs. Glendower Evans, who talked to him practically nonstop for three hours and sent him away with the names of a dozen more people. He interviewed them; then a dozen more, and another score given to him by Felicani. His sense that Sacco and Vanzetti were guilty of the crime with which they had been charged began to weaken.

Meanwhile, the Defense Committee grew; contributions flooded in, many from abroad, for Sacco and Vanzetti were becoming internationally known. All kinds of radical groups latched onto the case, seeking publicity, seeking some of the money. The Communists became particularly active; all on their own, without consulting the Defense Committee, they raised half a million dollars. The Defense Committee got six thousand of it; the Communists kept the rest.

On July 19, 1921, despite his oft-proclaimed faith in the court of public opinion, Fred Moore filed a motion for a new trial for Sacco and Vanzetti on the grounds that the "guilty" verdict went against the weight of the evidence.

On December 24 of that year, Judge Webster Thayer denied it.

6

Snow fell, that Christmas Eve. All over the Commonwealth, from west to east: not a heavy snow, a blizzard with fierce, destructive winds; rather a light, steady, softly accumulating snow, picturesque, benevolent. All over the Berkshires, the mansions of Stockbridge and Lenox, the hamlets tucked away up in the hills; over the Connecticut River Valley and its broad fertile acres; on across the old frontier towns, Deerfield and Groton and Lancaster; on to the seacoast, down over the frozen cranberry bogs of Carver and Plymouth, down to the islands, Nantucket and Martha's Vineyard, all across the thickly settled suburbs around old Winthrop's City Upon a Hill, up and down the broad, handsome avenues of the Back Bay, up and down the narrow, crooked streets of the North End and Beacon Hill: a beautiful snow, people said, just the way it should be. Sifting down onto the ancient tombs of the Old Granary and King's Chapel burying grounds, whitening the Common and the Public Garden, edging the brownstone lintels and doorways of the mansions along Commonwealth Avenue and Marlborough and Beacon Streets—a Christmas snow, a celebration of the season.

In the house in Louisburg Square, which Lyman had bequeathed to his son Winslow, the annual Christmas Eve party that Lyman had initiated years and years ago was in full sway. The parlor was brightly lit, a Christmas tree in one corner, a throng of a hundred people, laughing and talking, filled with the joy of the season. Edwin Jackson Revell stood to one side, holding a cup of eggnog and watching the company, most of whom were more or less related to him.

His wife was talking to Mrs. Winslow, and his two boys, Avery and Stephen, were with their cousins at the piano. There was old Judson, Violet's father, fit as a fiddle, getting acquainted with Winslow's youngest; and John, the astronomer; and Violet, who would later lead them all outside for the caroling; and Frederick and his handsome brood, and his mother, too, Cousin Isabella, as striking as ever in a green velvet dress and a diamond choker.

Suddenly there flashed across Edwin's mind a vision of the two men whose lives, whose fate, had occupied his thoughts for the past five months and more. He saw them sitting in their cells. He wondered what kind of Christmas celebration the Massachusetts prison system allowed. Probably not much.

"Edwin. Have you had the news?" Augusta stood at his elbow, looking very grim.

"About the motion being denied? Yes."

"On Christmas Eve, of all times! How cruel! When Mrs. Evans called me to tell me, I couldn't believe it."

"The second motion will win. Or the third."

"Perhaps. Perhaps. What I don't understand is, why does Thayer have to hear motions on a trial he conducted? Isn't that a conflict?"

"Are you questioning the wisdom of the Massachusetts system of justice?" As he spoke, he realized with a little stab of amazement that that was exactly what she was doing.

"Of course I am. That system convicted two innocent men. It is a system that no longer works—if it ever did. It is a system that is unjust—like the system in Washington, D.C. Remember? During the suffrage fight when they arrested us and put us in that filthy jail?" She shuddered. "There were rats in that jail. I still have nightmares about them. And then we went on a hunger strike, we said that we were prepared to die rather than go on living without full citizenship, without the right to vote. And they force-fed us, Edwin. I imagine you have never been subjected to that particular form of torture. They tied me down, and shoved a tube up my nose and down my throat, they forced hot gruel through that tube, it made me gag and try to vomit, so that I almost choked to death, and I believe that they would have let me die, I really do, except that they were worried about the bad publicity, bad enough as it was when the word got out about what they were doing to us. So that is your system of justice, Edwin. I will tell you frankly that I have very little faith in it."

"Augusta, I hope that you are not going to let this news spoil your holidays." She looked ill, he thought, shadows under her eyes, lines of fatigue and worry around her wide, expressive mouth. "There is nothing that we can do," he went on, "for the moment at least, and it is really too bad—" He caught Winslow's eye: Winslow, understandably, wanted people to enjoy themselves at his party; he did not want serious political discussions.

"Yes, there is," said Augusta. "We are going to start a petition drive, and tomorrow we are going to take Christmas presents to them, and for Sacco's family as well, he has a wife and child; his boy is named Dante, can you imagine? Professor Norton over at the College used to run a Dante Society. Dante the poet, dead for centuries, is acceptable, he is even a figure of reverence, but his latter-day descendants are reviled, persecuted—"

"Augusta, my dear." Winslow's rather dry voice grated on Edwin's ear. "Come and have something to eat before you go singing." And, with a nod at Edwin, of whom he was not fond, he led Augusta away.

People were putting on their coats preparatory to going out to carol. For form's sake, Edwin thought—for his children's sake—he would join them, at least for a while.

All around the square, with its snow-covered statue of Christopher Columbus—an Italian—candles flickered in the windows of the red-brick town houses. And now, as had become the custom, when the neighbors heard Violet and her flock begin to sing, they opened their doors, and many came out to join in, and slowly the little band of carolers became larger, making their way through the snow, singing their message of glad tidings: "O Come All Ye Faithful," and "O Little Town of Bethlehem," and "Good King Wenceslas," and, for the children, "Jingle Bells." Around the square and up Mt. Vernon and down Chestnut to West Cedar—all around Beacon Hill they went, and at many houses they were given cups of hot chocolate or eggnog, and everywhere they were warmly greeted, for this was Christmas Eve caroling on Beacon Hill—the most delightful tradition in the world.

Edwin, no singer, followed behind, enjoying the beauty of the scene, so beautiful that he felt as though he had stepped into a painting.

But all the while he carried in his mind's eye the image of Sacco and Vanzetti in their prison cells.

7

Eventually Edwin became obsessed with the case. He thought about it almost every waking moment. He worked ceaselessly. He could talk of nothing else. Without warning, upon the most casual greeting by an acquaintance, he would buttonhole the fellow and launch into a litany of argument and explication.

"Look," he would say. "Katzmann"—the prosecutor—"called a witness who swore up and down that Vanzetti was driving the getaway car. But *Vanzetti can't drive*! He never had a license!"

Or: "What about that cap, now? The one they picked up at the scene, the one they say is Sacco's? But it was picked up *two days* after the crime! After hundreds of people had trampled over that site! And it doesn't even fit him! He tried it on in the courtroom, he couldn't get it on his head!"

Or: "They had a witness at the inquest who testified that the man they claim was Vanzetti had a closely trimmed mustache. The witness was very particular about that. 'Closely clipped,' he said. Now you look at Vanzetti's mustache. Even allowing for the fact that three weeks went by before they arrested him, Vanzetti's mustache was never closely clipped. Why, that's the most luxurious mustache you ever saw! It couldn't possibly be the same man!"

Or: "What about the ballistics? Captain Proctor was very ambivalent about his identification of the third bullet, the one that killed Parmenter, and now he's filed an affidavit in which he renounces his testimony altogether. That bullet has been suspect from the beginning. Look at the identification mark on it—crude scratches, completely different from the others. Doesn't belong at all, I'd say."

Or: "Where's the money? Tell me that! They never found a penny! Nothing! Where is it, then, if Sacco and Vanzetti had it? Who'd they give it to?"

He became known as a crank; people began to avoid him.

The winter passed, and April, bright and brisk, came blustering in. People went about their lives. The Defense Committee did its work. Money came in; under Aldino Felicani's careful management, money was disbursed. Much of it went for legal fees: Fred Moore, in the years before they dismissed him, got over $100,000.

Sacco and Vanzetti sat in their cells for months—years—while new motions for a new trial were filed, and filed again. The difficulty was that Judge Thayer had to rule on all those motions, and so he was in effect ruling on his own competence. If he granted a new trial, he would in effect be admitting to some flaw in his conduct of the original.

People who knew Judge Thayer thought that he was not likely to do that. Especially since everyone knew how much he hated Sacco and Vanzetti—really despised them. He said so, all the time.

On October 1, 1924, Judge Thayer ruled against all the motions for a new trial. The verdict would stand, he said.

Shortly afterward, Fred Moore was fired.

8

"You saw Vanzetti?" Augusta's face was alight with admiration.

"Yes. We had a good talk." Edwin clasped her hands and then sat opposite her. They were in the front parlor of her house in Marlborough Street; she had not risen to greet him because she was in her ninth month of pregnancy, heavy and awkward. Because it had been a difficult pregnancy, her doctor had ordered her to stay in bed—something that Augusta had refused to do. So they compromised: she gave up all outside activity—all charity work, all social events, all thought of working for Sacco and Vanzetti—and he allowed her to get up for several hours a day.

"How was he? Depressed?"

"No, I wouldn't say that. He is of course perfectly well aware of the difficulty of his position. But depressed—no, I wouldn't say so. He is relieved, I think, that Moore is gone."

Jubilant would have been a better word. Vanzetti had smiled and nodded emphatically, "Yes, yes, that fella's gone. We got Mr. Thompson now, we should have had him all along."

A small man, surprisingly calm, whose expressive face showed his quick intelligence, he spoke English better than Edwin had expected, thanks, no doubt, to the faithful tutoring of the good women of Boston who had "adopted" the two men. Through the months and years of their imprisonment, these women had supplied them with extra food, gifts of clothing, lessons in English, and books and magazines to practice—everything that could be done to make Sacco and Vanzetti's prison existence even slightly less bleak, these women did.

Edwin had been surprised when Vanzetti had agreed to see him. Sacco, who was said to be increasingly bitter and withdrawn, had refused. Certainly Vanzetti had the worst of it in accommodations, so to speak, since he was incarcerated in the grim fortress prison at Charlestown, while Sacco stayed at the Dedham jail. This was because Vanzetti, before being found guilty in the South Braintree crime, had been found guilty in a previous matter, an attempted holdup that took place on Christmas Eve, 1919. Many people believed that, first, Vanzetti had been wrongly found guilty in that case, and second, had he not been found guilty in that case, he would never even have been indicted in the second, more serious crime, let alone found guilty.

It was about that first crime, the attempted holdup in December 1919, that Edwin began his questions.

"You have always claimed that on that day, the day before Christmas, you were selling eels door to door in Plymouth. And a number of your customers testified that you were in fact in Plymouth that day, and not in Bridgewater, where the crime took place."

"That's right." Vanzetti wore a slow, patient smile, like a teacher who has been over the material many times, who yet has the patience to help a laggard pupil.

"I find it—well, isn't it strange that you had so many witnesses, and yet the jury discounted their testimony?"

"No," said Vanzetti. "Not strange. All those people were Italians. They were speaking for me—another Italian. Mr. Katzmann—the prosecutor—made it seem like they was lying for me, because we are all Italians. That's what the jury thought."

"And there was no one else—no American—who saw you in Plymouth that day? Who might have testified for you?"

Vanzetti shrugged. "Guess not."

"Well, what about something other than alibis?"

"How you mean?"

"I mean evidence. Some physical piece of evidence that would prove that you did what you said you did. For instance—well, where did you get the eels? Did you buy them in Plymouth?"

"No. I got them from Fish Pier in Boston."

"You went there and bought them?"

"No. They sent them down."

"How?"

"Oh—American Express, I think it was."

"Well! There you are! Didn't you sign some kind of receipt to show that you received them?"

Vanzetti blinked, thinking hard. "I guess I did. I don't remember."

"I'm sure you did. I think we should check into it."

"All right," said Vanzetti. "You can check if you want. I don't think it will make any difference."

"But of course it will make a difference! If we can show that you were wrongly convicted for the first crime, then it will be that much easier to show the same for the second."

Vanzetti nodded. "Okay, mister. You can look. Maybe you'll find something, eh?"

There was an awkward pause. Then: "I wonder if you have any thoughts on the amount of interest your case has stirred up?" said Edwin. "I mean, not only your friends like Felicani, who is after all an Italian like yourself, and so his interest and that of other Italians is understandable. But you have a large group of supporters who are, ah, not Italian—"

"Yes," said Vanzetti. He nodded again but he did not smile. "They think we are innocent. They work hard for us."

"All over the world, in fact, there are people working for you—to see that you have a new trial, a fair trial. How do you feel about that? Are you surprised?"

Vanzetti smiled again, slowly, patiently. "Mister, ah, Revell, you understand, I am a peddler. I am very poor. I have certain political beliefs. I believe in the brotherhood of man. That is foolish, no? Look at the Great War. How many men die—for what? So on the one hand, I am not surprised that people work for me, for us, because you will always find some good people. But I am not surprised either that some people work against us, because some people will always refuse to see the truth. The truth is that we did not do that crime, I never did the other one either, and we got to get a new trial. You ask me, how do I feel?" He shrugged slowly. "I don't feel angry. Not anymore. I feel that maybe this was supposed to happen. Fate, you know? And maybe something good will come out of it."

When Edwin came away from the interview, he was dogged by the feeling that perhaps Vanzetti, at least, was preparing himself for martyrdom. He put the thought to Felicani.

"You think so?" said Felicani. "No one said that to me before. You mean, he's given up?"

"No. I think he still wants to fight, still wants to be free—or, at least, to have a fair trial. But he also seems to be preparing himself—and this is under-standable, psychologically—to lose."

"You mean, to die?"

"Yes. To die."

"Don't say that, Mr. Revell. That kind of talk don't do no good. We got to believe we'll win, or we can't keep on."

Edwin spent the next few weeks studying the trial transcript in William Thompson's State Street office. Thompson was a distinguished and very con-servative member of the Boston Bar who had come into the case after Fred Moore was fired.

As Edwin read the transcript, he discovered a record of unbelievable incom-petence on the part of Fred Moore; of gross pandering to nativist bigotry on the part of Katzmann, the district attorney; and of shameful prejudice against the defendants on the part of the judge, Webster Thayer. All of which would have seemed to ensure the two accused a new trial, save for the fact that the new trial needed to be granted by Thayer. Few judges would have wanted to admit error in such a notorious case.

However, aside from everything else, Edwin thought that there was one glaring, incontrovertible piece of evidence—or lack of it—that should have set-tled the case at once, with or without the hundreds of pages of other testimony pro and con. Finally he spoke to Thompson about it.

"The fingerprints," he said.

"That's right," said Thompson.

"Where are they?"

"Don't know. State Police have 'em, probably."

"But—why weren't they introduced at the trial? Surely, if the police had taken the fingerprints of Sacco and Vanzetti from the getaway car, that would have settled the case then and there."

"That's right." Thompson smiled sourly.

"And so if the state *didn't* introduce the prints—if Katzmann didn't intro-duce the one solid piece of evidence that would have clinched the case—what do we infer from that? That the prints the police took from the car were not Sacco and Vanzetti's? That not one of them matched?"

"Right again," said Thompson. "Katzmann couldn't introduce the prints be-cause they proved Sacco and Vanzetti *had nothing to do with the crime*! I don't have to tell you that if those prints that they took from the car had matched Sacco and Vanzetti's—if just *one* had matched up—that would have been Katzmann's first ex-hibit. Now this is a case that has aroused international attention. All over the world people know about Sacco and Vanzetti. Most of 'em want the Commonwealth of Massachusetts to set those two men free. Katzmann's under a lot of pressure, because a lot of people think he got a guilty verdict without proving it. Don't you think if he had had those matching prints, he'd have settled the matter once and for all and introduced 'em? Instead, he *never even mentioned 'em*. Funny, isn't it?"

"So why didn't Moore know that Katzmann had proof positive of his clients' innocence?"

"Because in Massachusetts, my friend, the prosecution isn't obliged to turn over its evidence."

"So there is no way Moore could have introduced those prints so the jury would have known about them?"

"Oh, sure. There's a way. He just didn't use it, that's all. That man isn't fit to do a simple real estate closing, let alone defend a murder charge. Now, the State Police captain who took those prints off the car was William Proctor. All Moore had to do was, when he had Proctor on cross, was to *ask* him about 'em! That's all! Any first-year law student could'v'told him that! But did he do it? No! He was too busy aggravatin' Judge Thayer by walkin' around the courtroom in his stockin' feet. In June, mind you!"

"And you can't introduce the fingerprints in one of the motions?"

"No. The law says they have to come in in a trial. Just one reason out of all the others we need a new trial—a whole new ball game. Then we'll finally get those two fellows a proper defense—something that they haven't had yet."

9

Edwin began having nightmares—or, rather, one nightmare over and over. He was in a crowded, poor part of the city, a place with narrow streets and pungent smells and a babble of foreign voices. After a while he realized with a little shock that of course it was the North End. It was nearly dark, a drizzly day, trails of fog wisping around the corners of the old red-brick tenements. And he was running. At first he didn't know why—running as fast as he could up one little street and down another, picking up speed—yes, hurry! Hurry! Don't let them catch us!—and then he realized that he had companions in his flight, and they were shouting something in Italian that he couldn't understand.

Sacco and Vanzetti—that was who his companions were. The two accused, the two condemned. They were at his side, struggling to keep up, slipping on the wet cobblestones—hurry! Faster! Panting, his lungs hurting, breath coming hard—around this corner, and then around the next—

Always, he woke up before they reached their destination. He did not know what that was, except that it was someplace safe, someplace where the police, the warden, the judge and jury could not get them. But they never got there. Running for their lives, terrified that they would be caught— No!

"Dad?"

He struggled up from sleep. He was alone: he had not shared a room with his wife for years. He saw a figure silhouetted in the light from the hall: his son Stephen, age fourteen.

"Are you all right? You were calling out—"

He was fully awake now, and sitting up. "Yes—yes, I'm all right. I must have been dreaming. I don't remember. Did I frighten you? I'm sorry."

Stephen was a thin, rather nervous boy, a student at the Boston Latin School. He had often had nightmares himself, when he was small.

"Come in," said Edwin. He patted the bed. "Sit down. Did I say anything coherent?"

"No. That was the odd thing." Stephen perched on the bed, shivering in his pajamas.

"Here—you'll catch your death." Edwin reached for his warm woolen robe at the foot of the bed and gave it to the boy. "So you couldn't understand anything?"

"No. Just a scary kind of—I don't know. Sound."

"But you've never heard it before?"

"No."

"Well. I'll have to tell my unconscious, or wherever it is that nightmares come from, to be more careful." He patted the boy's arm. "Go on, now—take the robe with you, back to sleep. School in the morning. How's it going?"

"All right. Mr. Knightley's giving us a test on the subjunctive tomorrow. I don't think I'm going to do very well."

More than once he had thought that the boy should go away to school. The atmosphere at 25 West Cedar Street was hardly homelike; he was away more often than not, and his wife Ruth had long since given up any pretense of maternal concern, devoting most of her time to one church committee or another. It was the housekeeper—a dour, if competent, Nova Scotian—who kept the place going. The older boy, Avery, had just started at Harvard, and was living there, which made life all the more lonely for Stephen. Well: they'd talk about it, and perhaps he could go to Andover or St. Mark's.

After the boy left, Edwin couldn't go back to sleep. His little bedside clock said four-thirty. It was November: the dark of the year, no dawn until after seven. Nevertheless, after a while he got up and put on his clothes and went down to the kitchen, where he made himself a pot of tea and a couple of slices of toast—early breakfast. These he carried on a tray to his study at the back of the first floor. He'd been working for a week on a new pamphlet for the Defense Committee. Now, reading over it, he thought that it was not forceful enough. It lacked punch. He'd have to do it over—or give it to someone else to do. He'd not have trouble finding someone.

On the other hand, he didn't want to find someone. He wanted to do this himself. He glanced at the calendar: November 18, 1925. Any day now the appeal would be taken to the Supreme Judicial Court of Massachusetts. Four and a half years the case had dragged on—five and a half since the two men were arrested.

It was a long time to sit in a jail cell, particularly if you were innocent.

10

Later that day a convicted murderer named Celestino Madeiros confessed to being a member of the holdup gang at South Braintree. His accomplices, he said, were the Morelli gang of Providence—a criminal crew well known to the authorities. Sacco and Vanzetti had had nothing to do with the crime, he said.

William Thompson was too busy to investigate and verify Madeiros's confession; he asked Roscoe Pound, the dean of the Harvard Law School, to recommend someone for the job. Pound suggested Herbert Ehrmann, a young graduate now practicing in Boston. Ehrmann believed that Sacco and Vanzetti were probably guilty.

Soon, however, he changed his mind. Right away he found out that Madeiros, previously impoverished, had acquired a large sum of money shortly after April 15, 1920—the day of the crime. He also found the four other members of the gang who fit witnesses' descriptions of the robbers far better than Sacco and Vanzetti did. He found the blond driver; he found the member of the gang who had spoken English—previously identified as Sacco, now identified as Joe Morelli, who was practically Sacco's double. Since Morelli had been born in America, he spoke pretty good English, while Sacco spoke it haltingly and with a heavy accent.

Further, Ehrmann found the probable weapons used in the crime; he found the way in which the Morellis learned when the payroll would be delivered; and he found a motive, which was to get funds for the defense of previous crimes.

In short, he amassed more evidence, and more credible evidence, against the Morellis than the state had had to convict Sacco and Vanzetti.

On May 26, 1926, William Thompson filed yet another supplementary motion before Judge Thayer, based not only on the Madeiros confession and Ehrmann's findings, but upon the fact that the prosecution had suppressed evidence—witnesses against Sacco who had by now changed their stories.

On October 23 Judge Thayer denied the motion.

On October 26 the *Boston Herald*, a newspaper whose editorial opinions reflected its conservative Republican readership, published an editorial on the Sacco-Vanzetti case:

> As months have merged into years and the great debate over the case
> has continued, our doubts have solidified slowly into convictions . . .
>   The question was not what a judge may think about it [the Madeiros confession] but what a jury might think about it. . . .

In short, said the *Herald*, Sacco and Vanzetti should have a new trial.

The following spring the *Boston Herald* won a Pulitzer Prize for that editorial. Shortly afterward the Supreme Judicial Court of Massachusetts upheld Judge Thayer's decision: there could be no new trial based on Celestino Madeiros's confession and Herbert Ehrmann's new evidence.

Some people thought that the SJC had been unhappily influenced by an article by Felix Frankfurter, a professor at the Harvard Law School. The article was not only a passionate defense of Sacco and Vanzetti, it was a ferocious attack on Judge Thayer, whose most recent opinion, said Frankfurter, was a "farrago of misquotations ... honeycombed with judicial errors, and infused by a spirit alien to judicial utterance." The article appeared in the March *Atlantic Monthly*; in April it came out as a book.

The decision by the SJC came down on April 5. On April 9 Sacco and Vanzetti were taken in chains to Judge Thayer's courtroom in Dedham, where he sentenced them to die in the electric chair during the week of July 10 in the year of our Lord one thousand, nine hundred and twenty-seven.

The two men were permitted to make a statement. Sacco, never completely comfortable in English, said, in part: "I never know, never heard, even read in history anything so cruel as this Court ... And Judge Thayer know that I am never been guilty...."

Vanzetti spoke longer. He, too, maintained that he was innocent, not only of the South Braintree crime, but of the Bridgewater crime as well. Then he mentioned one of his heroes, a radical thinker who had himself spent considerable time in prison for his beliefs: "Eugene Debs say that not even a dog that kill the chickens would have been found guilty with the evidence the Commonwealth have produced against us ... We have proved that there could not have been another judge on the face of the earth more prejudiced and more cruel than you have been against us ... We know, and you know in your heart, that you have been against us from the very beginning...."

And then Sacco again, one last cry of despair: "You kill two innocent men!"

11

Time was running out now. At the office on Hanover Street, Aldino Felicani exhorted everyone to work harder. "We got no time!" he would say. "We're up against the clock now! Two, three months we got! Hurry up!"

On May 4 the Defense Committee presented to Governor Alvan T. Fuller, former car salesman, a request for executive clemency. Governor Fuller immediately began to investigate the case; however, no record of his investigation could later be found.

In order to escape blame for his decision, whatever it was, he appointed a committee to study the case also. His verdict would be based on theirs.

When Edwin heard that news, he was for the first time in many months genuinely cheered.

"That's it!" he said. He slapped Felicani on the back and smiled widely at the others in the room. "They'll do the right thing."

No one smiled back.

"Who are they?" said Felicani.

"The committee? Oh, they are the best. The very best. The president will be the chairman, I imagine—"

"What? The President of the United States?"

"No, no. The president of Harvard. Abbott Lawrence Lowell. You could not find a more honest and honorable man. And Judge Grant—and the third member is Mr. Stratton, the president of MIT. So you see, this could not be a better group. And of course when they review the case, they will recommend a new trial. No question about it."

He was not really surprised that the Defense Committee was unenthusiastic. Lowell was, after all, a member of the same "Establishment" that had refused these many years to grant justice to the two accused.

"Do you know him—this Lowell?" asked Felicani.

"I've met him once or twice, yes. A starchy fellow, but straight, as straight as they come. He defended a socialist professor when the Board of Overseers wanted to fire the fellow a few years back at the height of the red scare. If Harold Laski went, Lowell would go, too, he said. So you see, he'll be fair. And the two others will follow his lead."

"Why?"

"Because he is Abbott Lawrence Lowell. If I may borrow a phrase from my cousin John, he has a gravitational pull that Stratton and Grant cannot resist. You'll see—it'll be all right."

He could see that they still did not believe him. He himself was convinced that this was the turning point, at last, in their long and bitter fight to see Sacco and Vanzetti released—or, at least, given a fair trial.

12

In June, after the Lowell Committee had been appointed but before it had begun its work, Governor Fuller paid a visit to the convict, Madeiros, at the Charlestown prison. He offered Madeiros a reprieve from the electric chair if Madeiros would retract his confession to the South Braintree robbery-murder.

Madeiros refused.

13

The summer of 1927: already a warm day, and by noon, when Edwin was scheduled to attend a march in front of the Statehouse on behalf of the two men, it would be broiling. Perhaps he would not cover it. Perhaps he would have lunch instead at Jake Wirth's with an anarchist acquaintance from New York, up to Boston to cover the case for an obscure anarchist newspaper.

Accordingly, shortly after twelve he and his acquaintance were seated at a table toward the rear, just getting started on their meal of sauerbraten and dumplings, when another journalist came in: Frank Stewart from the *Globe*. At Edwin's invitation, he joined them. He was, he said, fresh from a conversation with a Harvard person—no further identification forthcoming—who had filled him in on Abbott Lawrence Lowell. All was well, he said: Lowell was a fair man, and his committee would see that justice was done to Sacco and Vanzetti.

Edwin was about to agree when the anarchist shook his head vigorously. "You fellows are mistaken if you think Lowell will save those two," he said.

"What do you mean?" said Edwin.

"Why, man, don't you know about him? He was one of the founders of the Immigration Restriction League. Remember that? Wanted to keep everybody out who wasn't a certified Anglo-Saxon. Those people believe in the Master Race. They believe that folks from Southern and Eastern Europe are racially inferior. Now you tell me, how can a man like that deliver a fair judgment on two Italians? And Jews, too," he added. He ate rapidly while he talked, as if he didn't have many square meals; Edwin was paying.

"Oh, that old story—" Edwin began.

"Not an old story, my friend. He had a tremendous fight with Professor Frankfurter, didn't you know? Over the quotas for the Jews. So now Frankfurter comes out with this wonderful defense of Sacco and Vanzetti. Really brilliant. And do you think that all of a sudden Abbott Lawrence Lowell is going to embrace this pushy Jew and say, 'Yes, yes, you are right about this'? No matter what Frankfurter says, Lowell is going to oppose it. If Frankfurter says the earth is round, Lowell will have to say it is flat. He must say it, you understand, for his own psychological peace. He can never agree with Frankfurter on anything—not after that fight. I think Frankfurter would have done better to say they are guilty. Then Lowell could oppose him and set them free." The anarchist turned to Stewart. "Will you print that in the *Globe*?"

"Not on your life, buddy."

"Why not? You afraid of the great Abbott Lawrence Lowell? What's that little poem? 'Lowells speak only to Cabots, Cabots speak only to God'? They're so close to Heaven, you afraid of them?"

Stewart, who loved a good gossip as much as any newspaperman, was vaguely offended. Like most Massachusetts people, he liked to bask in the reflected glow of the Brahmin caste. It gave him a little class. If he traveled to other parts of the country—which he never did and never would, but if he did— people would know that he and Abbott Lawrence Lowell inhabited the same little corner of the universe.

"Listen, friend," said the anarchist, "that man hates Jews so much, he was opposed to Brandeis going on the Supreme Court. Can you imagine? Louis Brandeis? That brilliant man? Sacco and Vanzetti are going to die because of anti-Semitism, mark my words. And Lowell himself is a failed lawyer, you know. He couldn't make it in the law, so he went to Harvard to teach. Old alma mater took him in. And now he sits in judgment! He's handling a criminal case, and he's got two men with him who don't know any more about criminal law than he does—"

"Robert Grant is a judge," said Edwin.

"Of what? Probate Court? You got to be kidding me. And Stratton—why, he's just a little nothing. I don't care if he is the head of the Massachusetts Institute of Technology. He's just a yes man for Lowell. I heard that Lowell asked to have him. Could'v'had anyone he wanted, he picked that nonentity. Yessir. Lowell may be a bigot, but he's not stupid. He'll get what he wants. Wait and see."

"And what might that be?" said Stewart.

"Exoneration." The anarchist smiled at his two companions as if he were delivering only good news.

"For . . . ?"

"For the Commonwealth of Massachusetts, of course. You don't think after all this time that he will allow any conclusion that will admit that the Commonwealth of Massachusetts, the grand old Bay State, made a mistake?"

Despite the warmth of the day, Edwin felt a little *frisson* of dread ripple up his spine.

"One final bit of information about your precious Mr. Lowell is that he has consistently opposed child labor laws. He thinks that if you prevent a child from working ten hours a day in a factory, you violate the right of property." The anarchist showed a grim smile. "Not the sort of fellow I'd want holding my life in his hands, eh?"

"I've got to go," said Stewart.

The anarchist eyed him coolly. "Print what I told you," he said.

"Never."

"You're afraid."

"Damned right I am."

"And your editor is afraid, too."

"He certainly is."

The anarchist snorted in contempt. "At least you admit it." He signaled for the waiter. "Another order of sauerbraten here!"

14

"My God! Listen to this!" Felicani burst into the Defense Committee office one hot afternoon not long afterward.

"What, Aldino? What is it? Calm yourself, it is too hot to run."

But he could not be quieted. "They found the receipt book!" he shouted. "Mr. Ehrmann found it! Can you imagine? After all these years? In somebody's attic over on Commercial Street!"

"Where is it now?"

"Mr. Ehrmann has given it to the governor's lawyer."

"Well, you better make sure the Lowell Committee sees it as well."

This was important—crucial: the long-missing, concrete proof that Vanzetti, as he had claimed, had taken delivery of a shipment of eels to sell on December 24, 1919. Therefore, if he was selling eels in Plymouth on that day, he could not have attempted the first crime—the aborted holdup in Bridgewater—the conviction for which, his partisans believed, had led to his indictment for the second crime, the robbery-murder at South Braintree.

Not guilty of the first, not guilty of the second—splendid!

It was late, very late, but now new hope flared up. This was a gift from God! A portent—ah, now it would come right and the two men would be freed.

15

On July 25 the Lowell Committee heard the last of its witnesses—by no means all the witnesses it might have heard, but enough to give the impression of having done its work. That afternoon, President Lowell handed to his secretary a draft of the committee's opinion to type up. On July 27 the final report was delivered to Governor Fuller.

On August 2 U.S. President Calvin Coolidge announced that he would not run for a second term in the 1928 election.

On August 3 Governor Alvan Fuller, who had presidential aspirations of his own, was scheduled to announce his decision: would he, or would he not, grant executive clemency to Sacco and Vanzetti?

It was a hot day, and very humid—the kind of day when people longed for the icy blasts of winter. The red-brick city soaked up the sun's heat and radiated it back onto the suffering citizenry; even along the shore, at South Boston and Dorchester or across the bay in Revere and Winthrop, there was no relief.

In the morning the newspapermen gathered in the governor's anteroom, or in the corridors of the Statehouse, or they sprawled on the lawns of the Common across Beacon Street. Slowly the hours passed. Fuller was not in his office; no one knew when he would appear. Edwin looked in and after a few moments went away; he was too tense, too apprehensive, to wait with the others, playing cards, gossiping. He needed to do something—anything. Lacking any other occupation, he began to walk.

He went across Beacon Street and down the steps to the Common; then along the Mall to Charles Street and across to the Public Garden. The city seemed about to melt in the heat. Few people were about, and those who were looked ready to drop. He sat on a bench beneath a tree and mopped his perspiring face. Damned if he wasn't ready to take off his jacket and collar and tie, he thought; he didn't care what rules of propriety he might violate. A tall, heavyset man was coming down the walk toward him; Edwin needed a moment to place him, but then he did.

"Hallo, Harry."

He was sure that if he had not spoken, the man would have ignored him and gone on; he knew perfectly well that Harry Trowbridge, Augusta's husband, did not particularly like him.

"Morning, Edwin. Keepin' busy, are you?"

"Moderately. How about yourself? I thought you folks always went to the country for the summer." When he had last seen Augusta, in June, she had said that they would be making their annual journey to Harry's parents' farm in Petersham the following week.

"We do. The girl's there now, with Mother and Father." That was Winifred, their daughter. "Augusta insisted on coming back to town, and I insisted that the city is no place for a child in the middle of summer. This damned case—you're involved with it, too, she told me. I'll be glad when it's over. No place for a lady, messin' about with all those wops."

Harry Trowbridge was a decent enough man, but unimaginative. Edwin had never understood what Augusta had seen in him.

"You mean that Augusta is at home now? This morning?"

"If she hasn't gone gallivantin' off somewhere with that Glendower Evans woman. I blame her, y'know, for leadin' Augusta into this thing. She's been a perfect pest, that woman has. Well, it's all comin' to an end now, isn't it?"

Edwin allowed himself a smile. "Harry, your wife is not only a splendid human being, she is one of the most independent-minded women I've ever known. I don't think that Mrs. Evans could have persuaded her to do anything she didn't want to do."

Harry shook his massive head. "It's not right, y'know. Really not right. Women messin' about in murder cases. It just isn't ladylike. Well, I'm off. Regards to your family."

Within five minutes Edwin was at Augusta's door. The maid showed him in to where Augusta was sitting in the little back garden.

"Why didn't you tell me you were in town?" he said.

"I was going to. I was with Mrs. Evans all day yesterday and the day before. I did call you once, as a matter of fact, but there was no answer. What's going on?"

"Nothing. The reporters are all up at the Statehouse, waiting for Fuller's decision. Has Mrs. Evans been to see them?"—"them" being the two prisoners, as Augusta understood.

"Yes. Sacco wouldn't see her. But his wife went in. She said that he is resigned to it."

"To the electric chair?"

"Yes."

"And Vanzetti?"

"Mrs. Evans took his sister to see him. As you know, she has come over from their village."

"Yes."

She was silent for a moment. Then: "Edwin . . ."

"Yes, my dear?"

"They are going to die, aren't they?"

"I'm afraid so."

"In spite of everything."

"Yes."

"There is nothing that we can do."

"Apparently not."

She sat very still, her tall, rangy frame too big for the small iron garden chair. Her fist was pressed against her lips as if she were trying to keep herself from crying.

"I can't believe it," she said. "After all these years of work, people all over the world begging us not to execute them, so much support for them—after all of this, they are still going to die. Nothing has changed. All we ask is a new trial, and somehow the law won't allow it. The law—the law! What good is the law when it allows two men to die without a fair trial? Edwin, can't we get to Governor Fuller somehow, make him understand? Or if not to him, then to someone? Surely between us we know someone who can stop this atrocious judicial murder. That's what Mrs. Evans calls it, and she is right."

"I don't know Fuller at all," said Edwin. "And as for—"

"You know, there *is* someone," Augusta said suddenly.

"Who?"

"Cousin Frederick."

"You mean, because he sits on the Board of Overseers?"

"That's right. He is one of the few people connected with Harvard who has some power over Abbott Lawrence Lowell. Or influence, at least."

Edwin had a sudden memory: Frederick at fifteen, made miserable by his schoolmates' taunts about his mother's portrait. Edwin had helped Frederick— had been glad to help him—but they'd never been close afterwards.

"I hardly think that Frederick Griffin Revell would be sympathetic to this case," he said.

"I hardly think so, either." Augusta tapped her fingertips nervously on the glass-topped garden table. "But it's worth a try, isn't it? If Fuller denies the appeal, perhaps someone could make Frederick understand that Harvard and Cambridge and Boston and all of Massachusetts are going to look very bad if Sacco and Vanzetti are killed."

She watched to see his reaction. "Do you think that you could do that, Edwin? Convince Cousin Frederick to persuade Mr. Lowell to change his opinion?"

"If his opinion has gone against them."

"Which I believe it will. Don't you?"

He did not have the heart to answer, but he thought of the day that he had dined with the anarchist, and of that man's bitter assessment of Abbott Lawrence Lowell's mindset.

"Edwin. Will you go to Frederick? Will you talk to him? After all, what can he say? Yes or no? And if there is a chance in a thousand that he will say yes—"

"All right. I will talk to him. But let's wait until we hear Governor Fuller's decision. Perhaps he will surprise us."

Accordingly, Edwin took his leave of Augusta and went back to the State-house to join the waiting reporters.

Around six o'clock some of them sent out for sandwiches. A while later it grew dark. A palpable tension filled the air.

Shortly after eight there was a flurry of activity in the corridor, the sound of men's voices. Everyone in the room stood up—not as a sign of respect, but the better to have a look, toss a question.

Fuller walked in at a brisk clip, followed by his secretary, MacDonald, and two other men—bodyguards, thought Edwin.

"Say, Governor, what'v'you decided?"

"Governor! Are they saved?"

"Mr. Fuller! Can you give us a statement, sir?"

But Fuller paid them no heed; he scurried into his inner office, his companions close behind, and MacDonald firmly closed the door. The newsmen relaxed again, started up their card game again, but with a little more attention to the clock now: time was running out. Fuller had said, "August third." Only a few more hours left, now. Time running out—for them, for Sacco and Vanzetti.

Nine o'clock; ten. Edwin sat in a straight-backed chair tipped back to the wall, his eyes shut against the glare, half dozing in the dreadful heat—and yet he did not doze. His mind was racing—sifting back through the months and years that had been devoted to this case, to these two obscure men who now, for better or for worse, had become world famous. How many hours . . . ! Days and weeks and months of effort, letters and petitions and court appeals, the talents of hundreds of people, money donated, time and energy freely given, tears shed, Rosina Sacco weeping for her husband—Felicani had said that two days ago, when he drove her to Cardinal O'Connell's summer residence in Marblehead to take tea with the cardinal, she had wept going in and wept coming out, and very probably she had wept the entire time, twenty minutes or so, that she was permitted to see His Eminence. Felicani couldn't say for sure because he himself was a devout atheist and had refused to accompany her and Vanzetti's sister, just come from Italy, into the house. In any case, O'Connell had given them no help; he would never speak up for two atheist anarchists.

Shortly after eleven the door to Fuller's office was thrown open and Mac-Donald emerged carrying a stack of sealed envelopes, each bearing the name of a newspaper. The correspondent from the *New York World* was first to tear his envelope open. He found the crucial passage on the last of the five pages. Running into the corridor, he shouted to the waiting telegraph operator, "They die!"

In the sudden tumult as the reporters stampeded to the telephones, Edwin stood numb, hardly able to comprehend the news. And yet it was news that was not unexpected—news for which he had tried to prepare himself, ever since his anarchist acquaintance had enlightened him about Abbott Lawrence Lowell.

"They die!"

Impossible—and yet in the end he had known it, had known that Fuller could never allow them to live.

In less than a minute the room was empty. Fuller did not emerge from his office. He had done what everyone thought he would do. Now Sacco and Vanzetti were one step away from the electric chair, and the only thing that could save them was some extraordinary appeal—which undoubtedly would be taken—to some high court, either state or federal.

"They die!"

The words echoed in Edwin's head as he made his way downstairs. Outside, the heat had barely dissipated; no cooling breeze came off the water. The city lay dark and quiet before him. He stood at the top of Beacon Street and gazed down its length. Then at a rapid clip he started down the uneven brick sidewalk toward the Back Bay.

16

Earlier that same evening, Frederick went to dine with Isabella. Ordinarily by that date he would have joined his wife and children at Northeast Harbor, where he spent every August, but a matter of business had detained him in town for a few days.

Isabella awaited him in the courtyard. Tall wrought-iron candelabra stood in the archways. The flickering shadows of their lighted candles gave the place the atmosphere of antiquity that Isabella wanted it to have; they also provided a light sufficiently dim to make her look at least ten years younger than her age, which, as he knew, was seventy-seven. His wife disapproved of Isabella; no woman of that generation had the right to wear face powder and rouge and lipstick, she said. But Isabella had never cared what people said about her, and she certainly did not care now.

"Frederick." With the aid of her gold-knobbed cane she stood to greet him. Her fine features were hardly blurred by age; her brilliant eyes still looked out on the world with wisdom and clear sight. Gently he kissed her cheek.

"And how are you, dear Mother? You look splendid as always. Will you come up to Maine with me on Saturday? Get away from this heat? It was perishing in town today, I'll tell you."

"Yes, I imagine it was." She motioned him to a seat near the fountain, and the footman brought a silver tray of cocktails. Frederick sipped his martini and nodded approvingly. "Very nice. O'Hanrahan's doing all right by us, I must say." He referred to their supplier, a valued personage in these days of Prohibition. "Now. What about it? Will you come?"

She shook her head. "Thank you, dear Frederick. But no. I am happiest here. And as you see, these thick walls keep the place really quite cool."

"Just like Venice."

"Exactly. Just like Venice. The Italians, you know, have been living with intense heat for centuries—millennia. We can do worse than imitate them."

They dined on cold cucumber soup and broiled chicken and raspberry tart. They enjoyed each other's company tremendously; neither of them had ever forgotten that he had been, as it were, a specially chosen child, as adopted children always are.

After they had their meal in the dining room, they returned to the courtyard for their espresso. She reached out and took his hand. "Dearest Frederick," she said. "Mind you get the portrait of Catherine from Winslow. It is a perfect example of seventeenth century limner's art. You were meant to have it, you know. I can't think why Lyman didn't give it to you when you turned twenty-one."

Frederick laughed. "Uncle Lyman's the one who went to England to research the pedigree. You didn't expect him to give up something as valuable as that portrait, did you?"

"But you were meant to have it. Certainly you should have had it when Lyman died. Winslow has no right to keep it, and I shall tell him so."

"I don't think—"

"I've put it in my will that you shall have the Copleys. My own portrait—the Sargent portrait—must stay here, of course. I've provided an endowment so that this will be a museum always, and that portrait belongs here. But the Copleys must be yours, and it is all written out so that you will have no trouble taking them."

"And the other as well?"

"Why not? With you they are safe. God knows what would happen to them if someone else has them."

"Dear Mother. Why do you trouble yourself about this tonight?"

She smiled at him. "I don't know. Sometimes I feel that—well, that time is running short."

"Nonsense. Don't talk rot. You're healthier than I am."

"Possibly. But in any case, no harm done. Just make sure you get that picture."

They talked for a good while longer, and so it was after eleven when Frederick returned home to Commonwealth Avenue. He let himself in with his key. Only two maids had stayed in town, and he had told them not to wait up. His house was considerably warmer than Isabella's. He went into his library at the back of the second floor to open the tall windows. He thought he might sit up for a while, since he was not tired; in fact, he was oddly edgy. Strange, to have had his mother talking like that about the portraits. He didn't like such talk—didn't like to think of the day when he'd have to accept her loss. He couldn't say "death." And in any case, she wasn't—

He lifted his head to listen. He thought he'd heard the front bell. Surely not—at this hour?

He stepped into the hall. There—again. Some scapegrace, perhaps, having his fun. Or a madman. Certainly he wasn't going to answer at this hour, nearly midnight.

Now came a pounding—heavy, demanding—and someone calling to him by name. "Frederick! Frederick, are you there? Open up!"

So he had no choice but to go down, unlock—"

"Thank God you're here! Listen, I have to talk to you." And without a by-your-leave, Edwin pushed his way in while Frederick closed the door behind him. He had a sudden sense of foreboding: this would be a difficult interview.

"Where? In here?" Edwin gestured toward the darkened front parlor.

"No—come upstairs." Abruptly Frederick turned on his heel and led the way up. Despite the older man's kindness to him, long ago, in the matter of Isabella's portrait, Frederick had never been particularly fond of Edwin. He considered him to be dangerously unstable, a wild-eyed radical, writing books about the shame of the rich when in fact the rich had nothing at all to be ashamed of.

Edwin was too nerved up to take a seat. He paced the room as he spoke, pausing only to jab the air with his finger, usually in Frederick's direction, to make some particularly urgent point.

"The governor has handed down his decision," he said.

"His decision—"

"On Sacco and Vanzetti."

"Ah." Of course, thought Frederick: why else would Edwin come to him in the middle of the night? Not for cousinly affection, that was certain.

"They are to die."

Frederick did not know what to say, and so he said nothing. He lifted his shoulders in a little shrug. He did not want to get into an argument—not here and now, not with Edwin—and certainly not about Sacco and Vanzetti.

"I came here to ask you to do something to save them."

"To save them? But they have been found guilty, have they not? By a jury?"

"After an unfair trial before a prejudiced judge."

"And by the Lowell Committee as well?"

"The Lowell Committee was flawed from the start. And they did not have all the evidence. They found wrongly. And Fuller based his decision on theirs, and so Fuller found wrongly as well."

"My dear fellow, you make tremendous leaps—"

"*Listen to me.* The question is not whether they are guilty. Do you understand?"

"No, actually, I'm afraid I don't."

"The question is not any longer, whom did Sacco and Vanzetti kill? From now on, the question will be, who killed Sacco and Vanzetti? Do you see? They are on death row, they will die within days—and *they did not have a fair trial*! And that is why I am here tonight. To ask your help, not for their sake, but for the sake of the Commonwealth of Massachusetts. Don't you understand? Sacco and Vanzetti are no longer on trial. Now it is the Commonwealth of Massachusetts that is on trial. And if we let them die we will all be guilty of murder!"

The echo of his voice hung in the hot, still air. Not a breath came from the open windows; Frederick thought for a moment that perhaps he should shut them, if Edwin was going to go on shouting—

"Frederick, listen to me. We are the same Family, you and I—the same blood. That is important. We have our disagreements, but we understand each other."

No, thought Frederick, we do not. I do not understand you at all.

"Three centuries ago, now, our ancestor Bartholomew Revell came across with the Pilgrims—with the Pilgrims, Frederick! That means something, doesn't it? Of course it does! To me it means that we have a special obligation to this place—this little commonwealth that our flesh and blood helped to bring into existence. This is our place, Frederick! No other place in the world but this! And we are responsible for it, don't you see? We cannot let it—or its people— commit this terrible wrong. For if they do, they will commit it in our name as well. And forever after we will have the shame of it on our souls. Like the name of Pontius Pilate, the name of Massachusetts will stink in the nostrils of decent men—forever! Alvan Fuller has washed his hands of the case, and he has done it in our name."

"Alvan Fuller—Pontius Pilate— Really, Edwin, I must say—"

"Once before," Edwin went on, relentless, "we allowed ourselves to be ruled by our own worst instincts—to be ruled by all that is narrow and bigoted and afraid. The witchcraft, Frederick! We did that—the people of Massachusetts did that, their leaders did it in our name—and we have never lived it down, and we never will! And I am begging you—I am begging you, Frederick, to help to prevent another miscarriage of justice such as that. I grant you Sacco and Van-zetti have been found guilty. But it was not a fair trial, any more than the witchcraft trials were fair, and the Lowell Committee was not a fair committee, and now we must act quickly to see that justice is done, or it will be too late."

In the quiet night the two men stared at each other. Each felt that he was seeing the other for perhaps the first time. They bore the Family resemblance, of course, but beyond that their very different lives had marked them so that they might not have been related at all. Frederick, the younger by ten years, looked twenty years younger—twenty-five. And Edwin lacked the usual Family look of spit-and-polish. He was a little ragged around his edges; he had the look of the newspaperman about him, he had moved too long in those somewhat disreputable circles.

"What would you have me do?" Frederick said at last.

"Go to Lowell. You know him, you are an overseer, and besides, you see him all the time at the Somerset. But more important, I understand that Benjamin is courting his wife's niece." Benjamin was Frederick's eldest son, recently graduated from the Law School. "Go to him and ask him this: did he see the fingerprints from the car? And did he see the receipt book from American Express? Just ask him that. And if you bring back the answer I expect, I can handle it from there."

"You know as well as I do that Abbott Lawrence Lowell would never speak to me about this case," said Frederick. "He is a pillar of probity—a man of honor. He would judge it a gross violation of procedure—not to mention ethics—to speak to me, an outsider, about this most delicate and sensitive—"

"You can at least try. If Lowell won't speak to you, go to Stratton, go to Grant!"

"My dear Edwin, I can see how upset you are. But if I understand the case correctly, the governor's decision was the final appeal. So it is too late—"

"No! It is not too late! As long as they are alive, it is never too late!" Edwin's voice broke; he paused to mend it. Then, more calmly: "I have worked on this case for years now. And I have often asked myself, why this tremendous resistance to giving Sacco and Vanzetti a new trial? What are we afraid of? That they will be found innocent? That that will show that we were wrong the first time around—that the judicial system failed? But the judicial system is made up of men, not gods. Of course they will fail from time to time. But let them not fail in such a monstrous and irrevocable way!"

Frederick was silent. His expression was one of great sadness, but there was disapproval there, as well.

"Listen to me," Edwin went on. "I don't know how to put it to you any plainer than this. If those two men die, your beloved Massachusetts will be guilty of a crime far greater than anything Sacco and Vanzetti ever did. Do you understand? It is for Massachusetts' sake that Sacco and Vanzetti must have a new trial. And if you want to argue the point, it is proof of their innocence that the state is afraid to re-try them, for fear they will go free. They must be given another chance!"

Frederick paused before he replied; he wanted to choose his words carefully. Because now he was about to say something that he felt needed to be said, and yet Edwin looked so very distraught, that Frederick feared that the wrong words would set him off.

Carefully, as if he were speaking to a child, or perhaps to a person whose mind was not stable, he said, "Do you not think, cousin, that people's confidence in the judicial system has been shaken far enough? If a new trial were granted, do you not think it would be harmful to the population's very necessary trust in authority? It is important to people's faith in the stability of our institutions that the case be ended, once and for all. Because if people lose their faith in the systems that rule them . . ."

Frederick was not a timid man, but now his voice trailed off as he saw Edwin's reaction.

"You mean—and I think you do mean—it is better that Sacco and Vanzetti die than that confidence in the Massachusetts judicial system be further shaken."

"I wouldn't put it quite so—"

"Yes! You would! That is exactly how you would put it!"

"I simply mean that—"

"I know what you mean." Edwin took a deep breath. "God help you," he said. He turned toward the door.

"Edwin." Frederick crossed the room in two strides and held out his hand. "I am so very sorry. No hard feelings?"

Edwin swayed a little. It had been a long, difficult day, very hot, emotionally draining. He realized that Frederick wanted to shake hands. Well, Frederick could go to the devil.

He held on to the doorknob; he stared intently into Frederick's blue, blue eyes—so like his own, and yet they did not see the same things, they saw different worlds.

"One last thing," he said.

In response, Frederick smiled a condescending little smile full of false hope—the smile one gives perhaps to a dying child. "Yes, cousin? What is it?"

Edwin paused. He wanted to get it right. "Remember this," he said. "Remember it always: If we kill them, they will live forever! Do you understand? They will be immortal!"

And then he was gone, out into the hot, still night, and Frederick was left alone to try to understand what he had said.

17

Sacco and Vanzetti were now scheduled to die on August 22.

On August 8 Lawyer Thompson filed an eighth motion for a new trial, based upon the prejudice of the trial judge, Webster Thayer. Due to the quirks of the Massachusetts legal system, this motion had to be argued before the judge whose prejudice was its subject. Not surprisingly, he denied it.

On August 16 an appeal for a new trial was made to the Supreme Judicial Court of Massachusetts.

On August 18 the justices wrote their decision, put it into a safe, and left for their vacations with instructions that the decision was not to be made public until they were well away. To no one's surprise, they denied the appeal.

On August 20 and 21 Sacco and Vanzetti's lawyers hunted down vacationing justices of the United States Supreme Court. They needed to find one Justice— only one—who would grant a writ of certiorari. The writ would stay the execution, and would grant permission for the case to be heard before the full court in the fall.

First they went to Oliver Wendell Holmes Jr., who was summering in

Beverly, on the North Shore. Holmes was perhaps the most revered public man in the United States, wise and just and fair. He turned them down.

Next they went to Louis Brandeis. Brandeis, too, had his wide circle of admirers. He was known as a just and liberal man who had often, as a lawyer in Boston, fought for the rights of the underdog.

Brandeis turned them down also: not on the merits of the case, but because his wife had contributed to the Defense Committee. There was, he said, a conflict of interest. He could not involve himself.

Then they turned in desperation to the President of the United States, Calvin Coolidge, who was vacationing in South Dakota. The president's secretary said that Coolidge felt he had no standing to interfere. He could not come to the phone because he was tired from fishing the previous day.

Finally, on Sunday the twenty-first, two more Supreme Court Justices were found: Harlan Stone and the Chief Justice, William Howard Taft. Both refused to issue a writ.

There was, it seemed, no place else to turn.

18

Right up until the last minute, Sacco and Vanzetti's partisans kept on trying to save them. A young lawyer from Pittsburgh, Michael Musmanno, had come to Boston to help in the case some weeks earlier. Now he went early on the morning of August 22, a Monday, to inquire if the governor had acted on five affidavits that had been delivered the preceding Saturday. The governor had not yet done so. Musmanno then went to petition a superior court judge to grant a stay of execution. The judge said that he had no power to do so. Musmanno then took a petition for a writ of habeas corpus, prepared by a group of volunteer attorneys, to the federal district court, but the judge declared that he found no federal questions involved in the case and therefore denied the petition. Two of the volunteer lawyers then went to Supreme Court Justice Oliver Wendell Holmes, not for the second, but for the third time to appeal for a writ of certiorari, and for the third time he refused to issue it.

Meanwhile, Musmanno returned to the governor's office. He spoke to the governor personally. Like everyone who had done that, he had the sense that the governor did not fully understand the crucial details of the case, not to mention the larger issues. Finally the governor told Musmanno to go to see the Commonwealth's attorney general. If he recommended a reprieve, the governor would grant it.

The attorney general said that he could see no cause for a reprieve, but he would think about it. Musmanno reminded him that time was short: the men were scheduled to die at midnight, and it was now after eight o'clock. The attorney general said he was aware of the time.

When Musmanno returned to the governor's office, he found Sacco's wife and Vanzetti's sister. They had come to beg the governor for mercy. Musmanno offered to serve as their interpreter.

The women went on their knees to the governor. He may well have been embarrassed at this display of emotion, so un-Yankeelike. In any case, he rebuffed them and said that he could do nothing. The women screamed and fainted. Congressman Fiorello LaGuardia of New York helped to take them out. As they went, the governor's secretary, MacDonald, wanted to know what all the fuss was about; the men were just a couple of wops, he said.

Musmanno went back to ask if the attorney general had given his decision on a reprieve. Not yet. It was ten-thirty P.M. Over in Charlestown the condemned men waited. Around the world hundreds of thousands of people waited. The attorney general of the Commonwealth of Massachusetts thought about the case some more, this troublesome case of the shoemaker and the fish peddler—naive, innocent anarchists, dreamers of the brotherhood of man? Or dangerous red radicals, a gun in one hand and a bomb in the other?

At eleven o'clock the attorney general sent in his decision. A moment later the governor informed Musmanno that the attorney general did not recommend a stay of execution. And so, said the governor, that had to be his decision also. He depended on the opinions of legal experts: it was not his responsibility if the two men died.

Over in Charlestown the prison was an armed camp. Eight hundred police guarded the building, aided by machine guns implanted on the rooftops and searchlights scanning the skies. No one went in without a permit. In Boston every street was guarded by auxiliary police, constables, or Pinkerton guards. Governor Fuller had a bodyguard, of course, and his automobile showroom full of shiny new Packards was given a special detail. Of course no public gatherings were permitted that night—not in Boston, nor in Charlestown, either.

At the Defense Committee, Edwin waited with the others. Nine o'clock came and went. The room was quiet except for the muffled sobs of those who waited. Nine-thirty; ten. At last, unable to bear the tension, Edwin went out. He walked back to the Statehouse, he looked in at the governor's office, he spoke to Musmanno, and then he went away.

In the warm summer night the air was filled with murmurs and rustlings, as if the city itself were a living thing, restless as it awaited release from this long torment. Edwin felt a sense of terrible futility as he went—exhaustion, despair, a depression so black that it might never lift. Down Beacon to Dartmouth, over Dartmouth to Copley Square, the vast bulk of the library offset by the intricacies of Richardson's Trinity Church, Old South anchoring one corner, the S.S. Pierce castle anchoring the other. It was late: the bells were ringing eleven.

Any minute now Sacco and Vanzetti would die.

A party of merrymakers emerged from the Copley Plaza Hotel. Probably they had never heard of Sacco and Vanzetti. They screamed with laughter as they piled into their open touring car and roared away. Edwin paused; then he turned back, heading over toward Augusta's house on Marlborough Street. It was very late, but surely she'd be up, no one could sleep this night. Unless Harry had insisted that she return to the country.

When he reached the house, he saw that it was dark. Nevertheless he ran up the little flight of brownstone steps and rang the door bell. And only then did he see the note tacked to the door—a small white card. He lit a match to read it:

Edwin:
We are all at the Parker House. Come if you can.

A.

Downtown at the hotel, Mrs. Evans had hired one of the meeting rooms, and there he found Augusta and thirty or so others, a radio on the table, several telephones.

"Edwin! I'm so glad you came. Have you been to the Statehouse?"
"Yes."

She did not need to ask if he had any hopeful news. There would be, this night, no hope, no reprieve—nothing save the inevitable killings.

The clock on the wall said 11:55.

People sat in little groups of three or four, but they did not talk. Each one seemed preoccupied with thoughts too painful to be spoken.

Edwin sat with Augusta and two women whom he did not know. From the radio came the agitated voice of the newscaster over at the Charlestown prison: "We are waiting now for the official word, this is an amazing scene, the entire area is brightly lit with floodlights, we have a tremendous crowd held back by the police, you can hear shouting in the background, but most people are quiet, waiting, waiting—"

Suddenly, in the Parker House room where Edwin and Augusta and the others waited, the lights dimmed. For a moment they were taken by surprise, not understanding. Then someone shrieked—"Oh, my God, they've done it! That was the power surge for the electric chair!" And someone else screamed, and someone else—

Augusta gripped Edwin's hands so tightly that her rings bit into his flesh. She said nothing, just held his eyes with her own, her face frozen, blank . . . An endless time.

Someone sobbed; someone prayed.

The lights brightened.

The room was quiet, everyone waiting for the next dimming.

It was death, that sudden dip in the lights, draining off the power to send the voltage through the body of a convicted man.

"Ah!"

Celestino Madeiros, who had tried and failed to take the blame for the South Braintree crime, and who had been found guilty of another murder, went first to the electric chair that night.

Sacco's turn came next. Because he had been fasting, his body had lost the salt and fluid that conduct electricity, and so he had to be given an extra voltage.

Then it was Vanzetti who was led to the execution room, strapped in, blindfolded. Before he died he stated once again his innocence. By twelve-thirty he, too, was dead.

In the next few hours the news of the executions was flashed around the world. In New York, in Union Square, fifteen thousand people waited to hear Sacco and Vanzetti's fate. When word came, a roar of anguish went up that could be heard for blocks. In other cities in America, and in London and Paris and Rome and Berlin, in countries all around the world that night, people wept and raged and vented their anger, attacking American embassies, defacing American monuments, burning American flags. For that night, and for months and years afterward, the name of America bore the hatred that was in fact directed against the Commonwealth of Massachusetts, which once again, as it had done three centuries before, had found it necessary to kill those who were perceived to be its enemies.

19

The telephone awakened him. He had fallen asleep around dawn; now, glancing at his watch, he saw that it was after eight. For a moment he was disoriented; he forgot that this was the first day after Sacco and Vanzetti's execution.

"Edwin? It's Augusta. I wanted to make sure that you were all right. And to say good-bye for a while. I'm going back to the country."

"Yes—yes, I'm all right. I walked for a while after I left you, that's all. You're not staying in town for the funeral?"

There was a little pause. Then: "Harry doesn't think I should. And since I've tested his patience pretty far already, I don't want to aggravate him further."

"I see."

"So come and have a cup of tea with me in the fall, will you?"

"Yes—yes, of course I will. Good-bye, Augusta."

"Good-bye. And thank you."

"We did everything we could, you know, my dear."

"I wonder. That's what haunts me. Was there some one thing that I should have done, or you, or Mrs. Evans—one thing that might have saved them?"

"I can't imagine what it would be. Now we must get on with our lives. I hope you don't brood. You have your child, your life to live . . ." With that prig of a husband, he thought. Too bad!

"Are you going to do a book on the case?" she said. "You should, you know."

"I hadn't thought—"

"Yes. Oh, Edwin, you must. And perhaps I could help you with it." She gave a little laugh—a healthy sign, he thought. "I could even learn to type, if you wanted me to."

"Well, perhaps." And now that he admitted the possibility, it was immediately obvious to him that he would do what she suggested. He would begin to interview people at once, he thought, while memories were still fresh—and painful. It would be difficult, reliving it all; and yet if he could bear to do it without too much heartache, it was a splendid project—a fitting memorial to the two men. "Yes," he said. "Yes, I probably will. And of course you can help me."

"I'll see you in the fall, then."

"Good-bye, my dear."

20

It rained on the day of Sacco and Vanzetti's funeral—poured and poured, the heavens weeping, buckets of rain to spoil the funeral procession that the Defense Committee had planned despite the wishes of Sacco's widow and Vanzetti's sister that no further exploitation of their loved ones take place.

After the autopsies, the bodies were taken to Langone's Funeral Parlor, where they were embalmed and put on display. In the next few days at least a hundred thousand people came through to pay their respects. The funeral was scheduled for the following Sunday because the most people would be free to attend on that day. The committee had planned to have a band in the procession, in the Italian custom, but the police forbade it. They had planned to have the coffins carried through the streets, but the police forbade that also, and so the coffins went in a hearse. Felicani and his crew distributed armbands, black letters on red cloth, and told people to put them in their pockets; wait for the signal to put them on, he said.

The procession was to go from Langone's on Hanover Street to the crematory at Forest Hills cemetery, some eight miles away. Police were everywhere along the route, ready for trouble. The mayor of Boston, James Michael Curley, ordered road crews to dig up the street in front of the Statehouse so that the mourners would not be able to pass by the hated Governor Fuller's domain. As the procession wound through Scollay Square, people noticed the *Nation* magazine displayed at newsstands. Its cover read: "Justice Underfoot." Some men bought up all the copies and began handing them out. Now Felicani gave the signal, and all at once the armbands came out and were slipped on: JUSTICE CRUCIFIED, they read, repeated a thousand times, flaunted in the faces of the police.

Despite orders from the organizers to keep moving, the marchers now found their way blocked by a line of trucks. As they negotiated this obstacle, the mounted police charged them, clubs flailing. Many people were hurt. The rain kept on falling. Hostile onlookers booed and hissed. By the time most of the marchers reached the cemetery, the cremation had taken place. The ashes were mixed and put into three urns; later they were divided further. Today no one knows how many urns there were, or where they all are. It is known that one is with Sacco's family; at least one is with Vanzetti's family in Italy; and one is in the Sacco and Vanzetti collection in the Boston Public Library.

And so in the end the question became what Edwin Jackson Revell said it was, not "Whom did Sacco and Vanzetti kill?" but "Who killed Sacco and Vanzetti?"

And of course the answer was, at least for some, "The descendants of those Puritans who killed the witches, who killed Mary Dyer, who killed the Quakers—and who began by killing Ann Hutchinson, as surely as if they had hanged her, when they sentenced her to banishment in the wilderness; the fact that she survived for a while was no thanks to the ministers of the Massachusetts Bay Colony."

By the time of Sacco and Vanzetti, that Puritan mentality—that rigidity, that intolerance—had had three hundred years to refine itself. It did not, in 1927, bear the rough, blunt face that it had worn three centuries earlier. But it had survived; of that there could be no question.

Nor could there be any question that, having survived into the brave new world of jazz and flappers and post-war angst, Puritanism had become something of an anomaly, and a ludicrous one at that. Its most perfect expression, perhaps, was to be found in the New England Society for the Suppression of Vice, popularly known as the Watch & Ward.

This organization kept strict vigilance over the public morals; nothing got by them. For instance, the year after Sacco and Vanzetti's execution, a memorial service was held. One speaker, a well-known social historian, Horace Kallen, said that Sacco and Vanzetti, like Jesus Christ, embraced an anarchy that grew out of the love of man. Kallen was arrested for blasphemy—an act nicely reminiscent of the days of Winthrop and his fellow Puritans. Not long after that, Upton Sinclair published his book on the case, which he called *Boston*. Now, Sinclair was a troublemaker from 'way back, one of the original muckrakers, never afraid of a fight. So he and his publishers were delighted when *Boston* was banned in Boston. The publicity was tremendous. By that time, in fact (1929), to be Banned in Boston was a national joke and the answer to a publisher's prayer. Theatrical works, too, could reap benefits from this phenomenon: the playwright Eugene O'Neill, a sometime resident of Provincetown and a founding member of the Provincetown Playhouse, saw his play, *Strange Interlude*, banned in Boston in 1928. He and his producers picked up and moved it to Quincy, several miles to the south and reachable by trolley, and there it had a tremendous run.

As for the Sacco and Vanzetti case, it went on and on; it survives today, although it is true that with every passing year there are fewer and fewer people who remember; or whose parents remember; or grandparents. Hundreds of books and articles have been published both in America and abroad about the two Italian immigrants, and songs, and poems, and plays. Ben Shahn made a famous portrait; someone else made a documentary film. Sacco and Vanzetti lived.

One little footnote to the case gave grim satisfaction to their partisans: Alvan Fuller did not run for President after all. When his name was brought up in one of the smoke-filled rooms of the Republican National Convention, a powerful senator from the West commented that he didn't think that the Republican Party wanted to spend the next four months defending the execution of Sacco and Vanzetti. But in 1929, with the Republican Herbert Hoover in the White House, Fuller put out the word that he wouldn't mind being appointed Ambassador to France. When the French government heard this, it informed the State Department that Fuller's life would not be safe if he took the post. So Fuller stayed in Massachusetts.

3. AMERICAN BEAUTY

1

"Oh, Cousin Isabella, it is too horrible!" It was Fanny, Mrs. Winslow Revell, pouring out her troubles to the Family's grande dame. "Think of the scandal! Everyone is talking about it! Cousin Violet is simply being irresponsible! Taking up with a man—and that particular man—at her age!"

Privately Isabella agreed, but she was not about to say so, for she did not like Mrs. Winslow. She sipped her tea; she listened to the soothing sound of trickling water from the little fountain. The two women sat under one of the side arches of the great central court of Isabella's palace; it was not one of the public days, and so Isabella had her palace to herself.

"I mean, he's young enough to be her son!" Fanny went on; and then went on some more, but Isabella had stopped listening. Her thoughts drifted back to a time when she and Theo were the subject of shocked, outraged Family deliberation. And in the end it had worked out splendidly; they had been very happy.

But of course that had been different. They had reconciled two feuding branches of the same family—but that had been the point, they *were* the same Family, and so in the end it had turned out well.

She came back. Fanny was still talking: ". . . simply go to her in a delegation and bring her to her senses." Fanny was a plump little thing, just thirty-five but already seeming middle-aged. Isabella had always felt a strong loyalty to Winslow and Fletcher and Augusta because they were Lyman's children, and Lyman had been a great help to her all his life; but she was not sure whether her sense of obligation went so far as to include Lyman's children's spouses. Augusta's husband, Harry Trowbridge, was a dear, of course; but Fanny . . . Well, she'd never been terribly fond of Fanny, truth to tell, and she did not now like to hear her criticizing Violet. Who was, after all, a Revell by birth, not marriage. That made a difference.

Isabella set down her delicate porcelain cup with a loud little *chink*. Fanny looked startled, particularly when she caught a glimpse of the vertical line between Isabella's brows. That line meant trouble; even Fanny knew that.

"There is, of course, one sure way to stop the talk," Isabella said.

Fanny felt a surge of relief. Winslow had said that Cousin Isabella would probably have some solution to the dilemma, and he had been right.

"What?" she said. "Please tell me, dear Isabella. What do you mean?"

"They can marry."

Fanny thought that she must have misheard. She was so shocked that for a moment she could not reply. And although Isabella understood well enough that this was no laughing matter, she could not repress a smile.

Later, Fanny told everyone who would listen that Isabella seemed to be losing her grip.

2

Violet had met him at the party for the completion of Revell Hall. He was the singer in the little band hired to provide the music. He was about as tall as she was, with curly brown hair and merry brown eyes and a careless joie de vivre about him that came—although she did not know it then—from having survived war and revolution and the loss of everything he had held dear: wife and child, parents and brothers and sisters, family fortune—everything gone, swept away in the whirlwind of the Bolshevik triumph.

The one great lesson that he took away with him from Russia as he fled across the continent of Europe was to savor every moment of his life because it might be his last. He knew that that was not a terribly profound rule to live by, but it suited him; it would get him through his days and—more important—all the long nights.

He came to America in the fall of 1924, and within a year he had learned passable English and had begun to make a little name for himself. He had started out in life, in St. Petersburg, as the younger son of an ancient, if impoverished, noble house. Needing to earn his way, he had become a lawyer. Now, in America, he did not want to study law all over again. He had discovered that he had a pleasant baritone, one night in a café in Paris, a haunt of Russian emigrés, when he had drunk too much vodka and accepted a dare to get up and sing. To his surprise, he had been a hit. Soon he joined up with a little band. When it came time to leave for America, he put down "musician" on his papers.

In Boston he rapidly built up a good reputation. He was handsome, he was charming, he always showed up for an engagement. Soon women began to leave little notes for him: invitations to become better acquainted. He seldom accepted. Contrary to appearances, he was deeply conservative. No decent woman pursued a man; and he was not interested in any woman who was not decent.

In the fall of 1925 he and his musicians accepted a job on the North Shore. The place was crowded, a noisy crew, but appreciative when he sang, quieting nicely to hear his renditions. He had discovered that many New England folks liked to drink intoxicating spirits as much as Russians did. This crowd had been well supplied by their bootlegger; the champagne punch flowed freely, and he saw a number of men with flasks.

At the first intermission he made his way to the table set up in the dining room and, very thirsty, quickly downed two cups of punch. He didn't like it much—too sweet—and he turned away to find, as he was sure he would, something more palatable. He was in a hurry because he had only a few minutes. Inevitably, he bumped into someone—a plain, thin woman just about his own height, who reddened with embarrassment even though the collision had been not her fault but his. He saw that he had caused her to spill her drink down the front of her blue silk dress.

"Oh! I'm so terribly sorry—" she began.

"No, madam. My fault. Please . . ." He withdrew from his pocket a white silk handkerchief; given the location of the spill, he could not offer to wipe it himself, but with a little flourish he handed the scrap of cloth to her.

"I think—oh, it's all right." She dabbed ineffectually at her dress. "Never mind." She smiled at him, and it seemed a very brave thing to do. Like most survivors, he was a quick study of his fellow human beings, and he saw now that this lady was indeed a lady, and a far cry from so many of her kind, what passed for aristocracy here in America, smug and hearty and athletic and entirely sexless. This one had a certain tremulous, delicate charm that intrigued him.

He took her hand and lifted it to his lips. If Alexander Korsakoff knew nothing else, he knew how to kiss a woman's hand. And instantly he knew that he had been right about her, for he felt her tremble—no, it was more than that, it was a deep shudder that emanated from the depths of her femininity.

And so, that night, it began—the most improbable love affair in Massachusetts since Sir Harry Frankland married Agnes Surriage, a servant girl, back before the Revolution. For a long time they kept it secret. Of course they knew what people would say: the young fortune hunter preying on the susceptibilities of a desperate old maid. Sometimes at night she would lie awake in her narrow bed in her room at the top of her father's house in Clarendon Street, and she would think about the surprising turn her life had taken, and she would think that perhaps it was not real. Perhaps she was imagining it all. Perhaps she had gone mad.

At first they were very discreet, meeting in out-of-the-way restaurants, driving into the countryside. Boston was a small town, and Violet knew many people there; like most Revells, she could hardly walk across the Public Garden without seeing someone she knew. So at first she was very careful. She told herself that she was only being prudent. With the unavoidable bitterness of an old maid, she told herself that sooner or later he would drop her; she wanted to save herself any unnecessary humiliation.

But he did not drop her. He sincerely loved her, and she, of course, adored him more than life itself. Often, when he kissed her, she thought that she must have died and gone to Heaven, and much of the rest of the time she existed in a golden state of bliss that she had never even dreamed of.

Eventually, inevitably, word of the affair got out. Some Family members didn't object, but others, like Mrs. Winslow, were terribly upset. Violet's father, of course, was the last to hear. It happened one rainy day in November, not long after Mrs. Winslow's anguished visit to Isabella, a little more than a year after Alex and Violet met.

Judson had spent the day at home. Shortly after two, the maid brought in the afternoon mail. Not much: a bill from S.S. Pierce, the announcement of a local artist's show at the Vose Gallery, an invitation to a reception on Beacon Street at the end of the month. And—a good quality envelope with his name and address printed in a rather awkward way, as if the person who had done it were unaccustomed to printing. He opened it and read:

Mr. Revell:
I guess you don't care about your daughter's reputation, but I can tell you, if she was mine, I'd give her a good whipping.

A Friend.

What on earth . . . !

He was terribly upset. What in heaven's name did this mean? Some madman? Or had Violet got herself into some horrible mess, afraid no doubt to tell him—?

His old heart was pounding hard, and his rheumy old eyes were sightless with tears. Drat! Where was she?

Half rising from his chair, heedless of the papers that went scattering from his lap, he yanked the bell pull. The few seconds that it took the maid to come seemed like half an hour.

"Miss Violet in?"

"No, sir."

"She say when she'd be back?"

"No, sir."

Which meant she'd be in for supper, else she'd have said so.

More than five hours. Impossible! He was too upset. He couldn't wait that long. Feeling terribly unsteady on his old pins, he went to the telephone and called up Isabella. She'd know what to do. She'd better!

Isabella, hearing the state he was in, sent her chauffeur to fetch him. Judson arrived at Fenway Palace shortly after three—panting, distraught, his imagination (of which admittedly he had not much) aflame with possibilities.

Isabella had thought to offer him tea, but now, seeing him, she knew that something stronger was called for. So she gave him a good quality whiskey that had only just come in, and settled herself to listen to what he had to say. She had a pretty good idea what it was.

"This came," he said, handing her the anonymous note.

"I'm surprised you didn't get something like this long ago," she said. Swiftly she scanned it and gave it back.

"Isabella—what do you mean?"

"I mean, dear cousin, that Violet has fallen in love. Don't look like that. It happens to us all, you know. It's rather sweet, actually."

"Sweet! What are you talking about? Who is it? Some fortune hunter, some lounge lizard crawling out from under a rock?"

"Not that bad. Do you remember the party we gave when she finished Revell Hall?"

He nodded.

"Well, the band, that night, had a singer. His name was Alex Korsakoff. And somehow, he and Violet—"

"A band singer?" She had never seen Judson so agitated. She was a little alarmed.

"Judson, you mustn't upset yourself, I grant you Violet isn't, ah, experienced in these matters, but he seems a very decent sort of fellow, and I think if you gave yourself a chance to get to know him—"

"A Russian band singer? A Bolshevik, for God's sake?" Judson had gone from red to white to red again.

"No, no, just the opposite. He lost his family in the revolution, he had to flee—he is some kind of minor nobility, I believe. Won't you meet him, at least? I could have you all to dinner."

Judson glared at her. "Don't tell me you intend to encourage this farce! Why, she'll be the laughingstock of North America before this chap's through with her! I don't understand why you don't want to help me get her away from him!"

Isabella contemplated him. Her eyes were still the brilliant blue they had been when she was a girl, and Judson felt their full force. "I'm fond of Violet," she said. "I think she deserves a chance at—well, at one of life's great experiences. Every woman should have one glorious love affair, don't you agree?"

He honestly thought that she had taken leave of her senses. He stared at her wildly, as if he had never seen her before. At that moment she was a stranger to him.

"Talk to her, Judson." Isabella reached out and patted his hand. "Let her go on with it, if she wants to. And give the young man a chance to prove himself. You might be pleasantly surprised!"

So he went home in a highly agitated state and waited for Violet to return. For the first time in his life he knew what it was to want to kill—in this case not Violet, of course, but her suitor.

He sat by the fire, his ears cocked for the sound of the front door. Shortly after six she came in. He had told the maid to bring her in directly, and so now here she was.

She knew, of course. They'd been so close for so long, and she knew that now the moment had come when she must tell him. Briefly her courage failed her, but then she remembered how she loved Alex, how he had come into her

life as if he had been sent by Fate, as if somehow their affair had been preor-
dained, and she smiled bravely at her father, and knelt by his side and put her
head on his knee as she had done ever since she was a child; and it was thus,
holding his hand, not looking at him, that she told him about the curious and
wonderful turn her life had taken this past year.

"And I'd like to bring him to Winslow's at Christmas, after you meet him,
Father. I'd like to introduce him to everyone, and take him caroling—oh, he'll
be magnificent, going caroling!"

Judson's eyes filled with tears then, and he took his hand from hers and
rested it on her hair; and so, in that wordless way, he gave her his blessing, and
his consent.

"Trust her," Isabella had said. "Trust her—or lose her."

And he knew that she had spoken the truth.

Alex and Violet were married the month after Christmas in a ceremony at
Trinity Church in Copley Square. A Russian Orthodox priest assisted Bishop
Lawrence, who presided. Because Violet knew that all Boston had gossiped
about her, she invited all Boston to the ceremony and the reception at the
Copley Plaza as well—several hundred people. Everyone said what an astonishingly beautiful bride she was. People knew that she was at least ten years older
than the groom, but this day, radiant, she looked his age exactly. She wore a
dress of pale blue, and camellias from the Fenway Palace greenhouses arranged
in her hair, and she carried a bouquet of pink and white roses.

Judson, in the end, was simply delighted: he went around bragging about
his son-in-law as if, people said, that young man was the Prince of Wales instead
of a déclassé Russian. No matter. It was the event of the season, the loveliest
wedding Boston had seen in years.

3

In the summer of 1930 Judson Abbott Revell presided at the opening of the
Museum of the American China Trade. This was a project that had grown out
of his attempt to save as much as he could of the old Great-Uncle Philip's place.
It had stood empty for a number of years after Philip died. He had willed it to
Roger, but Roger hadn't wanted it; and Roger's son William had been busy
with his work at the Perkins Institute and with bringing up his little son, John,
and he hadn't wanted it, either. At last they'd found a tenant, but the tenant
had stayed only a few years; and so at last Judson, who was known as the
Family aesthete, had given his promise to his father, the novelist Washington
Abbott Revell, that he would do what he could to salvage all of Philip's artifacts. "There are some things that will be quite valuable some day," Washington

had said. "And some day this city will have a proper museum. They'll be glad to have a treasure like this."

Washington, who had died not long after, had supervised the dismantling of Philip's house; then the land was sold to a speculator wanting to put up a block of stores. The tile wall around the garden was carefully disassembled, the bronze and porcelain artifacts were packed into wooden crates and neatly labeled, the embroidered silks were folded away in unbleached muslin bags, the rice-paper paintings securely wrapped—and all of them were stored in a warehouse in Brighton until some suitable showcase for them could be found.

After Violet's success with Revell Hall, she and Alex together had restored half a dozen other properties. The two of them were fast becoming recognized as experts. If you had an old house that was worth fixing up, worth bringing back to what it had been, Violet Revell was the one to engage—Violet Korsakoff, rather, and her charming husband Alex.

They were always on the lookout for good quality antiques with which to furnish their projects. What was more, Violet began to assemble as many Family pieces as she could find for her own collection. She talked to Family members, wrote notes to them, asked them to give her first refusal on anything that they might sell. After the stock market crashed in '29, and as the Depression set in, she came by quite a few valuable items. One time she discovered that one of old Francis Revell's great-granddaughters, her second cousin Euphemia, had a sewing table that had belonged to Great-Grandmother Abigail: an exquisite piece, mahogany and fan-pleated silk. She had gone to the woman, who was eighty-odd and very cranky, and begged her to sell the piece to her, Violet, her own dear second cousin; or, failing that, to leave it to Violet in her will. Out of spite, Euphemia had sold it to a dealer in New York, and Violet had had to track it down and pay an outrageous price to get it back.

One day Judson had taken them over to Brighton to have a look at Philip's stuff. They had been ecstatic—had urged him to make a special place for it. So when the old Thomas Handasyd Perkins place in Brookline came on the market, he went to half a dozen Family members and put together the necessary funds to buy it. They got it cheap because nowadays no one wanted a big old ark of a place like that. Winslow and the other Griffin Revells lived practically across the street from it in the summers, but in the winter they retreated to the warmth and convenience of their houses in town. And of course if old Lyman's place hadn't already been theirs, they never would have built one like it—too big, too drafty (even in summer)—too hard to run without servants. A Family was lucky to get even one or two servants nowadays, let alone a full staff.

And so now here they were, a sunny afternoon and two hundred or so of the top people in the city and the state: a grand opening party, even the governor had come, and representatives of other old China trading families, of course, and some who weren't China traders but were First Families all the same, Saltonstalls and Lodges and Sohiers and Russells and Cabots and Winthrops and Lowells and Lawrences and Quincys and Adamses—and here and there a few others, too, names like Rafferty and Dunne. Cardinal O'Connell was here, too, his chauffeur having driven him over from his grand new imitation Renaissance palace on Commonwealth Avenue. Most people, having had the tour of the Museum, were standing about the garden, where Philip's porcelain tile wall had been reconstructed; its soft greens and blues shimmered now in the sunlight, while nearby a smiling Buddha seemed to cast his approval on the day's festivities.

"Mr. Revell! Glad to see you, sir!" A handsome man whom Judson did not know came up to shake his hand. "My name's Shaughnessy," the man said. "Michael Shaughnessy. When I was asked to make a contribution to the Museum Fund, I had no idea that I was helping to create something so magnificent. And your daughter did it all? Is she here? I'd like to meet her."

Shaughnessy. Shaughnessy. Judson remembered complaints, years ago, about a ruthless ward boss who ruled the West End with remorseless honesty and unyielding hatred for the Yankees. This man was too young to be that same one. A son, perhaps?

"Ah, yes, over there. In the blue hat."

"Thanks."

But before Michael could get to Violet, he was stopped by a rather desiccated-looking man who touched his sleeve and then held out his hand and smiled. "Shaughnessy? My God, you look marvelous. Coming to the reunion, are you?"

Of course he knew at once who this was: Fletcher Griffin Revell, who once upon a time had invited him to a debutante party in the Back Bay, with disastrous results. He had heard that this particular Revell had suffered badly in the crash, and certainly he looked it: well-worn suit, frayed collar, hair in need of a cut, scuffed and rundown shoes. On the other hand, the Anglo-Saxon bloodline was running thin after three centuries of inbreeding; this man might simply be another eccentric son who didn't like to spend money on clothes. Most old families seemed to have at least one.

Michael spoke with what civility he could muster. "I wouldn't miss it," he said. Their twenty-fifth reunion was scheduled for the following week.

"Splendid! Splendid! How are you? I've got a boy in the class of '32, don't y'know. How about you? Any sprouts?"

To Michael's relief they were interrupted just then by a tall, thin, fortyish woman who looked very much like his interrogator, and was introduced, in fact, as his sister Augusta. At which point, since she wanted to carry Fletcher off, Michael was free to proceed to Violet. But the run-in left him with an unpleasant taste. He hadn't thought often of that cold January night when he'd taken his little revenge on a Revell youth's callousness, but once in a while it had come back to him, and he'd felt his anger all over again.

But his presence here today was not about anger; it was about getting on with his plan—and that meant being civil to these people for as long as he needed to be, at which point he'd be able to tell them all to go to the devil. But he wasn't there yet. He would have been willing to bet that by now he was worth a good deal more than some of them—and certainly that was true after last fall's stock market crash. He'd heard that Frederick Griffin Revell was as good as bankrupt. He himself had made his money honestly enough, for the most part, in the construction business. There had been swindles and cocka- mamie schemes enough these past few years as the roaring twenties roared on: Carlo Ponzi's pyramid scam, and the machinations of Ivar Krueger, the "match king." Krueger in particular had taken a lot of rich old Boston Yankees down with him, and in fact the firm of Lee, Higginson was now in bankruptcy thanks to the wily Ivar. Since he himself had never had the social connections to have been invited to participate in such deals, he'd stayed clear and run his business with a sure hand, until today he was the next best thing to a double millionaire.

"So now yer rich," old Patrick would say. "Now what?"

"Now, Da, we can do as we please. Young Michael's going to the Law School. Then he'll probably go to work for a firm in State Street—"

"Hah!" The old man would pound the floor with his stick. "Who'd have him, eh? They won't hire an Irishman, those old Yankee firms!"

"I know one that will," said Michael. His face was grim, and of course the old man saw it.

"What'd'y'mean?"

"I mean, I have one of the senior partners by the short hairs; I lent him money that he hasn't paid back. He'll do what I ask. The boy will be taken in, and he will be advanced regularly up through the ranks. If that is what he wants."

Patrick peered at him. "And what if it isn't, eh? He's told me many a time he'd like to go into politics. Remember how I always took him to the club? An' he'd tell me he'd like to be in an election, an' beat th'Repooblikkins!" And he would pound his stick again. "Mark my words, that lad's goin't'be th'governor some day!"

"Perhaps," Michael would say, not wanting to encourage the old man's fancies. "Perhaps he will, Da. We'll see. Whatever he wants to do, he'll do."

But he would think: *yes. He will be governor, else why have I spent my life preparing the way?* All over the Commonwealth of Massachusetts, people knew Michael Shaughnessy: giver to charities, performer of good works, paragon of civic virtue. And all for his son—for that fourth-generation Irishman who in Yankeedom would always be an Irishman. No matter. He would be a winner, as well.

The Depression deepened. Many families, previously wealthy, lost nearly ev- erything. The grand old Commonwealth slumbered. Most of the textile facto- ries had already gone south, where raw material was closer and labor troubles nonexistent. Now many of the remaining ones either closed or fled also. The mill towns were ghost towns. The state was very like a ghost state, haunted by its past, by the high drama of its glory days, its long-lost days of prosperity: the quiet seaside villages threaded by narrow, crooked lanes, the square, white captains' houses gleaming in the sun; the somnolent towns in the interior, white church spires rising against dark, wooded hills; the dusty country roads seldom disturbed by traffic. The wharves of Boston and Salem, Gloucester and Newburyport, once bustling, lay empty and quiet; along the shore were the hulls of rotting ships, and in the bitter winters of that decade, as times got harder still, homeless men dragged them ashore and tore them up for firewood.

It was as if people were waiting for something, anticipating the moment when the old Bay State would come back to life. But it was not to happen yet.

4

To everyone's surprise—but not to Violet's—Alex turned out very well. He gave up singing, of course, which for a while only gave strength to the rumors that he was a fortune hunter after all. But very soon he began to help Violet in her work, and even to guide her and counsel her, until it became apparent that this Russian had a passion for things American unmatched by the doughtiest old Yankee. Together, he and Violet hired architectural historians and Colonial historians and specialists in American arts and crafts, and they learned from them; together, they worked on the sites with the architects and carpenters; they went into courthouses and pored over old wills for accountings of furniture and household goods; and before long they became recognized authorities themselves.

For Violet, some of the best times were the days when they went exploring into the countryside: in pursuit of a Shaker chair, say, rumored to belong to a family out in Pittsfield, near the old Shaker village at Hancock; or a painting of a round-faced, black-haired little girl and her big, black Labrador painted by one of the so-called "primitive" painters. After a few years word got around that Alex and Violet would buy almost any primitive painting that came up for sale, and if the seventy-five or hundred dollars that they were willing to part with seemed an outrageous sum, almost highway robbery—well, people pocketed the money and told themselves that the Korsakoffs could well afford the price.

So the Depression years, which were so disastrous for so many people, were happy ones for Violet and her husband. He became increasingly patriotic, increasingly enchanted with his adopted land. "You see," he would say, "we are free here! Even in this bad time, no jobs, this is a better place than what I come from. Yes! And these things—these paintings, these pieces of furniture, even these charming little samplers worked by little girls—all of these mean America to me. They are simple and pure and direct—oh, I love them! I think they are wonderful! I can never get enough of them! This is a great country, you see?"

One day, walking across Boston Common, he saw a crowd gathered around a man on a soap box. The man was shouting, haranguing, and people were shouting back, some heckling, some in agreement. Alex stepped nearer. To his horror, he realized that the man was a Communist and that he was reviling the government—the American government. A Communist! Alex became angry; he, too, began to shout at the man on the soap box. And it was only through the greatest good luck that Dwight Abbott Revell happened to be passing, and so was able to restrain Alex from physically attacking the man. Communists! He knew what the Communists had done to his homeland!

In 1936 Isabella and her adopted son Frederick died within six months of each other—he first of pneumonia, and she of old age. It was whispered that Frederick had failed to recover from his illness because he (or his wife, Elinor) refused, that bitter winter, to spend the money to properly heat their house—that big, high-ceilinged old pile on Commonwealth Avenue.

One week after his estate was settled, Elinor announced that she was going to sell the Copley portraits, one of which was the famous "Bullet Revell," the beautiful Emilie Griffin Revell.

"That's impossible!" snapped Violet when she heard of it. "She can't sell those portraits! It's out of the question! Sacrilege!"

She went around at once to see Winslow. "We have to do something," she said. "We can't let those portraits go—not even to the Museum."

Winslow agreed with her, but—"A lot of people have been hit very hard, Violet, and they haven't recovered. I don't know who you're going to find to buy them."

"Well, I do," Violet replied. Judson had left her a reasonable sum—a million or so—when he had passed on the previous year, and she couldn't think of a better place to spend it. If, indeed, Elinor was fool enough to sell, which apparently she was. Frederick had lost pretty nearly everything, it seemed; well, Elinor was lucky to find someone in the Family who'd take the portraits off her hands—and at a good price, too, ten thousand apiece and worth every penny.

On the day that the transaction was made, and the Copley Revells made the journey around the corner to Violet's house in Clarendon Street, she and Alex stood arm in arm in the late afternoon light streaming into the front parlor—but not onto the wall where the paintings hung, she had been very particular about that—and gazed at the proud, handsome faces hanging now above the mantel. Someday, perhaps, they could go to the Museum: after I die, she thought. Not before.

Ever since her father had taken custody, as it were, of the silver sugar box found at Revell Hall, he had made arrangements to put it into a safe deposit box while he summered at Lenox. Now Violet took more space, took an entire vault, in fact, and hired a guard and an armored truck to take the rapidly growing collection at the Clarendon Street house into safekeeping every summer when she and Alex traveled to the mountains.

One year, detouring south in pursuit of a picture as they left Boston for Lenox, she and Alex found themselves in Whitman at dinner time. Fortunately, they were told, the Toll House Inn was nearby, charming and clean—and wonderfully good food, particularly the chocolate chip cookies which were an invention of the proprietress. Thenceforth, they always made the detour especially for those delicacies.

Violet loved Lenox. During the days, she and Alex would explore the back roads and the little hill villages, and every now and then they would come back with some treasure, even something as modest as an old basket or a child's painted sled. At night they sat before a fire, for it was often cool, and read and read—Alex was enchanted with Grandfather Washington's books; they conveyed, he said, the very essence of the young, free country.

Alex had a special friend at Lenox, an exile like himself, Russian also, who happened to be the conductor of the Boston Symphony Orchestra. And so in the summer of 1937, when some members of the orchestra offered a series of three concerts under a large tent, Alex and Violet went to every one.

During one of these, what seemed almost an act of God occurred when a violent thunderstorm erupted just as the orchestra was in the midst of an all-Wagner program. "The Ride of the Valkyries" was never completed that evening, but despite that misfortune, the cloud had a silver lining, so to speak, when Serge Koussevitsky decided that performing under a tent was not acceptable; he and his musicians must have a permanent home. So even in the difficult economic climate, $100,000 was raised almost immediately, and an elegant, fanlike structure, familiarly known as "the shed," was erected before the next season. It was built on an estate known as "Tanglewood," after the name that Nathaniel Hawthorne gave to the little red cottage nearby where he lived one winter while he wrote *The House of the Seven Gables*.

Koussevitsky was of course very pleased with the grand new summer quarters of the orchestra, and he decreed that the most suitable opening selection would be the Ninth Symphony of Beethoven.

As twilight fell around the mountains, the audience streamed in. It was a warm evening in August, and the breeze carried sweet country smells of green growing things, clover and new hay and late roses. Alex and Violet had seats in the fifth row on the aisle. They glanced around, nodding and smiling at people they knew; the shed was full, and there were many new faces, people who had apparently driven some distance to be here this night.

Koussevitsky strode onto the stage. As if on command, a great swell of applause rose up, and then the audience was on its feet, people cheering and calling out to him; the tall, commanding figure made a brief bow, tapped his baton, turned to his musicians and raised his arms, and gave the signal to begin.

The first notes floated out. The audience held its breath. They felt as if they were in some enchanted place, fallen under a spell of pure, exquisite sound that gripped their hearts and lifted their souls and took them, as it was intended to do, outside of themselves; and for that little while, at least, they were caught up in the mystery of this genius touched by the hand of God as indeed he must have been, and here it was now, his music unfolding before them in its inevitable progression; and for this little while they were permitted to hear it, and they felt, that night, that no matter what hardships life might bring to them henceforth, no matter what tragedies and disasters, they had had the wonder and the glory of this moment to carry away with them, to keep with them until they died.

Alex reached over and took Violet's hand. Outside the shed, beyond the lighted stage and the darkened auditorium filled with rows and rows of expectant faces, the golden August moon rose in the night sky.

PART VI

RENASCENCE

GRIFFIN REVELLS

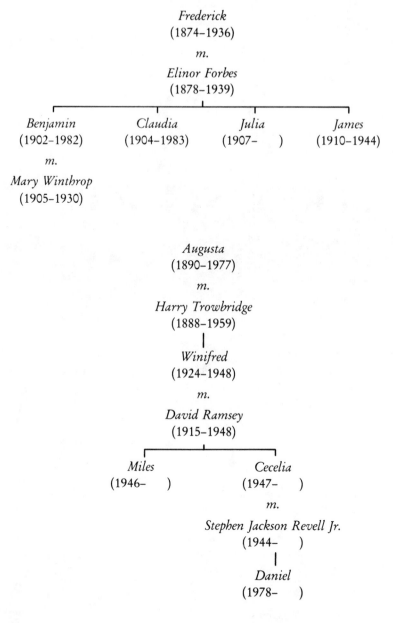

Frederick
(1874–1936)

m.

Elinor Forbes
(1878–1939)

| *Benjamin* | *Claudia* | *Julia* | *James* |
| (1902–1982) | (1904–1983) | (1907–   ) | (1910–1944) |

m.

Mary Winthrop
(1905–1930)

Augusta
(1890–1977)

m.

Harry Trowbridge
(1888–1959)

Winifred
(1924–1948)

m.

David Ramsey
(1915–1948)

Miles   *Cecelia*
(1946–   )   (1947–   )

m.

Stephen Jackson Revell Jr.
(1944–   )

Daniel
(1978–   )

GRIFFIN REVELLS
(Continued)

Guy	Roger	Daphne	Edward
(1913–1978)	(1915–1944)	(1917–)	(1920–1943)

Guy
(1913–1978)

m.

Josephine Perkins
(1920–   )

Adam
(1946–   )

m.

Kathleen
Shaughnessy
(1946–   )

JACKSON REVELLS

Avery
(1909–1969)

m.

Susan Winslow
(1913–1979)

Kenneth
(1935–   )

Stephen Sr.
(1911–   )

m.

Alice Fayerweather
(1919–   )

Stephen Jr.
(1944–   )

m.

Cecelia Ramsey
(1947–   )

Daniel
(1978–   )

ABBOTT REVELLS

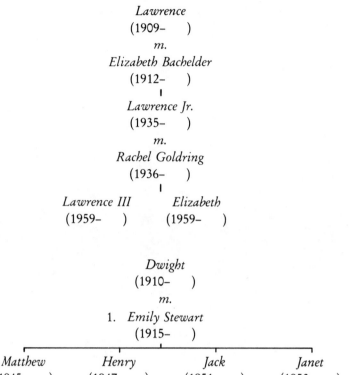

Lawrence
(1909–   )
m.
Elizabeth Bachelder
(1912–   )

Lawrence Jr.
(1935–   )
m.
Rachel Goldring
(1936–   )

Lawrence III   *Elizabeth*
(1959–   )   (1959–   )

Dwight
(1910–   )
m.
1. *Emily Stewart*
(1915–   )

Matthew   *Henry*   *Jack*   *Janet*
(1945–   )   (1947–   )   (1951–   )   (1953–   )
m.
2. *Dorothy James*
(1931–   )

SHAUGHNESSYS

Michael Jr.
(1912–1974)
m.
Marjory O'Neill
(1914–   )

Joseph   *Kathleen*   *Patrick*   *Thomas*
(1942–1967)   (1946–   )   (1947–   )   (1948–   )
m.   *m.*
Adam Griffin Revell   *Angela Paine*
(1946–   )   (1950–   )

In Wildness is the preservation of the World.

Henry David Thoreau

1. THE SCHOOL OF THE PROFITS

1

On Christmas Eve afternoon of 1964 Dwight Abbott Revell left work early and instead of going to his home in the pleasant suburb of Lincoln, drove into town. It was permissible for him to leave early because he was the president of the company.

"G'd-bye, Charlotte, Merry Christmas."

"Merry Christmas, Mr. Revell." His secretary was about his age, mid-fifties, and she worshiped him. He didn't mind. She worked harder because of it.

His offices and the adjoining plant were on the highway that circled the city, Route 128. So many businesses like his, technological spinoffs of one or another research project at the Massachusetts Institute of Technology, were located there that eventually Route 128 became known as "America's Technology Highway." Every year the traffic got worse.

A fine snow spat and hissed against the windshield of his Cadillac, and he switched on the wipers. Attend to his errand, back out to Lincoln to pick up his family, back to town to the annual Christmas Eve party and carol sing at old Winslow's—well, perhaps he'd call and tell Emily to bring them in on the train if the weather got too bad.

He parked at the Ritz and went into Firestone & Parsons' Jewelers. The clerk, a sleek young man whom he'd dealt with before, greeted him with an unctuous smile.

"G'd afternoon, sir. We're getting a little bit of weather, are we?"

"Just a little bit, yes."

"And what can we show you today, sir?"

He scanned the contents of the glass cases. He always needed to be careful, to balance the one against the other, to give just the right thing to each recipient. "Let's see that emerald brooch—no, the smaller one."

The clerk laid it on a black velvet pad. Dwight did not touch it, did not want to touch it. He simply looked at it, trying to imagine it reposing on his mistress Ilona's magnificent bosom. Her eyes were approximately that shade. And the diamonds surrounding it would match the earrings he'd given her last year.

"That's a really handsome piece," murmured the clerk. "Beautiful faceting. And the gold mounting is so much richer looking than platinum." He had oddly hooded eyes, so that even looking at you straight on, he seemed to be only half awake. Dwight had never liked him. Now, without responding, he turned back to the cases. The clerk knew that he always bought two pieces, every Christmas. "Let's see that one," he said, motioning. The clerk brought out a pearl brooch made of a miniature strand twisted round and round into a kind of lover's knot. "This is a very unusual piece," murmured the clerk, "and if I remember right, it would go nicely with the pearl earrings from last year."

Which was what Dwight had been thinking exactly; hearing the clerk say it made him momentarily want to refuse it, but it was three o'clock already, he had no time to waste. His wife Emily would like this piece; it was handsome and dignified and conservative, just as she was, and yet "different" enough to make her think that he had hunted a good long time to find it.

"All right." He nodded at the clerk, took out his checkbook, and began to fill in a check. He looked up expectantly, and after a moment the clerk gave him the total. It was five figures, of course, but a little more than he'd expected. No matter. It looked as if there were going to be a full-scale war in Vietnam, and that would be good for business.

While the two small boxes were wrapped in their gold Christmas paper, he stepped around into the Ritz bar for a quick martini. The room was empty. He sat at a table next to the window and watched the snow, thicker now, swirling down onto the bare-branched trees in the Public Garden. When his children had been small, of an age to read *Make Way for Ducklings,* Emily had often taken them on the swan boats around the little lagoon. He himself had never joined them because he was always so busy. And it had paid off, that hard work—to the extent that at Christmastime he could drop into the jeweler's and buy what he pleased without worrying about the cost. Sometimes he had wished that he had been able to spend more time with the children, particularly with his eldest son, Matthew, who now, at Harvard, seemed to be on his way to becoming a total stranger.

"Same again, sir?"

"No, just the check, please."

The wrapping girl, very efficiently, had put a slip of paper under each ribbon, identifying the contents. Now he took two small gift cards and envelopes and wrote the two names, the two messages, and put each envelope with its proper box. He'd never gotten them mixed up yet, no time now to begin. The clerk put the boxes into little individual bags; then Dwight put Emily's into his overcoat pocket and slipped Ilona's into the jacket pocket of his suit.

He went out, went along Arlington to Marlborough, and turned up Marlborough. It was snowing heavily now, the wind in his face, good thing he'd worn his rubbers. Not many people about. Through tall bow windows he saw Christmas trees, twinkling lights. Joy to the world, he thought. 'Tis the season to be jolly.

He didn't feel particularly jolly. He hadn't seen Ilona for a week. She would remind him of that fact. He would say he was sorry—which he was, undeniably. He wanted very much—*very* much—to make love with her in the brief time they would have this afternoon. Sometimes when he was in a hurry, as he was today, she grew sullen and resentful. Her green eyes would turn as hard as the emerald in his pocket, and her luscious mouth would go tight-lipped and she would pull away from him and let fall a few large tears—ah, yes. He knew the routine.

He felt his way up the snow-covered brownstone steps of her apartment house—like all the others, once a private home, now like most of them, cut up into small units. He pressed her bell; immediately the buzzer rang and he went in. She lived on the first floor, chosen because it was the most private. Usually she watched for him and had the door to her apartment open for him, but not today. So he tapped, and after a moment she came.

"Darlingk." She opened to admit him. She was wearing a new thing, a soft white wool dressing gown trimmed in ostrich feathers, high-heeled white satin slippers. On any ordinary woman it would have been a ridiculous outfit, but Ilona was not ordinary.

She pecked his cheek and glided away from his embrace. He was wet, his overcoat dripping. With a little moue of distaste she waved her hand toward the tiny kitchen. "Let it drip on the linoleum, darlingk. What a mess, hah?"

She had a fire going, started no doubt by the ever-obliging gent upstairs, and now she settled him in front of it and put another martini into his hand and sat at the opposite end of the sofa and smiled at him demurely—if a woman with her spectacular looks could ever be demure. Having expected recriminations for his absence, he was pleasantly surprised and at the same time a little apprehensive. What was wrong, that she did not scold him for neglecting her?

"So," she said. "How are you? What have you been doingk? And what have you brought me for Christmas? Something beautiful?"

"Not as beautiful as you," he said. It was the kind of thing he would never have dreamed of saying to Emily; with Ilona it just slipped out naturally. He reached along the length of the sofa; suddenly he wanted to get his hands on her, to feel her soft warm flesh.

But she shrank back against the sofa's arm, and on her expressive face he read the message: stop. He stopped. Something, definitely, was wrong. Perhaps if he gave her the expensive bauble that she knew he had bought for her, perhaps then he could discover what it was.

He fished in his pocket, pulled it out, and checked the tiny envelope. No sense in compounding the problem, whatever it was, by giving her the wrong thing, and the thing with Emily's name on it, at that.

Already her hand with its long slim red-tipped fingers was outstretched to receive it. Her face was the face of a greedy child. She curled her fingers around the box as if it were a live thing, as if it might escape. Then in an instant she tore off the wrapping, opened the box, found the velvet box inside which, when she flipped back the lid, opened to reveal—

"Aaahhh!" For a moment she simply gazed at it without trying to take it out. Then, very carefully, she reached in with forefinger and thumb, extracted it, and held it up. She flashed him a glance of triumph, as if somehow they had both just won something. Then, very carefully, she negotiated the little clasp and pinned it onto the shoulder of her white woolen gown.

"Oh, darklingk, thank you!" She blew him a kiss from her full, red lips. For a moment he missed a beat, failed to understand— *That* was her way of rewarding him?

"Ilona . . ." He was of course a gentleman, "a real chentleman," as she had admiringly said when they first met. So he would never force himself on her, of course he would not, but all the same, they had an understanding. Like every Revell who had ever lived, he expected fair value for his money, and just at this moment he was not getting it.

"I been meaning to tell you a long time now," she said. She had assumed an attitude of injured self-righteousness. "I don't think we make love no more."

She paused to see what effect this announcement would have. In the silence he was aware of the hissing and crackling of the fire, the glitter of the brooch against her shoulder.

"Would you care to tell me why?" he said. His voice sounded strangled. He felt as though the pit of his stomach had dropped away.

She shrugged; then she began tapping her long red fingernails against the back of the sofa. "It isn't working out," she said. "I got to think of my future, you know? I feel—not good. You never come, I got to hide here like I'm some kind of criminal, you won't even take me out to dinner because somebody might see us. It's no good. I'm sorry if I hurt you, but I got to get some other kind of life, you know? I don't want to just sit in this apartment and wait for you to come once or twice a month." She shifted her shoulders—her beautiful white shoulders—impatiently inside her robe. He stared at her, hardly able to comprehend what she said. She was dumping him! After he had set her up in this place, this very good address, bought her a wardrobe fit for a princess, never asked a thing from her except that she be there for him whenever he could get away to see her.

"I'm afraid I really don't understand," he said. "What are you going to do?"

"I'm going to get a job."

"A job! Can you type?"

"I don't need to. I'm going to help manage in a restaurant. The first Hungarian restaurant in Boston. Exciting, huh? You think they're going to like cold cherry soup in Boston?"

"A restaurant! Ilona, have you gone crazy? That's the most brutal work in the world, a restaurant! Twelve, fourteen, sixteen hours a day!"

She shrugged again. "I don't care. I got to do something, you know? I can't just sit here for the rest of my life, until I get old and ugly and you don't want me no more. You understand? I don't want to hurt you, but I got to look out for myself."

Never in his wildest dreams had he anticipated this development. Once in a while he had wondered how he might break off with her, if indeed he ever had to, which was a possibility that he hoped he would not need to confront for a long time. Now, incredibly, she had beaten him to it.

"Di-Di." She had never been able to say his name. "Listen to me. This isn't easy for me, you know. But I just think—"

"Who is he?"

"Who is who?"

"You have someone else. I know it. You don't expect me to believe that you would throw me over for a—for a restaurant!"

"I got part ownership, Di-Di. You know, I been saving, I been very careful." She stood up. "Oh, Di-Di." It seemed that she was sending him on his way. He couldn't believe it. Absolutely couldn't believe it.

Now she was holding out her hand. He stared at it. She was wearing a large ruby ring that had been his first Christmas present to her, five years ago.

When he tried to stand up he discovered that his legs were quite weak. He tried again. As he got to his feet he ignored her hand. The hell with her hand. The hell with *her*. Sending him away, after five years of—of—milking him. Like a goddamned cow, she had milked him all that time.

"Best of luck, Di-Di." She stood watching him as he lurched into the kitchen to retrieve his coat. His rubbers were by the door, but he did not stop to put them on. An undignified task, he would not perform it in front of her. Nor would he speak to her. Never again. Never, never again.

Five years, and this was his reward! Well, let it be a lesson to him. That was it: a lesson. A weird kind of Christmas gift. As he went out, he slammed the apartment door behind him so hard that he felt the building shake. In the little vestibule he got his rubbers on, and his topcoat. A lesson, yes. And he had learned it well. Despite the snow, he was going to drive home to Emily as fast as he could, and he was going to give her her Christmas present now, right now, and he was going to tell her that he loved her very much, which he did, and he was going to promise himself that never, never, never was he going to get himself involved with any hustling little whore again. Five years, for God's sake, and she sent him away as if he was a delivery boy!

He felt in his coat pocket to make sure that Emily's present was still there; then at a rapid clip, too rapid really for the snow underfoot, he set off for the Ritz garage. He waited impatiently while they retrieved his car. Then, faster than safety allowed on this wretched night, he set out for home. They would not, he thought, come back in for the party and the carol sing; instead, he and Emily could have a quiet supper together after the children were settled into their rooms—he had no idea what time they went to bed, but surely it couldn't be too late—and perhaps in the course of the evening he could manage to convey to her how grateful he was to her for always being such a good wife to him. Really, that was what she was: a good wife, faithful and true, and he was going to make it up to her, damned if he wasn't.

He had always been one of those tinkering geniuses. Yankee ingenuity, people used to call it. Before the war, when he was himself fresh out of the classroom, he had taught physics at MIT. He had a strong brain but a weak heart, and so he had spent the war years at MIT also. Along with a number of other men as clever as he was, he worked at the Radiation Laboratory. Despite its name, the Radiation Laboratory had nothing to do with radiation; rather, its staff devoted their talents to the development of radar—the single most important weapon in the victory over the Axis powers. At other labs at MIT during those years, scientists and engineers worked through pure research to develop other "weapons" in the fields of optics, photography, missile guidance, electronics—a brand new science—and navigation. Thus in their humble, sometimes ramshackle quarters, wooden structures thrown up behind the handsome granite university buildings, the men at MIT fought as valiantly in the war effort as did men in combat, if with less risk to their lives. And when the war was won, the technology that had helped to win it was turned to other uses, peacetime uses, pointing the way to the future, and a whole new generation of businesses was launched. Many of them, needing more room than crowded Cambridge had to offer, set up shop along Route 128, the "Miracle Highway" that circled Boston and Cambridge fifteen miles out. So many new MIT-spawned corporations started up in the decade or two after the war that some wag, mindful of the ancient appellation given to Harvard in the seventeenth century, dubbed twentieth century MIT the "School of the Profits."

Many other new, technology-based businesses in those years grew from the solitary genius of their founders. All of them together—Polaroid, Raytheon, Digital, Itek, Wang, EG&G, and hundreds more—succeeded in giving Massachusetts an intellectual and financial clout far in excess of its size or its insignificant position on the map. Break it off and let it float out to sea, a presidential candidate had once crowed. But that would have been stupid as well as impossible: the nation could not have sustained the loss.

Like many men of his type, nervous, brainy, a little "different," Dwight had never been very comfortable with women. His father, the famous John, had taught him that the greatest pleasures come from one's work; but John, busy in his observatory or traveling to spread his gospel of life on Mars, had never been a very attentive father, and so the lesson was imperfectly learned. What Dwight knew was that women, by and large, did not inhabit MIT; and that when, say, as an undergraduate he had encountered a young woman at one of the "mixers" that he infrequently attended, she would find out a little about him and then inevitably drift away. He never seemed able to develop any kind of permanent relationship with any of them. Not that he minded. His greatest joy always had been studying, and tinkering on the side. And when, during the war, he had met and married the pretty young woman who was the new Physics Department secretary, he had been as surprised as everyone else that she actually had consented to marry such an awkward, unworldly fellow as himself.

She had, of course, been amply rewarded, for in the post-war years the company that Dwight founded made everyone who owned even a little part of it extremely rich. The big house in Lincoln, a pricy suburb next door to Concord; the summer place on Martha's Vineyard; the household help; any material thing that she might want—yes, Emily was a lucky one, her friends had said, marrying so wisely.

Dwight, on the other hand, was increasingly unhappy. Years ago, he felt, his wife had ceased to understand him. When a well-meaning friend had introduced him to Ilona Nagy, he had undergone a revelation: here was a woman who would live *for him*. She had no interests, no occupation, no purpose in life except to wait for him to appear, and then, when he did, to do everything in her power to make him happy. He liked that: it had made him feel, uh, terribly masculine.

He realized now that he must have been deluded for a long time. She had been planning her escape, so to speak; and laughing at him behind his back, no doubt, for not suspecting her betrayal.

He turned off the main road to the narrow lane that led to where he lived. The house looked very pretty as he approached through the darkness, the snow falling in the light at the end of the drive, and the twin carriage lamps on either side of the front door with its Christmas wreath. It was a large, handsome reproduction Georgian colonial, not very old, but well built, a good amount of land, a good buy when he'd bought it just after the war.

He put the car in the garage and went in via the connecting door. The house was quiet, no one talking, no music from the children's rooms—and, now that he stopped to realize, no odor of dinner being prepared. But of course not: they thought that they were going to Winslow's, and he remembered now that Emily had said she wanted to give Cook the night off.

He left his rubbers in the mud room and went through the kitchen into the hall and put his coat in the closet. He slipped the little box into his jacket pocket. He glanced into the living room: no Emily, no fire in the fireplace, but the tree was up. They'd decorated it, as they always did, without him. Next year, he thought, he'd spend this day at home, helping to wrap presents, helping with the tree. Perhaps they could have an open house in the afternoon for the neighbors.

He found his wife in the library. She was sitting on the sofa, staring at the fire. She did not seem to have heard him come in.

"Emily?"

She gave a little start.

"Emily, dear. Merry Christmas." He bent over the back of the sofa to kiss her cheek. She seemed surprised. "It's a filthy night. I don't think we should go in to Winslow's. We can rustle up something for supper and have our own Christmas Eve right here."

He came around and sat beside her and took her hand. She looked at him blankly.

"I had a hell of a drive, but now it's all right, I'm home. What'v'you been up to, hm? Children keeping you busy?"

There were four, ranging from Matthew, the eldest, a sophomore at Harvard, to Janet, the youngest, in the seventh grade.

He patted her hand and wondered if she were coming down with something. It was unlike her to be so quiet.

And now that he thought about it, the house was unwontedly quiet, too. "Where is everyone?" he said—not that he wanted to see them at just that moment; he was glad of this little time alone with her.

"I sent them over to a party at the Websters'."

"Ah." It seemed an odd way to put it: not that they'd been invited, but that she'd sent them.

"Well!" he said heartily. "All the better. Nice to have a little time to ourselves, eh? Just let me get a drink. Want something yourself?" Usually she had eggnog ready at the holidays, but he saw no sign of it now, and in any case he did not like eggnog, he was happy to have another martini.

"No."

For a moment, as he poured, the image of Ilona's hard green eyes flashed across his mind, and he put down the glass so as not to spill his drink. Ilona was gone: done with. His future lay now where it belonged, here with his wife and family.

He returned to sit beside her. She continued to look not at him, but at the fire. He cleared his throat. "Emily. I, ah . . ." He sipped a couple of times and set the glass down on the tooled leather trunk that served as a coffee table. He slipped the little jeweler's box out of his pocket and set it beside the glass. She did not seem to notice. "Look—I was wondering—why don't we try to get away for a week or so after the holidays? We could take Fuzzy Peacham's house in Jamaica, he never goes down in January, and he told me the other day he hadn't rented it. Just the two of us, we could get a little sun, play tennis, swim . . . What d'you say? If you have any meetings, you could postpone them, surely." She served on a number of committees and belonged to a number of organizations; she was forever going to one meeting or another.

"Emily? Emily, are you all right?" He took her hand again, and now at last she turned to him, she looked straight at him. But with such an expression! Hastily, as if to forestall some disaster, he gave her the present, put the box firmly into her hand. "There," he said. "Why not open it now? Just a little token of my, ah, affection." He leaned toward her and tried to kiss her, but she pulled away from him. He was not a perspicacious man, but now all of a sudden, and not for the first time that day, he felt a little ripple of fear run through his brain, and a strong sense of déjà vu overtook him.

She looked down at the box. Then, without opening it, she put it back on the coffee table. "I can't take that," she said.

"What do you mean, you can't take it?"

"I—just can't."

"But why? It's your Christmas present."

She shook her head—a short, sharp, decisive movement. "It wouldn't be right," she said. "It isn't . . ." She paused, took a kind of deep gulp, and all of a sudden seemed to snap awake. She sat straight, turned toward him, and took both his hands in hers. He felt a premonition of disaster, and reflexively he held onto her very tight.

"Dwight, I have something to tell you. And I want to tell you now, before Christmas, so that I won't have to go through another holiday living a lie."

The room tilted and then slowly came back right again. She was speaking but he couldn't hear.

"What?"

So she said it again. "I want a divorce."

A loud roaring in his ears, he saw her lips move but he couldn't hear— "What?"

". . . far too long," she was saying. "It isn't healthy, to live without love. I'm like an automaton. I go through the motions, every day. But I'm sleep-walking. I don't even feel alive anymore. I just go through the motions, getting deeper and deeper into my rut. Not that it isn't a comfortable rut, mind you. But I'm not *alive*. Can you understand that? Oh, Dwight, you've been such a good provider. Really you have. And you've never been a drunk, you've never gambled, or run around with women . . ."

A million butterflies crashed around his stomach. He reached for his drink and knocked over the glass. Never mind. Neither of them made a move to clean up the spill. She went on talking.

"It's just, well, I really feel dead. And somehow I have to get back into the world, and *do* something."

"Do something." What an odd voice he had, all strangled.

"Yes. I'm going to law school."

"Law school."

"Yes. Isn't that exciting?"

"Law school?" What an odd voice, shouting very loud—"Law school? For Christ's sake, you're fifty years old! Where the hell are you going to go to law school?"

"At Boston University. They have a special program for what they call 'life-experienced' students. That includes women who've had the life experience of giving birth and rearing children, apparently."

There was an odd ringing in his ears. Deck the halls. Fa-la-la. She was talking again. "I've spoken with George Simmons." George Simmons was a good friend, a lawyer who specialized in divorce cases. "He says he'll work out some reasonable arrangement with you. I won't need much. They're going to give me a half scholarship and a part-time job. And as soon as I get through, I'll be independent. I don't want to be vindictive. You've always been a good husband. I have no ax to grind, to get every penny out of you that I can."

She stood up. She was a tall woman; she seemed to tower over him. He didn't even try to stand up as well; he simply stared at her, appalled.

"Well, Dwight, I want you to know that I have no hard feelings. I'm taking the children to Mother's for the holidays, I thought it would be easier on all of us. I'm going now to the Websters' to pick them up." And she turned and walked out of the room. Dwight sat in front of the fire, so numb that he was nearly in a coma. He felt as though he had been hit by a truck. He felt as though he'd fallen off a cliff. He felt as though he'd stumbled into a nightmare and couldn't get out, couldn't wake up.

After a long, long time he started to cry.

2

On a bright February day in 1965 the Family gave a party for Augusta's seventy-fifth birthday. Everyone was there, not only Family, but many others as well, university people and museum and literary and musical people—even some political people. Everyone who made a difference was there, and most of all, of course, that was Augusta herself.

She looked radiant, Cecelia thought. Cecelia was her granddaughter, a senior at the Winsor School. This afternoon she stood at the entrance to the great central court of Fenway Palace and greeted the dozens and dozens of people coming in. This was the event of the winter: newspaper reporters were there, and photographers, and even film crews from the local television stations.

A long line of guests waited to greet Augusta; it moved slowly because she insisted on talking at some length to so many of her friends—not necessarily Family, but people she had worked with over the years on various causes. Augusta Griffin Revell Trowbridge was a very political woman, a woman of many interests; on a day like this, when so many of them converged, she was nearly overwhelmed. She reached out now to embrace her cousin, Benjamin Griffin Revell—one of her favorites. She was nearly as tall as he, both of them with snow-white hair and bright blue eyes, so that they looked like brother and sister.

"Stay on later," she said. "I want to talk to you."

He pressed her hand and nodded. Impossible to talk in this crush—but he was glad he'd come; usually he hated affairs like this, but this one was special, as was the lady herself.

He looked around. He saw a number of non-Family faces that he recognized. Good: it was only fitting that they turn out for Augusta. She was a treasure—not only the Family's, but for all of Massachusetts as well. He saw the head of a well-known publishing house; two successful writers; several politicians; a newspaper columnist; three socialites whose families were nowhere near as distinguished as the Revells; and at least a dozen of the younger Revell generation. That Cecelia girl at the door looked to be doing well, handling herself with the aplomb of a seasoned diplomat. He liked the way she looked you straight in the eye—just as Augusta did.

One of the politicians was a former governor. The boy wonder, they had called him in his day; but his day had passed, and now he looked aged but not mature. They said he'd taken the President's assassination particularly hard. He was approaching, his hand outstretched. "Ben Revell! How are you?"

When Michael Shaughnessy Jr. smiled, he had all the fabled charm of his race, thought Ben. But he'd always thought Shaughnessy's smile had something ruthless about it, as well. The Irish were reputed to be merry, warm-hearted folk, but Ben thought otherwise. And in any case, he'd never liked Shaughnessy. They'd been on opposite sides of too many battles. So now he shook the former governor's hand politely enough, but no more than that.

"Mr. Shaughnessy." More than he could bear, to call him governor.

"Oh, come now, Ben! Why so formal? We're old adversaries, we can afford to be friendly."

But Ben knew too much about this man. "Good to see you," he murmured; and moved on, leaving Shaughnessy not a bit surprised. He knew that the Revells had no great opinion of him, and he felt the same about them, truth to tell.

Scattered through the crowd were some of the postwar generation of Revells: Miles and Cecelia, Stephen and Matthew, and young Adam, whom he didn't know at all—Guy's son, and since Guy was Augusta's nephew—there he was now, talking to the man who headed up the Athenaeum—that meant that Adam was her grandnephew. He was a handsome boy, with a strong resemblance—so quirky was heredity—to the Copley portrait of Ebenezer Revell that hung in Alex Korsakoff's front parlor over on Clarendon Street. Guy had been in the Foreign Service for years, and so Adam had lived abroad; he returned last fall to start at the College. Actually Stephen—Stephen Jackson Revell Jr., he was—was a little older than the others, born in 1944 because his father had been stationed in Washington during the war to perform some intensely secret task. Stephen was very tall, a little gawky, but he'd grow into himself in a few years.

Ben turned away then, surprised as he always was when the sudden grief gripped him; no matter how accustomed he was to it, it never failed to take him unawares. He had no children. His wife had died in childbirth in 1930, and the baby had died as well. He had never found anyone else. Ever since, when he was in the company of children or young people, he had been stabbed by the thought: those might have been mine.

A newspaper reporter was talking to Augusta: a dewy-eyed youth, looking no older than those young Revells. Ben edged nearer.

"It's always been a special delight," she was saying, "to have been born on Valentine's Day, and just one day away from Susan B. Anthony. You haven't asked me yet what my next project is, but I'll tell you anyway. I'm thinking of starting a campaign to make her birthday a national holiday. Isn't that a good idea? I mean, we wouldn't have the vote if it weren't for her, now would we?"

The youthful journalist looked at her blankly. Ben touched her elbow. "I think you need to explain who Susan B. Anthony is," he said. "She was born in Massachusetts, wasn't she? There you are—another local heroine." He spoke this last to the youth, who remained blank.

"Oh, for heaven's sake," exclaimed Augusta. "Don't tell me you don't know that. Why, any of my grandchildren or nieces or nephews can tell you about Susan B. She's the mother of us all. Go and look it up if you have to. I'm not going to tell you. Really! I don't believe it!"

She turned away from him in exasperation, and Ben could not help laughing. "That's not the way to get a flattering story," he said. "These press people are very sensitive. You have to be nice to them."

She gave him an icy-blue, withering stare. "No," she said. "I do not. And particularly not on my seventy-fifth birthday."

"I missed you at Christmas," he said.

"Yes. I just didn't feel up to it. I really didn't want to commit myself to this affair, either, but the young ones were set on it, and I thought, I'll get through it somehow. I'll even pretend to be surprised."

"You look marvelous." And she did, tall and straight, a good healthy glow from her post-Christmas weeks in Barbados. "Are you really going to start to campaign for Miss Anthony's birthday?"

"I doubt it. But it's a good idea, isn't it?"

But now they had to break off, lucky to have had even that, as Augusta was summoned to the center of the courtyard. It was bright with flowers forced into bloom, lilies and daffodils and azaleas and pots of ferns, the great open space warmer even than usual on this bitter winter day because of the crush of people.

Waiters appeared with trays of champagne; Ben was called to make a toast, and then Stephen Sr., and Dwight. Then old Winslow, eighty-seven his next birthday and hale and hearty, sprang to his feet and gave a gallant little speech, and when he sat down, Alex Korsakoff did the same in considerably more fractured English. In fact, there were so many people wanting to make a toast that Cecelia, who had helped to organize the event, didn't know who some of them were. She stood to one side, watching, glad for her grandmother that the day was going so well, but at the same time wondering if it shouldn't end, Gran would be overtired—

"She's splendid, isn't she?" It was Stephen Jr., one of the Jackson Revells, a senior now at the College, or perhaps he was only a junior, she didn't know. He was awkward and a little brash—to cover his shyness, Gran had said once when his name had come up, but Cecelia didn't think he was shy, he was just obnoxious in the way that so many Harvard boys were.

"Of course she is," she replied. "She always is."

"Even last summer?" he said. She couldn't believe anyone would say something so crude, and after what she hoped was a sufficiently scathing look at him, she edged away.

"Hey, I didn't mean anything." He was coming after her. Damn.

"It doesn't matter." She didn't look at him as she spoke, hoping he would get the idea. But like most Harvard boys—and Yale boys and MIT boys and every other kind of boy, for that matter—he was incapable of imagining that not every young woman was thrilled to talk to him.

"Want to go to a movie after?" he said.

"No, thanks."

"*Woman in the Dunes* is at the Brattle."

"No, thanks. I'm taking Gran home."

"You live with her, don't you?"

"Yes." As you know perfectly well, she thought.

"And you're in—what? Your last year? At—Winsor?"

"Yes." And then she saw that Augusta was speaking, and she turned her back on him, just flat out turned her back, she didn't care how rude he thought she was. If he was so stupid that he didn't know when to be quiet—

". . . to see you all today," Augusta said. "I have to tell you that for a few moments last summer I thought that I might never see Massachusetts again." Because she laughed, a few others did also, breaking the sudden unease. "And as I said to our young friend from the *Globe*, I'm thinking of starting a new civil rights campaign, for women this time. That's the only way I know to keep young. Now I want to thank a few people especially, and first of those are my grandchildren Cecelia and Miles." For a moment, as a little murmur of approval and applause went through the crowd, Augusta's vision blurred with tears. It was odd, she knew, but sometimes she thought of Cecelia and Miles as her children, and that made her feel guilty because it was like saying that Winifred had never lived, and of course she had lived, she had been very much alive right up until the end, when she and her husband had been in the wrong place at the wrong time, going home from a party one rainy night in the car out in Wellesley, a bad curve, a drunk driver plowing into them.

Someone was pushing Cecelia forward. She clasped Augusta's hand. "And Daphne and E-Liz, who organized everything so well. And dear, dear Alex, of course—Alex, where are you?"

He waved to her from deep in the crowd, and then he began to make his way to her, people helping him through, opening a path. He was nattily dressed as always, dark gray pinstripe and a burgundy silk handkerchief in his pocket to match his expensive tie. When Violet had died, several years ago, Alex had taken it hard. He had withdrawn into the Clarendon Street house, no one saw him for weeks at a time, he even missed a summer at Tanglewood. But now he seemed recovered at last, and he had been an enthusiastic helper for this party today.

"Dear Augusta—" He embraced her warmly. She had been one of the few Family members to favor his marriage to Violet, and he would never forget it.

And then Benjamin got up, and everyone hushed, because Benjamin was the most respected member of the Family. He had gone to war with fascists not in Europe, but in Washington, and he had won. Now he made a gracious little benediction, as it were, and they all lifted their glasses again, and drank to her again, and someone started to sing—not "Happy Birthday," thank God, but "Auld Lang Syne," and the melody carried them all along, made them all, briefly, one—and a damned good feeling it was, too.

And some of them thought, thank God we are not singing "We Shall Overcome," which really would have been too, too much.

Cecelia saw her brother Miles making his way toward her. He looked happy, which was a good thing because he'd been having a very hard time of it at Harvard, where he was a freshman. He'd been depressed for weeks, threatening to quit after he saw his first-semester grades, which were really quite bad.

"I guess everything is okay," he said.

"Everything's fine," she replied. "Relax. She's having a good time, that's the important thing."

"Do you think she was really surprised?"

Cecelia laughed. "Gran? Remember how she used to tell us when we were little that she had eyes in the back of her head? I remember always trying to get behind her when she was sitting down and looking to see those eyes back there. Of course she knew! And of course she would *say* she was surprised, because she wouldn't want to disappoint everyone who had worked so hard to surprise her."

"D'you think she'd mind if I left?" said Miles. "I have to meet with the section man for survey." Absentmindedly he gnawed his thumbnail. Cecelia felt sorry for him; he'd always had a difficult time in school, and now his first year at Harvard was destroying what little confidence he had left.

"No, I don't think she would. Go on," Cecelia said, throwing him an encouraging smile. Looking away, still smiling, she met Stephen's eye. To her annoyance, he smiled back. He looked better when he smiled, she thought—less obnoxious. On the other hand, she didn't want him to think she was encouraging him, and so she frowned and went to talk to Cousin Dwight and his son Matthew; everyone said Matthew was as brilliant as his father, and Cecelia had always thought that that was a heavy burden to put on anyone's shoulders.

"Hello, Cecelia. Nice party, my dear." Dwight had come in late and his hands were still cold, as was his cheek when Cecelia kissed it. Gran had said that they must be very nice, particularly nice and kind to Dwight, because while Gran could understand that his wife wanted to have her independence, or whatever, still it had been a blow to poor Dwight, her leaving so suddenly, and they must all help him through this difficult time.

"Thanks. Hello, Matthew."

"Hi."

And now they were singing "Happy Birthday" after all, everyone very jolly, and the caterer was wheeling out the trolley with the huge three-tiered cake on it, all yellow and white and green, beautifully decorated, and a single candle at the top.

Augusta, knowing the proper ritual from all the birthday parties she'd organized, closed her eyes, made her wish, opened her eyes, took a deep breath, and *blew*. Everyone applauded, oohing and aahing. Yes, Cecelia was glad they'd organized this party, after all the criticism Augusta had endured during the past year.

Everyone had a piece of cake, and then people began to go home. Augusta, having greeted each guest as he or she came in, was now attempting to say good-bye to each one also. She'd be exhausted, thought Cecelia, and she went to see about loading up the car with all the presents people had brought.

As Ben was going out, Augusta leaned in, and under the pretext of kissing his cheek, murmured, "Come to tea tomorrow, if you can. I want to change my will."

3

The previous summer, Augusta had joined the civil rights campaign in St. Augustine, Florida. Along with several hundred other demonstrators, she had been arrested. At her side had been her friend of many years, Mrs. Malcolm Peabody, the mother of the governor of Massachusetts and wife of the rector of the Groton School. The two women represented the very best of the New England character: high moral purpose, concern for justice, a willingness to fight for what was right, an active and unrelenting conscience. To others, of course, they represented the Devil incarnate—the Communist conspiracy which was still, in 1964, a tangible threat to the American Way of Life.

When she had returned home at last, she had been unrepentant. To Fanny, who could not hide her disapproval, Augusta said with some irritation, "Honestly, Fanny, don't you know anything? It was Henry Thoreau who inspired the Mahatma Gandhi, and Gandhi who inspired Reverend King. So how can we object to a philosophy that grew up right here at home? Thoreau went to jail for his beliefs, too, you know. They may be calling me a communist, but our very own ancestors were called traitors once upon a time. And that was far worse, don't you think?"

Fanny was not placated. She stared at Augusta, her face rigid with disapproval, and thought back over the years and years of Family tolerance of Augusta's deplorable eccentricity. Every family had them—eccentrics—but not many of them chose to act out on the public stage, as it were. As the newspapers were quick to point out, Augusta's arrest and imprisonment in St. Augustine had not been her first. They raked up all the old business of the fight to win the vote for women, the hunger strike and its subsequent force-feeding and public outrage. Fanny's granddaughter had just been graduating from Miss Hall's

School for Girls in Pittsfield, and she had been so embarrassed by the publicity that she had very nearly skipped the ceremony.

And some people remembered that Augusta had been involved in the Sacco and Vanzetti case, too, and had worked for a while as Edwin Jackson Revell's unpaid secretary when he was starting his book on the case. And in 1927—the year Sacco and Vanzetti died—the notorious advocate of birth control, Margaret Sanger, had come to Boston to speak, invited by the Ford Hall Forum and really they should have known better, such an outrageous, outspoken woman, and for once Mayor James Michael Curley had done the right thing when he issued the order that prevented her from speaking, on the grounds that she was inciting to riot. So Margaret Sanger sat on the platform with a gag around her mouth while Professor Arthur Schlesinger of Harvard read her speech. A little committee of women sat down front in a gesture of solidarity, and to Fanny's horror, Augusta was among them.

When Mrs. Sanger started to open birth control clinics in the 1930s, Augusta had been right there with her as well, and when the war was over, and a major fight was launched to legalize birth control in Massachusetts, Augusta—of course—had been in the thick of that doomed effort. Winifred had died around that time, and so Augusta had suffered a double loss, Winifred's of course by far the greater, and she had retired, as it were, to bring up Winifred's children, Miles and Cecelia, and for a long time she had remained blessedly quiet. But the civil rights struggle had fired her up again, and now here she was, a septuagenarian celebrity whose every action—unfortunately—would attract attention.

Fanny, who was Augusta's age exactly, thought that life was very unfair.

When former governor Michael P. Shaughnessy came away from Augusta's birthday party that cold February day, he told his driver to wait while he stretched his legs a bit. The sun was just going down, the temperature hovered around ten degrees. Leafless trees were silhouetted against the rosy western sky; the evening star hung low. In the morning he would go back to Washington and face a series of unpleasant decisions, issues that the President had asked him to deliver an opinion on. Half ashamed, he looked up now at the shining pinpoint and made his wish: "God help me to be right."

Once upon a time he had been considerably more self-assured. He had returned home from the war in late 1945 secure in the knowledge that God in His Heaven had allowed Good to triumph over Evil. The future stretched before him, limitless in its opportunities. He had rapidly impregnated his wife with their second child, and with her and little Joe, who had been born in 1942, he posed for a *Life* cover. It was the third most popular issue ever; it made him famous not only in Massachusetts, but all over the country.

"Now," said his father, "you've been given a great boost, what are you going to do with it? Go back to Lowder and Stritch?"

He didn't think so. A lifetime of corporate law seemed very dull indeed after three years of combat.

He sat in front of the dying fire and watched the old man watching him. His father had made a comfortable fortune in business so that his children could do as they pleased. He knew that his eldest son—this young man before him now, who had emerged unscathed from the war—had the potential to do anything he wanted. He could even—as astonishing as it might seem—be President some day. If he started now, with this tremendous boost, he might one day end up in the White House. . . .

So ran the father's thoughts, gazing on his son. Old Patrick, the ward boss, the saloon keeper, the vital and essential link between the immigrant and the fully acculturated sons and grandsons, had died before the war. He'd been delighted when Michael Jr. had gone to Harvard and the Law School—"We'll beat 'em on their own territory, by God!"—and he had accepted, if not approved, Michael Jr.'s decision to apprentice at one of the oldest and most prestigious Boston law firms. It was a position that was not offered gladly but that had come, finally, when Michael Sr. had had some plain talk with the senior partner about money loaned and not repaid.

"What about Ward Eight?" he said—a fitting place to begin, the Eleventh congressional district, Ward Eight the very heart of it, right where Patrick began and his father before him, the original Patrick who had come over in the famine years. A seat was going to open up the following year; it would be a good place to begin. They could walk the district together, he'd find some of his father's old cronies, some of the faithful old boyos to take young Michael around.

"I've heard that Jack Kennedy might go for it," said Michael.

"No! Have you really?" This gave the elder man pause. The Kennedys had far more money than the Shaughnessys. And young Jack, thin as a rail and as yellow as a ripe banana from the malaria he'd contracted, had about him nevertheless a real charm, a beautiful smile and a way with words—ah, yes, they'd have to battle it out between themselves in a primary, winner take all because the Democratic nominee in that district, Cambridge and Charlestown and certain Boston wards, had the election won for sure. A Republican in that district was a rare and endangered species, an oddity to be gawked at and then dismissed as irrelevant to the real business of life, which was politics, Democrat style.

"So I was thinking"—young Michael went on—"what about running for lieutenant governor?"

His father peered at him with new interest. "You don't say. Lieutenant governor. Now that's something I hadn't thought of. Who's running at the top of the ticket?"

"Oh, I think Sam Brigham will get the nomination, no question about it." Samuel Brigham was a member of a significant subspecies in the Massachusetts political landscape, a Yankee Democrat, a Brahmin born and bred who had, for some mysterious reason, chosen to join the enemy, which was to say the Irish

Catholic Democrats, and work against the best interests of his class. Tom Eliot, over in Cambridge, had been such a one: architect of the Social Security system for President Roosevelt, one-term congressman until James Michael Curley red-baited him out of the seat.

In the end it had gone that way: JFK for Congress, Michael Shaughnessy Jr. for lieutenant governor on the Democratic ticket. Often, that summer and autumn of 1946, Michael had thought that he had the better of it. He traveled back and forth, up and down the state, and really for the first time saw it in all its stunning beauty. He remembered one afternoon in particular: perhaps his sensibilities had been sharpened that day because only the day before his wife had given birth to his first daughter, whom they had agreed to name Kathleen for his mother. He was driving to a rally in Springfield. On a whim, on such a glorious October day, he told his driver to turn off the main highway and to follow a narrow, two-lane road that meandered north, through farmland and meadows bounded by stone walls and interspersed with patches of forest, tall pines, and then daubs of brilliant color, red maples mostly, and the rich brown of the oaks, the deep blue sky above, weathered red barns, snug white farm-houses, then a village with its neatly kept green, a bandstand, some handsome white eighteenth century houses spaced out around, or perhaps columned Greek revival, and the church with its tall white spire. And then out into the country again, stopping at a roadside stand to buy a peck of apples and a jug of fresh cider, taking a drink right there, the afternoon shadows lengthening across the empty dun-colored fields, a chilly breeze coming up with a foretaste of winter—best get on our way, he'd said, we're late as it is. And then on to the rally, the crowd cheering him far more than they did Sam Brigham, cheering Michael Shaughnessy Jr., the war hero, the role model for a generation of American men. Even out in rural Massachusetts, where most folks were Protestant and (mostly) Republican, his religion and his Irishness and his party affiliation hadn't mattered. They loved him; Brigham said later that it had been Michael who won the election for them, pulling voters into the Democratic camp. And then when Brigham, a doughty old liberal, had gone to Washington to sit in Presi-dent Truman's kitchen cabinet, Michael had succeeded to the governor's chair, and he'd acquitted himself well. He was particularly proud of the battles he'd won over birth control and over a mandatory loyalty oath to be taken by all state and local government employees. He'd succeeded in banning the former and requiring the latter—and a good thing it was, he thought with a smile, that it hadn't gone the other way around.

Now, years later, on the night of Augusta's party, he arrived at his home in Jamaica Plain just before dinner. His wife was still out, but she'd left him a note: a letter had come from Joe, she'd put it for safekeeping on the dresser in their room. From somewhere upstairs he heard the sound of music, that awful new stuff by those moppets from England called the Beatles, and laughter as Kathleen talked on the telephone. Kathleen was a big talker. She could even talk him around, if she'd a mind to.

He hurried up. Joe was with his unit in South Carolina. Michael thought that Joe probably didn't know what was going to happen in the next month or two. Already, one of the President's senior advisors had strongly recommended that they start to bomb North Vietnam. Michael had supported the recommendation. He had thought briefly of Joe, had thought that if the war were going to be escalated, Joe would surely be sent over, just as he himself had been sent to England and then the Continent in 1943. War was war; men had to go to fight. He hadn't quite been able to formulate the next thought, which was that many of those men didn't come back.

"Hi, Daddy." She startled him, darting out of her room like that. She gave him a hug and a kiss—"Oooh, you're *cold*! "—and the news that her mother had been detained at Aunt Rose's who was much worse, sinking fast, and so she, Kathleen, in consultation with the cook, was going to manage dinner, broiled scrod, canned baby peas—all right?

She was small and quick, red-brown hair, bright brown eyes, a joy to him since the day she was born, when he'd been campaigning for lieutenant governor. He'd always told her that she'd brought him luck.

"Anything you say, love." He released her and smiled to himself as he watched her run downstairs. She was in her first year at Emmanuel, a Catholic women's college in the Fenway, not far from Isabella Revell's palace. Next year she'd probably want to live at school. He'd miss her terribly—more, if the truth were told, than he missed Joe, whose letter awaited him.

You knew from the moment they were born that one day you would lose them, he thought, but it never got any easier.

Benjamin Griffin Revell dined that night at his club and thought, not for the first time, that he should get up a committee to hire a new chef. Afterward he chatted for a while with a couple of the members who, although approaching senility, nevertheless remained faithful to him. It had not always been so. Some years before, at the height of the McCarthy red scare, almost no one in the Whalebone Club spoke to him, and those who did, did so very curtly.

He hadn't cared, particularly. He'd had a job to do—face down the demagogue Joe McCarthy, who had everyone in the entire country terrified with his damned lists of Communists under every bed. And when they'd wanted a hardheaded nonradical straightlaced Republican lawyer to do the job, Ben Revell had gotten it. WITCH KIN FIGHTS WITCH HUNT, the headlines had screamed. He hadn't minded. Better him than some poor wretch who hadn't the financial wherewithal to have his practice ruined—for that was what had happened, he'd lost clients by the dozen, and only because he'd been able to draw on his trust funds had he not gone bankrupt.

All that had been ten years ago, now. It seemed longer. He remembered Michael Shaughnessy's fury at him for opposing McCarthy. Shaughnessy had called him an anti-Catholic bigot, a Papist-hunting Puritan in the mold of his ancestors—oh, it had gotten nasty, all right. Yet the man had spoken to him very civilly today. He must want something, thought Ben. Or perhaps he had simply been moved by the occasion to put on a cordial face. Ben didn't trust him. He could charm the warts off a toad if he wanted, but he was still Michael Shaughnessy Jr., grandson of the ward heeler, the scourge of the goo-goos. The Irish—and the Yankees, too, he supposed—had a race memory as long as your arm.

The next afternoon he went around to Marlborough Street, to Augusta's, and listened to what she had to say.

"I was wrong, you see, to leave both properties jointly to both children," she said—"children" being, of course, her grandchildren, Miles and Cecelia. "I've talked it over with them, and we've agreed that it makes much more sense to leave this place entirely to Cecelia, since she's a city girl, she's never enjoyed the country. And Miles, as young as he is, knows already that what he wants is to buy a lovely boat, and he'll dock it at Marblehead, of course, which is convenient to Revell Hall." She'd taken over the old place during the Depression, when Winslow had been hurting badly and the expense had been too much. "He thinks he might like to live there year 'round in fact. So I told them I'd indulge myself by giving each of them what they want. Can we do that?"

"Yes, my dear." He smiled at her: she had everything worked out so neatly, in such a sensible way. "We can do exactly as you wish."

4

Despite Cecelia's less than welcome reception, Stephen Jr. called her the following week. "*Woman in the Dunes* has gone," he said, "but they've brought back *Hiroshima Mon Amour*. It's pretty good, I saw it when it came out originally. And we could go to an early show and have something to eat afterward."

Cecelia had had only three dates in her life; one of her minor crises, in fact, was the problem of whom to invite to her Senior Dance in May. Winsor was an all-girls school; she'd met boys several years earlier at dancing class, and she knew the brothers of some of her friends and the friends of her brother Miles; and occasionally the school held joint affairs with boys' schools, Roxbury Latin or Belmont Hill or Rivers; but like most of her friends, Cecelia was without a steady boyfriend. Both she and her grandmother thought that this was an acceptable state of affairs; she had many hours of homework every evening, and on the weekends as well, and she knew that in good time—when she was in college, perhaps—she would eventually find a boyfriend or two. Some of her friends were already thinking of marriage, but marriage, to Cecelia, was an unimaginable state—like being President, or the Queen of England. Like many girls her age, she conducted a fantasy love life; her choice of a lover was Richard Burton, whom Cecelia longed to rescue from the clutches of Elizabeth Taylor.

Stephen Jackson Revell Jr. was no Richard Burton, but he did have one advantage: he was an older man. So she said yes, she'd go out with him. Her grandmother approved—largely, Cecelia thought, because Stephen was a member of the Family. "He's a very decent young man," Augusta said. She paused for a moment; then: "I knew his grandfather, Edwin."

Something in her voice made Cecelia look up. "Tell," she said.

"He helped us in the Sacco-Vanzetti case," Augusta said.

"The what?"

As always, Augusta felt a little shock—a twinge of self-reproach—when Miles or Cecelia showed their ignorance of something that had been vital in her life. If they didn't know about the Inquisition or the Edict of Nantes—well, that was one thing. But not to know about things that their grandmother had lived through—that was her own fault, for not teaching them.

Stephen, when Cecelia got to know him, turned out to be not so bad: not as obnoxious as he had first seemed, and not as awkward, either. She discovered that what he wanted, mostly, was an audience. He had all kinds of ideas that he wanted to try out, to talk about, and by talking (she thought), to get them straight in his own mind. So they would go to a movie—Stephen's favorite pastime—and then they would go somewhere for a sandwich and they would talk, or rather, Stephen would talk and Cecelia would listen. Sometimes she got bored, and then she would turn down his next invitation or two, but eventually she would relent and go out with him again. Or sometimes they would go home, to Cecelia's house on Marlborough Street, and Stephen would talk to Augusta as well.

"He thinks you're much more interesting than I am, Gran," Cecelia said, laughing. "Especially when he starts to talk about politics. He told me you're the most interesting person he's ever met. Good thing I'm not jealous."

Augusta laughed, too, but of course she was pleased. Stephen soaked up ideas and information like a thirsty sponge; and to her delight, he not only had heard about Sacco and Vanzetti, he actually knew something about the case. And he knew about the suffrage fight, and about the fight over civil rights—all kinds of things, he knew about. "I think he's splendid," she said to Cecelia: and wanted to add, hold on to him if you're smart. But she didn't; Cecelia was too young for such prodding.

Cecelia invited Stephen to the Senior Dance that May, and shortly afterward she went on a tour of Europe with a dozen other girls and three tour leaders—her graduation present from Augusta—and in the fall she went away to college at Mt. Holyoke—not very far away from Boston and Cambridge, but not terribly convenient either.

So she and Stephen drifted apart—not that they had ever been very close. She wasn't sorry to have known him, though, because in the next few years, as the war in Vietnam heated up, Stephen Jackson Revell Jr. became one of the most vocal—one of the most radical—student leaders of the antiwar movement. By that time he had graduated from college and was enrolled at the Divinity School; however, he dropped out in the middle of his second year to devote himself full time to the antiwar cause. His name was often in the papers; his picture, also, and sometimes on television as well. Cecelia let it be known, ever so casually, that not only was he distantly related to her, but that she had actually dated him for a while; to prove it, she showed around photographs of herself and Stephen at her Senior Dance.

"And I'll tell you what is really funny," she would say, "is that Stephen always got along very well with my grandmother. They used to love to talk politics together. Sometimes I'd get sleepy and go up to bed, and there they'd be. Talking, talking—and now look. My grandmother's picture is in the papers, too. *Again.*"

Not long after Cecelia went away to college, Augusta had become an activist once again. She had, she announced, recovered from her sojourn in the St. Augustine jail the previous year; she was ready to get back into the fray again. What fray? Why, whatever one seemed the most pressing.

She had done this by joining a disarmament group that had turned its attention to the war in Vietnam and in a rather decorous way was protesting it. Augusta was always urging them to take more radical action. She often mentioned her adventures in Washington, D.C., in 1917 when she had chained herself to the White House gates in the fight to get the vote. Eventually, as the war went on and on with no end in sight, people began to pay attention to her, until by 1967, she had formed a little offshoot group called "Out Now." She and some of the other members often went to Washington to lobby Congress and to protest and demonstrate; a well-known news photo of the time showed Augusta, age seventy-seven, chained to the White House gates, dressed in white just as she had been decades earlier, getting arrested. Many newspapers dug up the earlier pictures of her, and the ones taken of her when she was demonstrating in St. Augustine, as well, and printed them all. It was an eye-catching little feature, although many Family members were not pleased at the unwelcome publicity.

Augusta knew perfectly well that many of her relatives disapproved of her, but she didn't care. "I am expressing my freedom to dissent," she said. "If I understand the story correctly, that is what great-great-grandfather Ebenezer fought for in the Revolution." She was really impossible, people said; they hadn't the faintest idea what to do about her. Stubborn old woman!

One day she had what she thought was a pretty good idea; before she acted on it she talked it over with Ben.

"I'm going to talk to Michael Shaughnessy," she said. "He's gotten to be one of the President's closest advisors, even though he doesn't hold any office. But from what I understand, the President has a little group of men whom he consults fairly frequently, and our former governor is among them. Don't you remember, he came to my birthday party? I can get in to see him, at least, even if he won't listen, any more than he listened during the birth control fight."

"I've heard that he's very hard-line," said Ben. "He wants a clear-cut victory, won't settle for anything less. Unfortunately, thanks to Joe McCarthy's purges, we don't have a single person in the State Department who speaks Vietnamese or who knows anything about the country."

Augusta gazed at him triumphantly. "So you admit I'm right to oppose the war," she said.

Ben couldn't help laughing, even at such a serious subject. "I admit that you, dear Augusta, in true New England fashion, will always act upon your conscience. You know Cousin Violet used to tell me that her grandfather was a great friend of Henry Thoreau's. He was the original civil disobedient, wasn't he? Wouldn't pay his poll tax in opposition to the Mexican War?"

"That's right," said Augusta. "But you know, it gets even more interesting, because Thoreau influenced the Mahatma Gandhi, and Gandhi influenced Martin Luther King. And King is with us now, he's come out against the war. He's going to march in the next big demonstration."

"Oh? When is that?"

"At Easter. In New York."

"It must take a lot of work to put on one of those things." As Ben spoke, he realized that he had never thought about it. "It's like a theatrical production, isn't it? A kind of show? The kind of thing Reverend King's been doing all these years in Birmingham and Selma—a political show, theatrically orchestrated."

"That's right," said Augusta. "You know, he took his Divinity degree at Boston University, and while he lived here—just imagine it—we of course never knew he existed. But he got to know a really remarkable man who long ago used to be the minister at the Congregational Church over in Newtonville until they fired him for taking part in union organizing and textile strikes in Lawrence. And it was that man, A. J. Muste, who introduced Martin Luther King to the writings of Gandhi. They say that everything that goes around, comes around. It seems to be so, doesn't it?"

Ben smiled at her again. She was a perfect type, he thought: a doughty old Yankee woman setting herself up against the world, acting on her conscience. True, in the matter of the war, many Massachusetts people were on her side, and indeed the same universities that were the source of the state's richest resource—brainpower—and whose alumni, including Dwight Abbott Revell, profited mightily from defense contracting, were also hotbeds of student unrest and increasing protest against the war.

The next week, Augusta went to see her old nemesis, the former governor of Massachusetts, now an advisor to the President.

"Mrs. Trowbridge! Good to see you!" He did have that certain Irish charm, no doubt about it, but she thought he looked tired. For a few minutes they chatted pleasantly about inconsequentials. Then, with a certain amount of condescension in his voice, he said, "Now. What was it you wanted to see me about?"

"I wanted to talk to you about the war," she said.

He was surprised at that, and his first instinct was to smile. This dowager, this proper Bostonian grandmother—worrying about the war, when she should be at home crocheting antimacassars!

"Oh, yes? And what about it, may I ask?"

"It's wrong. We should get out. You know what Senator Aiken of Vermont said. Let's just say we won and then leave."

"My dear lady, it is hardly that simple—"

"Not now it isn't, because we've been so stubborn. We never needed to send in all those men, never needed to begin all the bombing, the napalm, the defoliation."

He stared at her. He was not accustomed to hearing elderly women discuss the details of combat.

"You see," she went on, "I think that one of the problems is that a lot of the so-called experts in Washington are too isolated from the rest of the country. They really don't know how people feel. Now you are a politician, you've run for office and you know how to talk to people. First of all, I think you should suggest to the President that public opinion is beginning to shift. People are uneasy. They aren't yet fully convinced that we should get out, but they are beginning to be uncomfortable with what we're doing. I think the President should know that."

"Mrs. Trowbridge, the President, if I may say so, has the best advice in the world. I say that in all modesty, for he has advisors who are far more skilled than I am. I don't need to name them; you know who they are. They are the best brains in the country. They are the real experts, men who know better than any of us how to conduct this country's affairs. And if those good men say that we must stay in this fight until Ho Chi Minh is whipped, then I for one am ready to accept that verdict. Trust me, madam. As someone so eloquently put it, there is light at the end of the tunnel. We can see it. Soon— possibly within the year—we will be standing free, out of the tunnel and in the bright light of freedom for that brave little country! You know, I don't like to get personal, but I have a son fighting over there. My oldest boy. He is in the Air Force. Now do you think I'd let my own son fight that war if I didn't think it was, number one, a just war, and number two, a winnable war? I don't think any father would willingly send his boy to die for a lost cause, do you? To die for nothing?"

After that there was really nothing more to be said, and Augusta, accepting temporary defeat, went away.

The following month news came that Captain Joseph Shaughnessy's plane had been shot down and that he was missing and presumed dead. Augusta sent a note of condolence to his father.

But the incident made her all the more determined. Like a candidate for office, she traveled the length and breadth of the state, organizing against the war. She became widely known; features were written about her in the newspapers, and someone came to her and interviewed her for a book about politically active American women.

The Family threw up its hands and finally, at long last, resigned itself to her troublesome existence.

6

"Good morning, gentlemen. And, ah, two ladies, is it? All right. Now here is what we are going to do. We are going to hold the scalpel like this—you see? Any lefties? No? Good. Now watch. We grasp the scalpel firmly and we cut straight down and then off to either side. These folks have been embalmed, so there shouldn't be any blood to speak of. Nice clean cuts like this. Now lay open the flaps and begin to see what you are looking for.

"Just follow the diagram. You will see that latex has been injected to help you—red in the arteries, blue in the veins. All right? Everybody clear on the procedure? There's a shortage of corpses, so you've been assigned in pairs. It's not as bad as it used to be, when students had to buy corpses from the resurrectionists—grave robbers. These bodies have been willed to us, donated to us by their, uh, owners, and I will remind you that they must be treated with the greatest respect. The greatest respect. Everybody have their lab dissecting book? Just look at the first page, it's all there, what you are supposed to do, the procedure, what you are supposed to see. It's really very simple. Memorize as you go, that way when the test comes, you'll be ahead of the game. Memorize everything. Memorize the connections, the three-dimensional relationships, so that you can describe where each nerve and each blood vessel goes. All the bones, all the muscles. What you will have at the end is a wiring diagram of the nervous system. Everybody got their kits? Scissors, scalpel, forceps? All right. Now go to your assigned tables, please, and begin."

Kathleen Shaughnessy looked across the corpse at her partner standing ready to begin. He was tall, blond, very handsome; but more than that, he looked oddly familiar. She was sure she'd seen him somewhere, and yet if she had, she'd certainly remember, he was so striking.

He held out his hand. "Adam Revell," he said.

She took it; he noted that her handshake was as firm as any man's. "Kathleen Shaughnessy." She had bright warm eyes and red-brown hair and a fair sprinkling of freckles; she seemed very sure of herself, not uneasy like some of the others—as if this was the place she was supposed to be. And now as they prepared to start work, she felt a little shock of recognition as her memory jogged: she hadn't seen *him*, but she'd seen a John Singleton Copley retrospective at the Museum a couple of years ago, and one of the paintings had been of a tall, blond, handsome man named something Revell, Ebenezer perhaps, and he'd looked almost exactly like this person across from her.

"You can go first," he said. He took it as bad luck to have been assigned one of the two females in the room. He'd have much preferred a man. He didn't feel too sure of himself, and a man was more likely to be of help. Women were notoriously laggard in the sciences.

"That's all right," she said. "You go on."

He was relieved. At least he'd have a stab at it, so to speak, before she could mess it up. His uncle Herbert, who was a distinguished heart surgeon, had explained to him the importance of a swift, clean cut. It was always that first cut that got to you, he said, and you have to train your mind to disassociate from the horror . . .

He grasped his scalpel, turned his full attention to the sheet-draped corpse with only the arm exposed, only the one place where he had to cut, dry and gray and shriveled, almost like a mummy—

He got halfway and stopped. He felt a little sick. The room, a bleak and dreary chamber, smelled overpoweringly of formaldehyde. He put down his scalpel and rested both hands on the metal table to steady himself. He felt his stomach turn over, and he gritted his teeth to keep it down. He was suddenly drenched with perspiration, and his knees had gone to water.

He didn't faint—not quite—but he did need to find a stool and sit down for a moment and put his head between his knees. He was glad to see that he wasn't the only one; two other fellows were sick, too.

Later, when people asked Adam and Kathleen how they met, they were always happy to get the big reaction when they said, "We met over a corpse when we were both students at the Medical School." People loved that story; Adam and Kathleen became famous for it. But they never told how he got sick and she didn't.

Her father, the former governor, had not been happy when she'd announced that after graduating from Emmanuel, she wanted to go to medical school—and to Harvard at that.

He'd stared at her, astonished. "What'd'y'want t'do that for?" he said. "Why don't you just get married and settle down and give me a dozen grand-children?"

"Oh, Daddy." She'd read *The Feminine Mystique* and *The Second Sex*, and while she wasn't about to declare her independence completely, she did feel the first stirrings of unrest in her rather inconspicuous bosom. She put her arms around his neck and kissed him, and of course it was no contest, he'd never been able to deny her anything she had her heart set on. Her mother was always the disciplinarian, had needed to be, because he was home so seldom, many late nights in the corner office in the Statehouse, and then, later, always down to Washington, committees, consulting, people wanting his time. Before he'd known it, his children had grown up. His wife had never complained. She was a sweet, forgiving, long-suffering woman—and strict with the children, he couldn't fault her for that at any rate. She'd done a good job with them.

He'd sent Joe to Harvard, of course, and Patrick was there now, as well, hanging on by his toenails, according to the dean. Tom had opted for Yale, which had been happy enough to have him; Tom was a sharp, sharp lad, the closest of any of them to Grandda the famous ward boss. But for a girl to go to Harvard was a problematical thing, and to the Medical School . . . He felt very strongly that she would learn things there that no decent woman should know.

"Darlin', you don't want to do that," he said in his most coaxing voice. "Really you don't."

"Yes, I do." She had stared at him fixedly, her eyes so steady that he got a little qualm in his stomach.

"But—why? All that blood and disgustin' anatomy—"

"I think I'd be a good doctor. I *want* to be a doctor. I may get married, I may not. But I want to be a doctor first. And if I do get married, I intend to keep on working."

He remembered his father's stories of Mary Margaret O'Donovan Shaughnessy. The overwhelming impression he'd carried away was of her absolute stubbornness and determination to survive. That death grip on life, so to speak. And now here it was all over again right in front of him, in this slip of a girl who was, in fact, behaving most outrageously, arguing with him, defying his superior wisdom of what was best for her—

"What if I say absolutely not?" he said. He was just testing, genuinely curious to see what she'd say.

"Aunt Jane said she'd stand me to it."

"She did, did she? Whew! I don't have a chance, do I?" Jane was his sister, a well-off widow, childless and always very good to all her nieces and nephews. "Does she know she's not to interfere between a father and his daughter?"

"She knows me." Kathleen smiled, sure of victory now. "I said I'd take a job and save up until I had enough, but we agreed that by that time I'd be so old I couldn't do all the memorizing. So she'll stand me to it, and I'll pay her back when I'm done."

He gave her a hug. How he loved her—this bright little thing who now all of a sudden was a woman grown, charting her own course! At some level of his understanding, he knew that if she had been docile and undemanding like her mother, he wouldn't have loved her so much. It was the Irish in her that got to him, the outrageousness combined with the lethal charm—his own Irishness, in fact, but so very different in a woman.

"I'll think about it," he said.

"Thanks, Daddy." She threw him a triumphant grin and went off about her business, both of them more or less comfortable with the outcome of their interview.

They didn't talk again for a while; and before they could get back to it, the word came about Joe, and after that nothing was ever quite the same again.

Shot down—but at least they'd recovered his body, not like so many who were never found, leaving their families in the agony of not knowing for sure what had happened. She'd never known him very well, her older brother; he was always about his business. But whenever she'd had a bit of time with him, he'd been very nice to her. She was sorry now she'd never gotten to know him better.

She'd cried all night, the night after the funeral, everyone weeping all through the mass, the flag-draped coffin, the reporters—how her parents had endured it, she would never know; they looked dreadful, so quiet, as if they'd been mortally wounded themselves, as indeed they had.

Not for some weeks did she bring up the subject of medical school again, and when she did, it was in a very different way, not coy and challenging, but subdued and matter-of-fact: I have to get the application in, remember we talked about it, I'm sorry to bother you about it, sorry to bother you about anything, but it has to be done now, there's a deadline.

She wondered if in medical school they'd teach her a remedy for the pain she saw in her father's eyes. Such enormous pain—probably there was no help for it, you had a pain like that and either you cured yourself or you died.

She'd been afraid that perhaps he would start to cry, or to try to tell her about Joe, and she didn't want to hear about Joe, not just then, it was too soon, and certainly she didn't want her father to start to cry, what in God's name would she do if that happened? But he didn't do either; he just nodded in that terrible detached way that he'd had ever since he'd had the news. And so she'd sent in the application, and she'd been accepted, and the hand of Fate—truly, it was that—led her to Adam Griffin Revell.

She'd never known anyone quite like him. He had about him a self-confidence, a sense of the lord of the manor walking the land—she couldn't quite put it into words. It wasn't just that he was rich, although of course that might have been part of it. But it was more than that; as she got to know him, she discovered what it was.

"You people have been here forever," she said to him. "No wonder you behave that way."

"What way? And anyway, you make it sound like a crime."

"No, I don't."

"Yes, you do. It's just your Irish inferiority. *You* people came over two hundred years too late. We got all the land, the shipping, the factories—"

"Ah, but we got the votes." She laughed. She didn't mind his talking that way. Not for nothing was she her father's daughter, her grandfather's offspring. She had her own confidence about this place—this little corner of the nation where her ancestors and Adam's had coexisted so uneasily.

Over the winter they fell in love. Adam realized that more than anything, he wanted to marry her. He also realized that given who she was, and what she was, she might never agree to marry him.

On the evening of the day they finished their last exam of that first year, he took her to dinner at the Ritz. They sat at a table by the tall windows overlooking the Public Garden. It was twilight, the lights coming on, people strolling in the warm spring dusk. Adam touched his pocket where he had put the small ring box. The waiter hovered solicitously; he had served many young couples on their engagement evenings, and he recognized these two as another such.

As soon as they ordered, Adam reached across the table and took Kathleen's hand. "Marry me," he said.

She'd known the proposal would come, but not quite so soon. Nevertheless, in her forthright way, she was prepared to accept his offer. Her father, she thought, would perhaps not approve, but she'd work him around somehow. She pressed Adam's hand. "All right," she said. "I will."

He took out the ring box and opened it, holding it for her to see. Both he and Kathleen were oblivious to the smiles and sympathetic glances thrown their way by the other diners, some of whom had themselves become engaged in this very room.

"Go on," he said. "Try it on."

She took the box, took out the ring, put it on. It was a diamond solitaire, two carats at least. It seemed impossibly large, but it was so finely cut that it did not look vulgar.

"Does it fit?" he said.

She held out her hand and he took it to inspect. Yes: it fit perfectly.

He had never been so happy in his life. "Waiter!" he cried. "Champagne!"

7

When Kathleen told her father that she had promised to marry Adam Griffin Revell, Michael reacted with a cold fury that shocked her, frightened her—she'd never imagined he had it in him to be so angry.

"I told you right off, you had no business going to medical school, and certainly not to Harvard Medical School," he said. He had gotten very thin since Joe died, and he'd always been pale, so now, even though he was not yet sixty, he suddenly looked drawn and ill—an old man, she thought. His hair was nearly white. "And now look—you come to me and you tell me you're goin' to marry one of 'em—one of those damned Harvard people. Well, young lady, you'd better think again, because if you do, it'll be over my dead body."

She was appalled; she had no idea what to say to him. He had always loved her so dearly, doted on her . . . How could he turn on her like this?

She spent the day in her room; that evening she went to her aunt Jane and announced that she would take that tuition loan, after all.

"I'd like to meet the young man," said Jane. She was fond of her brother, but she knew, as Kathleen did not, how unforgiving he could be.

Shortly afterward she went to see Michael. She was a small woman, sweet and plump and middle-aged, but at that moment, fighting for a niece whom she dearly loved, she was as hard and unyielding as an old Boston Irish ward politician calling in his favors.

"Michael Shaughnessy, you're behaving like a fool," she said. "These young folks have nothing to do with the bad old days, and you know it. Adam Revell seems to me to be a perfectly fine young man, and he's obviously crazy about Kathleen. He says he agrees to having the children brought up in the Church. What more do you want?"

The next week, Kathleen never knew how, Michael agreed to meet her fiancé. In the interim, Adam had his own battle with his parents, who were not happy at the idea of having their grandchildren brought up as anything but Episcopalians. But after a time they came around, and the following year Adam and Kathleen were married.

By that time Cecelia had graduated from Mt. Holyoke, broken off a stalled romance with a young man from Chicago, and taken a job in the public relations office of the Museum.

Stephen, of whom she had been moderately fond, but no more than that, had long since disappeared from her life. In the end, she thought that she had been right about him after all: he was awkward and gauche, and more to the point, he had become so wrapped up in the Movement that he'd had no time for any personal life at all.

Like Augusta, he had become an antiwar activist, but on a much bigger stage, for Stephen Jackson Revell Jr. had been one of the half-dozen national leaders of that vast wave of anger that was known as the Movement against the war in Vietnam. He had enrolled at the Harvard Divinity School in 1966, but he dropped out the following year to help organize the demonstration at the Pentagon; from that point he chose, as he put it, to find God through action rather than study. He had been on the road much of the time, sleeping on living room sofas at the homes of the faithful, moving from city to city, campus to campus, organizing, talking, arguing, speaking to big rallies, speaking to two or three key people. All the time, as his face became better known, his appearance was changing: he dropped twenty or thirty pounds, so that he looked gaunt, half starved; his hair, in the fashion of the day, grew down to his shoulders, and by the summer of '68 he had grown a beard, as well, with which to confront the authorities at the Democratic Convention in Chicago.

No one in the Family heard from him except, once in a while, his parents. In 1968 at the annual Christmas party at Guy's house in Louisburg Square, which once had been his father Winslow's, and before that his grandfather Lyman's, Augusta caught sight of Stephen Sr.

"How is young Stephen?" she said.

"Busy," he replied; she thought that many parents, particularly Revell parents, might not have welcomed inquiries about a son who was more or less notorious, but Stephen Sr. actually smiled a bit, and nodded in a positive way. "I spoke to him last week. He asked to be remembered to you, by the way. He said to thank you for all you've done for the cause."

Augusta laughed at that, pleased. "It's very little, comparatively, but tell him I thank him, all the same. If he ever has a spare moment, I'd be glad to hear from him. He can call me collect. We used to have some good talks when he was dating Ceil."

She didn't really expect to hear from him, but then one rainy night in November, almost a year later, the week after a huge antiwar mobilization in Washington, her telephone rang and it was Stephen Jr.

"I hope I didn't disturb you," he said.

"Not at all. How are you? I saw you on the news last week at the demonstration."

"Did you? Great."

"It looked like a splendid day. And your speech was very good, what I saw of it. I'm sorry I couldn't come, but it would have been impossible."

"I know. But you were there in spirit, I understand that. I'd like to see you, but I won't be able to."

"Where are you?"

"I'm still in Washington. But I'm leaving day after tomorrow. I'm going to India."

"India!" She was shocked; for a moment she couldn't think of a reply.

"Yes. It's time."

"Stephen, I don't understand that, but you are an intelligent young man and I'm sure you know what you're doing."

"Let's just say that I'm burned out. I've been organizing pretty nearly full time for almost three years. And this trip is—well, you might say it's a continuation of divinity school. A different kind of divinity, that's all. I think that the East has a lot to teach us, and I think it's time that I started to tend to my own soul again."

"Good luck, dear boy. Send a note, if you have time."

"I will. Thanks, Cousin Augusta. My best to Ceil. How is she? Not there, by any chance?"

"No, she's out this evening, but she'll be pleased that you called." Not really, Augusta thought, but no harm in telling a white lie. "She's fine, working at the Museum."

And so he went away, and no one, not even his parents, heard from him for a long time.

8

"We have a real opportunity here," said Dwight, "and I think we should consider it very carefully."

A June day at Revell Hall: golden sun spilling over green velvet lawn, the grand old house gleaming white with a fresh coat of paint, roses blooming, and peonies, and bright yellow lilies. In the distance the sea sparkled in the sun, dotted this Sunday afternoon with scores of sailboats out of Gloucester and Marblehead. Some of these folks here today would have been on the water as well, had it not been for the urgent summons that Dwight had sent out.

He glanced at Augusta who, as the eldest surviving member of the Family—and not incidentally their hostess this day—sat in a position of honor in a big old wicker chair under the shade of the green-and-white-striped awning that had been set up over the food tables. The second Mrs. Dwight, whom he had married not long after his divorce from Emily became final, had hired a new caterer; the food had been excellent, if a trifle precious.

Augusta was listening to something that Ben was saying to her privately; looking very spiffy in a white summer suit, he was leaning over and speaking into her good ear. She nodded once, twice, then she laughed.

Dwight cleared his throat. People were chatting with each other; no one paid him any particular attention. He caught his wife's eye; she threw him a brilliant smile and then nodded and raised her hand, as if she understood exactly what his problem was. She went to the food tables, found a spoon, and began banging against a metal bowl. In a moment there was silence.

"First of all," Dwight said, "let me start again by saying that I appreciate your giving up your Sunday afternoon to be here. If I hadn't thought that this was an important question, I wouldn't have asked you to come."

He paused and looked around. They were all paying attention now, all hundred or so of the Family who had come up to Salem to hear what he had to say.

For a moment he tried to see them as an outsider might: a handsome, prosperous group, the Family resemblance very strong: a tall, blond, wholesome-looking bunch, very, uh, American-looking. Some folks, he knew, would argue with that appellation: America is many different looks, they would say, white and black and brown and red and yellow. In any case, whatever you wanted to call them, the Revells were a fine-looking bunch. He was sure—if he could convince them to go through with it—that they would look perfectly splendid on film.

Which brought him to the subject of the day.

"You all know my son Jack. Some of you may know that while he was at Harvard, he had a friend whose father is a senior executive at CBS. Now it just so happens that CBS is looking for an appropriate Bicentennial project. It's 1974 and those things creep up on you fast. They want to, uh, finalize this so that they can begin."

There was a slight pause. Then: "Begin what?" said Augusta.

His wife had suggested that Dwight talk to Augusta privately before this meeting today, but he had decided not to. Perhaps, after all, he should have.

"Ah, that is what I'm getting to," he said. It was a hot day, even here by the water, and he was perspiring heavily. "The thing is, they want to do a film about us."

He smiled broadly, for just the thought of the project gave him shivers of delight. A TV show—about the Family! But as he looked around at them now, all peering at him without a trace of the enthusiasm that he thought he should see, he felt suddenly terribly deflated. So he tried again. Perhaps he hadn't made himself clear.

"Let me just tell you what they have in mind," he said. "They want to do—oh, I don't know, five or six programs, a series, really, about an American family. And not just the family here and now, but how it came over, where it settled, what happened to all its members—that kind of thing. And of course they were ecstatic when they found out about us. I mean, we came over on the

Mayflower! What could be better than that? And we can trace our line directly, we fought in the Revolution, and in the Civil War, and financed the railroads, and bought stock in Bell— Perfect! And not incidentally, the action, so
to speak, takes place right here in Massachusetts. Already the CBS people have
done a scouting expedition, and they agree that this is wonderfully photogenic
territory. They're dying to do it."

Ben stood up. "Excuse me, Dwight. Let me get this straight. They want to
come in and do a five- or six-part documentary on the Revell Family? And this
documentary will be in large part a historical examination of the Family—how
Bartholomew came over with the Pilgrims, how Ebenezer worked with Samuel
Adams, and so on."

"That's right."

"Don't forget the Salem witch!" someone called out.

"And Catherine Mayhew Revell's captivity!" called someone else. "That
should be good for a few laughs."

Dwight frowned. He did not like irreverence in any form; behind his back,
people called him stuffy. However, he was so rich that it didn't matter how
pompous he was.

"What would it mean for us in terms of cooperation?" Kenneth Jackson
Revell asked.

"That's a fair question," said Dwight, "but I can't give you an answer.
They will do a considerable amount of historical research, they'll probably
want to photograph interiors of people's houses, the Copley portraits certainly,
Cousin Isabella's Museum, and this place. They'll interview at length; they may
present all the historical stuff with pictures to illustrate what we're saying on
camera. I don't know."

"Wouldn't want costumed actors running about," said Ben's sister Claudia.
"That's awfully tacky, don't you think?"

Dwight shrugged. "These are details, and I simply can't tell you," he said.

"But they are the details that will determine how we decide," said Augusta.
She was sorry that Cecelia was not here; she would have had some pertinent
thing to say. "I don't like it," she went on. Everyone turned to look at her.
They respected her enormously because she was the oldest living Revell—the
oldest in captivity, as she liked to joke. "I think we're opening ourselves up
to—how long? *Two years*—of intrusion into our private lives, disruption, inconvenience—and for what?"

"But we'd be on *television*," said one of the teenagers in an aggrieved tone.

She understood. To the younger generation, you didn't exist unless you
were on TV.

For a long time, that afternoon, the issue went back and forth, but in the
end it was obvious to Augusta and everyone else that the overwhelming majority wanted to do it. Dwight had intended to call for a vote, but he decided not
to, so as not to rub in the fact to Augusta that she was on the losing side.

"Well, what about it?" he said at last. "Shall we make it unanimous? Augusta? We need your help, you know. We really can't do it without you."

A little pandering, a little sop to her not inconsiderable vanity. She smiled a wry, tough smile. She had been in too many political battles not to know when she was beaten. "All right," she said. "I'll cooperate—up to a point. But mind you—only up to a point!"

And so began the production of what turned out to be the most popular Bicentennial special, *One American Family*. When the producers found out that one of the Revells had married an Irish girl, the daughter of the former governor, no less, they were delighted. So then the Shaughnessys became involved, and the house on the Jamaicaway by the pond, near James Michael Curley's house and with shamrock shutters just like his, had a place in the story as well. But when the producers wanted to go to the West End to film the Shaughnessys' American beginnings, even as they had filmed the Revells' origins in Plymouth, they were stymied, for the West End was no more. In what had become a classic example of how not to do urban renewal, the West End had been torn down. Since the late 1950s, huge, hideous apartment blocks had stood where once the narrow streets of Patrick's ward had been, buildings that would have looked more at home with the Stalinist architecture of the USSR than side by side with Bulfinch and Victorian Boston. For years after the West End was destroyed, sociologists studied the people who had lived there; they found that many of the former residents who had been forced out had died before their time, sooner than people of comparable sex, age, class, and race. And many of those who lived suffered depression, alienation—they never felt right again, never felt at home anyplace else.

So the West End was out; but of course much remained. Before the end of that summer, television cameras were prowling through Revell Hall, and through the magnificent rooms of Cousin Isabella's palace on the Fenway, and at Frederick's on Commonwealth Avenue—now, alas, sold and cut up into apartments, but much of the original woodwork and plasterwork remained— and out at Alex Korsakoff's place in Lenox. One of the Jackson Revell boys was to begin at Harvard in September, and so they went along with him, much to the amusement of his classmates; another was starting his senior year at MIT, and he, too, had a camera and crew for companions. They sailed with Kenneth off Martha's Vineyard; they went with Dwight into his plant and filmed what could be filmed— not much, for a good deal of it was secret Defense Department work. They came to Thanksgiving dinner at not one house, but half a dozen; they came, of course, to the traditional Christmas Party at the Guy Griffin Revells' on Louisburg Square. They had luck, that Christmas Eve: a soft, photogenic snow drifted down over Beacon Hill just as the caroling began, and later everyone said that those were some of the most beautiful shots in the series.

At the Museum, they photographed several pieces of Jedediah's silver: a great salt, twin to the one at Harvard; and a pair of tankards and several candlesticks and a baptismal font made for King's Chapel. Then they sat Augusta in an elaborately carved, high-backed great chair, to one side of the Freake limner's portrait of Catherine Mayhew Revell. Augusta held a copy of Catherine's account of her captivity, and at the signal from the director, she began to read:

"It was on a night in November, nearly winter, when we heard the savages' drums in the forest, and feared greatly for our lives. We prayed all the night, but at dawn they attacked. Their hellish cries filled the air, their firebrands came down on the roof, and as we ran out to save ourselves, they fell on us. . . ."

To the reconstructed village at Plymouth, to Salem to Revell Hall and a nod to the witch trials, and a grand Family banquet at the hall, all the good old New England dishes, clam chowder and baked beans, cod cakes and turkey with cranberry sauce, blueberry muffins and corn bread and Parker House rolls with wild beach plum jam, New England boiled dinner, johnnycakes and maple syrup, a dozen different kinds of apples, some fresh, some baked into pies and pan dowdy and dumplings, dozens of lobsters, and the finest codfish poached so gently that it looked like a vanilla soufflé. They none of them had ever seen so much food in one place, and as the camera panned lovingly down the long laden tables, they wondered if mere photographs could convey the mouth-watering aromas and tastes.

Then the crew went back to Boston, the old city sparkling on a brisk autumn day, back to capture the tombstones at Old Granary, Bartholomew's and Jedediah's and Benjamin's, all of them, until the middle of the nineteenth century, when they had started to be buried at Mt. Auburn. And then the Massacre circle in front of the Old State House, and then to Old South, and on to Faneuil Hall, abuilding now with a really remarkable development that was being closely watched all around the country, shops and restaurants in the old Quincy Market buildings.

It was, in short, a wonderfully picturesque and photogenic series, and only the faintest trace of bitterness crept in when old Michael Shaughnessy, the former governor, said a few words about his grandfather, and about his great-grandmother, and tried in the brief time allotted him to convey something about the life of an Irish servant girl in a Brahmin family in the years before the Civil War. But then his time was up, and the scene shifted to his daughter Kathleen as she and her husband Adam Revell took the viewers to the Medical School, and then to the Ether Dome, as Adam spoke about what had become a world center of medicine—not Harvard alone, but the medical community that had grown up around Harvard.

And then their cousin Matthew came on with his father Dwight and took the camera to the Pakachoag Golf Course in Auburn, outside Worcester. There, a granite marker on the ninth fairway pointed out the place where in 1926 Dwight and *his* father, the famous astronomer John, had watched as Robert Goddard had launched the world's first liquid-propelled rocket—the first step on the long trail that would lead eventually to the moon and beyond.

For comic relief, one day the crew went on an automobile ride with some of the Abbott Revells through the narrow, twisted streets of Boston, more or less along the route taken by Goody Sherman's sow, or the cowherd coaxing along his flock. But such an expedition did not give the full flavor of a drive in Massachusetts, and so the crew went along as the Revell driver soared along Route 128, then north on 93, then back down Route 3—a dangerous bowling alley of a road—and back in along Route 9 to the Friday-afternoon suburban rush of Newton and Brookline. By the time the ride was done, the cameraman was pale and trembling, and the assistant director had cramps in his hands from hanging on so tight to the passenger strap. Whew! These people really winged it! In Massachusetts, apparently, a yellow light was a signal to speed up, and a red light a challenge to ignore. Passing on the right, weaving in and out, never look back, never give an inch, do what the natives called a Massachusetts left whenever you needed to, speed up when you came to that peculiar Massachusetts institution, the rotary, a joyride round and round and never get off, just like poor Charlie lost on the MTA, "Oh, he never got off, no he never got off . . ."

Another time, just for laughs, they had someone stand up and answer the question: Where would he park his car if he were so unwise as to drive into Cambridge?

The answer, of course, was that he would "Pahk the cah in Hahvahd Yahd." For some reason, people in other parts of the country seemed to find this particular phrase hysterically funny.

And then they went up to Lowell and Lawrence, and the stark, stunning images of the vast red-brick mill buildings, sadly neglected now, deserted, weeds and rubble choking the canals that had been like arteries carrying precious water—waterpower—to turn the great wheels that powered the looms—the engine of that Second Revolution that transformed the nation as much as had the first.

In the spring they brought in extra crews so as to capture both the Battle of Concord and Lexington, and the Boston Marathon. (One of the Jackson Revells ran; in a field of more than two thousand, he came in 573rd.) A few weeks later they went to graduation at MIT. As a little sidebar, they did three minutes on the number of MIT-spawned companies that made money for the Revells, even as the Family textile and shipping operations had done a century before.

The next day, Stephen Jackson Revell Jr. came home. He'd sent word in the spring that he was about ready to do so, but he didn't know, he said, exactly when he'd leave for Boston.

He walked into his father's house on West Cedar Street at nine o'clock in the morning, a Saturday morning, both parents at home—*"Stephen!"*

He was thin—so thin!—and his skin was deeply tanned, so that his blue eyes stood out startlingly in his long, lean face, and his blond hair was bleached to a pale yellow. But it was neatly trimmed, and his beard was gone. He trembled a little as they embraced; he was tired, he said, all he needed was a good rest, he'd be himself again.

But he was not: he was never that again. Whatever it was that he'd experienced in India—whatever he'd learned, whatever he'd suffered—he'd come back a changed man. Not so angry; not so impatient; not nearly so dogmatic.

"My goodness, Stephen, I hope they didn't turn you into one of those gurus that they have over there, just sitting around all day and meditating," said Augusta when she saw him.

He laughed; he was delighted to see her, delighted that she'd lost none of her spunk.

"No," he said. "They didn't do that."

But exactly what they did do, he did not—or could not—say.

After they'd talked for a while, he asked after Cecelia. She was in France, Augusta said, helping a well-known writer on food and wine with his next book. Stephen said nothing more about her, but Augusta thought he looked disappointed.

It was coming down to the wire, now, in the filming of *One American Family*, time running out, time needing to be saved for the spectacular finish. So when Stephen Jackson Revell Sr. suggested something that perhaps ought to be included, the television people were not terribly receptive.

"Who?" said the chief field producer.

"Sacco and Vanzetti."

"Sounds Italian. You got Italians in your family, too? We can have a regular United Nations."

"No, no, nothing like that. It was a famous legal case back in the twenties." Stephen, a tall, athletic-looking man in his mid-sixties, paused for a moment to swallow down the lump that had suddenly risen in his throat. They were on Boston Common: a very warm morning in June. A few tourists wandered about, looking for the Freedom Trail—a broad red stripe painted on the pavement that led past the Statehouse, King's Chapel, Faneuil Hall, and other places connected to the Revolution. The Family had been assigned to the television crew in turns, and this week it was the Stephen Jackson Revells' turn. They were preparing to go up over Joy Street to the back of the Hill to film the old African Meeting House as part of the Abolitionist Daniel Jackson Revell's segment. As a little prologue, the cameraman had just shot the Shaw Memorial across from the Statehouse: the gallant captain and his Negro regiment. Daniel had had nothing to do with Sacco and Vanzetti, of course, but his grandson Edwin had written the definitive book, had interviewed everyone, even Alvan Fuller, even President Lowell.

"I beg your pardon?" said Stephen.

"I said, did Sacco and Vanzetti do anything photogenic? Any good location shots we could use? Who were they, anyway?"

Just a couple of wops, he wanted to blurt out.

Suddenly he had to turn away; surreptitiously he wiped his eyes. He had been too young to understand, of course: his father's long absences, his mother's grim celebration that rainy Sunday in August 1927. And then six months or so later his father had gone away for good. To Switzerland: Stephen and his older brother had traveled across, in the summer of 1931, to visit with him. He looked awful. His hair was nearly white, his face deeply lined and aged, his eyes bloodshot. He was just finishing the book. He showed them the huge stack of manuscript—dog-eared and coffee-stained and mottled with cigarette burns, the typewriting scratched out and written over.

He had been drunk most of the time. Well, not exactly drunk, but hardly sober. He had seemed unconnected to the world; he was somewhere else. His sons had been uneasy in his presence, glad when their two-week visit was done. He had tried, at the end, to speak honestly to them: had apologized for leaving them, had begged them to understand why he had done so, had sworn to them that he loved them very much. He had cried, that last night—an embarrassing moment. A few months after that they had word that he had died. Stephen had never been sure whether he'd killed himself or died of what had seemed to be a broken heart.

"Dad?" It was Stephen Jr., loping down the Long Path in his familiar Revell walk, long-legged, loose-limbed, with the air of a man completely at home, a man who knew in his bones—in his genes—that this was his territory.

The director eyed him with interest. He looked extremely photogenic, although of course you never could tell until you got the picture. At the beginning of the project the director and his crew had looked at everyone in both the Revell and the Shaughnessy families and had made some tests to decide who should appear on camera. Augusta was wonderful, as was Benjamin, and Kenneth, and the Abbott Revell twins, and several others, including Stephen. Stephen Jr. had at that time still been in India; in fact, before this morning, the television people had never laid eyes on him. Now they experienced that familiar click in the back of their brains, impossible to ignore: use him if you can. So it turned out that there were two narrators for the Abolition segment filmed that day, and when, the following week, they went out to Concord to do Walden Pond, Stephen Jr. was with them.

They parked in the car park across the road and walked down to the pond, past the little beach where there were only a few swimmers because school was still in session. Then, with the crew grumbling about their heavy burden of equipment, they went along the narrow path around the water until they reached the cairn of stones where Henry David Thoreau had had his famous little cabin in the woods. One of the Abbott Revells read selections from *Walden*, and then Stephen read *Civil Disobedience*. This had not been a scheduled part of the program, but when the director realized who Stephen was, he readily agreed to the young man's request. It went very well, accomplished in one take. The swimmers were too far away for their cries to intrude, and only every now and then did the camera need to stop for a passing airplane. Deep in the woods, birds twittered at the unaccustomed intrusion; an occasional trout broke the surface of the water; a lizard sunning itself on a large, flat rock, scuttled away from the interlopers. There were no deer now at Walden, as there had been in Thoreau's day, but otherwise the landscape was more or less as it was. In a rapidly changing world, it was pleasant to report that it probably always would be that way: unspoiled, as near to wilderness as you could get not half an hour away from the city.

The next week they celebrated the Bicentennial. A parade of tall ships six miles long rode up the harbor. On the flood tide, the USS *Constitution* sailed out to meet them and lead them in to dock. When the moment came, she would fire her guns, one round per minute. The last time her cannon were fired using real cannonballs was before the Civil War, when she had been chasing illegal slave ships. The Queen of England was coming, too. The descendants of the revolutionaries loved this, even if their Irish brethren did not. It would be, in short, an extremely photogenic day. Given their special place in the history of the city, the state, the country (not to mention the needs of the producers for exciting footage), the Revells—or one of them, at least—really had to be included in the day's festivities.

It would be absolutely splendid, everyone said: a descendant of one of the leaders of the Revolution meeting the Queen, the representative of the royalty against whom he had rebelled.

"All right," said Augusta—and of course it had to be Augusta; who else would it be? "I'll do it. I'll meet her, and I'll make polite conversation. But I won't curtsey! I'm too old, for one thing—I'd topple over, for sure—and I'm too much of a small-D democrat, for another."

At that the director began to worry. He knew that sometimes old people said outrageous things—perhaps to show that they were still alive, he didn't know. But he didn't want to risk ruining what would be a really tremendous opportunity, the Queen, for God's sake . . .

He needn't have worried. Augusta even allowed herself to be made up for the occasion. She wore a lovely blue dress, and her freshly coiffed white hair sparkled in the sun. It was a Sunday—a beautiful day. The Queen and Prince Philip came out of Old North Church, where they had attended Episcopal services. The previous year, the President of the United States had come here to light what he called a "third lantern for freedom." During that same trip he had gone to Concord on Patriots' Day. Some diehard Massachusetts rebels booed him because he had pardoned his disgraced predecessor, thus keeping up the grand old state's tradition of dissent. But no one booed today: everyone was ecstatic to see the Queen of England. Now there was a little ceremony in which the pastor of Old North, Reverend Dr. Golledge, presented the Queen with a replica of a silver chalice made by Paul Revere for communion services at the church. The Queen said something gracious. They all posed for the photographers, who went crazy. Then the television crew got its shot, and also a shot of the wildly cheering crowd, and the moment passed.

At the luncheon that followed, no cameras allowed, Augusta sat opposite the Queen and next to the mayor of Boston, a charming, *charming* Irish American whose late father-in-law, "Mother" Galvin, had been one of the better-known politicos of his day. The menu included cranberry soup, poached yearling silver salmon, and hearts of Boston lettuce. The Queen seemed oblivious to the heavy security all around, made necessary by the depth of Irish nationalist sentiment in Boston.

Then the party proceeded to Samuel Adams Park behind Faneuil Hall to watch a parade of ninety-eight costumed militia troops from all over New England. Those who were in a position to observe said that the Queen's pleasant, attentive expression never wavered. Augusta, on the other hand, became tired halfway through, and so Ben and Stephen Sr. took her home.

She had performed splendidly, they said: the television producer was very pleased.

9

In the fall, after the best of the foliage but before the snow, Cecelia came home.

Augusta had been dozing in her chair by the fire on this chilly October day, but now at the sound of her granddaughter's voice she came awake and out of her chair before Cecelia could come into the room.

"Gran!" She brought the cold in with her, and her fresh, sweet scent, her strong young arms in a fervent embrace.

"No—wait—let me see you." Augusta pulled back. She wanted to be sure that this was real. For the past few nights she'd been having bad dreams— premonitions that Cecelia wouldn't get back in time. But no: here she was, glowing with health, a little tired from the flight, perhaps, but otherwise well.

"What is it?" Cecelia said now. "Don't you recognize me?"

"I thought you might not get here in time."

"In time for what? Oh, Gran, don't be ridiculous, for heaven's sake don't greet me with gloom and doom—"

"It's not gloom and doom. I just wanted to see you again, that's all. And you're just in time for the documentary. It's starting tomorrow night."

"Starting? You mean it goes on and on, like one of those *Masterpiece Theater* things?"

"Something like that, yes. They tell me it's quite good. We haven't seen it, of course."

It *was* good. More than that, it was wonderful. The critics loved it. The audience loved it. The sponsors loved it. The people of Massachusetts, having weathered a bad post-war recession in the early seventies, and now saddled with what people saw as confiscatory taxes, were absolutely delighted with it for showing all the best that their doughty little state had to offer. Most of all, the city fathers of Boston loved it, since for the past two years their fair little city had been wracked by the torments of forced busing, and held up to national shame as enraged whites showered down hate on black children and order was maintained only by virtue of armed riot squads. The Pulitzer Prize for spot photography that year went to Stanley Forman of the *Boston Herald-American* who snapped the shutter just as a furious, shabbily dressed white youth attacked a black man, a man dressed in a three-piece suit, a man obviously not about to make trouble, a man obviously being unjustly set upon, attacked him with a flagstaff used as a lance, the sharp tip of it pointed at the black man's midriff, and from the flagstaff dragged Old Glory, dragged, appropriately enough for such a terrible moment, on the ground, the youth's face distorted with hate—oh, that was a picture, all right, to see the shame the Stars and Stripes were put to.

So the city fathers were glad of this good publicity. It made Boston, and indeed all of Massachusetts, look like a civilized place again.

Cecelia had not wanted to be part of the documentary, but she enjoyed watching it. When the rather exotic-looking Stephen Jackson Revell Jr. came on, she let out a little exclamation of surprise. "My God," she said. "Is that that drip?"

"Drip?" said Augusta in mock horror. "When was a Revell ever a drip?"

And she joined in Ceil's laughter.

In the days following the broadcast of *One American Family*, Augusta Griffin Revell Trowbridge became a full-blown celebrity. By the end of October her fan mail had grown to a thousand pieces a week. She was swamped—overwhelmed. She hadn't the faintest idea how to deal with it.

"You should demand that the producers pay for a secretary," said Cecelia one morning when the mailman had just delivered a big carton of letters onto the doorstep. "I mean, you can't be expected to answer every one of these, can you? And many of the writers are not just simple well wishers, either. They want complicated genealogical information, or recipes, or advice . . . They seem to look on you as a national treasure, Grandmother, and a public resource as well. I mean, I was glad to type a few letters at the beginning, but this is ridiculous."

In the end the producers, happy with their hit and not wanting to be accused of hastening the death of its star, provided a desk in their Boston offices, hired a pleasant, middle-aged temporary, and gave her several standard replies which she was at liberty to use as she saw fit. Each week she made a sampling of perhaps twenty of the most interesting letters and brought them to Augusta to read and dictate replies to if she wished.

Augusta's celebrity went beyond thousands of pen pals, of course. She was invited to appear on several television talk shows, one of which was broadcast nationwide; she was interviewed for ten newspaper pieces and three magazines, including a long biographical piece in *The Ladies Home Journal* and—the ultimate—a *People* cover. Some members of the Family thought that this was an incredibly vulgar way to end her long semi-public career, but of course they could do nothing to prevent it.

"They are just jealous," said Cecelia soothingly as she sat with Augusta at the dining room table sorting through the latest batch of fan mail. "Pay no attention to them. I think this is the greatest fun in the world. And I wouldn't have missed it for anything."

"How is First Night?" said Augusta, putting down the letter she had been trying to decipher and rubbing her tired eyes. "Is everything on schedule?"

"Hardly," laughed Cecelia. "But it's coming whether we're ready or not, so we might as well enjoy it."

One of the reasons for Cecelia's return had been a summons from a friend who had had an idea for a public celebration of New Year's Eve, a kind of giant outdoor festival of lights, with strolling players and indoor performances and friendly crowds thronging the streets and making them safe, all of which was to culminate in a gigantic fireworks display at midnight. Some people thought it a splendid idea; others thought it madness. Cecelia thought that it deserved a try. With her friend and two other staffers, she spent twelve or fourteen hours a day, now, trying to organize the event, to make sure that it had a reasonable chance of success.

From time to time, during those busy weeks, Stephen's face floated up briefly into her mind. What an attractive man he turned out to be, she would think; so different from what he was ten years ago. But then the telephone would ring, heralding some new crisis, and she would forget him again.

On Christmas Eve afternoon Cecelia left her office at noon. She did a little shopping—a very little—and now she sat comfortably with Augusta by the fire, relaxing, drinking tea. It was beginning to snow. In a few hours they were expected at the annual Christmas party at Guy Griffin Revell's in Louisburg Square. Perhaps, she thought, Augusta shouldn't try to go out in a snowstorm— no, certainly she shouldn't—and if Augusta didn't go, she would stay here with her.

She was aware that Augusta was watching her. She smiled. "Hello, Gran."

"Hello, yourself. Everything all right?"

"Of course. I was just wondering if the printer will have the programs ready on time—the schedules of events."

They heard the door bell ring. The door to the hall was closed because of drafts, and so they could not hear the exchange between the caller, whoever it was, and the housekeeper.

The door opened; the housekeeper looked in. "Mr. Stephen Jackson Revell, ma'am, and Mr. Stephen Jr."

Augusta brightened. "Of course. Bring them in." And to Cecelia, "You don't mind, do you, dear?" The girl had an odd look on her face, as if she didn't know whether she was amused or annoyed.

"Of course not," she said, and then they were in, and she couldn't say anything more.

Stephen Sr. had always admired Augusta—it was the rebellious Jackson blood in him, he thought—and never more than these past few months. So he had gotten up a kind of scroll, a graceful little message of all their admiration for her, and he had gone around and gotten everyone to sign it, even those who had carped at her recent high visibility—a long, rolled-up thing, and when he looked out and saw the snow, he guessed that she might not get to Guy's that night. It was only a little way away, down Marlborough and around the Garden and up to Louisburg Square on the Hill, and of course she would be chauffeured—but not on a night like this. There was too much of a chance that she might slip even in the few steps from the house to the car, or going up the steps into Guy's.

"Hello, Ceil." Young Stephen took both her hands; his were cold, but his smile was warm, he seemed very glad to see her. "A long time," he said. "How are you?"

"Yes," she said. "A long time." Odd, how she didn't want to let go his hands, cold as they were. "I'm fine, thanks. Very well, in fact. And you?" My God, she thought, he really has changed—he's an entirely different person, looks different, sounds different, he's *gorgeous*. She suddenly felt a little awkward, which was not what she was accustomed to feeling, not at all.

"So here it is, dear Augusta," said Stephen, "with all our love. We are very proud of you—you've been simply splendid, and we wanted to tell you so."

"Stephen, this is—I don't know what to say," said Augusta; and, indeed, she didn't.

He laughed. "We were sure you wouldn't. That's one reason we did it. Come, now, cousin. Admit it. You love this new role you've taken on. We just wanted to let you know that we're pretty pleased with you as well. I met someone the other day, and when he heard my name, he said, 'Oh, I say, are you related to that Augusta?' It put me up a notch or two, I can tell you."

They all laughed, then, and relaxed a little, and Augusta said that she'd unwind the scroll later, she didn't want to spill tea on it, but they must stay for a bit, and perhaps they would be so kind as to walk Cecelia up to Guy's, since she herself was most certainly not going out in this storm.

Which of course they were happy to do. And later still, when everyone left to go caroling, Stephen took Cecelia's arm and held her back a little from the main body of the group, which over the years fluctuated but which, with neighborhood additions, almost always went over a hundred. The snow had ceased some time ago, and now a half-moon hung above the gabled rooftops of the narrow brick houses that lined Mt. Vernon Street. In its light, she could see Stephen's face—kind, concerned, attentive, admiring—all the things one wanted a man to be, so different from what she'd thought he was when she first knew him. So they walked a little behind the others, humming a bit, comfortable in their silence.

Then he said, "You missed being in the documentary."

"Thank God. I don't photograph well."

"I'll bet you do."

She clutched his arm to keep from falling as she negotiated an unshoveled crossing. When he had her safely across, he stopped and put his arms around her. In the distance, around the corner, the carolers were singing: "Hark the Herald Angels sing . . ."

And then he kissed her, and the music that she heard was altogether different.

They were very warm, the two of them, but even so, the night was cold and soon Ceil was shivering.

"Come on," he said. "Let's go eat."

"Where?"

"I imagine the Parker House is open."

It was. They sat side by side on a banquette and talked and ate and talked some more. At some point Ceil called Augusta to let her know where she was, and with whom, so that Augusta wouldn't worry.

Augusta's response to this piece of information was: "Wonderful!"

"Why wonderful?" said Ceil. The telephone booth was hot and stuffy and smelled of strong perfume spilled perhaps by some previous telephoner. She wanted to get back to Stephen. To get back—and not to leave him again. Ever. But still, she wanted to know: "Why do you say that, Gran?"

"You know why," said Augusta. Ceil could hear the smile in her voice. "Have fun," she added. "I'll see you in the morning."

Later, Stephen walked her back to Marlborough Street; later still, he walked home. Ceil crept up to her bedroom adjoining her grandmother's and made herself a hot water bottle (Augusta religiously turned down the heat at night) and crawled between the freezing sheets and lay awake all night, thinking. What she thought was that in the past twelve hours—in just that short time—her life had changed, had completely turned around, and she was happier than she had ever been.

Augusta usually spent Christmas at Ben's on Mt. Vernon Street, and of course Ceil, happily returned to the Family once again, went with her. But midway through the afternoon, when dinner had just finished, she excused herself and walked down the hill and around the corner to Stephen Sr.'s on West Cedar Street.

"Hello," she said, and it was as natural as anything, as if she'd always been with them, with that particular branch of the Family.

That night, she and Stephen went to a Christmas concert at Emmanuel Church. The next day Stephen came to the First Night office to help out. Less than a week, now, and still a thousand details needed to be tended to. No matter. They'd make it. That night he took Ceil to Durgin Park for dinner. The next day he helped her again; the next night they went to Locke-Ober's. Ceil laughed and said she'd have to start watching her waistline; Stephen laughed and said he'd watch it for her.

And so, in no time at all, it became obvious to everyone, not least themselves, that they were seriously in love. For the most part people were pleased; those who had frowned upon Stephen's activism in the sixties were happy that he had calmed down. And of course, who better to marry than one of their own?

On New Year's Eve, which from then on in Boston was known as First Night—and a tremendous success it was—Stephen waited until the fireworks were going off, much sound and light, and then in the middle of the display, he asked her to marry him.

And on Augusta's eighty-seventh birthday they were married at Isabella's palace.

2. WALDEN II

1

"I don't believe it!" Cecelia, shocked and very pale, took the newspaper that Stephen thrust into her hands and stared at the story and its accompanying photo: NORTH SHORE LANDMARK TO GO CONDO.

"Believe it," said Stephen. "The part I have trouble with is that he never said a word to anyone about getting rid of it—let alone about selling it to a developer."

"It" was Revell Hall; "he" was Cecelia's brother Miles.

Cecelia shifted uncomfortably in her chair. She was eight-and-three-quarters-months pregnant, unable to eat, unable to sleep, unable to put her feet up to rest because she suffered agonizing leg cramps—miserable, in short, and in no mood to hear bad news about her brother.

"They're going to do a 'tasteful' five-unit renovation of the main house," Stephen went on, "and twenty-five town houses 'in the spirit of the original.' Can you imagine? Twenty-five town houses on that property? They won't even have room to park their cars. Clever boy, that brother of yours, pulling this off without a hint to anyone."

At eight o'clock on this June morning it was already very warm. Cecelia wiped perspiration from her forehead and looked again at the newspaper. The story was beginning to sink in: her brother Miles, to whom their grandmother Augusta had willed Revell Hall in good faith that he would cherish the property and in turn will it to a descendant of his own, had instead sold that patrimony for a mess of pottage—how much?

"Two million," said Stephen. "And look who the developer is. Tom Shaughnessy. His father was governor, back in the forties. And *his* father had a construction company, I think. This fellow's sister is married to Cousin Adam

669

Griffin Revell. Looks like he can't get close enough to the Revells, wouldn't you say?"

"No," Ceil said. "I wouldn't." She let the paper drop. "I don't want to think about it anymore." She tried to smile at him and almost succeeded. They were in the breakfast room, formerly the conservatory, which opened out onto the tiny, brick-walled back garden of the Marlborough Street house. She loved this house that Augusta had left her, and she had thought that Miles was as happy with his bequest as she was with hers. Apparently not.

Stephen watched her anxiously. He took her hand, but she was too hot, too uncomfortable to have her hand held, and so she took it back. They had been married a little more than a year. When she announced that she was pregnant, they had both been delighted. Worth it to get a baby, she thought now; but only just.

"Wherever Gran is," she said, "I hope she's not aware of this. She'd turn over in her grave if she thought somebody was going to condo-ize Revell Hall."

She thought for a moment. "I suppose there's nothing we can do," she said.

"I'll talk to Cousin Ben, but I think not. It is Miles's property, he can do with it what he wants."

The following week their son was born. They named him Daniel Jackson Revell for his great-great-great-grandfather. He was a fine big baby, healthy and alert. In late July, when he was six weeks old, they took him to Nantucket for the remainder of the summer: to the village of Siasconset, where Stephen Sr. had had a cottage for many years. Stephen Jr. had not been there for a long time—not since before he went to India—but he had many happy memories of childhood summers running the beach, bicycling out past the moors, and, when he was old enough, earning pretty good money at one summer job or another in Nantucket Town.

So now while his mother happily tended her new grandson, he and Ceil walked the beach and tried not to think about what Miles had done. "I don't care if he is my brother," said Ceil angrily, "I'll never speak to him again!"

Given new sense of purpose by the birth of their son, they talked instead about what they wanted to do with themselves for the rest of their lives—or for the next few years, at least. Since his return to Massachusetts, Stephen had been working for a grassroots group dedicated to the preservation of the environment, but after his heady days at the cutting edge of the antiwar movement, this was tame work indeed. So when Stephen Sr. heard that the Harpooner House in town was for sale at a good price, he asked them whether they'd be interested in buying it and fixing it up and becoming innkeepers. "You'd have to work only half the year," he said. "So you wouldn't be marooned out here all winter. That's when folks go crazy, February on Nantucket."

That evening they went to the Opera House for dinner. Later they walked down Main Street to Straight Wharf. It was the beginning of August: the height of the tourist season. The sidewalks were thronged with sunburned, contented-looking people eating ice cream cones. Along the wharves many luxury yachts were anchored; along the narrow streets all around, pricy boutiques were open to catch the late trade. And yet, despite the activity, the lights and the crowds of people, it was all very low-key, nothing gaudy or tacky. In her modest and unassuming way, and despite the shift from whaling to touristing, the "Gray Lady of the Sea," as she was called, had managed to maintain a certain dignity. On the entire island of Nantucket there was not one traffic light, not one neon sign. Buildings were put up according to a strict code: unpainted shingles of either cedar or white pine that would weather to the island's color of fog-gray. Like a strong-minded New England lady of a certain age, Nantucket would not be trifled with; she would keep her integrity no matter what. Certainly she would never become, say, another Coney Island.

They walked around to look again at the Harpooner House: a modest place tucked away on Hussey Street, but with a good-sized yard. It was quiet here away from the crowds, and now, in the darkness, with the fog creeping over the island, the foghorn at Brant Point sounding its mournful cry, the sharp salt smell in the night air, it seemed as though they had escaped to the past; and for the moment, at least, it seemed not a bad place to be. Both of them in their different ways had been actively involved in the events of their time; now, with their child born, it seemed right to draw in a bit, pull back, make their nest, let the world and its business take care of itself for a while.

The next day they signed a purchase and sale agreement. The inn had eight rooms, all of them needing redecoration. The roof leaked; the plumbing was uncertain. Nevertheless: "This is right," Ceil said. "Perhaps not forever—but for now, yes."

They spent the winter fixing the place up. The next summer they were ready for guests. They had plenty; they almost never had a vacancy. Little Dan thrived on the island; he grew rapidly, and was a great favorite of the guests, many of whom turned out to be yearly repeaters and, more important, friends. Many of them had seen *One American Family*; they were charmed by the idea that their host had been part of it.

Stephen was not sure that a semi-famous innkeeper on an altogether famous island was what he had in mind to be, but there was nothing else, for the moment, that he wanted to do. He had tried once before to play a part on the great stage of events, and he had found it both painful and difficult; and if in the end "his side" won, it had been at such great cost, at the sacrifice one way or another of a good part of his generation, that he was not sure that the victory was worth the price.

So he was content to stay on that small, barren, exquisitely beautiful island save for a few months in winter when they went back to town to catch up on the world; and one night, looking in on his small son sleeping peacefully curled up clutching a well-worn bear, he had a little epiphany: after wandering literally around the world trying to find tranquility and happiness, he had returned to find it at home. The fact that this was a cliché did not bother him at all; what mattered was that it was true.

He leaned over and kissed little Dan's forehead; then he went out to the small room that served as both living and dining room to find Ceil, and he kissed her as well. She understood: she returned his embrace. For both of them, for a while, it was enough.

2

And then all of a sudden, almost before anyone could tell how it happened, the old Bay State transformed itself from its previous incarnation as a place of depression and high taxes into a lusty, burgeoning economy. "Taxachusetts," people used to jeer. In the oil patch of the Southwest, during the oil shortage of the early seventies, people had sported bumper stickers that read, "LET THEM FREEZE IN THE DARK." Now no one was freezing, and no one was in the dark, either. Something exciting was happening. The renaissance of Boston had begun with the Prudential building in 1965 and continued through the Lego-block new city hall in 1969; it came to blissful climax with the opening of the Faneuil Hall/Quincy Market complex in the Bicentennial year. Dozens of other new buildings had gone up as well, and not only in Boston. All over the state, things were stirring. You could almost watch her coming back to life. Lowell got some state money and some federal money and then some private money, and before anyone knew, the old red-brick city on the Merrimack was transformed from a terminal case into the first Urban National Park. Canal barges carried tourists past the giant mill buildings now filled with the new businesses of high technology, and uniformed National Park Rangers lectured on the long-gone Yankee mill women. Worcester renovated its magnificent old Mechanics' Hall and then built nearby a new state-of-the-art performance arena. Stockbridge established its Norman Rockwell Museum in memory of the artist who had lived there for many years, and had a hit on its hands from day one. Old Sturbridge Village had never been so busy, its costumed guides introducing a way of life—nineteenth century rural—that was as foreign to many of its visitors as life on a South Sea island. In summertime, in the Berkshires, you could hardly get a ticket for Tanglewood, or Jacob's Pillow, or the Williamstown Theater. Plimoth Plantation was nearly overrun. Faneuil Hall and Quincy Market had more tourists than Disneyland.

In 1977 the governor issued a proclamation on the fiftieth anniversary of the execution of Sacco and Vanzetti. It stated that their trial and the subsequent judicial reviews had been "permeated by prejudice." The Republican leader of the State Senate, a Yankee, promptly sponsored a resolution, which the Senate passed, condemning the governor for "casting a dark shadow" over the Commonwealth's judicial system. No matter. Times had changed. In 1977 Sacco and Vanzetti would never have been tried, let alone convicted and executed. By 1977 Massachusetts had a very different reputation from the one it had had fifty years before. Now the pendulum of history had swung, and the state that had been among the most "conservative" had acquired a reputation for being one of the most "liberal"—a dirty word, for many people. And not only "liberal," but downright cantankerous—as if her people were marching to Henry David Thoreau's "different drummer." Nowhere was this more glaringly apparent than in the presidential election of 1972, when Massachusetts was the *only state* to vote for the Democratic candidate. A year or so later, when the victorious Republican was brought down in disgrace, folks from Boston to Stockbridge sported a bumper sticker that read, "DON'T BLAME ME, I'M FROM MASSACHUSETTS." Early in the 1980s a prominent Texas Republican was asked whether he had ever been to a Communist country.

"Yes, I have," he said.

"Which one, sir?"

"Massachusetts"—this with a wink and a leer, a smarmy wordless message: those folks up there are so far left, they're downright un-Amerricun!

But such little digs were mere mosquito bites on a radiantly healthy body. Things got better and better. For a while there were boom times in the old Bay State—a technology-driven prosperity that people called the "Massachusetts Miracle." Like the Industrial Revolution that had preceded it a hundred and fifty years before, it was a product of Yankee ingenuity—a spinoff of all that concentrated brainpower.

Massachusetts became the trendiest place in the nation. By 1985 there were more yuppies per square foot in the Back Bay of Boston than any place on earth. Many of them had gone to college or graduate school in Massachusetts and liked it so much that they stayed on. They drove rents up and salaries down, but they also gave a powerful energy to the old place—a sense of urgent life.

3

One summer in the late eighties, people had a look at the future, and they did not like what they saw.

All spring, the weather had been dry, so that by June, when summer officially began, the place where heavily populated eastern Massachusetts got its water, the Quabbin Reservoir, was only two-thirds full. Strict rationing was put into effect: no cars washed, no lawns watered, no swimming pools filled. People grumbled, but the government put on a heavy barrage of propaganda, and by and large the rules were obeyed.

June was a hot month, and July was even hotter. Towns that had to rely on well water rather than reservoirs began to consider even stricter rationing as the wells began to go dry. The entire northeastern United States suffered under a heat wave that showed no sign of letting up. Brownouts happened more and more. The government asked people not to use their air conditioners, but when those people went into freezing shopping malls and then went home to toss and turn in their stifling bedrooms, they were unwilling to obey. The bureaucrats in charge of energy policy explained that when their computers had made their forecasts some years before, they had assumed full power at both the Plymouth and Seabrook nuclear power plants. But Plymouth—always unreliable—had been down for months, and Seabrook had never had more than a five percent trial run.

Day after day the temperature stayed above ninety degrees. A new phrase entered the language: "the greenhouse effect." It meant that the planet was warming up. The ozone layer that protected the earth from the sun's lethal rays was being destroyed. Already it had at least one large hole in it, and all of it was thinning. And the same pollutants that were destroying the ozone were also creating a lethal cloud of smog over most of the nation's cities—a cloud that, this broiling summer, could not be dissipated. And it was not just cities. People traveling to Martha's Vineyard and Nantucket on the ferry boats were dismayed, as they pulled away from the shore, to see a brownish-yellow cloud over Cape Cod, where the main commercial highway, Route 28, often resembled a parking lot.

When those vacationing motorists reached their destinations, many of them, capering down to the beach to dive into the surf, were halted by the sight of—ugh!—indescribable filth, medical waste and sewage and God knew what all. In Boston Harbor nauseated cameramen photographed cancerous fish that had lived and died in the chemical soup that lapped the wharves where granite warehouses had been transformed into expensive condominiums and much fancy new construction had gone up. Whew! What a smell!

Out across the country, that presidential year, the Republican candidate was red-baiting—or rather, Massachusetts-baiting—his way into the White House. He put out the word that his opponent, who was the governor of Massachusetts, was somehow by virtue of that fact less than patriotic. Only a man who was unpatriotic would want to govern such a hotbed of subversion as the Bay State. The Republican was a native of Milton, a few miles south of Boston, but his handlers kept quiet about that inconvenient fact, and the press never brought it up. He was practicing the "Devil" theory of political discourse: the man who can identify and vilify a devil—any devil—will win. Massachusetts herself had played this game often enough. Sometimes, as for Cotton Mather, the Devil was just that—Satan incarnate. Other times the Devil was the British Parliament, or William Lloyd Garrison, or the famine Irish, or labor agitators, or the IWW, or "reds," or Sacco and Vanzetti, or—often enough—good old Harvard. One of the Republican's henchmen, in fact, put out the statement that people who lived in certain parts of Massachusetts like Cambridge (home to Harvard) or Brookline (the governor's town) were even less patriotic than other Massachusetts folk. He knew it, he said, because he used to live around those parts.

Once upon a time the Devil had been in Massachusetts, and people had died because of it.

Now the Devil was Massachusetts herself. No one died, but a good many people were symbolically tarred and feathered.

It was an ugly time.

4

"Say, friend! How do I get to Walden Pond?"

August 11, 1988. Temperature 97 degrees. Humidity 89 percent. Smog alert: air quality unsafe.

The question is shouted from the open window of a van with Iowa plates to the open window of a scarred and rusting vehicle that is a battered veteran of Boston's traffic wars. They smolder side by side in adjacent lanes of stalled traffic on the Central Artery, a huge, ugly scar of a road built in 1958 on green iron girders above the water side of the city of Boston, thus effectively cutting her off from the sea that had for three centuries been her life's blood.

Thirty years before, the Central Artery was an expert's solution to the problems of Boston traffic. Now it had become a hideous eyesore, impossibly clogged from dawn to long past dark, fatally clogged like a damaged artery through the city's heart. There were many skilled heart surgeons in this world-famous medical center, but no traffic surgeon who could relieve the city's deadly congestion. Boston had the distinction of being the birthplace not only of the American Revolution and the Parker House roll and the system of mutual funds which were originally called "Boston funds," but also of the condition, in full flower this hot day, known as "gridlock." It was said to have happened for the first time on New Year's Eve afternoon, 1963, about four o'clock, when traffic in the city ground to a halt. Every intersection was blocked by competing lines of cars, each unwilling to give way for the other; no one could move. Eventually, some genius unsnarled the jam, but it had been a close call; people might have been stuck there for the rest of their lives.

"Say, friend! I just want to get to Walden Pond! Isn't it out in Concord?" The Iowan's face is dripping perspiration, his children are restless and cranky, his wife unforgiving of his stupidity which has landed them in this mess—a mess from which, apparently, there is no escape. She has never heard of gridlock, but she knows a disaster when she sees one.

"Walden Pond!" The Bostonian laughs. His thin florid face breaks into a thousand wrinkles. He turns to the friend sitting beside him. "He says he wants to go to Walden Pond!" The friend begins to laugh also. Walden Pond! That's rich!

The Iowans gaze helplessly at the landscape. In the middle distance they see the lower stories of the new glass and granite towers of downtown Boston glittering faintly through the grayish-yellow cloud that sits on the city like tangible malaise from the mind of an angry Mother Earth. Up ahead a truck has overturned, spilling toxic waste. In Dorchester, this day, a band of youths has rioted because they cannot dip their toes into the filthy water of Boston Harbor. Eleven beaches in and around Boston have been closed due to washed-up medical waste—syringes, bags of blood, dead laboratory rats—and sewage overflow. By midnight tonight the city will record nine deaths from the heat.

Walden Pond? Walden Pond? Who in this nightmare, this urban Hell, has ever heard of Walden Pond?

Say, friend! How do I get there?

Walden Pond is two miles outside Concord on the Walden Road.

Or it is a place in men's minds anywhere on earth: a leaving-behind of life's cares, a voyage into the wilderness, into a verdant region of the heart that all men long for. Thoreau called it "the eternal imperative of freedom." And since we cannot all go there, we celebrate Henry Thoreau, who did it for us.

Some men shook the dust of civilization from their feet and headed West. Some men went a'whaling. Henry went to Walden Pond instead, and made it immortal.

So now Walden glowed in people's minds like those other sacred places, like Avalon and Atlantis and Stonehenge, Delphi and El Dorado—a symbol of something infinitely precious, a touchstone for our deepest instinctive needs.

You *can* get there from here. But it is a journey that gets longer all the time as Walden recedes, shimmering, glimmering, a fathomless glacial pool deep in the woods, an enchanted place ever more precious as we encroach upon it. It is a place where the mourning dove coos her welcome to the dawn, and shy forest creatures come to drink at the water's edge, and the woodchuck rambles through the trees, and the solitary goose, honking, swoops across the autumn sky searching for his flock, and finds them, and sails off among them in that magnificent undulating V.

"In Wildness is the preservation of the World," said Thoreau.

And if wild Nature is our Great Mother, and if we foul her waters and pollute her air and destroy her forests and slaughter her species into extinction— if all these things are so, then let it be at Walden that the rescue begins, let it be at Walden that men and women together begin the long struggle back.

Who killed Mother Earth?

No mystery there: the most dangerous creature on Earth killed her—Man.

Say, friend! Walden Pond is where I want to go!

5

"What is it?" said Stephen. "Something wrong?"

His cousin, Matthew Abbott Revell, grinned in a shamefaced way. He was nearly as tall as Stephen, a year or two younger, but so different that he seemed to be from another family: a face that was neither handsome nor strong, weak eyes hidden behind thick glasses, a nervous habit of biting his thin lips.

"Yes," he said. "Something is very wrong."

He's gone and gotten some poor girl pregnant, thought Stephen, and she wants to marry him. If ever there was a man who was a confirmed bachelor, Matthew Abbott Revell was it. Supported by his father Dwight's seemingly limitless fortune, he'd drifted from one interest to another; now, in his forties, he was a familiar figure in Concord, Massachusetts, where he lived in a pre-Revolutionary house complete with a restored Colonial herb garden and a secret hiding place for escaped slaves traveling on the Underground Railroad. He'd written and self-published several pamphlets on Concord's history, and on the strength of those he had a reputation for being vaguely literary.

Stephen waited. He'd never known Matthew well, and he had been surprised at the invitation that had come for himself and Ceil and Danny to spend Columbus Day weekend with Matthew in Concord. They no longer wintered on the mainland because Danny, age ten, needed to be in school, and so they were glad enough to come over even for only a few days. It was the height of the foliage color, and as they walked through the woods, the sunlight filtered through red and yellow leaves to cast an almost iridescent light. Overhead, the sky was that deep October blue that came annually with the turning of the leaves; as Stephen looked up he saw, high above, a diving hawk. There was little sound: their footsteps on the narrow dirt path, the occasional "caw" of a crow; the wind rustling through the forest.

They came to the cairn and stopped: the little pile of stones at the head of the miniature bay where Henry David Thoreau had built his one-room house. Ceil and Danny had stopped to examine something along the way.

Matthew pulled a couple of apples from his rucksack and handed one to Stephen. "I come here a lot," he said. "Sometimes I feel—I don't know. A spirit. *The* spirit. It's amazingly quiet here, for a place so close to civilization. And I think, if I listen hard enough, I'll hear Thoreau playing his flute."

He flushed a little. He was very shy, very reserved; ordinarily he did not make such confidences. But he needed Stephen's help, and he was trying to approach him as best he knew how.

Stephen held up his hand: listen. A melodic trill of birdsong.

"There," Stephen said.

Matthew nodded enthusiastically. "That's right. I mean, this place has a kind of presence about it, you know? And in the summer, when they're swimming down at the beach—well, that's all right, I guess, although I know people in Concord don't like it, they think the beach attracts all kinds of riffraff. But I don't mind. But what I'm saying is, all those folks kind of destroy the atmosphere. So I like to come down here to this end, and just sit on this rock and think about Henry David, and every now and then I'll hear—something. I know it may sound crazy, but—"

"No," said Stephen. "It doesn't sound crazy at all." He saw a flash of bright blue some way back along the trail: Ceil's sweater. "So what's wrong?" he said, munching his apple. "You wanted to talk to me about—"

"Yes," said Matthew. He had been gazing at the pond; now he turned to meet Stephen's eyes. His expression was agonized, Stephen thought. Something very serious indeed was on his mind.

"They're going to build an office park and two hundred and fifty condos," Matthew said abruptly.

Out toward the middle of the pond a fish broke the surface with a little *plop*! Wind riffled the tops of the trees; the sun was warm, but in the shadow of the pines the air was cool, harbinger of the long cold months ahead.

"Who is?" said Stephen. "Where?"

"Right here at Walden Pond. An outfit called Continental Development from Dallas has proposed the office park. And a couple of local fellows, if you can believe it, want to put up the condos. The offices will be on Brister's Hill, which is literally a stone's throw—seven hundred yards—away. Thoreau used to go there to pick huckleberries. Nineteen acres, they've bought. It'll have parking for more than five hundred cars. Can you imagine what that will do to this place?"

"And the condominiums?"

"They're going to be on Bear Garden Hill. That's over there." Matthew waved his arm. "A little farther away, but not much. It's still all land that Thoreau walked, that he loved. It's still—desecration."

"Can't they be stopped?"

"I don't know. Apparently the town has to allow the condominiums to be developed because of some quirk in the law. They'll have low-income units, and Concord, of course, doesn't have enough low-income housing, not enough to meet state requirements, at any rate. What used to be the Thoreau family's house in Concord was sold last year to a private party for just under a million dollars, can you believe it? And it's nothing magnificent, just an ordinary New England frame house. They may be able to scale back the development somewhat, but I don't think they can stop it. But in any case the offices are the real danger. They'll be much more destructive to the environment. A hundred and fifty thousand square feet, can you imagine? The traffic, the pollution, the absolute ruination—"

"And the town of Concord has approved this?"

"Apparently."

"They want the tax money."

"I suppose they do."

"So what are you going to do about it?" Stephen was beginning to understand why Matthew had summoned him.

Matthew flushed a little, as if he had been asked to reveal some shameful secret about himself. "I don't know," he said. "I've tried to talk to a few people, but I'm not very good at convincing anyone about anything. You have to remember that people in Concord, by and large, don't like Henry Thoreau. They never did. He was always eccentric—although you know as well as I do that there are more eccentrics in the town of Concord than anywhere else in the country, so it isn't that exactly. It's that he was, ah—"

"Lower class?" said Stephen. "A surveyor and a manufacturer of pencils, rather than a textile magnate or a China merchant? Not a genteel literary man like Emerson?"

"That's it. They looked down their noses at Thoreau. They called him a drunk, which he certainly wasn't. Said he stole their pies cooling on their windowsills. They could never understand why anyone with a perfectly good Harvard education would just drift through his life without any purpose—"

"Or none that they could see, at any rate."

"Right. None that they could see. And of course all the time he was writing the books and essays that would make him immortal—a prophet. That's what he really was, I think. A prophet. Not only on civil disobedience—well, you know about that, don't you, from the war?—but on Nature as well. That's really what is coming into its own, I think. His writing on Nature. You know, he said, 'In Wildness is the preservation of the World.' Isn't that perfect? When everything's getting so built up—including this place, it looks like—we need to remember: 'In Wildness is the preservation of the World.' "

Matthew's face was a study in despair. "Stephen, I want to ask you to help. I do have a few people in Concord who've volunteered, but we don't know exactly how to proceed. And I remembered that you were such a moving force during the war, and I thought perhaps you could at least advise us."

"What exactly is it that you want to do?"

"We want to stop this development. Both of them, if we can, but certainly the offices."

Stephen nodded. "I don't blame you. I'd want to stop it, too, if I lived here. Don't they realize that Henry David Thoreau is a world figure? I'll bet people come from all over to see this spot. And isn't there a Lyceum or a Thoreau Library or something?"

"Yes, that's right." Matthew looked considerably happier. "Only the other day they told me they had a visit from some Germans. And someone from Sweden, I believe. And do you know who came last year? The Mahatma Gandhi's nephew! That's right. Isn't that amazing? The town of Concord has a resource here that they just won't recognize. Of all the people who lived here, Thoreau is by far the most famous—and the most important. Stephen, I'm so glad you understand. I knew you would. And if you could just give us some advice, we'd be so grateful to you—"

"Wait a minute. Wait a minute." Stephen held up his hand. "I do understand. Of course I do. But what you're going to try to do is—well, it's very difficult. Continental is a big company, you said. They'll have the best lawyers, tie you up in court for a long time, cost you a lot of money—a fight like this can be a killer."

"I know. Do you think I haven't taken all that into consideration? But we just can't let them come in and ruin this place, can we?"

"People in Concord don't seem to care."

"That's right. They don't, a lot of them. So we need to save them from themselves. They have no idea how bad they'll look, all over the world, when people find out that they've let Walden be destroyed. Do you know what one of the selectwomen said? She said that Thoreau was just a hippie, and that if he were alive today, he'd probably be put away. Can you imagine? 'Put away'—that's what she said. His ideas were 'way-out,' she said, and 'not very modern now.' Can you *imagine?*"

"No," said Stephen, laughing. "Really, someone said that?"

"That's why we have this problem," said Matthew. "Because people can't see beyond the end of their noses. And that's why— Listen, Stephen. We really need your help. I have a few people here who are going to put up some kind of resistance, but none of us has any experience at organizing a protest. And that's what we're going to have to do, no question about it. Organize a major protest, get media attention, bring in people who will donate money and time and energy. And you've done all that. I remember during the war—"

"No."

Matthew looked like a small boy who, for no apparent reason, had just been slapped across the face.

"Matthew, I can't. I simply can't. I have a family, I have a business to run, all kinds of responsibilities. I don't think you know what it is that you're asking."

"Well, I do in a way. I mean, I know it would be a lot of work. I'd help as much as I could, of course. But I'm not asking it for myself, Stephen. I'm asking for the sake of Walden Pond. For Walden Woods. All this." As he waved his arm, they looked down the path to see Ceil and Danny approaching. When they arrived, clutching handfuls of leaves and acorns and other found treasure, Stephen briefly reiterated what Matthew had said. Ordinarily Ceil's face was expressive; now, he saw, she was careful to show no reaction. He was not sure what that meant.

"I know it's a lot to ask," Matthew said to Ceil. "But think what it would mean to lose Walden. Just think!"

"I can't," she said. "It would be—well, it would be unthinkable, wouldn't it?"

For a moment Matthew thought of asking Ceil to help him persuade Stephen. But then he thought better of it. This was something they would have to work out on their own.

And so he said nothing more for the rest of the weekend; only when Ceil and Stephen and Danny were taking their leave on the Monday did he say, "You will think about what I said?"

"Oh, yes," said Stephen. "I'll think about it."

He was, Ceil thought, rather abstracted on the ferry trip across Nantucket Sound. Ordinarily he was busy with the boy, pointing out landmarks, chatting with the other passengers. But now as he stood at the rail, watching the horizon, he had an expression upon his face that, for once, she could not read; and he didn't seem to want to talk to anyone.

6

The week after their visit to Concord they picked up the paper one day to see that three gray whales, late in making their annual migration south, had been trapped in the ice at Point Barrow, Alaska.

For days the world held its breath as the trio of leviathans struggled to get free. By this time whales had been hunted intensively for more than two centuries, and most people were aware that whales—all kinds of whales—were an endangered species. Many people had great affection for whales, seeing in them, perhaps, a symbol of Nature in her most primeval aspect. For some years now there had been an active conservation effort to save the ones that remained.

Now, on the nightly television news, the world saw the three creatures lunging up from their tiny holes in the ice, pushing their big, barnacled snouts into the air, desperately trying to breathe. The sound of their laboring lungs was caught by the microphones and relayed into millions of homes; and it was that sound, more than any other thing, that aroused the public's sympathy. Lunge wheeze *splash* . . . lunge wheeze *splash* . . . Why, those whales are going to drown! We have to do something! We have to save them! Cut a channel! Get an icebreaker in here! Hurry!

Amazingly, the United States had no icebreaker. As the world watched, a growing cadre of conservationists tried everything they could think of to break the ice and free the whales in some other way. Nothing worked.

By the end of the second week of their captivity, public sentiment was at fever pitch. Do something! Anything! The cameras sent pictures of polar bears lurking, waiting for the chance to kill the whales and eat them, kept at a distance only by the hordes of humans standing around helplessly on the two-foot-thick ice, close enough to touch the enormous gray barnacled snouts coming up, over and over but always more slowly, desperately trying to breathe.

Finally one morning only two whales surfaced; the third was never seen again.

The public was in agony. *Save those whales!* The President sent his heartfelt good wishes to the would-be rescue workers: our hearts are with you and our prayers are with you also, he said. By now hundreds of media had descended on Point Barrow in a kind of feeding frenzy. Environmentalists who had worked for years to arouse the public to save the whales, or save the elephants, or save the oceans, were incredulous at the onslaught of attention that these individual creatures, as affecting as they were, had managed to generate.

But the media knew how to milk a good story when it saw one, and so it continued to give the saga a large play, and the public therefore continued to be enthralled at the stark, life-and-death drama being played out on the arctic wastes.

And then like a deus ex machina, help arrived: a Soviet icebreaker, the *Vladimir Arseniev*. In only a few hours it cut a channel through the ice. At last the whales were free—two of them, at any rate.

"Thank heaven," said Ceil when the happy news came. "I'm not sure I could have stood the tension any longer."

Danny, no fool, heard the sarcasm in her voice. "Didn't you care about them, Mom?"

"Of course I cared. But I'm not sure I cared as much as everybody else seemed to. I mean, look at the animals that are being slaughtered all over the world—including whales—that we never hear about. What about them?"

"But that's the point," said Stephen. "That's exactly why these three aroused so much feeling. Because they were three specific creatures, not a statistic of thousands. Everybody feels bad about the thousands, but they also feel powerless to do anything about them. Here, on the other hand, you had three creatures—and very appealing creatures, as odd as it seems—that deeply touched people's hearts. A specific hook on which to hang all their concerns about the environment."

"Like Walden Pond," said Ceil. It was not a question, although as she said it she cast a quizzical glance at him. They were walking. It was a cold, gray afternoon at the end of October. As they came out toward the moors, they were hit with the full force of the wind gusting from the northwest. Ahead stretched the miles of moorland, gray this day like the sky, blessedly empty, saved from development by a number of determined Nantucketers who had formed a trust to buy the land for conservation.

"Stephen? I said, like Walden Pond."

"I heard you."

"Have you changed your mind?"

"No."

So well did he know her, so well understand her every unspoken thought and feeling, that at once he knew that she was not entirely satisfied with his answer.

So he said, "Do you have a problem with that?"

And for just a moment too long she didn't reply.

"Ceil? What's wrong?"

"Nothing."

"Yes. Something is. Are you trying to tell me that you want me to—I don't know, start a big crusade? For Walden Pond? Have you been talking to Matthew?

"No. Of course not. And no, I'm not trying to tell you anything. I just—"

"What?" It was unlike her to be inarticulate; that alone raised a warning flag.

"I really think that Matthew was right when he said that you are one of the few people who could take on a job like that. You have the experience, the contacts—"

"They've all gone their separate ways. Some of them are dead."

"Still. You could do it if you wanted to."

"Which I don't."

"You're absolutely positive."

"Yes. I'm absolutely positive. Ceil, what is this? Are you trying to get me to do it? Do you have any idea what that would mean—to us, to the business, to our very own little family which right now is a terrific family, I think it's the best family I've ever seen, but if I go off on something like this, you know as well as I do what kind of strain that puts on people. It's like being in politics, and that's something I wouldn't wish on anyone."

"All right. I'm just asking."

"I have the impression you're persuading."

"No. Honestly I'm not. I just want to be sure that you are sure that you don't want to do it. Because if you don't, someone will. And you'll be watching him—"

"Or her."

"Or her, right—on television, and you'll be reading about him/her in the newspapers, and I don't want you to think, 'That should be me.' I don't want you to begin to resent staying here with us."

"Instead of . . . ?"

"Saving Walden."

"Or saving more than Walden."

"That, too."

"Like the Earth."

"Yes."

"That's a tall order."

"Yes."

"A big job."

"The job of a lifetime."

"Right. And I'm not going to try to do it."

"That's final?"

"That's final."

They had gotten to where Eel Point Road branched off Madaket, a good long walk, and so without saying anything more they turned around and went home.

7

Shortly into the New Year word came from Washington that Congress had voted itself a pay raise. Public opinion polls showed that politicians were held in low esteem; what was more, the public, rightly or wrongly (wrongly, thought Stephen) believed that congressional salaries were high enough, particularly when they were measured against the average worker's pay. So the public, encouraged by radio talk shows all over the country, worked itself into a great lather over the issue, and demonstrated its displeasure by mailing tea bags to members of Congress. Tens of thousands of tea bags flooded in to congressional offices—hundreds of thousands.

People in Massachusetts, still smarting from the insults they had suffered during the election, had some grim satisfaction at that. Tea bags! When the American people wanted to protest something, what did they do? Why, they harked back to the Revolution, that's what! And you couldn't get away from it, that meant the Boston Tea Party! All over the world, people knew about that: they knew that if you wanted to protest, your weapon was tea.

Wonderful!

In very short order the pay raise was defeated.

From time to time Stephen and Cecelia heard from Matthew. He would give the latest report on the project at Walden: it was going to go through; it was temporarily halted; it was on again—definitely on; halted again and now the subject of a lengthy traffic study.

After each conversation with Matthew, Stephen would go for a long walk and then return to the inn to retreat to his little office. From behind the closed door Ceil and Danny could hear the sound of his typewriter. They knew that he was not tending to business, for all their business was entered into their computer. This sound was his clackety old Selectric.

One day in March, a mild, springlike day with the breath of summer on the south wind, Matthew called and gave what was for the moment the final word: the project was on, definitely on—the study had been canceled, the last appeal filed. But there was another piece of news almost as interesting. Continental Development Corporation had been sold to a group of investors headed up by—are you ready for this? said Matthew—Cecelia's brother Miles, and the fellow who'd bought Revell Hall from him, Tom Shaughnessy. The Shamrock Corporation, they called themselves. Tom was the son of the former governor, and an in-law to the Revells because his sister Kathleen had married Adam Revell, Guy's son. Rumor had it that the marriage was not happy.

As Stephen put down the phone and turned to look at Ceil, she said, "What's wrong?" He was pale—suddenly haggard-looking, as if someone had knifed him, perhaps.

And when he told her, she felt the same way. Her own brother! Collaborating with the man who'd helped him ruin Revell Hall! Of course, she'd never visited the place after Miles had sold it, but one time she accidentally saw a picture of it in the newspaper, rows of cookie-cutter "town houses" where once the gardens had been. A man who would do that, even if he was her own brother, would do anything.

Stephen spent a restless night. The next day he went to Boston. No, he said to Ceil, he didn't want company. He'd be back in a day or two.

All the way across the sound on the ferry, he brooded, and scribbled in the little notebook that he always carried, and brooded some more. The captain, who knew him well, saw that he didn't want to chat, as he often did, and so he left him alone. Wintertime, the captain thought: wintertime on the island could do a powerful job on people.

At Woods Hole he caught the bus. When he got to Boston he walked rapidly across the Public Garden, struck as he always was by the city's beauty. He was headed for West Cedar Street, where his parents still lived in the house built by his great-great-grandfather Daniel. The Abolitionist. The man who'd taken on the whole world in company with his friend Garrison. The fanatics. The men who would not compromise in the face of the evil that they saw.

But such determination, such devotion, had its price. Stephen knew what it was. He had, once, begun to pay it. Now, with a wife and child whom he loved more than anything, he wondered if he could pay it more—pay it again.

And yet if he did not, what would he bequeath to that child? A blackened, poisoned planet unfit for habitation of any kind, human or otherwise? Water not fit to drink, air too poisoned to breathe, the ozone layer gone, people frying in the lethal rays of the sun, a slow, agonizing death of all life on the planet, Man the destroyer, the killer of his own species and every other as well?

He was so lost in thought that he narrowly escaped death at the hands of a Boston motorist rounding the corner from Charles Street into Beacon. Careful, he thought; in order to do anything at all, you have to stay alive.

His parents were not home. He left his bag and a note and walked back to Beacon Street and the Somerset Club. Although he could easily have qualified for membership, his political convictions would never have allowed him to join. Now, as he mounted the granite steps, Boston Common at his back, the State-house up the hill, the world of his birthright all around him, he felt suddenly alien. He had been inside the Somerset only once before, when he was in college and the guest of an elderly uncle. Now, suddenly, he felt that he was going amongst his enemies. Well: that was all right. He'd step on many more toes than these before he was done.

He had luck: Miles was in, the steward said. While Stephen waited, he looked at a small bulletin board that held, among other notices, a list of delinquent members with overdue bar bills. Miles's name was on it.

"Stephen, old boy! Good to see you! Come in—come in. Judd will take your coat, come along to the bar, just in time for a drink. How goes it?" Miles came down with a smile on his face, hand outstretched. Ceil's hostility over Revell Hall had saddened him; he had never imagined that she would take on so about what was, after all, only a piece of real estate. Selling Revell Hall had been the smartest thing he ever did—the start of his very own fortune, his break from dependence on Family trusts. She'd had no right to take on so. But now apparently she was going to be friends again, and she had sent good old Stephen to start the process.

They settled themselves in worn leather armchairs by the windows overlooking Beacon Street and the Common. Just now as the lights were coming on, it was a lovely view, such a quintessentially Boston view that for a moment Stephen caught his breath and smiled to himself. This precious place, this Massachusetts . . . !

"So—now!" Miles began; but before he could continue, their attention was diverted by an elderly man, obviously a member, who approached them wringing his withered hands. His face was drawn up into a rictus of agony; when he spoke, it was only to get out his words through clenched (and obviously false) teeth.

"I say, Miles! Pardon for butting in, but I really must know. Did you mean what you said at the meeting this afternoon? Fight them on the beaches, fight them in the hedgerows, all that? Good old Churchill, what? Had a real way with words, didn't he?"

Hastily, Miles introduced him to Stephen. "Yes, Parkman. I did indeed mean it. You have my full support on the issue."

"Thank God." The old man bobbed his head and stifled a sob. "Knew your father, y'know! And your grandfather! Splendid!"

After he had turned away, Miles laughed, a little embarrassed perhaps. Or perhaps not. "We had a knockdown and drag-out fight this afternoon. Members' Committee. Some of them want us to admit women. But I don't see how we can. Not possible. Not in my lifetime. This is a place where you can really, ah, let your hair down, don't you know. If you have any, that is." He laughed again, embarrassed again perhaps, and passed his hand over the top of his thinning thatch. "The city licensing person is a woman, unfortunately. She's threatening to take our food and liquor licenses away. Says we're discriminatory! But I told her myself, I said, we've let in three Irishmen and one, uh, Hebrew in just the past year. And old Alex Korsakoff was a member for years. How could we be discriminatory if we let in a Russian? I said. But of course on the other hand, that's the whole point of having a club, isn't it? To be, uh, discriminatory? I mean, it isn't as if the women couldn't do the same thing. Let them have all the clubs they want, I say. But leave us alone to have our own little gang, don't y'know. A place where a fellow can pick his own chums, doesn't have to watch his language. Sometimes we get to roughhousing in here, I don't mind tellin' you. That's a good way to get to know a chap, a little roughhousin'. Now how could we do that with women around, I ask you?"

He shook his head at the unraveling of civilized society as he knew it. He was two years younger than Stephen; he seemed decades older. "But that's neither here nor there, is it?" he said. "What brings you here? I'm glad to see you, by the way. Been too long. Be sure to give Ceil my love."

"Walden Pond," Stephen said.

"Beg your pardon?" For an instant Miles did not understand, but then his face brightened. "Ah—right! Walden! It's going to be wonderful! You know, if you wanted a little piece of the action, I could probably cut you in—brother-in-law and all that—"

"No. I don't want a piece of the action. I want—" He couldn't think of a tactful way to say what he had to say, and besides, they were beyond the point where tact had a place. "I want the project stopped."

Miles was so shocked that he sat speechless for a moment, his mouth hanging open. Stopped—?

"I don't follow," he said then.

"Stopped. As in—cancelled. Walden Pond's no place to put a big new development, and you know it."

"On the contrary, it's an excellent place. Think of the stationery."

"The what?"

"The stationery. You know—tenants in the building can put on their business letterhead, 'The Offices at Walden Park' or some such thing. It'll be a terrific selling point. You sure you don't want to come in on it? I could speak to Tom Shaughnessy, he's the brains of our little group, I'm sure he'd be glad to—"

"No, Miles, I don't want to come in. I want it stopped. You don't realize—"

"Wait a minute. Wait a minute." Miles's friendly smile had vanished, replaced by a scowl. "Who the hell are you to come barging in here and tell me what you want?"

"Miles, I'm telling you that if you go ahead with this project, you will have nothing but trouble."

"Now you're threatening me! I don't believe it!"

"I'm not threatening you. I'm trying to warn you, that's all. Walden Pond is an international symbol of Nature. Everyone knows it was where Thoreau lived. It's a special place, don't you see? It's possible that there would be so much bad publicity that people wouldn't want to have an office there. Did you ever think of that? You might not be able to sell what you build."

Miles stared at him, astonished. "You *are* threatening me. Yes, you are! Incredible!"

Stephen had tried to keep his voice low, but now Miles spoke louder and louder, and Stephen realized that people were staring.

"Listen to me, Stephen, because I'm only going to say this once. I am partners with Tom Shaughnessy. We are going to go ahead with the project at Walden. If you don't think that I'm serious about this, I'll prove to you that I am. Every penny I have is tied up in this project! D'you understand? Every penny! I'll grant you I made a lot when I sold Revell Hall, but I lost a lot, too, when the stock market crashed in eighty-seven. And what I have is riding on this deal. So don't come in here with your demands and your lectures on Nature and Henry Thoreau. Because you're wasting your time. I can't back out now. I'll go bankrupt if those offices aren't built."

After that, of course, Stephen saw what a fool's errand he had undertaken, and he got out as quickly as he could. It was dark when he found himself on Beacon Street once again, with a brisk wind blowing up the hill from the west. A cold night, he'd walk for a bit and then have dinner with his parents. They were good people, never condemning him in his days of exploration, so to speak. In fact they'd been rather proud of him, he thought, for fighting so hard against the war. Now, tonight, he'd throw a few ideas at his father, who had as hard a head as anyone in the Family. Get a little perspective. If he planned to do something, he had told himself over and over again, it had better be something that would work. Talking to his father would help him to decide what that was.

Dinner was pumpkin soup and roast chicken. They chatted easily of Family affairs, a new show at the Museum featuring some of Alex Korsakoff's American collection, the prospects for the summer season on Nantucket.

Then, with the coffee, he made his announcement. "They're going to build an office park at Walden Pond," he said.

His parents were horrified—shocked into momentary silence.

Then: "A what?" said his mother. She was a member of the Audubon Society.

"An office park. One hundred and fifty thousand square feet, parking for more than five hundred cars."

"But—that's ridiculous. The Town of Concord will never allow—"

"They already have."

"But—Why, I'll call Dorothy Brisbane right now. She's very active in Concord affairs, she's on the Library Board and the Conservation Commission—I can't imagine that she'd ever go along with such a thing. That's sacrilege! An office park at Walden Pond!"

Stephen Sr., who had been a lawyer all his professional life, was less shocked than his wife at this evidence of human frailty and greed. "Who's behind it?"

And, when Stephen told him: "Miles! And young Shaughnessy! Strange bedfellows. But then they've had dealings together before, haven't they? I suppose the great-grandson of Patrick Shaughnessy is only too happy to get his hands on another piece of Yankee property. Too bad it had to be this particular piece. And, as your mother says, it's really unbelievable that the town of Concord doesn't take better care of its treasures. Doesn't Cousin Dwight's boy live out there?"

"Yes. As a matter of fact, he's asked me to help stop it."

"And?"

"That's why I came up today." And he told them of his disheartening interview with Miles at the Somerset. "He was—I don't know—completely out of touch with everything."

"Hm. Too bad. So old Thoreau is going to have his place spoiled, eh? That's a shame. He's quite a world figure now, isn't he? Prescient. And one of our better writers, I've always thought. I'm not sure he's ever had enough credit for that. Well, well. It really is foolish of them out there to destroy his place. It's a perfect symbol of the wilderness. The whole business of saving the wilderness is becoming more and more important, isn't it?"

"That's really the point," said Stephen. "I've been sorting it all out, the business of man vis-à-vis the wilderness. It's interesting the way our view of it has shifted. The history of this country is the history of our relationship with the wilderness. In the beginning, in the seventeenth and eighteenth centuries, the wilderness was something to be feared. Its two most powerful symbols to those early settlers were Indians and wolves. We managed to kill off both of those, and by the eighteenth century we had begun to tame the wilderness. Then, in the nineteenth century—Thoreau's time—as the Industrial Revolution took hold, the wilderness came to be increasingly valued and idealized: the Romantic writers, the back-to-the-land communes, and of course Thoreau's writings. At the end of the century, men like John Muir saw the need to begin to preserve the land, and they made the beginning of the National Park System. Even then people realized that the wilderness was finite, that it needed to be protected from the most dangerous animal on the face of the planet, which is man. And now, nearly a century later, our view of the wilderness has changed again. You see how that view shifts as our situation becomes different down through the years? Now in the late twentieth century, now at the eleventh hour when it is nearly too late, we finally come to see that the wilderness is something infinitely precious, something to be cherished not only for itself, but for our very salvation and survival. You see? Now we understand at last—and perhaps too late—that *the wilderness is our life.* 'In Wildness is the preservation of the World,' said Thoreau. When it goes, we go with it."

Then: "So what are you going to do?" said his mother. She gazed at him trustingly, as if she expected him to give her without hesitation a five-point plan.

The room was quiet save for the cozy crackling of the fire, welcome on this cold March night.

"I don't know," he said.

"You don't know *yet*," she corrected him.

She was right, of course. He didn't know—yet.

8

Two days after Stephen's return to Nantucket, an oil tanker as long as three football fields went aground on Bligh Reef near the Alaskan port of Valdez and ruptured her hull and her containment tanks. By the time the spill was contained, more than eleven million barrels of thick, black Alaskan crude had been poured into the pristine waters of Prince William Sound. It was the worst oil spill—the worst ecological disaster—in American history. The shoreline for miles around—hundreds of miles, eventually—was coated with oil, marine life fouled, the salmon fishery destroyed, seals and otters and water birds caked and suffocated.

That year Danny had a class in current events. He came home from school very upset about the *Exxon Valdez* disaster.

"Mrs. DelGuidice said that it could happen here," he announced at the dinner table. "No one would want to come here, would they, if there was crude oil all over Surfside Beach?"

"That's right," said Ceil dryly. "Not to mention the damage it'd do to the ocean."

"So why do we need that stuff anyway?" said Danny.

"What? The oil?"

"Yeah. Look at this." He pulled from his notebook a photo clipped from a newspaper, a picture of an oil-caked bird. "That's awful," he said. "Mrs. DelGuidice said this bird would probably suffocate. I think that's really horrible. I think we ought to take the president of the oil company and cover him up with oil like this and see how he likes it."

"Well," Ceil said, "I'm sorry for them up there, but I must say, I certainly hope it doesn't happen to us."

"It did happen to us," said Stephen. "It's just that it happened to us four thousand miles away instead of in our back yard."

"Well, yes, of course. But you know what I mean."

None of this, they saw, made their son feel any less worried. He finished his meal in silence and shortly went to his room. When Ceil went to check on him an hour or so later, she found him asleep—but fully clothed and with the light on, a book open on his chest: *The Call of the Wild*.

She had a sudden, painful thought: And what of the wild will there be for him? And for his son after him?

What are we doing to him? Condemning him to a slow death on a poisoned planet?

The next morning Stephen and Ceil were in the little breakfast room, having their second cup of coffee as they always did after Danny left for school. It was early April: too early for the annual rush to get ready for the summer season. Now he put down his two-day-old *New York Times* and looked across the table at her: his wife of more than twelve years. Her hair was the Family color still, bright gold, but sun-bleached from their years on the island; and her skin, pale from the winter, had more than a wrinkle or two. She was not beautiful in any conventional sense, but to him, of course, she was. He could not imagine living without her. She had become, as it were, his other half. It was as if her heart had attached itself to his; if it were torn away, he would bleed to death.

"What?" she said. She laughed a little self-consciously under his scrutiny. "What is it?"

He shook his head. He couldn't put it into words.

Later she found him puttering, repairing a broken windowpane. That was unusual: he didn't like such jobs, and generally he left them to the enterprising young man who contracted with them to undertake repairs and upkeep.

Later still, when she looked for him to walk downtown with her, she discovered he had taken his bicycle and gone off without telling her—an unusual thing, too.

When they both returned home, and he was shredding the lettuce for the salad while she put together the beef casserole, he did not volunteer to tell her where he had been, and she did not ask. She knew that he was wrestling with something—struggling with something; moreover, she had a pretty good idea of what it was. Time enough, she thought, to let him talk about it when he's ready.

The next day they had another call from Matthew. A national magazine had done a paragraph on Walden and the proposed office park, and Stephen's name had been mentioned; Stephen knew this, of course, because he had given the story to the reporter. Matthew had had several angry calls from his fellow townspeople wanting to know what the devil Stephen was up to.

"What should I tell them?" said Matthew.

"The truth," said Stephen. "Just tell them the truth, that's all. That we're doing for them what they should be doing for themselves."

After Stephen hung up, Ceil said, "Do you think it's hopeless?"

"What? Do I think what is hopeless?"

"Saving Walden."

"No. I don't. I think they have a pretty good chance, in fact. It's the other that will be a bit tricky."

"The other . . . ?"

"The Earth."

"Ah. Yes. The Earth." She laughed a little, nervous, unsure of where he was headed. The *Earth*! "Saving it, you mean."

"That's right. Saving it—taking it back. Because that's what we have to do, isn't it? We have to take it back. Take back the Earth."

The instant he spoke, she saw—and she knew that he saw it as well—a placard lettered with those words: "Take Back the Earth." The placard was multiplied a thousandfold and waving in a demonstration. Because that was it—that was the phrase that every demonstration had to have, the crucial, activating words that served to unify every protest that hoped to grow beyond protest into a full-fledged movement.

Take back the Earth.

He looked at her. And in that moment she knew, even if he did not. He was going to do what Matthew wanted him to do, but that would be just the beginning.

Take back the Earth.

"You know, I've been thinking," he said.

"I never would have guessed."

But he was in no mood for sarcasm.

"Everything started here," he said.

"Everything started where? What are you talking about?"

"I'm talking about the Pilgrims. The Mayflower Compact. The Revolution. Seventeen seventy-five. And that other Revolution that nobody knows about, sixteen eighty-eight. And the Industrial Revolution—and the Abolitionists—

"I mean, when you stop to think about it, an enormous amount of energy and ideas have come out of this place. This one small state with no particular natural resources except people. It was all *ideas*—Yankee ingenuity, if you will, combined with a certain sense of activist morality, the same urge that made the old Puritans mind everybody's business for them. Am I making any sense?"

"A little," she said. She smiled at him as if he were a clever child. "A little. I understand what you're getting at."

"You do? Then perhaps you could tell me."

She contemplated him. "It's very simple. You're getting ready to leave us for a while."

After dinner Stephen had a long talk on the telephone with Matthew.

9

Stephen spent the summer on the telephone or brooding over his computer, which now had begun to serve a dual purpose. While Ceil and a young hired couple took care of the inn, and Danny, at eleven, was pressed into service as well, Stephen surrendered himself to what rapidly became an obsession: *Take Back the Earth.*

Amazing, he thought, how people remembered him: some from his environmental work; more from what he thought of as the old days. He had only to identify himself to, say, a fellow who now sold insurance in Des Moines, and the memories would come pouring out, the Pentagon, the Chicago Democratic Convention in '68.

He began to construct that most basic of political tools, a Rolodex whose dozens of cards were filled with names and addresses and telephone numbers (and now, fax numbers) of people who would help. People who would raise money, people who would organize, send out mailings, make hundreds of phone calls, hold meetings in their homes.

With his computer he tracked and catalogued and contacted every environmental group in the country. There were thousands: from the large and well-known, like Greenpeace and the Sierra Club and the Wilderness Society and Friends of the Earth, to small pickup local groups fighting, say, a toxic dump or the illegal filling-in of wetland.

Or an office park at Walden Pond.

In early August, as if to renew his sense of purpose—although renewal was hardly necessary—he went up to Concord to visit Walden again. Matthew went with him. They parked in the parking lot across the road and made their way down to the little beach. It was another scorcher, 95 degrees at noon, and humidity at 85 percent. The trees around the pond looked dry and dusty, their roots exposed along the eroded path, and Stephen saw a handmade sign tacked to a fence: No Cookouts. No Smoking. No Fires of Any Kind.

A raucous crowd was at the little public beach this day, so many people that you couldn't see a square foot of sand. The water looked scummy; algae floated on the surface, pockmarked by scraps of candy wrappers and cigarette packs and—yes, he was sure—used condoms. Some of the girls in the crowd were topless. What his mother used to call "unfit language" echoed in the hot, still air. Everyone looked sweaty and dirty and mean. The two cousins set off along the path toward Thoreau's place. Not far along they came upon a couple fornicating on the little strip of sand by the water. On the other side of the path, in the woods, the nearly unbearable rays of the sun glinted off several empty beer cans.

At Thoreau's they saw a vision of the sixties: a dozen or so people in what used to be called "hippie" style of dress, or undress, one of them wearing a skirt made from an American flag, tie-dyed undershirts, beads, sandals, headbands, were sitting under a large sign that read, SAVE WALDEN POND. Banners hung limply in the still air, as did the smell of marijuana. They had been here for the past week, Matthew said, and had gotten a mention on a local television newscast and a paragraph in the Concord paper. They vowed to stay until all danger of the offices and condominiums had passed; they were prepared to throw themselves under the bulldozers if necessary. They called themselves the "Henry Davids."

Stephen chatted with them for a few minutes. They were, he thought, harmless. Ineffective, but harmless. They hadn't the foggiest notion of how to achieve what they wanted, which was, in the short run, the rescue of Walden Pond, and in the long run, the salvation of the Earth.

But the sight of them reminded him that if he didn't want to leave the issue to people like that, people who meant well but lacked both the knowledge and the resources to do the necessary job, then he needed to get back to his computer and his telephone, and finish what he had started.

"How's it going?" said Matthew when they were on their way around the pond again.

"All right. I've instituted a kind of gigantic conference call for next year. We'll set the date—July twelfth, next summer—Thoreau's birthday. Then we can begin to get out the information that people will need."

"D'you have a—a watchum'call it? A motto?" said Matthew.

"You mean, like 'Bring the Boys Home Now'? Or 'Stop the Bombing'?"

"Yes. Like that."

"I'd thought of 'Take Back the Earth.' "

"And the day itself will be known as Thoreau Day."

"Right."

"And what are you going to do?"

"Not sure yet. Something telegenic."

They stopped. They were at a place where the ground shelved away down to the water, making a private miniature beach. As if by mutual consent, they stripped and dove in. Here, away from the public beach, the water was remarkably clean, and delightfully cool because Walden was a kettle pond nourished by underground springs. For perhaps ten minutes they splashed and swam, and then, refreshed, they clambered out and dried themselves with their shirts and pulled on their chino pants.

"D'you think old Henry David did that?" Matthew said, laughing.

"Oh, I'm sure he did. Probably with a friend," Stephen replied.

"D'you want to stay over tonight?"

"Thanks. But I need to get back."

"You saw what you wanted to see?"

"Right. What I wanted to see—and what I didn't."

"Meaning . . . ?"

"Those folks back there are having a little protest, right? And certainly they mean well, their hearts are in the right place and all that. But who cares? They aren't going to accomplish a damn thing. They can sit there at Walden Pond till Hell freezes over—never mind the pond itself—and no one will give a hoot. The offices will be built, the condominiums occupied without a hitch."

He was right, of course. That fall, the Henry Davids, who were part of a small but growing band of activists called "ecoterrorists," realized that their protest was having no effect. They grew restive and then desperate. One fine day in early November they broke camp, picked themselves up, and marched on the town of Concord. The town had always been populated by Yankees—no-nonsense types, who certainly had no time in their busy schedules for a band of do-nothings who were suspiciously like their eponymous saint, Henry David Thoreau. He, too, had had long lacunae in his career, times when he seemed to be doing nothing but walking in the woods instead of keeping his nose to the grindstone.

The Henry Davids marched down Main Street. Then they went on to the Concord town offices. Paying no attention to the startled protests of the secretary, they marched right in. The town administrator, who had been reading a computer printout, looked up in surprise. He had time only to emit an outraged squawk before they seized him and tied him up and got on the telephone to the media to announce that they had a hostage here, and that they would not let him go until the projected offices and condominiums were canceled.

The crisis lasted for about forty-five minutes, and then the police came in and broke it up and made some arrests. And that was the end of the Henry Davids.

10

That winter, Stephen held a series of meetings around the country. At each one he listened as people voiced their anger at what was happening to the planet. Chernobyl, Bhopal, Three Mile Island, Rocky Flats, Love Canal, the *Exxon Valdez* spill, the loss of the rain forest—all of it unnecessary, all of it threatening their existence. Yes, he would say, yes, that's why I'm here, I need your help because together we can turn this thing around.

Sometimes, on the other hand, even as he solicited their support, he felt constrained to remind them that everyone could do his or her little bit, that it was not all big corporations or governments that were to blame. To a concerned young woman hoisting her baby on her hip, for instance, he tried as tactfully as possible to point out to her that she should stop using "disposable" diapers, which were not in fact disposable at all, but were a major source of unbiodegradable garbage. She was annoyed at first, having her good intentions flung back in her face, but then she agreed and promised to start using a diaper service.

Because of his old contacts, he was able to reach many people who were still politically active, or at least still active in some kind of social concern—

that whole big bulge in the demographics that was the baby boom generation, a generation that had grown up accustomed to seeing political action, who thought nothing of energizing themselves if the cause was right, and what cause was ever more right than this one?

They were always entranced by his opening remarks, in which he told them of his walk around Walden Pond one golden day in October. Although some of them had visited Walden, most had not; but everyone had heard of Henry David Thoreau, and everyone had at least some idea of who he was and what he stood for.

"Freedom" was what he stood for; and "Civil Disobedience"; and most of all "Walden" and the wilderness, the wildness that was the preservation of the world.

"If they can destroy Walden Pond," he would say, "they can destroy the Earth. For Walden symbolizes the Earth. It *is* the Earth. I ask you to help to save it—and the Earth as well."

He was a persuasive speaker. Everywhere he went, to Chicago and Denver and San Francisco, to Seattle and Fargo and Memphis, to New Orleans and Atlanta and Richmond—everywhere, people were fed up with watching the planet die. They joined up in droves; he had never seen anything like it. Organizing against the war had often been difficult, sometimes not so difficult; once or twice, after some particularly egregious and genocidal action on the part of the military, it had even been easy. But never had he experienced anything like this. It was as if he had tapped into a gusher of public anxiety and fear and anger that was just waiting to be channeled into some action. Everyone wanted to do something to help save the Earth. They shared his anger and his very real sense of urgency: Now! We must act now! Next year or the year after will be too late! We have a decade at most, and then we are finished. Where are the politicians? Where is the leadership? Hurry! Sign here! Contribute! Lay your body on the line! Give me your time, your energy, your donations, and with your help we can finally at this eleventh hour begin to bring her back, our Mother Earth, to bring her back from the brink of extinction!

He would arrive home from these organizing trips tired and sometimes hungry, but always with a sense of elation, a sense of urgent purpose being fulfilled, which worried Ceil even as it heartened her. She felt, at those times, that she was losing him—had lost him already, in fact, to a harsher, more demanding lover than she could ever be.

"Hello again." She put her arms around him and laid her warm cheek against his cold one. He had just come off the ferry. It was a cold February night and they were forecasting a nor'easter. Thank heaven he'd made it in time, she thought.

He pulled back to look at her. So well did he know her familiar, beloved face, so well did he know her every mood, her every thought, that now instantly he saw trouble, even though she had not told him. "What is it?" he said.

She laughed to cover her nervousness. "It's—I really hate to bother you with it, but I called Ted Wilson, and he said—"

"For Christ's sake, Ceil. What're you talking about?"

Ted Wilson was the Nantucket police chief.

"He said, try to keep him talking and signal to Danny to run next door and call the phone company to trace the call."

"Who, for God's sake? What are you talking about? Has someone been making crank calls?"

"More than crank. Last night and the night before. Both times he threatened to kill you if you didn't stop organizing."

During the war he'd been tailed by the FBI. They'd tapped his phones, trailed him on his journeys, planted informers in his committees and provocateurs in his action groups. He'd gotten used to it after a while: even joked about it. You're just paranoid, people would say when he told them. Ah, but remember, he'd reply. A paranoid is simply someone who knows all the facts. And they would all laugh. And he would look across the room and meet the eyes of that new fellow who'd shown up last week, a good reference from someone in Cleveland, say, and a thorough knowledge of whatever it was he was supposed to know. But his hair would be too short or his clothing not quite right, or his education deficient in some telling way. He'd never read Kafka, perhaps. Who? Kafka, man. You know. Good old Franz K.

"Does Danny know?"

"No."

"Good." He smiled at her, pretending unconcern. In fact he was very concerned indeed. Not surprised, though. He'd known from the beginning that at some point somewhere along the way he'd ruffle some feathers. It was a sign of success, in a way, that someone considered him enough of a threat to go to the trouble of calling.

Unless, of course, it was just a lone nut. No connection to any corporation whose profits would be imperiled by stringent environmental laws.

Just some solitary cuckoo. He'd spoken to groups large and small all over the country. Anyone could come to them. He was easily traceable, the inn's phone number listed, of course.

"Look," he said. "Perhaps you should, ah—"

"What?" she said. "Go away? But I can't. Danny's in school. And besides, why should I let myself be disrupted, not to mention the two of you? I'm staying right here."

He agreed. And as it happened, no more calls came. But the incident stayed in the back of their minds, a small grain of irritant: be careful!

11

"A march! To where?"

"Oh—to First Encounter Beach on Cape Cod, I think. And in fact it won't be a march. We begin at Walden Pond to take advantage of that symbolism. It's better to do it all in one day, so we'll have a bus caravan to the Cape."

His parents had come to spend the weekend. It was April: getting down to the wire. Stephen Sr. was amazed to hear his son's plans, about which, until now, he'd had only the most general idea.

"And what will you do when you get there?"

"Oh, we'll commemorate ourselves, and tell the world it began there—and at Walden, of course."

"What did?"

"The move to take back the Earth."

"That's a pretty pushy slogan, when you stop to think about it. Who are you to demand to take back the Earth? Take it back from whom?"

"From the people who are losing it."

"Some of whom are us."

"Right. We have met the enemy and he is us, as Pogo used to say."

"Come on. You aren't going to start a new movement on a saying of Pogo."

"Why not? It's just the kind of thing someone in my generation would do. Whimsical, yet very very serious."

"But what are you going to *do*, Stephen? What exactly?"

"We are going to present to the governments of the world a program for action. There are dozens of groups, and hundreds if not thousands of highly trained people, experts in their fields, who can put together such a program; it is our job to mobilize a movement to focus the world's attention on it. We are going to present our plan, a ten-year plan to bring down emissions, save the ozone layer, reverse the greenhouse, save the oceans, change people's habits— that's the bottom line, we have to change the way we live in the developed world, and we have to either pressure or beguile the undeveloped world to develop in ecologically sound ways—"

"Telling people what to do? Pushing them around? That won't get very far."

"These fellows are the cream of the crop. I said, just give me the best possible plan of action. We won't get it, but it'll be something to start from."

"But I still don't understand. What *exactly* is it that you intend to do?"

"I intend to hold the politicians' feet to the fire until they do what they must—what these experts say they must—to reverse the direction we're going in. File the necessary legislation—and enforce it—to clean up the planet."

"And you think you can do it. You think the public will support you."

"I know they will. This is one issue where the public is way ahead of the politicians. We've done poll after poll that shows that people are fed up with the lack of leadership on this issue. They *want* to be asked to sacrifice. They *want* to be told we're on a war footing. They'll cooperate. They may howl in protest, but they'll cooperate. They need leadership, and they haven't been getting it."

"Until now."

"That's right."

"And what happens after the march?"

"After the thousand marches, it's not just this one. All over the country—all over the world, for that matter—people are going to be celebrating with us. That's what it is, too, don't forget—the first celebration of Thoreau's birthday. From now on, of course, Thoreau Day will be an event every year, bigger and bigger. At any rate—what happens next? Why, next we start to implement our program. Draw up legislation, have it introduced. Local, state, national. The politicians' feet are going to get very hot."

His father did not reply at once. He was thinking of his own father, the ill-fated champion of the doomed anarchists. That same father had once told him about his own grandfather, Daniel the Abolitionist. He'd been trying to describe some quality about him—some intensity of purpose, some wild dedication visible in his eyes; and now he saw it here in his son all over again. Right down through the Family: how had it skipped him?

But what he was hearing today was something far bigger than either Abolition or Sacco and Vanzetti. And therefore, of course, the possibilities of failure were all the greater.

"Stephen."

"Yes."

"I don't want to discourage you—and of course I realize that I couldn't do that, not when you've come this far. But why do you think you can succeed?"

A movement caught his eye: Ceil had come to the door and stopped, not wanting to interrupt. She held her finger to her lips, and he understood: she wanted to hear the answer, too.

Stephen nodded, not minding the question—welcoming it, almost, as a way to help him articulate what he thought.

"For two reasons. And in any case, the question has to be, succeed at what? At saving Walden Pond and Walden Woods from development? Yes. I think we can do that. It won't be easy, but I think we can, once we get public opinion aroused.

"The other half of that question is, can we succeed at saving the Earth? Can we take it back? And there again, I have to say yes, although perhaps not so confidently. But you see, for any movement to succeed, you have to have two things: the right issue, and the right time. They have to coincide. Now the issue has been here for years. The Club of Rome detailed it almost twenty years ago. But people weren't interested—or not interested enough to do more than do Earth Day and let it go at that. Now we've had two decades of absolutely incontrovertible evidence that we are killing the planet, and I think people are finally ready to do whatever has to be done to save it. We've been polling every month, and every month the figures go up. It's something like eighty-four percent now, answering yes to the question, 'Would you be willing to do whatever is necessary to save the Earth?' So I think we can succeed because we have the right issue at the right time. Notice I don't say *I*. I've helped to get this thing going, but anyone could have done it at this point. People are ready. They'll follow responsible leadership."

And now at last Ceil spoke up. "Do you know what Gran used to say? She used to quote Susan B. Anthony. 'Failure is impossible,' she'd say. That was when the women were trying to get the vote, and they'd had half a century of defeat. And then Miss Anthony would say, 'Failure is impossible!' And she was right. And it's the same now, of course. More so."

12

One mild day a woman about Ceil's age walked up the lane, pushed open the little wooden gate, and came down the path to the front door. Ceil was in the midst of the annual spring cleaning and getting ready for the summer season; this day she was washing the windows second-floor front, and so had a fore-shortened view of the visitor. The woman looked familiar, she thought, but she couldn't be sure.

The door bell rang. She was, for the moment, alone in the house: Stephen in San Francisco, Danny at school. They had a young woman to help with the cleaning, but her baby was sick this day and so she had not appeared.

"Coming!"

Hastily wiping her reddened hands on her damp jeans, Ceil stepped down from the ladder and hurried down the stairs. An early-bird guest, no doubt, hoping to find a room at off-season prices.

"Cecelia Revell. Hello. Do you remember me? I'm Kathleen. Adam's wife."

Like his father, Guy, Adam had been strongly in favor of the war in Vietnam—a real "hawk." But even more to the point, Ceil thought, was the fact that this woman's brother was Tom Shaughnessy—the man who had bought Revell Hall, who wanted now to build at Walden Pond, the man who was a partner of her own brother, Miles.

Ceil was aware of the sun warm on the front of the house, and the sharply etched configurations of the gray-shingled houses opposite against the bright blue sky. A robin red-breast was announcing himself with a fluting song; in the distance sounded the blast of the whistle as the ferry began the afternoon journey to the mainland.

After an awkward, too-long moment, she said, "Of course. Come in."

The visitor wore a handsome gray suede jacket over green cuffed trousers, a silk paisley scarf at her throat. Her curly red-brown hair was tucked under a gray beret; her bright brown eyes looked out at the world forthrightly with a touch of saving humor. She held out her hand. "Sorry to appear out of the blue like this. I saw a newsclip of your—of Stephen—on CNN yesterday and I just—well, I needed to get away. And so I thought I'd try my luck."

Automatically Ceil had stepped back. She'd never known this woman well, had never wanted to. Now she led her back through the hall, saying some meaningless thing that she hoped was gracious. Would you like some lunch? Tea or coffee?

"I might as well tell you right off," said Kathleen, standing in the middle of the kitchen. "I've left Adam."

Ceil glanced at the clock: twelve-thirty. Good. Two hours at least before Danny was due home.

"I'm sorry," she said. It was an automatic expression of sympathy, not a felt emotion.

"I'm not," Kathleen said. "It was time." She spoke in a bright, confident voice; her eyes were steady, her smile determined. "We don't have any children, so that makes it easier." She sat down at the kitchen table. "I may as well tell you the whole story," she said. "Why I came down here like this, I mean. The truth is, I've not only left my husband, I've left one of my brothers as well."

Ceil busied herself making coffee. "Really," she said, for lack of anything else. She knew before Kathleen spoke which one it was.

"It's the Walden Pond project, of course." Kathleen sat very straight in her chair, a tribute to the nuns' strictness, her hands clasped on the table in front of her. "That's what got me interested, I mean. I went to one of Stephen's meetings last month in Worcester. I was so moved by what he said that the next day I went to see Tom and I just asked him point-blank if he wouldn't please reconsider. Just cancel the project, I said. You don't need Walden Pond. Find someplace else to build an office, I said."

"Did he listen?" said Ceil. She set out cups and saucers and plates. There was a cold ham in the fridge, she thought, and some salad, homemade rye bread and a few lemon sugar cookies.

"No. He told me to stick to my business, he'd stick to his." Kathleen laughed, embarrassed for her brother's rudeness. "And *then* I found out—" She flushed and looked away for a moment; then she came back. "I suppose I might as well tell you. I found out that Adam was having an affair, and everything just seemed to fall in on me, if you understand what I mean, and I felt so smothered and trapped, and I had to get out. A bad marriage, a—well, not a bad career, but I need to give some thought to where I'm going. And then I saw Stephen on TV, and I thought, this is it. This is what I want to do. I mean, I'm a doctor. And so perhaps I can help by giving expert testimony on the effects of acid rain on three-year-olds, or some such thing. I'd think a movement to save the Earth could use some doctors, wouldn't you?"

It was such an innocent-seeming question from an individual obviously competent and experienced in dealing with the world, that Ceil could not help laughing. "Yes," she said. "I would indeed."

My God, she thought; she's very nice. I think I even like her.

They talked for the better part of an hour—or, rather, Kathleen talked and Ceil listened. Every now and then she would interject a syllable or two, just to show that she was paying attention. She was aware that this was a therapeutic session for Kathleen. She didn't mind. Having discovered that she probably liked this new arrival into her life, she was content to get to know her in this way, listening, being there.

And then Kathleen fell silent for a moment. She gazed into the middle distance, thinking.

"Did you know," she said abruptly, "that my great-great-grandmother once worked as a servant for one of your ancestors?"

"No," said Ceil, surprised. "I didn't. Are you sure?"

"Pretty sure. But that's all I know for certain. About the details, I couldn't say whether they're accurate. If my grandfather were alive, I'd ask him. He'd know."

Ceil's curiosity was piqued. She'd ask Matthew, who was a genealogy bug. "What are the details?" she said. "True or not."

Kathleen laughed a little. "There's no way of verifying it, of course, but the story is that my great-great-grandmother got off the boat and of course she needed a job. And in those days the only job for an Irish girl was as a domestic, and even those jobs were hard to come by because the Yankees didn't want the Irish in their houses." She spoke with no animosity, Ceil noted, simply stating facts, no hard feelings, my race memory doesn't hold grudges if yours doesn't.

"So at any rate, my great-great-grandmother—her name was Mary Margaret O'Donovan then—my great-great-grandmother was lucky enough, or persistent enough, to land a job at this rich Yankee home. And you can imagine she was glad to get it, and she'd never do anything to endanger it. But within a few months she was fired—for stealing, they said. Of course none of her descendants ever believed it, not for a minute. She has a reputation in the family for being as smart and as tough as they come. Far too smart to lose a good job. She was widowed young, left with a flock of small children to support—and she not only survived, she did very well for herself. She was a dressmaker eventually, and very prosperous, too, relatively speaking. Did you ever read Oscar Handlin's book on the Irish immigrants of Boston? For every one who lived, he says, ninety-nine died in the most hideous slums. But Mary Margaret O'Donovan Shaughnessy survived."

They were silent for a moment, thinking, perhaps, of their good fortune at being born into a less difficult world. Then as if she was suddenly conscious of having talked too much about herself, Kathleen asked Cecelia to talk: about her life on the island, about the latest news of Stephen's success at raising an environmental army.

By the time Danny came home from school, it was as if the two women had been friends all their lives.

13

"Say, friend! How do I get to Walden Pond?"

All day and into the night they gathered, coming in twos and threes, picking up their information packets, their placards, their packages of trail mix

donated by a major environmental organization. Their tee-shirts were emblazoned with the movement's logo, a stylized drawing of Walden Pond and Walden Woods: 🌲. They had brought their sleeping bags, and they settled down
in the parking lot to wait for the morning when the buses would come to
"march" them to their destination. Toward midnight Stephen spoke to them,
thanked them for coming, for being so well behaved, for obeying the rules—
no liquor, no drugs, everybody clean up his own place, leave it as you found
it. In the morning, he said, he'd see them again before they all set off.

Stephen and Ceil and Danny spent the night at Matthew's house in Concord, although Stephen was there only briefly because he was patrolling, as it
were—an anxious general before the battle.

"You have to get some sleep," said Ceil. It was three in the morning; he'd
been out most of the evening, speaking to the arriving marchers, and had then
come home to briefly sleep. Now he was awake again, unable to rest. He remembered the old days, when he'd gone for what seemed like days without sleep.
Twenty years ago: it seemed more like a century. He'd been a lot younger then.

Before dawn he and Ceil had their breakfast. Matthew's kitchen opened
out onto a small flagged terrace surrounded by the flower garden to which he
devoted considerable time. Now the birds were awake, too, sending up a chorus
to greet the day; toward the east the sky was beginning to pale.

"This has always seemed—excuse the pun—the most unearthly time of day,"
said Stephen. She'd made him a plate of bacon and eggs and English muffins, a
good dose of protein and fat and cholesterol and carbohydrates to carry him
through, and now as she poured his coffee, she looked up at him and smiled.

"Nervous?" she said.

"No. Nothing to be nervous about."

"It's going to be all right?"

"Oh, yes. Definitely all right. Feel it in my bones."

"Which aren't as young as they used to be," she said, laughing.

"Young enough for this," he replied. He reached out and took her hand.

Matthew looked in. "Five o'clock," he said.

"Right." Stephen swallowed the last of his coffee and picked up his backpack at the door. Ceil would follow shortly with Danny and Matthew.

It was a cool dawn; the weather forecast, which in Massachusetts was not
always to be believed, had nevertheless called for a clear, dry day, a perfect
summer day. It was as if Mother Earth were giving them, one last time, her
best: so they could remember; so they could try to save her for their children.

Stephen went down the path to the street, where a driver in a Jeep waited
for him. They drove through the sleeping town like intruders in a dream.
Concord had not welcomed this production: having no special reverence for
Henry Thoreau or his memory, it had issued permits for the necessary encampment only when Matthew and a few other residents began to apply pressure—what kind, Stephen never asked. It was enough that they were being
allowed to start from Walden: their wellspring, an important symbolic gesture,
a crucial photo opportunity.

It was first light when they pulled into the parking lot. Down the road as far as he could see was a line of buses, while here in the lot were the big, bulky television trucks. Some of the crews stood around drinking coffee out of plastic cups—nonbiodegradable, but never mind; Stephen saw one group with their equipment heading along the path into the woods to Thoreau's cairn, to where the sendoff would be filmed.

And now as the sun came up, people were awakening, getting ready for the journey, rolling up their bedrolls, waving at him, recognizing him, "Hey, Stephen! Give 'em hell! We're with you all the way, man!" Some of the faces that smiled at him were sixties faces, beards and all; but many others were young—people born in the sixties, who had therefore not participated in its passions, people who came fresh to this cause, so much less divisive than the sixties causes had been.

He went along the path to the clearing. In the little knot of people already there he saw his assistant, Tierney, and several of his staff.

"Ready?" Tierney's face was drawn with fatigue, but he looked happy and expectant. The high point of his life had been the March on Washington in '69; he'd been looking for a repeat ever since.

"Sure. Let's go." Stephen signaled to the television reporters and the several newspaper reporters, and stepped up onto a rock that raised him a little so that he could see the people delegated to come to the site for the filming of the sendoff.

"Friends! Good morning on this beautiful day! This is the day we begin to take back the Earth!"

At his words a cheer went up from all around, the cameras swiveled to catch the crowd, the reporters scribbled.

"Are you with me?"

And the crowd shouted *"Yes!"*

"You are with me because you know what we must do."

"Yes!"

"And we must start to do it now—right here at Walden Pond!"

"Yes!"

"Friends, I say to you that Walden Pond is about to be raped. And we can't let that happen. Because the rape of Walden Pond is the rape of Mother Earth! So now, this day, Henry David Thoreau's birthday, we begin to save them both—to save Walden Pond, to Take Back the Earth!"

And now the response came full-throated, sure of itself, firm in its purpose: "Take Back the Earth! Take Back the Earth! Take Back the Earth!"

"All right! Let's go!" And with a flourish of the green and white banner that someone had thrust into his hand, he leapt down and strode briskly along the path to the road where the main body of the demonstration had begun to board the buses. The cameras got it all: a beautiful ninety seconds of film.

They set off. In all the days of Massachusetts, there had never been a more perfect day than this: a warming sun, a little breeze, deep blue sky, the lush countryside all around, the same that had nurtured King Nanepashemet and his braves, that had heard the warning cries of Paul Revere and the tramp of British soldiers.

As the sun climbed into the sky it caught their banners waving from the windows, the stylized drawing of Walden Pond, white letters on a field of green: TAKE BACK THE EARTH. Many of the demonstrators had brought homemade signs as well: "Rape Walden/Rape Mother Earth," and "Let Us Breathe," and "Life on Earth."

Someone started to sing: "This land is your land . . ." There were several formerly famous folk singers present, and you could hear their voices ringing out, strong and true, holding the melody together: "We Shall Overcome," they sang, and "Bread and Roses," and of course the grandest marching hymn of all, Julia Ward Howe's "Battle Hymn of the Republic."

Stephen was in an open Jeep at the front of the line. He wore a khaki shirt and trousers, and a large green button on his chest with the Walden logo in white. With him were Ceil, Matthew, Tierney, and three people from the steering committee. In the first bus just behind were Kathleen and Danny and two of Danny's friends whose parents had given them enthusiastic permission to join the march.

According to plan, the cavalcade stopped for a midday rally at Plymouth. Then, in late afternoon, they arrived at First Encounter Beach at Eastham, Cape Cod. They rumbled down the access road, which was called Samoset Avenue, and pulled into the little parking lot. The television crews were waiting. Halfway down the wide expanse of sand, a bonfire was built, ready to be lit. It looked like some kind of primitive dwelling. Beyond it were the pits dug for the clambake. Two supply trucks with the food stood at the far end of the lot. The tide was out, and here at this particular beach the tide went a far way, for a mile it looked to be.

Stephen headed for the little speakers' platform on the near side of the bonfire and climbed onto it to see the progress of the buses coming in. They were doing well; no gridlock. As they pulled into the lot, their passengers spilled out. They seemed in good spirits.

Tierney had gone to reconnoiter. Now he came loping up. "It's all right, they're coming along, no problems."

"Good." Stephen looked down the beach. Danny and his friends had already gone to run across the wet sand, hunting for treasures, exploring. Across the bay the sun was going down. Silhouetted against the rosy sky was the bullet-riddled hulk of an abandoned target ship, the *General James E. Longstreet*. A little landward breeze had sprung up, fluttering the banners and standards that had already begun to be planted in the sand like a forest of message-bearing trees.

And what was it like when you were here, Bartholomew?

He tried to imagine it: the empty beach, the wilderness, the knowledge that Indians lurked nearby, waiting to make their first encounter with the interlopers who had only the slender resources of the *Mayflower* to fall back on.

The day was still warm, but suddenly he shivered. From such small beginnings they had come; and now three and a half centuries later they gathered here to save the very wilderness that once had seemed so threatening.

"Stephen?" It was his old acquaintance Goldberg, once a fellow activist, now a reporter for the *Los Angeles Times*. "Great story you have here, man."

"It is. Glad you're going to get it."

Goldberg's handshake was firm, his eyes clear—unlike the last time they had met, Stephen remembered with a smile.

"How'd you happen to get involved?" said Goldberg.

"It's a long story."

"Talk to me later?"

"Sure thing."

The beach was filling up now. The sun hung above the horizon, a glowing orange disk in bright-edged purple clouds. The sea had taken on the mother-of-pearl iridescence that comes to it late on a sunshiny day. Later they would have the clambake. Already fires had been set in the baking pits, heating the rocks that would cook the lobsters and clams, potatoes and corn—all layered in seaweed, all tasting, when they were cooked, better than anything in the world.

Stephen took a deep breath, inhaling the familiar sour salt smell of seaweed and briny water and myriad ocean life. Coming in, they had seen a cloud of brownish-yellow smog lying over the Cape, but now, as he faced the direction of the bay, he saw that the air was clear. It was that magical hour when the sun in his majesty descended in clouds of glory into the west; and in the east rose the shining silver-gold moon, a nearly full moon tonight, carrying the evening star, bright Venus, at her shoulder. From somewhere in the distance came the faint clanging of a buoy bell; nearby, people had brought flute and guitar, and they played while a rich contralto voice sang the song that had been written as the new anthem of protest. The marchers gathered around. The young woman singing jumped up onto the platform and began again, and this time the crowd sang with her.

It was nearly dark now: time to light the bonfire—that ancient signal sent from mountaintop to mountaintop, a signal from the oldest days of mankind, from the days when the planet was not young but scarcely used, still fresh and pure and green for each generation born onto it.

Tierney handed Stephen the torch; and Stephen put it to the kindling at the base of the pyramid of stacked wood. Instantly it caught. For a moment the flames licked around the edges of the wood; then they suddenly roared up through the center, straight to the top, and people fell back from the tremendous heat of it, faces in a circle like faces from time immemorial, drawn out of the darkness into the light and the warmth: a little haven of safety from the dangers of the wild. Except that now the danger was reversed, the danger was to the wild, not from it.

Stephen leaped onto the platform and held up his arms. In the gathering dusk, silhouetted against the flames, he seemed almost a figure of myth—a tribal chieftain from ancient, barbaric times, perhaps, who, whatever else his failings, lived in harmony with the Earth, understanding that she nurtured him, and gave him life.

"Friends of the Earth!" He paused for the reaction that he knew would come: a cheer, a self-affirmation.

"We are here today to celebrate the birthday of the man who is our patron saint, Henry David Thoreau!"

Cheers and more cheers: "Happy Birthday, Henry!"

"And more important, we are here today to pledge ourselves and dedicate ourselves to the renewal of this Earth—our beloved home that we have so badly damaged. We pledge to her that as of today, the damage stops." (Cheers.) "We pledge to her that today, the renewal begins." (Louder cheers.) "We say to you, and to the nation that watches, and to the hundreds of thousands who partici-pate with us all across the land, that by the end of this century, to celebrate the millennium, we will have accomplished our purpose: to save this Earth, before we lose it forever!"

And now a huge roar from the crowd, a full-throated cry—"Take Back the Earth! Take Back the Earth!"

From his place above, Stephen stood panting a little, the electric energy from the crowd energizing him—that giddy, intoxicating feeling that comes from whipping up a throng, feeling their power surge over him.

One more time he held up his arms, hands open, his long, spatulate fingers stretched wide—an expansive gesture that included them all. They understood: they quieted for him.

He spoke briefly about the difficult task that lay ahead: he urged them to keep faith. He spoke to them as no politician dared to speak, for he told them the truth: that they had the power to determine their fate.

They began to cheer. He let them go on for a while, building their excite-ment. The bonfire crackled in the night wind. All around the circle of ruddy light he saw the round, vacant, devouring eyes of the cameras like a herd of Cyclops. Beyond them were his people, the devoted who had pledged their lives to this cause. Ceil was standing to one side of the front. He caught her eye and lifted his chin and smiled—a private greeting. She smiled back. She had never loved him more than at this moment. She shivered in the night wind, and not entirely because she was cold.

Now he raised his arms again. He had that gift, she thought: the gift of persuasion that makes men leave their lives of quiet desperation and unques-tioningly follow. She glanced back. She saw a thousand faces lighted by the glow of the fire. Their eyes were on him—on Stephen, who would, they be-lieved, tell them what to do, who would tell them how to save themselves. Whatever it was, they would obey. She understood that most people, incapable of leadership, longed for someone else to show the way. Someone good or bad— the luck of the draw. Or perhaps people got what they deserved.

Once again now they were quiet, expectant, waiting for his signal: *Show us the way, tell us what to do.*

"Friends! Disciples of Thoreau! We will save Walden Pond!" (Loud, pro-longed cheers.) "And when we have saved Walden Pond, we will save Walden

Woods!" (Louder cheers.) "And when we have saved Walden Woods, we will go on to save the Earth!" (Louder, longer cheers.) "I do not ask you to follow me. I ask you to follow Henry Thoreau, who lived in a different time, and yet who had a vision that grows with every passing day now in our time. And I say to you that we will honor that vision. We will do what he would have done! We will act before it is too late! We will take back the Earth!"

"Yes!" A long, deep roar of affirmation.

"Yes! We will do that! We will take back the Earth! Take back the Earth! Take back the Earth!"

He was like the conductor of a symphony now, moving his outstretched arms in a circular motion, leading them into it, and they were chanting it now, one great rhythmic chant:

"Take back the Earth! Take back the Earth! *Take back the Earth! Take back the Earth!* TAKE BACK THE EARTH!"

Building and building—one voice, one great heartfelt cry, one voice for the preservation of life on the home planet, their beautiful, endangered Planet Earth.

Because they must do it now. They knew that: understood it. Their days were fast running out. The Earth had existed since the beginning of time. Now it faced extinction almost overnight.

So they needed to hurry. Hurry! They felt the urgency of their task like a coldness in the bone—a deep, terrifying knowledge of their certain fate: to be dead, to be extinct on a burnt-out cinder endlessly circling its murderous sun. A hundred years hence, the last one alive on Earth would know who was to blame: twentieth century man was to blame. He was the one: the most dangerous animal on Earth, he was, and who could save him from his own destruction?

"Take back the Earth! Take back—"

From out of the darkness came a man running. He was yelling incoherently as he bounded onto the platform. The people there tried to stop him before he reached Stephen, but they could not. With a wild, angry cry he leaped at Stephen, and even though he was nearly a head shorter, he got his hands around Stephen's throat and held on in a death grip, *my God, he's going to strangle Stephen, get him off!*

And of course they did, a dozen men broke his killer grip and pulled him away, the crowd screaming, terrified—*my God, a madman, he nearly did it!*

Stephen rubbed his painful throat while someone took to the microphone to calm the crowd: it's all right, folks, he's safe, no harm done, let's all sing along now with Miss Mary McInnis, everybody join in!

Stephen sat trembling on the edge of the platform at the back, facing away from the crowd. The police had his attacker in handcuffs, taking him away. It had all happened so quickly that Stephen had only a glimpse of a maddened, enraged face coming at him, coming at him—

He couldn't stop trembling. Ceil sat beside him, holding his hand; she felt him shaking.

"All right," she said, "let's get you out of here. Do you think you can walk?

Or we can drive a beach buggy right up to the platform— Oh, Danny, Dad is all right, he's not hurt." For the child crouched behind them, not saying a word; she could see that his face was tense and fearful, his eyes wide with alarm.

But Stephen wanted to stay; he was all right, he said. So they stayed, and they had some of the clambake, and after a while Stephen was able to talk a bit. Ceil and Danny stayed close by him all evening, as if by doing so they could protect him from further harm. By the time Stephen stopped trembling, Ceil had begun; all the way to the motel where they would spend the night before going home on the ferry, she kept on shaking. Stephen held her in his arms until she went to sleep; he himself didn't doze off until dawn.

14

The attack on Stephen was news—big news—for two days. It guaranteed coverage for the Thoreau Day rally even more than the event itself. Thousands of well-wishers sent messages and contributions to the cause.

Stephen recovered quickly, nothing to recover from, really, except some bruises on his throat. His assailant said that he attacked Stephen because he had seen him on television and he remembered him from the antiwar days. He felt a strong compulsion to make contact, he said. He was judged mentally unfit to stand trial, and he was put into a facility for the insane.

"It wasn't my time," Stephen said to Ceil. For the thousandth time she sent a message of gratitude—where? She didn't know. On high someplace. Thank you God for sparing him.

The summer passed, and autumn came. The stock market fell a hundred points, and there was a 7.4 earthquake in Mexico, and a member of the President's cabinet was caught with a sixteen-year-old prostitute, and the Soviet Union offered yet again to halt the arms race.

Life went on.

And while it did, over the winter, Stephen watched the organization he'd created survive and prosper. As planned, each of the demonstrators on Thoreau Day had served as a nucleus of action, so that now the entire country and indeed much of the world was seeded with dedicated activists organizing protests, boycotts, pressuring fearful politicians, pressuring greedy and short-sighted corporations—all the unglamorous but necessary scutwork that had to be done.

On a mild April day when the wind came out of the south, lilac buds just beginning to swell, daffodils pushing up their slim green shoots, Stephen and Cecilia walked out along the Jetties Beach. Little foamy-edged waves—clean, no debris—rolled up at their feet. The wet sand was pinpointed with clam airholes. The two of them walked slowly, his arm around her shoulders.

Yesterday he'd had good news. Tierney had called to say that the Massachusetts Legislature, together with the other New England states, was going to pass a tough new set of antipollution laws—air, water, ground—everything. Tougher than federal laws, which were by and large a joke.

"They're scared, for sure," Tierney had said. "I saw the fellow from G.M., the lobbyist. He was mad as hell. They wouldn't even talk to him. He says this bill will ruin the industry, but of course that's what he has to say."

Ceil looked up at her husband and smiled. He stopped to kiss her. A sea gull dropped a clam on a rock to break it and get his dinner.

"We're going to win," Stephen said.

"How do you know?"

"Feel it in my bones. We're going to do it."

"Failure is impossible."

"Right."

"Which means, Danny will live to a grand old age and know that his children and grandchildren will have a chance, too."

"Right again."

She took his hand. The sea stretched before them, flat and pearly light, softly moving: our aqueous home from whence we came.

"He can take them to Walden Pond," he said.

"If it's still there."

"It will be. Matthew called this morning while you were out."

"Don't tell me! Stephen! They've pulled out!"

"Yes."

"*Ah*—that's *wonderful!* It means—it means we've won!"

"We've won the first fight, at any rate. The rest of it will hardly be so easy."

"But it's a beginning—a good beginning, a good omen."

"Yes."

He put his arm around her again. Fleetingly he thought of her brother. Miles would go bankrupt now, perhaps, and perhaps Tom Shaughnessy as well. Too bad, Stephen thought, and he meant it. Still. Couldn't be helped. Walden had to be saved, that was the important thing.

He took a deep breath, and they walked on. Ever since Thoreau Day he had felt reborn, and never more than this day, the wind freshening from the south, the empty beach stretching as far as they could see. The sky was milky blue, the sun warm and benign. Gulls swooped and screamed; sandpipers scurried across the wet sand, busily searching for sustenance.

Thoreau said this: "Rather than love, than money, than fame, give me truth."

And: "The light which puts out our eyes is darkness to us," he said. "Only that day dawns to which we are awake. There is more day to dawn. The sun is but a morning star."

Say, friend! Take me along to Walden Pond!

ABOUT THE AUTHOR

Nancy Zaroulis lives in Massachusetts with her family.

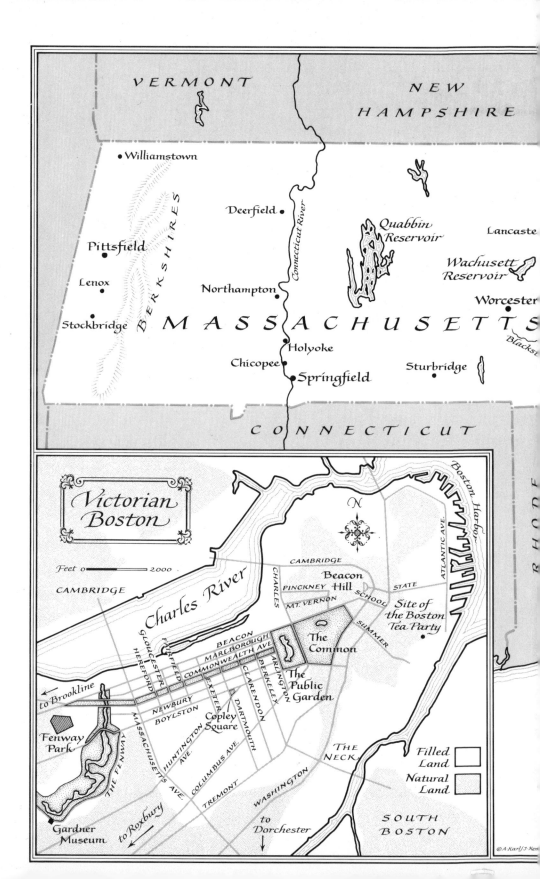